THE RELUCTANT PROPHET

TWO BESTSELLERS IN ONE VOLUME

THE WARNING
THE ULTIMATUM

T. DAVIS BUNN

A
JANET
THOMA
BOOK

THOMAS NELSON PUBLISHERS
Nashville

Published in Nashville, Tennessee, by Thomas Nelson, Inc.

The individual books in this omnibus edition were originally published
by Thomas Nelson, Inc., as follows: *The Warning,* Copyright © 1998 by
T. Davis Bunn; *The Ultimatum,* © 1999 by T. Davis Bunn.

Unless otherwise noted, Scripture quotations are from the KING JAMES
VERSION. Copyright © 1979, 1980, 1982, 1990 Thomas Nelson, Inc.,
Publishers.

Scripture quotations noted KJV are from the KING JAMES VERSION.

Scripture quotations noted NIV are from the HOLY BIBLE: NEW INTER-
NATIONAL VERSION®. Copyright © 1973, 1978, 1984 by the Interna-
tional Bible Society. Used by permission of Zondervan Publishing House.
All rights reserved.

Library of Congress Cataloging-in-Publication Data

Bunn, T. Davis, 1952-
    [Warning]
    The reluctant prophet : two bestsellers in one volume / T. Davis Bunn.
        p. cm.
    Contents: The warning—The ultimatum.
    ISBN 0-7852-6734-4 (hc)
    1. Bankers—Fiction. 2. Prophets—Fiction. 3. Depressions—Fiction.
    4. Women journalists—Fiction. 5. Washington (D.C.)—Fiction. I. Bunn,
T. Davis, 1952- Ultimatum. II. Title.

    PS3552.U4718 W37 2001
    813'.54—dc21   00-069554
                                                               CIP

Printed in the United States of America.

1 2 3 4 5 6 BVG 05 04 03 02 01

THE
WARNING

⊣∣ A NOVEL ∣⊢

T. DAVIS BUNN

A
JANET
THOMA
BOOK

THOMAS NELSON PUBLISHERS
Nashville

Published in Nashville, Tennessee, by Thomas Nelson, Inc., Publishers.

Unless otherwise noted, the Bible version used in this publication is THE
NEW KING JAMES VERSION. Copyright © 1979, 1980, 1982, 1990
Thomas Nelson, Inc., Publishers.

Scripture quotations marked KJV are from the KING JAMES VERSION of
the Bible.

Scripture quotations are also taken from the HOLY BIBLE: NEW INTER-
NATIONAL VERSION. Copyright © 1973, 1978, 1984 by the Interna-
tional Bible Society. Used by permission of Zondervan Publishing House.
All rights reserved.

This novel is a work of fiction. All characters, plot, and events are the product of the author's imagination. Any financial information or advocacy contained herein is purely fictitious.

Library of Congress Cataloging-in-Publication Data

Bunn, T. Davis, 1952–
   The warning / T. Davis Bunn.
     p. cm.
   ISBN 0-7852-7516-9 (pbk.)
   I. Title.
PS3552.U4718W37 1998
813'.54—dc21   97-40781
                                            CIP

Printed in the United States of America.

10 11 12 13 14 BVG 05 04 03 02 01

This book is dedicated to
Irven and Joanna Hicks
Twenty years ago, a young man ventured into
a Christian bookstore for the very first time.
Joanna introduced him to Christian fiction,
and Irven to contemporary Christian music.
Their patient sharing changed the course of his life.
He would once again like to say

Thank you,
Dear Friends

"Where there is no vision, the people perish."
Proverbs 29:18 KJV

⊣ ONE ⊢

Forty-One Days . . .

☐ The first Wednesday after Labor Day, Buddy rose from the nightmare like a drowning man fighting for the surface of the sea. Gasping and struggling and groping, he came awake with a hoarse shudder. It took a moment to get his breath under control before he could swing his legs to the floor and sit upright. He remained there, sitting on the side of the bed and gripping his chest against the sudden pain.

As he padded toward the bathroom, his wife asked quietly, "The dream again?"

"Yes." Buddy shut the door, stripped off his sopping pajamas, and washed his face. It had become a nightly routine. He glanced at the clock. Five o'clock in the morning. No chance of getting back to sleep.

When he came out, his wife was already up. He could hear her moving about the kitchen downstairs. He returned to the bath, ran himself a shower, and then dressed. The final words whispered through his mind the entire time, shreds of a dream which would not let go. *Forty-one days.*

He entered the kitchen to hear her say, "I'm calling the doctor first thing this morning. I want her to see you before you go to the office."

Buddy shook his head and finished knotting his tie. "What can Jasmine tell me about nightmares?"

"It's more than a nightmare, and you know it." Molly did not raise her voice. Molly seldom did. She was the quietest woman Buddy had ever known. But she held her opinions with silent conviction and protected her family with iron strength. "It's been more than two weeks now. Every night you wake up gasping and screaming and wet."

"She'll want to give me some pill." Jasmine Hopper was both their family doctor and a friend from church. "You know how I hate pills, Molly."

"Well, maybe this time you'll just have to take one." She turned to him and asked, "Eggs?"

"Why not." The wall clock read a few minutes to six. "I'll need something substantial to see me through to lunch."

"I spoke with Clarke Owen yesterday. Our prayer circle is going to start praying for you." She moved to the refrigerator and said as she returned to the stove, "Anne and Trish were over yesterday. They are going to talk with their Bible study groups and ask them to pray as well."

"For Pete's sake, Moll. You might as well have told the whole world." Clarke Owen was the assistant pastor and a close family friend. Anne and Trish were Buddy's two daughters-in-law. Good girls, but they did love to talk. "If they know, the entire town will be talking about it by dinnertime."

"A little prayer won't hurt."

"This is a whole lot more than a little."

"You're always so independent. Standing there as though nothing ever bothers you. Well, something is wrong, and I'm worried. I decided to ask almost everybody I know to help pray us through this."

Buddy stared across the counter at his wife. That was a very long speech for Molly. She was given to using one word where other women would use twenty, and to using silence most of the time. "You mustn't worry, honey."

"But I am worried. I see the way you hold your chest when you wake up. I hear how you gasp for breath, as if you can't get anything into your lungs." She brought over his plate and set it down in front of him. "Night after night I hear this. I know how you wake up soaked with sweat, how you have to lean on the wall to steady yourself when you rise."

"Aren't you having anything?"

"I'm too anxious to eat." She knotted the dish towel in her hands. The scar that emerged from her robe and covered the left side of her neck and chin was flushed with distress. "Promise me you'll call Jasmine today."

"All right." There was too much concern in her eyes for Buddy to refuse her anything. "But I'm telling you, nothing is the matter with me."

"And I'm telling you, there is. Are you having trouble at the bank?"

"Nothing to speak of." Buddy lowered his glance to stare at his food. "I'm not getting along with the director, but that's nothing new."

"You've had bad bosses before. None of them have ever bothered your sleep."

This one is different, he wanted to say, but he did not want to trouble her further. Besides, the new vice president responsible for their branch was not the reason for his nightmares. He was certain of that without knowing exactly why.

Buddy finished his breakfast in silence, accepted a topping off to his cup, and got up from the table. "I'll just go sit in the den for a while."

"Buddy—"

"If Jasmine can see me, I'll go by on the way to the office." He stooped to kiss his wife's forehead. "Don't worry, honey."

"But I do, you know." Molly gripped his wrist with surprising strength. She raised a gaze full of appeal. And fear. "I know you want to shrug it off and say this will pass. But it's gone on too long."

Nothing he could say would calm her fears. So he nodded and kissed her a second time, and left her for the quiet of the den and his morning Bible time.

☐

Yet when Buddy entered his den, it felt as though the nightmare was there waiting for him.

Living shadows seemed to creep out of the corners, whispering with the same voices that turned his spirit to jelly at night—voices he never clearly heard, except for those final words,

Forty-one days. But he knew whatever else they were saying was bad. Very bad indeed.

He started to turn and flee, but he was fearful that if he did he would never return. Which was ridiculous. The den had been his little corner of the house since before the boys were born. Yet now it was an alien place.

Buddy forced himself forward. The leather settee by the back window was his morning abode, and he was determined to conquer this silly anxiety and take his place. His big Bible sat on the side table. He fastened his attention on the Book and forced his legs to carry him forward. He almost fell into his seat. He set his coffee cup on the cork mat and then had to use his handkerchief to mop up what he spilled.

Buddy tried to still his shaking hands as he lifted the Bible. He was studying Genesis again, having decided to read the Bible from start to finish for the first time in years. He leafed through the pages, waiting expectantly for the familiar peace to arrive and his world to settle back to normalcy. Yet today it did not happen. Instead, the nightmare's lingering edges crept closer, the sense of foreboding so strong he could almost smell it.

He found his place and focused upon the page. What he found there so startled him that he clamped his eyes shut. Praying aloud he gripped his chest, trying to push the sudden clenching pain away.

□

The sky was pristine blue as Buddy drove the quiet streets of Aiden, Delaware. Yet a sense of thunder echoed in the distance. Buddy saw a neighbor wave at him, and he returned the salute. But he could not recall who it was. His mind remained fixed upon what had happened in his den. He stopped at a light and prayed once more. But this time there was a difference. The words seemed to come both from him and from beyond him. *Show me what this means*, he prayed. It was a strange experience to feel that the words were more than his own. He had never felt what others called a movement of the Spirit. Never seen any need, for that matter.

Buddy was a contented man, happy just to plod along with his own peaceable form of faith. Yet this brief prayer had come from somewhere beyond his own mind, for Buddy had no real desire of his own to know what was bothering him so. In truth, he simply wanted it to go away.

The car behind him honked politely, and Buddy opened his eyes to see the light had turned green. He gave a little wave and started forward. At that moment, the brief prayer popped back into his mind. *Father, show me what all this means. Show me what it signifies. Help me to see clearly what is intended.*

This time the prayer's impact was so strong that he was forced to put on his signal and pull over to the curb. He shut his eyes, wishing he could shut his ears as well. Once more whispers gathered around him. Once more he sensed reality being peeled back. The normalcy of his life was being stripped away.

With trembling fingers Buddy pulled the slip of paper from his shirt pocket. On it were scrawled the words he had found in his Bible that morning. His hands were shaking worse now than then.

That morning in the den the words had reached across and gripped him by the heart. They had risen up and magnified until he could see nothing else. The words had blotted out the sunshine, the birdsong, and the sound of Molly in the kitchen. There had been room for nothing but their pounding force. He had written them down, not only because he wanted to remember them but also because he needed to do something to nullify their impact.

Now Buddy was forced to prop his hand on the steering wheel to reduce the trembling while he reread the passage. There in the midst of his morning routine, halfway between his home and the bank, the words came alive once more. They reached across the distance, shouting to him with explosive force from the forty-first chapter of Genesis, a passage he had read dozens of times before and never noticed. Yet this time they drained the morning of color and sound:

> *God has shown Pharaoh what He is about to do. . . . seven years of famine will arise, and all the plenty will be forgotten in the land of Egypt; and the famine will deplete the land. So the plenty will not be known in the land because of the famine following, for it will be very severe.*

Buddy prayed once more. Anything to make this anxiety leave him alone. *Show me what this means.*

When nothing happened except an easing of the pain in his chest, he opened his eyes and put the car back in drive. As he put on his blinker and checked for oncoming traffic, he sent another quick prayer heavenward. This one asked God to keep him from going insane.

⊣∣ T W O ∣⊢

☐ "Okay, you can sit up now." Dr. Jasmine Hopper cut off the EKG machine. "How long have you had these chest pains, Buddy?"

"Hard to tell. Maybe a couple of weeks. No longer."

Dr. Jasmine Hopper was a woman of substance in every sense of the word. She was dark haired and big boned, with hands that would have suited a man, long-fingered and supple. She pulled the wires from their connectors, then began stripping the tabs and the tape from his chest. "Turn around and let me get to those on your back. Have you been under any undue pressure at work?"

"None to speak of."

Her gaze rested on him as she coiled the wires in a bundle. "What about at home? The boys doing okay?"

"The boys are fine, Jasmine. Their wives are fine. Their children are fine. Molly is fine."

"Something certainly isn't fine." She slid the long paper streamer through her fingers and tore it out of the machine. "No, leave your shirt off. I want to have another listen after I've studied the readout. I'll be right back."

The door closed behind the doctor. Buddy sat on the edge of the examining table. The room smelled faintly of some biting odor, sharp and clean. Buddy looked at his reflection in the long wall mirror. He straightened his shoulders and pulled in his gut. Even so, there was no escaping the fact that somewhere along the line middle age had sneaked up on him.

His black hair was graying but still pretty thick. Thick and straight, other than the bald spot at the back that he could usually ignore since he could not see it. He was a small man, standing just under five-foot-nine. His height had always been a disappointment, especially since his father had towered over the world. Six-foot-six his father had stood, and strong as an ox. Buddy had taken after his mother, a sparrow of a woman. It was hard to tell from whom he had gained his quiet nature, since both his parents had been tight with their words. But all his life he had wished he could have had at least a little bit more of his father's strength and height.

Buddy's father had come from the old country. That was how he had always referred to it. At the turn of the century, it was one forgotten corner of the Austro-Hungarian Empire. Then it was called Czechoslovakia for fewer than thirty years. After that the Nazis overran it and took all but the name. When Stalin assumed power he replaced one form of tyranny for another.

With democracy came independence, and the old country split in two.

Now the old country was Slovakia and the Czech Republic, and Buddy did not even know from which part his father's family had come. His father had almost never spoken of what he had left behind. His father had been nine when his own father, Buddy's grandfather, had pulled up the family and brought them to America. As far as Buddy's father had been concerned, it was America first and last. Whenever the old country had been mentioned in the news, Buddy's father had listened with a sort of bemused satisfaction, very glad in his silent way to be here and to be an American.

His father had been a handyman and carpenter and cabinetmaker. Buddy was the first of their family ever to graduate from college, the only occasion in Buddy's entire life when he saw his father cry. When Buddy had left for his new job at the then Aiden Bank, his father had been so proud he could have burst his shirt buttons. A picture of Buddy taken that first morning, dressed in his spanking new suit and tie, had stood on his parents' mantelpiece for as long as they had been alive.

"There is no indication whatsoever of any cardiac arrest." Dr. Hopper interrupted Buddy's musings as she shut the door behind her. She pulled the stethoscope from her pocket and fitted the earpieces into place. "Let's have another listen."

Buddy submitted to the quiet inspection, breathing as instructed. He was glad beyond words that his worst fear had proved to be groundless.

When she finally straightened, Jasmine went on. "I can't find a thing wrong with you."

"You don't sound very pleased about it."

"You say you've been having severe chest pains for the first time in your life. Generally this can be traced to some specific physiological change or new source of stress."

"I can't think of anything."

"Yet Molly says you've been having nightmares that leave you dripping wet and gasping for breath. Do the chest pains come with the dreams?"

"Yes." Able to be honest about it, now that it was not life threatening. His father had died from heart failure, keeled over three days before his sixtieth birthday. "Every night."

"You have had the same dream each night? For how long?"

"Just over two weeks." And each night the mysterious countdown continued. *Forty-one days.* But no need to mention that.

"You can put your shirt back on now. Can you tell me what the dream is about?"

"Ordinary things." Buddy hid his sudden discomfort by turning and reaching for his shirt. He ducked his head to fasten the buttons. "I'm in the bank and then on the street downtown. Nothing that should scare me."

"Try to remember. Did anything out of the ordinary happen the first day? The day of your first nightmare?"

Buddy thought back. "Well, yes, but nothing that serious. The monthly business forecast arrived. The bank subscribes to it; all the bank's managers receive a copy."

"Bad news?"

"No, as a matter of fact it was all good." Too good. That had been his reaction. Buddy recalled it clearly. Strange how he could have forgotten that until now. But that had been his reaction the *instant* he had read the headlines.

Inflation was back under control, the statement had read. Interest rates were on the way back down. Employment figures were stable, factory orders in good shape, consumer confidence sound, housing starts up for the third month running. It looked to be a banner autumn for the stock market and a great final quarter to the year.

But Buddy's response had been entirely different. The paper had seemed alive in his hands. And despite the rosy forecast, he had felt a rising sense of dread. It had seemed as though barriers separating him from the future were being rolled back, until before him lay only bleakness and sorrow.

He looked up to find Jasmine Hopper watching him closely. This was one of the qualities that endeared Jasmine to her charges and made them friends as well as patients. She would stand and wait with them, working not just to treat the ailment but also to find the cause. "Something bad?"

"No. Well, yes. But not . . ." He stopped. There was no way he could put into words what he had felt that day.

Her eyes narrowed at his inability to continue. "Buddy, I could give you a prescription that will help you sleep. But I don't think that's what you want."

"No," he agreed, definite on that point.

"Do you have a psychiatrist you could speak to? I could suggest one if you like."

His mouth opened and closed a couple of times before he could manage, "I don't think that's necessary."

"What about one of our pastors? Somebody you can trust with your darkest secrets?"

"Yes."

"Something is trying to work its way out. That's my guess. Talking to a trusted professional is perhaps what you need to put all this behind you."

"I'll think about it."

"I want you to do more than think. I want you to act." She moved for the door. "And if the chest pains grow any worse or start appearing at other times, I want you to call me immediately."

"All right."

"For that matter, make an appointment to see me next week, regardless." She nodded and gave a brisk smile. "Remember me to Molly."

⊣∥ THREE ∥⊢

☐ When Buddy arrived home that evening, his older boy, Paul, was sitting at the kitchen table. Somehow his father's height and strength had managed to skip a generation, bounding straight over Buddy's head and landing in his son. Nobody had any idea where his son had obtained his blond looks, however. Paul looked like a giant Swede—hair almost white, skin reddened by twenty minutes in spring sunshine, eyes the color of an early morning sky.

Jack, his second boy, was stamped from Buddy's mold. He had the same small build, the same intent air, the same dark hair and eyes. Jack was a lawyer with one of the local firms, a member of the town council, and a quiet bastion of their community.

Paul was as gentle as he was big. Both Buddy's boys were. Their gentleness had been a source of great concern to Buddy when the boys had been younger. Buddy had pushed them as hard as he could manage, trying to instill in them a need to excel and to do the most with what they had.

"Hello, Son."

"What did the doctor say, Pop?"

"Clean bill of health." But Buddy's eyes were not on Paul. They were on his wife. The scar that began just below her left ear and spilled down her chin and disappeared into her high collar was red as a beet. This was a signal of strong emotion. Anger, happiness, sadness, distress, joy—it did not matter. Whatever Molly felt, if she felt it strongly, was displayed the length and breadth of her scar. Molly was so quiet that this was often his only signal that she had been hit hard by something while he had been away. And right now it was blazing as if lit by an internal fire. "Anything wrong?"

"No, not wrong." Paul had a glow of quiet satisfaction about him. He set his mug down. "Mom tells me the dreams are still bothering you."

"From time to time." Buddy kissed his wife and studied her gaze. He saw a gentle joy in her eyes. He sighed silently with relief. Whatever had her so worked up was good. "But my health is sound, and that's what matters."

Molly asked, "And your heart?"

"Fit as a fiddle, according to Jasmine." He accepted a mug and seated himself across from his son.

"That's good, Pop. Real good. We've been worried."

"No need." He took a sip and gave thanks for the umpteenth time for having been blessed with two quiet and well-behaved sons. He did not know how they would have coped with loud or rambunctious children. He and Molly were simply not made for confrontation and anger. In their twenty-nine years together, he did not think he had ever shouted at her. Not once. It was just not their way. "Dr. Hopper wants to have another look at me at the end of next week, but she thinks everything is all right."

"I'm glad you talked with her," Molly said. "But I'm still worried about those nightmares."

He nodded, not wanting to go into that. He was glad his son was there; he was glad that something else in the air kept them from dwelling on what he still did not understand. "What brings you over today?"

Paul and Molly exchanged a look that filled the room with shared anticipation. Paul turned back to him and announced, "We've decided to expand. We're going to set up a second store in the new shopping mall."

This should have been the best possible news. Buddy had been after Paul for years to start a second shoe store. But his son was naturally cautious. Running one successful shop had been enough. Even when Buddy had walked him through the statistics and the calculations, shown him how he was being over-charged for his product, and pointed out to him how fragile his outlook was with just one source of revenue, his son had held back. Until now.

Yet Buddy felt none of the pride and satisfaction that he would have expected. Instead he felt a sense of danger.

Molly prompted Buddy with her words. "Son, that's wonderful."

Paul fiddled self-consciously with his mug. "I'll be coming in tomorrow to meet with you, Pop. I just wanted to let you know in advance that we're going to do it like you said. Keep our savings in place and borrow what we need, so we can write off the interest."

The words wrapped around Buddy in a veil of dread. "I'm not sure that's a good idea."

Paul's eyes widened in surprise. "But why, Daddy?"

It was the first time Paul had called him Daddy in years. Why, indeed? Buddy could not explain it, even to himself. Yet the dread continued to build, like floodwater rising to surround him. "I'm not sure now is a good time to saddle yourself with more debt."

His words were met with absolute silence. Molly slipped into the chair beside her son. "You've been after him for years to start that second store."

"I know I have." He rubbed his palms together, wiping away the dampness. He asked Paul, "Could you put off the decision for a while?"

"I suppose so." Paul was watching him strangely. They both were. "For how long?"

Despite his strongest efforts to keep it at bay, the pressure continued to mount. Once more an unseen force seemed to push at him and to squeeze his mind and his heart so tightly he could scarcely draw breath. "Two months," he managed. His voice sounded weak to his own ears. "Wait two months."

Paul looked frustrated. "And then?"

The idea popped straight into his head and exploded with the force of a skyrocket. Buddy said, "I've decided to sell the ridgeline."

Both his son and his wife gaped at him. "What?"

"Tomorrow. Those developers were back again yesterday. They want to build a hotel."

"But, honey." Molly's voice sounded as weak as his own. "You've always said that was for our retirement."

The ridgeline was a strip of land Buddy had bought soon after his first son was born. The bank had offered their employees low-interest mortgages, which had been a relatively cheap way for the bank to ensure employee stability. Instead of using the money to buy a larger home, however, Buddy had purchased the ridgeline from an aging farmer. The land totaled almost forty acres and overlooked the town and the interstate. Every year or so, some developer approached him with another deal.

"It's time to sell, that's all. We'll still have the cash." Buddy kept his eyes on his son. It was easier than meeting Molly's troubled gaze. "Wait two months. If you still want to go ahead, I'll lend you the money interest free."

Molly asked quietly, "What's wrong, honey?"

He could not put her off any longer. And he owed Paul that much, dashing his son's hopes as he had. "Nothing I can put my finger on. Nothing I can give any name to. But I've had the feeling for more than two weeks now that something is going to happen. Something bad."

There. It was finally out in the open. Words to clothe the rising dread. "Something awful," he went on, "an economic downturn or cyclical correction. I know everything looks rosy right now. And I feel like a fool for being so worried. But I am."

Buddy studied each of their faces in turn. "I have the strongest feeling that we're headed into the worst recession any of us has ever experienced."

He sighed with sudden release. The act of speaking had eased the pressure as inexplicably as Paul's announcement had brought it on. He steeled himself for their criticism.

Yet the ensuing quiet held none of the condemnation Buddy had feared. In fact, his son's face seemed to clear up and relax. Even Molly's concern eased.

Paul said, "It makes sense, Pop."

"It certainly does," Molly agreed.

Both of the men looked at her in surprise. Molly dropped her gaze. "Oh, I don't know the first thing about economics, but you'd be surprised what people say to a quiet person. Maybe they think they're safe, that I don't understand or won't repeat what I hear. And they're right. But I do hear things, and what I hear I take in. There isn't a single woman in my Bible study who isn't worried about money. Not one."

"It sure is strange," Paul agreed. "People have good jobs; they're making good money. But everybody's afraid."

"They buy things they don't want," Molly continued in her quiet way. "They go into debt and hate themselves for it."

"As if they can't control their own actions," Paul added.

"Or they sense that something is happening and feel powerless to do anything," Molly agreed. "Running faster and faster after something they'll never have."

Buddy stared at his wife in absolute astonishment. "Of all the things I might have expected you to say, this would have been the last."

"People are frightened of tomorrow," Molly said.

"I am too," Paul confessed. "I've put it down to nerves over starting another store. Like you said, Pop, everything *seems* to be fine. But what my mind says and what my heart tells me are two very different things."

There was a moment's silence before Molly asked her husband, "Does this have anything to do with those nightmares of yours?"

"Yes," Buddy replied, and he realized he was also admitting it to himself. "But it's not just the dreams. There have been other things. In the office, and during my quiet times."

Molly's gaze was level, deep. "Has the Lord spoken to you?"

Hearing the words he had been afraid to think left Buddy floundering. He opened his mouth, closed it, and finally managed, "I'm not sure."

⊣‖ F O U R ‖⊢

Forty Days . . .

☐ The nightmare came again just before dawn.
The dream was as bad as usual, the awakening as wrenching. Molly watched him rise, go to the bathroom, and return
wearing fresh pajamas. This time she said nothing; she only lay
her hand upon his shoulder as once more he settled into bed. But
as Buddy drifted off to sleep again, he thought he heard a hint
of murmured prayer.

The half-heard whispers remained with him through his
shower and breakfast and prayer time. He heard them again on
the way to work. They were there with him in the car, vague
murmurs that were more than lingering tendrils of a bad dream.
Yet try as he might, pray as he would, he could not seem to work
it all out.

□

Upon entering the bank Thursday morning, Buddy felt every vestige of the dream and the uncertainty disappear, which was strange, since the nightmare's first scene was always in the bank's main foyer. Even so, the night's distress was pushed aside by what he saw as soon as he walked through the big main doors.

Aiden was a middling town abutting the steep hills lining Delaware's inner border. It was too far from the big cities of Washington, Philadelphia, and Baltimore to have ever known the explosive growth that gripped much of the surrounding regions. Buddy had never minded. He had grown up here and had never wanted to live anywhere else. He liked the quiet attractive little town just the way it was.

The bank where Buddy worked was almost one hundred fifty years old. Seventeen years ago, however, the Aiden Merchant Bank had been taken over. The Valenti Banking Group had swallowed many such small banks, allowing it to dominate local markets. At the time, Buddy had been the bank's assistant manager and had wondered for weeks and months if he was going to keep his job. But Buddy had earned many friends within the local market, people who made it clear to the newly imported branch manager that their business would leave with Buddy.

In time, the incoming managers recognized that Buddy was the genuine article, a local man with local savvy. They sweetened his paycheck, for other banks were also seeking to make inroads into communities like Aiden.

A year later, Buddy was offered a major promotion and the chance to take over loan operations at another branch in another small town, one where they were having trouble making contacts within the local business community. Buddy turned them down flat. Eighteen months later came another offer. This time, Buddy told them the only way he was leaving Aiden was in a pine box. They got the message and left well enough alone.

But the Valenti group had a strict policy that each promotion required a move. Every man or woman on the rise thus came to know different divisions and different branches. And equally important was the fact that a person who was shifted around did not put down deep roots. Their first loyalty remained to the bank and not the community—which was exactly why Buddy refused to move.

This was also why he was so enraged upon entering the bank. These people were more than citizens of his hometown. They were part of his extended family. And Buddy's first glance was enough to tell him that one of his group was in dire trouble.

He had been concerned from the outset about hiring such an attractive and vivacious woman for the job of teller. But bank teller jobs were some of the lowest paid in town, and when the job market was tight, it was not always possible to hire people with families and thus greater stability. This was exactly what Buddy wanted in anyone who was going to be handling the bank's money day in, day out.

But Sally had seemed a proper kind of young lady, despite her bubbly personality and good looks, and the public liked her. Some of their older clients waited until she was free so they could stand and flirt a bit. Buddy did not mind in the slightest, so long as the bank was not too busy. After all, these clients' money kept their bank in business. If they enjoyed chatting with a cute young teller, that was fine and good.

But it was not a client who was making the teller's giggles ring like chimes through the bank's quiet air. Leaning across the partition that separated Sally's station from the next was the bank's new manager, Thaddeus Dorsett.

Since the takeover by the Valenti Banking Group, Buddy had endured eleven branch managers. Eleven in seventeen years. But Thad Dorsett was the first one since Valenti had itself been acquired by the famous New York tycoon Nathan Jones Turner. Thad Dorsett was also the first manager Buddy had ever genuinely disliked.

Thad Dorsett was a trader, imported from the financial markets of Chicago, the first one Buddy had ever met face-to-face. Buddy knew the bank now had a policy of promoting managers up from the ranks of their traders. And on paper this made sense. After all, traders were now responsible for more than half the bank's total profit. Buddy tried not to let Thad's background affect his thinking, but it was very hard. Buddy held a strong aversion to traders and all they stood for.

In their first conversation that previous winter, Thad's gaze had lingered on the silver cross in Buddy's lapel. He had smirked a little with the corners of his mouth, as though seeing the cross had confirmed something Thad had either heard about or expected to find. Then he had said, "You know, I actually attended seminary."

Of all the things Buddy had expected to hear from the new branch manager, this was the last. "You did?"

"One semester. Never even took my finals. I did it for dear old Dad, who was a preacher. And my grandfather. And the one before that, for all I know. It was all I heard about when I was growing up. This family tradition." His smile was larger this time. "But after I got there, I decided I'd rather serve mammon than heaven."

Buddy had felt like he had just swallowed a mouthful of quinine.

Now he walked across the lobby's parquet floor, under the huge brass-and-smoked-glass chandelier, and through the little gate separating the bank's office area from the main chamber. His secretary, Lorraine, was already at her desk. Her face was clamped into a harsh line, which was very strange, as Lorraine had one of the sweetest natures Buddy had ever come across. But she was staring at Thad Dorsett as he hummed his conversation across the partition to where Sally was smiling and setting up for the day. And Buddy remembered four months earlier, when he had come in and found Lorraine weeping bitterly at her desk, while Thad Dorsett whistled and chatted with one employee after another, pretending that nothing was wrong and that he had not just broken the heart of Buddy's secretary and very good friend.

Buddy walked straight over to where Thad was standing and said, "Can I have a word with you?"

Thad was slow in turning. The movement was a silent warning that he was not in a mood to be disturbed. He had a lot of moves like this, tight looks and silent signals. The branch employees were frightened by this outsider and normally kept their distance. But Thad also possessed a remarkable magnetism. Thad's gaze finally came around, and he said coolly, "It can wait, Korda."

But Buddy did not let him turn back around. He put an emphasis to his words, one he had not used since his boys had reached manhood. "*Now,* Thad."

Buddy walked back to his office. Passing Lorraine's desk, he exchanged a glance. Her eyes still bore the pain and sadness of a woman betrayed. Buddy stiffened his resolve. Which was helpful, because Buddy was no good at confrontation. He hated it, in fact. He would go around the block backward to avoid an argument. Yet there he was, picking a quarrel with his own boss. Buddy stood by his desk and watched through the glass wall as Thad approached.

Buddy's office was in the corner of the bank, with two walls of waist-high oiled wood and then tall panes of glass rising to the ceiling. Only the manager's office was completely enclosed. Yet Buddy loved the openness of his office, loved the way he could observe the entire operation. The glass, which had been put in when the bank was built, had beveled edges with hand-carved vines and flowers rising up each side. Over the past century and a half, the panes had gradually begun to warp. As Thad approached, his appearance waxed and waned, like a colorful apparition that was not entirely genuine.

Thaddeus Dorsett was the picture of a modern-day buccaneer, and he told anyone willing to listen that he was wasting his life away in Aiden. He was twenty years younger than Buddy and on the bank's fast track. His hair was dark and so thick it bunched and waved even when tightly slicked back. His face was angled and strong. His eyes were such a light green that in the morning sun they appeared flecked with gold. Thad had learned to use them well, and even now he opened them in a parody of innocence. "You had something that couldn't wait?"

Buddy had seen that innocent look before. It was Thad's way of covering a fast-moving mind. Sunlight streamed through the back window and turned Thad's eyes the color of a big cat's.

"The Valenti Bank has a strict policy against fraternization between managers and staff."

"Fraternization, what a quaint word." He cast a wide-eyed gaze about the room. "It suits you, Korda."

"I want you to stop flirting with Sally, Thad. It's a dangerous sport, and it disrupts the bank's smooth running."

"My, my. Aren't we on our moral high horse today?" Thaddeus Dorsett stepped closer, trying to use his superior height to intimidate. "In case you haven't noticed, Korda, you're speaking to your boss."

Buddy resisted the urge to step back. "If you don't stop this now, I'm going to report the matter to the head office."

"Report what?" Thad sneered. "That I was taking time before the bank opened to be nice to our newest employee?"

"I wasn't planning to report Sally," Buddy replied. "And I would substantiate my report with another one from Lorraine."

Like a veil dropping silently to the floor, Thad's round-eyed innocence slipped away. In its place rose a silent rage. Thad took another step closer, until Buddy could smell the coffee on his breath. His gaze was feral, his tone furious. "That's just the kind of spiteful attitude I'd expect from a backwater imbecile like you, Korda."

Buddy held to his course but could not keep the quaver from his voice. "Lorraine approached me last week about lodging a complaint, and I said—"

"I don't care what you've been sermonizing to your secretary." Thad wheeled about, stalked to the door, and stopped long enough to throw back, "For your information, Korda, Lorraine was chasing me."

Thad slammed the door hard enough to make the panes rattle. Buddy said to the empty room, "That's a lie. I was watching, you know." Then his strength left him, and he slumped into his chair. He hated confrontations. He really did.

A soft knock brought his head back up. Lorraine entered, her face wreathed in concern. "Would you like a cup of coffee?"

"Not right now, thank you." He glanced at his watch and rose to his feet. "I've got an appointment with some developers at their offices."

As he passed by Lorraine to reenter the main chamber, she patted his arm. "You did the right thing."

"I hope so," he sighed.

"Believe me, you did."

Something in her tone halted Buddy. He looked at his secretary and saw wounds that still had not healed. Lorraine went on, "He will do anything and say anything to get what he wants. Anything at all."

"I'm very sorry," Buddy said quietly.

"You know what they say." Her mouth twisted in a sad smile. "Big-city ways and small-town girls are a terrible mix."

☐

Buddy walked back through the bank and entered the day's gathering heat. The developers' offices were about two blocks away. When he had called that morning from home to say he was ready to sell the ridgeline, the developer had instantly replied that he would prepare the contract for him to sign. And the check. It was the smoothest real estate transaction Buddy had ever heard of. Odd how something like this could seem so strange and yet so right at the same time. As though his actions were guided by something far greater than himself.

As he crossed the street, the nightmares that were behind his decision to sell the ridgeline struck him with the sunlight. The only words that had been clearly audible returned to him, as though the whispers had penetrated the day and his wakened state. *Forty days.*

Buddy clasped his hand over his heart and hurried onward. He could not help but wonder how he had remained perfectly all right through such a confrontation with his boss yet now was being attacked by a dream.

□

"Don't even think about it," the voice on the other end of the phone commanded. "Put it out of your head."

Thad Dorsett stared out his sunlit window. "But Keith—"

"I'm telling you to forget it. Have you spoken about it with anyone else?"

"Not yet." The harsh tone confused him. Keith Wilkes was Thad Dorsett's chief sponsor within the branch. He was also senior vice president and the man who had personally hired Thad away from Chicago Mercantile. "Why?"

"Because you might as well shoot yourself in the foot as complain about Buddy Korda. Do you know how many branch managers he has ushered through since the original takeover?"

"Keith, the guy is so far over the hill he's sunk in the valley on the other side."

"Eleven. Eleven branch managers who are now senior executives. One of whom is now the bank's executive vice president, and another is a member of the board. All of them remember their time with Buddy as a real training ground. Do you hear what I'm saying? This guy may be as aggressive as a bath towel and a throwback to the last century, but he is also very well connected."

Thad had not expected this. "Keith, you don't have to work with the guy every day. He's a total waste of time."

"And I'm telling you that complaints like this will earn you nothing but enemies! Do you have any idea how hard I had to fight to get you this post?" Keith had to take a moment to get his impatience back under control. "We've been through this how many times? It's bank policy that every senior executive has to spend at least a year in a local branch. Buddy's branch has the lowest level of bad debts and the highest return on dollars spent. Staff turnover is low, morale is high, and business is growing."

"It's also like living in a crypt. This place has all the life of a funeral parlor."

"Then have yourself a few weekend trips to New York. I'm telling you, bank execs take a close look at your performance at the branch level. And being on Buddy's team is almost a guarantee of success."

"It's not Buddy's team, it's *mine*. And I want to fire the guy."

Keith's tone turned razor sharp. "You do that and the only way you'll restart your career will be through reincarnation."

"Can you at least shorten my assignment here?"

"I doubt it, but I'll see. In the meantime, put up with the guy. Laugh at his small-town ways. Everybody else does. But don't complain. It's suicide, I'm telling you."

Thad Dorsett kept his calm until the phone was back in place. Then he allowed his rage to build, a flood that turned his vision red. He hated being told what to do. Hated even more having his plans thwarted, especially by some small-town wimp in a suit straight from the fifties. Buddy Korda, what a name. With his starched shirt and dark tie, he looked like an undertaker and talked like a pallbearer. Never raised his voice. Never spoke back to him, not once, until this morning.

Thad was so angry he shook. A little fun never hurt anybody, and that's all he was after with these small-town girls. A little fun. Something to spice up the time until he could be up and out of here.

Thad bundled up the page he had been scribbling on, clenching it tighter and tighter until it was a solid ball the size of his thumb and threw it at the trash can. Nobody got in his way. Nobody. Especially not some assistant manager in Podunk, Delaware. He was trapped in a town nobody ever visited, much less called home. If he had known it was the bank's plan to stick him out here in the boonies for a year he would never have taken the job. A *year*.

Thad bounced from his chair and began stalking the floor. There had to be something he could do, someone who would understand. He stopped, staring sightlessly at the window. Perhaps he should contact Nathan Jones Turner's office directly. Spell it out. Thad was a trader, used to a trader's life. Cut him a break or risk losing one of their fast-track managers. Perhaps even talk to a couple of headhunters beforehand, make sure word got back to headquarters in New York. Something definitely had to happen. He was suffocating in this place.

⊣| FIVE |⊢

☐ Buddy was so tired that evening he could scarcely finish dinner. When Molly shooed him away from the table and ordered him to bed he did not object, not even when he saw the clock on the mantel read seven-thirty.

Buddy stopped to lean on the wall twice as he climbed the stairs. He undressed in a stupor. The doctor's visit, the quarrel with Thad, the daily bank stresses and strains, two and a half weeks of bad dreams and not enough sleep, the talk with his family and having his concerns finally out in the open—all the recent strains left him exhausted. He was asleep before his head hit the pillow.

There was no escaping the dream. Not this time. He was too tired. There was no normal drifting into the dream either. Buddy fell like a stone.

And yet, and yet. The dream was different this time. Very different. Sharper. More carefully defined. So crystal clear it did not seem like a dream. His every sense was heightened above the norm.

Not only that. The dream was no longer a nightmare. How he could be so certain the instant it began, he did not know. But it was not a nightmare anymore. At least, not a nightmare for him.

Buddy stood in the bank's central hall. Just like every other entry into the dream, he did a slow sweep of the grand old chamber. Only this time the scene was far more vivid. Dust motes danced lazy circles in the sunlight streaming through the top of the side windows. The blinds on the bottom halves of the tall windows were closed, as they always were until about a half hour before opening time.

Old Carl, the bank's morning guard, leaned against the wall just inside the main doors. He was no longer needed, what with the bank's modern security system. But Buddy had insisted that Carl be kept on, a bastion of the service and the heritage the bank stood for. In his dream Buddy raised his hand in a half wave but was not surprised when Carl did not respond.

What did surprise him, however, was the fact that Carl did not move at the sound of weeping. Generally he was on the spot whenever someone needed assistance, be it customer or clerk. But Carl just stood there, staring into space with a bemused expression, bemused and so shaken that his features made him look even more aged than he already was. His cap was pushed back on his balding head, and he stared across the chamber at nothing.

Still the weeping went on. Buddy made a gradual revolution. Everything seemed to be in slow motion, as though an invisible hand were guiding him, silently urging him to take everything in deep.

He saw that the wall clock showed ten minutes until opening time. Normally the venetian blinds would have been opened on all the windows by then. Yet the bank remained partly shrouded in shadows, while light through the windows' top half-circles sent beams of brilliance lancing across the room.

This was as far as he had ever continued in the dream. By this point, the sense of pressure had squeezed him from sleep like a seed shot out between thumb and forefinger. That tension was still there, but it was no longer directed at him. Which was very strange, for he could now sense a wrath behind the pressure.

His turning continued until the back half of the bank came into view. Lorraine sat at her desk, her eyes pressed into a handkerchief, her shoulders shaking hard. Buddy remained unmoved by this sight. Normally he would have rushed over and demanded to know what was the matter. Now he only continued to turn. And he realized that it was not only Lorraine who cried. Every one of the tellers was weeping.

The bank director's door was wide open. No one was inside. Nor was anyone in Buddy's office, which gave him a brief moment of relief. Even from within this protective cocoon, he would not have wanted to come face-to-face with himself in a dream, especially if he was to see himself crying. For somehow he knew a tragedy had struck. Not a dream affliction. Something real. Some cataclysmic event had buffeted the bank, and it was a genuine comfort not to find himself there sobbing with the others. It was very selfish. But it was also very true.

The slow circle continued until he faced back toward the bank's main doors just in time to hear the clock strike nine.

Carl pulled himself together enough to fumble with the lock. Buddy wanted to remind them to open the blinds and get ready for business, but he could not speak. He could only watch as the locks were released and the door slammed back, sending Carl sprawling onto the floor. The old man did not move. He remained where he was as a flood of humanity streamed inside.

Shouting, screaming, pushing, fighting, and clawing toward the teller windows. Hundreds and hundreds of people. People Buddy had known all his life, their faces distorted until they were strangers. Foreigners who were gripped by universal terror. They pounded fists upon the counter and teller windows, waved checkbooks and canes and papers in the air, screamed words that were lost in the crush as still more people pressed through the doors.

Buddy wanted to stay. He wanted to help, to find some way to calm them. He had never felt so horrified in his entire life. And yet, and yet. It was no surprise. Somehow he had sensed this from the very beginning. As though the instant the very first nightmare had attacked him, he had known this was what was behind it all.

Disaster.

But the invisible hand did not allow him to linger. Instead, he rose and floated over the crowd, passing through the tall main doors. Over the heads of those still fighting to get inside, across the street filled with even more people, beyond those who stood weeping and watching on the opposite sidewalk. On into the heart of his little town.

Aiden was as alien as its citizens. Gone was the cozy atmosphere he had known since childhood. Vanished was the feeling that here the world was a slower, kinder place. In its stead was an impression of *burden*.

The pressure was clearer because it was directed away from him. The force seemed to begin directly behind him, shooting out over his shoulders and his head, filling the world with wrath. Yet it was more than anger. It was an all-powerful force, filled with unimaginable sorrow. A strength so overwhelming nothing could stand in its path. Wrath and sorrow. Determination and vengeance. And it was here. In Aiden.

The roads were filled with cars that had simply stopped, as though the drivers had vanished and the cars had continued until something impeded their progress. Their doors were open and flapping in the hot autumn breeze. People clustered here and there, or moved aimlessly. In and out of doorways, up and down the sidewalks and the streets. Or they sat head-in-hand on the curb. Even from this height Buddy could see they were weeping.

□

"Buddy? Honey?"

He rose to a seated position and swung his legs to the floor. "It's all right."

In the bed beside him, Molly lifted herself on one arm. "Sweetheart, are you crying?"

He rose and shuffled toward the bathroom, wiping his streaming eyes with his sleeve. "It's all right, Molly. Go back to sleep."

He closed the door but did not turn on the light. He leaned on the wall next to the sink. There was enough light from the window to show his outline in the mirror. The clock on the shelf glowed, but his eyes were still too blurred to read the time. It did not matter.

He turned on the faucet and washed his face. There was no need to undress, for there had been no sweats with this dream. But it had not been a dream. Buddy did not know how he could be so certain about something like that. But he knew. This was no dream. It was a message.

The whisper came then, no longer simply a memory from the vanished dream. He heard the words so clearly they might as well have been spoken aloud. *Thirty-nine days.*

As he dried his face he knew what he had told his wife was totally, utterly wrong. Things were not all right. They never would be again.

⊣| SIX |⊢

Thirty-Nine Days . . .

☐ The limousine turned up Broadway and halted once more in midtown Manhattan traffic. Nathan Jones Turner fumed to his assistant, "The mayor has one. So does the governor. I'm more powerful than either one. If they don't think so, I'll be happy to put on a little demonstration."

"Sir, I've spoken to both their personal aides. There's some city ordinance that outlaws police motorcades for anyone except visiting politicians and dignitaries."

"They don't think I'm a dignitary? They think somebody from the other side of the Atlantic's got more clout than me? I'll show them just how much clout I've got if they keep me sitting here." He leaned forward and shouted through the half-open portal, "Get the lead out! You think I pay you to keep me sitting still?"

"I'm doing the best I can, Mr. Turner."

"It's not good enough!" He pounded on the armrest hard enough to make his assistant wince. "If you can't find a way to get me there faster, I'll find someone who can!"

To the driver's immense relief, an ambulance chose that moment to sweep around the corner, turning on both lights and siren. The driver eased over just far enough to permit the ambulance passage, then swept back inches from the rear bumper, cutting off a taxi trying for the coveted spot. He sailed down the block, the ambulance now forging a path for them both.

Nathan Jones Turner settled back. "That's better. Nothing I hate worse than sitting still."

"Yes, sir," the assistant agreed, pushing forward the file he held in his hands. "If you'll take a look at this—"

"Sitting still is for peons. You call the governor and you tell him that right to his face. Tell him if he's going to try to make Nathan Jones Turner sit still, he'll find somebody else sitting in his chair. You tell him that."

"Yes, Mr. Turner. Sir, you said you wanted to study the closing positions in Tokyo."

"I've read them already. Put that thing away." He drummed his fingers on the window. "You say they both refused me a police escort?"

"Point-blank, sir."

"Put them down for my box at the next Jets game. I'll have a word with them personally."

"Yes, sir. That'll be the season opener next week." To sit in the private box of Nathan Jones Turner, especially when the Jets finally had a chance to return to the Super Bowl, was one of the most coveted invitations in all New York. Turner was the team's largest shareholder, and he treated it like a personal fiefdom.

Nathan Jones Turner, the son of a middling Hollywood movie producer, had taken an inheritance of some ten million dollars and turned it into one of the largest privately held fortunes in America's history. *Forbes* magazine was consistently wrong in judging his wealth, but last year had accurately placed his stock and bond holdings *alone* at over a billion dollars. Besides that, he owned a hotel chain, a Wall Street brokerage firm, some Manhattan real estate. And the Valenti Bank.

His only two hobbies were his father's old movie production company and the New York Jets. He had been married five times to four different women and had fathered seven children, all of whom he had long since disowned. He was seventy-one years old and worked an eighteen-hour day.

He was pompous, rude, and tremendously overbearing. He could be courtly, however, when it suited him. He also possessed the ability to focus on a person with a force that people claimed was physically palpable. When he liked an idea he adopted it as an original thought. He managed to hold on to talent because he paid better than anyone else, but in return he expected his staff to demonstrate slavelike devotion. Dissent was an unforgivable error. The only person allowed to have a temper around Nathan Jones Turner was Nathan Jones Turner.

Most of his time he spent working from the Turner farm in Connecticut. Located just forty miles from Manhattan, the farm was a six-hundred-eighty-acre spread with almost a mile of coveted private beach.

But today's meeting required his personal presence. Nobody tried to transport the senior staff of a brokerage house away from Wall Street while the market was in session. Not even Nathan Jones Turner.

The Turner Building anchored the corner of Wall Street and Broadway. It had been built in the twenties, redolent of art-deco foppery, and was the second highest building in that part of town. Only the Chrysler Building was higher. Turner would have preferred to buy the Chrysler Building, but it wasn't for sale, and it didn't stand on Wall Street. He responded by pretending the Chrysler Building did not exist.

Greed might have lost much of its eighties allure elsewhere, but not on Wall Street. In today's financial markets, an investor could win or lose more quickly than a bettor at any racetrack or casino—and lose far more. This was the mad world of modern money, where billions changed hands every hour, and where gambling had become the norm.

This was the real reason Turner came here at all—to feel close to the action, to drink the energy, to get a sense of the market's pulse. It was as close as Nathan Jones Turner ever came to taking any drug. He neither smoked nor drank and seldom took anything stronger than an aspirin. When he felt the need for a fix, something to push him to a higher limit, he wallowed in the thrill of chasing money. And the power of controlling its course.

Before the limo pulled to a halt, three senior executives scurried out to welcome Turner. He ignored their greetings and marched straight to the elevators.

Nathan Jones Turner hated elevators. He managed to ride in silence by gritting his teeth and clenching his fists. His staff had long since learned that anything said during an elevator ride was not heard. So the ride was made in absolute silence. The one nice thing about riding with Nathan Jones Turner was that the elevator halted for nobody. The security guard responsible for the bank of elevators was on notice that if an elevator carrying Nathan Jones Turner stopped on any floor except the one where he was getting off, the guard was out of a job.

They finally stopped on the sixtieth floor and headed for the double doors at the foyer's far end. The secretary stationed there merely stood and smiled a nervous welcome as Turner and his entourage entered the lair of Larry Fleiss.

Larry Fleiss was one of the world's most successful traders. Which was why Nathan Jones Turner willingly paid him almost six million dollars in annual salary and double that in bonus. He was certainly nothing much to look at, and his personality was hardly any better.

He looked like a bespectacled slug, clad in a wrinkled white shirt and beltless trousers. He remained safely ensconced behind his huge U-shaped desk, not even rising for Nathan Jones Turner himself. Instead he glanced over, waved the entourage in, then turned back to his monitors. Someone on the speakerphone was shouting, "It hasn't changed positions since I was in your office."

"Yeah, well." Fleiss gave a laconic shrug. "You had the chance to say no before we got started."

Fleiss hit the switch and set down the coffee mug, his eyes tracking the group as they seated themselves. "How's it going, Mr. T.?"

"You tell me." Nathan Jones Turner tolerated such ill manners from no one but Fleiss. It was one of the prices he paid to keep the man behind the powerboard. That was Fleiss's name for his desk. The powerboard controlled the flow of the bank's and Turner's own money every day. Fleiss was rumored to spend more time at his desk than even Turner himself.

"Market's nervous this morning. Needs a tweak." Fleiss had the hoarse voice of an adrenaline junkie. His gaze constantly shifted back and forth, from Turner's face to the scrolling blue screen set in his side panel. The front of the blond-wood desk was bare save for a coffeemaker, two mugs, a pitcher of fresh cream, and an empty leather blotter. The desk's two long extensions, however, looked like imports from a flight control tower. They contained seventeen television screens, six phones with multiple lines, two computers, and a constantly scrolling news service. "Given a strong kick it could go either way."

"That's the same thing you told me last week."

"Nothing's changed, Mr. T. Everybody seems to be waiting for someone to tell them which way to jump."

Instead of waiting respectfully for Turner to respond, Fleiss punched a speed-dial number and demanded, "Anything happening post ten o'clock with your stuff?"

"No, looks like people have been kicked around too much." The voice on the other end shared Larry Fleiss's dislike for small talk. "The only sure bet is yen. It keeps falling like a stone."

Nathan Jones Turner kept his inscrutable mask intact. But inwardly he tasted bile.

Hastily Fleiss clicked off and tried to cover. "Problematic. Real problematic. People are just waiting for somebody to point out a direction."

"Is that—" Turner started but changed his mind. He turned to the others encircling him. "Leave us."

When the pair were alone, Turner went on. "Is that what's behind our own problems?"

"Partly. It's gotten worse since last week."

"I'm well aware of that," Turner snapped.

A tic surfaced under one eye. "Worse even since yesterday. The currency market's moving directly against us."

"Then get out."

"I've covered us as best I can. But the fact is, we're exposed."

"How much?"

"Down another eighty mil."

"*What?*" Turner half rose from his seat. "Since yesterday?"

"It's going to get worse before it gets better," Fleiss said. "Not much, but some."

"I thought you said we were covered."

"I've done all I can. If we got out now, we'd have to drop another thirty, maybe forty, before we could walk away. Any sale of that size would catch the market's attention. So what I did, I matched our sells with buys. Our floor is now set at twenty mil below where we are now."

"But if you've set a floor," Turner said, hating the sense of not having an adversary he could face and destroy, "that means we've set a ceiling as well, doesn't it?"

Fleiss's flabby shoulders shrugged once. "Best I could do. To stay uncovered is too risky. To cover means to cut off our upward chances, unless you want me to start all over and buy—"

"No." Turner resisted the urge to rise and throw his chair through the window, watch it fall upon unsuspecting heads sixty floors below. "What about the analyst who pushed us into this rotten mess?"

"It was an honest mistake. She's my best trader."

"Not anymore." Snarling the words, wishing he could destroy this worm as well, knowing he couldn't afford it. Especially not now. But he knew this analyst-trader was Fleiss's protégée. The one good thing to come from all this was finally having a reason to get rid of that woman. She had remained a barrier between Turner's spies and Fleiss. Turner hated the fact that he could not observe Fleiss's every move, observe and learn. Fleiss was a lone wolf, operating in solitary secrecy. The woman had been Fleiss's fire wall, keeping everyone else at arm's length. At least now Turner had a chance to move in someone who would report on Fleiss's tactics. "She's history."

A flicker of defiance, then a shrug of acceptance. "No problem."

"There better not be. I don't just want her fired. I want her destroyed." Good. Fleiss understood how close he was to the dagger himself. "I want you to make sure she can't get a job as dogcatcher in this town."

"You got it."

Turner took a breath, glad he had ordered the others to leave the room. "So what is our total exposure?"

"From this trade or overall?"

He gritted his teeth. The question burned like acid. "Overall."

It was Fleiss's turn to hesitate. A trace of fear appeared in those dead eyes, then, "Almost a quarter."

Two hundred fifty million dollars. A year's profit from all his nonfinancial operations lost in the space of one week. Turner rose and walked to the window. An unacceptable loss at an impossible time.

Until this present deal, Turner had never invested his own money into the futures markets. He was content to act as go-between, hiring the traders and taking a rake-off from every transaction. Turner saw himself as the shopkeeper who had followed the miners to the gold rush of the last century. He was the one who accepted their claims when the cash ran low. He was the man who stood on the front porch and watched them whoop and scream as they tumbled off the boat, staking money that burned holes in their pockets. He was the one who sold them everything they needed and turned a handsome profit at the same time. Then he watched them stumble back in after the money was gone, the claim had paid out, and they were down to their claim papers and their tools. He bought those as well, stowing them away for the next fool to take off his hands, taking his share coming and going, staying safely out of the fray.

Until now.

Turner rapped his knuckles on the glass, staring out at a fog-shrouded morning. The problem was the market, not him. He had stood by and watched traders turn fifty thousand into a million dollars, a half million into twenty, a million into serious money. The market was skyrocketing and people were making money hand over fist. Suddenly his own safe percentage had seemed too small.

Five weeks earlier, a luxury hotel chain had come up for grabs. He had always wanted to own a nationwide chain of first-class hotels. But the hotel market was booming like everything else, and it was a seller's market. The owners had stated that all bids would be cash only. No stock trades, no options, no bank paper. Cash.

The problem was, all of Turner's money was tied up in the other acquisitions. The only cash he had on the books was property of the Valenti Bank. And because it was a bank, its cash reserves were capped by federal law. He couldn't just dip into them.

He made a fist, wishing he could grind those bureaucrats into dust. Federal regulations on banking practices hung like a noose around his neck. "How are the pension funds?"

Larry Fleiss cleared his throat. "I'm not sure we should go that route again."

"Don't tell me the obvious." Turner kept his tone casual. "I want to know their status."

"Stable. No alarms raised."

"Good." Those pension funds were why he had acquired the Valenti Bank in the first place. Valenti was repository for seven of the largest corporate pension funds in the east. Like the big insurance groups, pension funds tended to spread their capital among a select group of investors. They were restricted to blue-chip investments and were left more or less alone. Pension funds sought security, not explosive growth. As long as the quarterly balance report showed steady returns, expectations were satisfied.

He had milked the pension funds for the cash required to buy the hotels. Strictly illegal, but that only mattered if he was caught. It was a temporary switch, or should have been.

Fleiss had come up with the plan of actually taking out *twice* what had been required. Half to pay the 50 percent down payment for the hotels. The other half for what should have been a surefire investment in futures options. Japanese yen, Fleiss's protégée had urged, it was time for a major upswing. A quick in and out, 100 percent profit in ten days was the prediction. Enough to slip the entire amount back into the pension fund and have the hotels added to his real estate portfolio. Everybody wins. Or they should have.

Turner walked back over and seated himself. He could not keep the sigh from escaping. "Whoever would have thought that the yen would do such a nosedive."

"If it's any consolation," Fleiss offered, "you've got the best of company. Word is that people took a bath up and down the Street."

"I didn't get where I am today being part of the herd," he snapped. "All right. Here's what I want you to do. Take out the same again."

Fleiss could not hide his astonishment. "Another three hundred million?"

"You hid it once, you can do it again." Masking his nervousness with customary harshness. "Only this time, you're going to find me a sure thing."

"Right." Fleiss resumed his customary stillness, watching and listening. "Whatever you say."

"What I *say* is this," Turner snarled, leaning across the desk. "You had better not let me down a second time. Do I make myself perfectly clear on that point?"

⊣‖ SEVEN ‖⊢

Thirty-Eight Days . . .

☐ Saturday morning, when Buddy told Molly that he wanted to spend his day in prayer and fasting, she did not object. Even so, he felt a need to explain. "I feel that the Lord has been close by. I know that may sound strange, what with the strain of the past couple of weeks. But that's how it feels. Now, anyway."

"I don't think it sounds strange." She was going to Bible study, dressed in her navy blouse with the high, frilly collar and her grandmother's cameo fastened at the neck. A light dusting of powder covered the worst of her scar not hidden beneath the blouse. "I'm glad you're doing it."

"You are?"

"It is a good thing to draw near to the Lord in confusing times. I'm glad to hear you say you feel like he's been close by. You need him right now."

He nodded agreement. "It's more than a feeling, Molly."

She did not ask what he meant; she did not pry. It was not her way. She simply said, "I'm glad."

When she was off and the house was quiet, he shut himself in the den. There was no need to ask to be left undisturbed. A closed door to the den meant he was to be left alone.

The den was a long room that ran the length of the house next to the garage. Elm wainscoting ran around three walls, a Christmas gift from his father. There was a big picture window looking out over the backyard. Buddy's desk was situated so that he could sit and watch birds flit from the feeder to the birdbath. It was where he did his morning Bible readings.

But today, when he sat down and picked up his Bible, the chair did not seem right, not fitting, in a strange sort of way, as though it had grown uncomfortable.

Buddy thought he understood. He slid down to his knees, and instantly the discomfort vanished. He pulled over the Bible, propped it on the seat of the chair, and read whatever caught his attention. He shut his eyes, prayed a little, but there was no sense of having much to say. He did not feel that he was there to talk to God. Rather, he felt that he was there to listen.

He settled on the Psalms and found a rhythm in reading a passage then shutting his eyes and letting the words sink in deep. Whenever his knees grew tired he stood up and walked around, carrying the Bible with him, stopping whenever he felt it was time to turn back to the Lord.

The hours passed. The outdoor Saturday noises dimmed, the birdsong and the dogs and the children and the lawn mowers. Now and then the phone rang, but Buddy felt no need to answer it.

Around midday his attention began to wane. He was down on his knees at the time, and it seemed the most natural thing in the world to stretch out on the rug and let the drowsiness sweep up and over him.

When he awoke the shadows were beginning to lengthen across the backyard. He felt mildly hungry, especially since he hadn't fasted in years, but not too uncomfortable. He went back to his knees, rubbed the sleep from his eyes, and reached over to reopen his Bible.

An authority seemed to descend upon him and the room and the day and the world. One that had been waiting just beyond his field of awareness, waiting for him to open his eyes and return to the position of prayer. One that was so strong the afternoon sunlight dimmed to insignificance.

The power was absolute, so strong that it could move with complete gentleness, speak in utter silence, and still dominate his being. In fact, had the power not been silent, Buddy knew with utter certainty that it would have shattered his mind.

He did not know how it was possible for silence to communicate in words. Nor did it matter. There was no room for objective questions. In that moment the silence spoke to him, and he heard with faultless clarity.

It is coming.

Buddy could not control his reaction. Sobs wrenched his body. Every dark shadow was illuminated, every failing, every mistake, every sin. All that he had not done, all that he had done for any motive but the purest. His whole life, his entire being, was revealed with perfect clarity. He was shamed to weeping submission.

At the same time, the power of Christ's sacrifice was incandescent. So far had his sins been separated from his eternal forgiveness that the Spirit saw them not. As far as the east is from the west, that was the distance separating his imperfections from the perfect One.

It is coming.

The sobs wrenched him still. He could not help it. The communication was planted within his mind and soul along with an absolute sadness. An immutable determination. Buddy had no doubt that the horror he had seen in his dream was indeed coming. He was totally convinced. It was indeed coming.

He raised his tear-streaked face to the unseen ceiling, and whispered, "When?"

Thirty-eight days.

He moaned aloud. The pronouncement was as powerful as the pounding of a funeral bell. Hardly more than a month. It was no time at all. "How long will it last?"

Seven years.

He clutched his chest, not in pain, but terror. Seven years of famine. Seven years of devastation. Seven years of need.

You must warn them.

"Who?" He could only manage a croaking sound, but he had no doubt that he was heard. He was not speaking aloud for the Spirit, but rather because the pressure required release. "Whom do I tell?"

All who will listen.

He almost cried the words, "What do I say?"

But there was no reply. Not this time. Instead the Presence began to recede, and with it the sense of overburdening sorrow. Buddy was instantly on his feet, aching with the absence of what was now disappearing. He raised his voice and shouted out the back window, "But why *me?*"

The response was a whisper, certain and steady and commanding.

All who will listen.

⊣‖ EIGHT ‖⊢

Thirty-Seven Days . . .

☐ As usual, Buddy arrived at church a half hour before the first Sunday service. He was both deacon and usher, and the group liked to gather for a little prayer time before the day began. Afterward he accepted his sheaf of bulletins and stationed himself by the side doors. This was as public a profession of faith as Buddy had ever cared to make—smiling and greeting the people, trying to make them feel welcome, having a friendly word for every newcomer.

Only today his smile was a little strained, his greeting not as heartfelt as usual. Each passing face seemed a silent accusation. Should he tell this one? And if so, how? Surely God hadn't chosen a man as shy and reserved as he was to stand up in front of the entire congregation.

"Buddy, how are you this morning?"

"Hello, Clarke. Fine, fine." Clarke Owen was the church's assistant pastor and a friend. When the old preacher had retired, they had passed over Clarke and offered the pastorship to a dynamic young man. Attendance and membership had rocketed as a result, but Buddy still preferred the quieter ways of the older man.

"No, you're not and don't fib on a Sunday." Molly stepped lightly up the stairs, halting next to Clarke. "Good morning, Pastor Owen."

"You look pretty as a picture this morning, Molly."

Molly blushed crimson. One hand reached up to hide the scar rising from her high starched-crinoline collar. But she forced her hand back down and clenched her purse. She turned to Buddy. "You need to talk with him."

Clarke stepped aside to allow people through the doors, then returned to say, "Why don't you come by my office after the service, Buddy? We'll have us a little chat."

□

Even before Buddy had settled in his seat, Clarke Owen asked, "Now what's this I hear from Molly about nightmares?"

"I've sure been having them." The church office on a Sunday after services was a good place for sharing confidences. Outside Clarke's closed door were the sounds of people hurrying off, sounds gradually replaced by the stillness of a big empty place. "Every night for more than two weeks."

"Do you want to tell me about it?"

Clarke was the perfect man to discuss this with, and Molly was a gem for having paved the way. He was a graying man in his early sixties, far too mild-mannered to have ever made a dynamic sermonizer. Yet he was adored by the parishioners, the one they always turned to in times of stress and strain. Clarke was a steady listener who knew the value of an open heart.

Even so, Buddy did not answer him directly. "What would you say if I told you I thought maybe God was giving me a message?"

Clarke leaned back and eyed him over steepled fingers. "Is that what you think?"

"I don't know." The calm was a comfort to his soul. Here he could be honest, and honesty was what was called for. "Well, yes. Yes, I think He is."

"Buddy, I've known you for how long, thirty years? You've been a deacon for most of that time. You've seen us through two building programs, loaned us the money, looked after our accounts, done just about anything we've asked you to. You never look for thanks; you never ask for the limelight. You are one of the most selfless servants I have ever had the honor of knowing."

Buddy looked askance at the pastor. This was the last thing he had expected to hear. "Clarke—"

"Hang on a second. You should know by now never to stop a pastor in mid-sermon. Now then. I know you to be a good husband and father. You are also known throughout the town as someone to approach with a financial problem. Half the houses in these parts are owned through mortgages you have personally written. You have the ability to help people see what they can and can't afford, and you do it without offending them or making them feel that you're prying or trying to take advantage. You're the only banker I've ever met who counsels people *away* from debt if they can possibly help it." Clarke allowed a small smile to break through. "Have I forgotten anything?"

"I feel like you've been talking about somebody else," Buddy replied. "Somebody I just wish I was."

"Natural modesty is a fine trait, so long as it doesn't keep you from being all you can be." Pastor Owen paused a moment and then finished, "Or all the Lord wants you to be."

Buddy stared at his old friend. "Does that mean you believe me?"

"I haven't heard what you think you've heard. But I have to admit that my natural inclination would be to say yes. If Buddy Korda tells me that the Lord has given him a message, and if the message stands up to scriptural inspection, I'd be inclined to accept it as truth."

Buddy found the same question welling up that had remained unanswered the day before in his den. "But why *me?*"

"Why *not* you?"

"Because I don't like people noticing me." The mere thought of it was enough to make his hands damp. He wiped his palms down the legs of his trousers and went on. "I'm a nobody, Clarke. I'm a second-rate bank clerk in a small town midway to nowhere. I don't know the first thing about talking to people."

"Ah. Now we're getting somewhere." Pastor Owen reached to the desk for his Bible. "We're really facing two parts to your question. The first part is why would the Lord choose you to receive a message from on high. The second is why would He want you to pass it on."

"I guess that's it." Relief was so strong it made his eyes burn. Not only was he dealing with a solid man of the church who believed him, or at least was willing to, but here was also someone who had the ability to put things into perspective. "That's it exactly."

"Fine." He handed Buddy the open Book, pointed to the bottom of one column. Start right there, First Corinthians, chapter twelve, verse four."

Buddy found his place and read aloud. "'There are diversities of gifts, but the same Spirit. There are differences of ministries, but the same Lord. And there are diversities of activities, but it is the same God who works all in all. But the manifestation of the Spirit is given to each one for the profit of all: for to one is given the word of wisdom through the Spirit.'"

"Okay. Now I want you to stop thinking of this as something that is going to make you declare yourself as an old-style prophet. Instead, see this as simply one more responsibility in your life as a believer. You have been given a *message*. And the message is for the *common good*."

Buddy saw where this was headed and tried to steer away from it. "You don't even know what the message is yet."

"Hear me out." Pastor Owen was not to be distracted. "Now, if the Lord has indeed given you the gift of a message, how can it be for the common good unless you share it?"

"It can't, I guess," Buddy mumbled.

"Exactly. How this is to be done is not for you to determine, do you see? If the Lord is truly behind this, then He will show you exactly where and how the message is to be shared. If He had wanted somebody who would have sprung directly into the limelight, appeared on television, and declared the message to the world, He would have gone elsewhere. If He has chosen you, then He has chosen you with some special purpose in mind. Simply keep your eyes and ears open, Buddy. He will open the doors if this is indeed His will."

Clarke Owen stopped there and waited long enough for Buddy to have a chance to object. When Buddy remained silent, Clarke asked, "Do you want to tell me what you think you heard?"

Buddy took a deep breath and let it out. He set both hands on the open Bible. He took another breath. "I think there's going to be a major financial collapse. An economic disaster. Followed by a time of commercial famine."

The pastor remained stock-still, his gaze steady. "When?"

"Just over a month." Buddy's voice cracked under the strain. He swallowed and tried again. "In thirty-seven days, the third Tuesday of next month."

Buddy waited for the soft voice to calmly dispel his fears, to echo all he had told himself through the previous night's sleepless hours. How it was natural in such unstable times to be worried. How things had often been far worse than now, and somehow disaster had been averted. How every economic indicator now said that things were good and getting better.

Instead, Clarke nodded once. A slow up and down, and then he said, "I think you should share this with the deacons."

"Clarke, no, I—"

"You know there's a finance meeting tonight. I want you to tell them what you've just told me." Before Buddy could object further, Pastor Owen lowered his head. "Now why don't we join together in prayer and ask the Lord to show us exactly why He has spoken to you, and what it is He intends for us to do."

⊣| NINE |⊢

☐ It seemed the longest afternoon of Buddy Korda's life.

As soon as lunch was over, he fled to his study. Sunday afternoons usually began with a nap on his couch, but today he started wearing a path in the carpet, pacing from the window to the door and back again. The idea of standing in front of the church's deacons and declaring he had received a message from on high was appalling.

Then a thought struck him. And he stopped in his tracks. His first smile of the day spread across his features. An expression of pure bliss.

Buddy walked over to his desk. He seated himself and pulled over his pad. He had always liked to have important points down in writing. He ignored the feeling that he was trying to make a deal with God. He was a banker and had a banker's eye for details. He simply wanted to get his understanding down in black and white.

A sign. That was it. He needed a sign before he gave himself up to this. A sign.

He wrote a contract, at least in his mind. On paper he simply put down a few terse words, numbering them one, two, and three. But in his mind it was set down as firmly and precisely as a loan document. He was asking for three signs. If a man as strong as Gideon could ask for two, then Buddy Korda needed at least three.

First, his darling shy wife would not only agree to go with him and be there in public at his side, but she would suggest it herself. Second, his wayward brother would not only return to the church, but he would offer to work with Buddy on this. And third, every single member of the finance committee would agree that Buddy Korda had received a message from God.

Buddy folded the paper and slid it into his top drawer. He released a contented sigh. If the signs did not appear, he was going to be able to walk away from this with a clear conscience. The first two signs were pretty impossible, but the third was straight from a fairy tale. The finance committee couldn't be unanimous over how much coffee to serve for the Wednesday night Bible study.

Buddy leaned back in his chair, thoroughly satisfied with the world.

□

He found Molly working in the kitchen. "You busy?"

"No more than usual."

"I think it's time I told you what's been going on."

His wife had a quiet way of moving, as though she wanted to pass through life without disturbing a single blade of grass. She glided over, pulled out a chair, and seated herself.

Buddy laid it out flat. No inflection, no embellishments. The nightmares and the pains and the Bible passage. He finished with the previous day's prayer time. Then he stopped and waited.

After lunch Molly had changed from her Sunday clothes to a housedress, one with a stiff collar that reached almost to her chin. All her dresses and blouses and nightgowns had high collars. They helped to hide her scar.

Molly was a naturally shy person. To have such a vivid scar only amplified her natural reserve, turning it into almost a phobia. She had spent much of her life hiding from public inspection. Even if Buddy had been determined to go ahead with this crusade, he could never have asked his wife to join him.

And yet, when she finally spoke she said, "I knew it was something like this. Even before you told Paul to wait with the new business, I knew."

"You did?" His voice sounded dull in his own ears. "How?"

"I don't know. But I did. And I knew it was something I was going to need to do with you."

Her eyes were brown, like her hair had been before age had turned it to strands of silver. Buddy stared into them now, looking straight into her heart. He felt shocked beyond speech.

"I've been praying about it all week. And the only thing I've felt come to me is how happy I've been these past few years, with the boys grown and busy with their own lives."

Buddy wanted to ask, What about how you are with strangers? What about the bad days, when you ask me to drive you to the shopping mall and walk around with you so you don't have to be around strangers by yourself? He wanted to ask her all these things and more, but not because he was interested in her response. No. There was too much honesty in Molly's words for him to be less than fully honest with himself. He wanted to push her away from where he felt she was headed.

"I was glad to be a mom," Molly confessed. "But I'm much happier being a grandmother. It means I can concentrate on being a wife again."

She had often said this to him these past few years. The words had come to be an intimate confession just between the two of them. Buddy waited for her to finish with something like, I don't want to leave this now. He even wanted to speak and say the words for her, because he most definitely did not want to be anywhere but here. Yet the words simply would not come.

She looked around the kitchen. "I like being just the two of us. I like being here with you at home."

He reached over and took her hand. He wanted to push away what he was hearing, what it might mean. But the love that welled up in him for his wife gentled away his ability to object.

"It's home the way we like it, quiet and cozy." She looked around again, sad this time, as though she was already saying good-bye. "I'll miss it."

He finally managed to force out the words, "We're not going anywhere." Yet even before the words were out of his mouth, Buddy knew they were wrong.

Molly did not answer him. Instead she simply reached over and placed her free hand on top of his. She sat there, looking around, looking at him, and then back again at their home. Her gaze was quiet and searching, seeing beyond the walls and the years, saying farewell to all that was and once had been.

Buddy hung his head. Never had the message seemed more real than at this moment. Nor the calling more dire.

Finally he rose from the table. Molly's gaze lifted with him. "Where are you going?"

He looked down at his wife. He answered, "I have to go see Alex."

⊣‖ TEN ‖⊢

☐ Buddy found Alex where his older brother spent every Sunday—at work.

Buddy drove under the banner announcing that the dusty lot was home to Korda's Fine Used Cars. He stopped and stared through the sun-dashed windshield to where his elder brother stood with a couple beside a car festooned with bunting and balloons. Alex was waving his arms about, which meant he was closing a sale. Buddy had spent a lot of time watching his brother and wishing things had turned out different than they had.

His brother was bigger all around than Buddy. Taller, wider, broader. Bigger smile, bigger hands, bigger heart. Alex Korda was one of those people who never learned to adjust to the real world. Buddy had known this long before Alex had gone through what Buddy had always called his change of life.

When Alex was eighteen he had fallen head over heels in love with a girl down the street. She, too, had claimed to love him, which was all the impetus Alex had needed. He had courted her and wooed her, or so everyone had thought. Especially Alex. Together they had set a date for the wedding. Two days before they were scheduled to be wed, the girl had left town. No word, no nothing for almost a month. Then a letter had arrived, and she had confessed to having fallen for a drummer in a band that had passed through town.

Alex had done exactly as she had requested, which was to walk over and pass the news on to her distraught parents. Then he had packed a bag and left town himself.

He had been drifting ever since. Oh, he had returned to Aiden six months later. But he had not been the same Alex. The smile was still there, the hearty voice and the friendly hello. But the man behind it had never returned from the horror of seeing his dream dashed on the rocks of reality.

There had been other women. A lot of them. And in between the ladies there had been an on-again, off-again love affair with the bottle. Three years earlier, Alex had finally sworn off the booze for good. He had joined AA and regularly attended the meetings. But he had never returned to church, never again set foot inside the doors, not even to see his two nephews get married. As far as Alex was concerned, when his fiancée had walked out of his life that day, she had carried God off with her.

Buddy sat in his car and waited for Alex to shake the couple's hands and send them inside to where his assistant sat ready to draw up the papers. Buddy reflected that there was still a chance he might get away with doing nothing.

Alex sprinted over to Buddy's car and opened the door. "You gonna sit there all day?"

Buddy climbed out and said what he did every Sunday. "Missed you at church this morning."

Alex gave his easy laugh, seeming to all the world a happy-go-lucky dreamer. "You're the second person who's told me that today."

This was new. "Who was the other?"

"Ah, now. That would be telling." He checked his watch. "Do I have the date wrong, or did we plan things different this month?"

"No, nothing's changed." One Sunday a month, Buddy came out and checked Alex's books. Another Sunday, he invited his brother for a family dinner. The other Sunday afternoons, Buddy simply telephoned for a long chat. They saw each other fairly often during the week, but the Sunday contacts were Buddy's way of reaching out. Buddy had been praying for Alex since Alex had disappeared, which was forty-four years ago. "I've got something I need to talk with you about."

"Come on inside then." Alex walked with the rolling gait of a big man. He was tremendously strong and possessed the jaw of an ox. No wonder the ladies swooned over him. Walking alongside, Buddy felt dwarfed by his brother and saddened by the missed opportunities. Alex had so much to offer the world. So much goodness. So much heart. Buddy found himself sighing a lot whenever he spent time around his brother.

Alex led him into the long trailer converted into an office. Couples were seated in front of both desks used by Alex's salesmen. Alex gave the entire room a cheery wave and led Buddy down the narrow hallway. The trailer smelled of antiseptic cleaner and old coffee.

Buddy followed Alex into the back room. On the side wall were three letters framed and hung like diplomas. They were from the sales managers of the three main car dealers in Aiden, all offering to buy Alex's stock and hire him as manager of their used-car divisions. He was that good.

Alex spotted the direction of Buddy's gaze and warned, "You're not going to start on that old thing again, are you?"

"No, that's not why I'm here." The fact that Alex was already on the defensive cheered him, and the fact that it cheered him made him feel guilty. Buddy shook his head to clear it. God knew him well enough to know that he would not want to take on the task of messenger. There was nothing wrong with being honest. And the truth was, he more than half hoped the signs would not arrive.

"What's got you so worried, little brother?"

So Buddy told him, in the same unadorned manner as he had used with Molly. Laying it all out, skipping nothing. He even paused a few times, waiting for Alex to give his big booming laugh and cut him short. The laugh was Alex's way of dealing with things he didn't like. The sound, as strong and dominating as he was, left little room for anything else.

But Alex did not laugh. His dark eyes seemed to deepen as he listened. No, listen was not the right word. He *drank* in the words.

When Buddy finished, silence filled the room. Which was extraordinary. Alex seldom permitted silence to linger when the two of them were together. There was too much chance Buddy would start in on all the things Buddy wished his brother would do, like make more of his life and his talents. And return to God.

Alex rose from his chair and walked to the room's only window. He stood with his back to Buddy, his fingers laced behind his back, and stared out at the yard full of cars. "I've got some news of my own."

There it was, the sudden change of subject, the move to something safer. Buddy was caught by the hope that Alex was not going to help him, then an accompanying twinge of guilt. "What's that?"

"Been wondering when I was going to tell you."

"Tell me what, Alex?"

One hand raised to part the blinds, as though Alex felt the need to get a better look at one of his cars. "That I've got cancer."

Buddy was on his feet before he realized he had even moved. "Alex, oh, my God, tell me it's not true."

"Wish I could, little brother." Alex angled his body away from Buddy's approach so that his eyes were almost hidden from his brother. Almost, but not quite. "Went in for that checkup you and Molly have been on me about. Look where it got me."

Buddy reached out his hand, stopped just short of touching Alex. "What kind is it?"

"I've forgotten the fancy name. In my lymph nodes." He grimaced toward the window. "Haven't been feeling myself lately. Nothing definite, just aches and pains now and then, here and there."

Alex had never been sick a day in his life. Just like his father. Buddy fought back a rising sense of nausea. He could not imagine a world without his brother. "Are they going to operate?"

"Can't. Wednesday they did one of those scans where they slide me inside a giant tin can, I can't remember the word now."

"MRI scan." And he had not been there. He had not even known. "Alex—"

"The stuff is everywhere, Buddy. Throat, under my arms, in my gut. Every lymph node has little bumps. They showed me." He turned around now, and let Buddy see what was there in his eyes. "I've got another couple of tests, and then they start me on chemotherapy at the end of the week. It doesn't look good."

Buddy did the only thing he could, which was to hide from the horror by taking his brother in his arms. Anything but stand there and see death's shadow in those dark eyes.

They held on for a long moment. When they finally released each other, neither could meet the other's gaze. Alex walked back around his desk, snuffling and wiping his face on his sleeve. "You know what I was thinking while you were telling me your news?"

"What?"

"That I wish there was something I could do to help."

The words felt like a stab to his heart. Buddy had to cover his eyes with one hand. "Oh, Alex. I feel like I've been the one to make you ill."

Alex huffed a short laugh. "What are you talking about now?"

"I made a bargain with God." The words were a moan. "I told him I'd go out there and warn the world if He gave me three signs. Molly would have to say she wanted to go public with me. You would have to offer to help out. And the entire church finance committee would hear me out this evening and say the message was real."

When his brother did not respond, Buddy looked up to find Alex grinning broadly. Alex asked, "Did Molly say she'd be there with you?"

"Right after church."

Alex's chest started shaking with silent laughter. "Sounds to me like you've done sunk your own ship."

"This isn't funny!" Buddy had to clamp down on his own case of shakes.

"Then why are you laughing?"

"I'm not. Well, maybe I am. It's better than crying, I suppose. Of all the things you could tell me."

"You don't know which surprised you more, me getting sick or me wanting to help, am I right?"

"How can you be laughing about this?"

"It's the way I've handled everything else in this crazy life."

"Crazy is right." How on earth he could be laughing was utterly beyond him. "Alex—"

"I want to help you, Buddy. I really do. I've been lying awake at night thinking things over. How you always said I wasted my life."

"If there were any way to take back those words, I'd do it," Buddy said vehemently. "I should've had my mouth washed out with lye."

"The words were true just the same. I want to do something good for somebody else." A trace of the shadow returned. "While there's still time."

"Alex, hearing you say those words is like a knife in my heart."

Instead of replying, Alex slid over a yellow legal pad, pulled his pen from his pocket, and started making notes. "We'll make this your command center."

"What, here?"

"Where did you plan on having it? You can't use the bank, that's for certain."

"I hadn't thought that far."

"Well, you'd better. They're not going to be very pleased to hear their manager start warning about a financial collapse."

"Assistant manager." But his mind was trapped by the realization that going public meant exactly that. "They won't be pleased at all."

"'Course, we're not planning on calling them up and telling them what you're doing in your spare time." He made rapid notes. "Anybody who wants to hear what you've got to say can call or fax us here."

Each word Alex spoke made the whole affair that much more real. "I feel awful."

"You look awful. You look like you need to go lie down before your third big sign comes true tonight." Which was good for another chuckle. "Boy, did you ever get it coming and going."

"Alex, I'd do anything—"

"Just stop right there. You didn't cause this illness." Alex raised his eyes from his note taking. "Did it ever occur to you that your God might have *suggested* these signs to you?"

Buddy did not know which was more startling, the thought itself, or to hear it come from his brother. "He's your God too."

"He might have known you'd need something like this to get you up and moving. If it's my time, well . . ." Alex stopped, momentarily silenced by the rising shadows. He pushed them back down and focused once more on his brother. "I want to help you do this, Buddy."

"Then you will." Buddy forced himself to his feet. "I'd better be going."

"Call me tonight when you get back." Another smile. "Tell me how it went."

"All right."

"Buddy." Alex waited until Buddy turned back around to say quietly, "There was something else I was thinking while you were telling me about this message. I was thinking that God couldn't have chosen a better man."

⊣| ELEVEN |⊢

☐ Buddy arrived at the church still numbed by his brother's news. He had left Molly teary eyed and heartsore, trying hard to put on a brave face for him. But she did not need to be brave. Buddy was too worried to care much one way or the other.

He entered the church's main conference room to an argument. One so unexpected that it almost shocked Buddy from his cloud. The church's two pastors were squared off at the front of the room. The others present clustered in silent little groups, staring in confusion.

Pastor Allen demanded of his assistant pastor, "You are *certain* this is a good idea?"

"Yes, I am. More than that, I feel it is divinely inspired."

Pastor Allen shook his head, clearly irritated. "I have to tell you, Clarke, I think this is unwise. Very unwise."

"You weren't there," Clarke Owen responded. He held to his normal, quiet tone, but he was equally firm. Equally unbending. "You didn't witness what I did."

"We have too full an agenda already, as you well know." Pastor Allen was a tremendously dynamic man in his mid-thirties, with an athlete's taut build and a movie star's even features. He dearly loved the Lord and approached the pulpit as he would a goal-line drive. He was definitely the force behind the church's revival and growth. He was also accustomed to subservience from his assistant pastor. "We have more than half the year's budgetary items to cover, and we're only two weeks away from presenting it to the church. Not to mention the shortfall in our missions goal. Something will have to be cut, and you know how hard a decision that is."

"Buddy will not need much time," Clarke responded. He seemed utterly unfazed by the pastor's determined arguments. His calm was unruffled, his stance relaxed. "All it took was a few short sentences to convince me."

"Convince you of what?" Pastor Allen ran an impatient hand through his hair. "That Buddy has something of such divine importance that we have to interrupt the church's monthly finance meeting to share it?"

"I could not have said it better myself," Clarke affirmed.

Buddy stood in the doorway, taking in one impression after another. The fact that they were arguing about him would normally have been enough to force him forward, to make peace between them. But today he could not do it. He felt shell-shocked, numbed by too much too fast.

There came another niggling notion, one that he did not at first recognize. Then it hit him with a start. The room was full. Hastily he counted the heads clustered at the room's other end. Fourteen. All fourteen members of the finance committee were present. He tried to recall another time in the twelve years he had worked with the committee when that had happened and could not come up with a single occasion.

Then he noticed the way they were standing. The committee members were drawn from the church's senior deacons and elders, along with a smattering of very large donors. They were people of importance within the community, people whose success and age generated solid confidence in their opinions. And since they all had opinions about everything, they argued all the time. They were a pompous, contentious lot, these committee members, and this was the impression of someone who loved them dearly. Talking about money and how to spend it often brought out the very worst in them. Only the leadership of both pastors working in tandem kept them in line—Pastor Allen leading from the front, Clarke Owen soothing from behind.

But today the normal lines of contention had vanished. The conference table was a long, slender oval stretching down the center of the room. Normally a group of seven or eight sat at the table, while any others chose positions on the sofas and in easy chairs that lined the side walls. These positions reflected their leanings; they seated themselves near the persons they tended to back.

Agatha Richards, a tall angular woman in her early sixties and widow to one of Aiden's richest men, headed one such group. She liked to see the church as spearheading a push to the farthest reaches of the earth. Every cent not spent on missions was reason for battle. To hear that her precious missions budget was to face a cutback was normally enough to have Agatha loading for bear.

Lionel Peters was the other powerhouse, a man who measured the church's progress by the height of its steeple. In his mind, the missions outreach should be restricted to what could be accomplished within the church's own buildings. He and Agatha genuinely loathed one another. And yet, and yet. Buddy stood in the doorway and watched the two of them standing side by side, their shoulders and arms almost touching. Like all the others, their eyes were fastened upon the two pastors. Who never argued. Who never seemed to differ in opinion on anything.

"I want you to give this up, Clarke."

"I would be happy to," his assistant pastor replied, "if I was not so certain that this was genuinely something that God was instructing me to do."

Pastor Allen reddened. He started to say something else, then he noticed Buddy standing in the doorway. His lips struggled to form a welcoming smile, but he could only manage a further tightening of his features. "Buddy, hello. Good of you to come." He turned so as to fasten his full attention on Buddy. "Clarke tells me that you have something of *vital importance* to share with us."

"I don't know if I do or not." Buddy recognized the pastor's appeal for support. But he could not give it. Not then. "If it is, I think that's something you folks are going to have to decide for me. Because right now I'm too drained to care."

Clarke walked over. "Are you all right?"

"No, I'm not." Sorrow hung like a leaden weight in his chest. He passed his hand over his eyes. "I just learned Alex has cancer."

The entire room drew a collective breath. They all knew the story of Alex. Many of them had grown up with it.

Agatha was the first to reach him. "Buddy, I'm so sorry."

The pastor was one step behind her. His concern was deepened by what he had just been saying. "This is terrible. How can we help?"

Buddy looked from one face to the other and saw the sorrow and genuine concern. "You're doing it now. Thanks."

"Come on up here." This from Pastor Allen. His former resistance had vanished. "Are you sure you're up to this today?"

"I just want to get it over with."

"Fine, fine." Allen guided Buddy into the chair he normally reserved for himself at the head of the table; then he motioned for everyone else to take their places. "Let's just bow our heads and have a moment of prayer."

Buddy lowered his head with the others, but did not hear the words. Instead, as soon as his eyes were closed, he felt a sense of peace. The words came instantly to his mind. *Heal my brother,* he prayed. *I'll do anything you want. Just make my brother well.*

He raised his head to find all eyes on him, the entire room waiting patiently. How long he had sat there he had no idea. He looked from face to face, wondering what on earth he was doing there at all.

Then Agatha Richards reached over and took his hand. She had never been particularly friendly to him in the past. Her family were grown and scattered, and she lived for her missions and her church. She had always viewed Buddy with suspicion, for he had sought to play peacemaker alongside Clarke rather than declare himself solidly for one side or another.

But none of the former distrust was in her face now. Her sight had started to weaken after her husband's death, and she wore bottle-bottom glasses that made her eyes look impossibly big. She gazed at him with brimming eyes, her hand gripping his firmly. Then Buddy recalled that it was cancer that had taken her own husband, and he placed his second hand on hers for a moment before rising to his feet.

Even when standing, he still had no idea what on earth he was supposed to say. So he simply laid it out. He cleared his throat and launched into it without preamble. How he had suffered through more than two weeks of nightmares. How he had seen the Bible passage about a coming famine come alive before his very eyes. How he had fasted and prayed and had received answers. How he had asked for signs . . .

Right then, before he could tell them what the signs were, a chair slammed so hard against the back wall that Buddy jumped. He turned to see Pastor Allen standing alongside him.

The pastor's head was upraised, his eyes clenched shut. He was swaying slightly, his arms outstretched, his hands rigid.

Pastor Allen was not opposed to movement of the Spirit, but he himself had never been a demonstrative man. His sermons were often punctuated by loud *amens* and occasional clapping, while many in the congregation sang with hands outstretched and faces upraised. He remained unfazed, simply accepting it and waiting them out.

But not now.

His entire body seemed to vibrate, shaking like a tuning fork struck by a divine hand. His neck muscles were so taut they stretched like wire cables beneath his skin.

Buddy took a step back and then caught sight of the assistant pastor. Clarke Owen was sitting beside his colleague, seemingly caught halfway between laughing and crying. He was biting his upper lip, rubbing one hand up and down the side of his face, up and down, his eyes never moving from Pastor Allen's face.

"Praise God!" Agatha Richards rose in trembling stages, her eyes staring up unseeing at the heavens. She reached one hand toward what only she could envision and cried again, *"Praise be to the Lord Almighty!"*

"Hallelujah!" Lionel Peters was up now on the table's other side, his voice charged with emotion. *"Hallelujah, Amen!"*

Buddy kept backing away from the scene until he was pressed hard against the wall. He watched as one after another of the committee members began to rise and call and shout and lift their arms and close their eyes. He felt nothing except shock. He could not be the cause of this. It was impossible.

Clarke Owen rose to his feet, the last to do so. Calm in a joyful way, clearly in control and yet guided with the others. "Brothers and sisters," he called, and gradually the hubbub faded. "Brothers and sisters, let us pray together and give thanks."

Hands were joined, and Clarke began the prayer. A low murmuring ran in waves around the chamber. Buddy joined his hands with the others, yet remained isolated and untouched. It was impossible that he had caused such a commotion.

The prayer went on and on. Buddy scarcely heard anything at all. Three words resounded through his mind, over and over, a litany spoken to the confusion he felt surrounding and filling him.

Heal my brother.

⊣| TWELVE |⊢

☐ As soon as he was home Buddy retreated to his den. It seemed a center of calm in the midst of the storm. He did not do anything; he merely sat at his desk with the Bible opened and unread before him.

Molly came in to say good night. She studied his face for a long moment and then brushed the graying hair from his forehead and kissed him and left him without speaking a word.

The night gathered, and more than darkness crouched beyond the reach of the room's feeble light. Buddy felt overwhelmed by all that had happened. He opened his top drawer and took out the list he had made. Could that have truly been only a few hours ago?

Almost in reply there came a whisper, a silent response. Not in words, not this time. But a signal that was understood just the same. Buddy caught a sense of urgent need.

He slid from the chair to his knees. The Presence gathered and intensified. He took no pleasure from it and little comfort. The future was too formidable. Too close.

"Make this cup pass from me," he said, speaking with eyes closed. Clasping his hands to his chest, pleading with all his might. "Give it to someone better prepared."

The response was as clear as it.was silent. A simple waiting.

He sighed, understanding the message far better than if it had been in words. He had asked for signs. They had been given. He was chosen. He had promised. He was called.

He wanted to make his brother's healing into another sign. Wanted to bargain. But he could not bring himself to do it. Why, he was not sure. But the wrongness was so absolute that Buddy could not negotiate. He could only beg.

He raised his clenched hands toward the ceiling, and pleaded, "Heal my brother. Please. Make Alex well."

The image was instantaneous in its arrival, as though waiting for this moment, ready in advance, prepared long before he was even born. It was that clear, that total.

Buddy saw his brother. Not with his own closed eyes. The image was far stronger than something of his own senses. He saw his brother in *entirety*. The Alex of all time appeared in his mind and heart—the young man, the brokenhearted lover, the fallen drifter, the drinker, the salesman, the hollow gourd who had turned his back on the church and refused to be filled. The hearty handshake, the empty laugh. The burly giant pasted around a life of chasing barren dreams.

With the image came a sense of seeing it not through his own memories at all. He was watching through wiser eyes, seeing a wholeness that was limited neither by time nor anything human. And with this observation came an overpowering sorrow. Anguish over a beloved child who had drifted away.

There was no time to give in to grieving. In fact, it did not feel like his own grief at all. Instead, his perspective began to expand. He did not retreat from his brother. Somehow he began to see Alex, and more besides, taking in the customers who came to Alex's lot, then all of downtown, then the entire town of Aiden.

The broadening did not stop there. The vista swept inexorably outward, carrying Buddy with him. No longer was there any question that he was seeing more than his own vision. No longer. The county, the state, the region, and onward. Farther and farther, on and on, until he was looking and feeling for an entire nation.

He did not stand at some great distance and look down upon his country. He was *joined*. The connection was *intimate*. Each person was there, each town and county and state and everything in between. How it was possible, Buddy did not know. But he saw both the individual and the total. And the sorrow would have overwhelmed him had the guiding hand not filtered it. For with the expanding vision had come a growing realization. It was not just Alex who was ill. It was not just for his brother that Buddy should be mourning.

The illness was an all-pervading malignancy eating at the very fabric of society. It came under a variety of guises, and was called by myriad names, but the source was the same.

The stain reached from shore to shore, from border to border. Buddy saw it all. He saw and felt a mother's anguish for a child who was slowly giving in to a deadly disease. He saw and wept for all the cancerous growths that had infected the body of his beloved country.

Here and there were islands of light, flickering candles of life. No words were needed now. No convincing necessary. For a reason that Buddy did not understand, he had been selected to speak with them. To carry the message and pass on the warning.

Suddenly the why behind his being chosen no longer mattered. The unspoken lesson had carried with it all the explanation he would be offered, all that really mattered. Buddy had been called. Despite all his failings and all his misgivings, no matter what anguish he himself might be facing in his own life, he had been *called*.

The perspective faded as quietly and gently as it had appeared. No indication of the force behind it, nothing of the experience's immense infinity remained. Instead, the room returned to focus. Buddy was back, and his life was changed forever.

The Presence whispered to him then, in words for the first time that night.

⊣| THIRTEEN |⊢

Thirty-Six Days . . .

☐ Monday morning Thad Dorsett entered the bank in a foul mood. He had taken his boss's advice and spent the weekend away. In Chicago, however, not New York. His first trip to New York would be as a king, not a weekend wanna-be. Still, Chicago held more than enough diversions to keep one returning veteran satisfied for a weekend.

Yet returning from the big city to Aiden, Delaware, was a bitter way to face another Monday. Thad grunted in reply to his secretary's cheerful greeting and poured himself a cup of coffee. His throat burned, his mouth tasted gummy, his tongue felt slightly furred. The insides of his eyelids seemed coated with sand from too little sleep and too many hours spent trying to have a good time. He stared out the bank's rear window, slurping his coffee and willing his body to wake up. The day outside was as grim as the town.

Thad was not so weary as to be blind to the way the bank's employees treated him, playing at being polite but not meaning a thing. He turned so that he could watch Sally at her till. Even she had started keeping her distance. He felt another set of eyes on him and looked over to where Lorraine sat behind her desk, watching him like a disapproving hawk. He stretched his tired face into a parody of a smile, but she did not even blink. No question who had been talking to Sally. As soon as he found a way to rid himself of Korda, that Lorraine was history.

Korda. The thought of that measly little guy getting in his way twisted Thad's uneasy stomach even tighter. And the way the others in the bank treated him, that was even more galling. Thad had seen it happen dozens of times. All the guy had to do was walk in the door, and every face in the place lit up. Like he was some kind of potentate instead of another small-town loser.

Thad couldn't stand to watch another of Korda's entrances. He carried his cup back to his office, saying as he passed his secretary's desk, "As soon as everybody gets here, have them come in."

□

Monday morning arrived dark and rainy. Buddy drove along streets he had known all his life, feeling as though he was saying farewell. He was not leaving, not yet. Yet the *when* no longer mattered.

He looked out his rain-washed windshield and saw his own future. The trees were still verdant with the weight of summer's leaves, but it was only a matter of time before autumn came.

Only a matter of time. Buddy listened to the windshield wipers snap back and forth, and wondered if there had ever been another moment when he had felt so helpless.

He arrived just as the bank's managers were filing into Thad's office for their regular Monday morning meeting. Buddy entered and slid into a seat in the far corner. He remained locked in his own private reverie through the report on accounts and outstanding loans. He said nothing as the previous week was reviewed. Nothing sank in very far at all, in fact, until Thad Dorsett rose and addressed the gathering.

"Interest rates have taken another rise, as all of you know. Or should know, if you're doing your job." He gave his dangerous little smile. "Unfortunately, too much of the bank's loan business is tied to fixed rates. This can only grow worse, as rates are predicted to go even higher. So here is what I want you to do. Make a list of all our customers with fixed-interest loans. Ignore the mortgages; we don't hold them anyway. Star all those who use their loan arrangements for rollover credit—the small businesses with salary accounts, that sort of thing."

Buddy was paying attention now. His focus was locked on the branch's manager, with his dark, swept-back hair and his tailored gabardine suit. Dorsett continued. "We're going to catch them in a double pincer. Starting today, no further increases on their loan balances will be permitted. And the rate of repayment will be increased by tripling their minimum monthly payments."

While this was still being digested, Thad went on. "Not only that, but we're going to issue each of these people new credit cards. We'll send them a personal letter signed by me announcing that as valued customers we are waiving our normal account charge and offering them our new Platinum Corporate Cards for free. With a twenty-thousand-dollar credit ceiling."

Buddy could remain silent no longer. "That's disgusting."

Thad did not seem surprised to hear from him. "No, Mr. Korda. It is highly profitable."

"Credit-card debt carries the bank's highest interest rate. Last week's rate hike pushed the accumulative over nineteen percent."

"Exactly."

"Those fixed loans and rollover credit accounts belong to our bank's oldest customers."

"Deadbeats who need waking up," Thad snapped, his face reddening.

"They aren't deadbeats," Buddy heatedly replied. "A lot of small businesses are being operated by the third generation of the same families. Businesses who started around the same time as this bank. They've trusted us with their accounts for over a hundred years."

"I remind you, Korda, that your loyalty should be to the bank and its policies. You—" He stopped at the sound of someone knocking on the door.

Lorraine poked her head inside, then said, "I'm sorry, Mr. Dorsett. But Mrs. Agatha Richards is here."

"Tell her I'll be right with her," Thaddeus Dorsett said. At the death of her husband, Agatha Richards had inherited three large companies and was now one of the bank's wealthiest customers.

"Mrs. Richards," Lorraine replied, "wants to see Mr. Korda."

Buddy felt as though he was propelled from his seat. "I'm going to write all my customers," he announced grimly, "explaining to them what's behind this scheme. I'll instruct them to destroy the cards and refuse to pay the increased minimum payment."

"Do that," Thad snarled. "Be sure to send me a copy. I'd be delighted to show our central office what sort of assistant manager I'm saddled with here."

□

"Can I get you a cup of coffee, Mrs. Richards?"

"No thank you, Lorraine." Agatha followed Buddy into his office.

"Mr. Korda?"

Hearing Lorraine call him by his last name was so surprising he turned back. "What?"

"Coffee?"

"No, no, I'm fine, thanks." He watched her softly shut the door, and wondered what had Lorraine acting so demure. "Why don't we sit over here by the window. What can I do for you, Agatha?"

"I just wanted to tell you how thrilled and moved I was last night."

"Oh." Buddy slid into the settee facing Agatha.

Agatha was not a gushy sort of woman. She stood an inch higher than Buddy but looked even taller, as she held herself rigidly erect. She gripped her purse in her lap and kneaded the top clasp with beringed hands. "I feel so *honored* to have been there at the outset. I've never been one to go in for gifts of the Spirit, but—"

"Agatha, please stop."

"I just can't tell you . . ." Her mind finally registered Buddy's quiet words. "I beg your pardon?"

"Stop. I don't know how to make it any plainer than that."
He knew he was being too harsh, but he could not seem to help
himself. "This is hard enough already without your gushing all
over me."

"Why, Buddy Korda." His words caught her totally off guard.
"I thought you'd be delighted."

"Well, I'm not." He could not bear to have her finish. "The
last thing I want is for people I've known all my life to start treating me like I was some kind of—" He started to say, some kind
of prophet, but stopped himself just in time. He finished lamely,
"holy man."

Before Agatha could collect herself, there was a knock on
his door. Lorraine timidly stuck her head inside and said, "Please
excuse me, Mr. Korda—"

"Not you, too, Lorraine."

"I'm sorry, what?"

"Never mind. Never mind."

"Reverend Owen and Reverend Allen are out here."

"Well, show them in." Buddy rose to his feet. Agatha remained
planted where she was, giving him an odd look. Buddy looked
at her and said, "I suppose you told Lorraine all about it."

"I didn't have to." Her gaze did not waver. "The whole town
is talking about you."

"Great. Just great." He walked over as the pair entered, and
offered them his hand. "Gentlemen. Come on in and have a seat."
He stopped Lorraine's question before it was spoken. "That will
be all, thank you."

He waved them into seats and sighed as he sat back down
himself. "What can I do for you?"

"Be careful what you say," Agatha said. "Buddy is in one of his moods."

"I do not have moods," he snapped.

Agatha Richards harrumphed. "Buddy Korda, I've known you all my life. And I know you can be the most quietly contrary man I have ever laid eyes on."

Buddy turned to the pastors. "Don't pay her any mind. She's the one who's being contrary."

"Now that is just not true. I simply wanted to offer you my help."

"No, you didn't." Buddy knew he should stop, but he did not feel able. "You came in here to sit at the feet of the wise man. Well, I'm sure not wise. And I'm not interested in your getting down on my carpet, no matter what the reason."

Clarke Owen halted Agatha's reaction with, "Actually, we came by for the same reason."

"If you really want to help me," Buddy snapped, angry despite himself, "you'd make this whole mess up and vanish."

Agatha was horrified. "You don't mean that."

"Oh, don't I?" Distress rose in waves. "Do you know what I hear when you start talking about last night? I hear the end of a life I've loved. Everything is about ready to be turned on its head, and I'm supposed to be happy. Now tell me exactly what it is that I'm supposed to be so all-fired delighted about."

There was a long silence, finally broken by Pastor Allen. "So you really think it's going to happen. This economic famine, I mean."

"Yes, no, I don't know." Buddy kneaded his forehead. "It's not only the famine I'm talking about. It's the *warning*. It's the fact that I've been chosen to go out and deliver this to people.

Only I don't *want* to go. Is that so difficult to understand? I *hate* traveling. I'm scared of airplanes. I don't like trains. My car is eight years old, and it's done less than twenty thousand miles."

He felt thoroughly unable to explain what he was feeling. His gaze landed on Pastor Allen who wore a troubled expression. Buddy said, "I sound ungrateful, don't I?"

"I should say so," Agatha huffed.

"Well, to be honest, I don't know what I have to be grateful for." Even so, the act of confessing was calming. He could feel the pent-up steam leaking out with his words.

"If you don't beat all." Agatha had difficulty finding the words. "Buddy Korda, the Lord has *called* you."

"That's right, He has. Now let's take a look at what exactly this calling is. I've been given a message of direst ruin. A seven-year famine is coming. That's my message. I'm called to go out and spread this message to anyone who will listen. I'm called to make myself a laughingstock in the business community, at least among those who won't believe me. And for those who *do* believe, I'll be bringing a warning that dashes every dream. I'll be telling them that their worst fears for the future will soon come true."

He felt like a deflated balloon, yet he was satisfied just the same. There was a genuine fulfillment in speaking the truth. And that was what he was going to do, he decided then and there. "I don't want this job. I didn't ask for it. I'm not a talker, and I don't like being noticed. The Lord's called me, and I guess I'm going to do what He's told me to do. But that doesn't mean I have to like it. Not one bit."

Agatha looked from one pastor to the other. "Are you just going to sit there and let him go on like this?"

Clarke Owen turned and waited for the chief pastor to speak. But Reverend Allen continued to study Buddy. Genuine uncertainty clouded his gaze.

For some reason, Pastor Allen's silence seemed to satisfy Clarke. He turned back to Buddy and said, "I have to tell you, Buddy, what I've just heard here only makes me more certain that the Lord has chosen rightly."

Agatha's mouth worked a couple of times, but no sound came out.

"Buddy, you're not a pastor. You're not called to lead a flock. You are called to give the world a warning. A message, Buddy. That is what the Lord intends for people to focus on. Not the messenger. Never the messenger. Do you see where I'm headed with this?"

"Yes," he reluctantly allowed. "Yes, I guess I do."

"Someone who wants to be the center of attention could very well get in the way of what God is intending here. He wants His people to hear a message, and to have it spoken with an authority that is so solid, so *certain*, that they will do as He instructs. They might not be anywhere near that certain if the message was to come from someone else."

Clarke paused for another glance at Pastor Allen. A knowing smile played across his features. "If the message came from someone with a talent for speaking and a heart for the stage, their attention might be on the *speaker*. But that's not what's intended here. The Lord wants people to focus on *Him*."

There was a moment's silence before Pastor Allen shifted in his seat and said quietly, "I agree."

The soundness of what he was hearing left Buddy locked in his unfolding destiny. "I'm so afraid."

"Well, of course you are," Clarke affirmed.

"Every word you say," Buddy went on, "brings my departure one step closer."

"Buddy, I'd like to tell you that you can go out and do your work and return home. I wish I could do that." Clarke placed his hands on his knees and leaned through the distance separating them. "But I can't. What I can say is that I'm proud of you. And I'm certain the Lord is too."

Pastor Allen rose slowly to his feet. "I suppose I'd better be getting on. I've got appointments back-to-back today. I just wanted you to know I'm behind you on this." His gaze fell not on Buddy, but on his associate. As Clarke smiled up at him, Pastor Allen went on, "Buddy, there's a meeting of the Businessmen's Bible Fellowship tonight over in Wilmington. They've asked me to speak. I think you should be there in my stead."

"I—" Buddy stopped as he watched Clarke reach out, grip Pastor Allen's arm, and squeeze it hard. His smile was exquisite. Buddy told them, "I don't know what to say."

Clarke dropped his hand and turned to Buddy. "Tell him yes. Let the Lord begin His work."

FOURTEEN

☐ The chairman of the Businessmen's Bible Fellowship in Wilmington, Delaware, tried hard to put a good face on it. But he was definitely unhappy with Buddy's appearance as their speaker. "We meet every Wednesday morning for a prayer breakfast. Once a month, we have these evening suppers. Usually it's on a Saturday, but we rescheduled to have our senator make the address—he could only come tonight. Then he couldn't make it, and Pastor Allen said he'd fill in. And now, well, I guess he had something come up too."

"No," Clarke said from Buddy's other side. "It wasn't like that at all."

"To be honest, I wasn't clear at all on why the reverend felt that we needed to hear Mr. Korda." He was leaning back in his chair so he could see Clarke, and paused long enough to offer

Buddy an apologetic smile. "Normally we get in some big speakers for these evening functions. The wives come, and we invite other people from the community."

"I am pretty certain," Clarke replied, "that you won't be at all disappointed."

The chairman looked as if he wanted to say something more, but settled on, "Maybe it'd be a good idea if you did the introduction, then."

"I'd be honored."

Buddy waited until the chairman had turned to speak with someone else, then muttered to Clarke, "I wish I was half as sure about all this as you are."

The room was part of a riverside wharf restoration project, with ancient timbers holding up the high ceiling. Every sound rebounded off the red-brick walls and polished floor. By the time everyone was seated and dinner was served, over a hundred people filled the long banquet tables. Every time Buddy looked up from his place at the front table, his stomach did flip-flops. A wave of laughter swept down one side, and it seemed as though the noise beat at him. Buddy pushed his plate away untouched.

Clarke set his utensils down and slid one arm around the back of Buddy's chair. "You'll do just fine."

"I wish it was over."

"I know you do."

"All of it. Not just tonight."

"Well, it's not. It's only just started. And you might as well get used to the idea and stop bellyaching."

The words were so surprising, coming from the quiet assistant pastor, that Buddy felt pushed an inch or two away from his anxiety. He stared at Clarke and was met by intense gray eyes. Clarke went on, "The Lord has chosen you, Buddy. You may not like it much, but it is still an honor. And more than that, what you have to say may be of vital importance."

Buddy gave a single slight nod. "You're right."

"Of course I am. God is not intending for you to go out and scare His church. He wants them to *prepare*."

Strange how being scolded could force him to a new level of calm. "There's a second part of the message about how to do just that."

"I did not doubt it for a moment." Clarke looked beyond him. "The chairman is going to call us to order."

Buddy sat through the opening remarks and the Bible reading and the prayer and the singing, scarcely hearing any of it at all. His heart beat a frantic pace. Finally Clarke rose at the chairman's nod and approached the podium.

"When I came to the First Christian Church in Aiden twenty-seven years ago, I did not know a soul. New assistant pastors are generally treated like a sort of third thumb at first—people don't have any idea what to do with them. Yet Buddy Korda went out of his way to make me and my wife feel welcome. In his own quiet way, he treated us like family. And that is exactly how we have considered him ever since. A member of our family."

Buddy's attention was caught by the side door opening, and he started at the sight of two people slipping in. His brother, Alex, was in the lead. Agatha Richards came in next. He stared as they slid into two empty chairs by the side wall. A more unlikely pair Buddy could not imagine.

"Buddy is assistant branch manager of the Valenti Bank in Arden. He has helped handle the finances of our community for more than thirty-five years. People tend to overlook him unless they need his help with something, because he prefers to stay in the background. To say that Buddy would rather not be up here tonight is like calling the Atlantic a fair-size puddle. But he *is* here, and he *does* have something to tell you. There is nothing I can say that will prepare you for his message, and so I am just going to sit back down and ask him to come forward. Buddy?"

There was some scattered applause and more than a little muted conversation as Buddy made his way over. He gripped the sides of the podium, feeling the grainy wood under his fingers. He looked out over the hall and remained silent. He was no longer afraid. That was not why he did not speak. He was silent because there before him in that sea of strange faces Buddy caught a glimpse of his own future. Traveling from place to place, passing on from church to Bible study to gathering, moving farther and farther from the town of his birth. Spreading a message of doom.

"Buddy." Clarke leaned over his empty chair, and gave his quiet smile. "It's all right, brother."

And suddenly it was all right. Perfectly all right. Buddy found himself abruptly sheltered within invisible wings of love, safe in the arms of the same Lord who had asked for his help. Buddy looked out over the murmuring crowd, and quietened them by simply starting with his story. How he had started having nightmares. How the Bible passage had risen up before his eyes. How the message had been given to him after a day of fasting.

He stopped there, expecting some back talk and mutterings. But the hall remained silent. Utterly still. So Buddy continued with how he had then asked for signs, looking directly at his brother as he explained what he had asked for. He felt anew the stab of pain over Alex's illness, an ache so deep that he caught his breath and stopped.

Which, as it turned out, was a very good thing.

A man seated at the center of the table to his right suddenly rose to his feet. It was a gradual change, almost as if the man was lifted up by invisible strings. But what raised the hairs on Buddy's neck was the expression on his face.

The man wore a look of blinding ecstasy.

One by one other people around the hall followed Buddy's gaze. The man remained as he was, hanging limply and yet erect. And as silent as the rest of the room.

Then it happened.

There came the sound of a rushing wind. A spark of joy so powerful it *leaped* from person to person and *rushed* through the room. From where Buddy stood, it looked like an instantaneous storm ignited the entire chamber. Some people remained seated, others rose and stood at their places. But no one spoke. Not a word, not a sound. Only the rushing wind. A deeply drumming crescendo of the power of God.

As swiftly as it came, it passed. In its place was a vacuum, interspaced here and there with the quiet sound of weeping. Buddy looked out over the crowd, waiting for people to resume their seats. He had not felt a thing. But he had seen it. And though he was sorry not to have had the experience anew, he was glad all the same. He did not think he would have been able to speak if he had been caught up once again.

"I have something more to tell you," Buddy said, and he waited until all eyes were once more fastened upon him. There was a new focus to the room, a desperate desire to hear what he had to say. Which was good. Because he then delivered the second part of the message. And that was far more surprising than the warning itself.

FIFTEEN

Thirty-Five Days . . .

☐ When Buddy arrived home from work Tuesday he was struck by a panic attack. Cars filled his drive and spilled out along the front curb. Then he recognized all but one of them and breathed a little easier.

He had hardly stepped through the doorway before he heard four voices squeal impossibly high and saw two white-blond-haired and two auburn-haired girls come racing from the kitchen. "Granddaddy!"

"A family gathering. Just what I need." It seemed as if the sun rose in his heart at the sight. "How are my princesses?"

He sank down and allowed himself to be engulfed by his four granddaughters. It was like trying to hold a basketful of wiggling puppies. Meredith and Macon belonged to Paul, his older son. They were almost exactly the same age as Jennifer and Veronica since Jack, his younger boy, had married while still in school, whereas Paul had waited to start his family. Buddy tried to envelop all four girls at once and wished there were some way to stop time from advancing. He would have loved to spend the rest of his days with these little angels, just as they were right now.

"You didn't hug me, Grandpa."

"Yes, he did. I saw him."

"Well, he didn't hug me enough."

"I cut my thumb. Will you kiss it?"

"I got an *A* on my coloring today. The teacher put it on the board for everybody to look at."

Buddy kissed the Band-Aid on one little finger, looked up to where Molly and his two daughters-in-law were watching and smiling, and said, "This is just the medicine I needed."

"Did you have a hard day?"

"Let's see." He rose to his feet, keeping his hands down low to hold the little forms close. "The entire morning was spent writing letters to three hundred customers telling them to oppose the bank's new credit-card policy. Then after lunch word filtered back to the branch manager about my speech last night. That's when things got interesting."

"Oh, Buddy."

"It occurred to me about then that it might be a good idea to take some vacation. I've got almost a month stored up." He looked at Molly. "I know we were planning to use it for that trip out West, but I don't think I could bear trying to handle the bank and this new work at the same time."

Molly gave him a quiet smile. "You were the one who wanted to go out West. Not me."

"I wanted to take you off somewhere."

"It looks like I'll be traveling with you now," she said, clearly at ease with how things were.

All six females were watching him—his two daughters-in-law and his four granddaughters—waiting to see his reaction. It was not the time to show worry. "Where are the boys?"

"Out back, keeping the company occupied."

"Company?"

"Wait, don't tell him yet." Trish was Jack's wife, as petite as Molly and as auburn-haired as her two girls. "I want you to see something first before you get all worked up." She raced back into the kitchen.

Buddy started to ask worked up about what, but the four granddaughters stuffed little hands in their mouths to stop their giggles and did excited dances in place. He put on his sternest face. "Jennifer, what on earth is your mother up to?"

"You'll see." She beamed up at him. "Something good."

"Veronica, you'd better tell me right quick."

"It's a surprise."

"I didn't have time to wrap it, Dad." Trish reappeared, flushed and flustered. "We just picked it up from the framer's on the way over here."

Trish did scrollwork and etchings for a number of the local shops. Buddy watched as she rushed over, hugging a frame to her chest. "What have you been up to, Daughter?"

This brought forth another paroxysm of giggles from the four little girls. Shyly, Trish raised the frame for him to see. "I hope you like it."

A simple, gold passe-partout framed three different pastels and bestowed a sense of colorful depth. At its center, words were scrolled in rich blue and edged in gold. They came from First Corinthians, and said:

Pursue love, and desire spiritual gifts, but especially that you may prophesy. He who prophesies speaks edification and exhortation and comfort to men. He who prophesies edifies the church.

"I'm very proud of you," Trish said quietly.

"I don't know what to say," Buddy told them all.

"We'll hang it in your den," Molly suggested.

"We're all proud of you, Dad." Anne, Paul's wife, was a statuesque blond whose warmth drew people like a flame. She gave Buddy a quick hug. "I'll go tell the boys you're here."

He looked up from the picture and asked, "What was that about company?"

"Alex called and asked if it was okay to bring him around," Molly replied. "I said yes."

"Bring who?"

"A reporter," she answered. "From *The Wall Street Journal.*"

□

"I find it surprising that somebody from *The Wall Street Journal* would come all this way to talk with me," Buddy said.

"I've been in Wilmington working on another story." He ground his cigarette in the house's only ashtray, which was why he was sitting on the back porch. Molly was allergic to tobacco smoke. "You know the Chemtel Corporation, of course, they're the biggest employer in this area. They were in the final stages of acquiring a local company."

"I think I heard something about that."

"The sale price was somewhere in the vicinity of a half billion dollars. This morning the chairman of Chemtel called it off. He gave several reasons, but he said in a private interview with me that the most important explanation was your speech last night."

"I see." Buddy was seated beside his elder son. Paul's silent presence was comforting. Alex sat at the picnic table's far end. From this perspective, it was easy to see how Alex's features had run like wax left in hot sunlight, weathered and wearied by crushed dreams and hard living. And now this illness.

Buddy glanced to where Jack, his second son, sat watching him from alongside the journalist. He could see Molly's face stamped there, her spiked features, her quiet watchfulness. Buddy felt immensely comforted by this gathering of family. Especially now. "Well, what would you like to know?"

"Do you mind if I record this?" The journalist's name was Chad, a sharp young man who spoke with only the slightest twinge of New York to his speech. His features were as crisp as his starched shirt. His hair was razor cut, his spectacles round tortoiseshell. His tie probably cost as much as Buddy's suit. He looked like every young New Yorker on the move Buddy had ever met.

Chad set the recorder on the table between them, checked to make sure it was running, and asked, "Could you tell me a little about what was behind your talk last night, Mr. Korda?"

"You follow the stock market trends more closely than I do. I'm sure you've heard anything I can tell you a dozen times before."

"Sure," Chad agreed. "But I was led to believe that there was something more behind your performance."

"It wasn't a performance," Buddy countered. "I simply shared with a group of businessmen my concerns over the future."

"That's not what I heard. From what I was told, you knocked them off their feet. Literally."

It felt to Buddy as though the family members were granting him their strength, giving him the capacity to say, "Are you a believer, Chad?"

"Am I a . . . ?" He adjusted his spectacles. "I'm paid to be objective, Mr. Korda."

"There is no such thing." Buddy felt the autumn sunlight beating down upon his shoulders. The warmth was magnified by the eyes on him. His two sons, his brother, all watching and helping in their silent way. "Objectivity is an excuse from those who prefer to keep life and faith at an emotional arm's distance. If you are not a believer, then claiming objectivity is a mask. If you are a believer, it will color every action, every thought, every feeling."

"Let's get this back on track." Chad leaned across the table. "We were talking about your speech last night. A couple of the people I interviewed were calling you a prophet."

"Then you'll have to talk to them about that." Strange that he was not the least bit troubled about all this. Chad's confrontational attitude rolled off him like rain on his car's windshield. "The Bible says that prophecy is for believers, not unbelievers. So unless you can speak to me openly as a believer, we will need to hold our discussion to market trends."

"Then let's just say I am a believer, for the sake of argument."

"There should never be arguments between believers," Buddy replied, not even needing to think it out.

"Okay, for discussion's sake, then." A trace of anger glinted through the spectacles.

"Then I would invite you to lead us in a word of prayer and ask the Lord to direct us forward," Buddy responded.

Chad watched him for a silent moment, his features tight. Finally he conceded, "You wanted to tell me something about trends?"

"Certainly. Anyone in banking is aware of current dangers. Or they should be. During the past five years, increases in stock values have added almost four trillion dollars to household savings. And this is extremely widespread, with more than half of all U.S. households owning stocks and mutual funds." Buddy had been watching these trends for years, and worrying for just as long. "The problem is, this is not *confirmed* wealth. This is *theoretical* wealth."

"If stock prices have risen and people own the stocks, then I don't see how this could be considered theoretical," the journalist countered sharply, still angered by his inability to steer the discussion as he would have preferred.

"It remains theoretical so long as people have not cashed in," Buddy answered. "They see the figures on their monthly statements, they watch how the values rise, and this affects their planning. But because they see how fast the stock values are rising, they *don't* cash in. Instead, they *increase their debt*. They borrow money to spend in the moment, expecting to be able to cash their stock holdings sometime in the future."

"That should make a banker like yourself very pleased."

"I can't be pleased when I see this debt based on false expectations," Buddy contradicted. "In this same period, household debt has jumped more than fifty percent, and today totals over *six* trillion dollars. This means if you measure the increase in stock prices versus the increase in debt, the net result is a *decline* in personal net worth of over two trillion dollars. This is an incredible shift, especially since it has happened so swiftly—in just five short years. Do you see where this is headed?"

"Suppose you tell me."

"People are not just increasing their debt to match the rise in their investment's current values. They are increasing their debt to match their *future expectations*. They are saying, the value of my investments increased by twenty percent last year, so it must do the same this year. I can afford this big new house or the brand new car."

Buddy shook his head, feeling the weight of this tragedy beating down with the sun. He was insulated from Chad and his petty anger, but not from the unfolding cataclysm. Not at all. "This is a horrific risk. Most households hold investments they can't easily use—life insurance policies, pensions, home equity, IRA accounts. This means that if there is an economic downturn, not only would they have difficulty meeting their debt payments, they could not pull out of these investments to cover their needs. They could lose their homes, their cars, everything. It is a recipe for disaster."

"But the market is in excellent shape," the journalist argued, clearly unaffected by Buddy's worry. In fact, he sounded almost bored. "The leading pundits predict another eighteen months of share price rises, minimum."

This was leading nowhere. Buddy rose to his feet and offered the young man his hand. "Then let's hope they are right. For all our sakes."

☐

Alex remained behind as the two boys saw the journalist to his car. He waited until the backyard was theirs before announcing, "That kid doesn't have the sense it takes to pound sand down a mousehole."

"No, that's not it." Now that it was over, Buddy felt drained. "He is an extremely intelligent product of our culture."

Alex started to object, then changed the subject. "Agatha Richards came by again. She wants to work with me. After today I think maybe I'll need the help."

"What happened today?"

"I got maybe two dozen phone calls from Lionel Peters alone. He's set you up with speeches from one end of the state to the other, including one later on tonight. I tell you, that man's on fire."

Buddy nodded, wondering why he was not more surprised than he was. "Any others?"

"Are you kidding? By five o'clock this afternoon when Chad arrived, I'd fielded thirty-seven requests for you to talk. Thirty-seven, Buddy. In one day. And the later it got, the farther away the calls came from. The word's beginning to get out. When I closed up, the phone was still ringing like mad. I just got tired of answering it."

Buddy turned back to look at his house. He could hear faint cries of childish laughter through the open door. "I guess it's started, then."

"I'll say it's started." Alex leaned forward, making the table creak under his weight. "Listen, Buddy. Agatha wants me to move downtown. She owns some big office building. Said she'd give me a whole floor. Secretaries, banks of telephones, the works."

"That sounds like Agatha."

"I don't want to move downtown, Buddy. I like it where I am. I know where things are. I know where I stand. Downtown, well, I'm afraid I'd let things get on top of me."

Buddy turned from the house, saw the fear and the appeal in his brother's eyes. "You don't have to do a single thing you don't want to do, Alex."

"I don't?"

"You're in charge of this. You handle it exactly the way you want."

"I don't have to do what Agatha says?"

"You don't have to do what anybody says. Most especially Agatha."

Alex leaned back, surprised by his brother's unqualified reaction. "Well, then."

"A project can't have two heads, Alex. You talk with Molly, you talk with me, then set this up however you see fit." Buddy could not say why it felt so right to speak as he did. But there was no room for questioning. Despite his fatigue, the peace that had stayed with him through the interview still lingered. "Just try to set it up so we're not crisscrossing the state. Make the meetings fit together as close as you can."

"You got it." Alex picked a splinter from the end of the table and then said quietly, "You know, while you were talking with that Chad fellow, I had the strangest feeling."

"I did too."

"The longer he talked, it seemed like the smaller and smaller he got. Didn't matter that he was from Wall Street. Didn't matter that he thought we were all packing just half a load. It seemed as though we were protected somehow."

"I felt the same thing."

"Last night during your speech," Alex started, then stopped to squint up at the sky. "Last night, I watched that thing happen. I saw Agatha get all worked up sitting right there beside me. And I didn't feel much of anything. Oh, a twitch I suppose, but not much more."

"I didn't feel it either, Alex. It doesn't mean anything. Faith is not about having rapturous experiences. It's about following Jesus."

"Maybe it didn't mean anything to you. But sure as chickens wear feathers, it meant something to me. It meant I wasn't doing what you said." His examination of the table became more tightly focused. "All my life, I haven't followed anybody but the wind. And every time the wind changes directions, so do I."

Buddy watched his brother, scarcely daring to breathe.

Alex looked up. "I don't want to follow the wind anymore, Buddy."

"You don't know how long I've dreamed of hearing you say those words."

"I'm gonna take these first steps slow and easy. That's just my nature. I need to understand where it is I'm headed." Alex exhaled a breath that sounded as though he had been holding it for years. "But it's time to start."

Molly appeared on the back porch. "Buddy, are you two going to be much longer? The girls are starving."

"You go ahead and start without us. We'll be a few minutes yet," he said, and turned back to Alex. "My brother and I need to have a little talk about prayer."

⊣‖ SIXTEEN ‖⊢

Thirty-Four Days . . .

☐ Wednesday morning Nathan Jones Turner leaned back in his padded chair, and stared out the window overlooking his estate as he waited for Larry Fleiss to come on the line. As soon as Fleiss answered, Turner demanded, "Found my sure things yet?"

"I'm working on it."

"Do more than work," Nathan Jones Turner barked. "I want results, and I want them fast."

"Things like this take time. I'll need a week at least."

"Do you have any idea what would happen if the Securities and Exchange Commission caught wind of what I've done with the pension-fund accounts?"

"It gives me nightmares." Fleiss paused for a sip from his ever-present mug. "There's one more thing. Small, but we need to discuss it. You seen today's *Journal*?"

"It's here in front of me."

"Take a look at page two."

Turner flipped open the paper and scanned the story about a Valenti assistant branch manager predicting a serious economic downturn. The reporter concluded with the effect Buddy Korda's words had had on derailing the Chemtel deal. Turner snorted his impatience. "So?"

"Doesn't look like much on the surface, I admit. But I've been worrying about it ever since I heard they were gonna run it."

"You knew about this yesterday?"

"Pal over on the *Journal* staff, he called me last night. Said the journalist who covered it was really shook up. The editors all thought it sounded a little wacko, but they had the space and decided to go with it."

"Quite frankly, I can't see any reason for the clamor." Nathan Jones Turner waved an impatient hand toward the strengthening sunlight. "An assistant branch manager finally realizes that he is going nowhere, that nothing in his worthless little life will be remembered ten minutes after he is gone. So he sets out to make a final hurrah."

"My brain is telling me the same thing," Fleiss agreed. "But my gut . . ."

Nathan Jones Turner had ample experience with Larry Fleiss's gut feelings. Fleiss seldom made mistakes, which made this last trade—the first Turner had ever taken a significant personal loss on—so galling. "What would happen if someone started pronouncing that the market was headed for a major correction? No, strike that. More than a correction. A significant downturn."

"You mean," Fleiss said, "someone the market really trusted."

"Exactly. Someone with a voice that people began to pay attention to."

"One word. Disaster." The only change was a tightening to the metallic edge. "It would be a case of wish fulfillment. People believe it, so it happens. We'd take a bath that'd cost us a billion. More."

"If what you say is true, this peon has to be stopped before he can wreak any real damage."

"You said it, not me."

"Do you know people who handle that sort of thing?"

"You mean, find some sort of leverage, force the guy to shut up?"

"I mean," Turner replied grimly, "whatever it takes."

―‖ SEVENTEEN ‖―

☐ Wednesday morning Buddy drove to his brother's car lot. The evening before he had delivered another speech in a nearby town, one of the events prepared by Lionel Peters. Buddy had then spent a restless night reliving the sight of another crowd coming alive while he felt nothing at all.

He and Molly were scheduled to begin their first longer journey that very afternoon, overnighting twice in hotels before returning home. The thought of taking to the road so disturbed him that he was pulling into the entrance before he noticed the difference in Alex's lot.

The multicolored flags still fluttered in the morning breeze, but their shadows fell upon an almost-empty lot. Buddy climbed from the car and looked around. A smiling Alex appeared at the office door. Perhaps it was just his imagination, now that he was looking for such things, but Alex looked a little paler than normal to Buddy. Yet his shirtsleeves were rolled up, and his grin was firmly in place. "Well, if it ain't the man of the hour!"

"Alex, what's going on here?"

"I did what the competition have been after me to do for years. I sold out to the highest bidder."

"You're going to work for the dealership?"

"Probably. We'll see about that later." He waved him over. "Come on inside. Who'd believe it could be this hot in September?"

When Buddy stepped into the trailer's air-conditioned cool, Alex went on, "Last night I decided I'd give myself full time to this. Yesterday was enough to show it's going to take all I've got to give and more. The Chrysler dealership called to buy me out, and this time I said yes. Shocked the guy right out of his skin."

Buddy was astonished at how easily Alex spoke about the empty lot. "I can imagine."

"My two salesmen are already over there. Taking them on was part of the deal. And my cars. They'll be over to pick up the rest this afternoon. I've got three months before they expect me to start. Figure that'll be enough time."

Alex caught Buddy's look, and hastily added, "Don't worry. I didn't tell them about my illness, but I was straight about everything else. They only pay for my inventory now, and I gave them more than a fair price. They're happy to do away with the competition. They've done well by it, no matter what happens."

"I'm glad you handled it the way you did," Buddy said, feeling a twinge of pain just the same. "Very glad."

"I've got to try to play it straight if I'm gonna do this for God." Alex's grand smile reappeared. "Who in the world would've ever thought I'd say those words?"

Agatha Richards appeared in the doorway and announced primly, "Certainly not me."

Even Agatha's big-boned frame and overly erect posture looked petite alongside Alex. He grinned at her. "Sure does dress up the old place though, doesn't she?"

"I'll say," Buddy agreed. Agatha wore a quilted jacket with gold buttons, a long navy skirt of rich velvet, and a double strand of pearls. Every hair on her graying head was set precisely in place, every gem on her fingers and in her earrings sparkled in the morning sunlight. "How are you, Agatha?"

"Busy." She glanced through her thick lenses at Alex. "I certainly could use some help."

Alex asked him, "Are you on your way out of town?"

"Molly's just finishing her packing." Seeing the sadness on his wife's features was what had driven Buddy from the house. "The speech still on for this afternoon?"

"And tonight. And tomorrow lunchtime." Alex grinned. "After that, things get sorta interesting."

"What do you mean?"

"I'll let the lady tell you herself." He gave her a mock little bow, and said, "It's your show, duchess."

Such a remark would normally have been enough to entangle the speaker with the sharp side of Agatha's tongue. But today all she did was adjust her spectacles and say quietly, "If you'll step this way."

She led them down the trailer's narrow hallway. The back room had been transformed. Alex's desk was pushed over to one corner. The little conference table occupied the middle of the room. The framed letters were stacked beside the desk. The walls were now covered with seven state maps.

Buddy did a slow circle. There was no need for anyone to tell him why all the little colored pins were stuck in the maps. Most of the pins were reserved for their home state of Delaware. But a few appeared as far away as Illinois. "Oh, my!"

"Calls are coming in from farther and farther away," Alex proclaimed.

"Word is spreading," Agatha agreed, her precise voice unnaturally quiet. "Buddy, I've had to make some changes."

"I agree with her, for what it's worth," Alex said. He could not have sounded prouder if he had invented Agatha himself.

"There's not enough time for you to accept just any invitation that comes in. And currently there is far too much backtracking." Another quick adjustment of her spectacles. "I have started calling the organizations back and asking them to come together into one large meeting."

"I'll bet that went over like a lead balloon."

"Don't. You'd lose your bet," Alex happily replied.

"Up to now, all have agreed. There are a few scheduling difficulties, but not many. The response has been, well . . ."

"Miraculous," Alex offered. His grin threatened to split his face. "No other word for it."

"One meeting per city," Agatha said firmly. "And the timing set up so your driving is kept to a minimum."

Alex said, "Now tell him the good part."

"Lionel and Clarke met yesterday afternoon with the coordinators for a series of nationwide revivals, where they bring in big music groups and a number of big-name speakers and lay it on all day long."

Buddy felt his legs go weak. "The ones where they rent a whole stadium?"

"We're talking forty thousand people," Alex cried. "Can you get your mind around that?"

"No." Buddy made his feeble way to the nearest chair and plopped down. "No, I can't."

The pair stared at him. Alex said, "I thought you'd be pleased."

"Well, I'm not."

"Your word is getting out," Agatha said. "This is a big opportunity."

"This is terrifying, is what it is," Buddy replied.

Alex and Agatha exchanged a glance. "Look," Buddy told them. "We've got to get one thing clear right up front. What is absolutely necessary among us is total honesty. Nothing else is permitted in this little circle. Is that understood?"

His sharp tone sobered them both. Agatha answered, "Yes, Buddy."

"Total honesty," he repeated. "Utter openness. We can tell one another everything, and do so with the assurance that our words will be met with love and support. This is far more important than any planning we might do, or any meeting you set up for me. Out there is a world of woe and discord. In here, among us, we need to be able to retreat and cast off the masks, and show one another exactly who we are."

Alex nodded somberly. "A team."

"Precisely. And I'll tell you with all the honesty I have that I do not want to do this. I don't want to travel. I don't want to sleep in strange beds. I don't want to eat packaged food. I don't want to shake the hands of people who will look at me like I've fallen out of the sky. I don't want people to think I wear wings and a crown." He felt the events-to-come crowding in on him until he drew short of breath. He grabbed his chest, willing himself to relax. "And I do *not* like the idea of standing up in front of forty thousand people. *Forty* strangers are enough to give me the shakes."

"Take it easy, Brother," Alex said.

Agatha asked, "Can I get you something?"

"No. What you can do for me is pray. And let me come in here and unload. And give me absolute honesty in return. Will you do that for me?"

"Anything," Agatha replied.

"You just name it," Alex agreed.

Buddy's shoulders slumped. Forty thousand people. The number was too big to comprehend. "Sometimes I feel that it's all just a dream. That I'll wake up tomorrow and it'll all be over, that I can go back to just being Buddy Korda. Comfortable and happy with my little life in my little town."

"You know what Pop used to say. 'God comes to comfort the troubled and trouble the comfortable.'"

"Do you know, I had forgotten that." Buddy found it nice to have a reason to smile. "Pop would be proud of you, Alex."

His brother's features slipped into hollow sadness. "Shame I had to wait until it was too late."

"It's never too late." Buddy glanced at his watch and rose slowly to his feet. He walked over and took his brother's bulky form in a firm embrace. "Never too late."

He released Alex and turned to the stiffly erect woman. It seemed so natural, so correct to sweep her up as well, and enfold her in his arms and say, "I owe you more than I could ever say, Agatha."

Her rigid form relaxed enough to hold him fiercely. "You don't owe me a thing. I'm not doing this for you at all."

He released her, smiled, and said, "Good."

□

It was fitting that a daughter-in-law and two of their granddaughters would be there to see them off that afternoon. Sad, but fitting. Anne stood with Molly by the car, while two little blond girls scampered around the big front lawn. Meredith was five and wise enough to let her younger sister catch her from time to time. Macon was four, and her progress was slowed because she insisted on running about while holding on to her floppy-eared bunny.

Buddy walked over, saw how the open trunk was full of suitcases and bags, and had to turn away. He watched the girls. "I don't believe I've ever seen a bunny as dirty as that one."

"It used to be pink," Anne agreed. "But that was six hundred washes ago."

Molly leaned over and allowed the little one to run squealing into her embrace. "That's all right, my darling. Your bunny likes to play in the dirt with you, doesn't he?"

Macon shrieked as though the hug tickled and then wiggled until Molly released her. Sunlight fell between the two grand elms and turned Macon's hair to sparkling platinum. Anne said, "I've told her that four years old is too big to be sucking her thumb anymore. Now I go in at night and find she's stuck one of those bunny ears in her mouth."

Buddy protested, "Look how the ears drag on the ground like that."

"I've given up worrying about where that bunny has been," Anne said.

Molly told her, "Your husband used to want to touch everything with his tongue. Learning to walk meant being able to get more to his mouth, and get it there faster."

"I remember that," Buddy said.

"Bugs, snakes, lizards, anthills, turtles, every puppy on the block, even the tires on Buddy's car. It went on for years."

"That man will never kiss me again," Anne declared seriously.

"They're little angels on the outside, but the dear Lord gives all children tummies of tungsten carbide." Molly wore a stiff blouse of dark ivory, with a lace collar that almost touched her chin. Her grandmother's cameo closed the neck, and from her pocket dangled her old-fashioned watch-pin. She lifted it to inspect the time and said to Buddy, "It's less than two hours to your talk."

Anne called out, "Come give Gram and Grandpa hugs."

The two little ones ran over, accepted the embraces with squeals and giggles, and then raced off to chase the sun. Buddy rose and saw the solemn light in Anne's eyes. His daughter-in-law said, "Paul told me to tell you that we're all proud of you, and that we'll be praying you through this, every step of the way."

Buddy started, "I wish—"

"Give everyone our love," Molly said, breaking him off. "We'll call once we get to the hotel tonight."

"Okay, Mama Korda." Anne hugged them and watched them climb into the car. When they started backing out of the drive, the two little ones waved and called and danced. Sunbeams and sorrow mixed in Buddy's eyes until he could not tell where the girls ended and the light began.

—|| EIGHTEEN ||—

☐ "Mr. Dorsett? This is Larry Fleiss."

Thad sat up straighter. "You're kidding."

"You've heard of me, then."

"Who hasn't." Larry Fleiss was a legend in his own time. A self-made trader, rising out of nowhere as all top traders did, going from strength to strength. "Is this really Fleiss?"

"The one and only. Have you seen today's *Journal*?"

"Afraid so." Thad gave a silent sigh. To be called by Larry Fleiss because of Buddy was the worst kind of insult. "Mind telling me why you're interested in Korda?"

"It's not the man, it's the article. If this talk of his is a fluke, it's a passing curiosity. But if it continues . . ."

"He could affect the bank's standing," Thad finished, loathing Buddy Korda anew. "If we can't control the ravings of one of our own, how can we be trusted to handle money on the Street?"

"I see we think alike." The voice sounded like a string plucked and sent buzzing over a tin plate. Of course. It had to be Larry Fleiss. His voice was as much a trademark as the man's ability in the markets. The metallic drone was a product of ten thousand market forays, putting hundreds of millions on the line and then watching the market spin. An adrenaline junkie. Fleiss went on, "I've heard some good things about you."

"You have?" Fleiss was one of the reasons Thad had joined Valenti. Here was a trader who was both fund manager and chief aide to the chairman of the board. Fleiss was the clearest possible signal that the sky was the limit. And the man had heard about *him*. "Heard what?"

"You're a trader with moxie. And you've got what it takes to rise to the top."

"Like you." Keeping his voice level, fighting down the excitement.

"Sure. What's your attitude toward this assistant manager of yours?"

"More fruit fly than manager. A wimp who's found his place in life." Thad cataloged the small-time habits, going through the recent conflicts and ending with the letter to the bank's top clients about refusing to accept new bank policies.

Fleiss's asthmatic breathing continued when Thad was finished. Then, "Sounds like somebody living in the past."

"The man is a throwback to horse-and-buggy days," Thad agreed.

"What do you suggest we do?"

"Strike directly." Thad did not need to think that one out. "Give Korda an ultimatum. Shape up or else. And if he doesn't drop this, we drop him. Chop him off at the ankles."

"I like your attitude, Dorsett. Think you can pass on the message from the front office?"

"With pleasure," Thad said with savage glee. "You can count on me."

⊣∥ NINETEEN ∥⊢

☐ Buddy drove up and over the hills west of Aiden. The change in altitude was just enough for the first hints of autumn to touch a few trees. They shone out from among their brethren, hinting at changes to come. Buddy took the drive slow and easy, trying to get used to the way things were. Hoping to find some breath of rightness to the new beginning.

Molly allowed him space and silence until they started down the slope's other side. "How do you feel?"

"Do you remember what your mother used to say when something riled her? She said she felt put upon." He took a steep curve. "That pretty much sums it up for me too. I feel put upon."

"It's funny," Molly said. "I was just thinking about Momma too."

He glanced over. Her face was tilted slightly, so that she could look out both the front and side windows. The scar that ran from her left ear downward was displayed in all its angry fullness. Molly went on, "I was thinking about the accident."

"Oh, Molly." This had to be a very bad day for her. Molly had not spoken about the accident in thirty years, not since the year before they were married.

"I was five, the same age as Jennifer and Meredith," Molly said, repeating the story he had heard just once before. "Momma was boiling bones on the stove to make marrow soup. The pot was boiling over. It was making such a mess. I had no idea how heavy it was until I tried to lift it off. It spilled all over me. Down the side of my face, down my neck and shoulder."

"I'm so sorry," he murmured, hurting anew for her. And not just because of the accident. Buddy ached over how the journey was already causing her such grief that she relived the worst time of her life. He was inundated with a desire to turn around and go home. Let the whole thing pass them by. Take the days left to them and just enjoy what was theirs. The temptation was so strong he felt little tremors run down his fingers and through the steering wheel.

"Momma was such a proper woman," Molly said in her own soft way. "She was a good person and a good Christian. But she was too concerned with what the world saw."

As suddenly as the tremors came, they passed. Buddy glanced over once more. This was something new. He had often thought the same things about Molly's mother, but had never spoken them out loud.

"Momma was devastated by what I had done. And so angry. I knew she was trying to hide her anger from me. But I knew.

She was *furious*. She shouldn't have been, and it didn't make any sense, so she refused to even see it herself. But she was so very angry."

One finger reached up and touched the scar. Buddy slowed so he could keep his gaze on her. Molly never touched her scar, except to powder it in the mornings. Watching her trace one finger lightly down the edge where healthy skin met the red-tinted scar tissue brought a lump to his throat.

"Momma stayed angry for such a long time. Probably not being able to admit she was furious even to herself made it last longer. At the time, all I knew was that I had done something terrible. And in my own way I understood better than she did. Momma was a *proper* lady. She was so concerned that the world thought good of her. And now her daughter had a scar that told everyone who looked at her that Momma was not a good mother, that she didn't look after her own daughter."

"You don't know that, Molly."

"I know the way she taught me to use makeup, long before other girls even knew what face powder was. I watched her take all my blouses and sew in embroidered collars that almost reached my ears. I learned from her how to set my hair so it would gather and spill over my left shoulder and hold it in place with bright ribbons, so attention would be taken away from my scar."

Molly dropped her hand, gathered it with the other in her lap. "I was so ashamed. I had disgraced my mother."

Buddy put on his blinker and pulled over to the side of the road. "You haven't disgraced anyone. Not then, not ever."

"But I did, you know." Her eyes were pools of grief. Deep inside, a little girl was still crying tears the woman no longer shed. "I saw it every time she looked at me. I was a scandal."

"Stop it, Molly, please." He reached over for her hands. "Look, there's still time if we hurry. I'll drive you back home. I can do this alone. There's no need—"

"That's not why I'm telling you this." One hand slid out to cover his. "I've let my mother's shame be a barrier for too long, Buddy. Coming to terms with this journey has brought up all the reasons why I've spent my whole life hiding. Oh, I know I'm shy by nature. But more than that is at work here."

Buddy leaned back but kept his hand in hers. He had no idea where she was going with this.

Molly looked out the light-streaked windshield. "For several years now I've been wanting to do something more. Something outside the church. I couldn't understand what it was or why I felt that way, but I do now. I wanted to grow beyond the barriers that I've let restrict all my life. I want to *grow*."

A flood of shame swept through him. He sat beside his wife of twenty-nine years feeling about two inches tall. Here he was, called in terms so vivid he felt as though his heart had been remolded in the process. And yet he was still looking for excuses to return to his comfort and his routines.

But his wife, who had a lifetime of quiet constraint to overcome, was willing to challenge her limitations for no more reason than a hunger to develop and the knowledge that he needed her. Buddy reached over and stroked a strand of wayward hair. "I'm so proud of you, Molly."

The words brought her back to earth and her quietly prim ways. "I didn't do anything."

"Oh, yes, you did." He stroked her cheek, let his fingertips run lightly over her scar. His wonderful, wounded little bird. "So much."

⊣∥ TWENTY ∥⊢

☐ Langston, Delaware, was a mill town. A forest of smokestacks lined the road, with high-tension wires for branches and billowing smoke for leaves. There was white smoke and black smoke and gray and brown and even one foul-smelling chemical factory with spumes of angry yellow. Molly covered her mouth with her handkerchief as they passed that one. The car's air conditioner couldn't begin to filter out the stench.

The church was in the border country between low-slung houses and the nearest factories. The exterior was red-brick dyed a dull gray by the soot. As they pulled up and stopped, they were surprised to see Clarke Owen wave and walk toward them. Buddy got out of the car, and Clarke called over, "How was your drive?"

"Fine." Buddy went around the car to meet him. "What are you doing here?"

"I'm your advance team. Hello, Molly. How are you today?"

"Just fine, Clarke. It's nice to see you."

Buddy demanded, "My what?"

"Somebody needs to travel ahead, make sure everything is up and running. Which reminds me. Three quick things." Clarke reached into his jacket pocket and came up with a palm-size mobile phone. "You need to carry this. The number is taped to the back, in case you want to tell somebody how to reach you. Be sure and remember to switch it off before you stand at a podium."

Molly stopped him from objecting by stretching out her hand and saying, "I'll take that."

"Number two. There's been a change tonight. We've been moved to a high-school auditorium. Seems there are more people wanting to hear you than the church could handle." He pulled papers from his inner pocket. "This is a contact number and address. This map shows both the auditorium and your hotel. Figured you'd like to stop by and freshen up after your talk here."

Before Buddy could form his objections, Molly said, "It looks like you've thought of everything, Clarke."

The assistant pastor gave a proud smile. "Trying, Molly. Trying hard."

"Clarke, I—"

Molly rounded on him and gave Buddy the same hard look she had used on her two sons. She said quietly, "Don't."

Buddy gathered himself. Molly rarely used that tone with him, but when she did, he knew to watch out. He clamped down on all he had to say.

Clarke glanced from one face to the other, then looked beyond them and waved over two people. "This is the couple responsible for the meeting here, Harvey and Gloria Rand."

The man was short and as florid-faced as his tie. "Saw you over in Wilmington the other night."

"We don't have a Bible Fellowship here in Langston," his wife interjected, showing more teeth than Buddy thought one mouth could hold.

"We like to get over there for the dinners," the man said. "Work business around those monthly meetings. Sure glad we didn't miss that one."

"It was positively thrilling," his wife agreed.

"We asked to hold the meeting here today because it's close to the factories. You're catching a lot of these folks between shifts." He waved an arm in the direction of the crowd that was streaming toward the church entrance. "You've got all kinds here, from secretaries to machine operators to vice presidents."

"The mayor said he'd try to make it," his wife added. "He goes to our church. I called him personally."

"Gloria has plastered notices all over town. She even tried to glue one on my forehead when I sat still too long." His grin turned a little nervous. "Are you gonna put on the same kind of show we saw in Wilmington?"

Buddy started to react to the nerves and the pressure with a sharp retort, something like, it wasn't a show. But again Molly's quiet voice was there first. "He most certainly is."

"Great, just great. Say, I don't believe we've met. Harvey Rand."

"I'm Molly Korda, Buddy's wife."

"Sure am glad you folks could make it today. Well, let's get on inside."

Buddy felt Molly's pressure on his arm and hung back. That look was back in her eyes. "Don't fight this, Buddy."

"I don't know what you're talking about."

"Yes, you do. All these people helping and making a big fuss over you. It's perfectly natural. And you need Clarke. What would have happened if you had gotten to Dover tonight and didn't know about the change of location?"

As if on cue, Clarke drifted back. "I almost forgot the third thing. Agatha Richards was supposed to tell you herself, but she couldn't work up the nerve. She is footing the bill."

Buddy felt like he was running just to stay up with the man. "What bill?"

"All of them." A merry smile slipped into view. "Every last one." He patted Buddy's arm. "I'm not going to hang around, much as I would like. I've got to get over to Dover and make sure things are set up for tonight."

☐

It was the noisiest crowd by far.

Halfway through the talk Buddy stood at the podium, feeling utterly empty of any sensation whatsoever. He waited through the shouting and the clapping and the talking and the weeping. He listened to one person after another call out an affirmation of what he had come to say. He watched the hands waving and listened to all the amens. Yet he could not have felt more isolated from the experience if he had been standing across the road.

And yet, despite his sense of disconnection, he also felt a rightness. He could not explain why, but he did. So he remained content to stand there and wait them out, because he certainly couldn't complete his message with all this noise.

As he waited, he observed. He saw the tiredness of day-in, day-out hard work etched into most of the features. He saw the scars and even some tattoos, evidence of life before Jesus. He saw the patched clothes and the tough, seamed faces. He saw stains beneath most eyes, as though the factory smoke had engraved shadows into their features. And he found himself feeling for them.

This was strange as well, for Buddy had nothing whatsoever in common with them. He had always had difficulty communicating with people like this. Even inside the bank, he had found it hard to talk things out, as though he was trying to translate his thoughts into a language he did not really know. The people would sit there, numbed by the strangeness and the feeling that things were out of their control.

Buddy had often recognized the helplessness in their faces as they sat there on the other side of his desk. Try as he might to make them understand he was on their side, he never really felt as though he was getting through. Yet they kept coming back to him and sending their neighbors. They came to him with their debts and their mortgages and their questions, and after every such meeting, he would sit back drained and feeling like he had failed once more.

When they were ready to look his way again, Buddy raised his arms and asked for quiet. Many chose not to return to their seats, but they did become silent. "I have more to say to you, and I ask that you pay very close attention." He was talking to them as he would if he was trying to explain a second lien. "This is going to sound complicated, but it's only because you don't know the words. I imagine if you took me into your place of work and tried to tell me about one of your machines, I'd be lost in fifteen seconds. You'd say things like flange and CNC panel, and I'd want to turn and run away."

"Me too, boss," called a deep voice from the back. "Me too."

He smiled with the laughter. "All right. You've heard me say there is a difficult time coming. And now I need to tell you the second part of the message. The part about how to prepare. Mind you, I'm not telling you what to do. I'm telling you what the message was. And I'm asking you to go home and pray about this. Pray hard. Then go and do what you feel called to do."

Then it hit him. Hard.

Perhaps because it was so unexpected, the power almost overwhelmed him. Suddenly he was not looking out over a group of strangers with whom he had nothing in common. He was *with* them. And they were *family*. And in their quietly intent faces he saw a need, a desperate appeal, an appeal to which his heart reached out in love and mercy, a feeling so mighty it felt as though a fist had clenched his throat shut.

Their lives were threatened by so many things beyond their control. And here he had come, to tell them of dreams and portents that threatened calamity. Buddy felt his entire being humming with an urgency to prepare against the coming storm. Not for himself. For everyone.

He did not know how long he stood there. They stood or sat and watched him, and they did not seem to be concerned about the silence. Buddy wondered if they could feel the vibrating energy, the sense of standing and hearing the clarion trumpet of heaven. He cleared the tightness from his throat and forced himself to speak. "The message is this: Take every cent you can spare. Go to a stockbroker you can trust."

He took great comfort from the calmness in his voice. To his own ears it sounded as if someone else was doing the speaking. "Is there a stockbroker in the audience?"

"Right here, sir." A man stood and waved. "I'm a broker."

"Are you a Christian?"

"I am." No hesitancy, no doubt. "Praise God, I am."

"Do you accept the message of today?"

"I've been feeling it in my bones for months."

Buddy nodded and pointed at the broker. "Here is one person you can work with. I'm not telling you to do it with this particular gentleman. What I *am* saying is that, if you feel led by my message, you need to work with someone who will accept your instructions and not talk you out of what you feel called to do. Because what I'm here to tell you would be considered very risky by a lot of people. As a matter of fact, some brokers would refuse to work with you at all. They would say that people who deal in options need to have a lot of extra capital. In other words, they need to be rich enough to be able to lose it all. Which you are not."

Buddy looked at the broker, waiting for him to object. But the man met his eye and nodded. Once.

Buddy turned back to the audience and went on, "There is a certain kind of stock transaction called a *put option*. It means you are predicting that the price of the stock will fall. It also means that you put as little as five percent down on the purchase. It is tremendously risky. But the gains are potentially very great.

"The intention here is to take whatever you can scrape together and make enough to see you and your families through the coming famine. The message is this: Take all you can and invest in *put options*. The options should be for shares in any of the nation's top twenty banks. The options should come due in three to five months.

"But you are not to wait five months. In exactly thirty-four days, you are to sell them all. No matter what the market may be doing, no matter what your broker may tell you. Sell them all.

"Half of all profit from your investment in put options should be given to your church," he concluded. "These funds are intended to help see the church family through this crisis. A group from the elders and deacons must be chosen to oversee the fund for as long as the famine lasts."

When he finished his talk, Buddy looked out over the crowded hall. The silence lasted a long time. Whether it was because the people were frightened by his announcement, or because they were caught up in the same quivering energy that he was feeling, Buddy could not tell. Finally the broker rose to his feet once more and proclaimed, "I feel the rightness of what my brother is saying."

"So do I," said a woman's voice from the back. "Right as rain."

Buddy could sense the audience's sudden restlessness, felt the power fading away, knew it was time to end this and move away. "Let us close with a moment of prayer."

TWENTY-ONE

☐ Molly drove all the way to Dover, Delaware, granting Buddy space and silence and an occasional comforting touch. Buddy sat in the passenger seat, watching the countryside and the busy road and the sunlight flickering down through the trees. Thinking was too much of an effort. Little flashes of thought or memory came and went but did not catch hold, like bubbles rising to the surface of water.

When she saw the exit sign, she asked, "Is it the first or second exit we're supposed to take?"

Buddy pulled the papers from his pocket and checked the map. "First."

She made the turn and asked, "How do you feel?"

"Fine. Drained, but fine."

"Will you be all right for another talk tonight?"

"I think so." What had happened in that church flashed clearly before his eyes. "It really felt right back there."

"It's nice to hear you talk like that. I want you to feel confident about what you are doing." She stopped at the intersection. "Which way?"

"Right, and then right again at the first light. The hotel should be on our left."

She checked both ways and pulled into the right lane. "You are God's messenger. You need to grow in confidence in your work and your message."

Buddy felt a trace of the same resonance he had sensed while up at the podium. *Grow into it.*

"You spoke with such authority up there. And I'm not just saying that because I'm your wife."

"I know you're not. I felt it too."

"It's time you accepted the importance of what you're doing and give yourself to it. Fully and without reservation."

Buddy waited until she had made the turn and pulled into the hotel's front parking area to say, "I'm glad you're here with me, Molly. So very glad."

☐

There was a message waiting for him to call Alex. He used the mobile phone for the first time as Molly checked them in. The little buttons were unfamiliar and left his fingers seeming too big and clumsy. When Alex answered, Buddy turned his back to the hotel lobby as he raised the phone to his ear. He felt very foolish. "I got your message."

"The bank called. Some guy by the name of Thaddeus Dorsett. One of those real smarmy voices, fake as white margarine." Alex snorted. "Sounded like somebody you'd like to shoot on sight."

"No, Alex."

"How about we just watch him trip on the rug as he enters the room. Bring him down a few notches."

"That is not a worthy thought."

"Well, he said it was urgent. Real urgent. Gave me his home phone, asked you to call as soon as you could." Alex read off the number, then asked, "Did Clarke tell you about the change of venue for tonight?"

"Yes. Alex, what is this about Agatha paying our bills?"

"Hang on a sec." The phone was laid down, and Buddy heard the sound of a door being closed. Alex picked up the phone and said, "Okay, now we can talk. It was her idea, Buddy. She came up with it all on her own."

Molly chose that moment to walk over and say, "The bill's already been taken care of. Do you want to go on to the room?"

Buddy nodded and followed her through the lobby as he said into the phone, "I can't accept this." Then he had to hit the brakes hard, for Molly turned and gave him a warning look.

"I told her you probably wouldn't like it. She didn't put up the fuss you'd have expected. More like a real wistful hoping."

Molly asked him, "Is that Alex? Are you talking about Agatha?"

He nodded. Alex continued, "She really wants to do this, Buddy. She said that she'd only be giving the money to God in some other way, that you have a divine message, and that she wants to do as much as she can to help out. A lot of stuff like that. I didn't have the heart to say no. I could have argued with her if she had gotten on her high horse, but not when she is like this. Sounded like she was pleading with me."

Molly told him, the warning still in her eyes, "Remember what we talked about in front of the church this afternoon? Let people help you, Buddy."

"It's fine, Alex."

Alex said, "It is?"

Molly continued, "You're not a banker here. You're not signing papers for other people's time and money. The only debts you have are with God, and those you'll never be able to repay, so you don't need to try."

He could not resist the desire. Buddy reached over with his free hand and hugged Molly close. He didn't care how silly he looked walking through the hotel lobby talking on the phone and hugging his wife. He said, "Alex, please thank her for me the very best you can."

☐

"Thad, this is Buddy Korda."

"Where are you?" The voice was tight, clipped.

"We've just checked into our hotel."

"We?"

"My wife and I. I'm on my vacation, as you may recall."

"No, you're not. I know all about your little escapades. So does the home office."

Molly's antennae must have been up and working, because she turned from her unpacking to walk over and stand by his chair. Buddy glanced her way as he said to the phone, "I see."

"No, that's your problem, Korda. You don't see at all. This is not some stunt you're going to be able to walk away from and forget. It has seriously damaged your career."

Buddy could see the manager's face there before him, the yellow eyes, the feral snarl unveiled. "My career?"

"What's left of it. If you want to have any job at all, you'll pack up and head straight home. Do not pass go, do not collect your two hundred dollars for the little talk you *won't* be giving tonight." The tone hardened to a surly growl. "Not if you want to have a job tomorrow."

Buddy felt the voice battering him, or at least trying to. Which was a surprise, because he positively loathed confrontation. Yet in this confrontation, which threatened the position he had given his life to, he was able to hold to his calm. "I see."

"You'd better. That is, if you're the *least* bit interested in holding on to your pension." A pause, and when Buddy said nothing, Thad continued, "That's right, Korda. There's more than just your own little job at stake here. Think about what you're doing to your family. And your own future security."

Buddy found himself searching for some sign of panic. His own lack of internal reaction was as bizarre as this conversation. "Well, thank you for calling, Thad."

His reaction threw off the bank manager. "This is the only warning you're going to get," Thad said, but the cutting edge had been dulled. "And frankly, if it had been left up to me, I wouldn't have given you this one. If you give your little talk tonight, don't even bother to come back to clean out your desk."

Buddy cut the connection and said to Molly, "The bank is going to fire me if I keep this up."

Molly's face was wreathed in concern. "How do you feel about it?"

"To be perfectly honest, I don't feel much of anything right now." He gave his heart another mental check and said doubtfully, "Maybe I'm just in shock."

"I don't think so." Molly sank to the edge of the bed closest to Buddy's chair. "Honey, have you been listening to your own messages at all?"

"Of course I have."

"I'm not so sure about that. Buddy, if what you're telling the world is true, five weeks from now, what shape is your bank going to be in?"

The thought pushed him back in his chair. The bank was going to collapse. It took a moment before Buddy realized he had not spoken out loud. The bank was going to go under.

His bank. That was the way he thought about it. He had given his adult life to making the bank's balance sheet and profit statement as sound as he could. He had served his community through his bank. It was as much a part of him as his eyes or his feet. And it was going to collapse.

"While we're on this," Molly went on, "have you thought about doing with our savings what you're telling others to do?"

"No," he replied slowly, his mind still caught by the earlier thought. It had been shown clearly, even made a part of his dream. But he had refused to see. His bank was going under. "The money for the ridgeline has been deposited into our account, I checked that before we left. Easiest transaction I've ever made. But I didn't do a thing with it. I guess I've missed that too."

"Well, you can worry about it tomorrow." She patted his knee. "Right now I want you to lie down and have a rest. You look exhausted."

□

Molly let him sleep so long he had to button his shirtsleeves and knot his tie in the car. It had been a curious slumber, leaving him more tired and woozy than before he had lain down, as though all he had done was give his body and mind a chance to reveal some of the stored-up tension. He had dozed in fitful bursts, tensing and jerking awake every few minutes. The same thought continued to course through him even when he was asleep. His bank was going under.

When they pulled up in front of the auditorium, Molly stopped him from opening his door by reaching over and touching his arm. "Are you all right?"

"It's a hard thing to accept, Molly. My bank is not going to make it. I can feel it in my bones."

"Would you listen to yourself?" she said softly. "Going out to pass on a message about turmoil afflicting the whole nation. You've just received word you're going to be fired for your troubles. And what are you worried about? The bank."

"A lot of people rely on us," he said feebly.

"Of course they do. Here." She reached into the purse beside her and pulled out a little note card. "I want you to have this."

"What is it?"

"A passage I thought of while you were sleeping."

Buddy turned on the interior light and held up the card. He read: "*A man can receive nothing unless it has been given to him from heaven.*" *John 3:27*

"I just wanted to remind you of what you already know," Molly told him.

"This is perfect." He reread the passage, looked up. "Thank you, Molly."

She turned shy. "I could do this every day if you like. Find a passage for you to take with you into your talk."

"I would like that," he replied, "more than I can say."

□

Clarke met them halfway to the auditorium. "I was just about ready to get worried."

"He needed to rest," Molly said firmly.

Buddy accepted the outstretched hand. "What are you doing about your duties in the church?"

"I asked for a leave of absence. The elders agreed unanimously. Even the ones who had not heard you speak that night said I should come help you." Clarke extended his smile to include Molly. "Maybe that's an indication of how vital they think my work is around the place."

"Don't you think that," Molly scolded. "Not for an instant."

Clarke said to Buddy, "Before we get started here, there's one thing. We've had some journalists show up tonight. I know who they are, at least I think I do. Should I let them stay?"

Buddy reflected a moment and could only come up with, "We don't try to keep anyone else out. I suppose we shouldn't start with them."

"I agree," Molly said. "Who knows? Maybe they will feel the Spirit and come to their knees and their senses."

Both men looked her way. It was not like her to speak her mind in public. Buddy reached over and took her hand. It was a good change.

Clarke went on, "A lot of them wanted interviews. I figured you'd be too tired to do it tonight. So I said anyone who wanted could show up tomorrow after breakfast. The television folk have been after Alex all day. They wanted to have you all to themselves, one at a time."

"No." Buddy did not need to think that one over.

"My sentiments exactly." Clarke motioned to his right. "Here comes the lady responsible for tonight. Mrs. Sandown, can I introduce Buddy and Molly Korda?"

"Such a pleasure, I just can't tell you." She was nervous and excited and dressed in a sharp businesslike outfit of navy serge. "My husband and I heard you speak at the Bible Fellowship dinner over in Wilmington. Well, more than heard. He's had to go to Boston for a sales meeting, but he helped me set this up. It's been amazing how willing the churches have been to get the word out. Nothing at all like what I might have expected."

The words no longer held the power of surprise for him. "I'm grateful for all the work you've put in."

"You have something important to say, Mr. Korda. I feel that everybody needs to hear it." She gave a nervous glance at the doors leading to the high school gym. "The reason why we needed to change venues is that we've had a surprising response from several African-American and Roman Catholic churches." She exhaled what seemed to be a breath she had been holding all afternoon. "And someone wants to video your talk. Not the press, we've already had it out with them. This isn't a circus. A member of my church works for the local television station, and I know he'll do a good job." Again the anxious waiting.

Buddy thought it over and decided. "I think that would be a good idea."

"There isn't that much time to get the word out," Clarke agreed.

"We'll ask that it be distributed only to churches, but you know how these things are." She twisted her hands together. "Do you think the Spirit will be with us like it was the other day?"

"I hope so," Buddy fervently replied. The people headed for the entrance doors in a solid stream. "I surely do."

□

Perhaps it was because of the sound that bounced off the hardwood floor and the distant ceiling. Perhaps it was because of the bleacher seating, or because of the size of the audience. Or perhaps it was simply because Buddy was so tired. Whatever the reason, it seemed as though the meeting would never end. Time after time he had to stop and wait for the noise to abate before he could continue. But he did not feel a thing. Not when people started crying and shouting and moving down the steps to stand in the middle of the gym and wave their hands in the air. Not when he reached the message's second portion and waited for the sense of authority to confirm his work. Nothing.

Whenever the noise forced him to halt, Buddy found his thoughts returning to the realization of that afternoon. His bank was going under. It was so strange that he had not really accepted this before. He had only thought of it in passing, like a stone skipping over the surface of a lake, not taking it in deep, not seeing what this meant.

He arrived at the final portion of his talk feeling that the evening had worked on him like a crowbar. His lack of vivid spiritual experience seemed to leave him not only empty, but exposed.

After it was over and Molly was driving them home, she asked, "Where do you feel like eating tonight?"

"I'm not hungry," he said dully, which was only part of the truth. He was tired, yes, but he was more bothered than tired.

She gave him a worried glance. "You need to have something, honey."

"I'll get a soft drink and crackers from the machines at the hotel. You can order room service." Buddy leaned back on the headrest. He did not even feel angry. Just grumpy.

He could understand what was happening. He had felt a glimmer of this in his prayer for Alex's health, then again in front of the church. He was being instructed to look beyond himself and his own concerns. But he didn't want to. Not the least little bit. If truth be known, the prospect was appalling. The sorrows and burdens of countless believers loomed before him like a great gaping maw. Ready to take him in and swallow him whole.

He felt Molly's eyes on him, and so he said what was there in front of him. The safe and selfish complaint, "I didn't feel a thing again. Not one thing. I felt like I was up there all by myself the whole time."

"Didn't you see the crowd?"

"Sure. They were there, and I was a thousand miles away." He sighed to the window. "When I'm up there and God is silent, it rattles me. I wish I had thought to ask for that as a sign. One that would continue for as long as this work does."

"Maybe God is keeping that back because it needs to be used sparingly."

"Why, Molly? Can you tell me that?"

"No, I can't. It was just an idea. Maybe we grow stronger through the silence."

"I don't feel strong. I feel drained." More than that. Buddy felt the burden of this new calling. The *challenge*. His horizons were being reshaped. And he didn't like it. Not one bit.

Molly drove into the hotel parking lot. She cut off the engine and turned to him. Buddy took that as a signal to go on. "I found myself growing jealous standing up there, watching my audience struck by the Spirit. Jealous and isolated."

"They're not your audience," Molly said quietly.

Buddy stared at his wife. "How do you have this ability of shaming me so quickly?"

Instead of responding, Molly opened her door and got out of the car. When Buddy was out, she said, "I admire you for asking these questions. I've never even thought of them. I never even thought I was good enough to deserve God speaking to me at all."

"You mean, you don't feel anything in these talks I'm giving?"

"Not a single, solitary thing." When they had walked to their room, she unlocked their door and turned on the light. After Buddy had shut out the night, she went on. "I've always simply accepted God's silence. The way others go on sometimes, well, I've assumed that's because He has something to say to them. But He doesn't need to say anything to me."

Buddy stood by the door. He felt slapped by the impact of Molly's words. Spanked for being a naughty child. That was exactly how he felt. Childish.

She looked at him. "Maybe what I need is to ask Him to speak with me. But I don't know how. Would you ask Him for me?"

"Of course I would." Hiding his shame over being so demanding. Having felt so much, received so much, his wife had never felt anything at all. "Why don't you sit in the chair?"

Buddy waited until she got settled and then walked over and placed both hands on her shoulders. He said aloud, "Heavenly Father, when I hear my wife speak, I hear the wisdom of one who would probably make a better messenger than me. Yet she has never felt the gift of Your presence move through her. And that is what I am asking for now. Breathe upon her, holy Lord. Make Your gentle Spirit move within her."

He stopped speaking. But the prayer continued within the depths of his soul. *Over and over I come to this place, Father,* he prayed. *All my life I have missed the mark. And I'm doing it again right now. I'm being selfish and demanding. I'm weak and afraid and unwilling to trust that You will be strong for me. I'm sorry to have failed You, Lord. Again. Shape me anew. Make me a servant who lives for You. Grant me the gift of selflessness. Do with me as You will, and show me how to obey.*

Buddy spoke aloud the final words, "In Jesus' precious name do I pray. Amen."

He felt the faintest breath across his face. A trace of motion, an angel's wing so soft that he could have easily ignored it and pretended it did not exist, save for the glory that infused his soul. He felt Molly's hands come up to rest upon his own. Warm peace flowed back and forth between them.

Standing over his wife of twenty-nine years, sensing with a wisdom that was not his own, again the unspoken lesson was made clear. How the time and the experiences and the love and the shared prayers had united them. They were one person, living out a single life in two bodies. Joined by the same gentle Lord whose power was so great it did not even need to be noticed. Whose presence was always there, always working, always loving, if only he would step beyond his own selfish barriers and allow himself to be lifted up upon the wings of heaven.

⊣∥ TWENTY-TWO ∥⊢

☐ Thad Dorsett drove through Aiden's darkened streets, impatient with everything about this town, even the night. For the thousandth time since being posted in this backwater, he wondered if he had made the right decision by staying with the Valenti Bank at all.

Most banks treated traders like tigers on a chain. They were tightly controlled and never given the chance to roam the jungle unleashed. Which was why Thad had leaped at the chance to join the ranks of upper management. Rumor had it that Nathan Jones Turner, Valenti's new owner, was planning to raise a few traders to board level and grant the profit makers real power. This was the only reason he continued to hold on to his impatience and make it through the horror of living in Aiden, Delaware. Thad felt as though he had been holding his breath for months.

When a stockbroker received an order from anywhere in the nation, he did not himself make the buy. He passed on the order to a person who handled thousands upon thousands of such transactions each day. The same was true for fund managers. Their buying and selling went through *traders*. Some operated from the floors of exchanges, such as the Chicago Mercantile where Thad had cut his teeth. Others worked from trading floors within large banks and fund groups. Traders sometimes operated on their own, working sums granted to them by people who trusted their savvy and knew that the time spent discussing a possible buy was time lost from the trade. These were known as *indies*. Most indies came and went like moths chasing flames.

Some people along the Street thought Nathan Jones Turner was insane to even consider offering traders the keys to the kingdom. But Thad knew better. Executive status meant faster access to capital. Speed was everything. Every day trades accelerated and rose in size. Going through various levels to gain permission meant losing out to the guy who could do it faster. Thad had lost out too often because his cap was set too low; his cap being how large a buy-sell order he could make without authorization from higher up the food chain. Thad wanted direct access to major funds. He wanted his name on the line and his deals to shake the Street. Gaining that clout was worth any price. Even enduring the straitjacket life of Aiden. For a while.

Thad Dorsett had come out of nowhere. That was how Thad described growing up in a suburb of Gary, Indiana. Son of a pastor and a doting mother, he had been trouble since before he could talk. He had more savvy than both parents combined. He understood things they would never grasp and tried hard to ignore. These days, the strongest emotion he felt for his family was impatience.

But he seldom thought of his family. It was a trait common to the trader breed. Whenever someone in the bank asked where he was from, Thad instantly knew he or she didn't trade. For a trader, the only personal history that mattered was the guy's last deal.

His parents would have loved Aiden, though. It had all the charm of a church picnic and about as much excitement. People around here lived life at one-quarter speed. He was being driven nuts on a daily basis.

Which was why he did not mind this present assignment. Not in the least.

At a quarter to one in the morning, Aiden's streets were as dead as yesterday's trade. Thad passed a patrol car and saw the cop's head propped on the backrest. Thad imagined he could even hear the snores. No question, this job would be a snooze.

Finding the doctor's address had proved harder than Thad had expected. Buddy's secretary had been no help at all, giving him a hard stare and demanding to know why Thad was asking for the doctor's name. Because, he had said, trying for nice, I need to complete records for the home office. Lorraine had looked at him standing there and said in a cold voice, "Then you'll just have to wait until he's back, won't you?" She had even taken her organizer home with her that evening. No question, Thad thought to himself as he scouted the empty night, she was definitely another on the way out.

Because of Lorraine's suspicions, Thad had been forced to spend the afternoon calling all the town's doctors. He had repeated a dozen times or so how he needed to make a follow-up appointment for Buddy Korda. He had known of the doctor's visit the morning of their argument and had seen Buddy clutching his chest for a couple of weeks up to the start of this latest mess. Which was why he was going to all this trouble. He had a hunch, nothing more. But traders learned to follow hunches. Good traders were known for the quality of their gut feelings.

Thad pulled into the parking lot and resisted the urge to blow the horn to see if he could maybe add a little risk to the exercise. He pulled his tools from the trunk and sauntered across the lot, feeling like the real Thad Dorsett was being released. The tiger unchained. He knew what he wanted for this. He could even see himself making the request. No, not a request. A payback.

The outer door gave the instant he slid his credit card through the crack and pressed down. Not even a dead bolt. Why bother, when people didn't break in? He smiled as he crossed the lobby, thinking of an ad he should place in the New York papers: *Take a thieves' holiday in Aiden, Delaware. Friendly people, sleepy cops, no alarms, special rates, package tours.*

The doctor's office was a little tougher, but not much. The plywood frame gave with the first tug on his long-handle screwdriver. He intentionally left signs of his entry. That was part of the plan.

He scouted the lobby, slid into the reception booth, checked all four walls, popped open the closet. He could not keep his grin from spreading. Incredible. A doctor's office without an alarm, in this day and age. Well, let this be a lesson to them.

He knew he should be hurrying. There was still the risk of a silent alarm. But something about the empty streets and the slumbering cop and the lack of a dead bolt downstairs left him feeling as if he could browse.

Thad felt the years slip away, sliding back into the nights of being a teenage juvenile delinquent again. He recalled how his parents had thrown up their hands in despair, especially after the police station started calling to ask if the reverend's son was home and in bed every time some young perpetrator disturbed the night. Those had been the days. Carefree and wild, leading a pack of wolves through darkened streets, nothing but fun and easy money, easy women, easy highs.

Seminary had been his own idea. Knowing he could not handle it for more than a semester, he nonetheless needed something on paper to balance out the rap sheet. Thankfully his dad's position had kept him from being arrested for anything serious. Still, there had been a list of misdemeanors stretching from joyriding to underage drinking to destruction of property. A semester of seminary was his way of whitewashing the whole deal, claiming to have turned over a new leaf. His parents' distrust of his motives had not bothered him at all.

Thad focused on the doctor's filing cabinet, which was solid steel with a security bar running down one side. But he knew how to ply the crowbar to spring the entire side. A lot of the old-style mom-and-pop shops used these places to hide their cash boxes during the week, and he had gotten to where he could jimmy a door, slide in, and spring a cabinet in thirty seconds flat. He ignored the clatter as the metal siding fell to one side. He pushed the files back, fiddled with the internal catch, and slid the security rod up and away. Good to know he hadn't lost the touch.

He tugged the cord controlling the blinds until enough streetlight fell inside for him to read. He riffled the files, quickly finding the one for Korda. Had to smile again. The guy's first name was Broderick. What a hoot.

Then as Thad read the last typed entry, he laughed aloud. He could not have come up with something more perfect if they had let him write it himself.

□

The call for which Thad Dorsett had arrived early at work finally came through a few minutes past eight the next morning. The metallic whisper gave no greeting, did not even bother to identify himself. "So did you get through to your man?"

"He's not my anything, Mr. Fleiss. But yes, I spoke with Korda yesterday afternoon."

"And?"

"And I did just like we said. Laid it on the line. Either straighten up or watch his job and his pension and his reputation disappear." Thad found it easier to discuss this on his feet. He pulled the phone cord free and began pacing. "Only I'm not so sure it did any good."

"He hung up on you?"

"No, he heard me out all right. But he just didn't seem to care. And since then I've learned that he went ahead with his talk." Thad gripped the phone hard enough to wring it dry, wishing it was Korda's neck. "Believe me, Mr. Fleiss, I was tough as possible. I did everything but crawl through the line."

"I believe you. And the name's Larry."

"Right. Thanks." Suddenly his hands were wet with relief. "You don't sound surprised."

"I'm not. Guys like that don't scare easily."

"Guys like what?"

"On a mission. You get them on the Street now and then. Fund managers and analysts who decide they've got the answer to all the world's worries. Usually it's a theory they've spent their lives perfecting. Every one I've ever heard of has had more holes than cheese from the land of snowcapped peaks. But this one beats them all." There came the sound of a noisy sip. "So what do you suggest we do?"

Thad liked the sound of that. What do *we* do. "I've already started nosing around."

"That's what I like to hear. Find anything we can use?"

"A lot." He felt like a bird riding high currents and catching the first sight of his prey. He was barely able to reign in his excitement. "His organization consists of an alcoholic brother working from a semibankrupt used-car lot."

"You've got to be kidding."

"Nope. Alex Korda, that's the guy. Oh, and a rich local widow as his part-timer. I drove by the place yesterday. He's got maybe ten derelict heaps sitting out front; he couldn't get fifty bucks for the lot."

"If this wasn't so worrisome, it'd be a hoot."

"Wait, it gets better." He took a breath. "Buddy was complaining of chest pains for a couple of weeks before all this started. So I managed to get inside the doctor's office last night. Took a look at his medical records."

"You don't say."

"Got them right here in front of me." Thad found breath hard to come by. As hoped, Larry said nothing about a doctor's records being strictly confidential or that it was illegal to read them. He struggled to keep his tone easy as he said, "You're not gonna believe what it says."

TWENTY-THREE

Thirty-Three Days . . .

☐ Buddy was halfway through his Bible reading and a second cup of coffee when he heard a little chiming. "Do you hear that?"

"It's your phone," Molly called from the bathroom. "Top of my purse."

He fumbled about, flicked it open, and said, "I'm not sure I like this thing one bit."

"You will." Alex sounded far too awake for this time of morning. "It'll grow on you like a third ear."

"Are you already at the office?"

"Been here for hours. Got so much going on I could start my own whirlwind." A chuckle. "Agatha beat me by an hour. Made the mistake of giving that woman her own key."

Buddy heard his brother's hoarse breathing and had to ask, "How are you feeling?"

"I'm fine."

"You've got to take care of yourself. Don't work so much—"

"Now look here." The voice turned flat. "You're not going to be pestering me about my health, Buddy."

"I'm worried about you."

"Well, you shouldn't be. You've got enough in your head already."

"Promise me you'll take care, Alex."

"I promise you I'll do everything the doctors tell me. There, how's that?"

"All right, I suppose."

"You're worse than Agatha for fussing." The tone lightened perceptibly. "That's some woman. She's been a big help, let me tell you. But my, she sure can talk. Got me agreeing to go to church with her some Sunday."

That brightened Buddy's day considerably. "This is good news."

"Can't hardly believe it myself. After you and Molly asking me year in and year out, here she just up and invites me, and I up and say, fine." There was the sound of pages rustling. "And now to business. I'm about ready to fax your itinerary to the front desk. You're gonna be one busy fellow."

"Are you leaving me time to breathe?"

"Wait, I think I've got that down here somewhere. Yeah, here it is. Thirty seconds for drawing breath, one week from next Tuesday."

"I can't thank you enough for all your help."

"And Agatha."

"Agatha too." He could still not get over that particular pairing. Agatha and Alex. It was like mixing oil and water and ending up with perfume.

"Take care, now. Agatha says to tell you she'll be praying for you through this interview."

Buddy cut off the phone and sat staring at nothing until Molly opened the bathroom door. She stood there in her robe, saw his expression, and asked, "What's the matter?"

"Nothing." A long sigh. "I was just missing my brother."

"He's not gone anywhere yet."

"That's pretty much what he told me. He said I shouldn't worry."

"Alex is right." She walked over and sat beside him. "I want to thank you for praying over me last night."

"I didn't do a thing."

"Well, you did and you didn't." She leaned over and kissed him. "You are a good man, Buddy Korda. I knew it the first moment I set eyes on you. I know it now."

They sat there sharing the moment until Buddy caught sight of the time. "I'm going to be late for the interview."

"You go ahead, I'm not coming. You can handle those press people without me. I need some quiet time with my Lord." She reached to the bedside table and peeled the first page from the hotel pad. "Here. I found this one for you."

Buddy accepted the page and read it aloud: "'Therefore gird up the loins of your mind.' 1 Peter 1:13." He looked up. "Just what I needed to hear. As always."

She reached around and gave him a squeeze. "Now go and serve Him well, my husband."

□

Buddy hesitated halfway across the hotel lobby. From where he stood he could see that the hotel's conference room was already full of lights set on metal stalks, cameras on tripods, cables, and people. He forced his legs to carry him forward.

Just inside the double doors, Clarke Owen was talking to a nervous man in a bright red hotel blazer. When Clarke spotted Buddy and waved hello, the man turned and stared, showing confusion when he did not recognize Buddy.

The room held a circular table with maybe two dozen chairs around it. Every seat was taken. At his appearance, the buzz of conversation continued. A couple of people watched Buddy's progress toward the front of the room. The others ignored him entirely as he squeezed past. He decided it was best not to hesitate or his nerves might freeze him solid.

"Good morning," he said loudly when he reached the podium, and there was a sudden flurry of activity.

"Wait a sec," called a voice from the back. Klieg lights flashed on, momentarily blinding him. "Okay, could we check your sound level?"

"My name is Buddy Korda," he said, speaking into microphones taped together like a bunch of metal asparagus. "Are we ready to go?"

"Okay on sound," the voice from the back said.

"Rolling," confirmed another.

"Go ahead, Mr. Korda."

Buddy touched the knot on his tie and wondered why he had agreed to this at all. It was far more intimidating than his talks.

At least there he had felt a sense of shared conviction. Here he felt nothing except apprehension.

And yet he knew what he needed to say. There was no question. All of the worries he had felt over the past several years suddenly solidified into a cohesive pattern.

He began without preamble, "Between 1925 and 1929, share prices roared up over four hundred percent. It was rank speculation. Yet newspapers around the nation proclaimed that an era of national growth and wealth had arrived. There was going to be a chicken in every pot. Everybody was going to own two automobiles. As long as a person had personal drive and ambition, the sky was the limit.

"Then, on the morning of October 29, 1929, the impossible happened. In a flash, the orders pouring into Wall Street made a 180-degree turn. Everywhere the only order was to sell, sell. It was the greatest market crash in history. Investors who had once counted rising paper profits were abruptly sent spiraling into very real debt."

Buddy caught several journalists exchanging weary glances. He noticed that no one was writing anything down. A couple of people standing by the back wall crossed their arms and leaned back, their faces falling into the shadows cast by the television lights.

Buddy plowed on, "For those who had money, the twenties was a time to get rich quick. Over a million Americans had money in the stock exchange, more than ever before. But most people didn't recognize it as such a good time. I'm not talking about the people who hit it big, the people living in uptown Manhattan with money to burn. I'm talking about the people living in small-town America. They had no idea this was such a grand time.

"I can remember one old-timer telling me he could hardly believe the news that America was on a roll, because his own family almost starved during the recession of 1923. But all the records show there was enormous growth in industrial production and personal wealth. But these are records, mind. After the fact."

He paused and then added, "Just like after this current period has ended, people may look back and say, oh yes, the nineties, they were *the good years.*

"Let me remind you of a few statistics about these current good years. While the number of millionaires has tripled in the nineties, the number of households without a job for more than a year has increased sevenfold. The annual rate of personal bankruptcies is *eleven times* higher than during the late eighties. The disparity between the nation's richest ten percent and the poorest twenty percent has more than doubled in the past decade. And most important of all, the income of middle America, the sixty percent just trying to make ends meet, has actually declined."

A laconic hand was raised. "Excuse me, Mr. . . ."

"Korda."

"Right. Are you telling me we're in for another Great Depression?"

"I know you've all heard the depression stories before," Buddy replied. "And that's become the problem. People aren't listening anymore. I'm simply telling you that it *could* happen."

A bored voice from the table's other side demanded, "But aren't you supposedly here to proclaim some prophecy of gloom and doom?"

"I'm simply telling you that a serious downturn could very well occur. One that might even be worse than the crash of '29." He was not getting through. Every notebook around the table remained as closed as their faces. "There are dozens of points I could make. But since we're talking about the stock market, I'll stay with that. Just as happened in the twenties, through the nineties we have seen an unprecedented number of small investors enter the stock market, either directly or through mutual funds. This has pushed the market higher than it has ever been before. Even higher than in the twenties, in terms of profit-to-price ratios.

"The market senses this imbalance. These days, share prices react hysterically to the smallest bit of news—a quarter percent rise in inflation, the smallest change in unemployment figures, the tiniest drop in quarterly profits. Factors that have no real effect on the economy are blasting the market like well-placed grenades."

A bored voice pressed, "Could we talk about your prophecy, Mr. Korda?"

"Let me just finish this point," he said, feeling sorrowful panic that he could not get them to sense the warning. "This nervousness is most dangerous because it could herald an extreme response to bad news. At that point, other factors may well begin an uncontrollable downward spiral.

"For example, most stock transactions are now controlled by computer. Price levels are electronically set to trigger a sell order. This is fine, so long as we are talking about a million small shareholders setting their own orders. But that is not the situation. We have enormous mutual funds now controlling sums that even ten years ago would have been unthinkable. In the early eighties, a hundred-million-dollar fund was enormous. Nowadays, that is less than what the top twenty funds buy and sell *each* day.

"So now we have these huge funds with gigantic share holdings. Their computers are flagged to issue a sell order *instantaneously*. They have to do this. Shares are traded twenty-four hours a day now, with the market in Tokyo opening just as Wall Street is closing. Markets in London and Hong Kong and Sao Paulo all trade in American stocks. All of them. There are limits now in place, which supposedly hold the amount of decline possible in these sell-offs. But they are limits placed *by each individual market*.

"So let us build a scenario, one which could all too readily occur. Bad news arrives. A sell order is launched, one so big it tilts other shares. This we know happens; it is well documented. One share price falling affects all others in that industry, which in turn drives down the Dow average. Other computer flags are raised at the Dow's overall drop. More sell orders are initiated. Other industries are affected, one after the other. The Dow drops like a stone, hitting the artificial limit set for that day. Then a mutual-fund manager, with four or five billion dollars at his disposal, decides now is the time to get out of the market entirely. He dumps their holdings. This is still possible. How? By transferring their sell orders to Tokyo, and then London, and then Frankfurt. Because all of these markets also trade in American shares. And each of these markets' daily floor levels are independent. So the funds continue to chase around the globe, with the panic growing each time their sell orders are halted by another artificial floor."

They were watching him now. Not taking notes, but at least listening carefully. And the cameras continued to roll. Perhaps some word of this might get out. Buddy looked at one face after another, willing them to listen, understand, and write of a need for caution. "The result, I fear, is that our market structure would collapse like a house built on sand and caught in a hurricane.

"I urge you to warn your audience. Get out of the market now. Get out of debt now. Be as ready as you can for a severe economic downturn." He waited then, steeling himself for questions that would drive attention away from his message. But before the reporters could gather themselves, he was struck by a silent urging, one he accepted with relief. "Thank you all for coming."

Reporters sprang to their feet. "Mr. Korda—"

"Wait, please, I want to ask—"

"That is all I have to say at this time," he said, thankfully reaching the door.

TWENTY-FOUR

Thirty-One Days . . .

☐ Saturday morning found them in a hotel in Williamsport, Pennsylvania, where Buddy was struck by three body blows in the space of twenty minutes.

First came the call from his doctor. As soon as Jasmine Hopper had introduced herself, Buddy started in on his apology. "I've been busier than a one-legged man in a polka contest."

"That's not why I'm calling. There's—"

"I'm feeling fine, Jasmine. Really. I'm sorry I didn't make another appointment. I've been so busy I forgot to call."

"Buddy, I'm not calling to ask about your health or your missed appointment."

"You're not?" At the sound of knocking, he carried his cellular phone over to open the door. Clarke Owen stood holding a bunch of newspapers. "Is something the matter with our children?"

Molly opened the bathroom door, her makeup powder in one hand and the pad in the other. Buddy looked at her as Jasmine said, "No, Trish has come down with what I suspect is a strep infection, but otherwise your family is healthy as far as I know."

Buddy swiveled the mouthpiece away and said to Molly, "Trish has strep throat, but otherwise everybody's fine."

"Is that Jasmine?"

"Yes." To the phone, "Why are you calling?"

"I got your number from Alex." She sounded extremely worried. "Buddy, there's been a break-in at my office."

"Jasmine, I'm so sorry." Scrunching up his forehead, he wondered why his doctor was calling to tell him about a burglary. They were friends, yes, but Jasmine Hopper was friends with half the town. "What can—"

"I wanted you to hear this from me first." She took a deep breath. "They were after my files, Buddy. *Your* file."

Buddy's gaze shifted from Molly to Clarke to Molly again. "My file."

"I've spent the past two days making sure it wasn't just misplaced." Another pause, then she went on worriedly, "Buddy, you were so tense at your last visit. And you were so insistent that everything was perfectly all right. These are classic symptoms of denial."

Everything fell into place. He took in Clarke's somber expression and the newspapers in his hands. Buddy said, "I understand."

"I wrote into your file that if the pains persisted, you would need to have a psychiatric examination." These words were spoken in an explosive rush, as though she wanted to get them out and over with. "I'm so terribly sorry, Buddy."

"You did what you thought was right."

"If these notes are passed to the press, we can prosecute."

Buddy decided there was no need to point out that the damage would still be done. Jasmine clearly felt bad enough already. "I have to get going, Jasmine. Everything is fine. Don't give it another thought. And thank you for calling."

Buddy cut the connection and said to Clarke, "Is it bad?"

"Bad enough."

Molly demanded, "What are you talking about?"

"*The New York Times* and *The Wall Street Journal* have both launched attacks at Buddy. Well, partly at Buddy." Clarke's expression became pained. "I'm so sorry."

"Alex," Buddy said. "They've gone after my brother."

"It's pretty rough. They talk about his alcoholism and his run-ins with the law, and they make his business out to be on its last legs."

Molly moved up to grasp Buddy's arm. "He must be beside himself."

Buddy lifted the cell phone and dialed his brother's number. When Alex came on the line, Buddy said, "Don't pay them any mind at all."

Alex's tone was edged by a new grimness. "If my ramblings have taught me anything, it's that I can't please everybody, but I sure can irritate the whole world at once."

"The more our message gets out, the more the financial establishment is going to attack us," Buddy said. "We've known that from the beginning."

"Seems to me you'd be better off if I was to retire and leave this work to better hands." There came a sound of hoarse breathing, of needing to take a moment to gather the energy to continue, "I'm not polished enough. I'm not a pro."

"If you quit, then I do too," Buddy said, gripping the phone so hard his hand shook. "And that's a promise."

"I'm carrying too much baggage to be much help to anybody." Alex sighed, weary at seven-thirty in the morning.

"That's not true, Alex. Not at all." Buddy found himself recalling something he had not thought of for years. The words had been repeated often by his favorite Sunday school teacher, the man who had brought Buddy to the Lord when he was fifteen years old. "Being the person God wants us to be is a victory over our past," Buddy recited from memory. "It means not just embracing His call, but also overcoming our limitations."

"God called you, Buddy. Not me."

"He's called us both. I know that in my heart of hearts."

There was a moment's silence, then, "You mean that, little brother?"

"We're in this together, Alex. And that's all there is to it." He reached into his jacket for Molly's card. "I want to read you something Molly found for me yesterday. It's from the twenty-seventh Psalm."

> *When the wicked came against me*
> *To eat up my flesh,*
> *My enemies and foes,*
> *They stumbled and fell.*
> *Though an army may encamp against me,*
> *My heart shall not fear;*
> *Though war may rise against me,*
> *In this I will be confident.*
> *One thing I have desired of the LORD,*
> *That will I seek:*

That I may dwell in the house of the LORD
All the days of my life.

When Alex had finally agreed to carry on and Buddy set down the phone, he tensed against well-meaning objections from Clarke. Instead he found himself facing a warm smile. Clarke told him, "That was a great thing you just did."

"It was beautiful what you told him," Molly agreed softly.

Clarke folded the two top papers he was carrying and dumped them in the trash can. "We sure don't need this mess."

"You two go on down to breakfast," Molly said. "I want to call and see how Trish is doing."

Buddy followed Clarke from the room and asked, "What are those papers you're still carrying?"

"One paper and one magazine." As they walked the hallway, Clarke showed him the cover of *Money* and said, "This came out today. Listen to what it says about you." He flipped to the page he had already turned down and read, "A mild-mannered, narrow-minded, small-town banker has hit the financial pond like a meteorite, and the tidal waves are still flowing outward. The question is, Whose boats are going to be swamped? If what Buddy Korda's increasingly convincing arguments say is true, it could very well be almost all of them."

Buddy accepted the magazine and slipped it under his arm unread. "If only there was some way for them to really listen."

Clarke glanced at him. "Time is pressing down on you, isn't it?"

Buddy nodded grimly. "More with every passing day."

□

Sunday they decided not to try and go home, much as both of them wanted to see the family and worship with their own church. But Sunday evening Buddy was scheduled to address a church gathering in Philadelphia, and the hours simply could not be found.

The following week, Buddy and Molly started early and traveled hard. On Monday they visited Camden and Trenton, New Jersey, before traveling Tuesday to meet groups in four different Connecticut towns. After overnighting in Bridgeport, they flew Wednesday to Providence, Rhode Island.

Like a stone dropped into a still and expectant pond, the ripples spread ever wider. People began approaching Buddy after his talks, introducing themselves, saying they had seen his video at a prayer meeting in Baltimore or a church luncheon in Chicago or a specially called gathering in Jacksonville, Florida. They told him how they had traveled six hundred, eight hundred, a thousand miles, just to hear what he had to say in person. Just to make sure the incredible power they had felt from the video or tape was really there. Just to shake his hand and thank him and say that without a doubt, he was a prophet called by God to warn the faithful.

Buddy endured these encounters because he had to. He masked his winces as best he could, especially when they looked at him with something like awe and wanted to hang on to his hand. He deeply loathed the sensation that they were trying to cling to him as though he were something holy. But he could not be rough with them. He could not turn and flee as he wanted. He had to accept and endure. It was the message that was important. He could do nothing that would take away from the power of the message. He could not.

Twenty-Seven Days . . .

☐ Wednesday morning, Larry Fleiss refilled his cup from the coffeemaker built into the left wing of his desk before swinging his Swiss-made leather and titanium chair around and scanning the screens. No major change, little action for that time of week. The Fed was scheduled to release its quarterly review of interest rates in two days, and the market was still trying to figure out which way the central bank was going to jump. He sipped from the cup, his fifteenth of the day. He averaged twenty before lunch, another two dozen by market close, an even fifty by the time he left. He went through a pound of Costa's best every day. He had long since stopped tasting much of anything.

Fleiss could not help glancing at the phone. There were nineteen lines into his office, plus the mobile and the two faxes and the six direct satellite hookups to the major overseas markets. But the phone he could not help looking at was the one linked to Nathan Jones Turner's office at the estate. He had spent all morning waiting for that call. He was supposed to have checked in with Turner an hour ago, giving him the word on a sure win. Which he did not have. But Fleiss had a hunch he knew where to find one. His gut told him so.

Only, if he was going to pull it off, he could not place this call himself.

He turned his attention back to the file, the only bit of paper on the desk's broad central dais. Thaddeus Dorsett. What a name. Still, he liked the feel of this guy. He flipped through the pages, already having committed the information to his prodigious memory. This was not an ordinary employee file. One of the changes Turner had brought to Valenti was a deep-profile investigation for all top managers. Fleiss was one of only three people permitted to see the information.

Thad's earlier delinquencies indicated a reckless spirit. This was good. Fleiss was not looking for somebody who was frightened by risks. And the way he had broken into the doctor's office, taken the guy's private records, and left the other files poking out as a warning—all this was very strong. Fleiss had probed a little after Thad had delivered his report, wanting the details, glad the guy did not pussyfoot around, but simply told him in an almost bored manner how he had obtained the information. Thaddeus Dorsett lived for the thrill. He knew the borderlands beyond law and legality. All this was good. Very good. Fleiss needed somebody like this. He needed him desperately.

Turner's firing of his top analyst-trader had wounded Fleiss badly. Fleiss needed a pair of legs, somebody to implement and to hunt and to be the face the Street saw. Somebody Fleiss could trust to be his man and his alone. The trouble with taking some-one from within the ranks of Valenti's trading arm was that Turner's spies were everywhere.

But finding the sure thing could not wait. Fleiss had spent the last week and a half hunting and worrying. But he had the entire bank's operations to cover as well. No. What was needed here was a number two who was not squeamish about where legalities ended and profits began.

Fleiss resumed his perusal of the file. He liked the feel of Thad Dorsett. It was one thing to trade for a year or so. Most could not take it longer than that. They burned up or burned out. But there was occasionally somebody who lived for the trade. Mar-ket junkies, modern-day privateers. Fleiss closed the file and tapped his fingers on the cover. Yes. He could very well imagine Thaddeus Dorsett was going crazy in that branch office.

When the phone finally rang, Fleiss had to stop himself from reaching out. One ring, two, then on the third he finally picked up the receiver and said, "Fleiss."

The querulous tone demanded, "Did I forget something? Was there a miscommunication somewhere? Weren't you supposed to be in touch already this morning?"

"Been busy watching the market."

"In case you have forgotten," Turner lashed out, "I do not like to be kept waiting. Not by anyone."

"You also don't like to be bothered." Fleiss was dancing on the razor's edge here. Since the exchange rate debacle, Turner had been viciously unpredictable. "I don't have a thing to report. If I don't have something to say, a call goes under the head of bothering."

"You're not paid to *report*. You're paid to find me a way out of this mess!"

"You told me to find you a sure thing. I'm still looking."

"Well, look faster!" Turner was breathing hard. Which was a warning in and of itself. The man was notorious for losing his cool in spectacular fashion. "Every day we wait is another day we might be discovered."

"I'm on it."

"You'd better be. This had better dominate your every waking thought and shape your nightmares." A moment's heavy breathing, and then, "I can't understand what is taking you so long."

"Middle of next week," Fleiss promised. "Soon as we figure out which way the Fed is gonna jump, I'll have a better handle on how to—"

"Do you know, are you the least bit aware, that I have to make the second *cash payment* for the hotels at the *end* of next week? And if I *don't* make the payment, I lose the *fifty percent deposit* I've already made! Of course you're not aware! How could you be? If you knew, you wouldn't be hanging about! Because if you *did* know, you'd also know that *I don't have the cash*!"

"Middle of the week," Fleiss repeated, and decided now was the time to strike. "Listen, about the *Journal* article."

"What?" The anger switched to confusion. Turner was not a man used to having the conversation's direction dictated by anyone else. It threw him off balance. "I don't—"

"The article about one of the bank's employees. That Korda guy. There's been a follow-up. And some of the other news services are taking notice."

"I fail to see how you can be so fixated on this worm when we are faced with a total fiasco!"

"Like I said," Fleiss persisted. "There's a risk here. What if one of the pension funds decides they don't like how we're managing our people and we can't be trusted to manage their money?"

"You're talking nonsense." But the old man's tone held a trace of uncertainty.

"Any move of a fund would expose our illegal borrowings," Fleiss pointed out.

"All the more reason for you to get moving," Turner snarled.

"You told me to handle it," Fleiss reminded him. "I've found a guy at the Aiden branch. He's one of the traders slated for top management who is putting in his time as a branch manager. He's sharp, and he doesn't like this Korda guy any more than I do."

"Doesn't like who?" Clearly Turner's mind was only partly held by this conversation.

"The assistant manager, the one who's causing all the ruckus. This manager, he has a plan to take care of Korda. But he wants out. He's going crazy there in the branch. He wants to move back into trading." Fleiss kept it casual, making it sound as though it was no big thing. "Wants his own portfolio, the works."

"Well, if he can handle this problem, do it." Turner was still too distracted to pay much attention. "But I want you to concentrate on what's important here."

"Will do."

"I want *answers*. I want *results*. Find me a way out of this mess. And find it *now*."

Fleiss hung up the direct line, thoroughly satisfied. He then picked up another phone and prepared to make urgent arrangements for Thaddeus Dorsett to travel up to the Big Apple.

Twenty-Six Days . . .

☐ Thursday morning, Nathan Jones Turner's personal helicopter attendant met Thaddeus Dorsett as he came off the private jet at Kennedy. Thad accepted the attention as though he had known it all his life.

The amenities were exactly what he had always thought a private chopper should have—soundproofing so thick the rotors' noise was cut to a barely audible whine, newspapers and magazines still in their wrappers held in a chrome-and-wood stand, crystal decanters and a refrigerator in one corner, a smiling hostess to keep him company, two pilots, three color-television sets, and big windows through which he could look down as the Big Apple swept into view, ripe for the plucking.

He had never before been to New York. It was not a confession Thad would have made to anyone. But early in his career, he had promised himself that there was only one way he would arrive in New York City, and that was in style. A winner. A big-time guy. A name.

He had made his mark in the Chicago dealing rooms, always hearing the extra edge that the New York guys held in their voices. They were top of the heap, and made sure that everyone understood this. The saying went, a trader never made it any-where until he made it in New York. Thad accepted the saying as fact. But he also knew that landing at the bottom in New York meant hitting hard and fighting mean. He had always figured he would battle his way out of the trenches where the competition was a little easier and the scars quicker to heal. Then he would arrive in New York with power and experience behind him and burn his emblem into the Street.

The pilot's voice sparked over the intercom. "That's the Turner Building to your right."

"I know."

"Oh," the stewardess said brightly. "Have you come in by air before?"

He did not respond. He did not want to share this moment with anyone. No, he had never come in by air, by road, or by any other way. But he had seen this picture before. Seen it and studied it so often it was burned into his heart, branded like all the desires that fueled his drive to get here.

The Turner Building was world famous. It was the area's sec-ond highest building and occupied the Street's most prestigious location. To its left was the Federal Building, where George Wash-ington had been sworn in as president. The Stock Exchange was a half block down Broad Street. The Federal Reserve Bank was a block in the other direction, just beyond the Chase Manhattan

Plaza. The Turner Building stood proud and imperious at the heart of financial power, surrounded by the biggest players in the world, fighting and scrapping for profit and position.

They used the chopper platform atop the Irving Trust Building, since the Turner's was crowned by an art-deco tower. Thad bid the chopper crew a distracted farewell and allowed himself to be led away by some Valenti lackey. He gave no response to the guy's oblique questions, knowing rumors would start flying as soon as the guy was back. How some young man from a branch in the middle of nowhere had been brought in on the old man's chopper and taken straight into Larry Fleiss's inner sanctum. Thad sighed with pleasure at the glances thrown his way as they entered the foyer, now dominated by Valenti Bank headquarters. This was better than he had ever imagined.

The Valenti Bank's trading operations, he knew, were spread over four floors, a total of 130,000 square feet. From this arena the bank generated almost 50 percent of its total operating profit.

Larry Fleiss's office was on the top trading floor, the sixtieth. Thad nodded as the guy held open the door to Fleiss's outer office. He smiled in response to the secretary's greeting and took a good look around.

The anteroom positively pulsed with luxury. Items scattered decorously about the room vied for his attention. The walls held two Degas watercolors and what appeared to be a Rembrandt sketch. The floor was rosewood, the carpet silk Esfahān. Side tables groaned under crowded burdens of crystal and silver. Thad found himself salivating over the thought of moving in.

Fleiss's interior office was refrigerated to within a degree or two of freezing. But Thad's involuntary shudder had little to do with the cold and everything to do with the man behind the desk.

Larry Fleiss looked like a human slug wearing a blond mustache and toupee. His skin was so white it looked blue, matching the milky paleness of his eyes.

Thad realized Fleiss was watching him, observing his reaction. So he kept hold of his poker face and said, "Great desk."

Fleiss gave a tiny lift to the edges of his mouth. His hand raised far enough to wave Thad into the seat. "Had it custom-made. I call it my powerboard." In person, the man's voice was even more eerie than on the phone, a metallic monotone barely above a whisper. "Forty-seven thou including all the toys. Even got a built-in sink."

"I want one." And he did. Thad wanted it all.

A single flicker of approval. Wanting another person's toys was definitely something Fleiss could identify with. And handle. "How are you doing in your branch, what's the name of that town?"

"Aiden." He did not need to think that one through. "Dying a slow death."

"I can imagine." The voice was utterly toneless, a single rasping note so emotionless that it sounded machine made. "I suppose you want out."

There it was. Finally. His ticket out of slumber land. But he was nothing if not a trader. And a trader never accepted the first offer. "No thanks."

Fleiss blinked his surprise. "What?"

"I want it all." Forcing his voice to remain bland. "The gold ring. A job in HQ. A book all my own." A book was a trader's personal trading capacity. The larger his book, the greater his clout in the market. "Two-fifty ceiling. Euromarkets and currencies included. Bonus linked directly to my own profits, not the bank's."

"Two hundred and fifty million ceiling. Interesting." Fleiss turned away. He ran a quick glance over the screens, automatically checking the market's frantic pulse.

Thad felt a sudden terror over the thought that he might be turned down. He fought down the desire to backpedal and accept less. Fleiss reached for his mug and glanced at him over the lip. He lowered the cup and hit a button with its edge. A lid on the desk's left-hand ledge slid back, and a gleaming coffee system rose into view. It was all there—a stainless steel sink and spigot, matching coffeemaker and grinder and utensils.

"Add a desk like yours to the list," Thad said approvingly.

A flicker of humor came and went. "Good to know we think alike."

The thrill was electric. "Does that mean yes?"

"I'm looking for a new number two. Are you interested in the job?"

"Answer directly to you?" Thad could scarcely believe his ears. "Are you kidding?"

"I never kid about trades."

"Then the answer is yes."

"Okay, but first you've got to pass the test." Fleiss spooned beans into the grinder, waited until the whine had ceased, and poured the black dust into the maker. The room was flooded with the perfume of fresh-ground coffee. "Find me three sure things."

That was a no-brainer. "Buy the next three Treasury issues."

"No can do. I want a minimum twenty-five percent instant return."

Thad laughed out loud. "There's no such animal."

"There'd better be, or you go back to hibernating in Aiden."

Thad watched the man rinse out the pot and fill the machine with water. "You're actually serious."

"I told you, I never joke about the market. Three sure things, Thaddeus Dorsett. Find them and the job is yours." He waved a hand toward the unseen trading floor. "Have somebody out there find you a desk. You've got forty-eight hours."

"Great." Unexpectedly, he did not feel dejected. Impossible simply meant it had not been done before.

"Wait a sec." Another button was hit, and another panel slid back. An upright filing tray rose into view. Fleiss flipped through the headers, pulled out a red-flagged file, and tossed it across the desk. "Have a look at this."

"What is it?"

"The last trade of the lady who had the job before you." Fleiss turned back to his screens. "I gave her the same assignment. She failed. Learn from her mistakes."

─╢ TWENTY-SEVEN ╟─

☐ Wall Street was all concrete and bustle and noise. Even on the brightest day, sunlight remained as out of place as a stranded tourist. Sunglasses were used in all weather, however, especially by traders. After sixteen hours spent in front of flickering trading screens, with fluorescent lamps spaced out over acres of trading floors, eyes found even the cloudiest of days to be outrageously bright.

The mountains of Wall Street were home to their own brand of trolls. Only here they were dressed by Valentino, driven by Porsche, fueled by liters of caffeine. They hoarded their gold and guarded it with bloodthirsty vengeance. They substituted hand-held faxes and satellite links for broadaxes, but they were trolls just the same. They even had their own language. Sunlight scared them. Fresh air was as alien as a moral code.

Thad waited in the window table of a deli across the street from the Turner Building until the lunchtime flood began. He closed the file he had been studying and crossed the street. He fought his way through the careless throng and rode an empty elevator back to the sixtieth floor. Instead of going right and entering Fleiss's outer office, he turned left, pushed through the double doors, and entered the war zone.

Even with half the traders at lunch, the scene was one of barely controlled bedlam. The floor was eighty yards square and home to four hundred electronically wrapped trading desks.

Traders roared and shouted and jostled and wrote and signaled. Paper fluttered like confetti. Sweating runners raced from the desks to the communication booths rimming the war zone. Each desk had four video monitors and six phones. Overhead were triple banks of more monitors showing the latest trading positions from dealer floors around the world. Above that flashed news service bulletins on lighted tracks that swept around all four walls.

Eight bored bicycle messengers stood in line at the receptionist's desk, waiting their turn and staring out over the pandemonium. Thad walked straight up to the harried receptionist and declared, "Larry Fleiss told me to find a desk."

"Yeah?" She did not even look up from signing the messenger's sheet. "Well, nobody's told me a thing."

"Take it up with Larry. In the meantime, where's your duty roster?" He spotted the clipboard and pulled it up.

"Hey! Get your hands—"

Thad stopped her with a look. The look where the frustration and the rage from six *months* imprisonment in Aiden all came through, leaving no need to raise his voice as he said, "I told you. Take it up with Larry." He shoved the roster back at her, stopping just before it jammed into her stomach. "Now, one more time. Where is the closest free desk to Larry's door?"

She gave him an uncertain glance, checked the page, and said dully, "Try one forty-two."

"Perfect."

"Hey!" This time without the edge. "You got a name?"

"Indeed I do," Thad said, moving away.

He found the desk without asking, which was good. He had no intention of talking with anybody. Let them come to him, and in their own good time. He dropped the file, managed to scout the room without seeming to, and spotted the table used as a dumping ground for the financial forecasts and business dailies. He walked over, scooped up a double-handful, and moved back to his desk. *His* desk. Just thinking the words gave him a rush.

Eyes tracked his every move. Totally normal. Anybody new was a threat. Thad opened the first forecast bulletin and scanned the crowd with overt glances. Even without looking directly, Thad could spot all the typical characters. Over there was the girl who brushed her hair continuously and stared at her reflection in the compact mirror taped beside her central screen, as she chattered on two phones. Farther down the aisle was the guy who chewed his way through three combs a day. Next to him was the cigar chomper, not allowed to light up, so he mangled a stogie or two per session. The man who used his tie like a noose, tightening and loosening it in constant jerks. The woman who balanced a tennis racket, or bounced it from knee to knee, pretending she could still run through six sets. The woman who scooted continually back and forth across the aisle on her wheeled office chair. The guy who chanted the news as it flashed along the overhead screen, not even hearing it himself. The pair who compared lies about women and big nights between trades. All the frayed nerves of veteran Street people.

By the time the lunch hour ended and the tension heightened into a full-throated roar, Thad was moving smoothly into the pattern and the patter. He sat like a stone idol before his own bank of screens, tracing the market's movements and listening as the other traders scurried.

He knew he was being inspected; he knew his first move would be watched by four hundred sets of eyes and tracked on screens here and in every other office of Valenti right around the globe. The mystery guy. New to the scene, vetted by Larry Fleiss himself. Not even a hello to the floor manager. Not even a nod to the other traders. The size of his first trade would inform the others of his authority. Thad was determined to make it a whopper. He sat and felt the rusty adrenaline faucets squeak slowly open again.

He perused the file of the last trade by Larry's former top trader and whistled at the size. Almost eight hundred million dollars in yen options spread over a ten-day period. He did not need to check the screens to know the bank took a hit on that one. A big hit. The yen had been dropping steadily, contrary to every pundit the length and breadth of the Street.

He then browsed the financial newsletters and the business dailies. Thad was not looking for answers. If these news sheets contained surefire wins there would be no losers. As it was, the Street was littered with the corpses of traders who had followed sage pundits down to their last bitter nickel. No. Thad was looking for *questions*. Where was the market's attention? What was hot? The biggest action would be focused on the fad of the moment.

Yen. The Japanese currency seemed to be on everybody's mind. Why did it keep falling? Some of the experts claimed it was interest rates, others the Tokyo market, still others the rising U.S. economic forecasts, more still the instability of the Japanese government. Taken together, the sages sounded like a group of New York taxi drivers discussing football.

Thad turned his attention back to the trading file to study the positions the bank had taken more closely. He was still at it when the red light at the top of his phone began blinking. Traditionally, this was the link between every trader and the floor manager or chief trader. Thad grabbed the handset and gave an overloud bark. "Dorsett."

"Hey, sport, tone it down." The rasp could belong to only one man. "What looks good?"

"Not a lot. Franc and mark Euros are bouncing all over the chart."

"Yeah, the market's had a bad case of the heebie-jeebies for weeks. How about the yen, it moving?"

Thad knew the overly casual question was a test, but he was ready; he had watched it ever since reading the file from Larry's former number one and the trade that ended her run. "There's some big money pushing yen all day. In and out. Two big players at least. Could be central bankers on the sly, trying to turn it around."

"What's your feeling?"

"It's too low," he said, knowing he was going out on a limb, especially since that was exactly the basis upon which the last fatal trade had been made. "Way too low."

"Come up with anything yet?"

In four hours? Who was Fleiss kidding? "Working on it."

"Deadline's been moved up. First thing tomorrow, in my office. Be ready." Larry hung up.

□

Thad Dorsett left the Turner Building in the breathless moment between evening and night. No need to stay any longer. He knew what he was going to tell Larry. Hanging around would only tempt him to give in to worries, which was death for a trader. Thad pushed through the outer doors and glanced up. The sun had set, light was fading, and the little strip of sky visible between the buildings was awash in rosy hues.

As he started across the plaza fronting the bank, a voice behind him called, "Mr. Dorsett?"

"Yes." Warily he backed away from the slender man in the dark uniform. He could never be too careful. Not here in New York.

"I'm Jimmy. Your driver."

"My what?"

"I've been assigned to be your driver, Mr. Dorsett." Taking no notice at Thad's surprise, he pointed at the suit bag Thad was carrying. "Is that all your luggage?"

"Yes." Reluctantly, Thad allowed the stranger to take his grip. He had only brought one change of clothes, not expecting to be here longer than a day. "Where are you taking me?"

"Wherever you want to go, Mr. Dorsett." The man started down the broad marble stairs toward the dark stretch limo parked in front of the bank. "But you've got a suite reserved at the Plaza. Maybe you'd like to stop off there first."

"You don't say." Thad allowed the driver to open his door, and he slipped into the backseat and smiled at the leather-lined space. When Jimmy was behind the wheel, he said, "Go down Broadway, will you?"

"Sure thing, Mr. Dorsett."

He sat back and enjoyed Broadway as it unwound about him. The garish carnival of night was gradually waking up. He felt as though it were all coming alive to welcome him.

This was the way to live in New York. No jamming into subways filled with a solid wall of flesh. No cringing over the dictates of a boss frightened for his own job. No struggling to live with impossible city prices on an impossibly tight budget. None of that. Thad sighed and settled himself deeper into the luxury. He was made to see life from the backseat of a limo. It was his destiny.

When he had just been starting out, he had heard somebody say that it was time to move to New York when one didn't need to ask the price of anything. Thad slid his hand over the limo's walnut paneling, and decided that the time had almost arrived.

TWENTY-EIGHT

Twenty-Five Days . . .

☐ The telephone's red light was blinking when Thad Dorsett arrived at his trading desk Friday morning. He did not bother to pick up the receiver; he just walked back through the doors and into Larry's office, feeling eyes follow him the whole way.

Larry greeted him by waving a hand at the seat opposite his desk and saying, "Okay, let's have it."

Though he had steeled himself for this moment, still his hands were suddenly slick with sweat. His chance to grab the ring and rise to the top depended on the gamble he was about to take. Larry had demanded three surefire trading deals. No limits, no defining boundaries. Just a guaranteed profit.

Thad took a breath and then began with, "We could make a major trade and arrange to front ride it." Then he stopped.

Fleiss blinked slowly, his only reaction.

Thad gave him enough time to object and then plowed on. "We've got control over large pension funds. Arrange for them to buy a block of stocks. Several stocks, because we couldn't make more than a quarter-point off each buy without alerting the SEC's watchdog group. We precede the fund's purchases by acquiring these stocks ourselves through dummy corporations. Ones far removed from the bank. Then we sell the shares on to the portfolios after tacking on a hit."

Thad watched Fleiss retreat behind his mug. Only the tiniest flicker of his eyes gave any indication of the intense thought being given to his suggestion. This in itself was a good sign. Very good, in fact, as it meant the idea was being taken seriously. Despite the fact that front loading a trade was highly illegal, Larry was earnestly considering the possibility.

Front loading a buy meant that the stocks bought for a customer actually were drawn from another account—an account controlled by the trader. This meant the trader could tack on an extra half-point or so per share and pocket the difference. On an actively traded stock, this much of a differential was found within every trading day. If questioned, the trader could simply claim to have caught the stock on the upswing. A 100-million-share purchase could result in a five million dollar instant profit. Front loading had been a favorite scam during the late twenties, when the market had heated up to the point where such frauds would rarely be detected. Pulling a trick from the history books might well work, at least once.

Thad allowed himself the first full breath of the morning and let his mind roam. Trading was the empire of the nineties. The futures market was transforming itself so rapidly that regulations and laws could not hope to keep up. Such trading was totally invisible to the common people, yet it was beginning to control their destinies like an economic puppet master. This was where Thad wanted to be, where he *belonged*, running a massive empire built on trading.

Financial trading knew neither borders nor loyalties. Patriotism was an outdated joke, as practical to a trader as a steam locomotive. Money circled the globe in an electronic sea, with tides and currents determined by the highest rate of return.

Windows of opportunity opened for seconds only. New information surged like geysers. Traders discounted companies before factories were built. They took their profits before the products hit market shelves.

They bundled Iowa mortgages and sold them to buyers in Paris or Calcutta or Baghdad. Computers were trained to fire off contracts as soon as enemy tactics were spotted. Millions were lost or gained in the blink of an eye. Cash was never touched. Zeros proliferated on daily balance sheets like goose eggs.

Larry shifted in his chair. "And the next alternative?"

"Door number two." The file remained unopened in Thad's lap. He had no need to review his notes. "We set a rumor in motion. You've got contacts at the *Journal* and other places."

Larry shrugged casual agreement. "So?"

"So at the next auction of U.S. treasury bonds, your connections report that the yen is so low and the Japanese banks are in such bad shape, they're not going to buy. Have the rumor start in London. Feed it through viable trading operations to your *Journal* friend so he's covered."

Thad waited. If his first suggestion was illegal, the second was totally outrageous. Being caught would stain the reputation of the entire financial community. Not to mention that it would result in felony charges and sky-high fines for all involved.

But all Fleiss said was, "How do we cover ourselves?"

Thad felt the band of tension around his chest tighten another notch. So close. "Both bond and stock markets will react, we go short in both. A one-time rake-off. Everybody knows the Japanese hold to the blue chips; we take short positions through other traders in different countries on the major utilities and federal treasury notes."

Again he waited while Larry mulled it over. Thad wondered if this was just an exercise or the real thing. What kind of pressure would push a major Street player to take such a risk? Thad could not imagine it, which was why he figured the exercise had primarily been to show one thing: that he was willing to go all the way and do whatever it took to succeed on the Street.

Another slow blink, a single nod. Then, "And the third?"

"The third." His breath quickened. "The third needs a little more work, so I can't talk about it yet. But it's good. And big. Bigger than the other two combined. And what's more, it's totally legit."

And more than that, it was too good to give up without being able to implement it himself. Thad had decided that in the sleepless hours of the previous night. He would give it up, but only in exchange for the gold ring. He readied himself for a battle over this and was determined not to give in.

But Larry did not object. "Okay. Good work." Larry gave another nod, then slid a folded newspaper across his desk. "Now take a look at this."

Thad picked up the paper and saw it was the business section of a Philadelphia paper. Then his eye spotted a name in the lead article, and he sank into the seat. "I don't believe it."

"Had it couriered up this morning by one of the branch managers. Seems your man Korda's got some of our local people running scared."

"Don't lay the goofball on me," Thad objected, reading swiftly. "Korda is not my anything."

The headline read, "Now Get Ready For A Real Bear." The lead paragraph began, "For months the market has been celebrating the longest running upturn in history and thumbing its nose at all those who predicted a downward correction of 10 percent or more. But Valenti banking official and economic pundit Buddy Korda insists otherwise. After addressing close to a thousand like-minded people at a standing-room only affair, Mr. Korda stated in an interview with this paper that . . ."

Thad slammed the paper back onto the desk. "They're calling him a pundit!"

"Keep it. Having that thing around gives me bile."

"Don't tell me you actually think there's something to what this wacko is saying."

Fleiss slid his cup around in a slow circle on the immaculate desktop. "You're a good trader, Dorsett. But you haven't been around the market as long as I have. The Street is as nervous as I've ever seen it. They're a wolf pack and have a pack mentality. The secret of my success has been in seeing which way the pack is going to move and beating them to the punch. I'm a loner, and loners can always get the jump on a group, so long as they're not ruled by fear."

He thumbed the switch that raised his coffeepot into view. Refilling his cup, Fleiss went on, "Right now the pack is waiting for a leader to emerge and tell them which way to run. At a more stable time, this Korda would be laughed off the stage. But at this point in time, he's a threat."

"I can't believe I'm hearing you say this."

"Believe it," Fleiss said. The words held a bitter edge. "If Korda can sway the investment habits of a thousand small investors, he can do it with ten thousand. If he does it with ten, it might become a hundred. And if a hundred thousand small-time investors react to his scaremongering tactics, there's a good chance Korda's prophecies will become self-fulfilling."

Thad felt Fleiss's words push him back into his seat. "You really think it could spread like that?"

"It's already started. The reason the Philadelphia branch manager contacted us is that they've been sitting there all morning, watching people pull their money out of savings and bank-controlled fund accounts. Customers who have been with the bank for years are closing everything down. Mutual funds, IRAs, savings, college trust funds, the lot. From what they've heard, it's happening at banks all over town. According to what they've been told, the money is being channeled into put options."

Thad worked it out and said slowly, "They're betting the market is going to decline."

"All because of something this Korda's been telling them in his talks."

"He can't be having this kind of effect," Thad exclaimed. "You don't know this guy. He hardly knows how to string a sentence together. I worked with him for the six longest months of my life and never heard him raise his voice. Not once."

"Well, he's found his voice now." Fleiss motioned with his cup. "I want you to go out there and stop him."

"What, me?"

"That's right. Do whatever it takes. Find out where he is and figure out something to stop him in his tracks. The Philadelphia branch has ordered one of their guys to follow Korda and find out where he's going to be on Monday and pass the information back to us here. I've spoken with security. They've assigned a couple of guys to go along and do whatever you tell them to do. They're downstairs waiting for you."

Thad stopped his objection before it surfaced. Deep within the folds of Fleiss's doughlike face, he could see the eyes watching, measuring, waiting. Another test, this one unspoken. If he refused, he would also be turning down the job. This was what Larry wanted, he knew, someone willing to do whatever it took.

Thad forced himself to shape the words, "You've got it."

Fleiss smiled for the first time Thad had ever seen. "Take a long weekend; enjoy your first taste of New York. Then hive off to wherever they're going to be on Monday. Work fast and stop this guy in his tracks, before this thing goes any further." A second smile flitted in and out of view. "In the meantime, I'll have the office next to mine fitted out for when you get back."

─┤ TWENTY-NINE ├─

Twenty-Three Days . . .

☐ Sunday morning found Buddy and Molly in the town of Altoona, Pennsylvania, just north of the Laurel Hills. The evening was booked with another talk, the morning was free for worship. Buddy was silent as he, Clarke, and Molly drove to the red-brick downtown church. There he endured the stares and the handshakes and the overloud welcome. He entered the church and slipped into the pew, immensely glad to be able to sit and relax and listen.

His first prayer was for himself, for strength and patience and the ability to see it all to the end. Buddy stayed there through the first song as all the others around him rose to their feet. He prayed to accept his Father's call fully. To stop his objections and his foot-dragging, and to strive to overcome his own limitations.

As he was about to raise his head again, Buddy found himself thinking of Alex. His brother felt so close it was as though he had suddenly appeared to sit there beside Buddy. A burning sensation came to his heart and his eyes. Buddy experienced a gradual *joining* with his brother. In that moment all the years of distress and all the problems he had endured because of Alex simply disappeared. The exasperation and the worry and the sorrow were no longer a part of him. In their place was only love.

Buddy leaned over so far his forehead touched his hands, which were clasped together on his knees. He felt Molly's soft touch on his back—comforting and joining with him, not needing to know what he was praying for, simply wanting to join with him.

He prayed for Alex. He prayed for a healing. He prayed that the healing would start in his brother's spirit and expand to include every part of his being. He prayed that Alex would rise and accept the greatness he had been born with, that he would rise and accept his Lord.

After the service Buddy felt himself much more calm about the attention directed toward him. His heart remained full, his peace intact.

They left the church and drove back toward the hotel. As they were turning into the parking lot, a pinging sounded from within the glove box. Buddy opened the lid and extracted the cellular phone. "Hello?"

"I wanted you to be the first to know," Alex said in greeting. His voice sounded even more hoarse than usual, as though roughened by an emotion he could barely contain. "I went to church with Agatha again this morning."

Buddy knew what was coming even before his mind had fully formed the thought. He felt his entire body squeezing tight, as though the sudden flood of joy was so great that if he did not clench up tight, he would explode. He shut his eyes and turned to the window. He simply said, "Yes."

"I took the walk, little brother. I did it."

His body was trembling so hard he could scarcely whisper the words, "Oh, Alex."

"I walked up and I asked the Lord Jesus to come into my life," Alex said, whispering himself now, forcing the words out around the emotion that choked him. "I confessed my sins, and I prayed for forgiveness, and I said that if it was His will, I wanted to spend the rest of my life being His man."

☐

Whey they came back from lunch, Buddy sat and pretended to read while Molly stretched out on the bed. He spent more time looking at his wife than he did his book. The travel had not just tired Molly, it had worn her down. For the first time since she had been sick with bronchitis two years earlier, Molly looked her age. She was drawn and thinner looking than before all this had begun. Yet there was an ethereal quality to her quietness, as though this, too, had been distilled by the road. She was suffused with a light Buddy felt with his heart, rather than saw with his eyes.

A half hour later she rolled over and sat up. "I want to go back and help out Trish. She's had this strep infection for nine days now. Her fever this morning was a hundred and four. Jennifer has a bad throat and a fever as well, and it looks like Veronica might be coming down with it too. Jack sounded exhausted when I spoke with him before church."

Buddy felt as though he had been waiting to hear her say the words. "I think that's a good idea, hon."

"I'm sorry to be leaving you, but not sorry to be going," Molly told him. "I need to see the leaves change color. Not these leaves. My leaves. I want to watch the elm in my backyard get ready for winter."

Buddy found himself worried that when she left, she would take the light with her. "I'll miss you."

Molly smiled only with her eyes, but it was enough. She seemed translucent, as though held to earth only by bonds of love. "I'll be talking to you every day."

"You'd better. I need to keep getting your Bible passages. They really help me, hon."

"I'm glad." She reached into her purse and came up with one of her little cards. "This is the one for your work tonight."

He accepted it and read: *Who knows whether you have come to the kingdom for such a time as this? Esther 4:14*

Buddy looked up. "This is beautiful. And scary."

Molly met his gaze with a calm brilliance, and quietly declared, "You are growing into a prophet."

The simple statement made him shiver. "I'm not so sure—"

She stopped him with a simple raising of her hand. Buddy halted, took a breath, and nodded acceptance. Molly went on. "Almost despite yourself, you *are* growing. I *see* it happening. Don't stand in the Lord's way, honey."

He did not need to ask what she meant. "It's frightening. And it hurts."

"The prophets of old were not happy men. They were forced to carry the weight of an entire nation." Her gaze was as quietly commanding as her voice. "But if you are truly chosen, as I believe you are, then the Lord must feel you are strong enough to bear up under the burden."

"I'll try."

"No, my darling." Molly reached over and took his hand. "You must *do*."

⊣| THIRTY |⊢

Twenty-Two Days . . .

☐ The security guys were about what Thad would have expected, silent and hulking and at first a little frightening. They wore matching blue blazers and crew cuts and had muscles so pumped up their shoulders remained bunched in permanent shrugs. He had asked their names and got mumbled replies he only half heard and instantly forgot. By the second hour of the early Monday drive, however, he had mentally designated them as Frick and Frack, his two silent shadows. They spoke a grand total of six words the entire trip down to Pittsburgh.

The bank's spy had done his job well. He was a nervous bespectacled kid by the name of Wesley Hadden, nine months out of MBA school and desperately eager to please. When Thad and the guards pulled in front of the Pittsburgh hotel, Hadden handed him a file containing Buddy Korda's movements over the next three days.

Thad endured the kid's business-school handshake and hearty voice, congratulated him on a job well done, and sent him on his way with a sigh of relief. He returned to where the security pair hulked, and laid out the plans he had formulated on the drive down. They accepted their marching orders with stony silence.

Thad went up to his room—the lousy hotel had only one suite, and it was being renovated. No matter. He would only be there one night. Then it would be back to the Big Apple and his office next to Fleiss. Vice president and number two trader in the Valenti banking empire. It had a nice ring. He stretched out on the bed, pleased with himself and excited about his plans.

It was a risk to stay in the same hotel as Korda, but Thad was not planning to move very far until this was over and done. Or lift a finger to do anything but give orders, for that matter. Having muscle at his beck and call wasn't all that bad a thing, when push came to shove. He laced his fingers behind his head and ran through his preparations one more time. If he had to be Fleiss's troubleshooter, this was the way to do it—separated from both the risk and the public eye, but close enough to revel in the action.

☐

The ache from Molly's absence kept Buddy company through the Monday afternoon drive. Clarke showed his usual understanding and drove in silence. The sun was a ruddy globe crisscrossed by power lines and road signs by the time they pulled into the Pittsburgh hotel parking lot. Buddy pulled his cases from the trunk and followed Clarke through the lobby and over to the reception desk, amazed that he had ever become so accustomed to the routine of checking in.

"Mr. Korda?"

Buddy looked up from signing his registration form. "That's me."

"Okay, you're in room two-fourteen." But before the clerk handed over the key card, he swiveled the form around so he could examine the signature for himself. He gave Buddy a sidelong glance, then passed over the plastic key card and said again, "Room two-fourteen."

"Thank you." Buddy walked with Clarke toward the elevator and said quietly, "What was that all about?"

"Word about you must be filtering beyond the churches." Clarke punched the button, entered the elevator, and glanced at his watch. "If we want to grab a bite before we head over, we'll need to meet in about forty-five minutes."

"Fine." Buddy walked down the hall, entered his room, dropped his bags, and went straight to the window. He swept back the curtains and flipped the window catch. He pulled, but could not get the window to open. Buddy was a fanatic for fresh air, especially in a strange room that smelled vaguely of disinfectant. He hit the catch a couple of times, but the window was jammed tight. He made a mental note to speak to the front desk about it, then reached for his cell phone and punched the number for Alex's office.

A familiar woman's voice answered with, "The Korda Trust."

Buddy dropped into a chair. "The what?"

"Mr. Korda, is that you?"

"Yes. Lorraine, what are you doing there?" But he knew the answer even before he formed the question.

"They fired me, Mr. Korda. Well, he did. Thad Dorsett. He's up in New York, and the notice came from the office of somebody at headquarters I've never even heard of before. But it was him, all right. I knew he'd be gunning for me."

"Lorraine, I can't tell you how sorry—"

"Don't let it bother you, Mr. Korda. It doesn't bother me. Agatha had already offered me a job last week. They need my help, and I love it here. She's promised me something permanent afterward." She paused and then added quietly, "If there is an after. Wait, here she comes now."

Before he could say anything more, the phone was handed over, and a cultured voice said, "Buddy?"

"Yes. I'm terribly sorry to hear about Lorraine being fired."

"Don't be. She's not. And my attorneys had a field day with the bank, warning they were going to file suit for wrongful dismissal. Got her quite a nice severance package. And we need her. Desperately."

Buddy found himself most comforted by Agatha's matter-of-fact tone. "What was it she said when she answered the phone?"

"Oh, the Korda Trust. My accountant filed the papers last week. We're spending quite a lot of money, and they wanted to set it up as a tax-deductible trust."

"Agatha, I don't like your spending so much on me."

"It's not the money. Well, it is, but it's not important. My accountant asked me to do it, and Alex agreed."

Buddy started to object and then remembered what Molly had told him about not putting up a fuss when people wanted to help. "Is Alex there?"

"No." A long pause, then more quietly, "He started chemotherapy last Friday. He goes in every third day."

Buddy felt himself drain away, all will, all energy, all desire. It was as if an unseen tap had been opened and his life was pouring out in an unstoppable surge. "How is it going?"

"He's handling it extremely well." A pause, then, "He was hoping we wouldn't even need to mention it to you. I suppose I shouldn't have said anything."

"No." Buddy tried to find strength to put behind Agatha's words. "No, you did right. He's my brother, Agatha. He shouldn't try to hide things like this from me."

"It wasn't hiding, really. He just didn't feel like you needed to worry about this along with everything else."

"It's fine. How is everything else?"

"Oh, we're moving right along here." But Agatha did not sound convinced. "Alex checked with everyone. Paul, Jack, the girls' families, me, Lorraine, Pastor Allen, the others at church. We've all bought put options through the same broker you've been using."

"That's good, Agatha." His voice sounded dull to his own ears. Poor Alex. "Please thank him for checking."

"Oh, dear. I was horribly wrong to tell you, wasn't I."

"Don't talk like that. You were absolutely right. How am I supposed to pray him through this if I don't know what's going on?"

She sighed long and hard. "I feel like I'm surrounded these days by all my mistakes and clouded motives."

"Agatha, I don't know what I'd do without you there, and that's the truth."

But it was as though she had not heard him. "You know when it hit me the hardest? Yesterday. Watching Alex go up to the front of the church. It felt as though I was seeing the most unselfish man I had ever met do what he was always destined to do."

"And you were the one who finally got him to church," Buddy pointed out.

"He went because I pestered him. He did it for me, do you see what I'm saying? And I did it for me too. Not for God. For me." Unshed tears filled her voice, but she forced herself to continue. "Just like I've railroaded the church, not allowing them to have my money unless they spent it on missions. Do you know why I've done that?"

"No, I—"

"Because my own two children have run away from God. No wonder, the way I bullied them at home. After Joe died, I used the children as a way to fill the empty days. I ruled their every waking hour, most especially on Sundays. I never let them build their own relationship with the Lord. Oh, no. I forced them to live according to *my* standards. And they did, at least until they were old enough to leave. One went to Berkeley and the other to the University of Hawaii, about as far away from home as they could get."

"Agatha, I'm so sorry, I didn't know."

"No, of course not. How could you? I pretended to all the world that everything was fine. Even when one joined a rock group and quit school and now spends his money on drugs and alcohol. And the other . . . Oh, I just can't stand the mess I've made of their lives."

"Agatha, even the Lord lost his first two children to the lures of this world. The perfect Father could not offer them freedom and then be sure they would hold to the proper course."

The sniffling slowly subsided. "I suppose that's true."

"Of course it is. You mustn't be too hard on yourself. Look at what you were up against, raising two kids on your own, trying to keep Joe's business going. You did the best you could. Yes, you made mistakes. We all do. But you cannot take their blunders on your own shoulders. Hurt for your children, yes; pray for them always. But accept that they are adults and free to find their own ways."

Agatha responded with a few moments of shaky breathing before she said, "It's strange how Alex has forced me to be so honest with myself."

"He is a remarkable man."

"Yes, he is." The words came easier now, though the voice remained an octave lower than normal. "I've spent years condemning him. I owe you as much of an apology for that as I do him."

"You don't owe me a thing."

But she did not let him stop her. "I let myself be fooled by his exterior. I saw his size and his strength, and I classed him as a drinker and a brawler. He told me about his fiancée and how he never could seem to get over being abandoned."

Buddy was so surprised he had to pull the phone away from his ear and look at it. He brought it back to hear Agatha say, "Are you still there?"

"I'm here. I'm just amazed Alex told you about that. He never talks about it. Not ever. He's not mentioned it to me once in all these years."

That gave Agatha food for thought. Eventually she said, "It's nice to think that our working together has been good for him as well."

"More than just good." Strange how Buddy could be so worried over Alex and yet so happy at the same time. "Maybe talking with you about what happened released him to go forward and accept Christ."

"Perhaps you're right." Another pause, and then, "He's a wonderful man, your brother. He has the biggest heart and the gentlest spirit I have ever known in a man."

Buddy searched for something to say and finally settled on, "I wish there were some way to turn back the hands of time and have Alex meet you earlier."

"That is the nicest thing anyone has said to me in years." Agatha's voice found a new calm. "Maybe it just wasn't time. Not until now."

"Maybe not," Buddy agreed. "I'm glad you're there now, though. Very, very glad."

⊣| THIRTY-ONE |⊢

☐ Thad Dorsett must have fallen asleep, because the next thing he knew there was a knock at the door. He rose and checked his appearance in the mirror, straightened his tie, and swept back his hair. Then he opened the door to reveal the larger of the pair. "Everything taken care of?"

"Come on over to our room," the security guy replied, which for him was a full lecture.

Thad followed him across the hall, where the guy rapped twice, paused, then knocked once more. Instantly the chain was drawn back and the lock released. Thad followed him inside, but he halted at the sight of the two women seated on the sofa. He inspected them carefully, then said to the guard, "Nice work."

"I'm Dawn," the blond one said. She was beautiful in a hard-edged way, so long as Thad did not look too closely at her eyes.

She motioned to the redhead seated beside her. "This is Crystal."

"You're both perfect, is what you are," Thad said. He turned to watch a stranger erecting a camera tripod by the window. He demanded of the guard standing beside the closed curtains, "He knows what to do?"

"No problem." The stranger answered for himself. He wore a greasy ponytail and worked with bored efficiency. A battered metal case was flung open to reveal a huge amount of photographic equipment. He lifted a camera housing attached to a motor drive and fastened it to the tripod. Then he brought out the longest telescopic lens Thad had ever seen. He hefted it like a rifle and swung it around so the larger end was pointed toward Thad. The outer lens was the size of a dinner plate. "With this thing we'll get every wart and wrinkle in living color."

"You'd better." Thad turned to the second guard and asked, "You arranged things with the front desk?"

In response, the man turned to where his mate still stood by the door and said, "Lights." Instantly the room was bathed in shadows.

Thad walked over to where the guard was peeling back the curtains. He peeked through, excited by the voyeuristic power.

The hotel was shaped in a three-story U. The guard's room faced the narrow, inner courtyard. Overhead the sky was giving way to night. Thad followed the guard's pointed finger and saw a man knotting his tie in the mirror in the second-floor room directly across from their own. A moment's observation was enough for Thad to declare, "That's our man."

The guard motioned to the two women and commanded, "Over here."

They rose in languid motions, used to having men watch. The soft light from outside was kind to their calloused features. Thad pointed and said, "Over there. Directly across from us. What's the room number?"

"Two-fourteen," the guard tonelessly replied.

"Here," the photographer said, snapping the telephoto lens into place. "You'll get a better look through this."

Dawn leaned over, looked a moment, and said, "It's a snap."

Crystal then focused through the lens. She exclaimed, "Yeah, sure, I thought I'd seen him before."

All eyes turned toward her. Thad demanded, "Where?"

"His picture was in the paper yesterday. What's his name?"

"Buddy Korda."

"Right. That's the guy. Korda."

Dawn asked, "You read the papers?"

Crystal straightened from the camera. "Something about a speech or interview or something. Wait, wait, I remember now. The economy, am I right?"

"It doesn't matter," Thad snapped. Anger billowed in fiery waves. "All you need to know is do it when he's back from his meeting tonight and he's gotten ready for bed. Just move in and set it all up fast."

"Sure," Dawn said, weaving her way back to the sofa. "We got it, no problem."

"There better not be. You only get one chance. And remember, he's not going to want to let you in."

"I'm a big girl," Dawn declared.

"We both are," Crystal agreed, as indifferent as Dawn. "A guy like that won't stand a chance."

"And be fast with the clothes," Thad said. "We need these pictures to be hot."

"We'll be in and on him so fast the guy won't even know what hit him," Dawn promised.

"There's a bonus for getting it right," Thad said. It was going to be a real pleasure to bring Korda down. "A big one."

─┤ THIRTY-TWO ├─

☐ The talk had tired him out more than any he had attended up to that point. Perhaps it had been the size—well over a thousand people—but he didn't think so. The crowds were growing larger with every passing day. And there were television or video cameras at almost every event these days. No, it was probably the increasing sense of pressure and juggling so much all at once—coordinating and planning and arranging and cramming more and more into every available minute.

His head buzzed with confusing bits and pieces of logistics, keeping him silent on the drive back to the hotel. When they arrived, he bid everyone a weary good night and headed for his room. His feet seemed to stumble as he plodded down the hall. He fumbled with his keycard and tried in vain to open the door until he looked up and realized he was trying to get into the wrong room. That brought an exhausted chuckle. He was tired indeed.

He scarcely managed to get into his pajamas and brush his teeth before falling into bed. He was asleep before his head hit the pillow.

The pounding seemed to come from a long distance away. Louder and louder, until he was pushed upward by the noise. The door. Somebody was knocking on his door.

He forced his eyes open. "Who is it?"

The reply was indistinct, but it sounded like a woman. He rolled over, fumbled for the lamp, and blinked in the light. "What?"

"Room service!" The pounding continued.

He rolled out of bed with a groan. "Just a minute."

He padded over, switched on the main light, and said through the closed door, "You've got the wrong room."

"Look, this is two-fourteen, isn't it?"

He had to struggle to think. "Well, yes, but—"

"Then you've got to sign for this."

"Oh, this is ridiculous." He unlocked the door and swung it open. "I told you—"

But the women were already in the room. Two of them. Beautiful and tough and *strong*. He was guided away from the door by the blond, while the redhead shut the door and then moved over to sweep back the curtains. So fast and so utterly unexpected that he could scarcely draw breath, much less speak.

Finally he managed, "Look—"

"No, buster, *you* look." The redhead wore a leer as she reached up behind and began unhooking something. "We're a little gift from a pal of yours."

"A special something you'll never . . ." The blond dropped the hand holding his arm and took a step back. "Hey, you're not him."

The redhead stopped shrugging off her dress. "What?"

"Take a look." The blond's leer was gone, her expression hard as granite. "What's your name?"

"Clarke," he stammered. "Clarke Owen."

The redhead gave him an angry frown. "Where's the other guy?"

"The other bed's empty," the blond said crossly.

Suddenly he understood, and the realization hurtled him to full wakefulness. "We changed rooms." He was no longer stammering.

The redhead's expression turned savage. "*What?*"

"There goes our bonus," the blond said glumly.

"We changed rooms," Clarke repeated, glancing from one to the other. "He likes to have fresh air at night, and this window is stuck closed."

"Great, just great!" The beautiful face held an amazing amount of bitterness. "Come on, let's go."

"Sleep tight, honey," the blond said, following her friend from the room.

Clarke stood frozen to the spot, listening to his rapid breathing, running the sequence over and over through his mind. His roving glance caught sight of the curtains. He realized with yet another startling jolt why they might have opened the drapes. As he stood there, the curtain to a darkened window across the courtyard flickered once, and was still.

Clarke closed his drapes and moved back to the door. With trembling fingers he reset the bolt. Only then did he notice the empty screw holes higher up, and realize that someone had removed the night latch. He walked over to the desk, picked up the chair, walked back to the door, and jammed it hard under the knob.

He turned off the lights and went back to bed, as awake as he had ever been in his life. He wondered if he should even mention the visitation to Buddy and decided he had no choice. They would need to make careful arrangements in the future.

Sleep was a very long time in coming.

THIRTY-THREE

Nineteen Days . . .

☐ The week was one hard push. Tuesday morning they made the six-hour drive to Akron, Ohio. Wednesday morning they moved on to Zanesville. Thursday they traveled to Dayton. It was not what had been originally planned, but very little was these days. Buddy's message was spreading far faster than he could travel, and demands for him to speak grew by the hour. The press pestered Alex and Agatha continually. They called from everywhere under the sun, demanding immediate access. Agatha turned from cool to frigid, and even Alex responded to the television bullying with a stonelike hardness.

Though tired from the week's activities, Thursday found Buddy ready for another press conference. He did not particularly want to face the press and its hard-eyed skepticism again.

But with less than three weeks left, he would do anything possible to make sure his message was heard. Despite his fatigue, he was able to trust in his newfound ability to remain steadfast to the central message. Which meant he entered the hotel conference room that afternoon, waited for the television lights to come on, greeted the gathered press while his microphones were tested, and then launched immediately into his message.

"The idea that our economy will always continue to expand, that our government can fine-tune the economy and make growth a constant, is nothing more than a myth. A sad one." He saw the smirks around the table. Such intelligent people. So certain of their attitudes and their ambitions. Buddy persisted. "All of life is cyclical. We are born, we live, we die. The same will happen with every economic cycle. There has never been a straight-line economic rise. There never will be. If you were to chart out the movements of just the last twenty years, you would need a huge graph, because the peaks and troughs are so far apart. But in peak times we tend to forget there were ever troughs. We would like to pretend that they can't happen again."

"Mr. Korda." One of the skeptical young men leaned forward. "Are you saying that we cannot learn from our mistakes? Couldn't it be possible to ensure that the next economic downturn would not be so severe?"

"In theory, certainly. In reality, no."

"And why is that?"

"Because of human nature. Because of greed." He was losing them. He could see it in their faces. Mention a moral code and their minds went on autopilot. "There is a passage in the Bible that goes, 'O foolish people, without understanding, who have eyes and see not, and who have ears and hear not.'"

He glanced around the table, saw no indication that anyone recognized the passage, and with a mental shrug returned to the central theme. "It is fairly easy to recognize that our financial system is out of kilter. Too many of the people in charge of our banks have completely lost touch with the world beyond Wall Street. They live to trade, not to serve their customers. They are after fast bucks and quick profits. Banks accept trading risks that would have been utterly unthinkable just twenty years ago.

"People look at the Great Depression as though it caught the world by surprise. Well, it did, and it didn't. I've done some reading about that time, and I've found that people were worried about the dangers five years before the crash actually arrived.

"What concerns me now, as it concerns others, is how *many* things we have in common with that period. Two of these factors have been in the press recently, the air of frantic speculation and the overly high prices of stocks. But there are other parallels that greatly concern me. I want to mention just three of them here, the three that frighten me the most.

"Back in the twenties, banks could trade nationwide. They operated in as many states as they wanted. That meant when they began going under in 1930, their bankruptcies had a *national* effect. So in the thirties Congress passed a series of laws restricting banks to operation in just one state. Banks have been fighting to have these laws rolled back ever since.

"In the late eighties, the banks finally pulled the last remaining teeth from these laws, and now we are faced with a growing national banking network all over again.

"Second, until the depression, banks could print their own money. Supposedly this was backed up by the banks' gold reserves. But these reserves were not effectively monitored. Banks used these same reserves to back wild speculations in the markets. The result was, banks printed money backed by their good name, nothing more. When the market dropped, the banks' assets were wiped out, and their money was worth nothing.

"Banks today do not print money, but they *do* print paper credits. They print them, and they trade in them. The difference between today's paper and yesterday's money is only one of magnitude.

"Paper money is a *promissory note*. It is a freely exchangeable slip saying that when presented to the bank, the bank will produce gold or U.S. currency to cover that amount. Today's bank papers are promissory notes as well, only they're a hundred million times larger.

"Once again, these credit papers are used like currency to buy and sell businesses, support governments, cover mortgages, and run local communities. Once again, this paper is backed on nothing more than the bank's good name.

"And third, the twenties saw a huge upsurge in the amount of foreign capital flowing into the American stock and bond markets. Germany was still in ruins after the First World War, as was much of the rest of Europe. Foreign capital flowed into the only market that was booming—America. That was very nervous capital and was controlled by just a handful of huge foreign investors. When they felt the market had peaked, they pulled their money out. All at once, there was an unexpected drain with cataclysmic results. How do I know that this had such a terribly destabilizing effect? Because records show that this occurred on the Friday before Black Monday—October 26, 1929.

"Today, the Japanese market remains in severe recession. Their stock market is down *forty percent* from its level of just three years ago. Our interest rates are *nine times* higher than theirs.

"Today, Europe's economy is in turmoil. Germany and France are experiencing their highest levels of unemployment in fifty years. Their stock and bond markets are stagnant.

"Because of these and other factors, the level of foreign investment in the U.S. markets has never been higher. Once again, this is very nervous money. There is an extremely tense finger on the trigger. This gun is aimed directly at the heart of our own financial system."

□

Thad was a bitter man. Thursday morning he stared out the Dayton restaurant window as the lunch crowd began to arrive. The sunlight seemed to mock him and his anger.

"Something the matter with your food, hon?"

"What?" Thad swung back around and focused first on the waitress and then on his untouched plate. "Uh, no, I'm just not hungry."

"You're going to have to do better than that." She showed a weary smile. "Take a plate like that back into the kitchen, we'll both have to answer to the cook."

"Just bring me a coffee." He turned back to the window.

The two guards remained as silent as they had been all week. He did not mind in the least. For three days they had tracked Buddy Korda, always one step behind the man's erratic course. Plans seemed to change by the hour, leaving them utterly unable to set another trap.

Not only that, but Thad's blood was brought to a boil by the morning's papers.

The day before, according to several articles, a bulletin had flashed over the financial wires. One paper said it had originated in London, another Rome. Reuters and AP both covered it, however. The report stated that the Japanese were not going to bid on the next treasury bond offering.

Just as he had suggested to Larry Fleiss.

The response had been explosive. Bond prices had dipped by 18 percent in the space of an hour. Then a second rumor had surfaced. Because of the yen's weakness the Japanese were pulling out of stocks as well. The New York exchanges went into a paroxysm of selling, shedding one hundred ten points in fifteen minutes.

The effect was so shattering that the Japanese finance minister had been raised from his bed so that he could issue a personal denial.

The finance minister's statement had resulted in just as powerful an effect, only in the opposite direction. Bond and stock prices had soared, with the Dow closing 212 points above the previous day.

Thad ground his teeth in silent fury. Larry's jovial call earlier that morning had only poured salt in his wounds. The man had congratulated him on a great idea and crowed over the profits made by going in both directions and in both markets. Thad had forced himself to sound easy and amiable, but inside he burned with wrath over having missed the action. His idea, Larry's glory. All because of Korda botching their well-laid plans and then running across the country like a fox.

Well, this time they wouldn't fail.

When the cell phone chimed, he had it up and at his ear before the first ring had ended. "Dorsett."

It was Wesley Hadden, the kid on Korda's trail. He sounded terse, frightened. "They're giving a talk tonight at the Clarkstown community center."

"Great." Thad made swift notes. "Good work."

"They don't have hotel reservations yet." He almost bit off the words.

Either that or they were keeping it secret. No surprise, after the other night's fiasco. "If you hear something, call us back."

"This is the last time I need to report, right?"

"Probably." The kid's tone was unsettling. "What's the matter?"

A moment's hesitation, then, "I've been listening to Mr. Korda speak."

"Don't let it get to you."

"This is a lot . . ." The kid stopped, breathed hard, then demanded sharply, "Exactly how much longer do I need to hang around?"

"A day, maybe two. I'll let you know. In the meantime, stay on his case." Thad switched off the phone to find the two guards watching him impassively. "Tonight's talk is in Clarkstown. You know people there?"

"We can find them."

"Just a question of knowing where to look," the second agreed.

"Okay. Hire some muscle. Just make sure they can't be traced back to us. Can you do that?"

"No problem." Toneless, terse, not the least surprised.

"After the other night, they'll be watching for us at the hotel. So we'll make our move when he arrives for the talk. Make it look like a mugging."

"There'll be others around," one guard pointed out.

"So hit them too. I don't care."

The two hulks exchanged glances. "How hard?"

"Hard as you want. I don't just want him stopped. I want him running scared. Or I don't want him running at all."

□

They had learned to give Buddy a little time to rest and recuperate after a public meeting, especially the press conferences. Today, however, he scarcely had time to lie down before there was a knock on his door.

When he stood up Buddy felt like he walked into an unspoken message, as though it had been draped around his bed and he walked straight into it.

Buddy opened the door for Clarke. Beside him stood the young man who had attached himself to their group back in Pennsylvania. Wesley Hadden was employed by Valenti Bank, which explained the young man's nervous air; anyone working for the bank but associated with Buddy ran the risk of losing his job. Wesley had proved to be a great help to Clarke on several occasions, traveling ahead while Clarke himself remained at Buddy's side.

"There's a problem," Clarke announced.

Buddy nodded. He knew.

"Tonight's meeting was supposed to be in a community hall, but an electrical fire broke out last night. I've just come from there. It smells like burned cork." Clarke studied his friend. "You don't look the least bit surprised. Did somebody already tell you about this?"

Buddy started to deny it, began to correct himself, and then realized it didn't matter. "Take the car and get back on the interstate. Go to the next exit. Get off and stop at the first church you see. A pastor will be out front. Ask him if we can hold the meeting there."

"Get on . . ." Clarke stepped back through the doorway. "Are you sure?"

"Yes," he said. "Yes, I am."

Clarke exchanged a glance with Wesley, who was staring at Buddy in openmouthed bafflement. Clarke said slowly, "If you're absolutely certain, I guess we'd better be going."

"Take the contact numbers with you," Buddy said. "There isn't much time."

─|| THIRTY-FOUR ||─

☐ The breathless call came just as Thad Dorsett was checking into the Clarkstown hotel. He moved away from the reception desk as soon as he recognized the voice. "What's the matter?"

The kid tracking Korda reported, "They've changed the venue."

Thad felt awash in an icy fury. "You mean you got it wrong."

"I mean they *changed* it. There was a fire at the community hall last night." Wesley's voice was more than agitated. The guy sounded like he was approaching the edge. "If you don't believe me, go check it out yourself. I don't care."

"Calm down," Thad snapped, signaling to the guards.

"*You* calm down. I've had enough of this. I'm out, you hear me?"

"Sure, sure. Take it easy." Dorsett turned away from curious gazes cast his way. "Where are they holding the talk?"

"This whole thing is *crazy*. The guy hasn't done anything wrong. Why are you bugging him anyway?"

Thad felt another chance slipping through his fingers. "I'll discuss philosophy with you another time. Right now just tell me where the talk is going to be held."

There was a moment's silence before Wesley sullenly replied, "I don't know."

"You mean they're keeping it secret." He exchanged glances with the cold-eyed guards. Bad news.

"I mean, I don't *know*. Nobody does. Mr. Korda's told us to drive into town, stop at the first church we see, ask if we can hold it there."

"That doesn't make any sense." Now it was *Mr.* Korda. Now it was *us* headed into town. "Run that one by me again."

The kid did as he was told. "This is my last call. I can't stand this."

"You mean they suspect you?"

"I mean I don't know what's right anymore. It seemed so simple when I started. But now . . ." He cupped the phone, said something muffled, then came back on the line with, "I see Clarke signaling me." Another moment of raspy breathing and then, "I quit. That's all. I'm a banker, not a spy."

Thad punched off the phone, turned to the pair of guards, and said, "You're not going to believe this."

□

"Are you sure we're doing the right thing?"

"What, doing as Buddy said?" Clarke laughed and shook his head. "All I can say for certain is, when he spoke there in the hotel room, it was not just Buddy's authority that I heard."

Wesley Hadden was a slender young man with a preference for suspenders and overloud silk ties. He settled his tortoiseshell-rimmed glasses more firmly upon his nose, every gesture tinged with the same nervous air that pitched his voice somewhere near a whine. "But it doesn't make sense! I mean, we're three hours from what's supposed to be our biggest meeting yet, chasing all over creation following orders that sounded, well . . ."

"Crazy," Clarke agreed. "Totally crazy."

"So how can you trust him?"

"I'm not trusting Buddy. I'm trusting God, and trusting that Buddy got it right."

"Got *what* right?" Wesley spun his head around. "Wasn't that an exit?"

"Where?"

"Back there! That side road behind us."

Clarke squinted into the rearview mirror. "I don't see anything."

Wesley spun in his seat. "I'm positive it was an exit." He slumped back around. "So now we're even more lost than before."

"Wait, there's another exit up ahead."

"So what? Mr. Korda said take the first exit." Wesley shook his head. "What difference does it make? I don't believe any of it anyway."

"Okay, here we go. No big deal. We'll just swing around and get back on the interstate going the other way." But then Clarke squinted through the windshield, and slowed the car.

"What's the matter?"

"Right up ahead, see that?"

"It's a church, so what?"

"So there's a pastor standing out there in front."

"Where?"

"Right there. By the notice board."

"But Mr. Korda said the first exit! We're on the wrong side of town!"

"Come on, it won't take a moment to see if this is the right one after all." Clarke glanced at the young man seated next to him. "Is everything all right?"

"All right?" Wesley wiped at the sweat beading his forehead. "We're off riding around Clarkstown on instructions that don't make any sense at all, and you ask me if everything is all right?"

"Have faith," Clarke said mildly, inspecting the young man more closely. Something was definitely wrong there. "In times like these, we can only find answers with the help of faith."

□

After his talk, Buddy stood listening to the pastor continue to radiate excitement over the unexpected meeting. "I had just heard that our evening speaker was canceled. Hard to argue with laryngitis. I had decided to stretch my legs while my assistant started calling around." He laughed. "I have to tell you, when your friends pulled up, I thought it was a hoax. It was only the night before last that I heard about you for the first time. A group of pastors from the area had been invited to a friend's to watch your video."

Buddy listened with one ear, still drained from the evening's meeting. Despite the lack of notice, the hall had been filled to overflowing. The meetings so often were these days. Buddy shook the hands of the last to depart and noticed that Clarke and Wesley were standing in the corner, trying to gain his attention. Buddy waved them over.

"I can't tell you how moved I was by the video," the pastor went on. "So moved I almost doubted it myself the next day. You know how it is, being swept up one moment, then caught by doubt the next. But tonight, my goodness, I have never felt such an affirming flame before."

The pastor offered Buddy his hand. "It has been an honor, Mr. Korda. And I mean that sincerely."

"Thank you." He wondered why Clarke was still holding back. Then he noticed that Wesley's face was streaked with tears.

"I will see to it personally that tapes of tonight's talk are passed throughout our city. You can rest assured of that." He gave Clarke and Wesley a friendly nod and moved off.

Clarke waited until they were alone to announce, "Wesley has something to tell you."

"I'm a spy," he blurted out. "Valenti headquarters sent me to track your movements and report them."

Buddy found himself waiting for some internal reaction, but all he felt was tired. "I see."

Clarke demanded, "Report to whom?"

"A guy named Dorsett. Thad Dorsett."

"That name sounds familiar," Clarke said.

"He was head of our local branch," Buddy offered.

"In Aiden?" Clarke stared at him. "Your boss?"

Buddy nodded and said to the young man, "Thank you for telling us."

"They promised me a promotion if I helped." The young man seemed broken by his confession. "I didn't know, I didn't realize."

Clarke's eyes widened. "The girls, the ones who came to my room."

"That was part of this," the young man confirmed. "They wanted to find some way to discredit you."

"I understand." Buddy felt more worried about the young man than he was about himself. "All is forgiven."

"Not by me," Wesley groaned. "I can't believe I've tried to hurt you. I've listened to your talk four times now, and all I hear is somebody trying to help others. You're not getting anything out of this at all."

"Nothing except the joy of serving my Lord," Buddy said, forcing aside his desire to go and rest. "That is more than enough."

"I don't even know what you're talking about," Wesley confessed. "I've watched the others at your meetings, though. I know this isn't some mass hysteria. I *know* it."

"No, it's not," Buddy agreed. It seemed the simplest thing in the world, the most natural, to offer, "Would you pray with me?"

The young man looked at him, astounded. "You'd do that? After what I've just told you?"

"As far as the east is from the west," Buddy replied. "That is how far the Lord will separate us from our own sins, if only we will confess and repent and accept Him into our lives. How can I do any less?"

Wesley nodded his head. "Teach me, then. Show me how."

Buddy reached out to draw both Clarke and the young man closer. He bowed his head and said, "Let us pray."

─╢ THIRTY–FIVE ╟─

Eighteen Days . . .

☐ Nathan Jones Turner heard Fleiss out to the end, then demanded, "You say this Dorsett thought up the rumor business?"

"The whole idea was his," Fleiss confirmed, taking great pleasure in rubbing the old man's nose in it. Losing his former number-one trader still burned. "Netted us a cool seventy-five mil in one day's trading."

"Not bad." Trying as hard as he could to sound casual about it. But Fleiss knew. The old man was seething. "Can we do it again?"

"No chance. This was definitely a once-only deal. Had to pull every string I could to get the rumors and the timing down right. Cost us some change too."

"That still leaves us down a hundred and seventy-five million," Turner pointed out. "Not to mention what I need for the second payment on the hotels. Which, I need not remind you, is almost due. I managed to put them off a week, but it was tough." Even so, the protests lacked force. Fleiss had one-upped him. Turner hated that worse than losing money.

Fleiss responded with, "A week should be long enough. Got a couple of other things in the works."

"I hope so." A pause, then, "These come from Dorsett as well?"

"One of them. The biggest one."

"Incredible that such talent would be found in a local Valenti branch."

"Sure is." Keeping his voice bland, he decided now was the time to spring the final shock. "Oh, by the way. I've decided to make Dorsett my personal number one."

"I'm not surprised, with that sort of record." Holding to his calm. But Fleiss knew and Turner knew. Another person was being moved in to shield Fleiss from Turner's spies. "Where is the wonder kid now?"

"Tracking Korda."

"Who?"

"The thorn in our side."

"Not that doomsayer from the back of nowhere."

"The very same. He's starting to have an effect on the market."

"I don't care if he's doing handstands in the middle of the Exchange!" Turner was clearly pleased to have something valid on which to hang his anger. "We've got an *emergency* here. Does the word have any meaning to you at all?"

"Sure, but this is—"

"I'll tell you what this is. It's a waste of our time, and it's a waste of our valuable resources! Bring that man back."

"Listen, I'm worried—"

"Be worried about your future," Turner snarled. "Get Dorsett back on the trading floor. See what other projects he can dream up. Find out if he can save both your hides. And while you're at it, have him report to me. I want to meet this boy wonder for myself." Turner gathered his dignity like a cloak. "Fly him to Kennedy. I'll send the chopper. Today."

□

"Thad, this is Larry."

"Don't tell me you've already heard."

"Heard what?"

"Never mind." Thad rose from the breakfast table and carried the cell phone out into the hotel lobby. "I'm afraid we missed Korda again last night. Or at least the guys we hired did."

"Never mind that now. Where's the nearest airport?"

"There must be a municipal field outside the city. Why?"

"I don't even know where you are."

"Clarkstown. What's the matter?"

"I'm sending a jet down. Get out to the field now."

"Look, Larry, we're on this guy. It's just a matter of—"

"I told you not to worry about that. Leave the security goons on his tail. You get back here. The old man wants to meet you."

□

Early Friday morning they left Clarkstown for Flint, Michigan. Buddy had rested well and felt even more energized by the conversation he had had that morning with Molly. He waited until they had checked out of the hotel and started for the car to declare, "I'm going home this weekend. Molly's orders. It's for my health. She says she's going to shoot me unless I make it back."

To his relief, Clarke did not object. "I think we could both use a break."

Buddy reached for the cell phone. "I'll call Alex and make sure there's nothing that can't be rearranged." When he disconnected, Buddy was smiling. "They hadn't gotten anything firmed up for either tomorrow or Sunday. Amazing."

Clarke turned from the highway long enough to share his grin. "I can't believe anybody who's been through what you have would still find that word in his vocabulary."

"I suppose so. Anyway, they'll try to book us on the last flight out tonight."

"Sounds good to me."

Buddy settled back. "That was nice, praying with the young man last night."

"You know, Wesley is going to stay on with us," Clarke informed him. "He says we need to take a more careful look at security and planning."

Buddy shrugged. "We'll have to rely on God to protect us, same as always."

Clarke glanced over a second time. "You've changed, old friend."

Buddy did not deny it. "It's the Lord's doing, not mine."

The interstate traffic was a steady, aggressive rush. Buddy glanced through the morning's newspaper, but nothing he read held his attention. He settled the paper on the seat beside him and returned his thoughts to his family, anticipating the joy of seeing them again, spending a weekend together. And then, unbidden, came the old ache of worry over his brother. Buddy sighed and shook his head.

"What's the matter?"

"Alex."

"Oh." Clarke nodded slowly. There was no need to say anything more.

"We've always been so close," Buddy went on, wishing he could push the pain out with the words. "He was the one who named me. Alex was named after my father's father. When I came along, they saddled me with my other grandfather's name, Broderick."

"I never knew that."

"It's one of those deep, dark family secrets. Alex never could say it. He was four at the time, and already the most headstrong little fellow you've ever met. I had that on best authority—my mother. Anyway, he spent the better part of a day standing by my crib trying to get his four-year-old mouth around my name. Then he gave up and called me Buddy. I've been Buddy ever since."

Clarke took the first exit for Flint. When he had stopped at the light at the bottom of the ramp, he turned and watched Buddy for a long moment before saying quietly, "It's in the Lord's hands, friend."

"I know." A long sigh. "Some things are a little harder to leave in his care than others, though. Aren't they?"

The ache accompanied them through the the streets of Flint. When they stopped at a traffic light, Buddy looked out his window at a bustling scene, at people hurrying to-and-fro, caught up in worries and business and work. Construction workers in hard hats, steelworkers in blue factory coveralls, women and men in business suits, people young and old. A mother in the car next to them was tending to a baby in the backseat. Behind her a woman in what looked like hospital whites was talking into a cellular phone. He could feel Clarke watching him, and he struggled to put his emotions into words. "I feel like I'm beginning to catch little glimpses of what it means to see with God's love. I feel His sorrow for the direction the world has chosen to go."

The traffic light turned green. Clarke drove on in silence. Buddy continued, "There will be millions who blame God for this economic disaster when it strikes. But the truth is, He has given us laws and He has given us a Savior. If we had followed them more closely, we could have escaped this entirely."

"If only," Clarke said quietly. "If only."

"We have nobody but ourselves to blame. But knowing this doesn't make it any better." Buddy glanced out through the windshield. "I hurt for them, Clarke. I feel like the Lord is taking my worries over Alex and changing them, forcing me to feel a taste of *His* pain."

□

The seating area in the back of the chopper was empty this time. One of the pilots came back to usher Thad in, close the portal, strap him to a seat, and wish him a hurried welcome. Clearly they were under instructions to make good time. Thad sat back and enjoyed the plush surroundings.

The leather seats gave way to walls and ceiling carpeted in the same silky covering as the floor. Seats and walls and floors, even the frames surrounding windows and the triple television sets, were a calming pastel blue. It gave Thad the feeling of being both cocooned and cosseted.

As Manhattan's skyline swooped into view, Thad reviewed what he knew of Nathan Jones Turner. The man was flamboyant and loved the spotlight. Turner was tall and well-kept for a man in his early seventies, with deep-set eyes and a piercing gaze. He was known for his notorious temper and had the touch of a modern-day Midas. He produced movies and loved to parade around with starlets one-third his age. He owned three jets and a helicopter and hated flying. He had recently spent twenty-two million dollars on a Van Gogh. The man was a living legend.

Thad felt a twinge of unease as they passed over the Manhattan skyline and kept heading east. When a white strip of beaches disappeared behind them, Thad punched the intercom button.

"You need something, Mr. Dorsett?"

"Where are you guys taking me?"

"Didn't they say? You're being met by Mr. Turner."

He looked out the window, saw nothing but blue skies and empty blue sea. "He's got a secret island out here nobody's ever heard of before?"

"Better than that, sir. Much better." The helicopter did a slow bank to the left. "Take a look out your left portal."

Thad slid to the other side of the chopper, looked down, and gasped aloud. Beneath him was the largest yacht he had ever seen.

The pilot slid open the door separating the cockpit from the passenger quarters. A grin appeared beneath his aviator shades. "Most people do that the first time they see the boat. Gape like that."

"That belongs to Mr. Turner?"

"It does now. They built it for some sheikh who never picked it up. Turner bought it last year. Seventy-five meters, over two hundred and thirty feet. It's got about everything you could ask for in a boat. Swimming pool, diving submarine, satellite links, the works. Hang on, sir, we're coming in now."

The blond chopper hostess was there to lead him from the ship's flight deck. Only this time she was dressed in a bikini top and wraparound sarong. She led him down a set of teak stairs with what appeared to be gold-plated railings, and ushered him into a palatial-size living room.

A white-haired man rose from the leather settee, tossing aside the papers he was working on. "Mr. Dorsett. Glad you could join me."

"This is an honor." Thad did a slow sweep of the room. Anybody who went in for this kind of ostentatious luxury was looking for compliments. "And this is the most amazing place I've ever seen, on land or sea."

"Home away from home. Here, sit right down there. What will you drink?"

"Nothing now, thanks. Maybe later."

"Just say the word, and Doris will see to whatever you need." Nathan Jones Turner resumed his seat. He was a well-padded man, but the carefully tailored skipper's blazer and white trousers gave him a sleek look. "Folks told me that I should charter a boat, that I wouldn't have time to use the thing more than a couple of weeks a year. Waste of money, they called it. Know what I told them?"

"I have no idea."

"Told them to stuff it. Told them it was pride of ownership that mattered. Something most people don't understand. Or can't. Or don't want to, because they know they'd never be able to afford it." Nathan Jones Turner leaned forward and punched the air with one finger. "But *I* can. And I didn't want to *borrow* somebody else's boat. I wanted to *own* one of my own. Know how much it cost me?"

The air seemed to vibrate with the man's power. Energy pulsed from him, making a mockery of his age and his white hair. "A lot."

"More than a lot. A million and a half dollars a foot. Know what else? Got thirty percent knocked off because I paid cash. Cash on the barrel, that's the way I like to do business. Know why? Because I *can*."

Turner leaned forward again. He was always in motion, always tense and coiled, even when seated. "Only a handful of people in the whole world can command that sort of power. Not just power of money. No, sir. Power to *control* money. Have so much you can thumb your nose at the whole rotten lot. You understand what I'm saying?"

Thad felt as though he was sitting through a cannon barrage. The energy being focused his way was that strong. "I'm not sure."

"You stay there on the trading room floor, you sidle up to your trading buddy, and you'll make yourself a good salary. With bonus, we might be talking a million or more a year." Turner wiped it away with a sweep of his hand. "Small change. It's still a *salary*. What I'm saying, you want to ride free, you need a *base*. Forty, fifty million in your hand, then you can start thinking like a free man."

He was being sold. He understood that much. But why was still not clear. "Sounds good to me."

"Of course it does. You're a smart man. Couldn't have come up with that idea of yours unless you were smart." Turner inched closer to the edge of the settee. "The question is, how smart?"

"Smart as I need to be."

"That's good to hear. Because I asked you out here to make you an offer. A once-in-a-lifetime offer. A chance for you to rise above the masses and live life like it means something."

"I'm listening."

"You'd better be." Turner stabbed the air a second time, the jab so sharp Thad had to force himself not to wince. "From now on, you answer to me. You tell me everything that happens in Fleiss's office. Every last detail. What the man thinks, what he says, what he has for lunch. Everything."

"You want a spy," Thad said, finally understanding.

"I've got spies everywhere. I want me a spy who can think. Fleiss is losing it. He's past his prime. I want you to siphon off everything you can of his and get ready to take over the hot seat yourself." Turner bounded to his feet, waited impatiently for Thad to join him. "Think you can handle that?"

"Absolutely. I'm your man."

"We'll see. If you work out, we'll make every dream you ever had look like table scraps." Turner wheeled about and strode toward the stairs. "Take the afternoon off and enjoy the boat. If you need anything, you just ask Doris. She's good at getting folks whatever they want."

☐

The lobby of the Plaza Hotel looked pale and public after the ship's private luxury. Thad seated himself in the corner, dialed Larry's number, and said as soon as the man came on the line, "Turner did a number on me."

"What's that mean?"

"He wants me to spy on you."

"Hang on a second." There was a squealing sound, then silence. "Okay. I've got a gizmo here that interferes with bugs and transmission devices. Can't be too careful with the old man."

Thad sketched out the conversation and used the traffic passing through the lobby as his own personal reality check. Slowly he felt as though he were returning to earth from a money-clad dreamland. Strange to be thinking that while seated in the lobby of one of the most expensive hotels in the world, one where his own suite was costing the bank eleven hundred dollars a night. But after the yacht, those numbers were peanuts.

Larry waited until Thad had finished to say, "So what did you tell him?"

"I told him yes. Are you crazy? What choice did I have?"

"Then, probably none at all. Not if you wanted to keep your job." A moment of asthmatic breathing, and then, "Now is a different story."

"You got me out of Aiden and offered me my dream job." Only now the dreams felt constrictive. The power of Turner's words and his offer still reverberated. "I owe you."

"Good to hear. Well, Turner wants you back here in the office."

"Great."

"See you Monday." Another pause, then, "Thanks. You're the one with the chit to cash in now."

Thad punched off his phone, waved to a passing waiter, and ordered a drink. He had made the right decision to tell Larry. The man was sure to have figured out what went on. As it was, his options were still open. He had plenty of time to decide which way to jump.

Thad stretched out his legs and gave a contented sigh. No question about it. He was a man on his way to the top.

⊣| THIRTY-SIX |⊢

☐ It was after ten that night when Buddy and Clarke finally landed, but Molly was there at the airport to meet Buddy. She took one look at his face and enveloped him in a warm embrace. Buddy dropped his carry-on, saw Clarke accept a hug from his wife and youngest daughter, and closed his eyes on the world. Molly's arms seemed to draw the fatigue from his bones. "I want to sleep and never wake up."

"Soon," she promised. "But I told Trish we'd stop by."

"Molly, not tonight. Please."

"Everybody is finally well, but it's been hard on them. And Jennifer declared that unless she can see you tonight, she is staying awake forever."

Buddy sighed and nodded silent acceptance. At five years of age, Jennifer could be the most stubborn lady any of them had ever met. As he walked out to the car, he found himself perking up at the thought of seeing his auburn-haired angels.

Scarcely had he come through the door before his legs were enveloped by two pairs of eager arms. "Granddaddy!" Buddy lowered himself and embraced them before rising to greet his son and daughter-in-law.

He scarcely seemed to hear what he said or was said to him. What was far more important than the words was the simple joy of being back among his family, in the place where he most belonged on this earth.

Molly sat across from him, content to be where she could watch him enjoy their family. Buddy sat with a mug of lemonade in one hand, a ham sandwich in the other, and a smear of mustard on one cheek, listening to three conversations at once, as happy as he had ever been in his life.

"All right." Trish broke up the gathering with a clap of her hands. "Veronica, it's so far past your bedtime we might as well plan for tomorrow. You, too, Jennifer."

Veronica, the younger child, reached out her hands. "Take me, Granddaddy, take me!"

Buddy scooped up Veronica and started across the room. "Say good night, honey."

She nestled her face into the space beneath his chin, and waved five fingers over his shoulder. "Night-night, everybody."

His daughter-in-law started up the stairs behind him and murmured, "Be sure to notice the fish."

So he went into their room, settled his granddaughter on the bed, turned to the goldfish bowl on her desk, and exclaimed, "My, what lovely pets you've got there."

Little shoulders scrunched up in pleasure. "They're mine."

"Well, of course they are. Have you named them yet?"

"Oh, yes." A finger pointed vaguely at one of the identical pair. "That one is called Chili. And the other is Con Carne."

"Is that a fact?" Buddy glanced a question over to where their mother leaned in the doorway.

"What can I say?" Trish replied. "My baby girl is nuts about spicy food."

He went from one bed to the other, hugging Jennifer and Veronica close and listening to their prayers. When the lights were out and Buddy stood in the doorway with Trish, he found himself reluctant to go back downstairs.

"You should see yourself," Trish observed. "You look about fifty times better than you did when you got here."

"Of course I do." Buddy stayed where he was, staring down at the two night-clad figures in their little beds. "Right here is as close to heaven as I'll ever find on this earth."

□

Aiden had never looked lovelier than it did that Sunday morning. Buddy sat in his back garden watching the morning gather strength, feeling blessed by birdsong, sunlight, and every late-blooming flower. His empty coffee cup sat on the lawn beside his chair; his Bible rested open but unread in his lap. Everywhere he looked, he saw the divine.

"Buddy?"

He turned to find Clarke Owen slowly approaching with Molly. Clarke wore a strange expression. Buddy reached out a hand to his wife, and smiled a welcome to the assistant pastor, "Hello, old friend."

"I'm sorry to disturb you," Clarke said. "You, more than anyone else I know, deserve a day to yourself."

"Don't be silly. You're not disturbing anything. Pull up a chair. Both of you."

"I can't." Still, Clarke's countenance remained odd, as though the man was seeing him for the first time.

"I can't either," Molly told him. "I've just gotten a call from some people at church. They were wondering if I'd speak to the adult Sunday school classes this morning."

Buddy inspected his wife's face. He saw none of the old fear and uncertainty there, but rather a sense of calm resolve. As much for that as for the news, he said, "Molly, that's just wonderful."

"Not about your message," Molly went on. "It seems as though everyone has heard that by now. They wanted to hear my personal testimony." She hesitated and then added, "I was wondering if you would like to come with me."

Buddy did not need to think it over. "I'd be honored." He rose to his feet, very glad indeed that the morning's glory seemed to stay with him. He asked Clarke, "Is this what's brought you over?"

"No." Clarke hesitated before saying, "When I walked into the yard, it seemed as though I could actually feel the peace around you."

He started to say that it had seemed the same way to him, but decided that some things were best savored in silence. He glanced at his wife and accepted her smile and her knowing gaze. Buddy asked Clarke, "What did you want to see me about?"

"Alex has gotten a call from the organizers in Richmond. They wanted to confirm that you're still on for their rally a week from this coming Thursday."

"Of course."

"It's just," Clarke hesitated, then went on, "that's only five days before meltdown."

Buddy started back toward the house. "I realize that."

"Well. Fine." Clarke seemed to be looking for some further reaction. "They're estimating eighty thousand men will be there."

Buddy nodded acceptance of the news, more concerned with the grace that accompanied him back into the house. He said to them both, "Give me a second to get on a jacket and tie."

□

The feeling of being embraced by the morning held him throughout the drive to church. It left him quietly isolated even when people began coming over and greeting him and welcoming him back. Buddy seated himself and watched as Molly was guided toward the front of the largest chapel.

Once at the podium, she glanced down to where her husband was seated, smiled a greeting to those gathered before her, and began, "Throughout these weeks of watching my husband share his message, I have not had a single experience of the Spirit. For that matter, I have never felt much of anything throughout my entire life's walk in faith. But the absence has bothered me. Then one night while I was traveling with Buddy, I asked him to pray over me. Nothing happened that night either, but the next morning I awakened with a sense of having been granted a message cloaked in the mystery of silence, the same silence I have known from God all my life."

Buddy could scarcely believe his ears. He leaned forward, wondering if anyone else in the entire audience realized what an effort this was for his wife, what it cost her. Yet as he watched, he began to see that it was costing her nothing at all.

Molly's voice held to its normal quietness, yet the assuredness with which she spoke was utterly new. "I have spent a great deal of time over these past couple of weeks wondering just what this silence means. And I've come to recognize that it is not an absence of God. All I've had to do is look out over the auditoriums and churches and meeting halls and see that God is there with us. I've come to see God's silence as *essential*. It has also occurred to me that this is often the way God deals with us. In *essential* silence.

"Imagine, if you will, a grand heavenly orchestra. The conductor raises his baton. The entire orchestra is poised, ready, *silent*. God forms such an essential silence in us so that our ears can become more carefully tuned. We are being prepared to receive His message. We are being invited to still our busy minds and our hyperactive lives so that we can hear the heavenly host sing out in eternal glory, 'Hallelujah! Praise His holy Name.'"

Buddy fought back the misting which threatened to cloud his vision. He did not want to miss an instant of this. He gave the pews to either side quick glances, just enough to see that the people were concentrating with a rapt silence of their own. He turned back to the front. He was so proud at that moment that he felt he would positively burst.

"What God communicates in faith," Molly continued, "is far greater than by vision and rushing wind. My isolation from these experiences has been an immense blessing. Otherwise I might have begun to *limit* my faith by grasping for them. I might have started to live for the *experience* and not for God.

"A mystical experience is not the defining moment. There should be affirmation from others within the church. And the written Word of God must confirm." Molly stopped there. She reached over and touched the closed Bible beside the podium.

Buddy strained to keep his vision clear. It was strange how such a simple act as his wife reaching out and touching the cover of the Book could affect him so deeply. Yet she seemed to be reaching across the distance that was separating her from God simply by reaching for the written Word.

Molly raised the Bible and held it to her as she went on. "I did not want to join Buddy as he took God's message and went on the road. I have always loved my small town, my little responsibilities, my stable world. Yet God has drawn me out from my comfortable routine. He has drawn me farther and farther along His chosen path with His silence.

"My expectations were not enough. My horizons were too small. I said to God, I like it here. God said to me, I want you *there*.

"In accepting His message of silence, I have come to see a larger directive, one that has consequence for all of us. The ninety-fourth Psalm calls death the 'land of silence,' the place where God is absent. Yet Jesus goes into death, the farthest recesses of empty silence, to seek and to save. He has shown us that His love is greater than sin or eternal death. He accepts our darkness, our death, and our well-deserved everlasting silence upon Himself. Through Him we have been given the glory of never-ending life. Through Him we may hear the eternal song of praise."

Molly bowed her head and said, "Let us close with a moment of prayer.

"Lord Jesus, You are the light that drives out darkness and saves us from the endless silence. You are the light that draws us to holiness. Help us make this day a living hymn of praise. Teach us to appreciate the moments of silence, that we may better hear Your call."

⊣‖ THIRTY-SEVEN ‖⊢

Thirteen Days . . .

☐ Wednesday morning found them in Decatur, and that was where the storm started growing fiercer.

The previous Monday morning they had flown to Indianapolis, where Buddy had given a luncheon address that filled the city's largest church to overflowing. Then it had been on to Lafayette for a press conference, a speech, and a too-short overnight stop. Tuesday had started in Kokomo, then across the state line to Champaign, Illinois. A morning speech in Urbana, then a fast drive to Decatur. His luncheon address drew almost a thousand people. Buddy had long stopped thinking about the numbers.

The newspapers were becoming increasingly vociferous, such that Clarke did not even mention them unless he felt it was something important for Buddy to see. But after the Decatur meeting a man approached, introduced himself as a local broker, and asked if Buddy was planning on changing his dates.

"Of course not."

"Don't get me wrong, brother." The man was both sincere and nervous. "I've heard about you from a dozen different people. Today's gathering only made me more certain that what you say is right. But do you realize the date you've set is less than two weeks from today?"

"I am counting the hours," Buddy replied fervently.

"But the market is stronger than it's been in years!" The man pulled a handkerchief from his pocket and wiped his palms, then his face. "I've got people calling me from all over the state, friends I've known for years. They're selling everything they own and putting their money in options."

"This is good news," Buddy said.

"Is it?" Another swipe, and then he nervously stuffed the handkerchief away. "If the market doesn't move as you're predicting, and on the day you say, these people are going to lose a lot more than they can afford."

"Other than the fact that the Lord reigns in heaven above," Buddy replied, "I have never been as certain of anything in my entire life as I am about this."

"And the date is set?"

"In stone," Buddy confirmed.

The man gave a grim nod. He offered Buddy his card as he said, "Call me if anything changes, will you?"

Buddy watched him walk away, then he moved to where Clarke stood comparing schedules with Wesley Hadden. He asked, "What are the papers saying?"

Clarke shook his head. "I've stopped worrying about them."

"And you don't want to know," Wesley Hadden agreed.

"Tell me."

Wesley expelled his breath in a rush. "Well, the small-town dailies are split. Most of the editorials can be pretty hard on you, but every once in a while there's somebody who claims that you are sounding an all-important wake-up call. They've usually attended both a press conference and a gathering of the faithful. They talk about the evidence you give, but they also mention the power of your message."

"And the others?"

Wesley glanced toward Clarke before reluctantly saying, "The closer we come to the date, the worse they sound."

"Show him the cartoon," Clarke said.

Wesley looked pained. "Why?"

"He wants to know. Let him see it."

Wesley reached into his briefcase, pulled out a magazine, riffled the pages, and said, "It's in this week's *Time*."

One glance was enough. The political cartoon showed him in a long white beard and three-piece suit. The cross hanging from his neck was so big it dragged in the dirt. He carried a sign that said, THE END IS TUESDAY. Tuesday was crossed out, and Friday scrawled beneath it, and Monday beneath that, and on down until he ran out of room.

Buddy handed it back, gave a thin smile, and said, "It looks a lot like me."

"That's all you have to say?" Clarke was astounded. "This doesn't bother you?"

"Why should it, when we're seeing the crowds get bigger every day, and we hear that people are acting on the message?"

"No reason," Clarke agreed, exchanging a glance with Wesley. "None at all."

Wednesday evening they drove to the airport and checked in for a flight to St. Louis. Buddy could feel eyes watching him as they checked in. He tried not to let it bother him. The crowds were growing, the word was spreading, and time was running out.

As he went through the boarding process, Buddy reviewed their plans for the final days. Alex and Agatha were condensing as much as they could. Alex sounded increasingly tired every time they talked, but so did everyone else. Buddy's hurried conversation the previous afternoon with Agatha confirmed that Alex was doing as well as could be expected, and that his brother continued to hold up under the chemotherapy. Buddy let it go at that. The rest could wait until after. Everything had to wait until after. The countdown became an unspoken chant they all shared. Just thirteen days to go.

Christian radio and television networks were organizing live feeds to stations around the country. Alex had agreed without even discussing it with Buddy, hoping the message's power would carry over the wires and through the air.

They were working straight through this weekend; Buddy knew he could neither object nor beg for another time at home. It was a flat-out race from here to the finish.

□

Buddy settled into his seat on the airplane and was busy with his seat belt when a voice said, "Mr. Korda?"

"That's me." Buddy looked up to find two men in business suits and briefcases hovering in the aisle. "Can I do something for you?"

"You already have." The older man offered a meaty paw. "Just wanted to thank you for what you're doing."

Buddy accepted the hand. "Thank God, not me."

"I do, sir. Every morning and every night and sometimes in between."

The other man said, "I heard your message on a tape they played in our Sunday school class last weekend. I've never seen people get so excited over something on a cassette. Went out and invested every cent I had into put options, just like you said."

"That's good," Buddy said. "Now make sure your friends don't just listen, but also act. Tell them to remember the road to hell is paved with good intentions."

"I'll do that, sir. I surely will."

When the pair had shaken his hand a second time and moved off, Clarke leaned over and said, "Now is as good a time as any, I suppose. You've been invited to appear on national television. *Lonnie Stone Live* wants to do two segments with you, one next Thursday night and one the following Monday."

"Fine," Buddy said, and it was. "Tell them yes."

"Buddy, these television people," Clarke hesitated, then willed himself to say it aloud. "They want to set you up, then once the date has passed, they want to shoot you down."

"I don't care what they want." Buddy turned to meet his friend's gaze full on. "Thursday night and Friday morning of next week will be the last chance we have to get the message across."

Clarke mulled that over, then asked, "And the following Monday?"

"I have to tell them to take their money and get out," Buddy explained. "Before it's too late."

⊣ THIRTY-EIGHT ⊢

Eleven Days . . .

☐ By that Friday Thad was beginning to feel secure in his position, and much more at home in New York. He was still housed in the Plaza, still living as a visiting exec on the company's expense account. But that was about to change.

From his suite high in the Plaza Hotel, New York's mythical image seemed almost true. The skyscrapers looked factory fresh as they reached up with beckoning arms to wish him a good morning.

The sordid reality was all too clear, however, down at street level. Even from the back of a limousine there was no disguising the beggars, ten to a block. The crazies were also out in force that morning. Two weeks in the place and already Thad knew to waste no time on the dregs scattered everywhere, clogging every alley and doorway, hands out like a ragged chorus line, begging for change. Ignore them all. It was the only way to survive in this town. Live like they weren't even there. Thad had already decided the city burned so bright because the darkness ran so deep.

Even so, the view from the back of a company limo wasn't all bad. The street life was as entertaining as a new Broadway musical. New Yorkers were constantly auditioning for roles they had already won, where the world was their audience and the admission was free. Laughter was canned and loud enough to carry. Everything was done at full speed. People even relaxed in high gear.

The city's energy amplified the closer he drew to Wall Street. He spent the remaining minutes of the drive going over the documents delivered from his Realtor that morning. Thad had put in an offer on a brownstone at Ninety-third and Park. Those who lived closer in called this area the hem of Harlem. He didn't mind. It was still Upper East Side, and it was a building that would soon be all his.

The objective for most New Yorkers was to rise to a higher floor. The lower down one lived, the greater the threat of being impacted by too many other human bodies. So everybody was on the move, trying to go from the first floor to the fifth, from the fifth to the twelfth, from the twelfth to the penthouse. Then it was time to keep the penthouse and buy the weekend place in Connecticut, which was as far as most New Yorkers' umbilical cords would stretch.

Thad was still enough of an outsider to prefer a bit of green to a more spacious view, and so he was looking to buy a house. The place he had selected came with a postage stamp of a garden surrounded by a thirty-foot brick wall topped with electrified barbed wire. All the comforts of home.

Upper East Side was the place of wealth in action. For about thirty blocks north and south and four or five east to west, it was a high-rent island for the wealthy. The greatest competition was over making an elegant impression. Money was less critical than the time to spend it. The pets were as decorative as the paintings on the walls. Here it was possible to believe there was nothing wrong with either New York or the world. It was a great place to have money and want to flaunt it, which was exactly Thad's aim.

He set the real estate papers back into his briefcase as the limo pulled up in front of the Turner Building. Thad bounded up the stairs, gave the receptionists a quick greeting, ignored the myriad stares that tracked his movements toward the elevator.

Upstairs Thad stopped by his soon-to-be office and checked on the workers laying the new carpet. The old carpet had been fine, but he had changed it anyway, selecting the most expensive silk-and-wool spread he could find. It was good to give the office rumor mill something big to chew on. His private sanctum was a declaration of having arrived.

The contract negotiations with the Valenti lawyers had been predictably vicious. But Thad had stuck fast, and Larry had backed him up. In the end he had gotten everything he had wanted. The day after signing, a mysterious payment had appeared in his newly opened account. That same afternoon a courier had delivered a pound of beluga caviar, a new solid-gold Rolex, and a note from Turner saying, "Glad to have you on board." Thad reported the early bonus to Larry and then used it as down payment on his brownstone.

He entered the trading floor and did a quick scouting. Activity remained at the same fever pitch. Everybody was on edge, stretched by positions that shifted from tenable to terrorizing in the space of a few minutes.

A guy whose name he could not recall looked up from his calculations to grin as Thad passed. Thad slapped the offered palm and asked, "How's it going?"

"Awful. This market needs a daily injection of Tylenol. It's one giant headache. Been that way for weeks." He swiveled to track Thad's progress past his desk. "Hey, what's the scoop for today?"

"Not a chance."

"Come on, be a pal."

Thad arrived at the final desk before the door leading to Larry's private sanctum. He dropped his case and turned to grin at the guy and feast on all the other eyes following him. "If you need a pal, go buy a dog."

In fact, Thad was working on his third idea for Larry. It was a major deal, one that would have been impossible to get by the bank's senior monitors had the market been any less nervous. As it was, however, nobody was making much money and losses were mounting. The sort of alternatives he had offered Larry his second day here were one of a kind. There was no chance to repeat them, not without risking being caught by the SEC. No, what he needed was a new way to guarantee profits, one that remained within legal boundaries. Barely.

As it was, the trading floors were structured along fairly normal lines—equities, currencies, futures, options, and so on. Thad opened his briefcase and pulled out the copy of a file he had left with Larry the day before. His plan was not to add, but rather to restructure on a massive scale. What he wanted was to shake up the entire trading operation, to put his stamp on the bank and its future in a major way. The great secret of New York was, take a chance. Thad was planning to do just that.

The over-the-counter derivatives market was bigger even than the one for money futures, and far more dangerous. Here, companies could hedge against any risk they cared to name, and for any amount. It remained almost entirely unregulated, as it essentially comprised contracts between two private parties. The crowning glory was that it was also completely legal.

Thad had watched its rise for years. He knew this sort of legalized piracy could spell major profits for years to come.

Over the previous eighteen months, OTC derivatives had suddenly started growing at an electric rate. Even so, many banks were afraid to touch them—Valenti included. Thad proposed to change all that, drawing a hundred traders from other less profitable areas and concentrating them on these ventures. The bank's first entry had already started, a project Thad had managed personally in interest-rate swaps. He was two days into the deal, and the bank already had a paper profit of $2.2 million.

If his proposal was accepted, Valenti would soon be doing a roaring business in trades whose names were a foreign language even to most bankers—caps, flaws, spreads, captions, flawtions, spreadtions, and even more exotic fare. Caps set an upper limit on the interest rate paid. Swaps typically changed a fixed rate of interest for a floating rate, or vice versa. For clients it could be a cheap insurance—or an expensive gamble. For everyone seeking to cover a risk, there was another party looking to take a chance.

Most often, people in positions of decision-making power gradually became hooked into playing the derivatives markets like others did the casinos. Metal-working companies, pension funds, insurance houses, utilities, local city governments—all were involved and actively courted by the traders. It only took one person with a penchant for fast profits and the authority to sign checks to open the company to risks it would never in its wildest dreams consider taking in its normal course of business.

If things went wrong, the results could be horrendous. Orange County lost over two billion dollars in thirty-six hours on a derivatives deal gone awry. The largest German steel company went bankrupt after just one bad trade. The oldest bank in England lost more than a billion dollars through one rogue trader and was forced to close its doors after 250 years in operation.

These and a hundred other companies had vanished without a trace, more grist for the gossip mill that circulated among derivatives traders. Here this morning, bankrupt at midday, forgotten the same afternoon. Thad was not the least bit concerned. He had no intention of being on the losing end of anything.

The magic to OTC derivatives was, there were no rules. None. Traders related the price of oil to the value of the Japanese yen to the cost of unmined Indonesian aluminum. Not even the traders themselves understood some of the risks they were setting up. Nor did it matter, so long as they got in and out fast enough. All they needed to see was the potential to win.

And if they did win, the payoff was huge. Twenty million dollars on a quarter-million-dollar hedge, payoff time of less than three days. That sort of thing was commonplace. Those who tapped out simply vanished. Their places were taken the next day. There were always more people out there clamoring to take the plunge.

Wall Street had a name for these high-risk derivatives. They were called nuclear waste.

□

The red light at the top of his bank of phones finally blinked a half hour after Thad's arrival. He picked it up and said in greeting, "The market's gyrating like a kid's yo-yo."

"When this volatility finally gets a direction, it's either taking off like a shuttle launch or dropping like Niagara Falls," Larry agreed. "Every day we don't have a direction is just adding to the explosive tension."

"Still looking for a leader, just like you said."

"Right. Come in here."

"On my way."

When he arrived, Larry pointed him into a seat and said, "I like your plan."

"Just like that?"

He closed the file and scribbled on the cover. "Something this big will have to be reviewed by the board and okayed by Turner himself. But I want you to go ahead and start implementing the changes."

Thad could not repress his grin. "Fantastic."

"Just one thing." Fleiss reached for his mug. "Korda."

"I know." The morning's high diminished. "The guy's becoming a bigger nuisance with every passing day."

"The *Journal* called him 'a phenomenon' this morning."

Thad's gut took a bitter twist. "I missed that."

"On the editorial page. Responding to some press conference in the back of beyond, I forget what the city was called. Made the *Times* business page yesterday."

His gut tightened even further. "I missed that one too."

"Just as well. Apparently it was more of the same. The twenties all over again, a major drop on the way, stuff we've heard a hundred times before." Fleiss hit the button to bring his coffee apparatus into view and refilled his mug. "Only now he's getting national play."

Korda remained the only dark spot in Thad's rapid assent. "I saw he got a mention in *Forbes* this week."

"And *Business Week*." Fleiss shook his head. "The man's gone from being a clown to a menace."

"Just like you said."

"Yeah, well, being right but being in the red doesn't get a win. I got a call from the old man this morning. He wants to know why we haven't done anything about this guy. After he ordered me to drag you off the case last week, it was a little hard to take."

"But you didn't tell him that."

"No, what I said was you'd be back on it. Seems our goons from downstairs have had trouble pinning Korda down."

Thad nodded. He knew all about that. Wesley Hadden had become a turncoat. He was acting as a one-man security detail, on duty night and day. "Nowadays Korda's schedule is a national secret. His hotel and airline reservations are being made under block bookings. His movements are impossible to track in advance."

"Not next Thursday." Fleiss picked up the other piece of paper resting on his immaculate central table. "I got word from the guards this morning. There's been major advance coverage of some rally he's addressing. You heard about this?"

"No." Thad did a quick calculation in his head. "But next Thursday is only five days before Korda's going to disappear all on his own. The following Tuesday is going to arrive and the market's going to surge despite all his sour predictions. Korda will be good for one round of Jay Leno jokes before he's buried for good."

"Doesn't matter. There's too much chance he'll push back the date a week or so. That'd just give the cycle more time to build." Fleiss glanced at the paper in front of him. "Next Thursday Korda's one of the scheduled speakers at this rally in Richmond."

Thad rose to his feet, reached for the paper, and said, "I'll get started on the changes around here and then go take care of Korda personally."

"Stay well back. You're there only to make sure things get done right this time. I want to get Korda out of the picture, not to lose my number-one trader." Fleiss's flat gaze followed him to the door. "'Just make sure the man disappears.' Those were Turner's exact words. The man is to vanish from the face of this earth."

There was no way he was going to sit this one out. "Don't worry. In a week's time Korda is history."

THIRTY-NINE

Five Days . . .

☐ Thursday morning Buddy gave what he hoped would be his last press conference of the week. He spent the time between breakfast and the conference reviewing the whirlwind that his life had become. Their Friday and Saturday itinerary had called for St. Louis to Dallas, Oklahoma City, and Wichita, and then a long leap to Omaha and Des Moines. On and on, pushing harder and harder, moving farther and farther from home. Television lights and reporters had begun meeting them at the airports, and with each stop their questions became more mocking. Yet the crowds had grown ever larger, and the message's power had continued to resound.

Sunday had been Seattle and Portland; Monday, San Francisco and Sacramento and San Diego; Tuesday, a flight halfway across the nation to Little Rock. In his daily conversations with the home office, Alex and Agatha had sounded increasingly like robots. Every day Buddy heard more voices in the background, more telephones and excited chatter filling the spaces between words with his brother. Buddy had known better than to even ask what was going on. Wednesday had been Atlanta and Charlotte, and that night the drive to Richmond. The entire way up Clarke and Wesley had chattered excitedly over the Richmond rally scheduled for the following afternoon. Buddy had spent the hours drifting in and out of a strange half doze, never really connecting with anything that had been said. In their nightly conversation the previous evening, Molly had offered to join him for the final push. Buddy had told her not to bother. He missed her, but he could not ask her to endure the road. Besides, it would not be long now.

When Buddy arrived at the hotel's grand ballroom that morning, he discovered waiting for him a crowd of journalists larger than the first few groups who had gathered to hear his message. He did not mind the number. He scarcely saw them. All he could think about was that the countdown continued. Tomorrow was the final chance for people to make their investments. He wanted to pound the podium and scream the words with every shred of energy he had left.

Instead, Buddy found the words were there waiting for him when the television lights flashed on. He began without preamble, "Analysts are now saying that there is every reason for the market to sustain its climb for years to come." Buddy shook his head. "I have been a banker for more than thirty years. I can still remember the late seventies, when the Dow was stuck below a thousand for over three years. That particular generation of analysts claimed that the market had permanently anchored itself.

That was the expression of the time. It was permanently anchored, and there was no reason to believe that it would ever rise again.

"Now we are looking at a Dow that has broken every record a dozen times over. Now we in our wisdom can look down our noses and say how wrong they were." Buddy gripped the podium, leaned forward, and said, "But how will the next generation of analysts view our confident assessment that this unprecedented rise in the market will continue for years to come?"

He gave them a moment, hoping and praying that the message would get through. But there was no response from the field of faces, just a sense of staring out at silhouettes rather than people. "No nation on earth has ever experienced growth without downward slides. Never, in all of history. Why? Because there are too many factors underpinning any economic rise. We tend to forget them when all is going well. But the truth is, if two or three of these structural factors fall in tandem, there is every likelihood that the entire economy will decline as well.

"Let us talk about one of these vital unseen factors that help to hold up our economy—our nation's banking structure. Never in recent memory has the banking system been as unstable as it is now. And the reason for this is the current trading craze. It is, in my opinion, a cancer eating at the heart of our nation's financial system.

"Before I explain why trading is so hazardous, let us take a look back at the Great Depression. After the Crash of 1929 on Wall Street, the world's economies crumbled like a house of cards. Poverty struck like a worldwide plague. Nobody thought it could happen. But it did. Wall Street's collapse was caused by gambling, pure and simple. People borrowed to gamble, because the returns were great. The more they made, the more they gambled.

Their debts rose just as fast as their incomes, sometimes even faster.

"After the Crash of 1929, the government instituted financial reforms that were supposed to make this gambling impossible. And it stopped things for a while, or at least slowed things down. But now two related markets are sidestepping these laws. These are the new trading markets that I say hold a disastrous level of risk for all of us. One is called *futures*, the other *derivatives*. Ten years ago, the market in financial futures barely existed. This year, the Chicago financial futures market will have a turnover in excess of *fifty trillion dollars*."

Finally, finally, he saw a few of them stirring. A few were leaning toward their neighbors, a few were making notes. Buddy felt a note of desperation enter his voice. He pleaded, "These modern-day traders dress their actions in fancy jargons and glossy brochures, but the bare truth is that they are simply buying and selling *risk*. The world's financial underpinning is based on a gambling pit unlike anything seen since 1929.

"America's top five banks hold on average three trillion dollars in derivatives on their books, and from this obtain almost half their total profits. This means they hold *ten times* more in high-risk paper than they have in total equity capital. Ten times. These banks have no choice but to ride the tiger.

"The biggest worry for the banks is not that they might have gotten things wrong. No. The biggest danger is that they have customers who will lose big and then not be able to cover their losses. One such major loss would be enough to wipe out a bank's total cash reserves. That could happen in the space of just one day. The bank would be insolvent. Everyone who has placed their money in one of these banks, everyone who is relying on these banks to meet their own financial obligations, would lose every cent.

"Worse than that, the big banks do an enormous amount of business with each other. When it comes to derivatives, all of the world's major banks are holding hands. So if one starts to sneeze, they could all catch colds.

"If one major dealer could not make good on its commitments, a dozen others could be threatened. Another participant might then withhold payments. If that happened with a dozen, the system would enter meltdown.

"And the eruption could take place in three or four hours. This situation becomes much more serious because of how concentrated the wealth and this risk have become. One third of the world's total monetary wealth is controlled by just two hundred funds.

"In offices around the world, twenty-four hours a day, these fund managers hear the same news, hedge their bets with new risk derivatives, and prepare to jump at a moment's notice. Everyone is trying to catch the market swing and move in the right direction. Everyone is watching the other. Two hundred players is not so many that one can move with much secrecy. This means that if one jumps, chances are others will too.

"To have this much money all jump at once means that whatever swing the market begins to make will be amplified beyond all logic. A relatively small number of investors, mutual funds, investment banks, and Wall Street firms might see a new risk develop, and so they move together. The market reacts with a big dip. This notifies others of a move. The others rush out. The market dives. Panic ensues."

Buddy stopped. For once, the gathering of press and media seemed genuinely attentive. A voice from the back said, "Then what, Mr. Korda?"

"Go look at the newsreels from the thirties," Buddy said, wanting to weep with a sudden wave of frustration over his inability to do anything about it all. "Look at men selling apples on every street corner. Watch ten thousand people riot when fifteen jobs become available. See people harnessed to horse carts because working a man to death is cheaper than paying for hay or gas. Ask an old-timer to describe what it was like trying to feed a family. Then try to imagine what it might be like doing the same for your own loved ones."

⊣| FORTY |⊢

☐ Thaddeus Dorsett slipped the leather thong down tighter on his wrist. He had never held a cush before. That's what the guard had called it. A strange, soft-sounding word for something so deadly. The instrument was about a foot long, with a springy handle ending in a bulbous, fist-size club of steel and lead, all bound in leather to make it easier to hold and quieter to wield. Thad's other hand still burned from where he had slapped the weight down a little too hard. He whipped the handle and heard the humming sound as it sprang back, hungry and vicious.

The guards had orders not to use guns. Too much noise, and not personal enough. He wanted Buddy Korda to see who was doing this. He wanted the man to see what it meant to cross

Thaddeus Dorsett. He wanted Buddy's last few minutes to be full of terrifying regret.

The alley was perfect. Thad could not have asked for a better place to spring their surprise. There was only one route for Korda to walk the three blocks from his hotel to the Richmond stadium. One narrow road. What was more, the entire downtown sector was strangely subdued this Thursday afternoon. As though the entire city's attention was focused on the nearby stadium.

The stadium crowd had been loud and quiet in strange turns. Occasionally faint snatches of song or voices could be heard. Thad had watched the guards exchange nervous glances over this. Which was very strange. He would have thought those goons could be bothered by nothing at all.

A guard came sprinting back from the hotel, confirming that Buddy had not left his room yet. The guards had brought in some extra hands to handle anybody who was unfortunate enough to walk to the stadium with Korda. Thad observed them leaning against the alley's opposite wall, a trio of goons with the dull-eyed blankness of people who would do anything for money.

Thad's blood surged at the thought of finally getting his own. "Remember," he hissed, "leave Korda for me."

No one bothered to respond. He had said the same thing a half dozen times already.

Thad checked his watch once more, wondering how much longer he could stand the waiting.

The guard by the alley's entrance chose that moment to turn and wave his hand over his head. They were coming.

Thad's heartbeat surged to an impossible rate. He glanced at the faces around, saw no sign of tension or excitement or anything beyond hard-edged boredom.

He accepted the black stocking mask handed out by the security guard. Thad watched how the others shifted the masks around so that the eye- and mouth-holes pulled down correctly. He felt a strange, stomach-twisting surge at the thought of what those guys had done to make this motion seem so natural. For himself, the mask felt tight and sweaty.

His breathing sounded overloud in his ears as he started toward the alley's entrance with the others. Up ahead, the guard raised his hand, the fingers extended, the thumb cocked back onto his palm. Four. There were only four of them. A piece of cake.

His heart pounded like a blood-soaked gong in his ears. He raised the cush, ready to pounce as soon as they appeared. The road stretched out empty and void in front of them. He heard the scratch of approaching footsteps, the murmur of quiet voices.

Out of nowhere, a fog drifted in and enclosed them, a mist so thick he could not see the wall he was touching. One moment all was clear and ready, and the next he could not see a thing. One of the thugs grunted in surprise. He heard someone else hiss for quiet.

If anything, the mist grew thicker, tighter. Breath was hard to come by, as though milky fingers were reaching out and closing around his throat. The feeling was so strong that Thad reached up and ripped a larger hole in the clinging mesh, clearing it farther from his mouth. Still, it was tough to draw a decent breath.

The footsteps were almost on them. Thad stepped forward, wanting to be the first to strike.

Shadows coalesced in the fog, but from the *opposite* direction. They were coming from the *stadium*. Thad backed up in alarm. The shadows followed, far too tall to be Korda and his men. They looked like warriors carrying shields, which was impossible. Shields and clubs. Or swords. Warriors standing a full foot taller than Thad, and broader than the goons.

A guard jostled him on one side. Or perhaps it was one of the thugs, backing up with him. Thad pulled off the mask. He could not breathe in this mist. Then he felt a wall behind him. He must have swerved sideways in the mist. Then the wall *moved*. Thad spun around and felt his heart squeeze shut at the sight of another shadow *behind* him. This one was bigger than the others, a behemoth looming over him, the club raised over his head longer than Thad was tall.

"*We're surrounded!*" The shriek was alien, even though he could feel it rip from his own throat. "*Run!*"

"They're everywhere!" The guard's voice was as hoarse as his own.

"Get me *out* of here!"

Thad felt a burning sensation on his hand, as if acid were seeping off the leather strap. He peeled skin off his wrist with his fingernails in his terror to get the cush off.

He dropped to his knees. Yes. That was the answer. Get down low and let the others take the heat. He sank lower, crawling and scrabbling on his belly through the damp filth coating the alley.

He heard shrieks and cries behind him. The sounds only made him crawl faster, through the blinding mist, wriggling on his belly so hard his clothes were shredded by the gravel underneath, finally catching a glimpse of light up ahead, as if he was approaching the end of a suffocating tunnel.

Thad gasped a sob and stumbled to his knees. His fine Armani suit was drenched and filthy with tatters flapping from his elbows and knees. He did not even notice. He scrambled to his feet and fled in terror.

⊣‖ FORTY-ONE ‖⊢

☐ Richmond that Thursday afternoon was experiencing a late heat wave. But it was not the temperature that made Buddy stop as he walked up the concrete runway and entered the stadium. Beneath a brilliant sun spread the largest crowd he had ever seen, much less addressed. Every seat in the bleachers was taken. Faces and colors spread out in every direction until they became distant blurs.

The playing field itself was lost beneath a seething mass of bodies. From the thirty-yard line back stretched row upon row of folding seats. Between them and the front stage, thousands of people gathered and stood and knelt and prayed.

Clarke moved up alongside. "Is everything all right?"

"Fine." It was a noisy, joyous, fervent cauldron of people and spiritual power. The Spirit was there and moving among the family of believers. "Just fine."

"Mr. Korda?" A harried young man wearing a badge and carrying a walkie-talkie scurried over. "Greg Knowles. Great that you could make it." He took Buddy's arm and began leading him forward, down the stairs and across the single patch of green not filled with bodies. "There's one more speaker before you. He'll be about a half hour, maybe forty-five minutes. We like to leave time for the Spirit to move at will."

"I understand." Buddy mounted the stairs, shook a couple of hands, and seated himself on the stage's back row. Strange that he could look out over such a gathering and feel no nerves. His fatigue and travel stress had gradually eased. Here and now, the outside world could not enter. Here and now, he was home.

When it was his time to speak, a distinguished gray-haired minister known throughout the nation gave the introduction. "By now, most of you have heard of Buddy Korda. This past week the press has been full of reports about how this one man has begun to have an effect upon the stock market. How there has been an unprecedented buying of futures options by people who would otherwise never be expected to enter this high-risk market. Huge numbers of people. Phenomenal numbers. That is the word I have read over and over this week. *Phenomenal*. It is phenomenal, the papers and the television pundits say, that one small-town banker can have such an impact upon people. They claim that it is simply a sign of the times, that people are nervous and willing to follow anyone who claims to know where the market is headed.

"Well, I am here to tell you that I have heard a tape recording of Buddy Korda's message. And after that I saw a video. I imagine that many of you out there have. And both times I was completely thunderstruck by the power of God moving through this man.

"We have a bank of television cameras out here in front of the stage today. Those of you who have attended our gatherings know this is not normal. But from what I have learned in a conversation with his home office this morning, today is the final day of Buddy Korda's message. Tomorrow is the last day we can act on his advice.

"I have every confidence that his message is correct, so much so that I have put all of my savings into something I did not even know existed before last week—something called put options. I am staking my reputation and my family's savings that Mr. Korda carries a message from God. And if his message is correct, Monday is too late. Brothers, hear what I am saying. More important, listen to Mr. Korda himself. And if you agree, if you feel the Spirit's direction, then I urge you to act. That is why the cameras are here. So that as many people as possible can hear and act." He turned and nodded toward Buddy.

Buddy approached the podium and the bank of microphones, greeted the crowd, and began. "I wish I could leave unsaid what I'm up here to tell you. Because what's most important is what you've been hearing from the speakers before me, that Jesus must reign in your minds and hearts. He is truly the way, the truth, and the life.

"But I can't stop there. Not today. I feel called to be where I am. Yet what's important is what you hear the *Spirit* say to you, not what words I speak. Remember that. I need to be the

Lord's messenger, and you need to hear confirmation from the Lord, not from me."

☐

"This way, Mr. Korda. Here, let me take the towel."

"Oh, thank you." It was Thursday evening, and Buddy was in the Washington offices of CNN. As he removed the makeup towel from around his neck and handed it to the production assistant, he glanced around. Here everything seemed to run at double time. People did not walk, they scampered. Voices were tense and high-pitched. All the expressions looked vitally important, immensely serious.

Buddy allowed himself to be shepherded through a series of doors and into the side wings of a large soundstage. At its center was the familiar backdrop for *Lonnie Stone Live*. The production assistant pointed to a large screen situated to one side of the empty stage and said, "Mr. Stone is in New York today. You'll be able to see him on that feed. The questions will be passed to you through a speaker set in the desk, see it there?"

"Yes." Buddy felt nervous tension transmitted from everything around him. Cables littered the floor. People moved lights and cameras about, barely casting a glance in his direction. He was simply the day's product, to be spotlighted and handled and monitored, and then moved aside for whatever was hot tomorrow. There wasn't time for anything else.

"Okay, let's just fit your mike into place." The production assistant stepped aside as a sound technician clipped a tiny microphone to his lapel, ran the wire under his jacket, and gave him the control pack to slip into his back pocket. "Would you say something so they can adjust the sound level?"

"I have never been on television before."

"Fine. That's great." She returned a thumbs-up through the control room window and ushered him toward the desk. "All right, let's adjust your coat so it doesn't bunch around your shoulders." She gave the back of his jacket a hard tug and tucked it farther into his seat. "Try to hold to one position through each question, Mr. Korda. If you want to move, do so when Lonnie is talking."

"I understand." The makeup was constricting, and under the lights it left his skin feeling as though it could not breathe. "How long—"

"Eight minutes until you go on, and we will probably play this for five minutes today." She glanced at her clipboard. "You're back with us next week, do I have that right?"

"On Tuesday," he confirmed.

"You'll be an old hand by then, won't you?" She gave him a practiced smile and moved back beyond the reach of the lights. Immediately a camera rolled forward and fastened its great square eye on him.

Buddy gave a swift prayer for guidance and received the same response as at press conferences—a simple determined fore-knowledge of what needed to be said.

The minutes dragged on until the production assistant waved at him, counted down, and then pointed to the monitor. Buddy saw the seasoned smile and heard the famous voice say, "And joining us now from our Washington studio is Buddy Korda, a name that has become increasingly familiar, and in a remarkably short span of time. Mr. Korda, it's a pleasure to have you with us today."

"Thank you for having me."

"Mr. Korda, do I have it right that you are predicting a major economic downturn to strike sometime next week?"

"On Tuesday," Buddy affirmed.

"You'll excuse me if I say that it seems a little strange. The markets are booming. The latest economic figures, released just yesterday, indicate that the nation enjoys the best economic health it has seen in years." Stone picked up a sheet of paper and read, "Unemployment is down, wholesale purchasing is up, factory usage is at an all-time high. Today the market hit another record level, with the Dow climbing almost two hundred points." He let the paper drop. "It seems as though the economy is not agreeing with you, Mr. Korda."

"There are a number of factors that could change that almost instantly."

"So you are suggesting, are you not, that people who hear your message should risk everything they own by going against the market, flying in the face of every pundit on Wall Street, and betting the lot on the market falling? Isn't that right?"

"Yes."

"Are you perhaps interested in changing your deadline, Mr. Korda? Perhaps give yourself a little breathing space?"

"There is no need." Buddy looked straight at the camera and put as much emphasis as he could on each word. "The reason I came into the studios today was to urge those who have heard my message and feel it is true to *act*. Tomorrow is their last chance."

"The markets will be open for business on Monday as well," the interviewer pointed out.

Buddy shook his head. "Monday will be too late."

The interviewer gave his familiar, hoarse chuckle. "I wish I was as certain about anything as you appear to be about this. Tell me, Mr. Korda, do you have any idea just how far the market will fall?"

Buddy felt the door open. Not for emotional impact, but rather for a response. One given in astonishing clarity. "The Dow Jones average will close next week at less than nine hundred."

It took Lonnie Stone a moment to recover. "That is a drop of over eighty percent."

"Yes, it is."

"In one *week*?"

"That is correct."

Another moment, and then, "Mr. Korda, all I can say is, I hope you are wrong."

Buddy felt an overwhelming sorrow, a sadness for the people, the businesses, the nation. He shook his head. "I'm not wrong."

⊣‖ FORTY-TWO ‖⊦

Four Days . . .

☐ Friday morning Thad Dorsett returned to the office a broken man.

He sat at his console, watching the markets open with the speed of a grand prix roaring into action. He saw nothing but a blur.

He started when the red light at the center of his phone console began flashing. Thad sat a very long time, trying to formulate a plan, struggling to draw his shattered parts together. Then he reached and picked up the receiver and punched the connection. "Dorsett."

"So how'd it go?"

The question brought a first sign of hope. Clearly Fleiss had not caught the interview with Korda, which CNN televised nationwide. Thad ventured, "Not too bad."

"That's good, sport. Real good. The old man will be pleased." The voice sounded like a robot's voice in a human body. "Say, what happened to the two security guys? They never checked back in."

Thad heard the flatness of his own voice, knowing the dead sound matched Fleiss's exactly. "I guess they must still be celebrating."

"Yeah, well, they deserve it. Say, you seen the market this morning?"

"It's rising," Thad guessed. It had been setting new records all week.

"Like a skyrocket. We're going for the stratosphere, you mark my words."

"Time to grab hold and ride the bull." Thad mouthed the words, but felt nothing.

"You got it. Heard your new office is gonna be ready first thing Monday. You still moving into your brownstone this weekend?"

"Tomorrow," Thad confirmed, searching inside himself for a shred of pleasure over the coming step, the arrival of all his dreams. All he found was a gigantic void.

"Good timing, kid. Nothing I like to see better in a trader." Larry's chuckle sounded machine generated. "Well, back to the trenches."

"Right." Thad hung up the phone and returned to staring sightlessly at the flickering screens.

He would leave early, as soon as he was certain the market was going to continue its ride into the wild blue yonder. Monday would come soon enough, then Tuesday, and with it Korda's downfall. As soon as the world saw that Korda's predictions were wrong, Thad's failure to take the banker down would not matter.

He struggled to draw the screen's numbers into focus; he saw that the prices continued to rise. He sat back, deaf to the screaming pandemonium rising around him. His lie was indeed intact. The market was going to rise, and Buddy Korda was soon to be history.

FORTY-THREE

Three Days . . .

☐ The Saturday morning papers were vicious. The market had broken all records on Friday afternoon. The pundits who mentioned him at all made Buddy out to be a disgruntled former bank employee who had turned against everything and everyone.

The weekend editorials read like obituaries. They were putting his time in the spotlight down as another of those unexplainable aberrations, symbolic of how people preferred to follow their hearts rather than their minds. With words as brooms, the papers and the radio and the television all pointed at the market's continued rise, then swept Buddy Korda into the back room of oblivion.

Buddy did not budge from his backyard. At his request, Molly had gone out and returned with as many papers as she could find. She delivered them with a set mouth. When Buddy asked her what the matter was, she simply said, "Stay where you are."

The day was warm and the sunlight strong in a cloudless sky. Buddy felt the light reach down and work to release the cold and the tension and the weariness trapped inside his bones. Through the open windows he heard the phone ringing continually. It awoke him from his brief naps, jerking him awake with electric jolts. He would reach out, as though still in some distant hotel room, still pressed for time, still driving himself and his friends to bone-weary exhaustion.

And for what?

He knew what the phone calls were saying. He knew people were calling, panic-stricken over having done as he had said. As he thought the message from heaven had said. But did he have it right? How could he be sure that he had listened to the right voice?

He had no answers. His prayers felt like dust rising from the emptiness of a spent and overworked heart. God remained silent and distant. Buddy had nothing to offer those who called, or the few who stopped by. His little back garden was a refuge from the world.

Saturday night they disconnected the phones. Sunday morning Buddy brought his coffee cup outside and sat looking out over an unseen lawn.

He did not even turn around when he heard Molly's swift steps swishing through the grass. "Aren't you coming with me to church?"

"You go ahead." Buddy sipped at a cup long gone cold. "If Monday goes like Friday, I doubt I'll ever move from this garden again."

The expected reprimand did not come. Instead, Molly's hand reached over to stroke his cheek. "My poor man. You've given everything you have to give, and you're afraid."

"Terrified." Buddy swallowed hard, fighting down the terror and the despair. "What if I was wrong all along?"

Molly squatted down beside his chair, gripped his arm with both hands, and said, "It's not time to worry about that yet. One more day. Can you hold out that long?"

He jerked a tight little nod. "Say a prayer for me."

"I always do, my husband." She kissed his cheek and rose back up. "The children wanted to come over after church. I didn't have the heart to say no again today."

"That's all right." Buddy turned now, looked up, and stiffened. For the first time he could ever remember, Molly wore her collar open. The scar was partially covered with makeup, but it was still there for the world to see. "Honey, what are you doing?"

She gave the open collar a nervous pat, as though unsure herself if it was right. But her voice was quietly resolute. "I've hidden behind my walls for too long."

"Molly, I . . ." Buddy struggled to his feet. "Wait and let me get on a tie."

"No, you stay here and rest." Molly guided him back down. "This is something I want to do on my own."

□

He must have fallen asleep, because the next thing Buddy knew, Alex was dragging one of the other lawn chairs over next to his own. "How you doing, little brother?"

"All right." But Alex deserved more than platitudes. "Tired. Scared."

"Sure you are." Alex seated himself, reached into his Sunday blazer, and brought out a slip of paper. "Clarke asked me to give you this."

Buddy accepted the paper, unfolded it and read:

> The LORD lives! Praise be to my Rock!
>   Exalted be God my Savior!
>
> You exalted me above my foes;
>   from violent men you rescued me.
> Therefore I will praise you among the nations, O LORD;
>   I will sing praises to your name.
> Psalm 18:46, 48-9

Slowly, carefully, Buddy refolded the paper and inserted it into his shirt pocket. "I wish I was as sure as he sounds."

"I guess you'll just have to let us be sure for you then, won't you?"

Buddy looked in helpless appeal at his brother. "Are you really so certain?"

"More certain of that than I have been of anything in my life." Alex's eyes held a burning light, one that seemed to touch Buddy as not even the sun had been able to. "I have discovered a love that will never abandon me. And I know that you serve the Master. I *know* it."

Buddy took a breath, drawing in Alex's confidence as well. "This is like a dream."

"Wait, it's about to get a lot better." He turned to where Agatha was hesitantly approaching and reached out a hand in greeting while rising to his feet. She walked over, allowed Alex to slip his hand into hers, and gave Buddy a shy smile. Alex turned back and beamed. "Little brother, we've got ourselves an announcement."

Buddy felt it coming before he knew what it was. He struggled to rise from the chair.

Alex watched him with an ever-widening grin. Molly was hurrying over, wiping her hands on her apron. When they were all together, Alex announced, "Agatha is going to make an honest man of me."

"You're already honest," Agatha said, the edge totally gone from her voice. "But I have agreed to marry you."

Molly said for them both, "This is wonderful."

"I didn't want to ask her," Alex said. "Can't even say how many days the Lord has left for me on this earth."

"None of us do," Agatha countered. "But whatever days we have left, I want to spend them with Alex." She looked at him with shining eyes and said with strength and quiet conviction, "Whatever comes."

"Praise God," Buddy whispered. He reached out and gripped Alex's hand with both of his. "Whatever tomorrow brings, I now count this whole trial a grand personal success."

⊣| FORTY-FOUR |⊢

One Day . . .

☐ A rascal wind greeted Thad Dorsett as he stepped from his new house Monday morning. Grit lashed at his face and tried to sneak in around his sunglasses. The air was far too hot for October. His skin felt dry as parchment and his tongue overlarge for his mouth. He nodded a silent greeting to the limo driver and slipped gratefully into the back.

Though not yet eight o'clock in the morning, the financial district throbbed with tension and activity. The communities of Riverside and Soho and rejuvenated Tribeca divulged their battalions of Wall Street warriors. They marched in their legions, racing toward the battle zone.

Thad took the elevator to the top trading floor. He stopped in the doorway of his new office, surveying with deep satisfaction the wood-paneled expanse and navy blue carpet. Looking around the room, imagining where he would station his desk and the conference table, and seeing himself enthroned by the window went a long way to restoring him.

The weekend had already done much to renew his confidence and enthusiasm. His new house was fantastic. The move had given his exploits a new sense of reality. Other than a series of jarring nightmares, moving into the top realm had been everything he had dreamed of.

But the nightmares had been vile. Thad Dorsett had woken time after time, bathed in sweat, chased by fiends taller than the Wall Street skyscrapers. Last night he had decided to take no chances and had swallowed a double dose of sleeping pills. The nightmares had been reduced to vague phantoms that he had managed to push away. Most of the time.

As the din from the trading floor began to build, Thad entered the main hall and slid into his seat. His last day among the peons. His furniture was scheduled for delivery by mid-morning. On the desk in front of him was the folder containing the outline for his proposed changes. A note from Larry clipped to the outside said that the old man had given his approval.

Thad laced his fingers behind his head, leaned back, and returned greetings from people he scarcely saw. Hearing the envy and the awe in their voices helped make the day truly complete.

☐

At ten minutes to ten, Thad looked up as a sudden silence gripped the room. The floor manager had the ability to draw major news bulletins off the top board and flash them on every screen at every trading desk. If any news bulletin ever deserved being called major, this was it.

Maurichi Securities was the largest financial institution in southern Japan. It controlled a full one-third of Honshu Island's total wealth. It employed 39,000 people worldwide. It had over eight hundred offices, including trading operations in Sydney, Hong Kong, Calcutta, Paris, and New York.

Thad sat joined with all the other traders in stunned silence and watched the words race remorselessly across his central trading screen. The chairman of Maurichi Securities had called a press conference and announced that undisclosed positions on the international derivatives market had cost the bank nine billion dollars. The bank's cash reserves were depleted. The bank had no choice but to close its doors.

The moment seemed to stretch into eternity, frozen by a universal desire to ignore the bulletin, to refuse to accept what it meant. Then Larry Fleiss's voice crackled through the intercom, shrieking at a level Thad had never heard before.

"*Sell yen!*"

The trading floor erupted. Thad was grabbing phones and punching buttons and screaming with the others, dumping every yen-based position the bank held. Or trying to. Everywhere around the world, traders were scrambling to do the same. Thad's screens began flashing new rates so fast Thad could not find a strike price.

Fleiss's voice sounded overhead once more, instantly freezing the clamor. "Okay, listen up. We're getting a feed on the stocks and bonds held by Maurichi. They're coming up on your screen now. Dump them fast. Take any price."

Like most Japanese banks and security firms, Maurichi had concentrated its U.S. holdings within the range of companies known as blue chips. These were the largest and most stable earners within the American economy. Yet earnings and price-share ratios and future profitability meant nothing at this point. Maurichi would be forced to dump all its assets in order to meet as many of its outstanding positions as possible. Prices were going to hit the basement and keep falling. It was vital they get out, and get out fast.

By two o'clock in the afternoon the Dow had dropped 850 points from its Friday close. A thirty-minute breathing space had been imposed when the market was down 500 just before noon, but the instant it reopened the frantic selling resumed. By mid-afternoon the traders were hoarse, exhausted, and sweat-stained. Thad had taken to drinking tea laced with bourbon and honey to hold on to what voice he had left.

Ninety minutes before closing, the next nail was set into the coffin. The chief official of the Japanese National Bank issued a formal statement declaring his "grave concern" over the state of the U.S. market. Ten short words, but enough to transform the traders' panic into sheer unbridled terror. Ashtrays and coffee cups went flying in every trading room around the world as dealers sought frantically to unload anything and everything tied to the dollar.

The U.S. treasury secretary lashed back thirty minutes later in a hastily declared press conference, accusing the Japanese bank official of "shock tactics in idiotic revenge for his own financial institution's precarious position," and declared that the weight of the entire U.S. government would go into supporting the dollar and the American financial markets.

The markets reacted with a violent about-face. The dollar leaped from the basement to the attic, rising seventeen yen in seven minutes. The dollar climbed 20 percent against its low of the day, just 5 percent down from Friday's high. But the stock market continued to drop. There was nothing that hit share prices like uncertainty.

When the closing bell sounded, traders stumbled about like shell-shocked victims of a bombing attack. Thad staggered to the back pantry for another cup of something he would not taste. His feet scuffled through paper and tear sheets three inches thick. Two traders he knew vaguely were sprawled on the floor, phones dangling by their sides. As he picked his way over their limbs, Thad happened to catch sight of a Reuters news flash streaking overhead. The Dow's final position was down one thousand, four hundred seventy-five points. A one-day decline of 19 percent.

⊣| FORTY-FIVE |⊢

☐ The press began arriving about three o'clock that Monday afternoon. The first few teams had the temerity to ring their doorbell. Molly appeared on Buddy's behalf, quietly refused their requests for interviews, but said he would make a statement later.

That was enough to galvanize the gathering. By five the street was blocked solid from end to end with television vans. The police had been called in, the front lawn cordoned off, and a semblance of order restored. Molly had given permission for the media to position microphones by the front steps, but otherwise the throng was kept well back.

Still the crowd grew. People who drove found themselves parking as far as three blocks away. There was no need to ask directions, not even for those arriving from out of town. The steady stream of people all took the same route.

Buddy appeared at six. There was a stir of recognition, and instantly the bank of television lights switched on. Buddy stood on his top step, endured the flashes from the photographers, and simply waited through the screaming flood of questions.

He spent the time looking out beyond the horde of press to where the gathering continued to grow. He nodded to a few familiar faces. They, in turn, were silent, somber—the exact opposite of the journalists and their shouted, aggressive questions. He stood there and waited, content to look out.

Once the journalists finally accepted that he was not going to respond, the tumult gradually died away. When all was quiet, Buddy stepped up to the huge bunch of taped-together microphones. "I have an announcement to make," Buddy said. "I will not answer any questions, because I do not want anything to take away from the critical nature of this message."

A reporter shouted, "Will the market continue to fall?"

"I will not answer questions," Buddy repeated, and waited until he was sure the silence would hold.

Then he looked out to the cameras, bunched on ladderlike tripods behind the reporters. He focused all the power he could muster and said simply, "This message is intended for all the friends and brothers and sisters out there who have heeded the directive I was told to bring.

"This message is, *SELL*."

Buddy tried to look *through* the camera, wanting to communicate directly with the people, make them understand how vital this was. "Sell your put options *now*. Sell first thing tomorrow morning. There is no telling how long the market will hold together. Do not allow greed to hold you in place. Sell it *all*.

"Then convert everything you have, everything you can transfer, everything you can withdraw, *everything* into cash. Not cash in a bank. Cash in your hand. Gold would be good. If not gold, then dollars. But cash."

He waited through a long, silent moment, and then said again, "*Sell now*. That is all I have to say."

A voice from far back in the throng shouted, "Thank you, brother!"

"Thank God," Buddy replied, turning away. "Good night."

─╢ FORTY-SIX ╟─

☐ At Buddy's request, Alex called and simply informed the national networks that Buddy would respond via a feed set up at the Aiden television station, and would be interviewed by Lonnie Stone alone. They had no choice but to agree. By this point, Buddy Korda and his on-target predictions were making headlines right around the globe.

When it came time that evening to leave for the local station, they had to call in the police once more. A phalanx of bodies was necessary to clear a way to the cruiser assigned to take them downtown.

The car was just beyond the drive when a man wrestled his way through the cordon and threw himself on Buddy's window. Buddy backed into Molly as the man clawed at the glass and screamed, "You did this! You! You cost me everything!"

Two policemen pried the man loose, but not before he shrilled, "It's all your fault, Korda! I hope you hang!"

"Hold on tight, folks," came the laconic order from the front seat. The patrolman began steadily accelerating away.

"Don't pay him any mind, sir." The patrolman in the passenger seat turned around. "I heard you speak on a video my church played last week."

"We heard the Spirit is what we did," his partner corrected.

"Yeah, well, anyway, we went out and did just what you said, stuck it all in those put options."

Buddy tried to still his nerves. The man's contorted features felt branded into his mind. "Get out first thing tomorrow."

"Yes, sir, we've already got the message through to our broker. He says he's gonna do it for everybody who did like you said."

"He said we're gonna be millionaires by this time tomorrow," the driver added. The flashing lights turned his solid features into multicolored stone. "Can't hardly believe it. But we're gonna take half of whatever we get and put it in the church fund. Don't know what we'll do with the rest. Bury it in the backyard, I suppose."

"That's good." Buddy felt himself steadied by the policemen's solid assurance. "That's very good indeed."

There was yet another crowd waiting outside the television station. As soon as the patrol car slowed, press and television camera lights flashed on full. The second patrolman said, "Looks like somebody tipped them off we were coming."

"There's an underground garage around back," the driver said, flipping on his siren and plowing steadily around the building.

Through the back window Buddy watched a horde race behind them, shouting and jostling and trying to keep up.

Even before the motor was cut, a nervous figure appeared in the garage's elevator and frantically waved them over. The driver said, "Better head on out, Mr. Korda. We'll hold the fort down here."

"I'll just sit right here," Molly said, leaning over to give his cheek a kiss. "I think this will be a much nicer place to pray."

"The Lord go with you," the driver's partner said, as Buddy slipped out. "We'll be saying the words with your wife."

Buddy rushed over, spurred to speed by the noise pushing in through the garage doors. The young woman greeted him with, "Mr. Korda, great. We hoped that'd be you. New York has been calling every five minutes, asking if we could move this up."

"Let's go," Buddy agreed, watching the doors shut just as the first figures raced into view.

The woman raised the walkie-talkie she was carrying and said, "Have security get down to the garage. We've got a riot in the making. And don't let any of those people inside the offices."

Upstairs, Buddy's reception could not have been any more different from the last time he visited a television studio. This time, the station president was there to shake his hand, thank him for coming, usher him personally into the makeup room. He was asked if he cared for coffee, and was then informed that Lonnie Stone himself was on the telephone, wanting to discuss the program.

"There's no need," Buddy said, waving the receiver away. "Just tell him I'm ready whenever he is."

His progress to the studio was followed by silence and stares. Everyone stopped to watch, study, and observe, knowing without saying that they were witnessing something they would tell their grandchildren about—the passing of a real live prophet.

The hookup was completed while Buddy was still being placed into the seat normally occupied by the local news anchor. As soon as the monitor came on, he saw and heard the world famous interviewer say, "I see we're finally hooked into Buddy Korda at the local Aiden, Delaware, station. Thank you for coming, Mr. Korda. I have seen the second part of your message, as has almost anyone in this country who has a television. Would you care to repeat it here?"

"I would," Buddy agreed, and again focused with all the force he could muster upon the camera. "All those who have acted upon my message, for your own sakes, do not let greed rule you now. Do not wait for the market to bottom out, hoping that you might profit even more.

"Others must be able to cover these obligations in order for you to gain from your investment. Tomorrow afternoon the people holding your paper will begin to fold. Therefore I tell you, *get out now*. First thing tomorrow morning, sell every put option you are holding. Convert it into cash and gold. And give thanks to God."

There was a moment's pause, a breathless hush that extended far beyond the monitor and the camera and all the shadow figures gathered just beyond the lights' reach. Finally the interviewer asked, "Are you saying that the market is actually going to crash, Mr. Korda?"

"I am making no more predictions. It is too late for that. I am simply telling these people to *get out now*."

"Too late?" Lonnie Stone adjusted his glasses, leaned across the desk, and said, "The president has announced a press conference for a half hour from now. He is expected to place the entire weight of the Federal Reserve and the United States Treasury behind keeping our markets open and stable. Would you like to change your position?"

"Not at all. Everyone who has taken heed of my message and purchased put options is urged to sell everything as soon as the market opens, and convert all their holdings to cash and gold."

"What about those who did not do as you said, Mr. Korda? Do you have any advice for them?"

"Yes, I do." Again Buddy forced all the power at his command upon the camera lens. "The kingdom of God is at hand. Repent. He who believes in the Son has everlasting life."

He stopped, half expecting to be cut off, but the production staff were all locked in the same breathless silence. So Buddy kept his gaze steady on the camera and went on, "Those who focus upon the world see these happenings as all that matter. But those who follow the Lord Jesus know that these events too will pass. They are *not* the end, not even the beginning. For the Scriptures tell us that all this will pass away, and in its place will come that which is more glorious than anything we can imagine. The twenty-fourth chapter of Matthew's Gospel tells us, 'And He will send His angels with a great sound of a trumpet, and they will gather together His elect from the four winds, from one end of heaven to the other.'"

Buddy paused again, this time simply to give thanks for the chance to serve, for the chance to have seen all that he had, for the opportunity to have grown as he did, and for it now to be drawing to a close. Then he finished with, "The door is open, the Lord is waiting to receive you. Come and join the living."

FORTY-SEVEN

Meltdown

☐ The next morning, chaos struck like a physical blow as soon as Thad Dorsett entered the trading room. Through the night, U.S. stocks had continued to trade around the globe, falling in every market worldwide. When the New York Stock Exchange began trading, the Dow Jones opened 917 points below the previous day's close. Trading was suspended for almost an hour. When the market reopened, it continued to fall steadily.

That afternoon, the market went through a brief rally. Then came the bad news. The Chicago Merchant Bank, the nation's eleventh largest, was closing its doors. Traders raced through the book, checking their positions on anything that might have been tied to Merchant and for which payment was now frozen. The result was grim despondency. Merchant's tentacles spread through the entire market structure, from options to currencies to every stock market to Fannie Maes to gold futures. The Chicago exchanges had bundled a huge amount of their trading work through them.

When the red light began flashing at the center of his phone console, Thad wanted to stand and flee. He picked up the receiver as he would a snake. He could only think that Fleiss would accuse him of lying, of not taking care of Korda as he had claimed. "Yeah?"

But clearly Fleiss had decided there was no time to waste on the past. "Take a look at our position. I'm putting it up on your screen now. Second channel. See it?"

"Yes." Thad stared at the screen, unable to believe his eyes. The numbers Valenti Bank were sustaining on the debit side were too big. These current positions were impossible to sustain. "What happened?"

"We hit the iceberg, is what happened." Fleiss's customary hoarseness was worn down to a leathery whisper. "We're gonna make the sinking of the *Titanic* look like a toy boat going down in a bathtub."

Leveraged positions that yesterday had made perfect sense now threatened to push the bank over the brink and into insolvency. And not just his own bank. "This can't be happening."

"It's happening, all right. Unless something major takes place and we find a way to hide the dirty linen until it does." A moment of heavy breathing, and then, "It's not just us, for what it's worth. I've been checking around. The whole market's sliding toward the falls."

The fingers holding the receiver felt numb to the elbow. "What do you want me to do?"

"Do what that Korda character's been saying. Go short. Buy every put option you can get your hands on."

Thad kept staring at the screen. "But we don't have the collateral."

"You think I don't know that?" The hoarse tone rose to a shrill whine and then subsided. "We're so far in the hole it doesn't matter any more. Buy everything you can. Bet the load on the market heading farther south. Pledge anything you can think of. I'm giving you everybody on the floor. No limits. Buy as fast as you can."

Thad sat staring at the silent phone until he spotted the floor manager hustling over. He stood, loosened the knot on his tie, and prepared for battle.

□

Finally at two-thirty the SEC chairman stepped in and closed the exchange. Trading was suspended on all the nation's markets. A breathing space was declared.

But none of the traders moved.

A half hour later, London and Paris opened. They promptly responded to the growing crisis by closing down all markets for twenty-four hours. Tokyo was deluged by so many conflicting orders that it had no choice but to follow suit.

Traders finally departed for the night with shattered nerves and shell-shocked expressions.

When Thad walked out on the street, his limo driver was nowhere to be found. He found himself too overwhelmed to care. He walked the length of Wall Street, seeing his own dread mirrored on every face he passed.

⊣| FORTY-EIGHT |⊢

☐ Buddy spent most of Tuesday in the back garden playing with his grandchildren, visiting with his family, and making idle chatter with Alex and Agatha and Clarke Owen and a few others that Molly permitted through the front door. The police kept the cordon in place, although by now most people had other, more critical things to fill their days. Even the number of journalists dropped to fewer than a dozen.

From time to time they returned to the living room, where they watched the drama unfold on CNN. The reports grew steadily grimmer. Even when the news flashed of a sharp rise in the market, not even the announcer seemed to believe that it would continue. Business reports from the balcony overlooking the New York Stock Exchange showed unbridled bedlam on the floor below.

When news broke of the Chicago Merchant Bank closing its doors, the normally unflappable business reporter looked ready to cry.

"Buddy," Clarke called from the door. "You're still coming to the worship service tonight?"

The church had decided late the previous afternoon to hold a meeting that evening. Before Buddy could decline, Molly appeared in the kitchen doorway and replied for him, "He'll be there. We all will."

"Good." Clarke gave him a single nod. "See you around seven."

When the door had closed behind him, Buddy turned to his wife. "Molly . . ."

"Don't you even start." She planted her hands firmly on her hips. "This is the church that raised you and stood by you through it all. You need to go, Buddy. It's time."

"Daddy!" Paul, his older son, called from the living room. "Get in here quick!"

He and Molly raced across the hall and stopped where his two sons and their wives stood before the television. He heard the business reporter announce, "Unconfirmed reports claim that it is not just Chicago Merchant facing dire straits this afternoon. According to sources close to the management, if the Valenti Bank were forced to cover all its trading liabilities today, it would be short almost seven billion dollars. A spokesman for the bank has called this ludicrous scaremongering. However, the bank had no comment regarding the accusations that it had lost heavily in tradings over the previous three months.

"On a related development, word is just coming in of a catastrophe at sea. Billionaire Nathan Jones Turner, owner of Valenti Bank, has reportedly fallen overboard and disappeared. While no one at the bank or at Turner's Connecticut office will either confirm or deny the reports, the Coast Guard did receive a frantic Mayday call from the Turner yacht, reporting a man lost at sea. We will have more on that as it comes in. We return now to our coverage of the Valenti Bank."

The camera panned out over the looming edifice of the Turner Building. The announcer continued, "Like many U.S. financial institutions, the Valenti Bank has poured massive amounts of its own and its investors' capital into the futures markets. During this recent era of rapid expansion, Valenti's worth has skyrocketed. However, sources claim tonight that this increased valuation was used as a basis for further highly leveraged tradings in what are known as derivatives."

The camera's perspective switched back to the reporter's face. "If what our sources claim is true, apparently this bubble is on the verge of bursting. What is certain is that given the current state of the market, Valenti's stock and bond assets are plummeting in value. This has undermined the bank's deposits, which in turn hold up its outstanding loan balance."

Molly said, "I don't think I understood any of that."

Buddy did not take his eyes from the television screen. "The bank is in trouble. That's really all you need to understand."

The announcer concluded, "Such a shortfall would only be aggravated by the rumored losses in the international currency and futures exchanges. Whether or not this institution can survive, if the rumors are indeed correct, is anyone's guess. This is Alicia Newstone for CNN News, reporting from Wall Street."

Molly's gaze followed Buddy as he backed slowly away from the television. "It's happening, isn't it?"

Buddy could only nod. The weight of sorrow for all those he had not managed to touch threatened to crush him.

⊣∥ FORTY-NINE ∥⊢

☐ Such was Buddy's distress that he kept his face lowered the entire trip to the church. He had not wanted to come at all, but Molly had insisted. The rest of the family tried to hide their unease with small talk. Buddy scarcely heard them.

Then Molly turned a corner and exclaimed, "Who are all these people?"

From the backseat Trish asked fearfully, "Is it a riot?"

"They look too well dressed for that," his son Jack pointed out. "And too calm."

Buddy raised his head and saw strangers milling about, surrounded by a darkness as complete as that which shrouded his heart.

"Look, Mom, the guy with the flashlight. He's waving you to the curb."

"We can't be expected to park here," Molly cried. "We're six blocks from the church."

Buddy squinted and focused on the man. He was indeed pointing them into a parking space. He heard his son say, "We've never had to park this far away."

"Where are the others?"

"Right behind us, Mom. I see them."

Molly cut off the motor. "Stay together, everybody. I don't like the looks of this."

Buddy opened his door and sighed as he got to his feet. The crowd was noisy but in a disjointed, comfortable way. Buddy sensed no threat. "Come on, everybody."

Then he jerked his head back as a light flashed into his eyes. "Buddy?"

"Point that thing in another direction, will you?"

"Sure." The flashlight dropped away, but the voice raised to a shout. "It's him!"

"Where?" A hundred voices eagerly picked up the chorus, demanding to know where he was. Then a hundred more. Buddy felt the first inkling of real fear. Then Molly was moving up beside him, taking his hand, and calling back, "He's right here."

Alex stepped up on Buddy's other side. "Make way, everybody! We've got a date with God!"

The man with the flashlight moved up in front of them. Buddy recognized him as Lionel Peters, the fellow church elder. "We've been waiting for you folks to get here. Come on, Buddy, I'll make a way for us."

The crowd did not press against them. Instead, they opened up a path toward the church and simply stood and watched as Buddy and his family walked through. At least at first.

Buddy turned a corner and spotted the distant shining steeple when the first woman crossed the invisible line. In the flashlight's glare her face was streaked and shimmering with tears. She grabbed his arm and cried, "Bless you, Brother Korda."

That was enough to burst the dam. People began flowing forward, reaching across, patting his back, his arms, trying to grab his hands. A thousand voices shouted thanks, cried in glory, yelled messages that were lost to the night.

Buddy allowed Molly and Alex to keep moving him forward, numb with shock.

Then they turned the corner, and Buddy realized what he had seen up to that point was only the tip of the iceberg.

The six-lane intersection in front of the church was packed solid with people. As was the lawn surrounding the building, the church steps, and the parking lot. Shouting and crying and waving, the noise was a commotion that followed them across the street and pushed them up the stairs.

Buddy caught sight of Clarke helping a group of young men arrange loudspeakers around the front pillars. He waved in Buddy's direction and pointed overhead.

Buddy looked up, and saw that a hand-painted banner had been strung from the eaves. It read: *The stone which the builders rejected has become the chief cornerstone. This was the Lord's doing. And it is marvelous in our eyes!*

Alex pressed his face close enough to Buddy's to be heard. "Ain't this something?"

Buddy turned to his brother and was greeted with resolute hope. "Who are these people?"

"Friends!" Alex shouted back.

Molly pressed close to his other side and said, "It is the harvest of your work, my husband. I am so very proud of you."

Alex settled a powerful arm across his brother's shoulders and pressed him up the stairs. "Come on, let's go praise the Lord!"

THE
ULTIMATUM

⊣‖ A NOVEL ‖⊢

T. DAVIS BUNN

A
JANET
THOMA
BOOK

THOMAS NELSON PUBLISHERS
Nashville

Copyright © 1999 by T. Davis Bunn

Published in Nashville, Tennessee, by Thomas Nelson, Inc.

Library of Congress Cataloging-in-Publication Data

Bunn, T. Davis, 1952–
   The ultimatum : a novel / T. Davis Bunn.
     p. cm.
   Sequel to: The warning.
   ISBN 0-7852-7086-8 (pbk.)
   I. Title.
PS3552.U4718U48 1999
813'.54—dc21   98-53794
                                            CIP

Printed in the United States of America.

5 6 7 8 9 BVG 06 05 04 03 02 01

"All duty lies in 'Come, follow me.'"
REV. ALEXANDER MACLAREN
(1830–1902)

⊣‖ PROLOGUE ‖⊢

☐ For Linda Kee, as for most people, it had been a winter of fierce winds.

Eighteen months had passed since the economic collapse, enough time for people to yearn for the good old days. Enough time for a new American president to be voted in and hold office for three months. Enough time for absence and lack and unanswered need to become normal.

Linda remained locked in numbness by the events of that day. She had been walking for hours, trying to come to terms with being fired. She had never been fired before in her entire life. She was thirty-one years old, and had been working at one job or another since she was fifteen. She lived for her job. She hardly knew anything else except work. And now she had none, and did not know where to find more. In one brief afternoon she had gone from being a person on the verge of fame and notability to just one more unemployment statistic.

Linda Kee stopped at the crossing and tried to read the street sign. She had lived in Washington, D.C., for nine years, long enough to know most downtown streets by their buildings. But the strange wind which had blown that entire season flung fistfuls of grit at her face. In the eerie twilight lost behind semipermanent clouds, she could scarcely see where the sidewalk ended and the pavement began. The same wind had blown all winter long, neither hot nor cold, moaning beneath ever-present clouds. Yet there had been neither rain nor snow, no relief from the dry dust storms. Just this same lamenting wind, sapping a person's strength and will to fight. Now it was late March, almost April, and still the winds blew, dry and fierce and constant.

As Linda stood on the curb, the dirt struck her like stinging slaps, punishing her for a lifetime of mistakes. Whatever it took—that had been the rule by which she had shaped her life. And look where it had landed her, lost in a city she thought she knew, every hope and goal permanently out of reach.

Darkness was gathering, a gloom only partly dispelled by the streetlights and shop windows. Cars rushed back and forth in front of her, hurrying to leave the city and the coming night behind. And she had nowhere to go.

Linda stumbled across the street and found herself at the foot of broad stone stairs. A respite in the wind granted her a single glimpse ahead, enough to see she stood at the entrance to a church. Then the wind bore down on her, blowing so hard it robbed her of all her remaining tears. She had no choice but to climb the stairs.

Three times she had come to God in her life. Once as a child because it had been expected of her and family pressure had been too great to resist. A second time the year after she had graduated from university, drawn by the happiness she had seen in the eyes of a friend. That period had lasted almost a year, until faith and ambition had done battle in her mind, and faith had been vanquished, she thought irretrievably. The third time was just last year, in the midst of a difficult, lonely time, when a fellow worker had shown her a peace she thought lost from the world forever. She had started attending church with his family, even began attending Bible studies. Then had come yet another choice, another turning, another step along the path to her goals. The same goals that were all torn from her now.

Linda was far from surprised to find the doors open, not even with the nation's capital in the clutches of a period when all doors were locked and all windows barred. She was gripped by the sudden sensation that her years of mistakes and wrong turns had somehow been leading her here. To the open door of a church, in a night and a storm without end.

Slowly she walked down the center aisle. Behind her, she heard the heavy door squeak and moan and finally click shut. The chamber was cast into gloom. Only one light burned, a soft glow focused upon the nave. Linda walked toward the front of the church as if in a dream.

But she was not dreaming. Nor would the howling winds vanish upon awakening, or the night ease. They were real, as real as the comfort and the peace she felt entering her heart.

She found herself thinking of the colleague who had invited her to church in those weeks following the economic meltdown. Clarence Ives was the kind of guy who never pushed, never pressured. Yet some days, in that dark period after the market crashed, Clarence's calm words and ready smile had been as threatening and pressuring as anything Linda had ever known. Strange she would think of Clarence now as she walked down the center aisle of an empty church. Strange he would seem so close, as though his friendship somehow had a part in all that had brought her here this night.

Linda stopped at the nave. She searched the corners of the church to see if anyone was watching, wondering where everyone was. She ran her fingers through her long dark hair, trying to draw some order to her wild day. Wild, yes. The night and the storm and the way she had been living. All wild. All wrong.

One by one she climbed the steps to the altar. By the sacristy Linda halted a second time. But the feeling was stronger now, as though a magnet had become attached to her heart. A magnet that drew her toward the light glowing upon the Cross. All about her the storm beat upon the windows, and moaned about the stone walls and the high roof. She stood at the storm's vortex, at the quiet center of the night and the tempest.

And somehow she knew that if she stepped forward and touched the foot of the Cross, her life would never be the same again.

─┤ O N E ├─

☐ When Buddy awoke he was standing in the middle of his bedroom, his hand outstretched to a door that was not there.

He turned back to the bed, the dream so vivid he had difficulty focusing on his wife. Molly was pushed up to a seated position, her eyes round and luminous in the streetlight streaming through their window. "Are you all right?"

He nodded. His mouth remained open, his breath coming in quick, hard gasps. Gradually his racing heart slowed to a more normal pace.

Molly remained where she was, watching him intently. Quietly she asked, "Has it started again?"

Buddy opened his mouth farther, but no sound came out. He looked back, wishing there were some way to recapture what now was lost. It had seemed so real. So incredibly, magnificently, beautifully real.

"Buddy?" When he did not respond, she pressed, "Is it another vision?"

Resigned to the loss, he said to his wife, "Not like last time."

Before she could ask more he walked into the bathroom. He washed his face, then stood there before the mirror. Even in the middle of a disturbed night, Buddy saw in his reflection a man who was aging gently. His small frame remained sturdy and trim, his hair graying but full. Buddy studied his reflection, and wished he knew of some way to hold on to that dream. The last tendrils still held such power he could feel the beat of angels' wings.

When he finally emerged from the bathroom, he found Molly still sitting up in bed. She watched in silent concern as he walked around and lay down and pulled the covers up to his chin. He stared at the ceiling, wishing he could recapture what now had been assigned to memories, to dreams, to a future he had never hungered for so much as right now.

Finally she asked, "How was it different?"

But it was lost. For now, for this moment, the dream and all that it had promised was gone. Buddy looked at her squarely now, his entire being aching from the toll. "This one was beautiful."

□

The next morning Buddy lingered over his coffee, taking solace from the daily routine. Molly hung up the phone from her morning talk with their elder son's wife; Anne was eight months and ten days pregnant and having a tough time carrying her third child. Molly moved at her normal pace, readying herself for another day of work; since the economic decline, she had helped Buddy over at the church. He watched her and wondered. More than thirty years they had been married, and still on mornings like this, his wife remained a mystery.

The first prophecy had begun with a dream, a year and a half earlier. The warning he had been commanded to tell the world had culminated in an economic meltdown, the nation's second Great Depression. The days and weeks of traveling and speaking had shattered the life they had loved so dearly. Molly had always been a very quiet lady, born into shyness and raised in a home where mistakes and sad accidents had left her afraid of almost everything new. Traveling with her husband had brought Molly into the public eye for the first time. Yet she had accepted it as a challenge sent from God, and responded with a determination that had shocked Buddy. But since the furor surrounding Buddy's prophecy had died down, Molly had returned to her homelife with quiet satisfaction. Nowadays she lived for her grandchildren and her church.

Buddy half expected that having another dream fracture their night would send his wife into a tailspin. Yet here she was, humming as she fastened the high collar to her blouse and checked her makeup in the antique oval mirror hung by the kitchen door. The soft gray light of a cloud-covered morning entered through the kitchen window and rested upon Molly's silver-brown hair like an angel's hand.

Buddy asked, "How is Anne?"

"Same as yesterday. Counting the hours. Her back bothered her again last night. She wishes she could sleep more, and the girls don't understand why she can't do everything they expect her to." Veronica and Meredith were six and four, two extremely active handfuls at the best of times. Molly caught sight of the way he was watching her. "What's the matter?"

"I was just wondering," he confessed, "if you were the least bit bothered by the dream last night."

"You were the one who had the nightmare, not me."

Perhaps it was the play of morning light, but Buddy had the distinct impression that his wife was actually smiling at him. "It wasn't a nightmare, Molly."

"There you go, then." She turned from the mirror, and the light seemed to follow her around. "Why should your having a good dream leave me worried?"

"Well, you were a little troubled the last time I had such a dream."

"More than a little. I was so terrified I didn't sleep a wink for weeks." Still there was no sense of anxiety. "I don't know anything that has ever frightened me as much as that dream."

His confusion heightened. "But you don't have any questions about what I dreamed last night?"

She watched him carefully. "Are you ready to tell me?"

"No," he said, faltering. "Not just yet."

"Just as I expected. Why should I press you to talk before you're ready?" His evident bafflement seemed to heighten her good mood. Molly walked over, seated herself beside him, and placed her hands around his. "Buddy, Buddy, I knew this was going to come."

Surprise over her words might have blown him from his chair, had it not been for the gentle grasp upon his hand. "You did?"

"Of course, my beloved little man. Did you really think God was going to use you once and let you go?"

"Well . . . I never . . . That is—"

"You were chosen for a reason. You served the Father well." She looked at him with eyes filled by sunlight and love. "Of course He is going to call upon you again. What has this been except a time of rest and growth?"

The naturalness of what he was hearing surprised him almost as much as the dream itself. "I guess I had always thought things would go back to the way they were before."

A trace of shadows from beyond the refuge of their little home crept in. "Things will never be the same again. You know that."

Sorrow made him drop his gaze. "Yes, yes, I suppose I do."

"Buddy, look at me." When he raised his gaze back to meet her own, she continued, "The world is full of need and want. If you have been given something that will help, you must go and shout it from the rooftops. Do you hear me?"

□

As soon as Buddy entered the church parking lot, he realized the news had preceded him.

Over the past eighteen months, the church Buddy Korda had attended since childhood had been transformed beyond all recognition. Part of Buddy's message had been a means by which individuals could prepare themselves and their families for the coming economic famine. Buddy asked in return that a third of all they received be tithed to the church. As a result, churches throughout the nation had experienced unsurpassed levels of giving. Churches like Buddy's had used these funds to become islands of refuge, stepping into vacuums created within the ailing nation.

Six neighboring businesses had gone under in the economic debacle. The church had subsequently acquired the properties in order to expand its outreach programs. The church-run school had quadrupled its enrollment, mostly with children on low-income scholarships. They were presently negotiating to acquire the motel across the street for additional classrooms. The church-run cafeteria served almost seventeen hundred breakfasts and more than four thousand low-cost lunches every day. Fifteen buses ran pick up services for the elderly and those who no longer could afford cars. There was a crisis pregnancy center, a training center, a jobs center, a teen outreach center, a sports hall, a coffee shop, two counseling centers, a housing center, and a business office. The latter was Buddy's chief responsibility, although he served from time to time in many of the others. The church continued to grow and extend its reach, trying desperately to fill gaps caused by the steadily contracting economy.

Buddy was thinking of none of this when he pulled into the church parking lot. Eighteen months had seen such an utter transformation of his little world that these things were taken more or less for granted now. What concerned him at the moment was the latest news airing on the radio. Manufacturing reported a decline in production for the seventeenth straight month. That morning the Justice Department had also released statistics showing a steady rise in crime, much of which was gang-related. Police forces across the nation were threatening to walk out on strike unless the ongoing series of staff cut-backs were halted. The president's chief of staff had this morning responded with a promise to set up a new task force to examine the issue.

Buddy spotted his brother limping toward the car, one arm waving as he bellowed out some song. Buddy opened his door and realized his brother was singing "Back in the Saddle Again."

Buddy rushed over and scolded, "You know full well you shouldn't be out here without a coat."

Alex allowed his little brother to take the arm not holding his cane and steer him around. "You gonna tell me what it was you dreamed?"

"Here you are, the end of March, and you only five months out of the hospital," Buddy went on. His hand gripped through his brother's jacket and felt the flesh of one twenty years older than Alex was supposed to be, and steered him back around. "It'll serve you right if you catch pneumonia."

"That's all right. Don't tell me about your dream." Alex made heavy going of the steps, but that did not diminish his good cheer any more than Buddy's reproach. "Why should your own flesh and blood know anything about what's going on?"

"I suppose Molly has come in and told everybody," Buddy lamented, helping his brother up the final few steps.

"Nah. She just told me and the reverend. And I didn't tell nobody but Agatha."

Buddy groaned aloud. Agatha was Alex's wife of nineteen months, and a woman who truly loved to be first with the news.

"It's your own fault, little brother. You didn't tell Molly not to tell."

Which was true. But it was not this fact that halted him at the church doors. Buddy stared down at the door handle, and felt a shiver of anticipation race through his entire being.

Alex peered at him through new spectacles, ones with lenses almost as thick as those of his wife. He had been diagnosed with cancer about the time of Buddy's first vision. He had endured three bouts of chemotherapy with two surgeries sandwiched in between. The cancer had gone into remission, but only after the cure had stripped Alex of eighty-five pounds and years of once-vibrant life. The only things that had truly survived his battle with the demon cancer were his love for God, his wife, and his brother. And his sense of humor.

Alex watched Buddy reach for the doorknob, then hesitate once more. "It had something to do with a door, didn't it? Your dream."

Buddy could not lie, most especially to his brother. He answered with a single nod.

"Boy oh boy." Alex had worked with Buddy through the entire episode of spreading his first message. "It's started again, hasn't it? Right here, right now. And I'm standing on the threshold with my brother, the prophet."

"Alex, please." Buddy forced himself to reach and grip and turn and open. Then he took an unsteady breath when he looked upon an empty church hallway. "It wasn't this door."

"Shoot." Alex waved his cane in frustration. "Then why'd you get me going? I was all ready for fireworks and 'The Hallelujah Chorus.'"

"I don't know what door it is," he said. Which was both true and not true. He knew the door. He felt it in his bones. Even so, the door was lost to him. For now.

Alex tried and failed to hold a matter-of-fact tone. "So what's on the other side?"

Buddy shook his head. That he could not say. Even thinking about it was enough to make his throat swell with the dream's aching power.

"All right. All right. Don't tell me. What business is it of mine, anyway."

Buddy forced down a swallow. "Exactly."

"I'm just another simpleminded lackey, good for nothing but step and fetch. Pitch hay and tote water. Answer the phone and write down the messages. Stick tacks in the map, carry the bags . . ." Alex paused, giving Buddy a chance to rise to the bait. When his younger brother refused to be drawn, he dropped his banter with a snort.

Together they traversed the hallway that connected the church to the new cafeteria. The church cafeteria was located in what was formerly an office supply store. The high walls were now painted white, the floors nicely tiled. All this was the work of trainees in the church jobs program, which also supplied most of the cafeteria's cooks. In all, the church employed more than five hundred staff now, far more than was actually required, making it one of the largest employers in Aiden, Delaware. The tumult echoing from the cafeteria signaled a typical Monday crowd, always the busiest day after being closed for the Sabbath. For many of the worst hit, the church cafeteria provided their one solid meal each day.

The closer they came to the cafeteria entrance, the more crowded the hallway became. Greetings were called from all quarters. Buddy felt glances cast his way, but these he had long since grown accustomed to ignoring.

Nowadays it was far easier to disregard the fanfare. In the early days people had driven hundreds of miles just to get a glimpse of him. As though the messenger was what had been important, instead of the message itself. Buddy told one and all the same thing: the only reason God had chosen such a nobody as himself was because He had wanted the message to be the focal point. The *only* thing that mattered.

The worst were those who came with questions he could not answer. The ones who had loved ones who were sick and dying. The ones who had lost everything in the sudden downturn. The ones whose children were going astray, joining the gangs that had risen in number and power since the economic downfall. The ones whose towns were withering on the vine. The ones who asked, What now? What does God say now? Buddy had no answers to give, except to reply that he had done as he had been called to do, and so should they. Have faith. Seek the Lord with all their heart. It was a feeble answer in the face of their pain and fear and want. But it was all he had to give.

Reverend Patrick Allen chose that moment to push through the doors leading to the newly expanded church offices. There had been a time when Patrick had seldom met a door without bursting through, as though he were still quarterbacking for Carolina. But no more. Now he entered the hall with a shove that showed little more than weary determination. Patrick Allen had endured eighteen terrible months, truly the most appalling times of his entire life. His wife had fallen ill the week after the nation's economic meltdown. She was gone almost before anyone knew her illness was anything more than the flu. Now Patrick lived for the church; the people took everything he had to give and still demanded more.

Patrick nodded as he passed Buddy and his brother, pulling his face into as much of a smile as he could manage. "Hello, gentlemen."

"You look tired, Patrick," Alex said. "Can't let yourself get worn down. Too many people counting on you these days."

Patrick did not respond directly. Instead he looked at Buddy and asked, "Did you hear we moved up the finance conference?"

"I'll be there," Buddy said.

"Good. We'll make it a point to be through in time for you to get to the auction this afternoon." Patrick turned away before Buddy could think of a protest. He hated the auctions, had forgotten it was his turn to attend. He stood and watched helplessly as Patrick continued down the hallway. The pastor stopped by one group after the other, speaking with such calmness that most people noticed his swift motions only once he had moved on. The man was still movie-star handsome, but worn down now to a taut and fragile edge.

Alex's arm kept Buddy from following the pastor down the long hallway. Quietly Alex asked him, "It *has* started again, hasn't it? God's called you back to the front line."

Buddy opened his mouth to deny it. To say the dream had not been like that at all. But the words were sucked from his lips and his chest long before he could speak. He stood there, his mouth open and working for what could not come, until he finally accepted defeat. As he shut his mouth he felt nothing but confusion.

Alex, on the other hand, looked at him with the broadest smile Buddy had seen in what felt like ages. "Boy oh boy oh boy oh boy," Alex said, tapping his cane in time to his words. "Hot diggety dog."

⊣ TWO ⊢

☐ The armed security guard waved his hand over the briefcase and ignored the pair of offered badges. "Good afternoon, Mr. Calder."

"Hello, Tom." He let the plastic ID badges drop down over his tie. "How's the wife?"

"Doing much better, Mr. Calder. Thanks for asking. The new medicine seems to be working fine."

"That's good to hear. You be sure she takes it easy." Royce nodded to the second uniformed guard working the OEOB afternoon shift. This officer was a new man; Royce read his name on the plastic breastplate and instantly committed it to memory. It was an automatic action after all these years, and one that had served him well. No telling when it might pay to be on a first-name basis with the little people.

Royce Calder joined the throng moving through the metal detectors and into the Old Executive Office Building. It was five months now since he had received his new assignment. He entered these portals as often as a dozen times a day, and still he felt a thrill over taking this first step into the realm of power.

The Old Executive Office Building, or OEOB for short, was only a few years younger than the White House itself. It was connected to the president's residence by both an overland garden path and an underground tunnel. The overland path went through two metal fences and a phalanx of security men and guard dogs. It was used by visiting dignitaries as a photo op, while the tunnel was used by all the staffers. Royce had come to know that tunnel very well over the past months.

His assistant bounced to his feet as Royce entered the outer office. Blond hair gleamed as he raced around his desk, the tagged file outstretched. "Don't stop, don't ask, just run."

"Don't tell me they moved up the afternoon conference," Royce moaned, the tension rising like he had hit a tripwire. Earlier he had turned off his pager for his monthly lunch with his son. The son he scarcely thought of anymore, except to meet with occasionally and send checks for his tuition. The son who despised Royce's political work and everything his ambitions had cost the family. Royce accepted the folder and vowed, "That's the last time I disconnect my pager for anybody."

His aide checked his Rolex. "You've got three minutes. Go. Go."

Royce bolted along the ground-floor hall and down the stairs and through the connecting tunnel. He only slowed as he approached the guard on desk duty at the White House end, which was when he realized he had forgotten to ask his assistant in which room the conference was being held. So he grabbed for enough air to say, "Morning, George. Would you happen to know where the committee's meeting today?"

The guard gave careful inspection to both badges—OEOB and the much rarer permanent White House pass—before giving the laconic response, "I believe I heard something about the main staff conference room."

"I owe you." Royce pounded up the stairs, and decided to take the front way. It meant threading through three groups of gawking tourists, but that was far better than having the working staff watch him race to a meeting with the White House chief of staff.

Royce Calder paused outside the conference room, took three deep breaths, straightened his tie, pulled down the lapels of his jacket. Then he walked in calmly, smiling as he passed the laughing cluster by the table's head. He slid into the seat directly across from the chief of staff's and willed himself not to puff. No one was to know he had sprinted. It did not fit with his label of unruffled calm.

Royce Calder's official title was Assistant Director for Domestic Policy. But the title was merely a tag for the public. To those in the know, Royce Calder was the *courier*, the top ranking official within the White House hierarchy representing the new party in power. He worked with both Congress and the White House, coordinating agendas and policy issues. He interfaced with powerful interest groups—which meant all who had money and were likely to invest in candidates or the Party. He was the man who arranged for Party bigwigs to meet privately with the president, to attend state banquets, to sit beside the power people, to sleep in the Lincoln Bedroom. In political parlance, Royce Calder was the get-it-done guy.

"All right, everybody's here. Let's get started." Ethan Eldridge sounded exactly like what he was, a misplaced New England banker. He had been President Gifford's best friend since their Princeton school days more than three decades ago. Ethan had followed his own father into the banking business, where he had shown a remarkable ability for making money. His one hobby was running the campaigns of his old Princeton friend.

When elected to the highest office in the world, the new president's first appointment had been Ethan Eldridge as the White House chief of staff.

"Who's starting today, Will?" He had a fussy manner and a nasal voice and eyes of Toledo steel—hard and gray and knifelike. "Go ahead, we've got a lot of ground to cover."

"Right." The deputy secretary of the Treasury opened his file and began droning, "Economic trends remain downward for this latest quarter."

Royce's neighbor muttered, "So what else is new."

"Unemployment jumped another four hundred and eighty thousand, standing now at eighteen point eight percent." The deputy secretary looked up and added, "Underemployment is where things really remain bleak. At best estimate more than forty percent of working adults feel that they are not fully utilized in their present—"

"All right, all right." When irritated, Ethan's nasal tone bit like a buzz saw. "We have gone through this. The president feels, and I agree, that the time has come to seek a positive slant on such data."

"Corporate bankruptcies are holding steady." With a doubtful glance across the table, the deputy secretary then added, "But since the number of companies is falling the trend does not look good." He flipped the page before Ethan could object and continued hastily, "Commercial construction starts are off another seventeen percent from the last quarter, but the downward trend seems to be slowing."

"Good, good. This is what we like to hear. Remember, people, our responsibility is to find a positive slant on what we send to the president."

Royce nodded in pretended agreement, but in truth he was no longer paying much attention. Years and years of sitting through committee meetings had taught Royce Calder how to split in two. The external Royce watched and listened and even took notes. To all the world he displayed the amazing ability to remain alert and focused through the most long-winded drone. He could even recite the last thirty seconds of whatever he had just heard like a constantly recharging tape recorder. Yet all the while, the internal Royce was a thousand miles away.

He used such times as this to calculate and scheme and design. Royce Calder did some of his finest plotting while pretending to listen to someone blowing a roomful of hot air.

Now he spent a few minutes reviewing what was to come, planning his moves like a chess grand master. He then focused back on the room, a quick check of the external world.

Treasury had given the floor over to the chief White House economist, who was continuing with the rambling of oppressive stats. " . . . Housing starts are down for the sixteenth month running. No surprise given the fact that foreclosures and personal bankruptcies are at an all-time high. The Dow appears to be holding stable at the twelve hundred mark . . ."

Royce retreated back into his secret recesses. While still in his first Washington position as aide to a freshman congressman, his boss had once told Royce that there was always a crisis brewing. Always. The key was to ride the problem like a wave, and come out on top. The congressman was long gone, but his lesson remained. Today's crisis was the economic meltdown. Royce's challenge was to find out how to ride it to his advantage.

Every successful campaign for high office required the help of outsiders. These political favors were like debts, to be paid off not with money but with the discreet use of power. Many of these favors were not granted directly to the candidate, since this would mean a line of responsibility that could be traced, uncovered, and exposed. Instead, most of the truly powerful favors were granted to the Party. During the campaign, the Party had received favors and soft-money contributions and endorsements and a thousand other essential bonuses that had helped catapult the new president into office.

Now it was payback time.

Allies considered Royce Calder a sort of power broker, the Party's top representative within the president's White House staff. Enemies considered him a mole, one with a venomous bite. There were as many enemies as allies, for Royce Calder had been at this game for a very long time. He had very few friends in the true sense of the word—almost none, in fact. Friends had the disagreeable habit of asking the impossible. Royce Calder did not like risks he could not control.

Something changed in the external world, a slight alteration in the flow of stats, something that caused the bell in the back of Royce's brain to ring. He brought the world back into focus, and instantly knew it was almost time to spring.

"The one continuing bright spot," the White House economist said, sarcasm dripping from his tone, "is church revenue."

"Amen to that," the man next to Royce wisecracked, and this time there were a few chuckles around the room.

"Over the past eighteen months, Christian organizations around the nation have experienced an enormous increase in the level of donations." He noticed the chief of staff's frown of impatience, as this was old news. The economist hurried on, "Their web of investments is extending in ever-greater circles. In Baltimore, Charlotte, Atlanta, Nashville, Indianapolis—the list grows longer every day—we estimate that the churches have become the largest noncorporate residential landowners."

"Churches as a group," Ethan corrected, but his look was as sour as the economist. "No single body or denomination has major sway."

"No, but the cash they're holding, the *wealth*." Royce's neighbor was an accountant, currently presidential adviser for tax reform. "The rest of the nation is suffering, and this tight-knit handful of people and churches is sitting pretty."

A momentary silence descended upon the group, something Ethan Eldridge seldom permitted. He preferred to hold these noncabinet conferences to a quick staccato, but there was a calculation to the silence, one Royce had come to know well.

In response there was a slight drawing back from the table, a reluctance to cast the first stone. Everyone there knew what needed doing. But it was also common knowledge that to make the move meant political suicide.

The situation had been brewing ever since the economic meltdown began, when a chance series of remarks by some unknown Deleware banker had led many people to invest against the stock market. Royce Calder remembered the banker's name. Buddy Korda. The man had shown the good sense to retreat from public view while still on top, instead of coming out with yet another prediction, one that would have inevitably failed. Korda was probably basking somewhere in small-town glory. Exactly what he deserved.

But the fallout from his prediction was still creating headaches in Washington.

The group of people who had invested as Korda instructed had afterward donated a *huge* portion of their gains to local churches. The figures were staggering when taken against the backdrop of a fall in disposable income across the rest of the nation.

"This much is clear," Ethan Eldridge finally said, his nasal voice showing clear irritation that no one else could be drawn into putting the matter forth. "We have a crisis situation at hand, one that is affecting the entire nation. Tax revenues are plummeting while social costs are skyrocketing. And at this very moment, a very few fortunate individuals have parked an excessive portion of their recent gains in nontaxable churches. They call it donations, and we, therefore, cannot touch this money. But to an old-fashioned New England banker like myself, I'd prefer to call it unearned revenue."

Now that Ethan himself had started the ball rolling, the economist was ready to give an indignant push. "Funds that, by rights, should be used to aid all Americans. Not just those who go to church."

Royce started to speak up, then decided to wait just a moment more.

The chief of staff's eyes flickered over him, as though the cadaverous banker with his tightly focused gaze had been able to peel back Royce's skin and peer into his motives. Royce met the man's gaze with his meekest smile, and waited.

The deputy secretary of the Treasury added, "The problem is, they're becoming a nuisance. They realize they're gaining power, and they want to use it. We can't rely on their outright loyalty anymore."

"It's outrageous." The White House counsel was a very attractive woman, save for her hard-edged features and what Royce called her Chicago attitude—abrasive and ready to do battle over almost anything, from her position on the presidential memo reading list to her seat in the White House dining room. "These people are flagrant abusers of the commercial plight afflicting our nation. They are using their ill-gotten gains to gobble up everything within reach—"

"Save your closing arguments for court, Counselor," Eldridge commanded. The woman bristled, but subsided, unwilling to go head-to-head with the president's number two. "All right. We are basically in agreement that the status quo is unacceptable."

"Absolutely," the economist concurred.

"Then the question now before us is, What do we propose to do about it?"

A gloom descended. The assistant for legislative affairs predicted, "The religious wing and their representatives in Congress would eat us alive."

"Murder us in cold blood," the Treasury man agreed.

"Crucify us," Royce's neighbor joined in. "Sorry. Bad joke."

Royce felt as though an invisible spotlight had swung over and was pinpointed upon him. He leaned forward in his seat and opened the file. In his mildest voice he said, "I've been doing a little research."

He shuffled papers and waited until all attention became focused upon him. Finally Eldridge said, "And?"

"In anticipation of this tide of events," Royce said, pretending to read from his notes, "I have caucused the finance committee members."

An instant's electrifying silence, before Eldridge barked, "House or Senate?"

Royce lifted his gaze to meet that of the chief of staff. "Both, actually."

"Both parties?"

"Well, yes, you see, that's where we have been making what turns out to be an incorrect assumption. Their constituents are suffering right alongside our own. Our opponents seem willing to back us."

Eldridge's gaze sharpened to match his tone. "What do they want in return?"

"An equal say in how these new funds would be utilized. Our support for their package of welfare reform. A few minor details."

"What you're telling us," Eldridge said, "is that you've gone out on your own and formed a consensus in both critical committees for us to push through legislation to tax America's churches?"

"Well, yes, I suppose I am."

The legislative liaison almost leaped from his seat with indignation. "You can't let him get away with this! This is so far out-of-bounds he might as well be playing on another field!"

Royce kept his gaze on the chief of staff. "It gets better."

"I'm listening."

"I pitched this as a taxation on *all assets*. The only thing we agree not to touch are the churches themselves."

A sigh of pure astonishment escaped from around the room. Royce felt like standing and taking a bow.

"All right." Ethan Eldridge closed the meeting as he did all staff conferences, with an open-palmed slap on the conference table's polished surface. "Thank you, everyone. That will be all for today. Royce, stay where you are."

But the legislative assistant was not done yet. He was a personal friend of the president from their congressional days, and so long as the issues were clearly defined along party lines, he wasn't bad at his job. "This is utterly outrageous." His jowls had turned a choleric red with rage. "I'll be taking this straight to the top."

"Save it, Harold," Eldridge snapped, not even looking up from his note-taking. "And if you go within twenty paces of the Oval Office without my express permission, I'll nail your hide to my wall."

"But—"

The chief of staff raised his gaze and silenced the former congressman with a single look. "Close the door on your way out."

When they were alone, Eldridge examined Royce across the table's expanse. "I've been wondering when you'd make your move."

Royce blinked and said nothing.

"I've heard stories about you for years. Chiller Calder, that's what they call you, isn't it? Not because of your calm either. Because of your way of sliding in the knife when your enemies least expect it. One quick stab, in and out, and you vanish into the shadows before they hit the ground."

Royce used the middle finger of each hand to line up his papers with exact precision.

"I don't have a thing against working alongside an assassin with ice for blood," Eldridge continued, smiling with his lips alone. "I couldn't have survived the banking world if I was bothered by such things. My only concern is whether your ambitions are in line with my own."

"In precise parallel," Royce said quietly.

"Because I could use a few good soldiers, people who have the ability to get things done." Eldridge leaned across the table. "I repeat what I said before. My concern is that we are thinking and walking and acting in tandem."

"I am very good at making things happen for my superiors," Royce said, putting a mild emphasis on the last word.

"All right. Here's your first test. In public I don't care what you hide or what you reveal. Your cards are your own." The gray eyes had the force of a surgeon's knife, probing deep. "But in private, I expect you to lay them all out."

"I understand."

"My guess is, you wouldn't have come in here with a few nods from the committees alone. You'd have canvassed your connections through the entire legislative arena. Now tell me I'm right."

"The first time."

"So how close are we?"

"In the Senate, two votes shy."

"Two votes are nothing. Two votes are something we can give to Harold so he feels like we've kept him in the loop. Two votes are pancakes and maple syrup on a cold day. Now let's hear the bad news."

"I couldn't do as much in the House because I didn't want word to get out." Royce accepted Eldridge's nod as the compliment it was. The House was a hotbed of conservatives with religious ties who would go for blood the instant they caught wind of such a move to tax their beloved churches. The Senate was a more understanding group, long used to compromise and better insulated from voters' ire by six-year terms. "I went through committee connections, and spoke to caucus leaders only. I can give you a hundred and fifteen votes for certain, another thirty-seven possibles."

"Which leaves us quite a bit short." Eldridge nodded. "I'm pulling you off the vote thing for the moment. I want you to develop a defense against the fire storm this is going to unleash."

"Fine."

"Give me something for the public outcry, and run it through the courts as well." Then Ethan leaned back in his seat. "All right. I'm listening."

For the first time, Royce felt a moment's uncertainty. "Excuse me?"

"You aren't doing this for the good of the country. I want to know what it is you expect in return." A finger stabbed the distance between them. "And remember. Nothing hidden between us."

Royce glanced down at his papers. The man was saber-sharp. He must be careful to never underestimate Ethan Eldridge.

"I'm waiting, Calder."

Royce took a breath. "Ken Oakridge is retiring."

"So?"

He raised his gaze. "I want his office."

"Ah." Eldridge gave a sharp nod of comprehension. "Everything has suddenly become very clear."

It was all about access. Royce had worked his entire life to be where he was right here, right now. Yet he remained blocked from the pinnacle. This president was almost impossible to see. President Bradley Gifford accepted meetings with virtually no one. He delegated all unofficial contact, and almost all meetings save for cabinet sessions and attempts to save crucial congressional swing votes, to his chief of staff. Which was exactly as Ethan Eldridge would have it. Royce Calder had no idea how much, if any, of his work actually arrived before the president still bearing Royce's own name.

Normally the Party's chief representative within the White House was accorded instant access. He was involved in almost every meeting that had to do with party matters, or reelection, or funding, or Congress—in other words, nearly everything that was not the exclusive bailiwick of defense or foreign affairs. But not with this president.

Ken Oakridge was the ailing chief of intelligence. The power of his position had steadily declined since the demise of the Cold War and the current economic meltdown. His assistant was slated to take over at the end of the month. To ask for Oakridge's office was a blatant demand for access.

The White House office staff was primarily located in the Old Executive Office Building. A few key staffers were granted offices in the White House basement. Other than President Gifford's own secretarial staff, only seven offices were located on the ground floor, one of which was the Oval Office.

Another was that of the chief of staff. Only two of the remaining offices looked out over the Rose Garden. Two.

Eldridge tapped one finger on the table. Up and down. The only motion in his entire frame. Finally, "I want one thing more."

Here it came. "Name it."

"I can't. I don't know what it is yet." A glint of genuine humor this time, a crinkling of the skin around those steely eyes. "You're delivering one impossible here and now. I want one more impossible. That's fair, considering what you're asking."

Royce had no choice but to repeat, "Name it."

"I'm a man of my word, Calder. You know that by now. I'll keep the office open, and I'll let it be known that I'm planning to assign it to you. Given the current state of affairs, we won't have to wait long before the next impossible surfaces." The humor vanished without a trace. "And in the meantime, I'm going to be watching you. Like a hawk, Calder. Like a very cautious bird of prey. And if you give me one reason to doubt your loyalty, I'm going to swoop down and pounce. And I won't leave more than a tiny stain."

⊣| THREE |⊢

☐ Buddy loathed auctions. None of the church's business staff liked attending them. But the work was vital, so they took the auctions in rotation. He dreaded the days when his turn came up.

"Lot eleven. Seventeen-thirty Hibiscus Lane, house and contents," the county employee recited. His voice was stripped of interest from handling two auctions a week, several dozen lots per auction. "Three bedrooms, living, dining, kitchen, half-acre lot, residential development, constructed seven years previously, occupied since new by current dispossessed, details in foreclosure documents supplied by First National Bank."

First National Bank of America was a fusion of banks from around the country. All of them had been so burdened by bad debts and failed bank-directed investments that only through federal intervention had they been salvaged. They were now part of a national bank governed directly by the Federal Deposit Insurance Corporation. Withdrawals were strictly limited, the rules tightening further with each passing month of increasingly bad news.

The county employee droned, "I have an opening bid for the house and all contents of twelve hundred dollars. Is there a second bid?"

Buddy stepped forward and offered the auctioneer a folded sheet of paper. Some of his staff preferred to bid in stages and follow the price up. Buddy hated prolonging the process one instant longer than necessary. Years of experience, both as a banker prior to the market meltdown and as the church's business director since then, had granted him a fairly solid idea of current market value. Buddy added 10 percent to his best estimate and offered it straightaway. He continually hoped someone at the church would object that his method was costing the church unnecessary funds, so he could quit going altogether.

A trio of men watched Buddy hand the paper to the auctioneer and muttered among themselves. Vultures, someone in the business office had once called them, and Buddy could not have agreed more. Two of them worked for out-of-state financiers; they were assigned to cover all the Delaware foreclosure auctions, picking up scraps from families' shattered dreams. The third had managed to escape being struck by the economic fallout, and he was striving now to become the area's largest landlord. Buddy had had ample experience with how he treated tenants who could not meet the monthly payments, often on houses they had once owned themselves. It was because of men like these that so many churches around the country had become involved in the property auctions.

As he returned to his place at the back of the throng, one of the vultures stepped into his path. "You're that Korda."

"Yes."

"Sure, I seen you around here before. And on TV." The man pulled on his trousers, trying to hitch them over his gut. "Which of you churches is the biggest landowner now?"

"I couldn't tell you."

"You guys are bound to be keeping score." A glance back at his fellows, sharing the smirk. "See which one's gonna come out on top."

"If you were offering a fair price and were willing to use your wealth to keep these families housed," Buddy countered, "there'd be no need for us to be involved at all."

The man snapped back, "You guys are gonna get your comeuppance soon enough."

Something in the man's tone kept Buddy where he was. "What are you talking about?"

"You just wait." Another glance to where the others were glowering and nodding agreement. "Think you church boys got it all fixed, well, this new administration in Washington is gonna straighten you out right quick."

A chill went through him. There had been rumors, scandalous remarks passed fearfully around the church meetings, things no one had been able to substantiate. "What have you heard?"

"You'll find out." A final glower and the man turned away. "The whole bunch of you is gonna be brought down hard, fast, and final."

The trio gathered and grumbled. Resentful glances were tossed his way as the auctioneer read off Buddy's paper, "I am offered eighteen thousand, six hundred and fifty dollars. Are there any higher offers? Eighteen six-fifty going once, going twice. Sold for eighteen six-fifty." He passed the sheaf of papers to the clerk seated behind his portable desk, hefted the next document, and read, "Lot twelve. Bulldozers and road-grading equipment, the former property of . . ."

Buddy shut out the litany of lost hope and shattered dreams. He filled out the forms, handed over his deposit, and hurried away, ignoring the angry grumbles that followed him from the hall.

Outside the bankrupt warehouse which the county had taken over for auctions, Buddy halted in front of four forlorn figures and announced, "It's all taken care of."

The man groaned in relief as his wife collapsed, weeping, into his arms. The older boy tried hard to remain stoic, but his younger sister was crying so hard she could scarcely shape the words, "Can we go home now, Mommy?"

"Yes." Buddy spoke the words around a jaw clamped tight. "The annual rent will be set just as we explained, at ten percent of the sales price plus taxes."

"I don't know if I can pay even that," the man mumbled.

"He lost his job," the woman explained. "The bank's even taken our car."

"We don't have anything else to sell," the man added.

"Come by the church's business office tomorrow," Buddy replied, searching the road behind them. Where was his backup team? "We'll try to help you sort something out. Do you have any groceries at home?"

"We'll see to that!" From the other side of the weed-strewn lot Alex slammed his car door and brandished his cane. "We got all that covered, little brother."

"Slow down, Alex," Agatha scolded, hustling to keep up with her husband. "You won't do anybody any good lying flat on your back."

"If you hadn't spent a half hour looking for your shoes we'd have been here in plenty of time." Alex huffed to a halt before the miserable gathering. "As if anybody in this crowd is gonna care one whit if her shoes don't match her dress."

"Oh, do be a good boy and shush." Agatha was a matriarch both of the church and local Aiden society. She was also Alex Korda's wife of one year and seven months. Nursing him back to remnants of good health had severely taxed Agatha. Yet through it all she had remained a bastion of the church relief group, there in answer to every need, paying for almost all of it from her own pocket. She still dressed the part, but as she had bought nothing new since the downturn her fine dark suit was frayed at the edges and her blouse was stained. Yet because her own eyesight was almost as bad as Alex's, it was hard to tell whether she even noticed. Alex certainly didn't.

Agatha carried a purse the size of a small suitcase. It landed at her feet with a solid thud. She opened her arms to the crying young girl. "Come here, dear one. It's all going to be just fine."

The girl flung herself at Agatha. The sight was enough to bring tears to her brother's eyes, but he fought hard for control. Agatha settled herself around the girl, enfolding her into a well-padded frame. She asked Buddy, "Did you win?"

"I wouldn't call purchasing a house from a foreclosure auction a win of any kind," Buddy replied, immensely glad to have them here with him.

"Don't quibble with me, Buddy Korda. I've had quite enough quibbling this morning from your brother."

Alex protested, "All I said was brown shoes would go fine with a blue dress."

"You did not and it never would." Agatha opened one arm in invitation to the wife. "How are you, Maggie darling?"

"Awful." She tugged her husband over so they could cluster with Agatha. "This is the worst day of my entire life."

"No it isn't. Not anymore." Agatha's briskness did nothing to mask the care and concern that shone from both her and Alex. Somehow their own suffering had transformed the pair into two of the most supportive people in the entire church. Whenever someone needed a listening ear, they sought out Alex and Agatha. Whoever was worried or frightened or damaged or alone, whoever needed someone to hold them or pray with them, the elder Kordas were there to show love.

"Last night might have been the worst," Alex intoned. "Or the day the sheriff arrived, I imagine that was pretty awful. Or when you lost your job, I bet—"

"Are you trying to make matters worse than they already are, Alex?"

"No, dearest. I was just saying—"

"I heard what you were saying." Drawing the trio tighter into her protective embrace, Agatha scolded, "You were standing there and listing all the horrid things you could think off. As if these poor people weren't hurting enough already."

Alex gave Buddy a very eloquent shrug. "Seems to me she was a mite more respectful before we walked the aisle."

Agatha shushed him with a look, then said to the family, "The house is still yours, dears. You have fifteen years to buy it back. Your rent goes toward the purchase price."

The husband looked not at Buddy but at Alex. "Is that true?"

"Come by the church office, I'll dig out the papers so you can read it for yourself. All down in black and white. Interest-free for the first five years."

Agatha stood there watching her husband, clearly waiting for something else. Finally she said, "Well?"

Alex glanced from her to Buddy and back. "Well, what?"

"I declare, Alex Korda, your memory is as bad as your vision."

"Oh, that." Alex cleared his throat, and announced, "I believe we've found you a new job."

The husband's face crumpled under the weight of his relief. "I don't know how we'll ever thank you."

"Thank God and help the next fellow in line," Alex said, waving his cane at Buddy. He was well aware of how much these times cost his younger brother. "You can get on back to the church, everything is under control here."

"Fine. I'll see—" Buddy stopped at the sound of a car racing up and screeching to a halt.

Reverend Patrick Allen leaned through the open window and waved urgently. "Buddy! Get over here!"

Something in Patrick's face drove Buddy's heart faster than his footsteps. He hustled over, bent down, and asked, "Is it Molly?"

"Get in, hurry, there's not a moment to lose." The pastor already had the car in gear. Before Buddy had settled into his seat, the vehicle was off and running.

Buddy offered a vague wave at the people he had left in front of the warehouse and asked, "What's the matter?"

"It's Anne." Patrick's face held to the same stone lines it had assumed in those dark days after losing his wife. "She's gone into labor."

Buddy felt a fist clench his gut. "The baby."

"Something's the matter." Patrick squealed his way through an intersection, wrestling the wheel with white-knuckle urgency. "They can't find a heartbeat."

─┤ FOUR ├─

☐ Patrick Allen followed Buddy through the hospital's main entrance, reflecting that this was about the only part of his job he genuinely loathed.

Pastoring a growing church through such times was definitely a job. A calling, most certainly. A passion, absolutely. A defining part of his life, so intertwined with his own spiritual walk that he could no longer separate the two. Trying to separate his walk into the work as pastor and the private worship of God would be as senseless as splitting breathing in from breathing out. He was a Christian and he was a pastor. He loved his work. It defined his life and his walk.

But it was also a job. And like every job, there were aspects that did not agree with him. Most especially visits with the sick. Most notably visits to this hospital.

He could not walk through these doors without recalling his own time of heartrending sorrow. He no longer asked or prayed that the wound would heal. He no longer even asked if this was the thorn that would always remain. After a year and a half, the loss of his beloved Alice was such an intimate part of him that it felt like his own heart, beating calmly and steadily and almost unnoticed. Except for times like now, when the beat of pain was disturbed, and it returned to the torrential pace that, for a time, he had thought would never end. And he was forced to feel anew the limb that had been cut from his tree of life and heart and family.

The hospital lobby was typical bedlam. Yet it had become such a commonplace scene for anyone who visited the sick, it no longer was cause for notice. The nation's physical health declined as steadily as the economy. Month by month the ranks of uninsured swelled. Many doctors in private practice were no longer seeing patients who could not pay for treatments in cash and up front. Which meant a growing portion of Americans could not afford a doctor's visit at all.

One of the new federal administration's earliest acts was an executive order requiring hospitals to treat all who came. This stripped clinics of the right to ask how payment would be made. To refuse anyone treatment, no matter how minor, was now a felony.

The result was perpetual anarchy.

The emergency room throng now spilled over to swamp the hospital's main lobby. Everything from common head colds to work-related injuries to the most serious illnesses were stretched out before him. Many of the staff wore white masks over their mouths and noses; over the past several months there had reportedly been outbreaks of TB and dysentery in some of the larger cities. These were rumors quickly quashed by the government, but still the fears lingered. The scene reminded Patrick of old war movies, with doctors and nurses and pastors and volunteers moving among the clamor and the throng. Babies screamed. Mothers wept. People moaned and called for help.

Buddy stopped and stared about him in stunned confusion. Patrick Allen placed a hand on his shoulder and guided him forward. He knew just how Buddy must feel. The first sight of a hospital these days was enough to stop anyone in their tracks.

Patrick guided Buddy past the reception desk where frantic people pressed three deep around its entire length. Together they walked down the hall, lined on both sides with patients on stretchers and portable beds. A local priest gave him a weary greeting as he passed. Although Associate Pastor Clarke Owen and his team had taken on most of the church's hospital duties, Patrick was still here often enough visiting parishioners that he knew almost all the doctors and clergy by their first names.

They went up to the third floor, walked down the long corridor with its relative quiet, and entered the maternity ward. As soon as Buddy pushed through the doors, Molly was up from the bench and rushing toward him. The scar that rose from her blouse to spread across her neck and chin burned a fierce red today. Patrick watched them melt together in an embrace that spoke of years and years of mutual support, and his lonely heart ached anew.

Paul, Anne's husband and Buddy's older boy, came over. He was a tall man, a throwback to Buddy's father. But today he was bowed so far over, Buddy did not need to reach up to draw him near. The three of them stood there in silent grief and love. Jack and Trish, Buddy's younger son and his wife, came over and offered Patrick the slow embrace of friends joined in sorrow.

Molly took a long unsteady breath, released her husband, and moved back a single step. The others drew near, until Patrick had joined with the family in a tight little circle. "The doctor came out a few minutes ago. It doesn't look good."

Paul gave the soft moan of a man who had never learned how to cry. Patrick felt the sound tear at his own heart's harshest memories, and he moved over to embrace the young man with all the strength and caring he could muster. He turned toward Molly. "How is Anne?"

"All the doctor said was, he hoped she would make it all right." The tears streamed unnoticed down Molly's cheeks. Her hands were now intertwined with Buddy's, and she leaned heavily against him.

"They wouldn't let me stay in there," Paul managed.

"It's probably best," Patrick said.

"But she needs me. I know . . ."

A silent signal drew them up and around. The doors leading back into the operating theater sighed back, and a very tired man walked through. He still wore surgical greens, and as he approached he stripped off his little cap, revealing prematurely graying hair. He walked straight over to Paul and said, "It looks like your wife will pull through."

"Thank God," Molly whispered. "Oh, thank God."

When Paul was not able to respond, Patrick asked for them all, "And the baby?"

"We've placed the child in an incubator to assist with the breathing." The doctor stared down at his shoes. It was all the signal they needed. In the corner of his eye, Patrick saw Trish lean her entire body upon her husband.

"The baby," Paul whispered, "is it a boy or a girl?"

"A little boy." When his words were greeted with silence, the doctor finished quietly, "We're doing all we can."

Paul moaned, "Can I see my wife?"

"She won't be coming out from under the anesthesia for a while yet. Give the nurses a moment to help her settle."

Because no one else was capable, Patrick said, "Thank you, Doctor."

The doctor nodded and turned away. When he was gone the tableau remained where it was, locked in the misery of being forced to accept the impossible. Reverend Patrick Allen waited with them, having learned that at such times no words were the right ones, nothing could be said to ease the burden. Silence and time and prayer were the only salves.

Molly finally was able to draw enough breath to say, "Let's all go sit down."

As they were walking together toward the plaid sofas by the window, Buddy halted in his tracks. Buddy Korda, a man Patrick had known for twenty years and more, a man who preferred nothing more than the quiet unseen corners of life, stiffened as though he had been hammered right between the eyes.

"Buddy?" Molly gripped his arm.

For a long moment Buddy stood stock-still, before finally taking a single, quivering breath.

Molly demanded, "Honey, is it your heart?"

"I'm all right." Buddy's voice sounded exhausted. "Help me sit down."

The others watched Molly help him over to the sofa. Buddy collapsed as though his bones had vanished with his strength. He sat there, staring at nothing.

Molly kept both hands gripped on his arm. "Do you want me to call the doctor?"

"I'm fine."

"What happened?"

"I'm not sure. I don't . . ." Buddy wiped his face with a shaking hand. "I have the strongest feeling that Anne and the baby are going to be all right."

There was a moment's pause, then Patrick asked, "Is that all?"

Molly did not look up from her husband to respond, "Isn't that enough?"

Patrick did not reply. He did not need to ask why he felt so disturbed by Buddy's seeming good news. No. What remained a mystery, however, was why Buddy looked sick with anxiety as well.

⊣| FIVE |⊢

☐ Royce Calder went straight from the White House staff conference to a meeting with officials from the Treasury on the Russian debt crisis, and from there to congressional subcommittee hearings on the FDIC's ever-expanding role. This was followed by some arm-twisting on Capitol Hill on two upcoming Party-sponsored bills, and then a rush back to the OEOB for a meeting with his own handpicked team.

As soon as Royce Calder returned to his office early that evening, he knew the president's chief of staff was a man of his word. His assistant rose to his feet as Royce entered and parodied a standing ovation. "Bravo to you, sir."

Royce played at confusion. "For what?"

"Put me out of my misery. Tell me you are taking me with you when you climb to the farthest reaches."

"Oh, that." Royce gave his quiet little smile. "It hasn't happened yet."

"When it does, then."

Royce examined the tall, delicate young man, and could find only genuine concern. "How did you hear?"

"*Everybody* knows about it. I've had about a dozen calls, all wanting to know if they can ride your coattails to the stars." Three months earlier, Elton Hardaway had been foisted on him by the top ranking minority senator, who had been surprised when Royce had not only accepted the man without a murmur, but actually thanked the senator sincerely. There was nothing that Royce liked as much as a good challenge. The young man had arrived sulky and disdaining the assignment to an unknown like Royce Calder, stuck in the boonies of the OEOB. A far cry from the eager assistant with the gleaming hair who now said, "I can well imagine they will line your path with palm fronds when you make your way over to the big house today."

Elton was from a powerful New York family, and favored hand-cut suits and solid-gold Rolexes. He had assumed his family connections and money and a degree from Harvard and three years working state politics would be enough to instantly grant him a position as a White House legislative assistant—LA for short. He had sought every quiet way possible to show his contempt for Royce and this indifferent posting.

At work, Elton had expressed a limp-wristed scorn with every motion. He had made passing over a telephone message an insult. Elton had spent his first few days punctuating Royce's every passage through the outer office with loud sniffs. He had swiftly become a favorite of the Washington cocktail circuit, and had made public his impatience to move closer to the throne.

Royce did not do what Elton had expected, which was to scream and shout and race to higher-ups with a demand that the laggard be transferred or shot, preferably the latter. Instead, Gladys and Jerry, Royce's two top allies within the OEOB, had stopped by several times. Patiently they had explained how getting fired was far from the worst thing that could happen. LA's come and go, they explained, and the proper question Elton needed to be asking was, Go where? They told the story of the staff assistant who had assumed he was protected by privilege, just like Elton, but was now counting salmon boats in the disputed waters off Washington state. A cold place to spend a winter, Royce's allies had said. A hard transfer to explain to Daddy.

Now when Royce entered the room, he was greeted with a bounce and a smile. Elton followed Royce into his office with pencil and pad at the ready, fresh coffee brewing in the alcove behind the door, the works. All without Royce having to say a word.

Royce headed for his desk and asked, "Are the fellows ready?"

"Straining at the leash."

"Tell them to come on down." After a moment's hesitation, Royce decided it was time to extend the invitation, "Why don't you join us today."

This was the weekly meeting of Royce's trusted cadre, all of whom had worked with him for years in one guise or another. They might have been separated by states or duties or allegiances to different houses of Congress, but they were first and foremost loyal to the only clan Royce knew, their Party. As with Royce, working close to this new administration was reward for a lifetime of fidelity. The power was finally theirs.

There were nine of them, three women and six men. None of them were particularly attractive or magnetic, which was to be expected. Anyone who had been blessed with television looks as well as the ambition and intelligence of these people would have gone in for elected politics.

The last to join them was Royce's number one, Jerry Chevass. His official title was Director of Public Liaison, which meant precisely nothing. Jerry came in with a box of jelly-roll doughnuts in one hand, a pile of papers in the other, both arms waving over his head like a pom-pom dancer making an entry. With his glasses down at the end of his nose and his gut bouncing with each step, Jerry Chevass looked like the clown he was. "All right, all right, let's hear it for the home team."

"Oh goodie, goodies," cooed Gladys Knight, Royce's second principal ally, known to one and all as Pips. She was a huge woman with a main-frame computer for a brain, a font of every statistic from baseball to barrels of Anchorage oil. "The gooiest ones are all mine."

Royce waited while Elton poured fresh coffee for everyone, Elton's way of ingratiating himself into this tight inner circle. As he freshened Gladys's cup, she rubbed the edge of his jacket between thumb and forefinger. "Nice," she said. "What is it, Armani?"

"Valentino," Elton replied.

Gladys turned to Royce. "Where do I get me one of these?"

"Oh, Elton is definitely one of a kind," Royce Calder replied.

Now that Elton was admitted to the clan, now that his loyalty was correctly focused, all past indiscretions were forgotten. After all, every one of them had stumbled at least once. Gladys raised her dimpled chin and gave the willowy blond man a cold smile. "Come up to the third floor, dearie. We're a much nicer bunch up there. Hot and cold running interns, no heavy lifting, light phone duty. Besides, the view's much better from my office. Royce's view of the big house is blocked by all those trees."

"Thanks," Elton replied smugly, and seated himself against the far wall, "but I'd much prefer the view from inside. Which is apparently where Royce is taking me."

Jerry Chevass asked, "So when are we moving home?"

"We're not, as far as I know." Royce held up a hand to halt the derision. "Any insertion into the upper ranks is contingent upon success with the matter at hand."

"You traded the tax bill passage for Oakridge's office," Gladys surmised. "Oh, you naughty boy."

"That and something more," Royce said. "Eldridge is a tough nut. I have to deliver not one, but two impossibles."

"That's what he called them, impossibles?"

"His very words."

"Then we'll just have to do like the marines," Gladys replied. "You know their motto. 'The difficult we do immediately, the impossible we do for a price.'"

"Okay, here's the play. We're now officially off the church-tax legislative count." Royce endured a moment of groans and comments about how Harold, the legislative aide, would muck up their hard work, then continued, "It's done, people. Let's leave it behind. We are now on two different issues. First, damage control with the conservatives in the House. Second, assuming we get the votes, maneuvering this new tax law through the courts."

"If it is challenged," Jerry murmured. "Which it will be."

"Let's leave the legal issue for a moment. I want to know how we can build a fire wall against the conservative backlash."

"Those religious gits are always getting in the way," Gladys griped. "Shame we can't just bring them out of the box when it's time to vote."

Royce gave them another moment for grousing over the Party's religious wing. It was a constant refrain. They needed the religious vote, counted on it in every close election—and what election wasn't tight these days? But the rest of the time they were shunned.

It was a fact of American political life that power was split in a way few people realized. On the one side was the public arena of politicians and political offices and campaigns and votes. The Party's religious wing was awesome in this stadium. They were driven by *issues,* and these days issues drove as many campaigns as candidates. As long as *issues* were at stake, the Party could count on their religious cohorts to work tirelessly.

But there was another side to politics, one that, thankfully, the religious wing rarely invaded. And that was *Party* politics. Thanks to the fact that issues were almost never decided upon within Party conferences, the religious wing steered clear. They had families to raise and values to uphold. Party politics was full of smoky backroom deals and playing one side against another—things the religious wing with their rigid attitudes could never understand. So rather than fight the establishment, they ignored it. Which suited people like Royce Calder just fine.

This was also why not one of the Party's cadre planted within the current White House regime was drawn from the religious wing, even though over *50 percent* of the votes that had propelled the current president into office could be claimed by that wing. The Party cadre was drawn from the Party faithful, people who had made a lifetime of Party politics. People whose first loyalty remained unswervingly focused upon the Party.

"Enough," Royce declared. "I don't need complaints. I need answers. How do we stop the religious conservatives before they attack?"

A young woman by the back wall suggested, "How about a counter-strike?"

"Won't work," Gladys declared flatly. "Too public."

"Gladys is right. We need something that will stop them without confronting them."

"Chop them off at the knees," Jerry agreed.

"Right. Something that will take the power out of their protests."

Elton spoke for the first time. "Like a traitor?"

"Wouldn't that be nice," Gladys said.

"Someone who sees the light and converts to our side," Jerry agreed. "I love it."

"But it won't happen," Gladys said. As the seniors in the room along with Royce, Gladys and Jerry customarily stood center stage. "They stick together like superglue."

"It's not a bad idea, though," Royce mused. "Maybe we could find someone inside their ranks whom everybody knows. Somebody who . . ."

Gladys was watching him and smiling. "I believe the lightbulb just went off."

"Maybe." Royce felt that gut-tightening thrill of an idea that would work. "That man who made the prediction about the market meltdown and then disappeared into the boonies."

A trio of voices shouted, "Korda!"

"Buddy Korda," Jerry Chevass said, grinning now. "It's perfect."

"We know he likes the limelight," Gladys said. "Did you see that guy on CNN? All he needed was a staff and a beard and he could have popped right out of a Cecil B. DeMille movie."

Royce wanted to stand up and pace, but he kept himself firmly attached to the seat, and held his voice to the same soft-spoken tone. "So he liked the spotlight. He made his prediction. He disappeared. But everybody knows about him. The mystery man who came out of nowhere and warned of this economic collapse and vanished again."

"They played that tape of him again the other night," Gladys said with a sneer. "Only now they're accusing him of a self-fulfilling prophecy. The economists say he scared so many people they jerked the market out of its positive course and sent it into a tailspin."

"Makes sense," Jerry said.

"It doesn't matter." Royce had to let a trace of his smile into view. "What concerns us is how the religious wing still thinks this guy had a message from on high. So what we want is to see if we can get him down here to Washington. And have him meet with the president. One-on-one."

"Beautiful," Gladys conceded. "Nobody applies the pressure like our top guy."

"Are you kidding?" Jerry's voice had risen a notch with the excitement. "Forty years of politics, the guy is an international grand master at arm-twisting. This Korda character won't know what hit him. We're talking trampled down, totally flattened roadkill."

"What we want," Royce reminded the room, "is for the man to come out saying that the country is ailing and needs every spare dime in tax money it can find. And that it has been unfair for the churches to be a haven for those who profited from the decline to park their gains."

"President Bradley Gifford," Gladys said, nodding emphatically. "He's your man. He'll bring Korda around in about three heartbeats."

"Okay. Enough on that. I want you people to get together and prepare a second scenario. Something we can use as a fallback." Royce rose to his feet, signaling an end to the meeting. Then another thought hit him. "Elton, it was your idea. Perhaps we should let you call Korda and invite him down to meet the president."

The young man positively gleamed. "Leave it with me."

Gladys asked, "What about the legal angle?"

"I'm meeting with someone about that tomorrow." Calder turned to Elton, "Call Eldridge and say I need to see him. Urgently."

⊣∣ SIX ∣⊢

☐ Patrick Allen approached Buddy's front door for the first time in over a year and a half, yet had no idea whatsoever why he had come. Nonetheless he rang the doorbell and presented a smile when Molly opened the door.

"Hello, Patrick." Her position in the doorway held her halfway between the night shadows and the hall light. Her face was creased by the day's strains. "How are you?"

"Fine, Molly. I'm fine."

Her gaze pierced deep. "No, you're not. You're no more fine than I am."

He allowed his shoulders to sag. "I thought I was avoiding a visit here because of Buddy. Now I'm not so sure."

"So. Now truth is entering with you. That is good. We're all too tired and too worried to hold to anything but pure truth tonight." She pushed the door open wider and took a step back. "We've missed you. Would you like a cup of coffee?"

"Coffee sounds good, thank you." He followed her inside, disarmed by her frankness and her fatigue. "How is Anne?"

"Hold your voice down in here. We're keeping their girls, and I just got them into bed. They were as tired as two little ragamuffins." She led him down the hall and into the kitchen. "Paul just called from the hospital. Anne is resting. He didn't say, but I gathered she's had a hard go of it."

"And the baby?"

"Paul doesn't know." Molly revealed a glimmer of her woes. "I can only hope and pray what Buddy said about their recovery is right."

"We'll be praying for you."

"Thank you." She walked over and hugged him. Hard. "Oh, it's good to see you here again. It's been too long."

The feeling of her arms, even when he had been released, caused him to say, "You're not asking why I haven't stopped by before now?"

"I know why you haven't come. Why should I ask what I already know?" Molly walked to the cupboard and pulled down a cup. "A man from your congregation explodes into national prominence with a message from God. He usurps your position as head of this church, as leader. His message ends, and he returns home." As she poured his coffee, she went on, "Then a personal cataclysm erupts. Your wife falls ill. You beg him to intercede for you, which I am certain was one of the hardest things you have ever done in your life."

"Awful," Patrick murmured, studying this quiet woman and wondering if he had ever really understood who Molly Korda was. "Coming over here that night felt like I was tearing the soul from my body."

"Of course it would. Why couldn't you ask God for help yourself? But God had not answered your prayers, and your wife was dying, and you had to try everything." She set his mug down on the counter between them, slid over milk and sugar. "I'll never forget how you looked that night, never in all my life. Standing there on our front porch, the rain pouring down like the heavens themselves were weeping for you and for Alice and for this whole poor country. Your clothes were dripping wet, you didn't notice a thing. You didn't even come inside. You just stood there and you begged Buddy to speak to God for you."

"Not for me," Patrick whispered, sipping at coffee he could not taste. "For Alice."

"Yes. Of course. And what did Buddy do but stand there and say certainly he would come, he would lay hands on your wife, he would pray. But he could do nothing. He was no more or no less than any other servant here on God's earth. But he came because you needed him. He went and he came back late that night. And when I came downstairs, I found my husband standing in our front hall weeping for the first time in his adult life."

"I didn't know that," Patrick confessed.

"Crying like a baby. Weeping and saying all he ever brought anyone was bad news. He wanted no more of it, not ever." Molly blinked hard, pushing back the pain. "He didn't cry at Alice's funeral, you know. He had cried himself dry that night after coming back from the hospital."

"Molly . . ." He found himself unable to say anything. So many emotions jammed in tightly he could get nothing out. Patrick retreated behind his cup, then asked, "Is Buddy in his study?"

"Yes." As he turned toward the door she stopped him with, "Prophets are a lonely lot, Patrick. Especially out-of-work prophets. They are yesterday's news. Stale oddities." She fastened him with a pleading gaze. "You know what they say about friends? If you have a good one, you don't need a mirror. Go be a friend to my Buddy."

□

Patrick remained so rattled by Molly's words that he walked down the hall and knocked and entered and started straight in, as though Buddy was a friend of many years, rather than a quiet little man who came and went and scarcely disturbed the air in his passage.

Patrick shut the door carefully, then said, looking at his hand resting there on the knob, "I know this isn't a good time. But after seeing you in the hospital today, I knew it was either come and talk with you or not sleep until I did. Buddy, the news around the church today has left me waiting for the next bomb to go off."

He stopped and waited for the challenge. When Buddy remained silent, Patrick turned to face him. "I need to know, Buddy. Alex told me you had received another dream. A message. Is that true?"

Buddy remained seated by the unlit fire, staring at the empty space with eyes as sad as any Patrick had ever seen. The months had taken their toll on Buddy as well. He was not stooped, but he bore his weariness like an older man, submitting to it in silence, hoping the strength would return. His hair was far more gray than dark now, and the lines of his face sagged with his shoulders, bowed and burdened.

Patrick closed the distance between them, halted by the chair on the coffee table's opposite side, and said, "Buddy?"

"I don't know," Buddy mumbled to the fireplace and the ashes. "I just don't know."

"You don't know if it was from God, or if you can tell me?"

"If I'm not certain it's come from God, *should* I tell you?" He turned his anguished gaze toward Patrick. "How do I know if it's God's word? How can I tell?"

Patrick felt for the chair behind him, not wanting to take his eyes from Buddy's face. "This is the last thing I expected to hear from you."

"Why, because I had a message before? What difference does that make now? Does getting it right once mean I'll never have it wrong?"

Patrick found himself relaxing by degrees. "Not necessarily. But your hearing so clearly before makes me more confident about what you might be hearing now."

"*Might* be hearing." The words pushed his gaze back to the fireplace. "But what if I'm wrong?"

Patrick Allen eased himself back in the chair. Forced himself to push aside the fact that this was God's messenger who was revealing his human side. He forced himself to *listen*. And what his heart said in that first moment of listening was that what he heard was not Buddy's deepest concern. "What makes you think you might have misunderstood?"

"I . . . That night . . ." Suddenly he could no longer remain still. The tension plucked Buddy up like puppet's strings. "I had a dream."

Patrick waited, and when Buddy did not seem to find the strength to continue alone, he offered, "Your first message started with a dream, do I remember that correctly?"

"That's right." The study was not wide enough to permit much pacing, yet Buddy jerked through three quick strides to the back window. "This one seemed so powerful, I thought, well . . ."

"You thought it was starting all over again." Patrick found he could express that thought without the dread he had felt on the drive over. He was not speaking to a prophet here. He was speaking to a frightened member of his flock. A man who desperately needed a friend. "You thought God was calling you."

"Not right then, in the middle of the night. Well, not consciously." A quick turnaround and Buddy paced to the bookshelves. "When it happened it was so intense there was nothing but the experience. The next morning, Molly was actually the first to suggest God was calling me."

"And Alex?"

"Alex. He asked me point-blank. I wanted to deny it because if I didn't, he'd climb up on the church roof and shout it to the world."

"A joke," Patrick said. "Good. I'm glad to hear you've still got your sense of humor."

"It's not humor. It's fear. Sheer solid blue funk. Am I listening to the wrong voice here?"

Patrick checked his immediate response. He was gripped by a powerful sensation that this was not the genuine question on Buddy's heart. It seemed to him that not even Buddy knew why he was so disturbed. As though it was easier to fasten upon this uncertainty than to search more deeply and see the true reason for his fear.

Patrick found himself feeling closer to Buddy in that moment than he ever had before. "Tell me the dream, friend."

"My dream." The words turned him around and headed him back toward the window. He stared blindly at his own reflection and beyond that, the mystery of night. "I was standing before a door. A closed door. One I knew. The door, I mean. I knew it instantly. But now that the dream is over I can't find it." Buddy closed his eyes and leaned his forehead against the pane. "Hour after hour I wonder if maybe the reason why the door can't be found is because I wasn't good enough. Because of all my failings I couldn't just find the door and open it."

Patrick started to protest, to point out that this was not the same fear Buddy had spoken of earlier. But even before the words were framed he settled back. The same listening heart told him *this* was not the central point either. Buddy was throwing out one worry after another, as though fleeing what he truly feared by seeking something else to fret over. "Buddy."

Something in his voice turned the smaller man around. "Yes?"

"God is well aware that we are all human. And inadequate." Patrick wanted to probe further, yet felt not so much held back as *cautioned*. So he simply asked, "Is that the dream?"

"Not all. I reached out and opened the door. And there before me was . . ."

Buddy made his way over to the chair opposite Patrick. Slowly he seated himself, and said softly, "There before me was this beautiful, glorious sense of *hope*. I think a person was standing there, but I'm not sure. What I remember most is not the sight but the feeling. Since all this started, I have never felt such a sense of comfort and healing. It felt like, well, like an invitation. Like a promise." Buddy waited through several breaths, then added,

"Then when I woke up I had the strongest feeling that I was being called to Washington."

"The capital?"

Buddy nodded, and the fear in his voice and his eyes seemed to multiply with each movement. "But I still haven't found the door." The words began rushing out. "Maybe it doesn't exist. I've been wondering about that. Maybe it was just symbolic, and I need to find the answer. Spend more time studying the Scriptures."

"I think . . ." Patrick hesitated at the sound of the doorbell. "Do you need to answer that?"

Buddy shook his head. "Molly will see to it."

Patrick waited for the sound of Molly's footsteps. He recalled stories from people who had visited the Kordas in the meltdown's early days. Back when national attention was still turned his way, back when Buddy had been heard to describe his own front door as a nightmare come to life. For weeks Buddy had hidden inside his study or at the back of the house, emerging into his own garden only around dawn or twilight.

Alex had been in the worst throes of chemotherapy then, and Buddy had taken to disguising himself in long raincoats and droopy hats and sunglasses and lying under blankets in the backseat as his sons drove him to the hospital and back. Two months after the economic crash, when attention had been pulled away by multiplying crises, Buddy had finally returned to church duties. He had refused to speak about his mission or his message. If asked he would simply walk away. People learned not to discuss it anywhere near him. Patrick had observed all this from a distance; he had wanted nothing to do with memories of those times. Nothing at all.

Patrick filled the waiting with, "Do you have any idea why He might want you to travel?"

"None at all. I don't know a soul in Washington." Buddy halted as the doorbell rang a second time. "I hope the girls don't wake up. Did Molly go out?"

"The last I saw she was back in the kitchen." Patrick watched the worry lines grow across Buddy's forehead, and offered, "I'll go see who it is."

Buddy showed genuine relief. "All right."

By the time Patrick had risen and crossed the study, the bell had sounded a third time. Patrick opened the study door and called, "Coming!"

Buddy appeared in the doorway behind him and called, "Molly?"

"I hear her voice in the kitchen. Maybe she's on the phone." Patrick started across the hall.

But as Patrick reached for the knob, a voice called out from behind him, "Wait!"

Patrick turned back. The question forming in his throat was halted by the look in Buddy's eyes.

Buddy stared at his own front door in shock and awe.

A light tread moved quickly from the back of the house. Molly appeared by the stairway and asked, "Did somebody call my name?"

Patrick kept his gaze on Buddy as he asked, "You didn't hear the door-bell?"

"It hasn't rung," she protested.

"Three times," Patrick replied.

"It can't have. I was on the phone, but I know I would have heard it." She turned to her husband, "You won't believe who that was. Somebody at the White House, they want you to come down for a conference." The doorbell sounded again. "Oh my."

Buddy crossed to the door, then hesitated a long moment before gripping the handle. "It's here. Right here. The whole time I was coming and going and never even thought it was my own door . . ."

Molly exchanged a wide-eyed look with Patrick, then they both turned to watch Buddy open the door.

Patrick craned to see over Buddy's shoulder. Before them stood one of the most striking women he had ever seen. "M-Mr. Korda?"

"Yes." Buddy opened the door wider. "Please come in."

"I'm . . . My name is Linda Kee." She remained nervously fastened to her place on the doorstep. "I don't even know what I'm doing here."

She was in her late twenties, perhaps early thirties. It was hard to tell. She was a mélange of colors and races. Her long hair flowed like a jet-black river over one shoulder. Her skin was the color of a permanent tan, neither Hispanic nor Caucasian but rather somewhere in between. Her pronounced cheekbones gave her face a distinct Oriental cast, yet her eyes were the most piercing blue Patrick had ever seen.

He also had the distinct impression he had met her before, which was ridiculous. Because Patrick was absolutely certain that if he had ever been introduced to this woman, even in passing, even for the tiniest instant, he would never in all his days have forgotten her.

Buddy backed away from the door and repeated, "Please do come in, Mrs. Kee. Did I say that right?"

"Yes. Kee. But it's Miss." She was tall and willowy, extremely attractive and equally intelligent. And very familiar.

Buddy asked, "Why are you here?"

"I wish I knew." Hesitantly she took a single step across the threshold. She gripped her purse with both hands, holding the clasp so tightly her knuckles glowed white. "I was in a church and I went up and touched the foot of the Cross, and I didn't *feel* anything but I thought, I thought . . ." Her astonishingly shaped eyes moved from one face to the other, begging for someone to say it all made sense. "I remembered how my father said he had seen a video of your talk and invested some money, and now two of my brothers are out of work and they're living from this money. And as I stood there, it seemed to me that I *had* to come up and thank you."

She looked down at the hands gripping her purse and mumbled, "You've probably had thousands of people do the exact same thing and you're fed up with them. The entire train ride up here from Washington I have been asking myself what on earth I'm doing."

"Washington." Buddy seemed to deflate over the word. Patrick pulled his gaze away from the young woman to stare at his friend. The look of ancient sorrow had returned to Buddy's gaze. "Of course. Washington."

─┤┠ SEVEN ┠├─

☐ "Thank you very much for giving me a lift."

"It's no problem. I'm going in this direction anyway." That sounded coldly formal, so Patrick added, "My sons have basketball practice tonight, and their school is right up the street from the motel we've booked you into."

"It was nice of the Kordas to invite me to stay. But it looked like they had their hands full with the grandchildren." Linda Kee glanced out her side window. "I'll need to stop this knee-jerk reaction of mine of pulling into whatever hotel is nearest whenever I grow tired. I've been on the road so much and for so long, it's hard to change. But I need to start saving money."

Patrick glanced over, saw nothing but the long dark hair as the woman kept her face turned toward the window. He detected the new sorrow in those words. "You've lost your job?"

"On Friday." Linda kept to as matter-of-fact a tone as she could. "I lived for my work. That's all I had, all I knew. Now I don't . . ."

Patrick stopped at a light and glanced over. Linda Kee turned to reveal those strange eyes with their Oriental slant yet colored sapphire blue. He still could not get over the feeling that he knew her from somewhere. "Excuse me for asking, but have we met?"

She hesitated a long moment, then said, "I don't think so." Another silence, then, "I feel like such a fool. Coming all this way and not even knowing why. Pressing myself on Mr. Korda when they've got sickness in the family and you—"

"I've got two teenage kids who are probably starving by now," Patrick finished for her. "Have you had dinner?"

"I don't think I even had lunch."

"Why don't you join us for dinner. That is, if you think you can stomach the table manners of two teenage boys eating pizza."

"Pizza sounds fine." She tasted her first smile of the journey. "And I've got a lot of experience handling teenage boys."

"Younger brothers?"

"Five of them. And all of them have kids of their own now. I've got eleven nieces and nephews."

"Wow."

"Yup, I'm the disgrace of the clan." But the words were spoken without the quiet sorrow of before. "My family has pretty much given up on me."

Patrick drove past the church and turned into the high school's rear parking lot. "Perhaps I should say this before the marauders strike. You said it seemed foolish for you to come up to Aiden today." He hid his hesitation by leaning forward and searching the night for two familiar silhouettes, then decided that he was revealing no confidences by saying, "Buddy has been called down to Washington."

That snapped her around. "What?"

"The White House telephoned just before you arrived." Two forms broke off from the cluster of kids and parents by the gym's back entrance and came racing over, backpacks bouncing on their shoulders. "They want him to come down and take part in some conference."

The boys spotted the passenger and piled into the backseat. "Hi, Dad."

Patrick swiveled around and said, "Good practice?"

"Great." The younger boy grinned. "I got my first slam dunk."

"Right," his elder brother scoffed. "Only because Tim Rughers boosted you six feet in the air."

He aimed a lazy slug at his brother. "Did not."

"Enough already. Jeff, Scott, say hello to Linda . . . I'm sorry, I've forgotten your last name."

"Kee. Linda Kee." She turned around and offered the boys a brilliant smile. Patrick found himself jealous that they were the recipients of that incredible flashing smile—and surprised he would feel anything like that at all. She asked, "Which is which?"

The two boys had suddenly become incredibly well-behaved for a pair of hyper teens, sitting upright and staring ahead, rather than turning their seats into combat trampolines. The elder offered, "I'm Scott. He's Jeff."

"It's nice to meet you both."

Patrick shrugged off their sudden quiet as merely their reaction to seeing their father seated alongside an attractive stranger. "How does pizza strike you two?"

"Pizza sounds fine, Dad." That was Scott. The younger boy said nothing at all. Another mystery. Simply mentioning pizza was usually enough to send Jeff into low-altitude orbit.

"My sons would eat pizza three times a day if they could," Patrick explained to Linda. He returned the wave of another parent and pulled away.

Linda nodded as though that made perfect sense. "If there is such a thing as a pizza addict, I would certainly qualify."

Scott offered, "Jeff once tried to make pizza ice cream in the blender."

"That's nothing," Jeff countered, finally finding his voice. "When Scott had his tonsils out, he asked the doctor if they could put pepperoni in the drip."

Patrick smiled, happy to see them responding so well to having a stranger in the car. Usually they were resentful of people imposing themselves on the little private time they managed to have. "I have to warn you, sitting at a table with my two boys and a pizza is dangerous business."

"Dad calls Jeff his walking grenade," Scott explained. "He doesn't eat a pizza, he explodes into it."

"And he says *you* can scarf down a whole deep-pan pizza without swallowing," Jeff countered. To Linda he went on, "Dad says Scott is the family's own personal human Hoover."

"When I was a kid," Linda said, "I used to practice mouth-stretching exercises just so I could get a whole slice of pizza in at once."

Through the rearview mirror Patrick caught a glimpse of Scott and Jeff exchanging grins. Something that had once been such a normal part of their lives that he scarcely gave it a second thought. Now, he found the sight attached to so many memories and so many absences that a hole was branded right through the center of his chest.

He pulled into the restaurant's parking lot and cut the engine. The three passengers were up and out as if they were attached to springboards, Linda clearly enjoying the sparring contest. Patrick sat there a moment, trying to get his breathing back in line with his body. As he slowly crossed the lot behind them, he found himself wondering if the past would ever stop pouncing on him like this.

When he finally entered the restaurant, he found the boys standing and grinning beside the hostess's stand. "Where's Linda?"

"She wanted to wash her hands." Scott resembled his father, at fifteen years already touching six feet and sporting a cleft chin and solid shoulders. It disturbed Patrick more than he could ever say to enter the school and hear some young girl describe his older boy as a hunk. Scott was dressed in shirt and sweater and chinos, only the effect was lost by the clothes having been stuffed in the bottom of his gym locker. He gave his dad a look of wonder. "Where did you *meet* her?"

"At Buddy and Molly's."

"She's *great*," Jeff offered. Jeff was so much like his departed wife that there had been moments in those early days when Patrick had found it difficult to even look his way. Jeff was slighter in build and far more sensitive than his older brother. Alice had been the one to make Jeff bloom, urging him to accept his nature and not feel called to follow the crowd. Alice had introduced Jeff to opera and classical music and art museums, things that had never entered Patrick's orbit. Alice had encouraged Jeff's voracious reading habit and found a retired English professor who had been willing to tutor him. For months after the funeral, Patrick had been terribly concerned if Jeff would pull through at all. Which was why it was genuinely shocking to hear his younger son express with true delight, "This is totally unreal. We're going to have pizza with Linda Kee."

"Wait 'til the guys hear about this," Scott agreed.

Patrick stared at his boys in confusion. "You know her?"

His sons exchanged a look of pure astonishment. Scott demanded, "You don't recognize her?"

"I don't *believe* this," Jeff said.

"Recognize who?"

Scott gaped at him. "Dad, come on."

Jeff gripped his stomach in a parody of mirth and gave a rolling ho-ho-ho.

Scott said, "Dad, think a second. *Linda Kee*."

Patrick stared at his younger boy, tried to remember the last time Jeff had shown mirth in public. Years. It had to have been years. "I'm thinking as hard as I can and I'm drawing a total blank."

Jeff was ho-ho-ing now so hard he had to support himself on the hostess's stand.

"This is totally unreal." Scott gave his father the kind of look possible only when a teenager is observing an adult caught acting like an adult. "Dad, the television. The news. Washington."

Recognition slapped Patrick Allen upside the head. That was exactly how it felt. Which was why, when Linda pushed through the rest room door and started toward him, Patrick was standing there with his mouth hanging open.

"Look at Dad," Scott said, catching his brother's glee.

Jeff was laughing too hard to respond. Patrick said to Linda, "I feel like such a fool."

"This is great," Scott said. "Dad didn't recognize you."

"It's all right," Linda said, holding to the poise that could only come with long duty in the public eye. "Really."

"I can't believe I asked if we had ever met," Patrick said.

"Look how red Dad is."

Patrick allowed the hostess to take them over to a table. When they were seated and the menus deposited, he said, "About six months ago they started insisting that it was CBS News or nothing at all. I thought it was a school assignment or something."

"Dad always was a little slow," Jeff said, which was enough to start off another bout of ho-ho-ing.

"Then whenever Peter Rudd mentioned Washington, they started cheering," Patrick continued. "That was when I finally caught on."

Linda gave the boys a little half-smile. "Glad to know I've had a positive effect on your education."

Jeff pointed and said, "Look, look, it's the smile!"

Patrick had to agree. That's exactly what it was. Linda Kee had this signature way of signing off whenever she was reporting, usually with the White House or Capitol Building in the background. She would look straight at the camera and draw up a smile that canted her features slightly over to the right. "You'd better be careful, this is the point where my two sons start howling at the moon. Smiling at them now could be a serious case of overkill."

Their waiter chose that moment to come over. "Hi, my name is . . ." He stared at Linda, the smile still in place, and his hands dropped to his sides. "Oh, wow."

Scott said to Jeff, "Is this the greatest or what."

The waiter said to Linda, "It's not really you, is it?"

Jeff beamed at the poor guy. "Sure is."

Scott added, "And our dad didn't recognize her."

The waiter dragged his attention to Patrick. "You've got to be kidding."

"I thought we were here to eat pizza," Patrick said, trying to sound cross.

"Right." The waiter raised his notepad, but his eyes had tracked back to Linda. "You know what you want?"

Patrick warned her, "Prepare yourself for the worst."

Scott and Jeff said in unison, "Two deep-dish pizzas with pepperoni, sausage, Canadian bacon, sweet corn, and extra cheese!"

"They've been practicing that a lot," Patrick explained.

"That sounds perfect," Linda said. "Make that three."

Scott and Jeff exchanged delighted beams. Patrick sighed his defeat and said, "A thin-crust cheese pizza and a green salad."

"Dad's on a sort of permanent diet," Scott explained.

"Which is supposed to be kept a family secret," Patrick reminded his son.

The waiter wrote without looking anywhere but straight at Linda. "Drinks?"

The order for colas went straight around, then as the waiter departed Scott predicted, "The state that waiter's in, we'll probably wind up with tuna and mushroom pizzas with extra anchovies."

Linda turned to Patrick. "It's a shame my sponsors don't count teenage boys as their ideal marketing audience." She explained to his sons, "I was fired this week."

The two boys looked positively stricken. Scott said, "That's awful."

"They can't do that," Jeff protested.

"Afraid they can," Linda replied. It cost her dearly, but she managed to hold on to her matter-of-fact tone. "I was the last hired, and there are cutbacks everywhere. Even in the Washington bureau of CBS News."

Patrick excused himself. As he made his way through the room, he noticed heads emerging from the kitchen doors. When he returned he found more and more attention being turned their way. To his surprise, he found he did not mind.

A far greater astonishment awaited him upon his return to the table. As he slid into his seat, he realized the boys were talking with Linda about their mother. He was so shocked he pushed back from his seat, wanting to put more distance between himself and the table. Granting him a space to sit back and observe. In the eighteen months since the funeral, his boys had found it difficult to speak about Alice's passage even with him. And yet here they were, Scott nodding and looking somber yet calm, as Jeff said, "The hardest thing about it was how fast everything happened. I mean, it seemed like one day she was talking about the flu and the next she was going into the hospital."

"Everybody's been real nice about it," Scott offered. "At the church, I mean."

Linda turned a very sad face his way and said, "I'm so sorry."

Patrick found a sudden lump in his throat, one he had trouble forcing down, which was as strange as everything else about this entire discussion. Having one more person express sympathy over their loss should not affect him; it seemed the whole world had stopped by at one time or another to offer condolences.

She seemed to understand his silence, for she turned back to the boys and said, "You both seem to be handling it extremely well."

"It's been really hard," confessed Jeff.

Patrick stared at his son. That had to rank as the understatement of the year. Jeff had stopped speaking at all for almost two months.

"Sports have helped too," Scott offered. "Jeff made the high school junior varsity team this year."

"And Scott is a starter on the varsity."

"This has to be basketball. The high school football season's been over for what, three months?"

Jeff and Scott showed genuine pleasure that she would know such a thing. "Dad used to quarterback for Carolina."

"The Tarheels. Wow. Champions of the Atlantic Coast Conference so many times they've stopped counting." To Patrick she explained, "My first job after doing journalism at Rutgers was as sports girl for a Boston radio station. Quarterback at Carolina. I am definitely impressed."

"Just to set the record straight, I never rose above second string," Patrick said.

"He started over half the games his senior year," Scott said.

"The first-string guy got hurt."

"He got an offer to play for Atlanta," Jeff piped in. "But he had already heard the call of God."

The words were enough to turn Linda around. She inspected the boy so closely, Jeff asked, "Did I say something wrong?"

"Not at all." But her voice had gone quiet once more. "I suppose it's just, well, I'm not used to having people talk about God like He was sitting here at the table with us."

The silence was finally broken by Scott, "I guess that's what's gotten us through. Thinking God stayed right here with us through everything."

"Closer than a brother," Jeff added. "Right, Dad?"

Patrick had to drop his head. Hearing his sons speak the words struck him hard. He had never felt as proud of them as he did at that moment. He said hoarsely, "That's exactly right."

The waiter returned with their pizzas and drinks. Or rather, he returned leading a line of every waiter and busboy in the restaurant, each carrying something as an excuse to walk over and get a closer look for themselves. It seemed to take forever for them to set down the pizzas and the colas and the salad. Patrick did not object because Jeff and Scott returned to their beaming pride. Linda shared a special look with them, one that brought dimples to her cheeks even though she didn't really smile. It left both boys blushing as the waiters retreated. Once more Patrick felt a tiny stab of jealousy over being left out of that look.

When they were alone once more, he asked Scott, "Would you like to say the blessing?"

His boy bowed his head and intoned, "Father, thank You for this really great night, and for our family, and for this great meal, and this great company. Bless this food. Amen."

Linda raised her head and said, "I feel honored to be included in that."

Patrick warned, "You may want to retreat to another table."

"Dad," Jeff protested.

"I may be slow off the mark," Linda replied, lifting her knife and fork, "but when it comes to pizza, I like to think I can finish with the best of them."

Patrick refrained from making any further comments when both boys followed her lead and picked up a knife and fork. If her presence was going to finally cause them to use table manners around pizza, he was all for it.

Linda hummed her delight over the combination of flavors, bringing enormous grins to the faces of both boys. Patrick could not remember the last time he had seen so many smiles at their table. She then turned to him and said, "It's not all that surprising that the administration would want to have Buddy Korda down, when you think about it."

"I'm not sure I follow you."

"Sorry. I was going back to your saying the White House had issued him an invitation."

This news shocked the boys so, they actually stopped eating. Scott recovered first. "President Gifford invited Mr. Korda to the White House?"

"Not exactly," Patrick replied, then asked Linda, "What did you mean about it not being surprising?"

"Think about it a second." Her face seemed to gel before his eyes, settling into lines that spoke of intelligent perception joined to tough insight. "The churches are becoming a force to be reckoned with, thanks to Mr. Korda's prediction and their new financial strength. You've heard about the status churches have as landowners?"

"Who hasn't."

"There is bound to be a horrific backlash within the administration to a shift in the power structure. What the administration will want to do is minimize opposition to whatever step they decide to take. The best way to do that is by *splitting the opposition*. And the best way to accomplish this would be by suggesting that someone from inside the church ranks might actually be sympathetic to the government's plight."

"Like Buddy." Patrick found himself recognizing her pattern of speech from television. She spoke in a way that dealt concisely with complex issues, boiling the salient points down to a few tight comments. "You're saying he shouldn't go to Washington?"

"I'm saying he should be extremely careful. Especially over whom he allows near him in any photo ops they arrange. And especially over what he says in front of the cameras." She was struck by a thought that pushed her back in her seat. Her eyes widening, she asked, "Do you think that's why I'm here?"

"I'm not sure. It might be. I'm not even sure I should be commenting on what might be occurring in relation to God speaking to His prophet."

They mulled that over in relative silence, until Linda sighed and leaned back from her plate. "I can't recall the last time I have enjoyed a pizza this much. Or a meal."

That brought another delighted glance between the two boys. Jeff then asked, "Dad, what makes a prophet?"

Another surprise in a night of many amazements. Jeff rarely asked him anything to do with faith these days. He listened whenever Scott posed a question. But almost never did Jeff show any interest of his own. "God calls someone to be His messenger."

"Sure, I know that. I mean, how does God speak? Does Mr. Korda talk with Him like I talk with you?"

"I'm not sure I could even begin to tell you the answer to that. But if you were to ask Mr. Korda, I'm certain he would tell you himself." He saw disappointment flicker over Jeff's features. Patrick forced himself to slow down, to treat the question with dignity.

He tried again, speaking as gently as he knew how. "God speaks to man in many different ways. Sometimes in dreams, sometimes in visions, but most of the time through His written Word."

The fact that Patrick was trying hard to explain was enough to raise Jeff's face back up. "But Mr. Korda didn't get his messages just from reading the Bible, did he?"

"No, I genuinely believe Buddy has received a divine message from on high."

"But what does that *mean?*"

He felt more than saw Linda's intent examination, but he kept his gaze fastened upon his son. "There are as many answers to that as there have been messengers. If you like, we could study the prophets together, and I'll show you what I mean. But there is one thing I think all of them would have in common. I can't say this for certain, but I am pretty sure I'm right. Can you think what that might be?"

Jeff paused a moment, then shook his head.

"One of the early prophets was a man by the name of Elijah. He was living through a very difficult time, probably a lot like what we are going through right now. And after a while he went out into the desert just to get away from everything. Even though he was a prophet, he felt like God was very far from him. Out in the desert, he asked God to speak with him. And God did just that.

"We are told that there came a hurricane, but God was not in the loud winds. Then there was an earthquake, but God was not there either. Nor was He in a storm that followed. Then, when Elijah was about ready to give up all hope, there came a tiny breath, quieter than the softest whisper. And that is where God was found."

Patrick leaned back in his chair, lost in the telling. "Bible scholars have always had a problem translating this point. The words in Hebrew read 'noise,' followed by 'silent.' And just to make sure the message is absolutely clear, these two terms are followed by the word *tiny*. God was to be found within a *tiny silent noise.* Here in this invisible breath of the unspoken, Elijah found his faith renewed. A voice so soft it could easily be missed. One that could only be heard because Elijah was listening with all his might." He examined his son, this boy resting on the verge of manhood, one he loved more than life itself. "This is what marks all the prophets in my opinion. They focus their attention upon the Lord. They are ready to heed His call. They *listen.*"

The silence stretched around them for a moment, before Linda finally said, "That was very nice."

He showed her a bashful smile. "I'm sorry. It's an occupational habit. Preachers like to sermonize."

"You weren't sermonizing." She turned to Jeff. "Did you think he was lecturing you?"

Scott made a face. "Maybe a little."

"But that's okay," Jeff added.

"I don't think he was sermonizing at all. You asked a question, and he gave you an answer." She turned her attention back to Patrick. Her full attention. And the look in her eyes warmed him right down to his toes. "A very beautiful answer indeed."

EIGHT

☐ For Buddy, the night was full of shapes and whispers and fears.

When the hands on his clock reached the pinnacle of night and began leaning toward the unwanted dawn, Molly finally turned to him and said in a voice utterly void of sleep, "You need to get some rest."

"I can't."

She pushed herself up in bed. "Roll over and let me rub your back."

"It won't do any good, Molly."

"Now who is sounding like a sulky four-year-old? Roll over and hush."

Buddy bunched his pillow up with a few hard punches, then lay down on his belly. Molly began stroking his back, drifting caresses that instantly made his eyebrows feel heavy. He tried to fight it, but he couldn't. He said to the night, "I remember when you used to do this with our boys."

"Shh, not so loud, you'll wake up the girls."

He spoke more softly, "Do you remember how it always seemed like if one boy got sick, the other one came down with something too?"

"It didn't just seem that way. It was." She began scratching between his shoulder blades, light strokes that made his whole body feel as if it were floating. "Whatever one got, the other caught. And then you'd come down with it. As if two moaning boys weren't enough, you had to get your share of attention too."

"I never."

"Husband, I am telling you as one who has lived and loved you for more than thirty years, you are the biggest little boy I have ever met."

Buddy smiled into his pillow. "I suppose senility had to strike you some time. Pity it's so soon." When Molly popped him on the ear, he finished, "Ow."

"I don't suppose you remember getting stomach pains when Paul had his appendicitis."

"Of course I remember. It was the worst case of indigestion I've ever had. I don't know when I've been so worried."

"Or how you went down with a sore throat and a fever when Jack had his tonsils out."

"How could I ever forget that? The doctor wouldn't let me see my own son when he was in the hospital."

"Little boy I said and little boy I meant." She moved up and began massaging his neck, her fingers running from behind his ears up to the base of his skull, kneading away all the tension. "Now why don't you tell me what's really bothering you."

Buddy stared at the lights flickering behind his eyelids, and said into his pillow, "I'm so scared, Molly."

"That I can certainly understand."

"You've read the prophets. You probably know the Old Testament better than I do. You know why God sent His messengers down to the seat of kings."

"Because He had a message for the leaders of the nation."

Buddy raised up and swiveled around. "Not a message, Molly. A judgment."

"Lie back down."

"A judgment, Molly. A condemnation. God sent them down because He was planning to inflict woe and misery on them."

"I'm not going to tell you again, Buddy."

He made an exasperated noise, but flopped back on his stomach. "This poor land has already suffered through so much. How can I go down there and tell people that things are going to get even worse?"

"You don't know that."

"It doesn't take a genius. Go take a look at Jeremiah." Buddy felt the burden of woe and suffering press down upon his heart. "And it's all my fault. I was the one who warned them last time. What's going to happen when I go down and tell them there's even more trouble in store?" He shook his head back and forth, pressing his head deeper into the pillow. "I hurt for them, Molly. I hurt for every single person who has been struck by misfortune."

"I know you do."

"I feel their pain. I feel like it has been branded upon my very heart. I feel it so much it hurts to breathe." Buddy was very glad the pillow and the night hid his burning eyes. "I know we've gone astray. I know we've done wrong. I know all this, but it doesn't make any difference to how I feel. I love this land, Molly. I love it so much I feel like I'm going to be crushed sometimes by everything that's happened."

"Did you ever think," she said, her voice as soft as her hands, "that was exactly why the dear Lord chose you to speak for Him?"

"I don't care. I wish it was somebody else. I always have. I hate being put into the limelight. I hate having to make people more worried and more afraid and more hurt than they are now."

"Buddy, pshaw, listen to what I am saying. How can you be so sure you're being called to say something bad?"

"I just told you. Read the prophets and you see—"

"I've read the prophets, same as you. And I know that it is not pain and anger and misery and judgment behind what the Lord has to say. You know that as well. Tell me what the Lord says above all else. Can you do that?" When Buddy did not speak, she continued, "It is a plea for repentance. Above all else, the Lord wishes to give us salvation and hope and love. Now isn't that true?"

He offered the pillow a small nod. Listening hard now.

"Think about something else. Didn't your last message start with a nightmare?"

"A terrible one," he agreed, shivering at the memory. "Horrible."

"And was it bad this time?"

"No." The first faint shred of hope surfaced within him. "It was wonderful."

"So don't you think you might at least try and hope that maybe He is sending you to offer them something good? Something that speaks of healing and hope?"

Once more Buddy found himself caught by the simple wisdom of his wife. He spent a long moment thinking that over and concluded, "You would make a much better prophet than I."

"I'm right where I belong, of that I am certain." Molly was silent for so long her next words seemed to drift from the quiet slumber reaching up to claim him. "In the midst of our struggle, when God seems so fiercely distant and we feel so vulnerable and exposed, we must remember one thing above all else. God is constantly desiring to draw us nearer to Him. His instructions, His laws, His Word, His Son, His Spirit—all of these things have one purpose in mind. One. In every moment of every day, from the first moment to His glorious return, in all of time, God is seeking to call us home."

⊣| NINE |⊢

☐ Tuesday morning, Patrick Allen reached for the phone even before he was fully awake.

He set it down again, rubbed his face, and sat on the edge of his bed, wondering what had gotten into him. But the feeling was still there. Not that he should give this man a call. Rather that he should call him *now*. He *must* call.

He went into the bathroom, washed his face, then walked down the hall to the little guest bedroom Alice had set up as his office. Her smile was there to greet him, in the oval silver frame on his desk. He smiled back this morning, caught by a swift memory of how nice the evening before had been. As he reached for his private directory, he glanced at the clock and hesitated once more. But the sense of immediacy was just as strong. He looked up the number and dialed.

The phone was answered on the first ring. "James Thaddeus Wilkins here."

"James, it's Patrick Allen."

"Well, now." The rich black voice rolled down the line. "If this ain't a pleasant surprise."

"I hope I'm not disturbing you, calling at six-thirty in the morning."

"Not at all. Not at all. Twenty-eight years as a postman leaves habits hard to break. If I'm not outta bed by five, I feel guilty all day long. How are you, brother?"

"Pretty good," Patrick confessed after a moment's internal reflection. "Matter of fact, I'm doing better than I have in a long time."

"Now this is certainly a fine way to start the day. Do you feel like the Lord's healing hand is upon your heart?"

"I don't know, James. I really don't."

"It's all so new a feeling," Pastor James Wilkins suggested in his deeply sonorous voice. "So new and so strange you're almost afraid to believe the worst of the grief might be behind you."

Patrick squeezed his eyes shut. The man often showed a remarkable ability to touch the nerves. "That's it exactly."

"Well, all I can say to you this fine morning, sir, is praise the Lord. Yessir, praise His holy name. Let us hope this is just the beginning. A new day is dawning in your life, and with God's help you will rise to walk and serve Him with joy once more."

Two years earlier, a pastoral retreat had ended with a call for each attendee to prayerfully seek out a brother or sister in the audience, one who might in time become a confidant—a mirror to help see all the things that remain hidden from those closest to them. Awkwardly, Patrick had risen to his feet with the others, embarrassed to meet the eyes of those he passed, unwilling to be the first to stop and say, "Okay, let's talk." As they meandered around the great hall, the speaker continued to say that even pastors had times when they needed a secret confidant, someone who was far removed from the pastor's normal ministry and circle of friends.

No one had been more surprised than Patrick when his feet had stopped abruptly in front of a tall black man with a face as seamed as a winter field. His own fumbling words had been met by stern reserve from James Thaddeus Wilkins. After Patrick had traded cards and shaken the man's hand, he had turned away in genuine relief.

But three months later, during Buddy Korda's sweep through America, Patrick Allen had received a telephone call from the New Jerusalem Church of Washington D.C. Many pastors had called to ask if Buddy Korda's message was for real. But James Thaddeus Wilkins had telephoned for an entirely different reason.

He had told Patrick that he had seen Buddy on a video, then driven to Richmond to hear him speak. And he was calling to ask if Patrick was handling this all right. Patrick had bluffed, asking what James Thaddeus was talking about. "You know exactly," Wilkins had replied. "I'm asking you if you're able to stand strong and fast while the Lord is raising up a prophet inside your own congregation."

When Patrick had found himself unable to respond, Wilkins had continued, "It can be a mighty hard thing, finding yourself stripped from the podium."

Patrick swallowed hard, and confessed, "It's awful."

"Don't I know it. Don't I just know it's a trying time. Tell me now, has he pushed himself up as somebody wanting to run the church?"

"No." He was able to answer that clearly. "Buddy Korda is not that kind of man."

"And does he still show you proper respect?"

"Every time we meet."

"Then you need to remember that even while the spotlight might be turned his way for now, it is *your* ministry that helped to raise up this man. Do you hear what I'm saying?"

"I do," Patrick had said, feeling at that moment closer to this stranger than he did to many of his closest friends. "I do indeed."

"The logic inside you is gonna say, we all serve the same Lord. But don't you deny the fact that you feel like maybe the Lord should've chosen you instead. That's human, to want to be chosen. Accept this feeling as *real,* turn it over to the dear sweet Lord above, and remember that even Jesus Himself knelt down that fateful night and washed the feet of those He was sent to save."

Patrick had written down those words and carried them around with him. Afterward he had spoken with James Thaddeus Wilkins every week or so until the economic meltdown. After that, they both had been too busy for much conversing. And then Patrick's wife had become ill.

In those dark nights of descending into the cauldron of helpless agony, James Thaddeus had stayed there with him, calling two and sometimes three times a day, being the one to whom Patrick could say anything, shout and rail at God when the prayers of healing went unanswered.

While the nation slid into turmoil and the church faced the gravest crisis since its consecration, and his family was being torn up at its roots; while the congregation desperately needed his strength and he had two young boys who threatened to fall apart in front of his eyes, James Thaddeus had remained the one person with whom Patrick felt he could be the weak and frightened and shivering man he was.

The morning his wife died, Patrick had emerged from Alice's hospital room, as empty of life as the corpse lying there on the bed. He had allowed himself to be swallowed in the arms of his sons and close friends from church. His eyes had remained as dry as his bones, his heart full of nothing but dust and ashes. He had listened to his sons sob, watched the sorrow well up on faces he had known all his life, and felt as though he would never know anything but emptiness for the rest of his barren days.

Then a tall, dark figure had pushed his way through the throng, and suddenly James Thaddeus was standing there before him. The seamed features were wet by the storm of sharing what Patrick could not let himself feel. The black man had not raised his hands to embrace Patrick. Instead, he had stood there before Patrick and shown him how a pastor, a leader, and a man of God could weep.

He did not express his condolences, did not make offers of help. Instead he had rumbled in that deep bass tone, "Don't you hold it in now, son. Don't you dare. Storms will either make you bend or make you break, you hear what I'm saying?"

"My life is over," Patrick had said, his voice already dead to his own ears.

"Part of it, yessir, I do surely know. Part of it is now in the Lord's hands. But another part, you're standing there with your arms wrapped around what is still with you, still living, still needing."

Patrick shook his head, trying to keep him out. The man's words tortured him. They drew him from where he wanted to go, down into the impossible sorrow, down into the darkness, down with his beloved wife.

James Thaddeus had seemed to understand, because he went on, "She ain't down there, son. You know that as well as I do. She ain't there. You can't let yourself fall down in the grave with what ain't your wife anymore. She's up in heaven, singing praises to the God who still needs you here on earth."

"I can't," he whispered.

"I'll tell you what you *can* do. You can weep. You can let it out. You can bend and you can wail and you can lay it out on the altar of sorrow. Cry out to the Lord how you can't handle this alone, and let God's healing hand rest upon your life."

☐

Patrick traced a finger around the edge of the oval silver frame holding his wife's smiling face. He turned away from the picture and the memories and tried to focus upon what was in front of him in the here and now. "Buddy Korda has had another vision."

"Oh my." James Thaddeus had the ability to turn his reaction into a chant. "Oh my."

"Yes. He doesn't seem to know what it is, other than the fact that he has been called down to Washington."

A pause, then, "I suspect it must be a big one."

Patrick nodded, the words confirming what he had not wanted to admit even to himself. "He also received a call from the White House to attend some conference down there. He's planning to go today. And last night a young lady showed up unannounced at his door. Linda Kee."

"Should that name mean something?"

"Linda Kee," he repeated, and found himself smiling as he recalled the previous evening. "CBS News."

"Of course, on the television—a right attractive lady. Is she a Christian?"

"She gave me that impression, yes."

"Then I would say that all this adds up to a mighty strong affirmation. Wouldn't you?"

"Yes, I think so. We had dinner last night, my boys and I and Linda Kee. She thinks there might be some trouble brewing over Buddy attending anything that might be connected to church business."

"Don't matter what anybody thinks." Firm now, certain as his walk, James Thaddeus continued, "The Lord has called Mr. Korda to come. We must help him obey. You coming down with him?"

Patrick's breath caught in his throat. "Me?"

"You were there, I take it, when this message arrived?"

"No. But later." He shivered anew thinking of the moment in the hospital ward.

"And you were there for this woman's arrival?"

"Yes."

"Well, son, it seems to me the Lord's done this with a purpose in mind for you as well."

"I had thought I'd call and ask you to sort of host him around Washington."

"I know that's what you *thought*. But what I'm telling you is maybe the Lord has something else *planned*. Now how does that rest on you?"

Patrick mulled it over, then admitted, "You may have a point."

"I expect Mr. Korda's gonna have himself a place given by the government. You come on down, plan on staying over here with us. We got a couple of grandchildren in and out; their mommas have gone back to work. You don't mind a passel of kids underfoot, do you?"

"Not at all. Thank you very much for the invitation."

"Mister Buddy Korda and Miss Linda Kee coming to Washington to do the Lord's work. Yessir, the White House won't know what hit 'em." James Thaddeus enjoyed a good chuckle. "Be nice to see you again, son. Drive careful, now. And remember me to your fine boys."

□

Patrick called the motel, planning to leave a message for Linda, only to hear that at that moment she was standing in front of the reception desk. The receptionist passed over the phone, and a very hesitant voice said, "Hello?"

"It's Patrick. I hope I'm not disturbing you."

"Oh, no!" He thought he heard a sense of genuine pleasure in her voice, making the phone in his hand shiver slightly. "This is amazing. Nobody knows I'm here, and while I'm checking out all of a sudden there's a call for me."

He found his face stretching into the unaccustomed position of a genuine smile. "I've phoned a friend down in Washington. Somebody who might help and be there for Buddy in all that's coming."

"Is he in government?"

"No, he's a pastor."

"Oh." A swift moment of thinking, the intensity of her intelligence showing in the clipped words. "That's probably a good idea. Give him someone to turn to."

"Actually, I was also thinking that, well, I may be driving Buddy down and if you like you could come—"

"That would be wonderful."

The sincerity in her voice caused his smile to broaden even farther. "When would you be ready to leave?"

"Oh, I'm ready now. I've been up for over an hour. Years of rising at dawn and chasing deadlines have left me unable to lie in bed even when I don't have any reason to get up."

"Why don't you come over and join us for coffee?" Surprising even himself by the invitation, he added, "That is, if you can stand watching my boys get ready for school."

☐

When Scott came downstairs wearing a sleepy expression and yesterday's T-shirt and a pajama bottom, he did a totally electrified bug-eyed scramble at the sight of Linda Kee seated at the kitchen table, having coffee with Patrick. There was the sound of thunder overhead as he bolted back up the stairs, slammed open his brother's door, and raced into the bathroom. A second series of bumps and thumps joined Scott's, and in less than ten minutes two fresh-faced wide-eyed young men came rushing down the stairs. They wore pressed slacks and clean shirts, and their combed hair was doused with so much water it dripped on their shoulders.

Patrick looked at Linda and said, "Please come back again soon. I would pay good money to have this happen every morning."

"Hello, guys," she said, smiling for them all. "How did you sleep?"

She received shy mumbles in reply, and the two boys slid into their seats and sat there, staring at her, clearly trying to work out whether this was a dream or really happening. Linda Kee joining them for breakfast. Patrick knew exactly what they were thinking: How were they going to get the guys at school to believe this one?

Patrick asked, "Cereal or eggs?"

"Cereal," they chorused, and Jeff added for good measure, "Please."

Patrick rose and fished out bowls and boxes and milk, since clearly they were not moving. As he poured cereal into their bowls, he said, "Think maybe you two could get along on your own for a couple of days?"

This brought them around. "Sir?"

"I talked with Reverend James Wilkins this morning. James feels I should travel down to Washington with Buddy and help him get settled." He poured in milk and carried over the bowls and spoons.

A new light dawned in Scott's eyes. He asked Linda, "Are you going back with Dad?"

"If he's offering." Another smile for him. "I'm sure it would be nicer than taking the train back by myself."

The look Jeff and Scott gave their father over the rims of their bowls left him too uncomfortable to stay silent. "I'll just be gone one night."

Linda rose to her feet. "Could I use your telephone and call my answering service? I've been waiting to hear about a new job."

"Sure. Use the phone down the hall there, you can shut the door and have some privacy." When she had left and the kitchen was theirs, the boys' gaze did not waver. Finally Patrick demanded, "Okay, what?"

"Way to go, Dad," Scott said.

"This is about Buddy Korda, guys. Not Linda Kee."

"Sure." Jeff lifted his bowl and slurped out the remaining milk. "Right."

"Boys, come on. Give me a break." But his protest lacked steam. "We're talking about something very important here."

"I'll say," Scott agreed. "Can we come?"

"Can you . . ." Patrick halted his knee-jerk denial. The idea had merit. "What about school?"

"Come on, Dad," Jeff pleaded.

"Yeah," Scott agreed. "We go in and tell the principal, 'Hey, we've got a chance to go to Washington, D.C., to help Buddy Korda deliver a message from God.'"

"'And with Linda Kee,'" Jeff reminded his brother. "Don't forget that part."

"Right. Do you really think he's going to say no?"

Patrick looked from one boy to the other. "Do you two stand in front of the mirror practicing that innocent look you give me, or does it come natural?"

"Strictly natural," Scott confirmed.

"We inherited it from you," Jeff agreed.

"What a completely horrible thought," Patrick said, and meant it sincerely.

TEN

□ "Come in, Royce. Good to see you again. Have a seat over there, we won't be long." Supreme Court Justice Harold Hawkins pointed him into a chair by the far wall, then turned back to the journalist. Royce smiled his thanks and settled in to wait.

The justices rarely granted interviews on the record. They had no need for such exposure, since they could never be stripped of office. Which meant they had their aides carefully vet all journalists, and met with only those who would ask the right questions and show the right respect—both in person and in print. The journalist seated before Justice Hawkins's desk was young, eager, and awed—a suitable receptacle for the justice's wisdom.

Harold Hawkins was wrapping up now, in a style that sounded just as pedantic as Royce would have expected from someone who was completely cut off from public opinion. "We do not examine cases for error," the justice intoned. "By the time a case reaches us, each side has already had at least two chances to present their arguments in front of lesser courts."

Royce made an effort to keep his smile internalized. *Lesser* courts. The man was so used to being top dog he had no idea how pompous he sounded.

"We look at the case strictly from the perspective of constitutional interpretation. All courts have the right to apply the Constitution to a case. The difference with us is one of degree. In the case of the Supreme Court, it is an *exclusive* focus."

Howard Hawkins waited for the journalist to catch up, then continued, "From ten million legal cases heard each year in the United States, thirty million counting traffic violations, about seven thousand wind their way through lower courts and request a hearing from the Supreme Court. Of these, only about a hundred are ever heard. One hundred from ten million."

The journalist cleared his throat and hesitantly inquired, "How do you decide which cases to take?"

"Ah, the alchemy of decisions." Hawkins bestowed a knowing smile upon the journalist. "Our power is derived as much from which we deign to hear as from the rulings themselves."

As Hawkins droned on about the procedure by which cases are filtered—four justices must agree to hear a case before it is placed on the docket for briefing and oral arguments—Royce inspected his surroundings. The private chambers of a Supreme Court justice were ideally situated for rubbernecking. The corner office spoke of age and power and quality. A fireplace in the far wall warmed the high-ceilinged room against the wind and unseasonable chill. Portions of two walls were given over to built-in bookshelves filled with legal tomes with gilt-edged bindings. The gleaming furniture was mostly from the Federalist period, as was the building itself, and the carpet was genuine silk Isfahan. The oil paintings were drawn from the same national archival treasure trove as those adorning the White House walls.

The side window looked across the huge marble courtyard to where the central fountain was blown to blistering spray by the storm and the wind. Beyond rose the Capitol on the Senate side. The Library of Congress loomed one block away through the other window. An impressive view of power.

Royce rose to his feet and gave his patented little smile as the journalist passed him and departed. He nodded his thanks as Justice Hawkins waved him into the newly vacated seat. "What can I do for you today, Royce?"

He had approached this man with court-related matters for over a decade, long enough to know Justice Hawkins had no time for small talk. Without preamble Royce said, "We are considering a bill that would permit a taxation of growing church wealth."

"Ah." A single nod, a keen glance. "If I know you, a mere consideration would not be enough to bring you over. You have it fairly wrapped up, don't you?"

"Not yet, but we're working on it."

"Good, good. It's high time the churches were reined in. They are beginning to think they actually wield some power within the national arena."

Royce settled back, satisfied that he had guessed correctly. He had three contacts within the Supreme Court, but Hawkins was the one he most often approached. Hawkins had been appointed so far back that few people could recall by which party. Supreme Court Justice Harold Hawkins had served the court through the reigns of four presidents. Twenty-four years of watching them come and seeing them go had left Justice Hawkins with the placid superiority of one far removed from the fray. Royce knew the justice considered these meetings mildly entertaining.

Vacancies in the U.S. Supreme Court came up very infrequently. Each of the nine justices was appointed by the president and confirmed by Congress. The appointment was for life, which was what had led Thomas Jefferson to once state, after the court had ruled against him, "The problem is, they never retire, and they never die."

One of the few points that pricked Justice Hawkins's placid nature was the rise of religious conservatism. He was a member of the old school, the product of a powerful industrial family and trained in the nation's finest educational institutions. As far as Justice Hawkins was concerned, the Party hierarchy should always remain a bastion of industrial might, conservative intellectualism, and privilege.

"Well, the foundations for a favorable ruling on such a tax are all in place," Hawkins mused. "Over the past decade the Court has ruled consistently against the church's invasion of the power structure. Legal encroachment into their sacred turf is already well under way. The Constitution is a powerful tool, when used correctly."

"We were thinking of presenting the taxation bill as a temporary measure," Royce offered.

"Good, good. A transitory loss of the church's tax-exempt status. A temporary levy, one wrought from the current economic crisis. Won't make any difference as far as our considerations are concerned, of course. But I'm sure it will make it more palatable to the electorate."

"You'd act on a constitutional challenge to such a tax?"

"Oh, I imagine something of this import will require a full hearing." He swiveled his high-backed dark red leather chair around, and mused to the window, "If I were in your place, I would go ahead and prepare the groundwork for such a legal challenge to emerge."

Royce nodded slowly. A brilliant concept. "Beat them at their own game."

"Precisely. Choose a place where you are bound to lose, somewhere in the Bible Belt would be good."

"I know of a judge we can rely on in Alabama. A real religious firebrand. He'd leap at the chance to make national headlines, rubbing the administration's face in the dirt. And he'll give his opinions a lot of play in the press."

"Perfect." Hawkins smiled to the window and the storm, distancing himself from his own comments. "A negative ruling by a bigoted lower court will polarize the entire populace. They will *want* us to overturn the ruling."

"All but the religious conservatives."

Justice Hawkins waved that aside. "You might as well assume they'll fight you. Do you have something in place to counteract their public attack?"

"We're working on that."

"Fine." He resumed his perusal of the gray clouds sweeping over Congress. "We'll make it known discreetly that we are watching the case as it moves on to the Court of Appeals. Have the U.S. solicitor general fast-track it."

"Can I tell him you said that?"

"Of course not." Justice Hawkins smiled as he rose and offered Royce his hand. "But do keep me abreast of developments, won't you?"

Royce accepted the hand, and asked, "Is there anything I can pass on to the powers that be if they ask for the Court's initial reaction?"

"The Court can have *no* reaction until the matter has been raised officially. However, you may tell anyone who cares to listen that this is a First Amendment matter, like all religious issues. And any decision related to the First Amendment must be workable for *all* Americans, be they Buddhist or Hindu or Muslim or atheist or agnostic."

"Or Christian," Royce added.

"Of course," Justice Hawkins agreed. "That goes without saying."

⊣‖ ELEVEN ‖⊢

☐ Patrick knocked on the Kordas' front door. When Molly appeared he said, "I was wondering if Buddy would mind having a little extra company for the drive down to Washington."

"I shouldn't think . . ." Her eyebrows shot up as Scott's and Jeff's heads appeared from behind Linda Kee. "Oh, my."

"Hi, Mrs. Korda," Scott said.

Jeff asked, "How is the baby doing, Mrs. Korda?"

"Come in, all of you." But her smile was so forced the scarred side of her face seemed to pull down, as though fighting hard to show a frown. It was enough to silence both boys and lower their eyes in impending defeat. Molly fastened her attention upon the woman at the back of the little line. "Hello, Linda. Everybody but Buddy is in the kitchen."

Patrick let them pass and waited until they had started down the hall. "This was a bad idea."

"No, no, it's not that." She seemed grateful for the chance to let go of her smile. "Oh, Patrick, I'm so worried."

"The baby," he guessed.

"They won't tell us anything." She twisted her hands in anxiety. "Paul spent the night sleeping on the floor in Anne's room. They won't give him any information at all."

"The hospital is totally swamped, Molly. You saw what it's like over there."

"Yes, we know, that's what everybody keeps telling us. But they should at least be able to say how the baby is doing."

"I agree." He pulled his lower lip out in thought. "Let me see what I can do. Can I use your phone?"

"Of course, come in here. Oh, we'd be so grateful. What—" Her query was cut off by a shout of laughter from the kitchen. The sound was enough to touch Molly's worry with a trace of a smile. "Alex is back there with the girls."

Patrick searched through his pocket diary, came up with a number, and began dialing. "Where's Buddy?"

"Upstairs praying. He's been at it since before dawn. When the girls got up and started making noise, he moved from his study up into our bedroom." Molly glanced at the ceiling overhead. "I only hope he was hearing God's voice about the little baby being all right."

"Why don't . . . Hello, is this the maternity ward? Could I speak to Dr. Kendrick, please. She's the new pediatric intern there . . . Yes. Thank you." Patrick waited until the familiar voice came onto the line. "Renee? This is Patrick Allen."

"Oh, Pastor Allen, hello." The newly licensed doctor sounded listless with fatigue. "Are you calling about the Korda baby?"

"The family is pretty worried," he said, keeping his voice light for Molly's sake. Renee Kendrick had been a member of their church since arriving in Aiden for her internship. As soon as Patrick had heard that a new doctor was among the congregation, he had sought her out. Having such personal Christian contacts within the overcrowded hospital system was crucial. "They can't seem to get any information."

"That's because there isn't any to give them. Are they there with you now?"

"That's right."

"I would be very careful not to give them false hopes, Pastor."

He worked hard to keep his face and voice calm. "What are you saying?"

A metallic squawking came through the phone. She said, "Hang on a minute."

Patrick listened as she lifted her pager and spoke tersely. Back on the phone, she told him, "I have to go. We've got another emergency."

"Can't you tell us something?"

"All we can say for the moment is the baby's heart has not stopped again."

"I see."

"Between you and me, Pastor, everybody here is just waiting for him to go. No matter what Mr. Korda might have said." It was the doctor's turn to pause. "I've heard the rumors. Did Mr. Korda really declare that the baby would survive?"

"That's right." Patrick wet his lips, wishing he could turn away from Molly's tight inspection. "Can't the parents see the baby?"

"We've been holding back only because the situation looks so bleak. Do you understand?"

"I'm not sure. Look, I've got to go to Washington, can I have someone else call later?"

"Like who?"

"Molly, Buddy Korda's wife. The grandmother."

"I suppose so. If you think she can handle it." The pager squawked again, and Renee's voice turned up a notch. "The little guy's got about two dozen needles and monitors stuck in him. He's the bluest baby I've ever seen. He's undersized and he's pinched up tight and he hasn't moved once since birth." Another pause, just long enough for the words to sink in. "It's your call, Pastor. If you want them to see the boy, have them page me, and I'll take them down to neonatal intensive care personally. But I've got to tell you, the mother had a tough time in the operating theater, and I'd think long and hard about giving her another shock. She's going to have enough to endure when . . . well, you think about it. Like I said, it's your call."

Patrick took his time, hanging up very slowly, trying to decide what he should and should not say. When he finally raised his head, Molly's gaze was steady. "Tell me."

"Molly, it's not good."

She was rocked, but not nearly as much as he would have expected. "I supposed it would have to be, since they haven't let them see the baby."

"They're afraid of giving Anne another shock . . . Apparently she had a harder time in the operating room than we thought." He took pen and paper from the phone table and scribbled. "This is my contact there, Dr. Renee Kendrick. Don't be put off by her manner, she's a good person and a strong Christian. She's also stretched to the limit." Patrick handed the information over with the warning, "Just be ready for the truth, Molly. She doesn't give the baby much hope."

Molly accepted the paper, her chin quivering as the words sank in deep. She then took a breath and steadied herself. Patrick actually saw the resolve settle in and take hold. "Patrick, that baby is going to be well. He is going to grow up strong and fit and fine."

It was his turn to be rocked. "You have that much faith in Buddy?"

"No," she said quietly, and then added confidently, "In God."

□

They entered the kitchen to find a different world, one of light and laughter and play. Veronica's white-blonde curls twisted and tumbled as she tried to dance around the table wearing Alex's spectacles. Her sky-blue eyes were turned to great wavering pools by the heavy lenses. She skittered over a floor she could not see, bouncing into everybody in turn, until she plopped onto the tiles and sat there squealing with laughter.

"I'm sure it's the funniest thing that's ever happened in this house," Alex grumbled, his own gaze weak and unfocused without his glasses. "Only I can't see a bit of it."

"His eyes might be bad," Scott announced, plucking the black-framed spectacles off Veronica and handing them back. "But Uncle Alex knew who Linda was straight off."

Alex blinked through the glasses, made an astonished face, and pointed across the table. "Why, that there's the world-famous Linda Kee."

Jeff found that hilarious. "Dad didn't know who she was even after we told him."

"I think it's about time we put that tale to bed," Patrick said, extremely glad that the gloom had not been permitted to follow him in here.

Then Molly asked Linda, "Are you famous?"

Which broke up everybody in the room, even Patrick. That was how Buddy found them when he pushed through the door. He looked around with such solemnity that it made them laugh even harder. Patrick just let it out, glad there was a reason to laugh in such times. So very glad.

Buddy said, "This is about the noisiest place I have ever tried to pray."

Molly said plaintively, "They are laughing at me."

"Go on, brother," Alex said, pointing across the table. "Tell your dear, sweet, addled wife who that lovely lady is."

Buddy looked down, and smiled a greeting to the blushing woman. "Hello, Linda. How are you this morning?"

Jeff shouted, "He doesn't know either!"

"Stop, please," Linda protested, blushing even more.

Buddy demanded, "Know what?"

"Linda Kee, Grandpa!" Veronica shouted. "The television news lady!"

"You didn't know until I told you," Jeff said.

"Did so! Did so!"

Buddy and Molly gaped at the woman with the rose-tinted cheeks and together said, "Oh my goodness."

It was enough to make them all laugh once more. So very, very good.

"Miss Kee, I'm so sorry." Buddy slid into the empty chair at the head of the table. "I've watched you every night and here you are, and I didn't even—"

"It doesn't matter. Really."

"Uncle Alex has been making us laugh," Meredith, Veronica's little sister, announced. She was just big enough to look over the rim of the table, and was tired of her older sister getting all the attention. "Go on, Uncle Alex, tell them what you told me."

"They already know all about my eyesight," Alex protested.

Veronica danced over to stand in front of her grandfather and almost shouted up at him, "Last night he kissed the cat and put Agatha out for the night!"

When she could be heard, Meredith added, "Aunt Agatha has stopped serving him alphabet soup because the letters are too small for him to read them anymore!"

"All right, all right, a little softer now," Buddy chided, but he was smiling too. "Linda Kee, my goodness, sitting right here at my table. Isn't that something, Molly?"

"It certainly is. Can I get you anything?"

"I'm just fine, thanks."

"She already ate breakfast with us," Scott explained proudly.

"And dinner last night," Jeff added. "We had pizza."

Patrick decided a little explanation was in order. "I called her at her motel this morning and asked if she'd like to have a cup of coffee before we got started."

"We?" Buddy looked from one to the other. "You're coming with me?"

"If you'd like."

"The boys too," Molly added, smiling at the two eager teens.

"Only if you'd like them to join us," Patrick said, then watched as the sad shadows settled back around Buddy's features.

Buddy said quietly, "I think it should be all right to have them along."

The pair looked at one another and did a swift *yes* in teenage tandem, before Veronica piped up with, "Go where, Grandpa?"

"Your grandpa needs to take a little trip," Molly said, reaching over to stroke the blonde head. "And we are going to stay here and pray for their safety and swift return."

"And for Momma and Daddy and the little baby," Meredith piped in.

"That's right, honey. They all need our prayers."

Buddy asked, "Any word?"

"We'll talk about that later," Molly said, smiling down at the little girls.

"All these people heading out," Alex said. "Looks like we'll need to take two cars."

Patrick watched Buddy reach for his brother's arm. "I need you to stay here and help Molly with the family, brother."

Alex puffed out his scarecrow chest. "What, you don't think I'm up for the journey?"

"No, no, it's not that at all."

"Because I'll tell you one thing, if the Lord calls my little brother, He calls me too."

"And me," Meredith added in her high, clear voice. "Don't forget me, Grandpa."

"I'll never forget you, honey," Buddy replied, but his eyes remained on his brother. "Alex, there is nothing more important that you could do for me than to stay here with Agatha and make sure the church prays me through this."

The man who had aged twenty years in the twenty months since Buddy's first message, released the tension in his shoulders. "You're sure you'll be all right down there in the big city?"

"With God's help," Buddy replied, reaching over to pat the thin arm. "With God's help."

TWELVE

☐ The road joining Aiden to the interstate rose through the surrounding hills. Because spring was so late in coming that year, the trees did not block their view of the Delaware valley so much as frame it. As Buddy looked down and observed the town nestled within the surrounding countryside, he felt as though all the worries and all the cares had no place in such a setting. The little town was too lovely to shoulder such times. It was his lifelong home. These people were his people. He missed them already.

Buddy remained trapped within his own desolate island of solitude and worry during the entire journey to Washington, D.C. He felt nothing but gratitude and relief for the company of Patrick and Linda and the boys. The truth was, he did not want to be doing this. No matter what Molly might say, no matter what he might logically tell himself about Scriptures and calling, he did not want to take the Lord's message to Washington.

Whatever he had to say, it was bound to spark dissent and anger and resentment and conflict. And he wanted none of it. He already felt burdened beyond what he could endure. A drive through Aiden's forlorn streets was all the mark of sorrow his poor heart could sustain. And no matter how he might argue with himself, he did feel as though the nation's trauma was his fault. If only God had chosen a better messenger, someone who could have made them listen when the warning was given, perhaps all this could have been avoided. If only the divine call had appointed someone more gifted.

Besides which, Buddy was worried about his daughter-in-law and the new baby. He wanted to be sitting in his living room with his grandchildren playing by his feet, waiting for word that Anne was getting well. That and nothing more.

An eighteen-wheeler blasted by them, shaking Buddy from his reverie in time to spot a road sign indicating they were twenty-five miles from Washington. He glanced through the side window and saw a sky that matched his mood, gray and borderless and threatening to rain at any time.

Scott and Jeff sat with Linda Kee in the backseat. There had been a minor riot when it had come time to decide who was going to sit in the middle, and thus next to the former newscaster. Patrick had wisely restored peace by promising to halt midway so they could switch places. It was Jeff's turn now, and not even Buddy's moroseness could silence him. "Are there a lot of blue-eyed Chinese?"

"Jeff," Patrick said, weary from the drive and embarrassment. "Please."

"Yeah, way to go, little brother."

"There's nothing the matter with asking her that. You don't mind, do you, Linda?" Jeff threw back.

"Of course not."

"See, smarty-pants? I bet you were wondering the exact same thing and were just afraid to ask her. Ow!"

"Enough, you two. One more outbreak and I'll put the luggage on the seat next to Linda and you two in the trunk."

"To answer your question," Linda said, restoring peace, "I'm only three-eighths Chinese. Can you figure that one out?"

When Jeff and Scott remained silent, she went on, "My father's mother was pure Fukienese, from a province in southeastern China. She emigrated to this country when she was very young. My father's father was half Chinese, half Hawaiian. The other parts are a real mishmash. I'm Puerto Rican, Italian, British; I even have one grandmother from Stockholm. Do you know where that is?"

"Sure," Scott offered. "It's the capital of Sweden."

"Our granddad's family is from Ireland," Jeff offered. "And our grandma was from France."

Suddenly an invisible hand seemed to pound the car. One moment they were rolling down the highway, the next it felt as though they were being slapped across the road.

Patrick fought for control, then slammed on the brakes and steered over to the shoulder as ahead of them a truck fishtailed across all three lanes. Buddy gripped the armrest and dash as yet another invisible fist blasted out of nowhere and hammered their car.

Scott cried, "What was *that?*"

"Wind," Patrick said tersely, gradually speeding up once more. "I'm sure glad we weren't driving alongside that truck when it hit."

"The Washington weather's been like this all winter," Linda offered. "It never really grew that cold, and we didn't have much in the way of rain. Just these strong winds, some of them gusting up to hurricane force. And dark clouds every day it seems—always like we're just about ready to have a rain that never comes."

"The weather in Aiden has been pretty bad this winter," Patrick said. "But nothing like this."

"Washington has had its own weather pattern all winter," Linda replied.

The wind moaned around their car, a low, menacing sound. Buddy felt a sudden foreboding and murmured, "Maybe we shouldn't have brought the boys."

"Why, Mr. Korda?" Jeff protested. "We've been in lots of storms."

Patrick cast him a worried glance. "They're good boys. They know to behave."

Buddy said nothing more, just sat and listened to the wind wail, and watched the midday sky grow steadily darker the closer they got to Washington. By the time they crossed the Fourteenth Street Bridge and the Capitol came into view, most of the cars around them had their headlights on.

Linda kept up a running commentary as she directed them toward Buddy's hotel. The boys were especially caught up in the capital's atmosphere. As they rounded Dupont Circle and started up Connecticut Avenue, Jeff asked plaintively, "Why are so many people standing around the park, Dad?"

"They don't have any work," Patrick replied tersely, clearly saddened and embarrassed for his country. "They don't have anywhere else to go."

"People don't have jobs in Aiden," Scott protested. "They don't gather like this."

"And look at all the police cars," Jeff pointed out. "There must be eight of them over there."

"People come to the parks and the traffic circles because it's safer than a lot of streets," Linda said, imparting the news as gently as she could. She looked forward at Patrick and asked, "Should I be saying this?"

"If they ask you a question, they deserve an honest answer," Patrick responded without hesitation. "It's the only policy I've found that works."

"All right, fine." Linda turned back to the boys. "Washington resembles a number of our big cities. There has been a huge rise in gang violence recently. People with nowhere else to go come to parks like this. There is safety in numbers."

"But why are the police here?"

"Because the city is worried that so many people gathered like this might riot," Linda explained, her voice carrying audible pain. "They are here to keep the peace."

Buddy wanted to beg her to stop talking. It felt as though acid was being poured into his heart's open wound. But all he could do was sit in his comfortable car seat and stare sorrowfully back at all the faces watching their progress down Connecticut Avenue. Every windowsill and every lamppost and every doorway contained a beggar. So many young faces, all made old before their time. All of them pointing the invisible fingers and shouting at him in silent agony, *It is all your fault.*

"It doesn't look like peace to me," Scott said. "They look pretty angry."

"Yeah," Jeff agreed. "Do you see how they watch our car?"

"They watch all cars," Linda said. "Cars mean the drivers have money. Out-of-state cars mean people who might not be so careful with that money. It's one of the problems with big cities these days. While a few people have managed to stay wealthy, most are a lot worse off. Those who have lost everything are angry. And every day more people arrive, hoping to find some kind of work."

The Hilton Hotel parking lot was flanked by a half dozen stern-faced security guards, all armed. They waved Patrick into the lot and resumed their careful scrutiny of the crowded streets. Patrick pulled into a parking space, and they entered the high-rise hotel in a tight and subdued cluster.

To their surprise, the hotel lobby was packed. Linda excused herself and walked toward a bank of phones by the side wall, moving easily through the jostling, noisy throng. The crowd was dressed in flowing multicolored robes and native Indian gear and saris and cone-shaped African hats. Men and women alike sported huge feather-and-silver creations hanging from their necks. Others had crystals tied by thongs to their foreheads. As Buddy carried his suitcase over to the check-in counter, a number of eyes tracked his movements. A wave of whispered comments drew even more attention his direction.

The smiling receptionist was clearly as determined as Buddy to ignore the watching eyes. "May I help you?"

"My name is Korda, Buddy Korda, I believe I have—"

"Oh, yes. Welcome to Washington, Mr. Korda. Your reservation is all in order." She passed a card over. "Would you be so kind as to fill in your address and sign there at the bottom? And do you have a car you'll be leaving in the parking lot?"

"No," Patrick offered from beside him. "We'll be driving over to stay with friends."

"Fine." The receptionist pushed a photocopied map across the counter. "If I could just ask you to take a moment and look at this with me, please. This is a map of our area of Washington. The hotel is marked with an X here; this is Connecticut Avenue."

Buddy could not help but notice the large blackened portion that began right behind the hotel. "What is this shaded area here?"

"That is the region known as Adams Morgan," the receptionist replied, holding to her brisk cheery tone. "The hotel strongly advises you not to go anywhere near there. We cannot take responsibility for the safety of anyone who chooses to do so, either on foot or in any form of transport. We also advise you to take extreme caution walking anywhere beyond the hotel grounds after dark. Never hail a taxi off the street. Always request the cab's number from the concierge when booking transport. Do you have any questions?"

"No," murmured Buddy, feeling as though he had been soiled by her cheery lament. "No questions."

"Then I must ask you to sign here at the bottom, which absolves the hotel of any liability should you or any others in your party choose to ignore these warnings. Thank you very much. And here is your key, room 517. Please be sure to double-lock your door and use your safety bolt whenever you are inside your room. Have a pleasant stay in our nation's capital."

Linda returned from the phones and offered, "A lot of Adams Morgan has been turned into a sort of shantytown by incoming homeless. Crime has been a real problem around here. The local gangs have become notorious."

Before Buddy could tell her to stop and not say one more thing, a tall black man stepped out of the crowd. He was dressed in a dark suit and starched white shirt and dark tie. His face was all angles and deep furrows, his eyes deep-set and powerful. Then he smiled at Patrick, and his entire face was transformed. "Hello, brother."

"James, you didn't have to come to meet us."

"Wasn't no problem. Wanted to make sure you all got in safe and sound." He turned his attention and his hand toward Buddy. "Mr. Korda, I can't tell you what an honor this is."

"Buddy, this is the friend I was telling you about, Reverend James Thaddeus Wilkins."

Buddy accepted the soft yet powerful hand, but found himself too distressed by what he had seen and heard to speak. He waited, knowing he was going to have to endure a flood of thanks over what he had done for the family or the church or the community of believers, as though his message had been something fine and good, rather than a herald of all the misery and sorrow that surrounded him.

But James Thaddeus Wilkins allowed his smile to slip away, and the dark eyes searched carefully. He leaned in closer, and said in a voice meant only for Buddy, "It's a heavy load you're carrying, isn't it, brother?" When Buddy did not respond, the pastor intoned, "Yes, Lord. A heavy load. Well, all I can say to you is you're not alone. No sir. Not even here, not even now."

He found the strength to both meet Wilkins's gaze and say, "Thank you."

"No sir, don't you go thanking me. Thank God. I'm here on account of serving the same Lord. Anything I can do for you is just another work I hope to someday lay upon the altar."

Reverend Wilkins turned to smile at Jeff and Scott. "Would you just look here."

"Hello, Reverend," they chorused.

"You boys surely have grown. Turning into fine young gentlemen. You making your daddy and your Lord proud of you in these hard times?"

Jeff offered an embarrassed yes, while Scott replied, "We're trying, sir."

"Got to be strong in these dark times. Got to be good and stand tall and shine for Jesus." He turned to the young woman standing beside them, and said, "My, my. Now isn't this just something."

Patrick said, "I guess you recognize Linda Kee."

"A pleasure to meet you, ma'am." He accepted her hand, and asked gravely, "Are you a Christian, Miss Kee?"

The solemn calmness behind the question seemed to widen her gaze, exposing her and leaving her calm as shattered as it had been the evening she had arrived on Buddy's doorstep. "I-I . . . Well, I try, Reverend. I guess that's about all I can say."

"Time for trying is gone, Miss Kee. Time for *doing* is here." Buddy heard no accusation behind the words. Nor did the eyes seem to condemn. More like the grave old man with the very deep voice was seeking to challenge. "Trying ain't enough in the here and now. You walk the walk alongside the Lord's appointed messenger, Miss Kee, you got to be *worthy.*"

"Yes. I . . . Yes." She turned to Patrick and said, "I just checked with my answering service. I've had a couple of calls about job interviews."

"That's wonderful."

"I have to go. Where can I reach you?"

"Just call this number right here, Miss Kee, they'll be staying with me." Reverend Wilkins handed her a card, then said to Buddy, "Before you go upstairs and we go our separate ways, what say we join now and ask the Lord to sanctify this moment."

THIRTEEN

☐ Royce Calder watched as yet another Silicon Valley executive rose from his chair and began spelling out his wish list. As with all the other company presidents who had spoken before him, the man spent a few minutes on platitudes, then turned to how the economy needed jump-starting, and the best way to do this was by the government buying more high-tech products, especially his own. Royce showed the gathering a quietly interested face, while internally he was busy calculating just how much the Party could garner from this little gathering.

The Old Executive Office Building's south wing was dominated by what had once been the State Department Library. The entire State Department had been housed in this portion of the OEOB until 1947. Since then, the State Department had doubled in size, and redoubled again, and a third time, and a fourth, and now was approaching its fifth doubling. The library now housed White House archives, legal tomes, and agency documents. But occasionally it also saw service as a very exclusive gathering point.

The executive from the San Mateo company finished to polite applause. The secretary of commerce thanked the gentleman, then introduced the next high-tech CEO, who rose to her feet and declared that President Gifford urgently needed to help her company dig itself out of the recessionary hole. Royce glanced around the room and calculated there was close to four million dollars seated around the broad oval table—not four million in personal worth, but rather four million in potential soft-money contributions.

Soft money was the grease that smoothed the campaign process.

Congress was very much aware of the public's desire to see campaign spending reined in. But Congress was also very much aware that the current state of affairs supported the people who had already gained office. Elected officials were able to use their status to raise more money. Elected officials could do favors for contributors. Elected officials therefore had more to spend, and thus could buy more airtime, and be seen by more people. A genuine limit on campaign spending would be like these same elected officials shooting themselves in their collective foot.

The result was that Congress continued to pass campaign reform laws, but only pertaining to money given directly to any candidate. This was a very shrewd move, and one that power-brokers like Royce Calder supported with all their might. It meant that people who did *not* hold office would have even more difficulty raising money, and whatever they raised would be held up to very public scrutiny. There were only three choices left to candidates seeking office. They could be personally very rich and spend their own money. They could try to run an old-style campaign based on personal contact with the public. Or they could be raised up within the ranks of their respective Party, which meant the Party had time to shape these candidates. It also gave the Party the power to support only those who had shown lasting loyalty. This was Royce Calder's favorite kind of candidate. The ones who could be counted on. The ones he could control.

So Congress passed campaign laws, but these laws did not touch *soft money*. This was money given to the Party.

This money could be passed on to those the Party chose to support. And the Party supported those candidates who in turn could be trusted to support the Party. It kept those in office, and those seeking election, tightly within the Party line.

It also meant contributors such as those attending this gathering were treated like the visiting royalty they were.

Though small in number, the "moneymen" dominated the Party's development of issues. They were soft-money donors. They carried the biggest stick there was.

Gatherings like this took place several times every month, sometimes more often. They were drawn together either by region or industry. Most of these Silicon Valley donors had been visitors so often the White House no longer held the same allure as for the first time visitor. They were scheduled to have a reception with President Bradley Gifford this afternoon in the East Room. For the moment, they were content to sit in the OEOB and gawk at these more unfamiliar surroundings.

The central table sat upon a Minton tile floor dating back to the middle of the last century. The coved ceiling was a full four floors overhead, the giant skylight permitting in a gloomy storm-clad light. The walls were intricately designed cast iron, supporting balconies of bookshelves and study alcoves.

Royce was drawn from his financial reverie as the executive pounded on the table to emphasize her final point. The sound echoed back and forth like distant cannon fire. Royce's eye was then caught by Jerry Chevass entering through the library's back doors. He was followed by Elton Hardaway, Royce's assistant. Both men wore tense, worried expressions. Royce ducked his head in apology to the secretary of commerce, then rose and joined the pair in a side alcove.

Jerry began with a whispered, "You're not going to believe this."

"I went over to the Hilton." Elton said, his voice quavering slightly with the excitement of being the first in the know. "I thought it would be a good idea to find out who was traveling with Buddy Korda."

Jerry's eyebrows lifted in a silent gesture to Royce. Royce nodded agreement, and said to Elton. "That was good thinking."

"Prepare yourself for a shock," Jerry said.

The blond young man took a moment to preen before leaning over to whisper, "Korda was met by a tall black man. I've asked around, but I still can't find out who he was."

"If we can't identify him, he's probably not too important politically," Royce said.

"Yes. But I *did* recognize the woman who arrived with Korda." Elton took a breath, then revealed, "Linda Kee."

Royce could not completely hide his surprise. "The television reporter?"

"Not anymore," Jerry said. "She was canned."

"Of course. I heard about that somewhere." Royce's gaze tightened. "This is not good."

"You're telling me," Jerry said. "Korda showing up with his own press relations official is a disaster. You think he knows what we're planning?"

"Impossible," Royce said flatly, hoping it was true.

"But a personal press attache, you know she's going to insist on being there when Korda meets the president."

"We can't have that." Anyone experienced with the Washington style of arm-wrestling would limit the impact they could have. Royce thought furiously, then came up with, "You say she was fired?"

"Last week. Budget cutbacks."

"Well, I can't imagine Korda's outfit paying her anything like what she used to receive from CBS." Calder turned to Elton, "You're sure she was actually traveling with the Korda group?"

"I saw her get out of the car. That's what caught my attention." Elton remained slightly breathless from the impact his news was having. "I was watching her when I recognized Korda. They drove up in the same car. Linda got an overnight bag out of the trunk. They talked with the black man at the reception desk, Linda made a call, then she left."

"All right." Royce made a swift decision, patted his pocket, and then realized, "I left my mobile on my desk."

"I brought it," Elton said, handing it over.

Royce glanced over, received a nod from Jerry. This guy was learning fast. "That was smart thinking, Elton."

"Thank you, Mr. Calder."

"Call me Royce." He punched in a number from memory. When the receptionist answered, he said, "Royce Calder for Mr. Satchell."

An instant later a voice boomed over the phone. "Whatever it is, the answer is maybe."

"I have a problem."

One of the most powerful political consultants in Washington, and as good a friend as Royce could afford, chuckled and responded, "Good, good. I always like to have White House personnel bowing and scraping."

"Linda Kee. Does the name mean anything?"

"You're asking a dedicated bachelor if he knows the most gorgeous reporter to ever have the brains to hold a microphone right side up? You've got to be kidding."

Normally Royce took mild pleasure from Rob Satchell and his humor. But not today. "I'm in a hurry. Linda Kee is proving to be something of a nuisance. She needs a job. Are you hiring?"

"Linda Kee has been fired by CBS?"

"Last week."

"Their ratings are going to take a nosedive." A moment's pause, then, "You want her placed in a position where she can be controlled."

"Exactly."

"That's a tall order. Seeing as how the world is currently in the second Great Depression of the century."

Royce kept his voice blandly soft. "I'm not asking for an economic report. I get enough stats from Treasury."

"I'm just pointing out—"

"No you're not. You're upping the ante. Fine. Name your price."

"This is getting better all the time." The chair squeaked. "All right, here's the deal. I've got a young candidate from Virginia. He's borderline in the congressional primary."

Royce felt a flush rise from his collar. "The man he's running against is a six-term veteran."

"Who is also ninety-seven years old and has slept through the past three sessions. Come on, Royce. You know full well it's time to cut the fellow off. He's snoring so loud, you can't hear the Speaker's gavel."

"All right." Knowing it would be hard, knowing it had to be done. "I'll arrange for one of the Virginia senators to endorse your man."

"And the governor."

"And the governor," he agreed through gritted teeth.

"And you'll loosen the Party's purse strings. We've got to get this boy some airtime."

"Done. But don't ask for anything else."

"Don't worry." Satchell gave a rich chuckle. "Tell you a secret, old son. I'd have hired her anyway." And he broke the connection.

Royce lowered the mobile, waited until he had his emotions fully under control. Then he gave his tight smile and said, "All right, that's done. Now take one of the limos and go pick up Korda. It's time to see who it is we're dealing with here."

Royce made his way back to his seat. As he smiled his apology to the secretary, he promised himself the pleasure of revenge. He hated people who caused him political trouble, who threatened the smooth running of the Party machine. Just as soon as they were finished with Korda, Royce was going to publicly squash him like a bug.

FOURTEEN

☐ Patrick Allen sat in the book-lined study of Reverend James Thaddeus Wilkins. He listened to the chatter and cries and the laughter drifting up from downstairs, and ached for what was no longer.

Upon their arrival his boys had been a little concerned by the noisy greeting. The downstairs hallway and front room had been a mob of strange faces, including three of the Wilkins children with their spouses and families, all there to greet the friend and pastor of Buddy Korda.

They all knew the story of how Patrick had lost his wife, he had seen it in their eyes. But no one had said a word about it. Even so, he and the boys had felt overwhelmed by the noisy welcome, with kids from diapers to college age scrambling around the big P Street vicarage.

Then one of the middle grandchildren had then walked over and inspected the two teenage white boys, who were standing there awkwardly holding their duffel bags. When his grandfather had introduced him as JT, he had grabbed the bag from Jeff and demanded, "Either of you know your way around a computer?"

There had been a visible relaxing of the atmosphere, and an exchange of glances between Patrick's two boys. Then Scott had replied, "Some."

"What about computer games, you ever played?"

"Sure," Jeff said.

The tall boy's gaze remained blank. "Space Invaders, Version Three, Galactic Division, ever come across that one?"

"I think I've seen it around somewhere," Scott replied, matching the bland tone.

But it was too much for Jeff. "Scott's the hottest space pilot in our school," he bragged.

Reverend Wilkins's grandson was utterly unimpressed. "Yeah, well, this here's the big city. You ready to go up against the best?"

Soon after the house resounded with cries and cheers and chatter, while Scott and the older Wilkins grandchild did serious battle across the universe's wide expanse. Patrick sat and recalled times when his own house had echoed with such bedlam. The place had become so quiet since Alice's passing.

Reverend Wilkins walked in, smiled down at Patrick seated by the window, and said, "Kids and computers. Only way I knew how to get them to stay more than five minutes was to put one downstairs in the living room. Still don't know if I did the right thing."

"I'd call it the retreat of a wise man," Patrick offered.

James Thaddeus eased his way down into the big leather chair opposite Patrick. "Fine boys you're raising, brother. Know what the younger one just told me?"

"That would be Jeff. No, I can't imagine what Jeff might have come up with."

"I asked him if he knew where his daddy was. Your boy, he said his daddy had gone off to visit with his momma." James Thaddeus rocked slightly in time to his words, bending stiffly from the waist, back and forth, emphasizing his words with a gentle bass cadence. "Gone off to visit with Momma, yessir, that's what he said, calm as if he was talking 'bout the weather. Said his daddy needed times like this, times to speak with his wife, the woman he loved. Yeah. Little boy growing into a young man, standing there looking at me and speaking the words calm and wise as somebody twice his age. Fine boys there, brother. Real fine. You done your dear Alice proud."

Patrick cleared his throat, and managed to say, "It shows how much he thinks of you, James. He rarely speaks about Alice at all. Even to me."

"No, that boy's grown from a boy to a man since I saw him at the funeral. Ain't spoken to him more'n three, four times on the phone. No, he sees how his daddy treats me, and because he's his father's boy he gives me the same respect." The nodding gradually stilled. "Yes sir, fine boys."

The moment called for the silence of friends, a sharing beyond words and time. The space caused by eighteen months since their last meeting was soon gone and forgotten. Finally James Thaddeus swiveled his chair around and said to the window, "Been spending a lot of time on my knees since you called. Knelt right by the window there, where I could see the lights of this poor, wounded city. And I prayed, yes, prayed as hard as I knew how. Asked my Lord to show me clear as the dawning day why you felt you needed to call old James Thaddeus, and just what He wanted me to do."

Patrick followed the gaze of Reverend Wilkins out the window. To his left the red-brick church anchored the corner. Trees stripped by winter's long storm ringed the park across the street. Their branches waved wildly, frantic supplications to the gray clouds scuttling overhead. A particularly harsh blast of wind shook the windows separating him from the storm and the winter and the city.

"One thing's come clear to me," James Thaddeus went on. "Just one. And that one thing is, Buddy Korda should not be left alone."

"I agree," Patrick said, speaking to the same window and the same city as James Thaddeus. "It feels like you are speaking words my own mind has been trying to tell me."

"That man is going to be standing in the face of the wounded beast," James Thaddeus intoned. "Gonna have a struggle on his hands, and he's gonna need the strength of others. People standing there alongside God's messenger, people praying for him right across this nation."

"I can think of a dozen people I should call right now."

"Got to be careful who we draw in here. Can't have folks who'll say yes, yes, then forget the promise soon as they set the phone back down." The rocking resumed, the quietly compelling voice preparing for the calls to come. "We need special folks here. People who will promise to stand fast, no matter what might come their way. People who will stand for their Lord."

"I hear you." Patrick found himself nodding in time to the older man. "What we're after is people who know how to *commit*."

☐

Buddy sat with the stiff hotel chair pointed toward the window. Outside the sky was shaded a hundred colors, all gray. The clouds roiled and tossed like waves upon an angry sea. His Bible lay closed on the table beside his hand. Every once in a while he reached for it, tapped the cover, then retreated. He had tried to read three times already, but the words seemed spoken from a thousand miles away. He had tried to call home, but the answering machine had responded. Molly was still over at the hospital seeing after their daughter-in-law. Buddy ached for her and his family.

From the hallway outside his door rose a constant clamor, people clumping back and forth, pausing to chatter or laugh or call greetings. The hotel held an almost carnival-like air, a bizarre sensation to have in such depressed times, but that was the feeling Buddy had. As though what he heard and saw held no reality to the world beyond the hotel's boundaries.

When the phone rang he rose with genuine relief, glad for something to pull him from the lonely reverie. "Hello?"

"Mr. Korda, great! This is Sol Goldberg. Hope I'm not disturbing you."

"No, I'm sorry, I don't—"

"I'm vice president of Paramount Pictures, Mr. Korda. I spoke with our contact over at the White House this morning, they told me where to find you. Amazing coincidence. I'm here in Washington, too, getting ready to put a big-ticket film into production. Staying down at the Mayflower." The man had a perpetually booming voice, excited and pressing. "Mr. Korda, I'll put it to you straight. My company would like to do a film of your life."

Buddy reached out a hand and leaned against the wall. "Excuse me?"

"Okay, okay, I know that's kinda sudden. You haven't signed with anybody else, have you?"

"You mean, for a movie? No, I haven't—"

"Look, I've got some of my people here with me. Could you just sit down with us, have a little chat? No harm in a chat, now, is there."

"There is no way—"

"Don't say no, Mr. Korda. You never can tell what kinda good might come out of something like this." Buddy's response had only accelerated the man's rate of speech. "Buddy Korda, the one person who saw all this coming and tried to warn the world. Who out there might want to hear your story?"

The question stopped him cold. "You mean, there might be a greater benefit drawn from this."

"Yeah, benefit. Sure. Exactly. So why don't we get together, have a little confab, see if maybe we can have a meeting of the minds."

Buddy searched his heart, wishing he had some sense of guidance. Was this tied in some way to why he was here? He felt nothing but the same empty silence that had surrounded him since his arrival. Defeat sounded in his own ears as he responded, "I suppose it can't hurt to meet."

"Exactly what I was thinking." Triumph rang in the man's tone, that and an urgent desire to close the deal. "You just stay right there, I'll get my people together and find our driver. Say, twenty minutes, thirty tops. Look forward to meeting you, Mr. Korda, having a little face-to-face."

Buddy set down the phone, wishing now he had refused to meet. There had been a number of such calls in the days just after his message had been delivered and the stock market had done its first nosedive. It had been one of the reasons why Buddy had stopped answering either the phone or the door. Even so, he could always tell when Molly had been pressured by another hard-driving agent or executive. She always returned from the phone with her mouth compressed into a single thin line.

When the phone rang a second time, Buddy grabbed for it, relieved that he could change his mind and cancel the meeting. "Yes, hello."

But it wasn't the executive. "Buddy?"

"Molly." Relief fought with regret. "Where are you?"

"Still at the hospital. I called the house and got your message off the machine. Who did you think I was?"

"Some Hollywood producer. I didn't even get his name. They want to meet."

The rejection he had been expecting did not arise. Instead, Molly asked, "Do you feel like this is part of what took you to Washington?"

"I don't know. I just don't know. I guess that's why I agreed to meet with him."

"Well, maybe that's a good idea."

"What's the matter, honey?"

There came the sound of a long breath over the phone. "I was hoping you wouldn't notice. You've already got enough on your mind."

"Molly, we've been married over thirty years, of course I'm going to notice when something's bothering you." He tried to keep his voice steady, but could not entirely quash the tremor of fear. "How's the baby?"

"Not good." The words were spoken quietly, void of hope. Defeated. "Not good at all."

Buddy leaned both elbows on the table, cradling his head in his forearms. "How is Anne?"

"Sweetheart, I'm not sure . . . You have so much else to think about just now."

"Molly, tell me what's happened."

"Anne just had a bad night, that's all."

"No, that's not all. Stop trying to protect me."

"You need to be strong now."

"How can I be strong when I'm worried sick over what I don't know?"

"Buddy, darling . . ." She stopped, said in defeat, "I never was any good at holding things back from you."

"Tell me, Molly."

"Neither Paul nor I could seem to get any answers. So finally this afternoon I asked Dr. Kendrick if she could do some checking for us."

"Who?"

"Renee Kendrick. Patrick's friend on the ward. She's a new intern here, and she goes to our church."

"All right." Buddy's chest was so tight he had trouble drawing enough breath to speak. "Tell me what she said."

"At least now we know what happened." Molly seemed to share his difficulty, for she had to stop and take a quick little breath after each sentence. "The day before yesterday, Anne felt the baby go all still inside her. She called the doctor's emergency line, and he had Paul rush her straight to the hospital. They did a CTG and an ultrasound and couldn't find a heartbeat. Wait, I wrote this down because I knew I'd need to tell you . . ."

There was the rustle of paper being unfolded, then Molly continued, "They couldn't find a heartbeat. We knew that much. They called in a neonatal pediatrician and rushed Anne to the emergency surgical unit and did a crash induction. That's when they don't wait for the patient to stop eating long enough to empty their system, they just anesthetize her immediately. As soon as she was under, they did an emergency C-section. Anne had started complaining of pains, I forgot to mention that, didn't I? Buddy?"

"I'm still here." His forehead rested on the table, his hands linked over the back of his head and the phone.

"She had contraction pains that started right after the baby stopped moving. But they couldn't wait to induce labor. Every second counted if there was any chance for the baby. Dr. Kendrick explained that this was a very rushed operation. From the time they had Anne under to the time they had the baby out was less than two minutes." A very ragged breath, then, "This emergency procedure is very hard on the mother. The doctor says it will take a while to know if Anne's recovery . . ."

"Oh, Molly."

"Wait a minute." Buddy heard the phone bang down on the counter, then the sound of Molly blowing her nose. The phone was lifted back up. "All right. The neonatal pediatrician immediately began an emergency resuscitation procedure on the baby. He had to use, wait, I have it written here, cardiopulmonary pressure. It means they had to knead the baby's chest. But they found a heartbeat and so they gave the little thing oxygen and moved him up to the special care unit."

Buddy had to take a moment to find the strength to ask, "Have you seen him?"

"This morning. Paul went with me." Another shaky moment, but Molly fought for control and won. "Buddy, the little thing isn't moving. They're having to ventilate him just to keep him breathing. He's stuck with so many pins and tabs and tubes he looks awful. Just awful."

"Honey, I'm so sorry."

"Paul took it very hard. I think that's probably what set Anne off. For a little while it looked like we might lose her too. But she's better now, and the doctor's given her something to help her rest. He made Paul take a pill, too, and they've set up a cot in Anne's room."

"Where are the girls?"

"Over with Trish and Jack. I'm supposed to pick them up this evening. Wait, I need to tell you the rest." Again there was the sound of paper rustling. "Dr. Kendrick told me that the baby's Apgar score was very bad. That's the way the hospital measures how flat the baby is, how little movement he has. A normal baby has a score of eight or nine, which means it's wiggling and crying well. Our baby scored just two, which means he could scarcely breathe and he wasn't moving at all."

"I understand." But he didn't. Not at all. It was not just the baby's ill health. It was the way God had let him down. How could he have been given such a terribly misleading message? There was only one answer. He had been listening to the wrong voice all along. But how could God have let the wrong voice speak to him? Wasn't he trying as hard as he could to be a good servant? Something was terribly, horribly wrong about all this. "I should be up there with you."

But Molly was too caught up in the telling to hear him. "There is a great concern there will be permanent damage from the baby having gone without oxygen to the brain for too long. He might even have cerebral palsy." Molly did not even try for control anymore. "We won't know for a few more months if he starts missing normal milestones. That is, if he . . ."

"I'm coming home, Molly. My family needs me."

"No, don't." But there was no force behind her protest.

"I don't even know what I'm doing down here."

"Serving God."

"I don't know what voice I've been listening to. How can these things be happening to us, Molly?"

Molly sniffed loudly and managed, "They're doing everything they can for Anne and the baby, honey. There's nothing more you can do for them by coming back right now."

"Of course there is. My family is hurting. They need me to be there for them."

"I don't know what to tell you. Just pray about this, all right?"

"Yes. Fine. I love you, honey. Give my love to Paul and Anne when they wake up."

Buddy hung up the phone and rose slowly to his feet. He would pray if he could. But right now desperation ringed him with an impenetrable wall that kept out everything, all light, all hope.

The phone rang. Buddy looked down at it, wondering if he had the strength to lift the receiver.

□

"Mr. Korda, great, just great. Sol Goldberg, glad you could fit us in."

"Mr. Goldberg. I'm sorry you came all this way. I really don't—"

"This is Tony Shaefer, head of our group's finance division. And Sal Collins, Paramount's number one feature film director. You mighta heard of his latest hit, *Final Showdown*. Number one on the charts right now."

The three men could not have been more out of place in the Hilton lobby. All three were smiling and polished and dressed in suits that clearly had been hand-tailored to fit their suntanned forms. Buddy replied, "I'm sorry, I haven't had much opportunity to get to the pictures recently."

"The pictures, hear that, Sal? When was the last time you heard anybody call them that?"

The director was a softer-spoken man, slender where Sol Goldberg was bulky. But he shared the executive's glossy look. Like a sleek, hybrid cat. "I've directed eleven features for Paramount, Mr. Korda."

"That's right, and every one a winner," Sol gushed.

The moneyman spoke for the first time, his voice as dry as his gaze. "Sol and Sal, you couldn't ask for a stronger team in Hollywood, Mr. Korda. Every picture they've done together has had great legs. That means they break strong and stay ahead of the pack. People are begging for a chance to buy into their next picture. I'm sure I don't need to tell you in times like these, financial backing is extremely hard to find."

"Why don't we get outta the rush here, take a seat. I tried to book us a conference room, but there's something big going on here, everything was taken." Sol took hold of Buddy's arm and guided him through the bustling hall. The crowd was even denser and louder than it had been upon Buddy's arrival, and even more strange in appearance. Colors swirled like a drunken rainbow as people mingled about them. A lady rushed by, trailing a scarf as large as a flag. Upon its brilliant purple backdrop galloped a golden dragon. The three Hollywood executives in their well-cut suits and collarless shirts and carefully groomed hair drew stares like magnets. But even more attention was focused upon Buddy.

Once they were seated in the leather overstuffed chairs at the side of the lobby, Sol Goldberg leaned across the low dividing table and went on. "Like I was saying, Buddy—you don't mind if I call you Buddy, do you? Great. Like Tony was saying, all the films Sal's done for us have had great legs. That means if we say we're going to do a movie of your life, you can put money on it. The film is gonna get done."

"That's a hard guarantee to find in Hollywood these days," the director added.

"Nobody else is in a position to offer you such an ironclad guarantee straight off like we can. They might say they're interested, but they'll spend years getting the package together. With Sal's latest film sitting there at number one for the tenth week running, what we say goes."

"Naturally," Sal added, "I'd take a much lighter hand to your story than I did with *Final Showdown*."

"Sure, sure, that goes without saying. I mean, on the one hand we've got gang warriors taking over a school and holding the kids ransom. On the other, we've got the man who tried to warn the world that everything was gonna take a dive."

Buddy found his attention focusing. "That's what your film is about? Gang warfare?"

"Not warfare, Mr. Korda. Not at all." The director's voice carried the polished smoothness of one well-prepped to respond to such questions. "My film is a societal statement of the effects of this current economic malaise. We're portraying the anger and frustration of an entire generation of materially deprived youth through the actions of—"

Goldberg broke in with, "What Sal's trying to say, Buddy, is a gang takes over this school and holds it for ransom. Then the greatest action hero in movies comes in and saves the day. You gotta admit, it's a bold idea. When Sal came to me with the concept, I thought, whoa, how come nobody's done this before?"

"I thought it up myself," Sal admitted proudly. "Our driver had the day off, the nanny was sick, my wife was busy with something or other, and I was sitting outside my six-year-old daughter's school waiting for her to come out. And like a bolt of lightning out of the blue, it hit me. A gang armed with everything from submachine guns to bazookas walks in and takes over the entire school. Seven hundred kids and teachers, all getting wired with explosives while the meanest teenage hoodlums you could ever imagine demand ten million dollars in cash. I mean, talk about terror."

"Nothing like operating with a genius, is there, Buddy?" Sol exclaimed proudly. "Fear is what works in this business. And Sal has struck gold with this one."

Buddy had heard enough. But before he could rise to his feet and break off the discussion, a great booming sound began resounding through the hall. In the far corner a pair of women were pounding on feather-clad drums. Several people joined arms and did shuffling steps in tight little circles.

Rising with Buddy, Sol came in close enough to shout, "Can you believe this? Look, why don't we go over to my suite at the Mayflower, get down to some serious discussions."

Buddy felt as if the drums were beating directly into the bones of his skull. "What is going on here?"

"What, you mean the drums?"

"No! I mean everything!" Buddy took in the entire lobby with one sweeping gesture. "Who *are* these people?"

Sol backed off and gave Buddy an astounded look. "You mean you don't know?"

"Know *what?*"

"These are fortune-tellers!" Sol glanced around, making sure his two colleagues were sharing in the joke. "I can't believe you hadn't heard about this!"

The film director leaned forward to add over the drums, "You've spawned an entire industry, Mr. Korda."

"Yeah, probably the only one in the country that's growing right now!" Sol found that hilarious. "Washington's full of these people. Everybody claiming to have a direct line to what's gonna happen tomorrow, and how to ward off all the bad stuff."

"I have to get out of here," Buddy declared. When they looked at him in astonishment, he raised his voice and said, "I am leaving—right *now!*"

"Mr. Korda, Buddy, wait! We'll go back to the Mayflower—"

But he was already sprinting for the reception desk. The woman standing behind it saw him approaching and set down the phone. She leaned across the desk and said, "Mr. Korda, I was just trying to call your room."

"I want to check out."

"What?" The drums chose that moment to stop. After the cheers died down, the marble-lined foyer echoed with the silence. "Oh, thank goodness. Somebody from the White House just called. They are sending over a car and driver to pick you up."

"I won't be here."

"They said . . . Excuse me?"

"Please prepare my bill. I'm checking out now."

"But Mr. Korda, they—"

"Right now."

"Yes sir." She keyed into her computer, read off the screen, "The White House is picking up your tab."

"Fine. Can you tell me the nearest place I can book a flight?"

"There's a travel agent just along the hall to your left at the back of the shopping arcade. Right next to the rental car agency."

"Excellent. Thank you." Buddy was already moving for the elevators. He felt the glares of the three Hollywood people, but did not even bother to look their way. Five minutes to pack and call Molly, then back downstairs and take the fastest way out. Buddy decided he would wait and call Patrick once he got back to Aiden. He stepped into the elevator and punched the fifth floor, then smiled at his reflection as he realized Molly would still be at the hospital. The bell pinged for the fifth floor, and Buddy was moving before the doors had fully opened. He could call home and leave a message. No reason at all to give his wife or his friends a chance to change his mind. No. He was headed back to the one place on earth he belonged, and nothing on earth would stop him.

Buddy Korda was going home.

FIFTEEN

☐ "I'm sorry, Mr. Korda." The rental car agent was a girl in her early twenties with a cheerfully serious air. "We just don't seem to have any cars available."

"Anything." Buddy strived to keep the panic from his voice. "It's an emergency. I've got to get out of here *now*." Then he remembered, and grabbed for his wallet. As he frantically searched through his little pile of plastic, he said, "Look, look, I have your special Honors Card. Here, right here." Actually it had been given to him when he was still traveling for the bank, but it was in his name, and for some reason he had never thrown it away. He pointed to the writing on the back and read, "It says I am *guaranteed* to have a car *at any time.*"

"Well, I suppose . . ." She keyed something into the computer console, studied the screen, and then said doubtfully, "We had a car come in last night, but the former renters left it on the street in gang territory and it's been totally trashed."

"Fine. I'll take it."

"Mr. Korda," she showed him a very concerned expression. "You seem like such a nice man. Couldn't you wait until tomorrow? I'm sure—"

"That's impossible."

"You really don't want this car. What about taking a plane?"

"Aiden doesn't have an airport, and all the flights to Wilmington are full. I checked."

"Well, a train then."

"There's a problem with the tracks. All trains going north have been delayed indefinitely." Buddy swiped a frantic hand through his already frazzled hair. He had spent the most frustrating ninety minutes of his life in the travel agency next door. It had felt as though every door in the universe was being slammed shut in his face. Buddy headed off the young lady's next suggestion with, "And the two buses scheduled for Delaware this afternoon have been canceled. Believe me, whatever you have is my only hope of getting out of town."

"How about waiting just a few hours? We're not expecting anything back until the morning, but you never can tell."

"I don't care how the car looks," Buddy assured her.

"I'll have to speak with our area supervisor." She picked up the phone. "I don't even know why I mentioned it. But it's so strange—I can't remember a time when we didn't have *anything*." She waited a moment, then said into the receiver, "Mrs. Atkinson? It's Betty at the Hilton. We have an emergency request from an Honors Card holder and all we have on the lot is the . . . Yes ma'am, the Explorer. Uh-huh, I told him. No, he says he can't wait." She listened a moment, studying Buddy's face, and finally gave him a nod. "Yes ma'am, I'll tell him. Yes, I have a waiver right here."

She hung up the phone and said, "I wish I could say you are in luck."

"I can't thank you enough."

"Wait until you see the car to tell me that. Could I have your driver's license and a major credit card? And please read and sign this waiver; it says you have been informed of the car's condition and accept it regardless. Or maybe you'd rather go see it first."

"No need." Buddy scribbled his signature. "I'm sure it's fine."

She began preparing the contract. "How long will you require the vehicle?"

"Just for today. I'll drop it off tomorrow in Aiden, Delaware."

She halted her work. "Are you aware there is an out-of-state drop-off charge?"

By that point Buddy was beyond caring. "Fine."

"Boy, it must be some emergency." She resumed typing. "I'm afraid I have to charge you full rate for an oversize luxury vehicle, and you'll need to take insurance and liability, that's not an option for a car in this condition because—"

"Whatever. Can you hurry?"

"Okay, almost done." She slid from her seat and walked to where the printer quietly hummed. She ripped the contract free and laid it on the counter in front of him. "Please initial everywhere I have made the *X*'s, and sign at the bottom."

Buddy started signing, then halted to exclaim, "Six hundred and twelve dollars?"

"I really think you should wait for something else to come in, Mr. Korda."

"No, no, fine, I'll pay." Buddy signed the contract and waited for his copy, then hefted his suitcase and demanded, "Where's the car?"

"Right this way, please."

He followed her out the door, trying not to think about all the money he had just agreed to shell out. The wind was harsh and warm and full of grit. It flung a fistful into Buddy's face, peevish and worrisome. Buddy squinted and clenched his suitcase tighter.

Then he spotted the car, and stopped in his tracks. "That can't be it."

"I told you, Mr. Korda. If it wasn't an emergency and if you didn't have that card, we wouldn't dream of letting you take this vehicle anywhere." The agent was holding her hair down with her right hand, the other gripping the contract against the blustering wind. "They really did a job on it, didn't they?"

The once-luxurious Ford Explorer was a mess. Every window was cracked, and the back window had been replaced by plastic sheeting lined with green tape. The exterior had been sprayed with jagged graffiti lettering. The side Buddy could see shouted in angry red and black, *Danger, Danger.*

"At least they left the tires," she said doubtfully. "That is, the police arrived before they could strip anything more than—"

"It's fine." He was growing more angry by the moment. He didn't care if unseen forces were pushing and prodding him to stay in Washington. He was going *home.* "Where are the keys?"

"In the ignition, at least they should be."

Buddy walked around to the other side, where the car's entire length shouted, *BACK OFF.* He snorted and opened the door and flung his bag inside. Then he had to take a step back at the smell. But because the agent was watching him and looking for a reason to call the whole thing off, he took a deep breath and plunged inside. The seats were ripped apart, the radio torn out, and the stench was simply terrible.

Buddy ignored the shards of cut leather jamming into his back, and held his breath until he could get the car started and power down the cracked window. With his first new breath he said, "Great. Just great."

"Uh-huh." She leaned farther back to avoid the pungent odor. "I'm sure if you'd just—"

"Thanks for all your help." He flung the car into drive, ignoring the grinding protest from the hood. "Bye."

Getting lost four times before he found the proper bridge across the Potomac only hardened his resolve. As did the hour-long backup at the ramp leading onto I-95 north. The truck that slewed across three lanes of traffic and almost removed the graffiti from his left side only stirred him to press harder on the gas pedal. By the time he hit the Maryland state border, Buddy was doing almost eighty miles an hour, and the steering wheel was shimmying so hard it blurred his vision. Buddy only gritted his teeth and hung on tighter. Nothing was going to stop him now. Buddy Korda was going *home.*

Yet he could do nothing about the sense of quiet tragedy that invaded his soul. His heart felt squeezed by a guilt so strong he could have stopped and wept there by the side of the road. But he was committed now. He was leaving all the misery of that great wounded city behind. He knew where he belonged, and it was not in Washington, D.C.

Then he crested a rise, and this time he had to slow down. He *had* to. For up ahead it seemed as though reality itself was splitting apart, tearing into bizarre shreds. Overhead the clouds were descending.

Not just *a* cloud. The entire *sky* seemed to be falling. Settling in feathery curling wisps, unfurling like great gray streamers, unwinding in soft calamitous mystery.

And then it began to snow.

Buddy looked out the window in dazed bewilderment. When he had left Washington he had been in a spring-weight suit and no overcoat. The sky had been gray and the weather blustery, but certainly no colder than he would have expected for a stormy April afternoon. Yet this was no final spring flurry. Flakes as big as the palm of his hand landed and clustered upon his windshield. And what fell upon the highway was sticking.

He turned on his windshield wipers—no, only the wiper on his side worked. And this one scraped and squeaked its way across the glass. The other wiper was a broken metal nub, waving like an admonishing finger at him through the windshield, urging him to reconsider his course.

Buddy rolled down his window, and a Siberian ice storm was flung into his face. A blast of wind ripped through the opening, rocking the car and causing him to wrench the steering wheel hard for control. The car lifted up on two wheels, slammed down hard, began sliding in the other direction. Buddy's eyes were open wide now, ice needles or no ice needles. He remembered his early training and pumped the brakes in quick little bursts, steering against the car's four-wheel skid, reducing both speed and the severity of the swerves. Gradually he regained control and steered over to the shoulder. He pressed down on the brakes so hard his thigh muscles bunched and quivered. He jammed on the emergency blinker and sat there, his breath coming in quick, high-pitched gasps.

Only then did he realize just how cold he was.

Tears of fright had spilled and frozen upon both cheeks. The snow still pushing through his open window was lying in white abandon across his lap and the dash. His left hand, the one closest to the open window, felt frozen to the wheel. Buddy unclenched his grip and pressed the button to roll up his window. The glass squeaked and shuddered and finally ground to a halt about halfway up. He turned and stared at the glass, then beat his fist on the panel and opened and slammed the door, then tried the electric button once more. The glass did not budge.

Buddy dug through his suitcase and came up with two T-shirts and a pair of pants. He bundled these up tightly and jammed them into the open slit. He had no choice. As cold as it was, it was either seal the opening or suffer frostbite on that side of his face.

He jammed the heater's temperature control all the way over to high. His hand was poised on the fan control, when he finally realized how quiet it had become.

He swiveled in his seat, but could not see anything because of the plastic sheeting for a back window. He tried to look through the side mirror, and that did not help either. Reluctantly he opened his door and rose from his seat.

The wind did its best to rip him from the car. He cupped both hands around his eyes and scouted behind and ahead. He could not see another car. In both directions, the major road artery running from Washington to New York was utterly, completely empty.

Already the vista looked like the dead of winter. Drifts leaned against tree trunks and piled high on branches. The highway was still speckled with black, but was swiftly becoming merely windswept white. Buddy slid back into his seat and slammed the door. He turned the fan on high, ignoring the putrid smell that blew out with the heat. He held his hands in front of the vent, waited until feeling had returned to his fingers, then gripped the wheel and put the car into drive. If anything, the snow seemed to be falling harder.

He kept his speed to 10 miles per hour, yet even with four-wheel drive the wind was pushing him all over the road. Three times in fifteen minutes, blasts almost flung him into the ditch. Buddy squinted around the falling snow and drove with white-knuckle determination. Fear was a beast burrowing deep into his gut, its cries all black and full of nightmare scenarios. If he did not find shelter, he was going to die.

When the snow-encrusted road sign appeared through the blizzard, Buddy could not help but cry out in relief. He increased his speed, only to end up in a four-wheel skid that slammed him into the highway's inside railing. Buddy did not even stop to recover. He jerked the gearshift into reverse, pulled away with a rending shriek of metal, slapped it into drive, and started off again.

Finally the second rest-stop sign wavered into frozen view. Buddy slowed his pace, the tires scrunching and sliding over the snow.

He almost missed the turnoff, it was snowing so hard. Buddy had to stop and reverse, not wanting to risk going over an embankment. Even so, fifty feet into the side road the car hit an icy strip and stuck. The wheels spun, halted, spun again. Buddy sat back in the seat, struggling against panic. He was going to have to get out and walk.

If he was careful, if he stayed on the pavement, he should be able to find the rest stop. He had no choice. If he stayed in the car he was going to freeze to death.

He pried loose his bundle of clothes, the outer segments snow-encrusted and frozen rock hard. He stuffed them back into his suitcase. If the rest stop was not heated he would have to wear everything he had just to survive.

The wind was blowing so hard it ripped the car door from his grasp.

Buddy rose to his feet, the suitcase gripped as tightly as he could manage, and forced himself to remain there a moment. He could not see three feet in front of his face. Even the hood of the car was lost from where he stood by the open door. His only hope was to aim in the direction the car was pointed, and use the wind at his back to help him navigate.

He started off. His back was burning and his feet in their business shoes were already turning numb. But the wind pushed and prodded so that he was fairly certain he was headed in the direction of the road.

He walked and he walked and he saw nothing but falling sheets of white. He could no longer feel his feet, and his back was growing so numb he could not tell for certain where the wind was coming from. Buddy stopped, shut his eyes and turned around, trying to make sure the wind was still straight to his back. But the icy needles seemed to rake at him from all sides, and his ears could hear nothing but a constant roar.

Buddy fought down a rising gorge of panic. He forced himself back around and kept moving forward. He had to go forward. The desire to turn around was suicidal. He had to find the rest stop. It was his only hope.

He found the curb by falling over it. He picked himself up and stumbled on, no longer certain which way he was headed, knowing only if he did not find refuge swiftly he would fall once more and not have the strength to get up.

He found the building by colliding with the redbrick wall. He backed up a step, sobbing with relief and fatigue, and traced his free hand along the comforting rough surface. He tripped around the corner, stumbling over a knee-high drift, and pushed through a door he could not even see. And entered into safety.

Buddy fell facedown onto the cold tile floor. He lay there for what seemed like hours, lost in the dark, trapped in the belly of this great white beast of winter.

SIXTEEN

☐ Patrick dialed the number, listened to it ring, and said to James Thaddeus Wilkins, "I don't believe I've ever dreaded a call like this one."

The reverend winced so hard his face seemed to fold down upon itself. "I hear you brother, I surely do."

"I suppose if she doesn't answer this time I'll have to call the hospital. But I sure hate bothering . . ." He was halted in mid-sentence by the sound of the receiver being picked up. To the sound of a familiar hello, he started in with, "Molly, it's Patrick. How are you?"

"Tired." She did not sound tired. She sounded exhausted. Her voice held the tinny quality of old-time movies, scratchy with strain. "Anne has been having a hard day, Buddy probably told you."

He avoided answering that by asking, "How is she?"

"She's still with us. She and the baby both. That's about all I can say right now." Molly turned from the phone and said, "Veronica, honey, don't pull your sister's hair. No, dear, it's her doll. I'm sure yours is up there on your bed. No, you can't have any more cookies, it's hours past your bedtime. Go on upstairs and brush your teeth and get into your nightie."

"I'm sorry," Patrick said. "I've caught you at a bad time."

"They're just tired. We've had a long day. How is Buddy?"

"Actually, that's why I'm calling. Has Buddy been in contact with you?"

"Not since right he arrived at the hotel. I just this second walked in the door. I haven't even checked my answering machine for messages. Why, isn't he there?"

"Would you mind just checking and seeing if he's called you? I'll wait."

She hesitated, then said with all traces of fatigue gone from her voice, "Hang on a moment."

Patrick waited and listened through several inconsequential messages, then stiffened as he heard Buddy's voice say in the distance, "Honey, it's me. I've had all I can stand of this place. I'm no closer to understanding what it is I'm supposed to be doing than I was when I got here, and I'm a *lot* less certain whose voice I've been hearing."

Molly murmured into the phone, "What on earth?"

Buddy's voice broke in with, "It's about three now. I can't get a flight out, everything's booked, and there's something the matter with the trains. I'm going down and renting a car and driving back. I'll be home as soon as I can. If Patrick calls . . . I love you, honey. Tell Patrick I'll call him tomorrow."

"Patrick, why would—"

Patrick found it necessary to wipe the perspiration from his forehead. "Molly, can you just wait and see if he's called you again?" They listened through several other relatively unimportant messages, including three from Patrick asking her to call him just as soon as she got in. Patrick said quietly to the reverend, "Buddy called to say he was heading home."

"Lord have mercy," James Thaddeus murmured.

When Buddy's voice did not reappear, Molly said tightly, "What happened down there, Patrick?"

"I wish I knew. We got into D.C. just after lunch. I stayed with Buddy until I was sure he had checked in okay, then went over to Reverend Wilkins's with the boys. When we came back to pick him up for dinner, the hotel said he had checked out."

"What? When?"

"That was, oh," Patrick checked his watch. "About four hours ago now."

"It's ten-thirty at night! How on earth could it take so long for Buddy to get home?"

Again Patrick dragged a hand across his forehead. "Have you heard about the storm that hit just north of here?"

"Meredith, go back upstairs and climb into bed. No, sweetie, I can't hold you now. Go on, I'll be up to tuck you both in shortly." A moment's pause, then, "Patrick, I haven't heard a thing. I've been at the hospital all day."

"They're calling it the freak storm of the millennium. It's been snowing in Prince George's County since about the time Buddy called you."

"Snowing!"

"I know it sounds crazy, but Molly, every road out of Washington headed north has been closed. They've had to get every snowplow in three states out of summer grease, and still they say I-95 won't open until tomorrow morning."

She sounded frantic now. "It's gotten cold here, but there isn't a hint of rain, much less snow!"

"I know, it's the same here. A cold wind, but no snow. Nothing." He shook his head at the reverend, who lowered his head in dismay. "Molly, we're stuck here in Washington tonight. Tomorrow, just as soon as they open the roads, I'll start back. If Buddy gets in, would you please call us here at James Thaddeus's home? Do you have his number?"

"I wrote it down here by the phone." She hesitated, then asked worriedly, "Do you think we should call the police?"

Worry sat like a block of ice in his stomach. "I suppose it can't hurt. Just to be safe."

□

Night turned into morning. By Wednesday afternoon, with still no word from Buddy, Reverend Wilkins felt compelled to call Molly himself. "Mrs. Korda? I don't know if you'll remember me, but my name is James Thaddeus Wilkins."

"Of course, good afternoon, Reverend. I met you at Alice's funeral. Patrick has told us what a help you were to him and the family."

"I hope I haven't caught you at a bad time."

"No, I took the girls over to the hospital so they could see their daddy, and we're back now for some lunch. Wait, let me get off my coat." Molly shed her scarf and coat and deposited them with her purse on the hall chair. "How are you, Reverend?"

"Ashamed, ma'am. Mortally ashamed and repentant. Which is why I asked Patrick to let me make this call."

"I see." Molly found herself rocking back and forth slightly, as though tiny tremors ran up the floor and through her frame. "So you still don't have any word about Buddy?"

"No, ma'am. None at all. That storm is still blocking passage for the highway folks. They been down the road a few times, haven't seen nothing at all. Not a single car. But it's still snowing so hard they can't fly over it, can't hardly drive through it. Strangest thing anybody's ever seen."

"Yes, they were talking about it on the radio as I was coming back from the hospital. A thermal inversion, I think they called it."

"Yes, I heard that talk too. Seems to me they're lots of smart people scratching their heads and trying to feel better by naming the Unnamed."

The tremors strengthened into a shiver. "You think God's hand is at work here, Reverend?"

"Yes, ma'am, that's exactly what I'm thinking. Yes, I do believe we are witnessing the hand of God settling upon our land."

Molly found herself relaxing, as though somewhere deep within a knot was gently being released. "I don't know, I just don't . . . To be honest, Reverend, I've been so worried about Anne and the baby . . . I put the girls to bed last night, then lay down for a moment and the next thing I knew it was eight o'clock this morning. And me still in all my clothes. I hadn't spent a moment thinking about Buddy. That sounds terrible, I know."

"No, ma'am, it sounds human." Reverend Wilkins hesitated, then said, "It also sounds like maybe God's hand was at work in your weariness."

It was Molly's turn to ponder. "Half of my mind feels so caught in a tangle of worries I don't know which way to turn. The other half . . . Do you know, Reverend, somehow what you've just said gives me hope."

"Me too, ma'am. Me too. Mind if I ask how your sick ones are doing? I know Patrick will ask."

"Wait a second." Molly settled the phone against her shoulder, and heard the girls playing upstairs and out of hearing range. She then said into the phone, "Anne is doing somewhat better today. She rested well last night."

"And the baby?"

Molly struggled to hold her voice steady. "The doctors didn't seem so pessimistic this morning. That's about all I can say."

"We've all been praying for them both. And for you."

"Thank you, Reverend. I'm most grateful."

"Gratitude ain't why I'm making this call." James Thaddeus sighed long and hard over the phone. "I feel like this is all my fault. The Lord called me to be there for your man. And I said yes, oh yes, amen, Lord. Tomorrow."

A sound came over the phone, one that might have been a moan. "Yes, I knew it was Him speaking to my heart, and He was saying not to leave your Buddy alone. And I said right away, 'Lord, let me just go back and see to my own first and I'll be right with You.'"

Molly bent over and brushed her coat and scarf and purse to the floor. She settled down onto the chair and said, "Don't be too hard on yourself, Reverend. I called Buddy right after he arrived in Washington. He needed my strength, but all I gave him was need and worry. I think that's why he drove home." The shivers returned. "I spoke to the police. They say they're doing everything they can to free up the road."

"Yes, ma'am, same this end."

"Do you think I should come down?"

"You'd be most welcome, Mrs. Korda. But to tell the truth, it seems to me you can do more staying there in Aiden to help the family. And praying."

"I am. Just as hard as I know how." The tremors finally reached her voice. "It's all my fault."

"No ma'am, excuse me, but it's not. And it don't help anybody or anything for you to shoulder a guilt that's not yours to carry."

Molly nodded to the opposite wall, but could not keep from saying, "If only I had given Buddy the confidence and hope he needed. I feel like I failed God as much as Buddy."

Reverend Wilkins sighed his agreement. "Seems so easy, heeding the call when it comes. Spent a lifetime telling my church to be ready, to stay awake, to listen for all they're worth. Then look at what I went and did. I'm making this call to ask your forgiveness."

"There's nothing to forgive, but I accept your apology." Molly tasted the words rising from somewhere deep inside, and decided they needed saying. "This will probably sound crazy, but in the moments when I'm not trapped by worry I have the strangest feeling that Buddy is all right."

The voice over the phone lightened perceptibly. "Do you know, ma'am, I've been having the same feeling. Yes, like there's a purpose, even here, even now. Every time I start to do my mourning and my moaning, I feel like the Lord is there, saying, 'Peace, be still.'"

☐

Thirteen years as the son of a pastor had taught Jeff that there were times to be himself and times to play the tortoise. With the worry of both his dad and Reverend Wilkins hanging in the air, today was definitely a time to remain hidden inside his shell.

A constant trail of children and grandchildren and parishioners and people from up and down the street paraded through the Wilkinses' back door. So many kids and adults Jeff stopped trying even to count them, much less figure out who was kin and who was just curious. A lot of dark faces appeared in the living room doorway to say hi and look him and Scott over. A lot. He was used to being stared at, used to people being nice to him because they wanted his daddy the pastor to think they were right with God and the reverend. And there were a lot of black families in their Aiden church—at least, a lot by the standards of other churches he had visited. But this was something totally new.

Nobody needed to tell him Reverend Wilkins was more than a pastor. He was leader of this community. Jeff was okay with that, his dad had taken on a lot of the same since the crash. But this was different. Here, people came and went in waves, asking for everything from recipes to advice about kids, marital problems, and money. Everybody seemed to know everybody else's business and talked about it as if it were the most normal thing in the world. Some of the things he heard discussed made he and Scott exchange wide-eyed looks.

There was always a pot of coffee brewing, always something simmering on the stove. The whole house smelled of bacon and turnip greens and coffee and fresh biscuits. Most everybody walked around with a plate in their hands and something in their mouth. Anytime he went in the back there must have been a dozen women in the kitchen cooking or talking or washing up, and everybody asking if he didn't want anything more to eat. In one of their few quiet moments Scott had confessed he was about ready to start waddling like a duck, he was so full.

The kids in the living room had settled into a sort of pecking order. The older one, the kid playing on the computer with Scott, was called James the Third. Or Thirdly. Or JT. His brother Gregory, also known as Little G, played chess on the coffee table with Jeff. Big G was his uncle, one of the largest men Jeff had ever seen. The man drove a taxi. Big G stood six-foot-thirteen and weighed as much as his Buick. His voice sounded like a bear growling from the back of a cave. He was also one of the most gentle men Jeff had ever met.

That morning Big G had come over and introduced himself, swallowing first Scott's then Jeff's hand in one bigger than a baseball mitt. He had then smiled as every child in the room had raced over to pile onto him, letting them climb up as though he were a flesh-covered mountain, clearly loving it. He had said to Jeff and Scott that since their daddy looked to be tied up most of the day, would they like to go for a drive and see the sights.

Gregory had wedged himself into his taxi, the wheel creasing his bulging middle, and toured Jeff and Scott and Little G and JT and Kitty around for a while. But all the homeless had made Jeff sad, and the buildings had not seemed to sparkle as he remembered as a kid, and all they talked about was the thermal inversion and where Buddy Korda might be. So finally Big G drove them back to the house, and they returned to their games.

There were a lot of other kids hanging around, some he was at least able to name. Kitty and Samantha played dolls back behind the television where the boys couldn't get at them. Reuben and Robert, twins with skin the color of sun-dressed honey, sprawled on the hook rug reading comics pulled from a chest kept behind the sofa.

Little G watched Jeff move his queen's knight and scoffed, "What you think you're doing, boy?"

Jeff had learned not to pay the words any mind. The night before, though his confidence had been shattered the first few games by Little G's constant scoffing. Then JT had leaned over and said not to worry about it, Gregory had a mouth on him was all. So Jeff had hunkered down and concentrated, and the next game he had whipped Little G six ways from Sunday, which had earned him a quiet little "huh" from the boy across from him. Jeff was two games up now, and feeling pretty good.

But as the day wore on, a sense of quiet gravity settled in on them all. It infected even the kids, the littlest ones beginning to fret and run for comfort to whichever adult was closest. Jeff's dad went out and came back with his overcoat all wet, which caused Jeff and Scott to exchange another of those looks, the kind they had developed for when they were in public and couldn't really talk.

The closer the afternoon drew toward dusk, the more people talked about the weather. It was just raining in Washington, but it was still snowing north of them. And all the roads were still shut tight. That news had heads shaking and people giving these soft little chants. People would nod and say nothing. Then someone else would say, "Lord, Lord, is this Your hand at work." Asking the question like it was a statement, not looking for an answer, sharing more with looks than the words.

About five o'clock, the police came for about the seventh time that day and had some more coffee and something to eat and left. Linda Kee stopped by soon after, looking worried and distracted both from the news and from all the difficulties she was having trying to find another job. Clearly her interviews were not going well, and it bothered her a lot. She did not stay long. Jeff could tell his father was disappointed with that, and for some reason he was glad about it, the one nice thing that happened all day long.

The adults remained in the hall and the kitchen, talking and worrying. From the little Jeff heard, there wasn't a single thing new to report about Buddy Korda being missing. Only now it was growing dark again. Every once in a while people would walk to the front window and look out and go, Umm, umm, umm. In the dining room there was a group praying pretty much nonstop, and more in the kitchen. James had the computer sound turned almost the whole way off, and the kids were growing quieter by the minute.

Around dinnertime the house emptied. Jeff's dad went upstairs with Reverend Wilkins and a couple of elders. Everybody else went home to start dinner. Mrs. Wilkins, a tall big-boned woman with her husband's quiet ways, was banging pots in the kitchen. Kitty and one of the boys went in to help her. The house seemed even more silent and worried than before. Jeff found himself missing the noise, and wondered if maybe some of the people hadn't been there earlier to help them through the waiting.

"Beat again," JT complained from the seat by the computer. He gave Scott a narrow-eyed look. "Where'd you learn to shoot like that?"

"There isn't much else to do in Aiden. It's just a little hick town, remember?"

"Thirdly got hisself whipped again," Little G chortled.

"Hush up, you. I don't see you marking down too many wins on your side of the table."

Scott set down his joystick and leaned back with a contented sigh. "I can't get over your grandfather having a primo computer like this."

JT shook his head and replied, "The way Granddaddy got this computer was, I pointed and he bought."

Gregory told Scott, "Granddaddy bought it so's we'd come over here and play 'stead of complaining how we wanted to go home."

"Granddaddy still hasn't found the switch to turn it on," JT confirmed.

Kitty appeared in the doorway and said, "Gran says everybody go wash up."

Gregory didn't look up from the chessboard. "I'm not hungry."

"Me either," JT agreed. "Feels like my belly's gotten bit by the same blues everybody's carrying 'round in here."

Scott nodded his head. Jeff understood exactly what they meant. The somber feeling had infected him too. Nobody was saying anything, at least not in here, but Buddy Korda's absence was everywhere.

The back door slammed and a boy's voice asked, "When we eating, Granma?"

All the kids made the same face. Kitty said, "Josh."

Jeff knew Joshua and didn't like him. He was the only grandkid Jeff didn't want to be around. Josh wasn't big, but he wore baggy clothes and multiple layers of sweatshirts and swaggered around talking loud. Gregory had said Josh's mother deposited him here a lot, and Kitty had added, "Yeah, a lot more than anybody wanted including Granma." Every time Josh walked into the room the little kids shrank up smaller and refused to look his way even if he shouted at them. Josh made a habit of glaring at Jeff and Scott and standing in the doorway muttering stuff they couldn't quite make out. Jeff thought Josh was scary, and didn't like to think what he might have done if the others were not there. Jeff had not been the least bit sorry when Mrs. Wilkins had sent Josh to the store.

But now he was back and Jeff heard the reverend's wife say, "Dinner is coming directly. Did you get all I asked for?"

"Nah. The grocer started giving me some lip and bad-mouthing me. So I told him, did he want our bidness or what? 'Cause he talk to me like that, I told the man he can take his bidness and shove it."

The whole room seemed to catch its breath. Gregory lifted his head and gave Jeff a round-eyed look.

Elaine Wilkins snapped, "What kind of talk is that?"

"You ast me did I get it all and I'm telling you."

Gregory said to Jeff, "Uh-oh."

Kitty agreed, "Josh is gonna get it now."

From the kitchen there came the sound of a loud *smack.* Then, "Ow!"

"Are you wanting a hiding? You must be wanting one, you come in talking like that."

"I was just telling you what the man said!"

"No you wasn't. You was talking street trash. Anybody talks street trash in this house is gonna get hisself a whipping!"

"I was talking better than you and Granpa talk all the time!"

There was the sound of another *smack,* and every kid in the front room winced in unison.

"Ow!"

"Look at this hand here. I've done hardened this hand upside the heads of six childrens and nineteen grandchildrens. You don't think I know how to use this hand, you give me more of that street trash and I'll just *show* you what this hand can do!"

Gregory said quietly, "Josh sure is dumb. Or maybe he's just stubborn."

JT murmured, "Dumb. Plain dumb."

"Poor Josh," Kitty said from the doorway, but she was grinning.

"But Gran—"

"You listen up, child. Your granpa don't talk no better 'cause he didn't have no *choice.* He done spent his young years walking behind a plow, then he raised your momma and your uncles and aunts by walking these here streets carrying mail. He walked eight hours a day six days a week, and studied the Bible all night. He didn't have *time* to learn to talk better. All so's you could stand here in my kitchen and talk this street trash to me, is that what you're thinking? Answer me, now."

"Pure plain dumb is all," JT repeated, but he was grinning too. One of the little boys reading comics let a giggle slip out.

A miserable voice said in the kitchen, "No ma'am, Gran."

"All right, then. Come over here and give me a hug. Now go get yourself a sugar cookie and get on out of here, I got dinner to get on the table. And don't you ever let me hear you talking no street trash, not ever again."

"You ask me," Gregory said, grinning at the chessboard now, "there's gotta be an easier way to earn himself a sugar cookie."

JT replied, "Yeah, but Josh, he's always got to do things the hard way."

Kitty was still standing in the doorway and grinning at the room. "Poor Josh."

Mrs. Wilkins called out, "Kitty, go tell your granddaddy to stop his praying and come get something to eat. All right now, who else is gonna help me eat this here dinner?"

JT rose to his feet. "Count me in on that one."

"Me too," Scott said. "I didn't think I'd eat for a week, but all of a sudden I'm hungry again."

Little G stood and carried his grin with him. "Yeah, ain't nothing like listening to somebody else getting smacked to raise a good appetite."

Kitty turned from the doorway and said, "Especially Josh."

⊣‖ SEVENTEEN ‖⊢

☐ Royce Calder liked to think of himself as a nice guy. He liked others to think of him the same way. He especially liked it when they assumed the quiet, small man was also meek and ineffective. Royce took great satisfaction in watching power seekers who reached out to pat his close-cropped head retreat without their fingers.

The quietness and the niceness were not acts. They were talents as carefully honed as his remarkable memory for names. They were *essential*. All part of what had elevated him from the dust of West Virginia to the heights of political power.

Royce Calder was the first generation of his family to claim West Virginia's capital as home. His mother's family had all been scrubland farmers, his father's clan all miners. His father was a dentist, a quiet man with a strong sense of absolutes—an absolute right, an absolute wrong, an absolute faith in God. Royce's three sisters and one brother all held to the same pattern as his parents, and theirs before them. But not Royce. By the final days of high school Royce had known he was made for better things.

His father's hometown was simply a stop sign on the state road, one marked by mining pits, a grocery store, mining company cottages, and a school that functioned as a church on Sundays. Royce's father had arrived in Charleston with two T-shirts, one extra pair of freshly laundered jeans, thirty-seven crumpled dollars, a full university scholarship, and a Bible. Royce's father had been the first of his family to pass the eighth grade. Royce's two uncles, great uncle and seven cousins all worked the pits. None of them had a thing to say that Royce Calder had ever found of any interest whatsoever. Their lot was to dig the earth. It was all they knew.

Royce's other grandfather had been a hardscrabble highland farmer in the realm of strip mines and sediment-clogged rivulets. As a child Royce had been forced to make the weekly trips into the hinterland, and loathed everything about them. The last time Royce had endured a visit had been the weekend before his eighteenth birthday. His grandfather had told Royce the best key to success was something in his past so awful he would do anything and everything never to do it again. It was the one thing of value Royce felt the old man had ever said. That autumn, Royce escaped from home with the speed of a greyhound chasing the mechanical hare, carrying with him a whole load of such memories.

For as long as he could recall, Royce had loathed his family's religion. As far as Royce Calder was concerned, the Christian religion was for people who were too weak to make it on their own. They wanted someone to make sense of their miserable lot, and they wanted company. Royce's memories of church were mostly of hard-scrubbed faded dresses and stiff, shiny suits and seamed faces and chapped, work-bloated hands. His father's insistence that all the children listen to Bible readings every night had been a source of dread all his young years. When Royce left for college, he had left every vestige of his religious upbringing behind. As far as Royce Calder was concerned, the worst thing about religion was how he had to drag those memories around all his life.

University politics and the Party's youth arm granted Royce a means of reinventing himself. By the time he graduated with honors in political science, Royce Calder had held positions in every class government, and knew for certain that elected politics was not his game. He had observed those who gained votes with ease, whose smiles magnetized the most reserved voter. Royce Calder was enough of a realist to know that this was one talent he would never learn.

But Royce was not someone who craved the limelight. He was quite happy to remain behind the throne. In his spare time, while working his way up in the Party's youth wing, Royce Calder had learned a vital lesson. Those who were voted into office were also voted *out*. But the bureaucrats, the men and women who wielded power in the name of those whose faces appeared on billboards and television screens, they were there to stay. That is, if they were careful, and if they watched their step.

Which was why that morning, as he sat across the desk from President Gifford's chief of staff, Royce Calder sweated as he confessed, "Buddy Korda has disappeared."

Ethan Eldridge's pen stopped its scratching progress through a rough draft of a speech the president was scheduled to deliver that afternoon. He stared across the desk. "Excuse me?"

"Korda. The man who made the prediction about—"

"I know full well who Buddy Korda is. His predictions cost my bank almost one-third of its total pre-meltdown assets. But never mind that," Eldridge snapped. "You say you lost him?"

"No. Not at . . . That is, I don't know."

Ethan Eldridge laid down his pen and leaned back in his chair. "All right. I'm listening."

"We put him into the Hilton. You know it's become a gathering place for the wackos trying to sell their services on Capitol Hill."

"Smart." Eldridge nodded. "I like it. Let him see he's just one of hundreds who claim they can tell the future, all without our saying a word. Very smart."

"Korda checked in, he went to his room. Just before he was to be picked up, my assistant called over. We were going to have an initial session with him the day before yesterday in the Naval Room." The Naval Room was the most ornate of the refurbished rooms from the OEOB's early days, a place intended to put the fear of power in anyone who entered. "But when he got there, Korda was gone."

Ethan waited, then, "And?"

Royce had no choice but to show his confusion. "We did a series of calls to his house. It wasn't until late last night that we finally reached somebody. It seems he's got a daughter-in-law who's in the hospital and she's—"

"I don't care if she's the newest addition to the petting zoo," Eldridge said peevishly. "Spare me the unimportant details and get to the issue."

"He's vanished. Nobody knows where Korda is. He left a message that he was going to rent a car and drive home. But he never arrived. We called again this morning. No word. Nothing."

"Did you say drive?" Eldridge's eyes widened. "The storm."

"That's what we thought. But it can't be."

"Buddy Korda has been trapped in the freak storm of the century." Eldridge gave his head a slow shake. "If it wasn't for the fact that we need him, I'd say good riddance to bad rubbish."

"We were going to notify the state police, then thought better of it."

"Absolutely not!" A sudden gust of wind whipped the garden outside Eldridge's window. The rose bushes would normally have been budding by now. But this was anything except a normal spring. Black, bare branches shivered and shook beneath a coal dust sky. "Can you imagine what the press would do if they heard the White House was behind Korda's coming down here and getting trapped in a blizzard?" Eldridge swiveled his chair around and stared out the tall windows. "A blizzard in April. You'd think the capital had picked up and gone to Oslo."

"We've set up a contingency plan," Royce offered, but his attention remained trapped by the view outside Eldridge's windows. The chief of staff's office was separated from the president's by a large antechamber holding four secretaries—two for each man. There was only one other office with a view of the Rose Garden. It was currently occupied by the soon-to-depart Oakridge. Royce felt the chance slipping from his grasp even as he said, "Should we start work on that?"

"No, not just yet. Find out what's happened with Korda, and do it discreetly." Eldridge swiveled back around. "I've got to say, as much as I despise the name, bringing Korda in was a work of genius."

The words were the one ray of light in an otherwise gloomy day. "Thank you."

"Your wish list is still intact as far as I'm concerned," Eldridge said, then revealed the gaze tight as a banker's vault. "Only make sure you bring this man in, and soon."

⊣ EIGHTEEN ⊢

☐ Buddy almost missed the second sunset entirely.
In his idle imaginings he had often wondered how he would manage being isolated. He had read of the work of Admiral Byrd at the South Pole, and studied the lives of men who had come to faith in prison and solitary confinement. He had decided he would probably fare pretty well.

But the reality was far different from his imaginings. For one thing, it was cold. Not dangerously cold, no, he did not risk hypothermia. But the interstate rest stop's heating system had not been made to withstand blizzard conditions. The temperatures never rose far above freezing, and the chamber's tiled floor and walls felt damp and clammy. Buddy was dressed in everything he had packed into his suitcase—four T-shirts, four pairs of socks, three pairs of slacks, three shirts, a sweater, and two suit jackets. The long line of mirrors over the sinks told him he looked like a weary sausage.

Going outside was not only dangerous; by Wednesday it was also impossible. That morning, he had attempted to call once more from the bank of phones—he had done so several times the night before, but the lines had been down and the phones dead. That morning, the snow had drifted up against the outer doors and sealed him in as effectively as bars on a prison cell. The rest room itself was ringed by high wired windows that he could crank open for frigid ventilation. Yet every time he did so he let in icy blasts of blowing snow. Buddy seldom opened the windows.

Three other factors made the isolation a truly miserable experience. The first was hunger. The rest stop's candy machine was broken, the snack machine empty. The sinks still gave water, so he was not in any danger, at least not yet. But by the end of the second day he was weak and hollowed.

The second factor was the utter loss of control. He had naturally read of this, the fear and pain of losing control of life's course was one of the psalmists' great agonies. But he had never expected it to happen to *him*. And never under such degrading conditions. Trapped in a highway bathroom by a blizzard in April! It was the kind of thing the nightly news would end with, something for the nation to laugh at before bedtime. Only now it had happened to him. He was too ashamed to be angry.

And the third dismaying factor was how distant God seemed. Never in his wildest fears had he ever thought he could feel so hopelessly, dangerously alone. He was not just isolated here in this rest stop. No. He was *convicted.*

Sleep came in fits and starts throughout the night and the day. He would curl on the frigid tiled floor using his suitcase for a pillow and sleep for an hour or so, every dream tainted by the smell of disinfectant. He would then awaken with the side he had been leaning on cold and cramped. Standing was agony. He limped in tight little circles, forcing the circulation back into his shoulder and arm and leg. He grew miserably tired of standing or walking and avoiding the sight of his own reflection.

He almost missed the second sunset because he had finally fallen asleep again. He had to wait until exhaustion would numb him from the discomfort and usher him swiftly into sleep. This time when he awoke he thought that perhaps it had grown a little darker outside, but it was hard to tell. Overhead the bare bulbs burned relentlessly as they had since his arrival—he could not find a light switch anywhere and had decided it must be located somewhere outside. The greenish light showing through the high narrow windows gradually grew darker, and finally Buddy accepted that he was about to enter his second night in this white-tiled prison.

His limping circle took him over to the sinks. He bent over and drank his fill. As he raised back up he was caught by the sight of his reflection. He had always been very conscious of how he looked. He liked to have his hair trimmed every ten days or so. He walked three miles at least four times a week, right through the winter. He did not own many clothes, but those he possessed were of good cut and quality. But as Buddy stared at himself while the light outside faded to another snow-bound evening, he did not see a responsible member of church and community. He saw a pathetic little clown.

This time, he could not look away. This time, he saw not only the gaunt-faced exterior of a lonely exhausted man, he saw the interior as well. The mirror showed the reflection of a heart hollowed by by his own selfish demands. He stood at the center of this calamitous misfortune not because life's harsh turn had slapped him down. No. He was here because he had chosen to walk away from God.

God had been silent, just as God was silent now. Yes, that much was true. But what right did he have to decide when God should speak?

He saw that now. That and how he had in truth not *wanted* God to speak. Why? Because Buddy knew in his heart of hearts that whatever God had wished to tell him, Buddy had not wanted to hear.

It had taken the impossible weight of these hopeless conditions to bring him face-to-face with his own dishonesty. The shame was so great Buddy could not even turn away. He looked into the mirror and saw two lifeless defeated eyes staring back at him. A face hollowed not just by hardship, but by humiliation. He had not *wanted* to hear God, not unless God had spoken what Buddy had wanted to hear. And when the words had not come to him as he had wished, he had turned and run for home.

Suddenly the burden of his own selfish nature became too great to bear. Buddy slipped down to rest his knees upon the cold tile floor.

He leaned his elbows and his forehead upon the sink. His ears were filled with the sighing whisper of snow-clad winds and the tinkle of a dripping faucet. He clenched his hands and his eyes, and in the darkness he sought words to apologize to the God he had shoved so carelessly aside. Every word he prayed felt empty, selfish and partly false. He remained there on his knees long after the feeling had drained from his lower legs. He could not find the strength to weep, as though even his tears would be tainted by his own deceitful purpose. He knelt and he sought meager words with which to ask forgiveness, until he could no longer bear his own weight, and he sank onto the dank floor.

☐

Buddy awoke to the sound of metal thunder.

He rolled over and groaned as tired, cold muscles contracted in a sudden spasm. Then the pounding halted and the outer door scrunched open and a voice shouted, "Anybody in here?"

Buddy was hardly able to croak a reply. He stumbled over, flapping the one arm that was not cramped from taking his weight upon the floor.

"Pete! Quick! We got us a live one!" A burly man in emergency yellow garb reached out gloved hands and said, "Take it easy, fella. That your car out there?"

Buddy almost fell into the man's arms. "Yes."

"Anybody else in here with you?"

"No. Alone." Now that it was over, he found himself able to manage only single-word responses.

"You been in here since the storm started? Have anything to eat? No? Man, you must be starved." When a second helmeted figure popped into the doorway, the man supporting Buddy said, "Go get the thermos."

"He okay?"

"Looks that way. It's not too cold in here. Half-starved, though."

"I'll see if we got any sandwiches left." Then Pete was gone.

The thought of food must have shown on Buddy's face, for the grizzled roadworker grinned and said, "Don't get your hopes up, man. What's your name?"

"Korda. Buddy Korda."

"We been pushing these rigs hard ever since it stopped snowing—oh, musta been just after one in the morning. I'm pretty sure everything's been all ate up."

But the snowplow operator was wrong. They found half of one limp baloney and cheese-spread sandwich, and two mugs of rich, supersweet coffee. Buddy sat in the snowplow's backseat and forced himself to eat slowly. But his hands trembled and the hot liquid sloshed over his fingers as he tried to drink. The men kept glancing in and grinning, proud of having brought him out alive.

Five minutes later the heavyset man who had first appeared in the rest stop doorway piled in behind the wheel and said, "Feeling better?"

Buddy found the strength to return the man's smile. "That was the finest meal I have ever had in my entire life."

That drew a laugh from both men. "Wait 'til my wife hears about that," Pete said. "She'll be reminding me every time I complain about eating the same old stuff day in, day out."

"Try going without food for almost three days," Buddy said, draining the last drop from the thermos top.

"No thanks. I think maybe I'd rather complain." Pete pulled out a mobile phone and keyed in a number. "There's gonna be lots of people wanting to talk with you."

"Me?" Buddy pulled the corners of the blanket tighter around him. "Why?"

"You kidding?" The beefy operator started the plow and wheeled back onto the highway. "A man gets trapped in a rest stop bathroom for almost three days. By a blizzard. In April. In Maryland. You're big news, man." He shook his head. "I've been pushing snow for almost nine hours and I still don't hardly believe it myself."

"You're the first guy we pulled outta this storm," Pete said. "Crazy, how busy this road usually is, but you're the only one we've found trapped."

"So far," the driver added.

His mate pressed the phone tighter to his ear. "Yeah, it's Pete. We found this guy in the rest stop just outside Andersonville. No, he's okay. Tired and hungry. Hang on, I'll ask." Pete turned around and demanded, "What'd you say your name was?"

"Buddy Korda."

As Pete repeated that into the phone, the driver said, "That name sounds familiar. You somebody famous?"

"No." But just as Buddy was saying that, Pete's shoulders stiffened and he came slowly around, clearly listening to something else on the phone. He said to the driver, "You know what? This is the guy."

"Who?"

"Korda. The guy. The man who came on television, when was it, last year and—"

"Sure, I remember now!" The driver turned with Pete to stare at Buddy. "You were the one with the message about doom and gloom, ain't that right?"

"Sure, my cousin, she and almost everybody in her church did like you were saying. She told me I ought to as well, but I said it sounded like crazy stuff." Pete kept staring as he said to the phone, "Yeah, it's him. I remember him from the television."

The driver said, "Don't seem so crazy now, does it?"

Buddy reached over the seat as Pete closed the connection. "Mind if I use that to call my wife and tell her I'm all right?"

"Sure, of course. Sorry, I should have thought of that myself."

"Thanks." Buddy stared out the window as they passed by the trashed Explorer.

"Looks like somebody did a number on your car, man."

"It's a rental." The words written upon the sides were still covered by the remaining snow, so only the cracked windows and plastic-covered back were visible. Forlorn and spent, its final mission accomplished. Buddy bent over the phone and coded in the number.

Molly answered on the first ring. The pleasure of hearing her voice again was sweet agony. He curled his frame over the phone, masking his reaction from the men in the front seat. "It's me, honey."

"Buddy!" Molly cried out to others with her, "Jack, Trish, it's Buddy!" Then back to him, "Oh, sweetheart, how are you, are you all right?"

"Fine. I'm fine. I'm better than that."

"Sweetie, I was so worried." Molly caught herself, the shaky tone audible even over the roar of the snowplow's motor. "No, that's not true. I was worried, but I was at peace at the very same time. But I don't want to talk about me now. Tell me now, are you truly all right?"

"Fine. Cold, hungry, tired. But fine. Truly."

"What happened?"

"I made a terrible mistake."

"What, I don't—"

"I tried to run from God's call." Buddy kept his body bent over his legs, even as the plow roared and bounced and scraped at the road's surface. The motor revved louder and he asked, "Can you hear me?"

"Yes, but what is that noise?"

"I'm riding in a snowplow. They're taking me . . . Wait a minute." He raised up and said, "Where are we going?"

The driver replied, "I don't know about you, but Pete and me are headed for home and bed."

Pete turned around and said, "We're going south. They said they'd be sending out a patrol car to take you wherever you want to go."

"Washington, D.C.," Buddy said, not needing to think about that for one instant.

"Isn't that where you were just coming from when you got stuck?"

"Yes." Buddy bent back over his knees. His eyes on the corrugated metal floor, he said into the phone, "Are you still there?"

"Yes, oh, it's so good to hear your voice again. Can you tell me what happened?"

"The Lord brought me face-to-face with who I truly am." He squeezed his eyes so tightly shut he saw colors. "He showed me all the weaknesses I can handle only with His help."

"Buddy—"

"I'll tell you everything once I'm back in Washington and settled somewhere."

"Back? You're going back there?"

"Absolutely. That's where He wants me, that's where I'm going."

"If that's what you think is best."

"I have to go, Molly. I have to."

⊣∥ NINETEEN ∥⊢

☐ The morning after Buddy's rescue, Linda Kee pushed through the elegant entrance halfway down the K Street corridor, and wondered what on earth had happened to her ambition and her drive.

Back when she had made the big switch to standing in front of the camera, a mentor had told her she should use such times of preparation to put on her game face. Like football players, he had explained, sitting on the bench before they ran into the stadium. They tightened the whole world down to the coming moment. They imagined plowing through all opposition and planting the ball right between the goal posts. If she did this, she would be ready to use every last shred of ambition and hunger and talent and desire, bunching it all together and tightening down the screws until the tension was so strong and the power so focused, *nothing* could stand in her way. Coming up a winner each time, every time. No matter what the cost, to herself or anyone else. Yes. That lesson had served her well.

But today, as she gave her name to the security guard and was directed to the elevators at the back of the lobby, she knew her game face was missing. Strange as it seemed, what most occupied her thoughts that morning was Patrick Allen.

They had spoken each day since her return to Washington. This morning, after sharing relief over Buddy's safe return, Patrick had asked about her job search. It had been a very frustrating few days, and having his concern on the other end of the phone had helped her mightily. Most of the meetings had been tentative at best. She had the distinct impression that many people had asked to see her more because they wanted to meet Linda Kee than because they actually had a job to offer.

This morning, Patrick had listened to her describe her upcoming interview and remained silent as she had explained both to him and to herself how working for a political consultant might be a good thing. This meeting was different, she had felt it in her bones. Patrick had replied that he would be praying for her. Yet instead of reassuring her, somehow the promise had hollowed her, leaving her unable to do more than simply thank the man. Patrick had then said he would have to return to Aiden that afternoon, he still had a church to run. Linda had felt the hollowness expand to fill her entire chest—four days in Washington and they had not managed more than a cup of coffee together. But she had not known what to say.

Patrick had hesitated a moment, seemingly as much at a loss as Linda. Then he had asked if she would like to join him for the weekend. The thrill she had felt had lifted her reply a full octave.

Now, as she crossed the polished marble lobby with its glittering artwork, Linda could not seem to get the pastor out of her thoughts. The tall, handsome man had been battered by his own personal storms, yet not defeated. Far from it. Somehow he had emerged from life's harshest blows as a deep and caring individual. His presence challenged her, forcing her to question both her actions and her motives. Without saying a thing, Patrick left her wondering if this job prospect was correct for her, even though she had no logical reason to think otherwise. Especially now, when a good job was scarce as diamonds.

As the brass elevator doors closed, Linda studied her reflection and wondered how this man she hardly knew, from a world utterly alien to everything she had lived for, could dominate her thoughts at such a crucial time. Despite her best efforts to focus on the here and now, she spent the entire ride to the top floor pondering the sudden realization that it was not Patrick alone, no matter what his own appeal. No. What was going on here was something far greater. As the elevator doors opened on the ninth floor, Linda once again found herself seeing the image of her reaching out, touching the foot of the Cross.

She entered the outer office of Satchell Consultants, gave her name to the receptionist, and endured the older woman's frankly curious stare. Linda crossed to the corner sofa and fell back on earlier times, pulling out her notebook and jotting down words and tag lines. Trying to prep herself into readiness.

She had never worked with Rob Satchell. But she knew of him. The highest echelon of Washington power was a tightly restricted crew, small in numbers and closed to outsiders. It possessed a careful pecking order and a rule book all its own.

Political consultants liked to stay in good standing with the press, especially television news. A favor given now meant airtime later for a candidate, helping to create a buzz around a new face, having him or her labeled as the next rising star. Television news was essential for deciding which candidate and which topic became that day's hot item. A top political consultant was not merely someone who knew the process and could steer a candidate. The real players, and there were only a half dozen in the entire country, were also power brokers in their own right. They made things happen. Keeping an inside track with the national news networks was all part of the game.

Satchell was a key source for the top correspondent at the Washington bureau of CBS News. Which meant hands-off to all junior staffers. Linda had gradually developed her own sources, and chafed under the restrictions and the pecking order.

She glanced around the reception area, pretending to take careful note of everything. The furniture was heavy leather and solid wood, reminiscent of a stodgy English club. Unlike the next tier down of political consultants, Satchell's walls contained not a single plaque or picture of the man himself with important people. If the visitor was not already aware that Satchell knew literally everyone in power, that person did not belong. There was an Impressionist print on the side wall, and what appeared to be an original Chagall sketch directly opposite where she was seated. The charcoal swirlings and half-formed figures mirrored her thoughts exactly.

The first time Linda had met Rob Satchell was at a high-society bash where Jay Leno's band had played. Someone in her group had pointed Satchell out as he moved toward the dance floor. "Watch this," Linda's friend had said. "Talk about the worm becoming a butterfly!" Linda hadn't understood the comment until the balding elephantine figure moved out and *dominated* the dance floor.

When the new president had taken office, they both had been invited to the top inaugural ball—she because of who had taken her, Satchell because of who he was. This time she had joined the envious throng of her own volition, and watched him dance the rumba with the new first lady, turning the elderly woman into someone as light and beautiful as a spangled cloud.

"Linda Kee!" Rob Satchell emerged from his office with hand outstretched. "Is it really you?"

"Certainly is." She rose to meet him, allowed her hand to be swallowed in a grip as big as the rest of him. Satchell was fifty-one years old and thirty-five pounds overweight. He wore expensive suits cut so baggy they fitted him like gabardine balloons. He was balding and bulbous and not the least bit attractive. Yet he moved with the grace of a ballet dancer.

"Can you believe this? I can't." He smiled the way a puppet smiled, all teeth and mouth and rosy red cheeks. "The sharpest newscaster in Washington and the sharpest looking, here in my little office!"

"Not so little." And not putting much behind her words. The man's gushing entry seemed to drive Linda even farther away from her normal brilliance and presence. "Thanks for seeing me."

"Are you kidding? The minute I heard CBS was letting you go, I said to Jack, 'Those boys have lost the last of their little minds.'" He did not need to turn around to ensure his aide had slipped up behind him. "Right, Jack?"

"Right as rain." The aide was an older man, polished and unremarkable. He reminded Linda of Johnny Carson's former sidekick, Ed McMahon. The perpetual audience for this political star. "How are you, Ms. Kee?"

"Good, Jack. Nice to see you." She used this as an excuse to remove her hand from both of Satchell's. She then stood and waited, her expression saying, "Well, you got me here, what now?"

"Right, sure, great. Come on this way." Satchell ushered her into his office, eyeing Linda uncertainly. Clearly her aloof calm was not the reaction he had expected.

She followed them into a corner office with a view of Washington Circle. In the distance was Foggy Bottom and all her old State Department haunts. The office was a finer rendition of the reception chamber, leather and inlaid wood and Persian carpet and heavy silk drapes. "Nice place, Mr. Satchell."

"Hey, it's first names all around, okay? Have a seat there. Comfortable? Good, good." The receptionist appeared in the doorway, and Satchell asked, "How will you take your coffee?"

"Just black, thanks."

"You know how we like ours, right, Gladys? Great. Great." The uncertainty remained as he turned back to her. "So what have you been up to since CBS did the number on your career?"

"Picking up the pieces." She startled even herself with this plain speaking. She would have thought the proper reaction would be something positive. Something to show she was still in demand. Linda looked down at her hands, gave her head a little shake. What had happened to her? How had a simple trip to Aiden, Delaware, changed her so?

She raised her head to find Jack watching her sympathetically. He said, "Hard to get started after a kick in the teeth, isn't it?"

She found herself liking the older man already. "I thought I was making all the right moves."

"You were, you were." Satchell took his aide's reaction as a signal, toned down his bonhomie. "It was the economy that misfired, not you."

"These are hard times," Jack went on. "I hear they're not finished making cuts over at CBS."

"Yeah, the blood's flowing everywhere." Satchell leaned forward, the leather squeaking under his weight, retaking control of the meeting. "All of a sudden the guy with a job is king, the others just numbers on a page."

"Which is why we're here," Linda said, finally finding her cue.

"Exactly! The economy may be in a tailspin, but politics is still big business. That's why we wanted to see you." He leaned back as his receptionist reentered and set out a coffee service of bone china. When they were alone again, he continued, "Our press officer is retiring. This isn't altogether a bad thing. We need a fresh face around here. Somebody keyed into the younger end of the demographic scale. An up-and-comer who can do more than liaise. We want an adviser."

Jack added, "Someone to help shape the candidate for the camera."

"I could certainly do that," Linda said, knowing it was the truth, wondering why she could not show at least a shred of excitement. "It's a discipline that has to be learned."

"Just like anything else," Satchell agreed, pressing hard. "We need an in-house expert to guide the new people. Mold them and public opinion. Work both sides of the coin—do you see where I'm headed?"

"You want me to help position them and polish them." She nodded slowly. "I can do that."

"Not to mention dress up our office, right, Jack?"

"What he means," his aide interpreted, "is we need somebody to be a face for the cameras."

"Right, exactly!" Shifting direction as Jack intended, Rob Satchell added, "These candidates, they're going to need a press spokesperson. Design the pablum for the masses, then feed it in fifteen-second sound bites."

"I would be very good at that," Linda said quietly. Searching inside herself, wondering why it felt as though she was missing something here. Something crucial.

"Which is why we want to offer you the position of press liaison," Satchell said, leaning over until his gut rested on his thighs. "But there's one condition. We don't want to take you on just so you run off to head the press office of the first big name we attach you to."

"We require a long-term commitment," his aide explained. "We need to be able to associate your name with ours."

Linda looked from one face to the other, but in truth she was more intent on examining what was lacking inside herself. However, she said the only thing that came to mind because they were waiting. "It would do my own career no good whatsoever to be seen as flighty. I have stayed with CBS since they first hired me, rising inside the ranks. There would be no benefit to changing my personal strategy now." The words seemed incomplete, so she continued, more for effect than desire. "Naturally, in return for my promise your own contract is going to have to demonstrate the same long-term loyalty."

The two men exchanged glances, and Satchell's aide gave a single nod. Satchell rose lightly to his feet. "Great, just great." He offered a hand, then enfolded hers in both of his. "I'll let you hammer out the contract details with Jack." He showed his brace of shining teeth. "Only keep in mind we're in a deep recession here. Our generosity only goes so far these days." He gave her hand a slow, meaningful shake. "Great to have you on board, Linda Kee. I look forward to working closely with you. Very closely."

□

Two hours later, when Linda emerged from her negotiations with Rob Satchell's aide, she had every reason to be satisfied. But as she shook Jack's hand and told the receptionist good-bye, she still felt as though the most vital parts of both the day and herself were absent. She spent the elevator ride arguing with herself. This was ridiculous. Not only did she have a job, she had the chance to turn around her firing and actually come out on top. The disaster had become yet one more step up the ladder of ambition and success. It was what she had been after all along, wasn't it?

Linda was halfway across the lobby when she was struck so hard by a thought it seemed as though an invisible hand reached down and turned her. Before she could talk herself out of it, she walked to the bank of phones by the side wall and dialed the long-familiar number.

The first ring was cut off by a flat voice droning, "CBS Washington."

"Hi, Attie. It's me."

"Linda?" The voice dropped the necessary prerequisite of all television receptionists—the power of the instant no. "Where are you?"

"Here. Washington. Is Clarence around?"

"Sure, I think so. Girl, what's happened to you?"

"Oh, this and that." She fought down a sudden urge to tell Attie about the night of her dismissal, about the church and walking forward to touch the Cross. Attie was a cynic's cynic, and would have used the news as gossip ammo. Ten minutes after she hung up, all the office would have heard how Linda had been dismantled by her dismissal, pushed right over the edge, wait until you hear what that girl went and did. So all Linda said was, "I've been offered a job."

"Whew, that's a relief. I mean, it's good you got the offer and a real relief that's not why you're calling 'round here."

"The ax is still falling?"

"Girl, it's coming down so fast all you see is this shining blur, then the screams start. Joe's gone as of this morning."

"No kidding." Joe Moranchi was the number two face, next up the ladder from Linda. "That's tough."

"No joke. We're down to seven people. Seven. From a high just last year of thirty-nine."

"What about you?"

"I guess I'm okay. They cut my salary, which is a pretty good sign. And I'm typing letters and doing expense accounts while I answer the phone with my third hand." There was a faint pinging in the background. "Speaking of which, my board's lit up like a Christmas tree. Let me see if I can find Clarence. Good to hear from you, girl. Don't you be a stranger."

Linda waited and wondered over what she was doing, especially since she had left CBS bitter and angry and promising never to have anything more to do with the old crew. The whole experience of her dismissal still tasted like ashes.

Yet as soon as she heard Clarence's voice, she knew why she had called. "Linda?"

Not only that, she knew why she had felt *urged* to make this connection. "Clarence, hi. How are you?"

"So-so. They've got me doing double duty. Story research *and* camera work."

"That's tough." Though Clarence was two years older than Linda and a father three times over, it was hard to think of him as anything other than a kid. A good, kindly round-faced kid. "How are you coping?"

"Trying not to worry. But it doesn't look good."

She did not need to ask what he was talking about. "They'd be fools to get rid of you, Clarence."

"These are hard times, Linda."

"You're the television version of a jack-of-all-trades. Editor, researcher, camera operator—you're one in a million."

"Seniority. That's the key issue. And I don't have enough." His smile was obvious, even over the phone. "Shame we're not the ones running things."

It was his favorite stock phrase. "What will you do?" Linda asked.

"Pray and hope and wait. It's not a total loss if they let me go. I haven't been home in time to see the kids before they go to bed all week, and things only look to get worse for the ones who hang on to their jobs. You've heard about the latest cuts?"

"Yes."

"It's all panic and heartache around here right now. I've even had a couple of people come in and ask to pray with me." Another smile. "At least I can be thankful for that."

Although Clarence Ives was one of the most talented and versatile people on the CBS staff, he was far from the most popular. His calm placidness was matched by an openhanded treatment of faith—not an acceptable posture within the highly charged atmosphere of television news. Linda had been one of the few people who had actually asked to work with the man, accepting both his ability and his faith with ease. She had been rewarded in many ways, and challenged in more. She had even started going to church with him and his family, finding there the love and ease she had never known within her own. Yet when she had abandoned the practice and taken yet another false turn on life's bitter road, Clarence had neither criticized nor judged. He had simply asked her to promise to call if she ever needed a friend. The words had bit like acid tossed upon the path she had chosen for herself.

"Clarence . . ." She stopped before she could tell him about the job offer. Standing there in the lobby of the K Street high-rise, she realized it was the least important of all she had going on. Linda restarted by saying, "I've met Buddy Korda."

"Buddy Korda, as in the man who predicted the meltdown?" Clarence was agog. "You're kidding me."

"I took the train up. Spent the night in Aiden and traveled back down to Washington with him."

"Linda, this is . . . Do you have any idea how hard New York's been after him for a *Sixty Minutes* segment? Especially these past few days."

"Yes, but that's not why—"

"Since they heard he got caught in the snowstorm they've been calling down here every half hour, asking if we've tracked him down. Is he all right?"

"As far as I know, he's fine. Do you have a minute?"

"For this? I've got all day."

So she told him. Standing there with the world going by, turning occasionally and staring at the rushing people, not a single smile to be found among the grim-faced crowd. All so worried. The day and the times had stamped themselves indelibly upon every face she saw. Outside the door two panhandlers asked for coins, a few more had set up feeble stalls selling cheap watches and sunglasses. Those with jobs and purpose to their stride hurried by, trained now to ignore the pleas that struck at them from all sides. She found it strange, how she was seeing this as though for the very first time, while she stood and told Clarence about the night of her own dismissal, and the trip to the church, and touching the foot of the Cross.

"I stood there afterward and waited, and nothing happened. So I went home. And the next morning I woke up feeling as though I needed to go to Aiden. You know my father had invested some money after Buddy made his prediction."

"Buddy's prophecy," Clarence quietly corrected. "Yes, I remember you mentioning that. I did as well."

"I didn't know that."

"I still remember the night I saw a video of his talk. I went home certain that I needed to do *exactly* what he had said. But the next morning I was, well . . ." His sigh rattled the earpiece. "Let's just say I listened to all the other voices telling me not to be foolish. The news was all so good, and my broker told me Buddy's investment instructions were extremely high-risk. I could lose everything, he said. So I did what I think most people ended up doing, which was to take only what I could afford to lose. The result is, I've got enough to cover our expenses for a few months if I'm canned, which is looking more certain every day. If I had done what he said, I'd be . . ."

"My dad says the same thing," Linda told him. "Look at it this way, at least you did something."

"Right." Pushing it aside, Clarence returned to the matter at hand. "So you met Buddy Korda. What is he like?"

"Quiet. Very quiet. Solemn and withdrawn. His daughter-in-law and her new baby are very sick, that probably has something to do with it." Linda found herself seeing not the afternoon and the people and the lobby and the gray scuttling crowds beyond the tall windows. Instead, she turned her back to the world and there upon the blank wall above the telephone she saw the Cross. Her hand reached out and touched the base once more. Only this time she felt a sense of power course through her. A purpose so strong she shivered. "I've been offered a job, Clarence. A good one. But all the time I was up there, I felt—I don't even know how to explain this."

"Like it wasn't right?"

"Something like that."

"Then it probably wasn't. Where is Buddy Korda now?"

"Still here in Washington." She checked her watch. "As a matter of fact, I'm late to meet the pastor who drove down with us."

"I have a feeling that you need to stay with Korda. A very strong feeling." Clarence was as serious as she had ever heard him. "Did he say anything about why he had come to Washington?"

"Not a word."

"Stay with him, Linda. And call me, okay? I'd really like to hear what happens."

"All right, I will. Thanks for listening, Clarence. Thanks, well, for just being there."

"I'll be praying for you. And for Buddy."

Slowly she hung up the phone, reslung her purse, crossed the lobby, and pushed through the outer doors. Instantly the wind lashed her with her own hair. She gripped it in the hand not holding her purse, and forged ahead. As she walked, she mulled over the realization that Clarence had not asked what would be the most natural question for a newscaster: Did Buddy give you an exclusive? As though that, too, was simply not important. Not here, not now. Going against all logic, two hearts speaking of what the world would never comprehend.

Perhaps that was what it meant to have a friend.

⊣❘ TWENTY ❘⊢

☐ "I didn't run away from Washington," Buddy quietly declared. "I was running away from God."

Patrick sat beside James Thaddeus in what the Wilkins family called their missionary quarters. The prewar brick house was split into three modest apartments, one per floor. The furniture of this ground-floor living room had a worn, cast-off look. The carpet was threadbare in places, and paint flecked from the room's high corners. But James Thaddeus had insisted this was where Buddy belonged. "No more hotels for God's messenger," the old man had demanded in his deep drone. "No more leaving him alone in the midst of shadows and worldly wraiths. We're gonna surround this man with a whole *host* of shields." James Thaddeus had repeated this over and over on the drive back from the police station. "We're gonna put him close to the hearth, build a circle of prayer and love right around God's chosen man."

Despite its dated appearance, the downstairs apartment had a cheerful air. A coal fire hissed and burned inside a cast-iron grate. The heating pipes pinged happily in the background. Outside big old-timey sash windows, a porch extended beneath the overhanging roof, lined by sturdy corner pillars of interlaced brick and stone. There was a sense of peace here, of comfort and kin. Patrick was glad he could leave his friend in such welcome arms, for Buddy had stated flatly that he was not returning to Aiden, not even for the weekend. His work and his call were here.

"I think down deep, even in my darkest moment of doubting, I think I knew it was God's voice I heard," Buddy went on. "But I also knew He was going to order me to do things I didn't want, and say things I wouldn't like. I was scared to death of what He had in store for me. Not just then. In my heart I think I've always tried to keep a part of myself aside. Tasting of His glory, and still keeping selfish hold of where I was going and what I was to do with my life."

James Thaddeus started to speak, then thought better of it. He looked over at Patrick seated on the fireplace's opposite side, and gave a single nod. *He is your friend. You speak.*

"You remember that night I came by your house," Patrick started. "I had the feeling there was something else bothering you. Something deeper. I couldn't put my finger on it then. But now I feel like we've finally reached rock bottom."

"Hardest part to solving a lot of problems is finding out what they are," Reverend Wilkins intoned. "Hard as hard can be to see what the heart don't want to admit to."

"Every time . . ." Patrick halted at the sound of a knock on the front door.

He watched as the door eased back, and Linda Kee stepped hesitantly inside. "Mrs. Wilkins said you were . . . Oh, Mr. Korda, hello."

"Afternoon, Miss Kee." Reverend Wilkins was already on his feet, drawing the other two men by his example. "How are you today?"

"Fine, I'm . . . I'm sorry, I'm interrupting something."

"No, please stay." To their surprise, this invitation came from Buddy. "I have the feeling that you are an important part of this. A vital part."

For some reason, Buddy's words seemed to increase her agitation. So Patrick asked, "How did your interview go?"

"I've been offered a job. A good one." But she only frowned in response to their congratulations. "Are you sure I should stay?"

"Absolutely, Miss Kee. Just you set yourself down right here." Reverend Wilkins offered her his own chair, then pulled up one from the dining room table for himself. When they were all seated, James Thaddeus said to Patrick, "You were about to start in on something important."

Patrick said to Buddy, "Whenever God revealed His word to the biblical prophets, there came alongside this a request for them to adjust their lives to Him. Not a command. An *invitation.* They were not His slaves. They were His colleagues in action. They had to *choose* to do as God was requesting. The decision to change was theirs and theirs alone."

Buddy nodded slowly, his gaze somber and inward. Patrick took this as a sign to continue. "Look at what the Scriptures say about Noah, Abraham, Moses, the prophets, even the disciples of Jesus. Whenever God called them, none were able to remain where they were or *as* they were, and still go where God directed. Their lives were changed by this choice to serve."

"Say it, brother," James Thaddeus intoned. "Say it loud."

"This is an especially hard message for you. You have already heeded His call once before. You know as well as anyone just how difficult it can be to have your life turned on its end by the Lord's request to serve," Patrick continued. "But accepting that this new adjustment will happen is critical. It means that the Lord is then able to mold you so that He can accomplish His will through you. Not the will that you would like to have, not the will that is comfortable to where you are and what you would like to have happen."

"No, Lord," James Thaddeus quietly agreed. "Not the comfortable. Not my will. No."

"We are then ready to heed *His* call, do *His* will. We are not just mouthpieces. Our actions become beacons in themselves. Our very lives become affirmations of His call. Hard as it may be, even painful at times, this is a critical part of His unfolding purpose."

Buddy's face was creased in pain as he stared into the hissing flames. Patrick looked over to Reverend Wilkins, and was rewarded with one final nod. He then glanced at Linda, and found her face a mirror of Buddy's. Patrick asked, "What's the matter?"

She answered with a quiet question of her own. "Were you speaking to Buddy or to me?"

"The man was talking to all of us," James Thaddeus replied. "Every single one of God's chosen flock."

Buddy sighed, placed his hands on his knees, and straightened slowly. "I need to stay here for the time being. My place is here in Washington now. Not in Aiden."

"Long as you like," James Thaddeus responded. "Just as long as you need to stay, this place is your place."

"I don't want to see anyone this weekend," Buddy murmured. "I need to remember what it means to listen with all my might."

"Nobody's gonna find you here, brother. Don't you worry none. Far as the world is concerned, this place is shielded."

"Thank you, Reverend." Buddy kept his gaze on the fire as he said, "I need to sit and wait for God to tell me what He has in mind."

☐

James Thaddeus Wilkins knew he was a man of many faults. If he were called this very day to stand before the throne and make an accounting of his gifts, he knew of only three he could claim for certain. First and foremost, he loved his Lord, his family, and his church; he tried to love the rest of the world, but failed more often than he succeeded.

Second, he knew he could preach; he could drive a message home that lasted longer than the start of Sunday dinner, and his words could bring people to their knees. This he knew for a fact.

And third, he had an eye to look below the surface.

It was this watchful eye and his listening ear that were in action now. He sat at his kitchen table, the morning paper opened but unread in front of him, waiting as Patrick first drove Buddy to the shopping center for some supplies and then took Linda by her uptown apartment for something she had forgotten. He sat and listened to the youngsters in the front room. There were six of them now, JT and Little G almost permanent fixtures since Scott and Jeff's arrival. Kitty was also spending a lot of time in there, mooning around the good-looking older white boy. The jury was still out on that one. And Josh, a big surprise there, had taken to sitting in the corner by the window. The boy was supposedly reading a comic they kept for the littler ones, but every time James Thaddeus stuck his head in the door, Josh was watching and listening, the same comic on the floor in front of him, the pages unturned.

Earlier that afternoon, the children had clambered all over James Thaddeus Wilkins when he had returned from his talk with Buddy Korda. Asking a thousand questions, all but Josh, and even he hung around the doorway, listening as hard as the others. My, but did the others have the questions. Wanting to know, Did Buddy Korda have a vision while he was trapped in the snowstorm? Wanting to hear what the police said, what Buddy said, and just everything. They had hit him upside the head with so many questions he almost forgot what he was trying to tell them and

Elaine both. But he did not correct them, and neither did his usually sharp-tongued wife. No. There was something special about their questions, more than just six hyper children wanting to shoulder into the talk of two grown-ups. When he got to the part about Patrick speaking of the need for choices, they got all silent and solemn, so much so that he and his wife exchanged a glance. Wondering just exactly what was going on here.

But as soon as he stopped talking they were just children again, heading back to the computer and the chessboard and the comics. Might as well not have opened his mouth for all the thought they seemed to give. That was just how he felt.

Even so, neither he nor Elaine said a thing about all the time the kids were spending there with the computer. And that was another curious thing. James Thaddeus normally did not hold to wasting time, and the hours they spent there in the front room, sprawled over the furniture and Elaine's best hook rug like so many sacks of suet, it sure *looked* like wasted time. But over and over again James Thaddeus found himself striving to look below the surface, as though a finger were coming down out of the sky and saying, Wait, search, *see.* So he did not say anything, and for whatever reason, Elaine chose not to speak either. Not a word.

Perhaps it was Josh. A change had come over the boy. James Thaddeus could not say exactly how he knew, but he was certain the change was there. The anger was gone. Josh sat and he watched and he listened, hiding like a hurt little animal there behind the rocker, watching the world through wooden bars, the same comic lying open there in his lap for two whole days.

Elaine and Harriet, Josh's mother, were busy making a basket of sandwiches for Patrick and his boys. Patrick had told her they would stop somewhere and break up the journey, but Elaine could no more let people set off on the road without food than she could let a young one come to the table with unwashed hands.

Linda Kee traveling with them back to Aiden, now, that was another mystery. There was another whole passel of questions to be asked about that one. But not just then.

No, right now James Thaddeus Wilkins's attention was caught by just about the strangest sound he had ever heard. A sound so strange it froze Elaine and Harriet right there where they stood at the counter.

The sound was of Josh asking a question.

"There's something I don't understand. How come we's the ones hurting when we's the ones believing?"

Elaine turned to Harriet. Their youngest daughter met her mother's gaze with eyes about ready to pop out of her head. Josh never asked anybody a thing. How could he, since he was the one knowing everything? Yes, Lord, everything there was to know, especially about anger and hurt and the pull of the street.

A silent surprise gripped the living room, same as the kitchen. It was JT who found his voice first. "What do you mean, Josh?"

"It ain't just them on the street who's done got burned by the bad times." Josh fumbled for words, but without his usual shield of bitter rage. "My momma and my daddy fought night and day. Momma saying, you didn't do like Granpa said and like Buddy Korda told us on the video, and you lost us everything. And my daddy yelling back, you better hush up now, or I'm gonna get mad. But my momma kept on 'bout how we done lost it all, and now what are we gonna do, all on account of him being such a stubborn fool."

Harriet clapped a hand to her mouth. James Thaddeus watched as his wife reached over and put one arm around her daughter's shaking shoulders. He wanted to rise and go join them, but right then he was too caught up, listening for all he was worth.

"So my daddy up and left us. And we's hurting. How come God didn't do a better job of protecting me? That's what I want to know."

The next surprise came when Jeff was the one answering. Little white Jeff, the boy with the wounded eyes. The one scared half to death by Josh when he first arrived. Now he was the first to find his voice and say, "Do you know who Baruch was, Josh?"

A moment's hesitation, then, "Know the name. That's about all."

"Baruch was Jeremiah's scribe. He complained to the prophet about how he was hurting real bad and how it didn't seem fair. I mean, he was the prophet's assistant and all, and he was spending his whole life helping to do God's work. How come God hadn't protected him from all the pain and misery?"

The two women turned to look his way. James Thaddeus slowly shook his head, knowing his own eyes were just as round as theirs. This was surely something to behold.

"Jeremiah had a message straight from God. The Lord said to Baruch, 'I won't protect you from everything. Not when My wrath is striking the world. But you won't be crushed. You will survive to serve Me.' That's what He said."

There was a long pause, then they heard JT go, "Huh." Just that. Then Kitty hummed, like the women in church, halfway between a yes and an amen.

Jeff went on, "I think about that a lot when I hurt bad, you know, 'cause our mother got called home."

Josh asked, "You done lost your momma?"

Scott was the one who answered now. "Two weeks after the market crashed. Two weeks to the day."

Josh again. "You lost your momma and you sit there still loving the Lord?"

Jeff now. The one causing his daddy such concern. "I hated Him for a long time. I wanted to hate Him forever. But my life was already too empty. I woke up one morning and I knew I couldn't do without Mom and God both. I needed one of them around to give me the love to keep going."

Another little punctuation from JT then, one more quiet "Uh-huh."

Then nothing.

The women seemed to breathe with one set of lungs, taking in all the air there was. They had time to wipe their eyes and release one another, then JT walked down the hall from the front room. The sound forced the three adults to stand up straighter and turn toward the kitchen doorway. JT came in to stand there in front of James Thaddeus, this boy fast growing into a young man.

"Granpa."

"Yes, son." Yes, yes, growing fast.

"Last night, Scott and Jeff and Little G and me, we was talking."

"I heard you." Four young voices in the bedroom down the hall from his, talking what seemed like half the night.

"Sir, we want to do something. Something more than pray."

He watched as Scott and Jeff and Kitty and Little G and Josh all gathered in the doorway behind their spokesman. "You talking about Mr. Korda, now?"

"Yes, sir. We all got the feeling something is gonna happen."

Scott chimed in, "Something big."

"We want to help him, sir." Standing there like a little man, shoulders squared, resolute and ready to be turned down, but asking just the same. "We want to go out and be soldiers for the Lord."

James Thaddeus chewed on his lip for a minute, long enough to get himself back into shape and ready. Which was long enough for the front door to open, and for Patrick to walk down the front hall and come in to stand looking down at him and the gathered children.

So James Thaddeus stared at the man and not the children, which made it easier to say, "Your boys want to come back down and help with the cause. I can't say nothing for their home life and their lessons, no. But I want to tell you that far as I'm concerned . . ."

He paused long enough to turn and glance over to where his wife was standing. Both Elaine and his youngest daughter gave him a quiet nod. He turned back and finished, "Far as we're concerned, both you and the boys are always welcome down here." He smiled at the young faces. "Yes, sir. Always welcome. This here is your home."

─┤ TWENTY-ONE ├─

☐ Patrick spent the first part of their homeward journey wondering what on earth had possessed him to invite Linda Kee.

His nerves seemed to have infected her as well, for Linda remained
silent and reserved. The only reason the trip could be considered a success
at all was the boys. Linda had insisted straight off that she wanted to ride
in the backseat, from where she could see everyone. For reasons Patrick
could not fathom, the boys both found that to be absolutely fantastic. There
was a minor skirmish over who would sit in back with her, quickly quashed
by Jeff proposing to start in front and trade places midway, surprising both
his older brother and his father with the offer.

The first hour and a half were spent reviewing the week: the storm,
the Wilkins household, Buddy's disappearance, and his return. Linda asked
the occasional question but said almost nothing else. Patrick spoke even
less. He remained acutely aware of her presence in the opposite corner,
and could feel her eyes sporadically resting upon him. Jeff spent the entire
trip twisted around in his seat, competing with Scott for her time and
attention.

Two hours into the journey, Jeff pointed forward through the gathering dusk. "Dad, look!"

He had already seen the exit. "No way."

"A Union 76 truck stop! You can't pass it up, Dad. You can't."

"Watch me."

Scott explained to Linda, "They serve the biggest hamburgers known
to man."

"Like this," Jeff said, holding his hands a foot apart. "And some of the truckers look as weird as video-game baddies."

Patrick said, "Which is definitely why we are not stopping."

"Linda would love it, wouldn't you, Linda?"

"I'm not sure I should weigh in with an opinion here."

"Absolutely," Patrick said, glancing at Linda in the rearview mirror. "I need all the help I can get."

"Anybody who grows up in California gets used to being around a little weirdness," Linda said, smiling for the boys. "Besides, I've never seen a hamburger the size of a dinner plate."

"You can't be serious," Patrick said, but the boys were already cheering and exchanging high fives. So he had no choice but to veer off and park beside an 18-wheeler and lead them into the Yankee equivalent of cowboy heaven.

The meal was all noise and country music and laughter. The hamburgers were so large Patrick and Linda could not finish the one they split, while the boys left little mountains of dough and cheese and limp fries on their plates. They then departed to explore the vast array of gimmicks and wizardry on sale in the adjoining store. To the strains of Loretta Lynn, the pair found themselves alone. Linda said, "Your sons are great, Patrick. Does anyone ever call you Pat?"

"Not more than once."

"Good. I've never been big for androgynous names." She wrinkled her nose. "Androgynous. That sounds terribly citified and snobbish, doesn't it?"

"It sounds intelligent." Patrick knew he had to say it, even though what would remain unspoken felt like the weight of Mount Everest bearing down upon every word. "Linda, there are going to be some comments made about you coming back with us."

Her smile slipped back into the recesses of her eyes. "I can imagine."

"I mean, the church, the women . . ." He avoided her calm gaze by glancing out over the tattooed ponytailed diners and linoleum and fluorescent lighting. He was paid to be good with words. "What I'm trying to say is, well . . ."

"People are going to point and talk and gossip. And you're worried to death about everything that might be said, and even more worried about what they might be thinking." She paused. "How am I doing so far?"

"Better than I could."

"I spent two hours ransacking my closet for the most conservative, boring, high-necked, low-hemmed outfits I could find." Her eyes crinkled at the edges. "To tell you the truth, it's got me more nervous than my first time in front of the camera."

"Then you understand why I can't invite you to stay in our guest room."

"With a church to run and two teenage boys to raise, are you kidding?"

"The church has an apartment for visiting missionaries and friends. I've called ahead and booked it for you to use."

"I'm sure it's going to be just fine," she said.

Patrick hoped desperately she was right. "Here come the boys, I guess we better be hitting the road."

Night had descended by the time they were back on the interstate and headed north. Jeff sat behind him now, a chattering, curious boy hammering Linda with questions about working in front of the camera. Linda's voice held to a steady calm as she described the roles of the makeup and production staffs, the choosing of location and the aiming at one word to be punched in each sentence. She walked them through lighting and camera and redrafting, how she held the microphone, the needling questions that became her trademark, the competition, the stress, the hours, the pressure. Patrick listened as her descriptions became ever more complex, and had the distinct impression that though she was answering the boys' questions, her words were meant for him. The thought warmed the night and the highway stretching out ahead.

There came a time of silence, and Patrick felt the night gather in around them. It was not a bad sensation. Not at all. More a sense of power assembling there with them. He found the hairs on the backs of his arms beginning to rise, as before a heavy thunderstorm.

Then Jeff asked, "Have you always been a Christian?"

Linda did not laugh, did not push the question aside, did not offer a quick response, which would have closed that topic off entirely. Instead, her voice lowered to a soft burr, one that only heightened the sense of the night listening along with him. "That is a very complicated question. Well, not the question, but the answer. Are you sure you want to hear it?"

Both the boys chorused in the affirmative. Patrick held his gaze on the road and said nothing.

"This is not something I have spoken of very often. I don't even think about it much. But something your father said to Buddy today . . ." She was quiet for a moment, as though the gathering force were a pressure upon her own heart and mind as well. "I have to ask that we speak here as friends. I think we are becoming friends, don't you?"

The way she said those words, and the solemn way the boys both responded, left Patrick's eyes burning. He did not answer aloud because he did not know what to say. But he nodded. Slowly, up and down several times. Friends.

"Sometimes a friend will share with another friend something that is a secret. Something that is hard to say. Those things are not to be talked about with anybody else. It is a gift. And this kind of gift needs to be kept in confidence. Does that make sense?"

"A lot," Scott said quietly. Jeff retreated into silence. Patrick glanced in the mirror as a passing headlight illuminated his son's face with eyes drawn into great round globes.

"My earliest memories are of religion. My grandmother used to care for us while both my parents worked."

Scott's voice was as hesitant as Patrick could recall hearing it. "Is it okay if I ask a question?"

"You can ask anything you like."

"Is this your Chinese grandmother?"

"Yes. She was Fukienese. She told us stories about what it meant to be a Christian. They scared me to death, those stories. I was four or five when she started, or maybe I was younger and those are the first times I can remember. But what I remember more clearly than the stories are the nightmares I used to have. Horrible nightmares. I have them still sometimes. They leave me feeling like I did when I was little, trapped inside something terrifying that was going to eat me alive."

Linda turned away then, the passing headlights showing a face drawn taut. It accented the Oriental cast of her features, the upward slant of her eyes, the straight nose, the tightly angled jaw and chin. The darkness tinted those blue eyes of hers dusky and more Oriental still. Different and alien and mysterious.

But she turned back, gathering herself and speaking with a gaze directed straight into the mirror, so that Patrick could not have any question whatsoever to whom she was speaking. "They frightened me terribly, those stories. Whole villages being wiped out by marauding soldiers or Communist insurgents or malignant local rulers. My grandmother would make me and my brothers sit and listen to tales of being forced to flee from their homes and land."

Linda halted. This time Jeff was the one to speak. "You don't have to tell us any more if you don't want to."

The tension seemed to drain from her. Just spilled away. Her tone softened as she reached over and touched his arm. It was the first time she had ever touched any of them. She said, "You two are some of the finest young men I have ever met. All I have to do is look at you and know what a wonderful mother you must have had." She turned forward and said to the mirror, "You must make your father very proud."

"They do," Patrick said, his voice tight in his own ears. "Very proud."

She sighed, the sound leading into words spoken in almost a singsong cadence. "My grandmother was fifteen and betrothed when they were driven from their village. The Japanese had started their saber-rattling, but had not yet invaded. The Communists were just beginning to make raids from the hills. The national government was headed up by an ancient woman who was addicted to smoking opium, and a puppet of a son. China was unraveling.

"A rival warlord had defeated the local ruler and was slaughtering everyone known to be Christian. My grandmother's most vivid memory of starting that trek was the sight of churches burning on every hilltop. My grandmother called them the funeral pyres of all her dreams. That day everything she had considered worthy and important in her young life was destroyed. I will never forget her telling me about this. Never.

"She and her family walked for nine months. All but she and her father died on the road—her mother, her aunt and uncle and three cousins, her four brothers, her fiance. All died. Her father brought her to Hong Kong, where he destroyed his lungs working in a sweatshop earning passage for them to America."

"So much pain," Patrick murmured, only half aware he had spoken at all.

"My grandmother never talked about forgiveness. Or hope. Or love. The only thing my grandmother talked about was the *cost*."

When his two boys seemed incapable of saying anything, Patrick offered, "I'm amazed you kept hold of any faith at all."

"I didn't. Not really." She met his gaze in the mirror, knowing what she said was shaming her. Saying it nonetheless. "Filial duty is very strong in a Chinese family. Even one that is only partially Chinese. I was taught obedience. My grandmother ordered me to be a Christian. So I was a Christian. At least to the outside world. I had my white Sunday dress and my little white socks and my polished black shoes. I went to church and I learned to sing the songs. I bowed my head. But did I believe?"

She turned away, unable to hold his gaze any longer. The road hummed and bumped around them. The night wind rushed by. The car remained quiet until Jeff finally asked, "Did you?"

Linda swiveled around so that she faced him fully. "I don't know. But what shames me is not that I didn't know, but that I didn't *care.* I didn't care enough to find out how much I believed and didn't believe."

Her gaze returned to the mirror. "When you were speaking with Buddy today, I discovered the cost of this indifference. I realized that all these years, I've run away from every chance I had to deepen my Christian life. As long as believing came easy, I was fine. Twice I came back, once through a girl in school, then through a dear, sweet man at work. I went with them to church until the next choice came up. Then I turned away. It was always easier to choose the world than to face what you said today, which I think maybe I recognized somewhere down deep. It wasn't just the *choice* that scared me. It was the fact that God wanted me to *change.* That was the ultimatum I could not accept."

"*Ultimatum,*" Patrick said quietly. "It's a good word."

"Why, Dad?" Jeff now.

"Because to choose God means to choose change. You cannot escape the fact that He will remold you. It is inevitable."

Linda retreated into her corner, her face showing just how much the confession had cost her. The car continued on in silence. Patrick searched the dark for something more to say, something that would show her how deeply her words had touched him. He heard Scott draw a ragged breath as he turned to face the front of the car, then he saw Jeff look from Linda to Scott and back again, and Patrick knew that he was not alone in how he felt.

It gave him the strength to say, "I can't tell you how much it means, your sharing that with us."

Linda gave her head a little shake, then leaned her forehead on the window. She sighed to the night and the past.

"I never knew it was like that." Scott was fumbling as badly for words as his father. "I mean, I've heard about all that persecution stuff, sure, but I've never known . . ." He looked in appeal to his father.

"Hearing about it from someone we know makes it live," Patrick offered, knowing it wasn't what needed to be said. But not finding the words to say it correctly. Not any. Feeling helpless in his utter lack.

"So many mistakes," Linda murmured. "I don't even know why I try . . ."

Through the rear window Patrick saw a tentative hand reach out. Jeff, the boy Patrick had remained fearful would never recover from the loss of his mother, dear sweet Jeff reached over and touched Linda's shoulder. He said so quietly Patrick almost missed the words, "It's hard to talk sometimes, isn't it?"

She nodded, her forehead sliding up and down the window. "So hard."

"I know. I remember . . ." Jeff let his hand drop away. "It helps to talk. Really. Not now. But later. It makes me feel like I can see things, well, clearer." He kicked the back of Patrick's seat. "That sounds stupid."

Which was enough to bring Linda around, and bring a small smile to her face. She reached out and said, "Come here, you."

Jeff slid across, cutting the distance between them until Linda could wrap one arm around his shoulders and hug him close. Not saying anything, either of them. Just sitting there in the dark. Headlights flashed past now and then, showing brief glimpses of the two of them close enough to share little smiles and the same wounded gaze.

"Dad."

Patrick started at the sound of Scott's voice. "Yes?"

"You just passed our exit."

He stared out at the next road sign, and had to admit, "So I did."

⊣❙ TWENTY-TWO ❙⊢

☐ Saturday midday Linda Kee stood in the Aiden church cafeteria entrance and wished she could find a friendly face. She felt eyes upon her everywhere. The boys were at basketball practice. Patrick had taken time to show her around and introduce her the best he could, but urgent calls struck at him from every side. She had insisted she leave so he could get to work. Now she regretted making the offer.

Linda pasted on what she hoped looked like a friendly smile and started forward. There were two cafeteria lines, both moving fairly swiftly, and soon she was just one more face waiting for food. The people around her came from all walks of life. Ahead of her stood a mother with two children and carrying a third. The woman tried to ease her shoulders without waking the baby in her arms. Linda offered, "Would you like me to hold the child?"

"That's the nicest thing anybody's said to me all day." She settled the infant into Linda's arms, then said, "My back's killing me."

"I can understand why. She's a heavy little girl."

"Yeah, Cathy could sleep through the Second Coming." The woman had the gritty look of one living rough. Her clothes were clean but so faded all the colors had long since drained away. She looked down at the elder of her two tousled boys and said, "Not like this one here. He's been having nightmares that like to wake the dead."

The little boy was embarrassed by the attention and slouched away from his mother's hand. But not far. As he backed off he kept a wary eye on his place in the line. Linda asked, "Are you alone?"

"No, thank the dear Lord. My man's out standing on some corner like half the rest of this town. Looking for work." The grimace pulled her features into unaccustomed lines, as though she was searching for an action long forgotten. "Ain't that a laugh. As if anybody out there's got any work to offer. But my Harry's gotta try. He's a working fool. He don't find something soon, he's gonna shrivel up and blow away."

The smaller of the two boys whimpered, "Momma, I'm hungry."

"I know you are, darling. Won't be long now." To Linda, "They take after their daddy, the both of them. Don't hardly never complain. But standing here waiting for food when they can smell it just up ahead is hard on a young boy's belly."

"Linda! Miss Kee! Talk about a sight for sore eyes." A vaguely familiar figure approached, leaning heavily upon a cane. He was a tall man with the strangest growth of red hair, like a wild bush that desperately needed tending. "Alex Korda. We met—"

"Of course, I remember now. You're Buddy's brother."

"—in his kitchen. Or I oughtta say, in Molly's kitchen. Buddy's just a visitor there like the rest of us." He squinted at the bundle in her arms. "I don't believe I recall anybody telling me you've got kids."

"I don't. That is . . ."

"It's my youngest, Mr. Korda."

"Of course, sure, I oughtta know that little angel anywhere. But with my eyesight I'm lucky if I can find my own trousers when I already got one leg inside." He cocked his head to find the best angle through his lenses, and inspected the weary mother. "How you doing, dear?"

She gave her head an exhausted shake. "Don't see how the days can get any longer than they already are. But they do."

"I hear you. That man of yours found work yet?"

"Few hours here and there. But nothing steady."

"You tell him to come see me. I'm sure we can fix him up with something a little more regular."

"I done told him 'til I'm blue in the face, Mr. Korda. But Harry says it's too much like charity for his liking."

"Charity!" Alex puffed up like a balloon with a clown's face. "You get him over here and I'll show him so much charity, come suppertime he'll be whimpering like a poor little whipped pup. He'll be so tired from toting bales and baling cotton he'll be begging for a little charity."

The smaller boy gave a little giggle, and Alex bent over to glower at him. "You got something to say to me?"

The boy was not the least bit frightened. He pointed one finger into Alex's face and said to his brother, "He's funny."

"Humph." Alex straightened slowly, pushing hard on his cane. "You tell your Harry to get himself over here, I'll show him just how uncharitable this crotchety old man can be."

"I'll tell him, Mr. Korda." The woman brushed hard at one cheek. "I'll surely tell him."

"Fine." Using his free arm, Alex eased the infant from Linda. He turned to the elder boy and said, "Come over here, son. Take her easy now. That's it. You see that silver-haired woman sitting there by the back door?"

"Yes, sir, I see her." The boy held his sister with the ease of one long used to baby-sitting duty.

"Her name's Matilda. She's got a lap that's just begging for a baby. If I were your sister's size, I'd crawl up there myself. You go give your sister to her and say Alex asked her to hold the little one long enough for us all to eat in peace. Run along now."

The woman managed the best smile of the day. "You're a saint, Mr. Korda."

"Words like that don't do a thing but show how little you know me." Alex patted her arm. "You be sure to tell Harry to come see me tomorrow. And I don't want to hear anything more about this charity nonsense."

Their way through the serving line was slowed by everyone behind the counters wanting to share a word and a smile with Alex. When Linda and Alex were finally seated, Linda said, "Everybody seems to be your friend."

"I'll tell you what it is." Alex unfolded his paper napkin and spread it in his lap. "I've walked right up close to death's door, I've knocked and told the grim reaper a how-do. It's left me with a lot of respect for those bearing pain. Yes sir. I think people see that in me and think maybe here's somebody who can understand what they're going through. You want me to bless this food?"

"Sure."

Alex bowed his head and intoned, "Father, we do truly thank You for this day and this meal. Bless all those who are going hungry today. Bless those who are looking for work, and those who have found some. Bless those who are worried, and those who are afraid. Bless us all. Heal this world. In Jesus' name, amen."

She did not know why his simple words would impact her so, but it took a long moment before Linda felt able to lift her gaze and say, "You were ill?"

"I've got cancer." His matter-of-fact way of speaking robbed the words of either shock value or a need to respond with sympathy. "I'm in remission, thanks be to God. But having cancer at my age is sort of like being an alcoholic. A body might stop suffering for this one particular day, but the shadow is always there." He spread a liberal portion of pepper over his entire plate. "I speak from experience on both those fronts."

"It's hard to imagine you ever having had a problem with drink."

"Yeah, well, that's on account of you seeing me only after the Lord started His work." Alex lifted his fork and tried to draw it into focus. "Is this spinach or turnip greens?"

Linda inspected her own food. "Spinach."

"It better be. Turnips and me had a parting of the ways a while back." He took a tentative bite and nodded. "Spinach. Safe again. My eyesight's gotten so bad I used one of Agatha's belts for a tie this morning." Someone called a greeting and Alex smiled without really seeing them. He asked, "Is Patrick not joining you?"

"He's tied up in some meeting."

"That man could be cloned and still be too busy."

Linda picked at her food, wishing there were some way to ask what she wanted without showing an improper interest. She glanced at the man across from her, with his thick lenses and awkward frame and wild red hair and walking cane hooked on the back of the next seat, and she decided that there would probably be no better place or time or person than here and now and Alex. "How long has it been since Patrick's wife died?"

If Alex found anything extraordinary about her question, he did not show it. "Coming up on eighteen months now. Two weeks after the market crash." He paused for a sip from his glass and a glance around the cafeteria. "I still remember the gravesite. Which is mighty strange, what with everything that's happened since then. But I remember it like we laid her to rest yesterday and not a year and a half ago."

She recognized his pause there as an invitation, and gave silent thanks for having decided to ask him. "It must have been a hard time."

"Sister, you've just spoken a whole truckload of truth." Alex was a remarkably neat eater for such a large and gangly man. His table manners had clearly been learned long ago, and learned well. "Hard as anything I've ever known, and I've known some hardship in my days."

She examined this strange man seated across from her. He seemed ancient in his birdlike ways, a poor, wounded creature who deserved to fly, yet never would again. "Did she die young?"

"Anybody who leaves behind two boys not yet grown dies too young. You noticed the shadows those boys carry?"

"Yes. Especially Jeff." The light burning in Alex's eyes spoke of timeless youth. Here indeed was a man who deserved to soar in laughter and ease. "I think they are two of the finest boys I have ever met." But because she did not want to speak about the boys, and because he was such an easy man to talk with, she asked, "Did you know Patrick's wife well?"

"Hardly at all. I'd only started going to church five, six weeks before she fell ill. No, I count her as a friend only because her story rests so clearly on the three men she left behind. And *them* I count as closer than friends. Brothers." He raised one hand and adjusted his black-rimmed spectacles. "You have any idea where I was headed with this?"

"Her funeral."

"Not the funeral. The gravesite. That's what I remember. The whole church was there, some in pretty good shape financially because they'd done like Buddy said, and others who'd lost everything. But they were all there. And every one of them was wailing like the sky had fallen. Weeping and calling out and shouting like they were the ones being laid down. Caught up in it so much I doubt they even knew they were making any noise at all. Only four people didn't join the commotion. Only four."

Linda found herself shuddering at the almost cheerful way he spoke. And yet not cheerful at all. Just light. Untouched, or perhaps touched so deeply he did not need to show it. "Were you one of them?"

Alex laughed, a youthful sound. "Bless you, honey, no, I was crying like my heart had broken. Which it had. Only not over this poor lady and her family. Over how it felt like we had gathered that day to bury an entire way of life. Which I believe is what was making all the others weep so. Whether they knew it or not. Yes, I truly do believe that."

Another shudder. She understood his words all too well. "Who was silent?"

"The pastor and his two sons and Buddy. I guess Patrick and his boys sort of knew what the people were about, and wanted to keep their own grief for a more private time. A time for them and Alice alone. That was his wife's name. Alice Allen. An angel called home before her time."

"And Buddy?"

Alex was silent a while. Then he turned and craned and asked, "Do I smell coffee? Can you see if they've got the urns out yet?"

"Yes, let me go get you a cup. How do you take it?"

"Thank you, that's surely nice of you. One sugar, no milk."

When she returned with two steaming cups, Alex was speaking to someone leaning over the table. Linda seated herself, waited until the woman had moved away, then repeated, "And Buddy?"

He lingered over his first sip, then set his cup back down with slow, deliberate movements. "I never did get up the nerve to ask my brother why he didn't cry that day. I guess maybe I was afraid he'd tell me . . ."

When he halted a second time, she leaned across the table and pressed, "Tell you what?"

Alex fixed her with a gaze that swam huge and sober behind his thick lenses. "Tell me it wasn't time yet to weep. Tell me that the Lord had something more in store, something even worse than what we're facing now. Like judgment." Slowly, Alex shook his head. "I didn't think I could handle hearing that just then. And when I stand in line with people like that dear woman with her unemployed husband and those poor tired little children, I *know* I don't want to hear him say that now."

□

When Patrick appeared later that afternoon, the first thing he saw was Linda in the center of a cluster of older ladies. They were part of the crowd that staffed the outreach center, nowadays a critical church function. But, oh goodness, those ladies could talk the ear off a statue. Linda looked up and gave him a smile that pleaded for him to free her from their clutches.

To make matters worse, Lionel Peters was at his elbow. The self-appointed watchdog of all church fiscal matters gestured toward Linda and said, "There she is, Patrick. You can ask her now."

As they approached, the group of seven or eight ladies opened to include them as well. "Pastor, this is just so exciting! A real live television personality—"

"Ladies, something vital's come up." Lionel Peters was a formerly successful businessman who made up for his short, chunky stature with an overlarge set of opinions. He was a difficult man at the best of times, and when he was worried he tended to accent his pushy nature with rude anger. "This just can't wait. Can it, Patrick?"

"I'm sorry, I thought our business meeting would never end," Patrick said to Linda, wishing Lionel would get the message and back off. "How are you?"

"Fine. I'm fine."

One of the elderly ladies exclaimed, "She was describing what it was like to interview President Gifford! Imagine, the president of the United States!"

"I was one of three dozen reporters crammed together on the White House lawn," she reminded them quietly, her eyes on Patrick. She asked him directly, "Something is the matter, isn't it?"

"I'll say." Lionel used his voice to silence the ladies. "Do you want to ask her or shall I?"

"Lionel," Patrick wondered if there was a Christian way for a pastor to publicly tell one of his congregation to back off. "Linda has no connection with this whatsoever."

"Maybe not. But she knows more about how Washington works than we ever will."

"All right. Fine." Patrick hoped the apology was clear in his gaze. "Lionel has heard a rumor that the government has something planned for the churches."

"Not rumor. Fact."

"Unsubstantiated, Lionel."

"Almost fact, then. Close. Too close for comfort."

Linda's gaze swiveled from one to the other. "Planned what?"

Patrick found it hard to even say the words. "That they have decided to revoke the churches' tax-exempt status and go after us in a big way."

The ladies let out a joint gasp. Lionel exploded, "Not just church *income*. Church *holdings*."

"According to Lionel's source," Patrick explained, "the government is planning to take a portion of all holdings beyond what is actually used for the worship service."

"Land, buildings, fixed assets, the works." Lionel found it necessary to wave his arms for emphasis. "Have you heard anything about this?"

"No." Linda looked at Patrick, then back to the smaller man. "But it doesn't surprise me."

That stopped them. "What?"

"Since the economic meltdown, the churches have held a disproportionate amount of nonessential wealth."

Patrick stared at her with the others. It seemed as though he could actually see it happen. She had changed from a newfound friend to someone he was not sure he knew at all. A person whose brilliance penetrated both their worry and their problem. Her features seemed to sharpen along with her concentration, until her gaze and her face all tightened into a beam that pierced whatever it touched.

"Nonessential wealth is the government's way of describing funds not required to meet daily needs," Linda went on. "It's the new catchword for this present crisis. In the government's view, they need to tap all sources of nonessential wealth to help restart the economy."

"But this is money that has been given in trust to us by our congregation," Patrick protested. "The surplus that has been donated since the crisis started is ours only because of how people acted on a message from God."

She shook her head. One swift movement. "That won't hold much weight in Washington. Their attitude will be, you have it and others don't. This money should be used to aid all Americans. Not just churchgoers."

Even Lionel's punch was deflated by her attitude. "They had their chance along with everyone else. They just didn't follow Buddy's message."

"God's message," Patrick corrected quietly.

"Rubbing the federal government's face in its own errors will only harden their resolve," Linda replied definitively. "Nobody likes to be reminded of their mistakes, most especially . . ."

She stopped, her eyes narrowing in thought. Patrick asked, "What is it?"

"I'll bet that's why they asked him down."

Lionel demanded, "Asked who down where?"

"Buddy Korda. The White House invited him to Washington," Patrick explained impatiently. Then to Linda, "What do you mean?"

"He gave the first prediction. I'm sure they're wondering if there's some way to get him to endorse their taxation plan."

"That's ludicrous!" Lionel scoffed.

"Don't be too sure. A night in the Lincoln Bedroom of the White House, a private meeting with the president himself, a bevy of Washington's finest carting out data on the current crisis—it can add up to incredible pressure to do what they want."

"Buddy would never do such a thing," Patrick said, hoping he was right.

"You would be surprised what people will agree to, when seated in the Oval Office with the president of the United States personally urging them to aid their country." Linda held to her clipped analytical tone. "Very surprised indeed."

Lionel turned to Patrick and almost shouted, "You've got to warn him! Better still, get him back up here. He doesn't have any business—"

"Buddy Korda is taking orders from nobody but God," Patrick assured him. "I just called down. He is in seclusion and has been ever since we left yesterday."

But Lionel was not ready to let go of his worry. He rounded on Linda. "How do we know we can trust what you're saying?"

One of the older ladies gasped, "Lionel Peters! I've never in all my born days!"

"Well?" With his fleshy jaw protruding, he looked like an angry pit bull. "She comes from Washington. She's been in the thick of things down there. How do we know she's not up here to spy on Korda?"

Before Patrick could recover enough to fry Lionel where he stood, Linda gave him a look. Just one. But the look was powered by eyes hard and fierce as blue lasers. "I do not lie, Mr. Peters. I am *certainly* not going to start with you."

"Get away with you, Lionel," one of the older women said, pushing her way in between them and planting an angry hand on Lionel's chest. "You ought to be ashamed of yourself, treating the pastor's guest like this!"

When Lionel started to protest, the lady shoved him once more, harder this time. "Go on with you! And don't you *dare* show your face in here again until you're ready to apologize!"

When Lionel had skulked off, the lady turned back toward Linda and said, "I can't tell you how sorry we are about this."

There was a chorus of agreement from the others. Linda looked at them, not yet ready to smile, but the icy fire was gone from her gaze. "Thank you."

"I have known that man all my life it seems, long enough to know that Lionel Peters is a trial."

"It's fine. Really." She looked at Patrick, her sharp intelligence in plain view. "Back to the matter at hand. If Buddy Korda has been scheduled for the main treatment, he's going to need someone to guide him through this. If this is truly what the White House has in mind, the pressure they could exert would be simply enormous. You have no idea."

☐

A light, misty rain was falling when they emerged from the church. The parking lot was ringed by light-filled buildings, and the puddles glowed dripping and yellow. The air smelled of wet chill and of earth. Linda took a deep breath and smiled at the thought that finally, finally she could taste a hint of coming spring.

Patrick fiddled with the church lock, turning the key carefully through three full rounds.

The news and the confrontation had turned him as gloomy as the night. "I can't tell you how sorry I am."

"It's okay. Nine years in Washington helped me grow a pretty thick skin." She stood under the entrance overhang and stared out at the gathering dusk. "One nice thing about that little dispute, the ladies were playing judge and jury with me before you showed up."

"I can just imagine."

"Did you see the way they said good-bye? I am one of the fold now. I passed the trial by fire." The smile slipped away. "I'm sorry. That sounded terrible, didn't it?"

"It sounded honest. I have no problem with honesty. I learned long ago that just entering the church portals does not transform humans into angelic beings." He squinted at the sky. "I left my umbrella in my office."

"It doesn't matter. It's more a heavy fog than rain. Let's just run."

They sprinted for the car. Once safely inside, Linda ran a hand through her hair, brushing off the droplets, shivering as Patrick started the car and put the heater on high. "I had a long talk with Alex today."

"Somebody told me they saw you with your heads together." He hesitated, then added, "Which brings us to an important point. If we go to any restaurant in Aiden, we are going to be talked about."

"That doesn't bother me, I'm the stranger here. Or are you thinking your own fears out loud?"

He hesitated, then answered slowly, "I'm not afraid."

"Good." Her smile slipped out again. "Do you have a favorite place?"

"My boys' tastes run strictly to steak and pizza. There's a nice Italian restaurant I haven't been to in, well, years. I don't even know if it's survived the crash."

"Let's go see."

As they drove quietly through the wet darkening streets, Linda found herself framing questions only to set them aside. She didn't really care to talk about his work of the day, as it would only bring the depressing present in more closely. And she didn't want to talk about Buddy and what had brought them together. She wanted to talk about them.

Patrick remained silent until they pulled around a corner, then he remarked, "Well, the sign's still up and there's a light in the window."

"Looks like this is our lucky night, then."

He pulled into the parking lot. "Four cars. I remember how on weekends you had to park two blocks away and wait an hour in line for a table."

Another dash for the front door, which tinkled as they opened it. A vast woman with gray hair pulled into a steel-colored bun brightened and slid from her stool. "Reverend Allen, what a nice surprise. Welcome, welcome."

"Mrs. Stefanelli, hello, I was so happy to see you are still open for business."

"Such business as there is." She pointed a chubby hand at the almost empty restaurant. "Four tables we have. Four. We used to have that many dishwashers and ten times the number of waiters."

"I remember."

"Now Papa cooks and my two eldest daughters help, and their men work out here with me. If you can call this work." She shrugged as she picked up the menus. "But what can you do. At least we have food on the table. And Papa has started baking his own bread again. He hasn't done that since we opened our first little storefront cafe, oh my goodness, that must be forty years ago."

She started a heavy gait toward the back. "But never mind that. Look, the nicest table in the restaurant, I must have been saving it for you and the lovely young lady." With a squint of concentration, she watched Linda seat herself. "I know I've seen you before. I never forget a face, never in all my sixty-eight years do I forget. Have you been here before?"

"I'm sorry, no."

"What is your special tonight?" Patrick asked, drawing her attention away from Linda.

"Chicken cacciatore. The cheese we have brought in by a farmer who's started making it in his own stone dairy house." She kissed her first three fingers. "The tomato sauce we are making from scratch. And the herbs we grow in our own garden."

"Sounds perfect," Linda said, handing back her menu unopened.

The woman gave Linda a final lingering inspection, then turned toward the kitchen. "Enjoy, the both of you."

When they were alone, Linda said, "Thank you."

"I can't imagine what it would be like to have a million strangers all think they know you."

"You get used to it." Somehow the words left her feeling as old as stardust. "If you've got the ambition to make it to the top in the news business, you learn to put up with a lot of stuff."

Patrick's gaze did a slow sweep of the cavernous room. "This place is so quiet, I wish you could have seen it two years ago. On the weekends they used to have these six old geezers, all from the old country, who would sit up on that little stage and play these tunes on fiddles and accordions. For a while you could think you'd been transported to Italy."

"It must have been very nice," she said, watching him.

"It was." His gaze seemed to open as he searched the shadows of memories. "Alice used to love coming here. She never had a chance to travel. It was one of the things we always promised ourselves, to get over to Europe. But we never went. First there was no money, then there was a little church to get going, then the boys came along. Her folks died young, and mine both passed on in our first years of marriage . . ." He stopped and focused upon her. "I'm so sorry."

"Don't be."

"I should never have . . . I'm so new at this I don't even know the ground rules."

"I don't mind. Really." She hesitated, then confessed, "Why do you think I asked you to choose a favorite restaurant?"

Patrick cocked his head to one side. "You wanted me to talk about Alice?"

"I want to know you," Linda replied. "How can I do that without knowing who she was?"

The dinner was slow and easy and comfortable, despite the fact that his wife seemed to occupy a vacant chair. Patrick spoke about the world that once was and never would be again, about a woman he had loved more than life itself, and lost. Linda found herself minding yet not minding, as though for her the evening was about coming to terms with the unseen partner, the one who would always be there and yet absent. The meal itself was delicious, the feeling at their table as poignant as the big empty restaurant. So many memories crowded into that barren chamber.

When they had reached the point of playing with the food left on their plates, Patrick said, "I can't believe we've spent the entire evening talking about me."

"I like it."

"But I've got so many questions I want to ask. About your work, your life." He smiled at her then, seeing her fully now, as though talking of his deceased partner had granted him space to breathe in more air. "About how you managed to stay single so long. Or have you been married before?"

"No." She had to stop herself from turning cold and snippish. It was such an easy thing to do when confronted with questions about her past. When forced to look at so much that shamed her. So many wrong turns. Instead Linda worked at a little smile and said, "Let's end the evening the way we've started. We can talk about me next time."

Patrick did not smile. He merely nodded, slow and steady, the movement taking in his entire upper body. "I like the way that sounds. The next time."

Linda forced herself to say the words, though she knew she risked destroying the evening and the sentiment. "Alex told me about the funeral."

"The worst day of my life," Patrick said, still nodding slowly, the only change to the tableau being a slight darkening of his gaze. A wound opening in his eyes that fell straight to the center of his soul.

"I'm so sorry, Patrick."

"Thank you." The nodding continued as he looked at her and at something else. Something internal. "There are two things I've gained from the horror of losing Alice. Two treasures. I call them that now, and that's what they are. I've struggled to keep hold of them when grief threatened to tear them from me, as hard as I've ever fought for anything in my entire life."

She leaned forward, started to take his hand. Something stopped her before she could reach out. Perhaps the same something which told her listening heart that he had seldom spoken of this before. If at all.

"The first treasure was learning how to listen. Before, I'd listen to someone only until I knew the answer. A pastor is forced to listen to so much. My defense from being overwhelmed was to find the solution, the response, and then raise barriers and shut out the rest. Now I've been forced to accept that I don't have all the answers and probably never will. Sometimes the best thing I can do for someone is to let them try to express the confusion and share with them the *lack* of answers."

He continued to stare at her, but he saw her no longer. His gaze was too tightly centered upon what he was exposing within himself. "The second gift was the gift of hurting. I don't say 'caring,' because I have always cared for my flock. But now I *hurt* for them. *With* them."

It was not what he was saying that wounded her so deeply, though the words themselves carried sufficient power to make her tremble. No. What threatened to strip away all her carefully contrived defenses was how honest he was at seeing himself. How utterly merciless, and yet how *compassionate.* Linda could not explain exactly how she knew, but there was a sensing so strong she knew without a doubt that Patrick had not only come to care for others, but to care for *himself.* To care so deeply that he had learned how to forgive both what was past, and what was yet to come. This honest clemency probed the recesses of her hidden heart like a lance. For she had never forgiven herself anything. Never. Mistakes were burdens she was meant to carry all her life. God might forgive her, for God was perfect—or so people always said. But she never could. Never. Linda sat and stared across the table, seeing the strongest man she had ever met in her entire life.

"Learning to listen and learning to care for the wounded by hurting with them," Patrick went on. "These were lessons I could have only gained by losing Alice. She left, and in leaving she prepared me to care for the crippled."

He stopped there, and Linda knew he would only be able to finish shaping his unspoken realizations if she prodded. Which meant emerging from the void of her own lack to say, "She prepared you for these times."

Patrick nodded slowly, the gaze deepening, the wound becoming utterly exposed now. "I just wonder, I know I shouldn't but I can't help . . ." He took a very shaky breath. "Had I been someone who was more willing to learn these lessons earlier, maybe she wouldn't have been called home."

Linda reached for him then. She took his hand and squeezed hard and willed what strength she had into him. "Patrick, there are few things in this world that I can be absolutely certain of. But I am utterly positive that your wife's passage was not your fault."

He released a breath broken by a year and a half of unspoken fears. "I hope you're right."

"I am. Believe me. I am."

They paid and left the restaurant, the silence between them filled with all that had been revealed. And all that was beyond the reach of words and of time.

⊣| TWENTY-THREE |⊢

☐ Buddy spent the weekend alone in the Wilkins' guesthouse. Most of the time was spent either seated before the fire or standing in front of the gray window. He watched the rain, he reflected, he prayed, and he listened. And for once, he found himself comfortable with the absence of any reply.

Friday evening and again Saturday morning he spoke with Molly, trying to explain his need for solitude. She did not like him being so far away. She did not understand how the snow-bound isolation was not enough. She missed him. She remained very worried about Anne and the baby. But she did not insist on him returning home. She, too, had heard the need in his voice, and loved him enough to share the need of his soul.

He turned to the Scriptures now and again, but more to bind himself to the Lord's path than to study the Word. After Saturday lunch he did not eat. He found himself hungry from time to time, but there was a rightness to this fasting. And the sense of rightness brought with it an ease. Mrs. Wilkins had brought over supplies, and Saturday evening she started to invite him to join them for dinner, but the words were halted before they were formed. Buddy actually saw it happen. The good woman stopped in mid-sentence so cleanly a hand might have been clapped over her mouth. She set down her covered dish and her groceries and walked back outside without saying anything more. Buddy understood perfectly. Somehow his threadbare haven did not welcome many words.

It was not a time for searching inside himself. Rather, it was a time for *silence*. Buddy Korda sat or knelt or stood or paced as the moment demanded.

No matter what his position, the quiet stillness remained. For the first time in his entire life, he was content to *wait*. Without expectations, without demands of his own.

All Saturday Buddy Korda waited upon the Lord. The longer he waited, the more each surfacing thought became a barrier, an obstruction holding him back from doing what he felt he was called to do.

Silence gathered with the night. By the time he finally went to bed Buddy felt as though each act had taken on a special singularity. He put on his pajamas and brushed his teeth with the utter absence of ordinary mental noise. There was just this one action. Just this one single solitary silent moment.

Then, with Sunday, there came the harvest-time.

☐

As far as Royce Calder was concerned, weekends were a loathsome habit invented by the slaving lower classes. He himself maintained rigid routines to fill the otherwise empty days. This Sunday, like every one he spent in the city, started with the brisk walk down to the local newsstand, where his thirty-two pounds of weekend magazines and newspapers were bound in plastic against the torrential downpour. Royce walked on to his favorite breakfast cafe, reflecting that the one nice thing about this incredible rain was how it kept the beggars from pestering him.

He nodded thanks to the waiter who bustled over to help him with his coat and hat, ignoring the glances and muttered comments from people who recognized him. In minutes he was surrounded by news from around the world. He claimed Saturday and Sunday were indispensable to his keeping up with world events. In truth, it was the best defense he could find against the barren hours.

The other tables in the stylish Georgetown cafe swiftly filled with the normal weekend club. A few couples blearily sought to bring the day into focus after watching a dawn from the wrong end. Another few tables were taken by single women with the hard-edged complexions of dedicated Washington workaholics. The majority of tables were filled with single men, uncomfortable out of their suit-and-tie uniform. The state of their sweaters was fairly good evidence of how long they had been living alone. Those with the coffee-stained fronts and frayed elbows had been divorced for years. It was mostly a silent crew, many of them hollowed by the empty day ahead, wishing they still had people to care for them. Unable to pretend they were happy, fulfilled, in charge. Yes, the room was full of dedicated weekend haters.

Royce accepted greetings from people all around the room. This was a Washington crowd; people here did not invade his private space although most knew who he was and what power he wielded. Even so, every time he raised his head, some face or another was looking his way, hoping for an excuse from Royce to meander over, twist his arm on one point or another. Royce kept his head down almost all the time.

He lingered over his final cup of coffee for as long as possible. The hours between his arrival home from brunch and his departure for whatever reception or dinner he had scheduled that evening stretched out sterile and dull. And there was always the risk that he would glance into his living room and see the empty mantel. The one where his wife had kept their collection of wedding photographs and baby pictures from his son's early days. Most of the pictures his wife had taken with her when she returned to Richmond, where all her family lived. The few she had left him, in a vague hope he might regret letting them go so easily, Royce kept in a box upstairs in the attic. He had not looked at them since the divorce. It was only on empty weekends that he thought about them at all.

When the inevitable could not be put off any longer, Royce folded up the last paper and selected the segments he wanted to take with him. The remainder he left for the waiters and later customers to peruse. It was a habit of such long standing the staff no longer even thanked him.

Just as he was sliding from the booth and looking for the waiter to ask for his bill, however, his mobile phone rang.

He flipped it open and punched the button. "Calder."

Rob Satchell started in with, "Hey, good buddy, it's your knight in shining armor."

Royce settled back into his seat. "Good morning, Rob."

The political consultant spoke with the fruity boom of a man who was always selling, always *on.* "Thought I'd let you know we set the hook just like you wanted."

"Linda Kee has accepted a job?"

"Spent two hours with my assistant wrangling over terms."

"This is good news." Royce squinted into the unseen distance. "Why did you wait until Sunday to call and let me know?"

A moment's hesitation, then, "To tell the truth, we've been busy watching the news."

"Ah." Beyond the rain-streaked window, a man's umbrella was caught by a sudden gust of wind and flipped inside-out before being ripped from his hands. The man stood and looked in astonishment at the impossible weather. Royce agreed. There had not been a single breath of wind all morning, and suddenly this. The man hunched his shoulders and made his sodden way down the sidewalk. Royce said, "You wanted to see whether she appeared on camera alongside Korda."

"Exactly. We can't risk hiring somebody who's jumped right off the political spectrum and into the rainbow of never-never land. You know what happens to people who get tagged as religious extremists in this business."

"They die a swift political death."

"Too right." Strange how the man could discuss the toughest of topics with a smile and a chortle. But this was Rob Satchell's trademark, taking political mud and making mud pies. "Anyway, she not only kept her face from the cameras, she hid Korda so well not even the morning chat shows could find him."

"I've just checked the New York and Los Angeles papers as well as ours. There's a lot of talk about Korda being caught in the blizzard, but nothing whatsoever from him personally."

"Not a pip. I heard two more people over at CBS lost their jobs because they couldn't track Korda down for a *Sixty Minutes* special." A moment's hesitation, then, "What say we give this another few days before sending Miss Kee the contract. Just to be safe."

Royce permitted himself a small smile. "Then I'm afraid we're going to have to retract our promise on the Virginia governor's support for your man. He happens to be a close personal friend of the congressman your candidate hopes to take down."

"You're a snake, Calder." Even this was said with a smile. Metallic, harsh, but a smile. "Anybody ever told you that?"

"All the time," Royce replied. "Was there anything else?"

"Nah, that'll do for today. You have yourself a nice weekend, now."

Royce cut the connection, but before he could set the phone down it rang a second time. He said in greeting, "Don't tell me you've decided to change your mind again."

"Royce? Royce Calder?"

"Mr. Eldridge." He straightened in his seat at the sound of the president's chief of staff. "I'm sorry, sir, I just got off the phone with—"

"Never mind that. I suppose you've seen the papers."

"All of them."

"Not a single quote from Korda. Don't you find that a little strange?"

"Yes and no." He decided there was no reason not to say, "Apparently Korda has hired himself a professional PR staffer. A former newscaster for CBS News."

"Ah. That makes sense. He's keeping Korda under wraps until the mockery has died down somewhat."

"Actually, it's a 'she,' sir. The consultant. But that would be my guess. And it seems to me that all this attention might actually be playing to our advantage."

"Yes, yes, of course." Eldridge's tight tone loosened a notch. "He's been brought back into the public eye."

"Precisely, sir. All we need now is to make sure he's not going to come out with something ridiculous—"

"That would make us the laughingstock," Eldridge finished for him. "Then as soon as this has died down a bit, we pounce."

"Exactly what I was planning."

"Good. That's very good, Calder. All right, sorry I disturbed your weekend."

Before he could respond, Ethan Eldridge had cut the connection.

Royce folded up his mobile and slid from the booth. There was no putting it off any longer. His lonely little house awaited.

─┤ TWENTY-FOUR ├─

☐ When Buddy arose to the gray Sunday dawn, he knew the Lord was near. Even before he opened his eyes, he knew.

He went through his morning routine in silent readiness. Anticipation was not what he felt; no, for anticipation meant he was *waiting* for something. His impression of the morning was not like that at all. Buddy sat over coffee with the Bible open before him, knowing that the Lord was not coming. No. The Lord was *here*.

Throughout the morning he continued the same lonely procession as the day before—kneeling, sitting, standing at the window, pacing the sparsely furnished front room.

Lunchtime came and went unnoticed, signaled by nothing more than the movements of the hands on a meaningless clock. Marking time in a world that meant less and less with each of Buddy's slow rotations around the room. He was hungry, but he could not eat. It was not proper. Not here. Not now, in this place and time made sacred by its joining to something far beyond time.

☐

Midafternoon found him standing once more by the window. He became enraptured by the falling rain. Droplets cascaded off the roof, thousands and thousands of liquid cymbals falling on the porch banister, on the ground, on the stalks of bushes still empty of leaves. Yet in the moment's growing stillness, each one became a jewel of God's making.

Each drop became a vision of perfection. Each one demanded his *total* attention.

Time slowed until it felt as though he could count a million breaths in the space of one falling perfect droplet. The music of water and wind paused then, held by the majesty of the Creator's entry.

Buddy did not weep, though he wanted to, if only to release some of the pressure in his swollen love-filled chest. No. What he did was release that breath, that moment, that perfect timeless drop of falling water. He breathed, and breathed again. And he accepted that he was no longer alone.

The stillness was not merely there in his mind. Not anymore. The stillness was now so powerful, so divinely potent, that he, and all he saw, had become connected to the eternal.

There, in the quiet of a silent house and a silent mind, God whispered to him.

☐

"Buddy? Mr. Korda?"

He blinked his eyes, focused, and realized he was looking up at Reverend Wilkins.

"Brother, are you all right?" The dark face was creased with worry. "Do you need a doctor?"

"No." His voice sounded rusty after two days of silence. "No, I'm fine."

"Slow now, let me help you up. Did you fall?"

"No, I didn't . . . What time is it?"

"Just gone five. Have you had dinner?"

Buddy started to pull his feet under him, then decided he needed to sit there on the living room floor a little while longer.

James Thaddeus gave him a curious look, then rose to full height and went into the kitchen. "Ain't touched nothing my wife fixed for you. You been fasting all weekend. Yes. And this after three cold and hungry days in a snowstorm. Look at this, one cup is all that's dirty."

A stern face poked through the kitchen door as Buddy rose unsteadily to his feet. "You didn't drink nothing 'cept that one cup of coffee, is that it? Man like you ought to have enough sense to know to drink lotsa water when . . ."

Something in Buddy's gaze halted the reverend's words. Buddy asked quietly, "Is Patrick coming back to Washington tonight?"

"He didn't say."

"He needs to come. Now. This minute."

The old grizzled head cocked to one side, observing closely. "I can call him directly if you want."

"Yes. Tell him . . . Tell him to come. And the woman, Linda Kee. She needs to be here too."

"I'll see if I can find them both." He crossed back to where Buddy stood weaving slightly. "Now you come over to the house and let my wife get something hot into you." But the grip on Buddy's arm remained light, respectful. "Even God's messenger has got to eat."

☐ The drive back to Washington was a quietly tense affair. Linda was not certain exactly what had transpired between Patrick and his sons, but smoke was still trailing from him as Linda and Patrick drove south. All he had said, when she asked what was wrong, was that sometimes the silent treatment is the hardest battle of all. Not to mention, he had added as he slammed his door and started the car, the stress of leaving a church before a Sabbath evening service when he was scheduled to speak.

Linda did not mind the silence. In fact, she welcomed it. Her thoughts remained caught up in all the weekend's emotions. Patrick's sermon that morning had unsettled her as nothing had in a very long time. So much so fast, she did not even know what to think.

Once they arrived at the city, Patrick followed Linda's directions and took the Fourteenth Street Bridge. The night and the entire capital seemed to weep with uniform weariness. Even the beggars around the Mall seemed defeated by the endless rain.

A black umbrella popped out of the church's back entrance before Patrick had pulled into the parking lot and stopped. They watched JT, tall and slender as a young sapling, sprint around the streetlights and the puddles. His face fell as he realized the backseat was empty. When Patrick opened the door and extended his umbrella, JT said, "You didn't let them come?"

"They have school, JT. You know that."

The boy said nothing more, just turned and called dejectedly back to where Kitty and Little G stood waiting just inside the door, "He made them stay behind."

Patrick waited until Linda had opened her umbrella and joined him to say, "It's the strangest thing. Scott and Jeff wanted this trip more than anything I can remember. But when I said no, they didn't argue, they just clammed up." He stared up to where the Wilkins grandchildren had disappeared from the doorway. "It's left me feeling worse than if they had argued. A lot worse."

Her response was cut short by Reverend Wilkins popping into view, still grappling with one arm of his raincoat. "Glad y'all made it," he said, rushing over and pointing toward the brick house across the street. "Real glad."

They fell into step beside him. Patrick asked, "Is something wrong?"

"Can't tell you that. Buddy didn't say a thing to me. Nothing 'cept how you two needed to get down soon as you can."

They crossed the street and rushed up the guesthouse stairs. Elaine Wilkins was there in the doorway to greet them with, "Got to stand over this man to make sure he eats proper."

"That's not true," Buddy protested, rising from the table.

Linda stepped through the door, and found herself unable to go farther. The room seemed charged with power. Not bad, not dangerous, just *mighty*. She looked from one person to the other, wondering if anyone else could sense it.

But Elaine merely took their umbrellas and coats, and said, "Got a call from Mrs. Korda this evening, after she heard how that man there done laid himself out flat from hunger."

"I didn't faint because I was fasting, Elaine. I've told you—"

"Lady said I was to make sure he got hisself two proper meals tonight and three more tomorrow." Elaine pointed back to Buddy's vacated seat. "You sit yourself right back down and finish your supper."

Buddy started to object, but Elaine's frown brooded no argument. He settled back, muttering, "I feel like I'm being fattened for Easter dinner."

Elaine turned to the newcomers and asked, "Y'all had yourselves something to eat?"

"We stopped on the way, thanks." Patrick walked over and sat down across from Buddy. "You fainted?"

"I'm not sure."

James Thaddeus said, "Came over this afternoon, found the man flat on his back here by the window. Out stone-cold."

"Ain't got no business missing meals," Elaine Wilkins groused. "God's man oughtta have the sense to know that."

Buddy rolled his eyes, but said nothing more until he was facing a clean plate. Elaine picked it up and walked into the kitchen, muttering something to the effect that a full-grown man ought to know when to stop and eat. Buddy said, "I know now what it is that brought me here to Washington."

Patrick nodded slowly. "Are you sure?"

"Yes." No need for emphasis. "I'm sure."

Linda found herself unable to apply her customary skepticism. She sat at the table between James Thaddeus and Patrick, sensing a room so charged with power the hair on her nape was ready to rise and sparkle.

To her surprise, Buddy turned to her and said, "I'm going to need your help."

She nodded slowly. Perhaps this was why the power was being applied to her. Somehow this utterly illogical thought made sense. The power was pointed in her direction, because this was not a time to stand back and observe.

"All right," she said faintly. It was time to *choose.*

If only she wasn't so fearful of falling yet again.

"Part of what became clear was that I need to hold myself apart," Buddy went on. "I cannot become caught up in the press of interviews and talks. I need to remain separate. I need to keep myself ready to hear God, if or when He decides to speak with me again."

Linda risked a glance at the others, and saw they were waiting and watching, no more ready to question Buddy's words than she was. She asked, "What do you want me to do?"

"I have a message. Something I need to put out on video, in case others want to hear it." Then Buddy said to the others, "I have the impression that the dispersal is not my responsibility. Not this time. I need all of you to help me with this."

James Thaddeus turned to Patrick. "Looks like it's time we put your idea of a council to work."

Patrick nodded agreement, then asked Buddy, "Can you tell us what the message is?"

"Not yet. Soon, but not today. First I need to have a meeting with a lawyer."

They took a moment to digest that before James Thaddeus said, "Any particular kind?"

"Someone who knows his or her way around the Constitution."

"Know just the man," James Thaddeus said, as though he had been waiting all along for this request. "Youngest deacon of my church. Don't hardly look old enough, but he's a fine man from a fine family. Got himself a case in front of the Supreme Court right this very minute."

Buddy accepted this with the calm of someone who had no doubt it would be so. To Linda he went on, "I need you to help coordinate all my meetings. Keep everyone but those who are truly essential at arm's length."

She blinked. "You want me to manage your schedule?"

"If that's what it is called, yes." He watched her carefully. "No one is forcing you to do this. I know it's a lot to ask, and if you would rather—"

"No." The sense of gathering force only intensified, a power that could not be denied. "No, it's fine. I'm happy to help."

Buddy visibly relaxed. "I don't know exactly what is going to happen. But I know there is going to be a lot of press attention turned my way. A *lot* of attention."

"I'm sure you're right." To the others she explained, "Being trapped in the storm has only intensified their interest in having him back in the spotlight. The man who predicted the economic meltdown, back with another message, caught in the century's freak storm, here in Washington at the White House's request. All of this is going to make for great play."

"That's exactly what we want to avoid," Buddy said, a sharp edge to his voice. "No play at all. Nothing can be allowed to take away from the message itself."

"I understand."

"No word about me, no interviews except those exclusively about the message itself. And about God. Nothing about me."

"That goes directly against the vein of every rule of solid interviewing. The message is not the story. The person is." She leaned back, understanding what was being asked here. "The only way that will be possible is if we package the interviews and hand them out. Have our own cameraman, an in-house sound and lighting team, and do it all ourselves."

Buddy watched her carefully. "Can you help us do this?"

Linda took a breath, feeling pressed from all sides. The past, the future, the mistakes she had made, the ones she feared she might make again. If only she had a little of their strength. But all she said was, "I know just the man."

□

Molly's voice held the clipped tone she used when the grandchildren had been caught doing something very wrong. "What's this I hear about you fainting from hunger?"

"Molly, I didn't—"

"Do you have any idea how foolish that sounds? A full-grown man with your responsibilities allowing himself to fast until he passes out cold on the living room floor?"

"It wasn't hunger," he protested, but quietly, because he knew she was no longer listening.

"I don't have time for this. I've got my hands full with a sick daughter-in-law, a worried son, a sick baby, and two children to look after." Molly paused long enough to draw a quick breath. "You listen to me, Buddy Korda. Are you listening to me?"

"Yes, dear."

"You are down there to do God's work. Not make yourself sick from bad habits and poor eating."

"All right, Molly."

"I've spoken to Elaine and she is going to make sure you eat three meals a day. And I don't want you giving her any back talk. Are you still listening?"

"To every word, dear."

"Silliest thing I've ever heard of. What on earth did you think you were doing?"

"Molly, I—"

"I let you go off like that because you said it was important. What's more important than your health? How could you do something like that, Buddy? I'm up to my neck with worry about our Anne, and I don't have time to mess with this!"

"I understand." When he was sure she was finally finished and ready to listen, he said, "Molly, the Lord spoke to me."

It took her a moment to let her irritation go. More subdued now, she asked, "What did He say?"

"I'll be talking it out in front of the camera tomorrow. Linda's trying to arrange for a professional to come in." That was all he was going to say just now. About that portion, at least. "Molly, there was a message for us. About Anne."

That caught her up entirely. "From God?"

"Yes. Honey, she's going to be all right. And the baby. We are to expect a complete recovery. Tell Paul."

"Are you sure?"

"Sweetheart, the hand of the Lord was upon me. That's why I fainted. It wasn't from fasting. I know this is true, Molly. We can trust in His message."

"Oh, Buddy . . ." Her voice broke then, as though his few words were the final weight to bend and snap her resolve. "Wait just a minute." There was the sound of her setting down the phone and rummaging through her purse and blowing her nose.

"Molly?"

"I just got back from the hospital. The baby . . . Oh, Buddy, the poor little thing . . ."

"Molly, trust me. No, trust God. And tell Paul he is to call the baby Josiah. The name means 'Jehovah heals.' King Josiah led reforms after his predecessors had taken Israel almost to the brink of ruin. Tell Paul it is a sign from God that all will be well with our nation, if only we follow His lead." He listened to the sound of Molly's quiet weeping. "Will you tell him that?"

"Yes." She sniffed hard, struggling for control. "I'll call him right now."

□

"CBS News."

Clarence's home phone had been busy, so Linda had decided to try the office. Sunday evenings were like any other time in the news business— tied to the same tight production timeline. But not usually for the receptionist. "Attie, hi. It's me. Why are you working Sunday evening?"

"The question you oughtta be asking is, 'Attie, when do you ever go home?' Girl, don't you ever check in with your answering service?"

"Not since Friday, why?"

"Jackson's been hunting you, is why. And when he couldn't find you he started making misery for me. Like I was responsible for you dropping off the end of the world."

Jackson Knowles was chief producer at the CBS Washington bureau, and her former boss. "I went out of town."

"Well, your timing ain't so good, is all I got to say. Hang on, let me see if he is around."

"Attie, wait. Can I first speak to Clarence?"

"Oh, honey, I hate to be the one to tell you." Her tone softened. "Clarence got canned yesterday. Came in to work Saturday, finished a double over-time shift, and was let go. Now that's hard."

"Poor man."

"Times are so hard, I just don't want to get up some mornings. Jackson's still around here somewhere—I know he's gonna want to talk with you. Hang on, let me see if I can find the man."

A series of clicks, and then the booming, ever-cheerful voice saying, "Linda Kee! My favorite rising star!"

"Funny thing to say to somebody you just fired."

He was a man of a thousand masks and voices, altering everything but his eyes. The voice played for sincere, almost dripping from the phone. "You know that was forced on me by New York. They took the pencil, drew a line, and said everyone below that had to go." Now for cheer. "But that's all behind us. And you know why?"

"Suppose you tell me."

"Because my ace reporter has come through for us once again! Tell me you're still in contact with Buddy Korda."

"He's in the room next to me."

"Great! This is just fantastic! Now tell me you've signed him for an exclusive interview!"

"As a matter of fact, he has just asked me to handle all his publicity and media contacts for the foreseeable future."

"And that is your ticket back to the big time! Did he really get trapped in that rest stop for the entire snowstorm?"

"Yes. But Jackson—"

"This is so big, Linda, New York is hopping up and down. Why did he come down to Washington, can you tell me that?"

"He has another message from God." Saying it out loud, the words became cheapened by who heard them. And in that moment she understood perfectly why Buddy was intending to insulate himself from the media.

"This is soooo good, Linda. A CBS exclusive, the nightly news followed by two, maybe three full portions on *Sixty Minutes*. Listen, we need to move while—"

"Not so fast, Jackson. This is not an exclusive."

"What? I thought you said—"

"I haven't had a chance to say much of anything. Buddy Korda does have a message and I will be filming it. But there is no exclusive arrangement. And *Sixty Minutes* is definitely out, at least for the interim."

A silence, then, "It's that Satchell Consultants, isn't it? Rob's already sewn you up with a contract. He's going to farm it out and you're taking revenge." Pleading now. "Linda, Linda, this is your old company here. What about loyalty, doesn't that mean a thing?"

"Absolutely." It meant so much the hunger was rising like bile in her throat, at direct odds with everything else in this room. Showing her just how weak she was. She had no choice but to break the connection with, "Give me a call in a couple of days, I'll make sure you get a copy of the interview. I have to go now, Jackson. Bye."

She disconnected, stood there tasting the air. The same sense of conflict she had known during Patrick's sermon that morning rose like a cresting wave. She had listened to that fine man stand at the podium, holding the packed church spellbound with the power of his preaching. And she had felt the ultimatum resonate within her, shaking her hard, urging her to *choose*. To *commit*.

The urging had terrified her so much she had been hard-pressed to remain in her seat.

She took a long breath and dialed Clarence's home number from memory. When the quiet man answered, she said, "I can't tell you how sorry I am."

"Thanks, Linda. You're a special lady." There was the sound of a door closing, and the laughter of children was muffled. "It's strange, but all day I've had this really powerful feeling that God's hand is at work here."

"I understand," she said, though the tremor passed through her voice like a tree shaken by invisible winds. "Maybe for the first time in my life."

"Ellen and I have been praying, and there's a church group that works with people who've just lost their jobs, sort of getting them through the initial hardship. We met with them this morning. Everyone seems to have such a sense of peace. I know it sounds crazy—"

"No, it doesn't. Really."

"—But we all have had this feeling that something big is about to happen." He paused, as though embarrassed by what he was about to say. "Something good."

"Clarence, do you still have some old gear?"

"You mean the cast-offs? Sure." Clarence's hobby was buying the news service's battered equipment, repairing it, and reselling it to local schools and freelancers. He did it more for the pleasure of working with his hands than for the money. "There hasn't been much demand for anything lately."

"I need you to light and film an interview." Linda took a breath, taking another fearful step, walking a path visible only to God, certainly not to herself. But walking it just the same. "Record the sound too. And do the edits. Professional quality. National coverage."

"No problem. It's not like I've got anything else to do. When do you need me?"

It was just like him not to ask about the money. Even now. "First thing tomorrow morning."

"Okay, sure. I can ask Ellen to see to the kids. Who are we working with?"

"Buddy Korda."

A silence. "You're kidding."

"He's had another message, Clarence." She had to stop for a breath. "I think it's starting. Whatever it is."

TWENTY-SIX

☐ Monday morning Linda led Clarence up the stairs and into the apartment's living room. It had stopped raining, but the early April sky was low and dark, promising more wet to come. Linda set down the camera she carried near the door, waited for Clarence to unload the pile of lighting frames, and then said, "Clarence Ives, this is Reverend Wilkins. We're in his church's guest house."

"It's an honor, Reverend."

"Honor's all mine, Mr. Ives. Linda's been describing you as a man of many talents."

"Call me Clarence, please. I guess I love my work."

"Always a good thing, yes. Friends call me James Thaddeus, that or just James if the first mouthful is too big." He gave the smaller man a careful inspection. "Linda also tells us you're a servant of our dear Lord."

"I try my very hardest to be."

"That's good, now." He smiled, and the dark face seemed to radiate light. "Hope you don't mind me asking. But we're gathering here at the Lord's call. Need to make sure all those in the circle are akin to the power of prayer."

Linda felt a wince run through her frame. If only she were stronger. If only she were better. If only she could choose correctly this time.

"Prayer is all that gets me through the day," Clarence replied calmly. "And I don't mind you asking. Not in the least."

Linda asked, "Where's Buddy?"

"We've done moved Mr. Korda upstairs. Seems to Patrick and me we're gonna have us a lot of comings and goings. Need a place for the public, and rooms where Mr. Korda can get off by himself." He gestured toward the space in front of the fireplace. "This be all right for you to set up?"

"Fine," replied Clarence, and started work.

"Mr. Korda will be down directly. Just now he's . . ." James Thaddeus stopped as a young black man clumped down the stairs and into view. He was dressed in a three-piece suit of gray worsted wool, white shirt, and dark tie. He stopped at the base of the stairs as though uncertain where he should go now. The reverend asked, "Everything go smooth up there, Elroy?"

The young man wore a bemused, awestruck look. "He knew exactly what it was he needed to have."

"That's all right, now." James Thaddeus walked over and patted the man's arm. "Don't you worry none."

The young man looked at the reverend without seeming to see him. "All I needed to do was make the wording in accordance with legal norm. Everything else was concise, exact, perfect." He looked back up the stairs, then said to Reverend Wilkins, "That man is a prophet of God."

"I know, son. I know." Another pat on the arm. "You go on over to the house, have Elaine make you something to eat."

"No, no, I've got to get back to the office. I'm arguing a case tomorrow morning." Another glance up the stairs, then, "You call me if there's anything else you need."

"I will, son. Don't you worry."

He crossed to the door, pulled it open, and said, "I mean, anything at all. I really want to be a part of this."

They continued setting up, aiming lights and the camera tripod toward an empty chair set by the cheery fire and the cast-iron grate. Reverend Wilkins remained busy with the phone, which rang nonstop. He took the calls at the dining room table, speaking in tones so low Linda could not make out the words. Twice when he hung up, Linda started to ask where Patrick was, but found herself unable to frame the question to such a stern-looking man.

But when the front door creaked, and Patrick walked through with bundles in both hands, she could not mask her delight. He returned a smile so warm and caring it twisted her heart. She walked over, and had to resist the urge to throw her arms around him. Here was the strength and sureness she lacked. She reached out and said, "Here, let me take those."

"No, it's okay, they balance each other." He walked over, set the bags down on the table, then allowed her to help him off with his raincoat. When she turned back around, she found Reverend Wilkins watching with an understanding, knowing look. She hid in the closet, taking time hanging Patrick's coat, until the blush had eased from her cheeks.

She turned to find Clarence and Patrick shaking hands. "I'm sorry, where are my manners?"

"It's all right." To Clarence, Patrick said, "Linda told us so much about you last night I feel like I know you already."

"Linda is a fine woman."

"Yes, she is." They both turned to look at her then, the tall handsome pastor and the slender cameraman with his wisps of fading blond hair combed over his central bald spot, sharing nothing but the look in their eyes. James Thaddeus observed them and her, then hummed deep in his throat. Linda found herself growing flush once more.

"Here." Patrick dug into the bag and came up with a cluster of mobile phones. He read off the back. "James, this one is yours. Do you know how to use it?"

"Been avoiding the necessity as hard as I can."

"Well, I think the time has come to break down and learn." He read the back of another. "This one's mine. Linda, here's yours. And Buddy's. And three extras, unassigned as yet. Clarence, I went ahead and got you one as well. You'll see there is a label on the back where I've written everyone's phone numbers."

Linda examined the phone in her hand with mixed feelings. It had been hard to give up her office mobile after being fired, very hard indeed. She had felt as though she had been passing back a badge of office. Now she eyed the new phone as though it were a physical sign of commitment. Another step down this strange unseen path.

"You been busy," was all Reverend Wilkins had to say.

"You don't know the half of it. I've called the first two dozen names on my list," Patrick replied.

"You beat me by three names," James Thaddeus said.

"And?"

"You go first."

Patrick smiled. "It's incredible. About half gave me the impression they'd been waiting for my call."

"Same thing happened to me."

"Did they offer you a contribution?"

"Almost every single one." James Thaddeus shook his head. "Here we are facing the hardest times I ever did see, and I got church leaders from all over the country wanting to know where can they send a check."

"It's not just money," Patrick said. "We need prayer and we need support for whatever it is Buddy's going to give us." He turned to Linda and went on, "My people are setting up prayer and support groups all over the nation, calling more people, leaders in and outside the church."

Linda looked down at the phone in her hand. "We don't even know what it is Buddy is going to say."

"Something important," Reverend Wilkins said. "Something big."

Standing there in the center of the tired old room with its frayed furniture, she suddenly felt as though she were being split in two. Half of her wanted to shout, "*Stop! How can you be so certain of what you don't know?*" The words seemed to rise until they threatened to choke off her flow of air. Even so, she could not speak. For there, alongside the familiar old call for logic and visible direction, was something new. Something she could not even describe. All she could definitely say, even to herself, was that somehow she shared the calm assurance of the others gathered there with her.

The top stairs creaked, and they all turned to look as Buddy descended into view. He wore a dark blue suit and was busy brushing the lapels as he appeared. He asked, "Do I look all right?"

Linda's professionalism took over. She walked over, pulled down his lapels, brushed lint off one shoulder, and straightened his tie slightly. "There." She turned back. "Buddy, I'd like to introduce our cameraman, Clarence Ives."

"Mr. Korda, I can't tell you what an honor this is."

"Call me Buddy, please." The blond cameraman was a full head taller than Buddy, but probably weighed less. Clarence's face was rounder, and the bags under his eyes more pronounced—a newscaster's occupational hazard. But the light in their eyes seemed to reflect one another's, and the smile that arose was of one accord. Buddy went on, "Thank you so much for helping us out."

"I wouldn't have missed this for the world." Clarence held out a lapel-mike and battery pack. "Have you ever used one of these before?"

"A long time ago."

"Slip this pack into your back pocket. Can you open your jacket? Great. I'll just hook up the mike like this."

Linda pointed at the single chair surrounded by slender aluminum lighting frames. "We did not know if you wanted to be alone, or if I should act as interviewer."

"No, this time I need to make a pronouncement."

Again, she was of two minds and two reactions. One side of her felt relief that she would not be required to publicly show her hand. The other side, however, was noticing something different. Something utterly unseen. For with the emergence of this small graying man with his quiet, gentle voice, something else had arrived. The same sense of power she had felt that morning was here with them again. Stronger now, pressing in with such force she felt humbled, as though the only place she truly belonged just then was on her knees.

Clearly the others felt it, too, for James Thaddeus said in solemn respect-fulness, "Is there anything we can do to help, Mr. Korda?"

"Pray," Buddy replied, and walked to the chair. He sat down, lowered his head, and said, "Pray for me now. For all of us."

Linda listened to the words with her mind split and warring, yet what she heard most clearly was the word that had resounded through her since yesterday's sermon. *Choose.* When James Thaddeus said the amen, she took a breath and did her best to dispel the remaining anxiety. There was only room for one voice now. Even if it was new, even if it was frightening.

Buddy waited through the lighting and the sound check with down-cast eyes, a little man surrounded by technology and bustle. Yet he was not alone. Linda could not question this. She could not doubt it, even if the old voice and logical mind might have liked to try. The power mounted with each passing moment, until one by one the movements of the others halted, trapped in the invisible amber of this gathering force.

"All right, Mr. Korda," Clarence finally said.

"Buddy," he corrected.

"We're ready whenever you are."

Silence gathered, and with it an electrifying force. One so powerful and so immense Linda felt as though the air had become trapped in her breath, the blood frozen in her veins. Not even time could proceed in normal fashion within this maelstrom of authority. The power of God arrived, and it *commanded.*

From within the locus of this force, Buddy raised his eyes and faced the camera. He began without preamble,

"The Lord our God has spoken to me.

"So long as we have known peace and stability and prosperity, we have been able to stand back and observe our country's slide away from God. But this is not a stable time. This is not a peaceful moment in our nation's history. Things are not good. People are hurting. Economically, socially, spiritually, America is facing a serious decline.

"We have the opportunity to reverse this descent into economic famine, and to do so now. This very moment. But this turning is possible only if we bind ourselves and our nation tightly to our Maker.

"America has arrived at a dividing line. Here and now, our nation must choose whom to serve. No longer may we straddle the chasm. God or mammon. Light or shadow. There is no other way.

"We must heal the rift between our nation and our God. Because we have defiled this land, one founded upon the worship of our sovereign Lord, God has been forced to withdraw. In His withdrawal, He has come to judge this people and found them lacking. We have brought this upon ourselves. Not God. We are guilty. But if the people will recognize the Lord's sovereignty, God will return and nurture His people.

"The Lord calls us to an act of public, national penitence. The Lord's enemies have used the highest law of this nation, the Constitution, to tear us asunder from our Maker. We must therefore use this same sacred text to rejoin what has been torn apart.

"We are called to add a new amendment to the Constitution of the United States of America. It reads as follows:

In accordance with the views of the Founding Fathers that religion and morality are necessary supports for the liberties this Constitution seeks to protect. Therefore, to promote the common good of society, no law or policy may limit the free expression of religious beliefs, nor the application of religious moral principles, in the public sphere."

Buddy paused a moment, then closed his eyes and said, "Father, the events in our own world are confusing and distressing. Enlarge our vision of who You really are. Help us to recognize You as our sovereign Lord. Cleanse from us the taint of choosing other gods. Fill us with a desire to live for You and in You. In Your great name's sake do we pray, amen."

There was a long moment of stillness as the force gradually retreated from the room. Clarence cut off the camera and the lights. One by one the others gathered there managed sighs of indrawn breath. Linda felt the power release its hold on her chest, but not her mind. As she walked forward to take the mike Buddy held out to her, she noticed the second voice, the one she had lived by for so long, was well and truly silenced. At least for now.

TWENTY-SEVEN

☐ While Linda helped Clarence disassemble the gear, Buddy spent the time staring out the front window. Patrick and James Thaddeus were galvanized into action by what they had heard, calling around and leaving messages with all the people they had spoken to earlier. As she worked, Linda heard the two pastors speak almost identical words over their phones. Yes, Buddy Korda had another message from God. Yes, they had heard it. No, they could not say what it was on the phone. They would send them a video. Of course they could supply more copies, how many? A dozen? Two dozen? Fine. Yes, the new message was important. Vital.

When they had finished the packing, Linda stood looking down at the videocassette in her hands. It seemed to hum at a very high note, one that could be felt through her fingertips and not heard with her ears.

Clarence came over to stand beside her. He looked down at the video she was holding, his expression equal parts reverence and awe. "I'll run by the house, pick up all the duplication equipment I have."

She nodded, watched him leave, then observed Patrick hesitantly approach the small figure standing by the window. "Buddy?"

"I was just thinking," Buddy said to the gray early afternoon, "I have not been out of this house for three days."

"We could go for a drive if you'd like," Patrick offered, asking a question with his eyes to Linda, who nodded. Of course she could guide them.

"Not 'til after Mr. Korda here has himself some lunch," James Thaddeus said, not even looking up from his phone and the handwritten list of numbers. "I ain't having another talk with his wife like the one yesterday. No sir. Not this man."

"A drive. Maybe I'm supposed to stay here . . ." He took a breath. "No. A drive would be nice. Wonderful. It's been years since I've seen the sights."

"Buddy, I'm sorry to bother you with this, but several of the people I've spoken with have asked about a rumor. They say that the government might be planning to tax the churches. They are wondering if you have any word as to what they should do, how they should respond."

Buddy felt as though he were shrinking inside himself, growing smaller than he already was. "I don't know these things, Patrick. I'm just one man."

"I understand," he responded, immensely patient. He glanced at James Thaddeus, who remained at the dining room table, cradling the phone in both hands and watching them intently. "I wasn't meaning to put any pressure on you, Buddy. I just felt like we needed to ask. That's all."

"I don't know anything, I don't *have* anything to offer you or anybody else unless God gives—"

It happened then. A swift rushing sensation, a whisper of something so powerful that if it had shown itself fully, Linda would have positively exploded. Every muscle, every atom of her being vibrated in harmony to the sweeping rush of angel's wings. A river of light unseen, a wave of sound unheard, a detonation of intensity. And it left. There and gone in the space of two heartbeats.

"Praise God!" James Thaddeus leaped to his feet, the cry wrenched from his throat. His hands were stretched out before him, palms upraised in supplication to whatever it was that had come and was now gone. *"Praise the Lord Almighty! Thank You, Jesus!"*

Buddy looked at Patrick and said in his same quiet voice, "There will be several such attacks. We of His church are to do nothing. Let the chasm divide us, let the attacks spur us to unite. And to act. But only as He has directed us. We must focus upon the act of binding our nation once more to our God."

"Thus saith the Lord," James Thaddeus intoned, his eyes now closed, his chin pointed to the ceiling. "Thank You, Jesus. Yes, Lord. Amen."

☐

"Washington is a lot quieter than I remember," Buddy said. "And dirtier."

Linda said nothing. She found herself trapped by astonishment over what she had just experienced. It reminded her of entering a room as a little girl, where her parents had been speaking with other adults. She could remember such times, walking in after everyone thought the children were in bed, looking in on some discussion and seeing expressions they seldom revealed to her. Adult faces speaking of things from an adult world, one different from that which she inhabited. That was how it felt now, sitting in the car and thinking back to the moment when Buddy had heard God's voice.

The room had held an intensity that was utterly alien to anything her mind had ever experienced. Although the moment had been wholly positive, she had felt like she was the usurper, as though all her troublesome thoughts were there on display. As though she did not belong to the group of believers who deserved such experiences. As though she never would.

"It's mid-afternoon on a workday and the streets are half empty," Buddy observed.

Patrick asked from the driver's seat, "Where do we go now, Linda?"

"Turn down Pennsylvania," she said from the backseat. "We can go by the White House, if you'd like."

"Yes, that would . . ." Buddy let his words trail off at the sight of the next block. The sidewalk broadened, and on the extra space a cardboard village had sprung up. The better-dressed pedestrians crossed the street to avoid the forest of outstretched hands that emerged from the boxes. Every inch of space was taken up with mock dwellings. "If I didn't know better, I'd think I had been transported to Bombay."

"Every day there are more homeless people," Linda said. "The police don't do much so long as they don't gather in key spots like the Mall or in front of the White House. They *can't*. Many of these people don't have anywhere else to go."

They stopped at a light, and two dozen children came rushing up. Some of the kids were so small their little hands could barely reach up to where the windows began. Buddy shrank back, so distressed he could not even speak until Patrick was able to pull away. Then he murmured, "This has to work, Patrick."

"I know."

"It *has* to." Buddy pointed at a long line snaking along the next block. "What's that?"

Linda started to say they must have opened a new soup kitchen, then she realized the people were too well dressed for that, and they were being protected by young men in gang mufti. Even before she saw the cinema's headline, she knew. The gang members acting as security explained it all. Her voice grated with a sudden flash of anger as she said, "It's the most horrid movie ever made."

Buddy read off the marquee, "'*Final Showdown*.' Somehow that name sounds familiar."

"It is exploiting the worst of this terrible situation," Patrick said, as angry as Linda.

"A teenage gang takes over an elementary school," Linda explained. "They hold it for ransom. A big action hero comes in at the last moment and shoots the bad guys and rescues everybody else. You don't want to know any more than that."

"What has been so infuriating is to hear the psychologists and sociologists claim it is a good thing," Patrick said angrily. "How this trash is a conduit for people to feel the rage and the frustration they might otherwise suppress."

"This is wrong," Buddy murmured.

"Be glad you haven't ever had to interview them," Linda said. "I was assigned to cover the film's opening. They had me—"

"No, this is *wrong*." Buddy turned to Patrick. "Take me back to the guesthouse."

"I thought you wanted to get out for a while."

"So did I. But I see now it's wrong." When Patrick put on his turn signal, Buddy relaxed into his seat. "I have to hold myself apart. I can sense this as clearly as anything I have ever known. I have to hold myself apart and ready, in case God wants to speak again."

Patrick glanced in the rearview mirror, but all he said was, "We'll have you back in no time."

TWENTY-EIGHT

☐ The Party's national headquarters anchored the congressional end of First Street. Its next-door neighbor, the City Club, was a slightly smaller twin, both nice but not overly ornate. They were stoic, strong examples of Georgian simplicity. The Chairman's office mirrored the building itself, very nice and very large, but neither so large nor so nice that it would suggest to any visitor that the chairman was seeking to hold an undue share of power.

The most notable aspect of the chairman's private chamber was his power wall. The power wall was a silent confirmation of who this person was—which in politics meant, who he knew. And this chairman knew them all. The chairman's power wall held dozens and dozens of photographs, *big* pictures, all signed. Past presidents appeared in many of them, followed by key members of both houses of Congress, and the current president. Shelves flanking the power wall were stacked with bronze eagles, ivory and gold Party figurines, models of jet fighters, and countless plaques.

Royce had served under nine different Party chairmen. The current one was no better or worse than the others. Jim Jenners was a former congressman from a state whose voting boundaries had been redrawn just prior to the last election. He and another sitting congressman, also from the Party, had suddenly been pitted against one another. His opponent was the senior Party member on the House Appropriations Committee. Being the less powerful of the two, Jenners had been asked to step aside. In return he had been offered the Party chairmanship. The soon-to-be-former congressman had looked at the three hundred grand per year salary, the promise of yet another plum position on corporate boards once he retired, and leaped at the offer.

Jim Jenners was a very distinguished fifty-four years old. The kids from his first marriage were all grown and gone. His new wife was seventeen years his junior and a former congressional aide. He gave great speeches on family values whenever required, but in truth he had little time for the Party's religious wing or their issues. He was smart with the press, knew all the major players on both sides of the political fence, was a scratch golfer, and had a voting record that shouted political expediency to anyone in the know.

There were four in the chairman's office that afternoon. Royce had brought along Jerry Chevass and his assistant. Elton Hardaway was there because it was time to begin rewarding the young man's growing sense of loyalty. Together they watched the video through to its end. When the image of Buddy Korda finally faded, the chairman treated them to a moment's silence before demanding, "Where did you get this?"

"Elton has been monitoring Korda's situation since he disappeared into the snowstorm. We found out he's been using a church in Georgetown as a base. Elton has been calling there several times a day."

The chairman glanced Elton's way. "I know your family, don't I? Fine people. Have you spoken with this Korda fellow?"

Elton shook his blond head. "They won't let anyone get near him."

"As soon as word got out where Korda was hiding, the press tried a frontal assault," Royce added. "They found themselves surrounded by hundreds of church members, all black, all singing, all keeping them back until the police arrived."

"First he gets trapped in the weirdest storm anybody has ever heard of," the chairman muttered to the blank screen. "Now this."

"This whole thing is a farce," Jerry declared, looking around the room. "Here we are, watching a guy fresh out of nowhere tell us they're going to enact a new constitutional amendment? It's insane."

"Korda's prediction of the economic meltdown was crazy too," Royce reminded the room.

"I agree," the chairman grimly said. "How did you get the tape?"

"Elton just went by and asked for it."

"They gave me a form to sign, just a photocopied sheet asking for the name of my church or organization." Elton smiled. "I claimed it was for the National Organization of Women. They were so busy they didn't even read it. There must have been a dozen people in line with me, and phones ringing off the hook."

The chairman stared at the empty television screen. "Imagine what this would do to our power structure."

Jerry looked from one face to the other. "Excuse me for injecting a little reality. You people cannot be planning to take this guy seriously."

His incredulity was exactly why Royce had brought him along. The doubter was required here, the cynic who kept them all firmly grounded. "We can't afford to do otherwise."

The chairman asked, "Has Ethan seen this?"

"I stopped by his office as soon as it arrived," Royce confirmed. Another surprise there. The president's chief of staff had shown no outrage over this turn of events. Instead, Ethan Eldridge had been genuinely relieved that Royce had pounced on this so swiftly. "He was the one who wanted you in on this. He thinks we should be prepared."

"Just in case," the chairman agreed.

Jerry Chevass gaped at his boss. "Just in case *what?*"

Royce answered for them both. "Just in case Korda hits it right a second time."

□

The second-floor dining hall within the City Club was as exclusive a power point as any visiting state dignitary could imagine. For Royce, it was more like a local cafe. Since his divorce he ate there many times each week— at least, he had done so until he was granted White House dining room privileges. Since then he used it for meetings that could not be conducted within the big house's rarified atmosphere. Such as the meeting this Thursday.

Across from him sat Rob Satchell, whose group was consultant to more rising political stars than any other consortium in the nation. Today Satchell's baggy suit had the slightly bunched and knotted fabric of a wool and raw silk weave, which made him look as if he were wearing a thousand-dollar burlap sack.

Satchell sat with his back to the room, which was the only way Royce could be sure to hold the man's attention. They had spent the first two courses reminding one another of favors done and received through the years. Royce understood Satchell very well. In fact, he admired the man. Satchell had managed to build himself a remarkably stable base within the constantly shifting sands of political campaigns. Over dessert Royce cut to the chase with, "I think it's time you make the move on your newest employee."

"She's not anything yet." Satchell's grin was infamous. His enemies said it was largest just before he stuck in the knife, but enemies were like that. "Hard to remember she's sharp as a two-edged blade, that's how good-looking she is."

"She certainly hasn't been showing such intelligence in her latest antics," Royce said, hoping he was first with this news.

The grin slipped away. "You've brought me here and stuck me in the farthest corner of the room to complain about something an almost-new employee is supposed to have done?"

"Not supposed to have. This is definite."

"Come on, Royce. She's not shown her face over at the Korda place. Nobody has. You ought to pin a medal on the lady. She's new to the political game, and still she's managed to keep a lid on something the press is yammering to get ahold of." He made a process of stirring sugar into his coffee, trying for unconcern. "How bad can this be?"

"Bad. She was the one who made the Korda video."

Satchell laughed out loud. "You're joking."

"I wish I were. My assistant did some sniffing around over there. The church ladies handling the video distribution told him straight-out. Linda Kee and another former employee of CBS News put together that message."

The humor vanished. "You sure about this?"

"I'm telling you, Rob. She is responsible for the videotaping of his latest prediction."

"Who would have believed the guy would come up with something like a constitutional amendment?" Satchell chewed on his lower lip. "Wonder where it's headed."

"So far the press has treated it as just another oddity. They play segments of Korda's earlier interviews, then talk about how the former banker has now become the unofficial adviser to the national government. Making fun of him. This has been good as far as we're concerned. Making light of the matter means the administration has not needed to respond officially."

"Yeah, I've been watching how the president's press attache has done his best two-step every time the press ask a question about Korda." The gaze turned keener. "You think it's going to last?"

"We can only hope." There was no need to share with Satchell the worrisome news coming in from the state Party headquarters, tales of how many religious state legislators and mayors and even a few governors had become caught up in the latest Korda move. Actually pledging their support to these new councils being established. No, there was no need to mention that at all.

Royce had become friends with Satchell through the oddest of circumstances. They had both been represented by the same lawyer for divorces that had been granted on the very same day. Royce's enemies liked to say that his marriage had broken up because his wife could only promise him one vote. Satchell and he had spent numerous evenings together, healing the raw wounds in a variety of bars and restaurants, exposing to each other the pain they could show to no one else. Royce trusted Satchell simply because they had traded secrets. It was something both men could understand.

"I can't be seen having anything to do with the religious wing," Satchell declared. "That goes double for my staff."

"The rest of your clients would vanish in a puff of smoke," Royce agreed. "You'd be painted as just another pariah."

"So why are you telling me this? I know it's not from the goodness of your heart."

"We want her to tell us what's going on."

"A spy." Satchell nodded. "Sure. I can go along with that. You think this is going to set off a fire storm?"

"You saw what happened the last time Korda started his jig. Pressure her. Get her to pass on everything she can about the movement."

"I'm supposed to see Linda at a reception tomorrow night. I'll call and make sure she's coming, then put it to her straight." The grin resurfaced, but this time it was tainted by calculating greed. "This is going to cost you."

"I pay my debts," Royce said, holding to his mild tone. "You should know that."

"And you're as good with the political knife as I am." Satchell patted his lips and folded his napkin along the ironlines, his movements delicate and precise for such a big man. "Speaking of which, do you have anything in mind for the lady once she's done with this?"

"Nothing particular," Royce quietly replied. "But I would be personally very grateful if you could arrange to have her land extremely hard."

Satchell gave a brilliant smile. "That would suit me just fine."

TWENTY-NINE

☐ "It's not ready yet."

"Linda," Clarence sighed his exasperation. "This is some of the finest work you have ever done. Either of us, for that matter."

Late Friday afternoon they sat side by side at what before had been the second-floor apartment's dining room table. That entire half of the room was given over to a mass of equipment. Cables writhed across the fraying carpet, across the kitchen floor, and out the back window to where the electrician had rigged a secondary transformer in the back lot. The side wall was one solid bank of editing and copying machinery, amassed over the week by Clarence. All the copying machines were busy making further renditions of Buddy's initial speech or sermon or message. Linda found she wasn't so sure what to call it anymore. Or exactly what she had experienced that day.

On Tuesday Buddy had been moved upstairs to the apartment under the eaves. The first floor was now a public meeting place, filled from morning to evening with people coming for conferences or videos or planning sessions or interviews for this work. The second floor held a private conference room in what had once been the back bedroom, and their own mass of electronics. The week had become as frantic as anything Linda had known in the news business. And a hundred times more worrisome.

On Wednesday the nation's press had confirmed both the new message and where Buddy Korda was hiding. National newscasters announced that Buddy Korda, the banker who had predicted the financial meltdown, had returned from small-town hibernation with an order for the nation to draft a new constitutional amendment. The White House press attache had then responded with a half smile and a mocking tone, saying it was the responsibility of every citizen to uphold the Constitution.

Linda walked over to the front window and stared out to where the press camped beyond the police barriers. The press and socio-journalists had weighed in against the message almost instantly. The first communication in over a year from the man who had warned of the economic meltdown could not be ignored. Television talk shows had condemned Buddy Korda's movement from the financial sector—which at least was his original background—into politics, of which he clearly knew nothing. The written responses had been equally vicious. Linda had found her hands trembling as she read the *Washington Post* editorial pages that week, feeling as though they were not attacking Buddy Korda, but herself personally.

Yet nothing they had said, no pronouncements or predictions that the whole thing would vanish in a puff of smoke, could slow the avalanche of interest that Buddy's message had generated. And every day it grew stronger.

Clarence interrupted her whirling thoughts with, "This is not just good, Linda. It's *ready.*"

Reluctantly Linda turned away from the window and conceded, "Maybe parts of it are okay. But the video needs something else to bring it all together."

"Everybody around here is wondering why we can't let them at least take a look at the rough cut. Which this isn't. It's finished and it's ready to roll." Clarence rubbed a weary hand through the remaining strands of blond hair on his head. He left them straggled and standing upright, so she could see how age and hard work had turned them almost transparent. He asked, "Not only that, do you know how many calls we received for this second video today alone?"

Linda had managed to keep herself hidden from the press only because of Buddy's strict instructions to avoid any direct contact, which had suited her right down to the ground. She had organized teams of church volunteers to staff the newly installed bank of telephones. The volunteers had taken the hundreds and hundreds of orders for Buddy's videotaped message. They had also handled the phoned-in press inquiries, using a blank stonewalling that had left the press snarling and frustrated beyond words.

Linda had spent much of this week doing what she was best at—filming. She had worked as hard on this video as she had on anything in her entire life. As long as she was working, she was safe. It was only at the end of each exhausting day, when she returned to her lonely home and thoughts, that she came face-to-face with the terrifying fact of what she was doing.

Linda walked back to the equipment-strewn table. "All this interest is precisely why we need to make sure this is word perfect."

"We received one hundred and thirty-seven orders for tapes today alone. Patrick told me before he left. And more than two hundred yesterday. Which for the week makes one thousand—"

Hearing the numbers only left her wishing she had somewhere to run. "Let's see it through one more time."

"There isn't any need, Linda. The thing is as good as it gets."

"One more time." She glanced at her watch. A quarter of six on Friday evening. The house was silent. Buddy had left with Patrick for a long-awaited weekend home. She had refused Patrick's gentle urgings to join them, saying only that she had an important invitation for that evening. Something she could not miss. Knowing she could not bear another weekend of being challenged by their strength and their faith. Not just then. "One time straight through. No pauses. We'll go home as soon as this is over. I promise."

She slid into the seat beside him, comfortable with a routine that had framed so many of her days, so much of her work. This was a normal part of any reporter-editor relationship, the two of them seated together before the viewing monitor, the tape in place, going over the film segment by segment.

Clarence punched the button to the video machine, a professional apparatus the size of a large suitcase and designed to run tapes of various sizes. There were numerous knobs unseen on consumer gear, permitting such things as a second-by-second splicing or altering the run of sound to image. But Clarence was no longer working the knobs and switches and feed-ins from the secondary machines. This time he leaned back in his seat, popped his pen into his mouth, and watched.

There was the normal five-second countdown, followed by the twenty-nine-minute tape's opening scene. As soon as Linda saw herself staring into the camera, the gleaming Capitol dome rising lofty and stalwart behind her, she knew why she was so afraid of releasing this tape.

"Hello, I am Linda Kee."

No follow-on afterward, such as, Linda Kee "for CBS News," or Linda Kee "for *Sixty Minutes.*" Nothing. Just her name. Her heart rate surged with the same punch of fear she had been feeling ever since she began work on the tape editing. She was in the final stages of doing her first full-length news drama, and she was terrified at the thought of anyone seeing the finished result.

"In the five days since Buddy Korda gave us his new message, more than four thousand requests have been received for the video. It has been played in churches, in homes, in state and city government offices, before groups large and small. Religious cable networks around the country have aired his words, and they have been played on countless Christian radio stations."

She found herself wincing at the word *Christian.* The stamp was there in the first minute of airtime. The taint that would never wash clean. This was not just a documentary. Not for her. It was a personal declaration. And once it went out, she would never be free from the stigma. Not ever.

"Eleven full-time telephone operators have been set up at the New Jerusalem Baptist Church on P Street, here in our nation's capital. For those who wish to call or write, the number and address will be given at the end of our broadcast. But we must ask that no money be sent."

That was another astonishing fact—how despite the hard times, money and offers of even more funds had come pouring in. Even before they knew how the money was to be spent, before they were aware of just exactly what was required, checks and cash were arriving.

On the screen, the dark-suited Linda Kee began climbing the stairs to the main entrance of the Capitol. The one day that week when it had not rained, they had rushed around filming the external segments. The brooding, dark sky seemed to cling to the congressional dome, heightening the tension she saw on her face. "The main questions asked by those who have seen Buddy Korda's new message and witnessed its power have been, 'What now? What do we do? How can we help?'"

Linda entered the halls of Congress, the camera walking right along with her. The intention had been to keep this sober but matter-of-fact tone as she *unveiled* the mystery of government. "Our purpose here is to describe exactly what you can do to make Buddy Korda's message a reality. We will walk you through a step-by-step process of how a constitutional amendment can be attained. What is required, what must be organized, and who you will need to contact. But first, let us begin with a word from the messenger himself."

Linda watched herself push through a set of doors and walk into the upper gallery of the Senate. Buddy Korda was seated in the front row, looking out over the august chamber. Another surprise there—how easily she had managed to arrange this shot. She had stopped by the congressional press office, expecting to be turned down. But the assistant press officer was a Christian who held Buddy Korda in awe. Her way had been paved in a matter of minutes.

Buddy turned exactly on time, as though he had been doing this all his life. No rehearsals, no second takes, as smooth and authoritative as the first time he had spoken there in the little church guest house. "A serious discrepancy has developed between our nation's course and God's law. The nation's highest bodies have sadly decided that, like the secular side of our society, God should no longer have a place within our government and legal system. The attributes our Founding Fathers used to define our nation's course are being steadily eroded, or cast aside entirely. Timeless concepts that bind us to the *absolutes* of God are being severed.

"These sections of our government apparently feel that we are no longer to be a nation under God. We are to be a pluralistic society. According to today's government and today's courts, we are to allow each individual to determine what is right, and what is wrong. No longer is there a place for the singular authority of an almighty God. To the detriment of our nation's future, they have decided it is within their power to reinterpret our nation's course, and set us upon a path of their own choosing.

"How can they do this? How can they usurp such power? Simply by usurping the position of God. No longer is there an acceptance of our One Lord seated upon the throne and ruling in final authority over us and our nation. The Holy Father is no longer afforded any more respect or acknowledgment than any other belief system."

The camera drew in closer, so that Buddy's gaze and the power emanating from his eyes filled the screen. "We disagree with this in the strongest possible terms. This nation was established with God as our beacon. As our *one* guiding light. We intend to reassert this, not as a belief, but as fact. The community of believers is called to action. And act we will."

The image faded to be replaced by a young black man seated at the central table in the Georgetown University law center's reading room. Although the building was new, it had been constructed in the neoclassic style, and reeked of legal authority. The table was surrounded by towering walls of teak, rising five floors with a spiraling mezzanine lined by books and reading booths and computer stations. From off camera, Linda heard herself say, "Elroy Tommkins is an associate with the law firm of Pickering, Chambers, and Olesson. He is a specialist in constitutional law, and has argued four cases before the Supreme Court. He is also a deacon of the New Jerusalem Church."

Elroy's only sign of nerves was a slight tremble to the fingers, which rose to adjust his round spectacles. Linda had decided to leave that in, showing the viewer that yes, even here we are human. She watched as Elroy began spelling out the requirements for passing a new Constitutional amendment. Using simple language, keeping the talk down-to-earth and action-oriented.

The standard way for a new amendment, Elroy explained, was for two-thirds of both houses of Congress to vote for the amendment, followed by three-quarters of the states. But Congress was unlikely to take this action. So they needed to concentrate upon the second alternative. A grassroots movement could bring forth an amendment through calling a Constitutional Convention.

Two-thirds of the state legislatures would need to vote in favor of this call. Once this happened, candidates would present themselves to be elected as convention delegates.

Elroy outlined the need to identify their local state representatives, and pressure them to bring this to the forefront of their agendas.

They switched venues twice with Elroy, trying to keep interest strong by moving from internal to external to internal again. He spoke at lakeside in the middle of the National Mall with the Washington Monument in the distance, the sky so dark and menacing it filled every word he spoke with quiet urgency. Then inside again, now at the foot of the Lincoln Memorial, the brooding statue looking down and watching as Elroy urged people to move fast, so that the process could be completed before the current legislative session was finished and momentum lost.

Then came three surprises, one after another. First, there was a federal district judge seated in her private chambers, speaking of the ramifications of what such an amendment would mean. She spoke with the same sincerity Linda had heard over the phone, the woman having seen Buddy's video and feeling an urgent need to call that very night.

Then, there was the state legislator who described the petitions they would need to gather, the need to go outside the normal lines of parties and affiliations. He spoke standing on the steps of the Virginia statehouse, the ancient building adding authority to the man's simple directions, urging them once more to act and act fast, while the momentum was strong and opposition not yet organized.

Then, there was the biggest surprise of all, the opposition party's congressman from the state of Indiana adding his own endorsement to the move. He described the political battles he had waged and lost since entering Congress, the frustration he had felt at his and his colleagues' inability to avert the nation's sliding course away from the divine.

From the powerful to the humble. The camera left the congressman's office to arrive in the study of Reverend James Thaddeus Wilkins. The man was a natural on camera. The deeply lined face appeared lit from within, sternness and gentleness in delicate balance upon his finely carved features. It had been a spur-of-the-moment decision, to ask him instead of Buddy to read the proposed amendment a second time.

When he had finished, James Thaddeus looked straight into the camera and said, "We have to realize one thing before we get started here. This is not a *political* issue. This is not a *Party* issue. This is not an issue of *race*. No. This is a *divine* issue. We are called by God to set aside every single problem that divides us, present and past and future. We are to do this by looking *beyond* who we are, to focus upon the One who unites us. Do not look to one another. Look to God, and walk together in harmony."

A single instant of staring back into those powerful dark eyes, then Reverend Wilkins's features were replaced by Buddy's.

Buddy said quietly to the camera, "The call is to be for a *single-issue convention*. And the convention is to be held in Philadelphia, where in 1787 our Constitution was originally framed."

Buddy Korda paused a moment, as though finished, but then continued with, "Those who will oppose you have diverted the expressed intentions of our Founding Fathers. They have decided their present opinions are more valid than all which has come before. Religion, in their eyes, is nothing more than a matter of personal expression. No longer is it to be the framework upon which our nation rests. Make no mistake, your actions will be opposed by these people."

Another pause, then, "In the sixth chapter of Daniel, those who attacked the prophet could find nothing to criticize about him or his work, *except his God.* Except for his daily walk of faith. They thought that by attacking his beliefs, they would strike at his greatest weakness. But in truth it proved to be his greatest strength. Let the strength of Daniel be our own during the days to come."

The image faded, and to the strains of the "Battle Hymn of the Republic," addresses began to scroll down the screen. Already groups had sprung up in seventeen state capitals, giving a place for people to call or write and volunteer. Linda listened to her voice-over requesting that people not call the Washington office unless there was a matter of universal importance, as they were already swamped with requests. She heard, but did not hear, for over it all she felt the pounding of her frightened heart.

Clarence stopped the tape, leaned back, and said to the blank monitor, "It's the best work we have ever done."

She no longer had the strength to object. Linda forced herself to rise and walk from the table.

"Linda?"

"I'll call you tomorrow."

"We need to make a decision here."

"Tomorrow." She was already on the stairs, fleeing with a fragile mask of calm that did not even permit her to look in Clarence's direction. "I've got to go change for the reception."

THIRTY

☐ The Canadian embassy was the newest in Washington, a concrete and glass structure separated from Pennsylvania Avenue by its own private plaza. When Linda had been part of the news team, and thus a working member of the social scene, she had received so many invitations to events like this one she had stacked them on her desk like playing cards. Now, as she paid the taxi and grasped the hem of her dress to start up the long stone stairs, she felt a sudden thrill. Perhaps she had not lost everything along with her job after all.

She handed her embossed invitation to the hulking security man and stepped through the metal detector, a common signal that high-powered people were attending. She smiled and waved at someone she remembered vaguely from earlier days, and stepped into the colorful, swirling crowd.

The embassy's three front chambers were purpose-built for Washington gatherings—big and high-ceilinged and separated from the embassy's working section by a steel security wall. As she moved from one marble-tiled room to the next, Linda found herself easily slipping back into the rapid-fire Washington chatter. She greeted faces she had met at a hundred such functions, made light of her departure from CBS, remained vague about her plans for the future. She spotted a pair of senators from opposite sides of the floor, now standing well away from their aides and using the reception for some serious horse-trading. Out of habit she found herself wondering what might be the subject of their intense discussion.

A voice from behind her said, "Bet you'd give a kazillion bucks to be a fly on the wall over there."

She turned slowly, preparing a proper smile for her future boss. "I left that work behind, remember?"

"You left the *job* behind." Rob Satchell was dressed in a double-breasted suit of midnight blue, so baggy she could have made flags from the flannel crumpled around his shoes. "But a lady who's fought as hard as you have for the brass ring, you never let the work go. Never. It's in your blood."

She glanced back to where the two senators stood arguing, oblivious to the crowd watching them. "Maybe you're right."

"I know I am—which makes your current actions truly bizarre."

That got her attention. "What are you talking about?"

"Come on over here where we can talk." He grasped her arm above the elbow, not hard, but possessively. Normally Linda would have used the breakaway movement every big-city girl learned early on. In her confused state, however, she allowed herself to be pulled over to the far side of the buffet table and into an island of relative quiet. Satchell went on, "You know why I had you invited here tonight?"

"You arranged the invitation?" Her unsettled feeling heightened, though she could not say why. "I suppose I should thank you. It's very nice to—"

"The reason was," he went on, as though she had not spoken, "I couldn't be seen talking with you anywhere in private. *Certainly* not around our offices."

She felt a stone lodge deep inside her middle, the same one that flattened her voice. "You're withdrawing your offer."

"That depends on you, missy." Rob waved his drink at someone who called out his name, but did not turn his hard gaze from her face. "What I need to know is, just how involved have you gotten yourself with the loony fringe?"

"If you are speaking of Buddy Korda, you are sadly mistaken," she said. Yet even speaking the man's name here in this gathering seemed to cheapen it.

"That's where you're wrong. Dead wrong, if you keep up with whatever it is you're doing over there." Rob Satchell moved over so that his back was fully to the room and his bulk blocked her from seeing anyone but him. "Let me give you an old war horse's view of the Washington political scene. There are two parties fighting for power these days. The baneful party and the stupid party. Neither one of them can be trusted."

"That's the most cynical thing I've ever heard."

"Sure it is. But it's also correct." He raised one manicured hand, weighed the air on his left. "The baneful party is a coalition of single-issue groups. The gay single issue. The abortion single issue. The black single issue. When it works, they stand up for one another's special interests. When it doesn't, they eat one another in the pit."

She crossed her arms. "I thought you might have dragged me over here to discuss something important."

"We are. Your career." The hand holding his drink raised to weigh the air on his right. "Now over here we have the stupid party. This one is filled with old-style conservatives who say that every problem known to the nation is the fault of government. Get rid of government and you enter some kind of perfect world."

He lowered his hands, taking a deep swig from his drink on the way. "The money people run politics these days. You should know that, you've been close enough to the fire to get singed. On the baneful side, one thing that keeps the single-issue groups bound together is their need for help in hunting down funds. On the other side, the conservatives with money think everybody should be happy just by paying lower taxes and having less government intervention. You with me so far?"

Linda took a breath, let it out, and then shook her head. Not over what Rob was saying. Over how she felt trapped here. Caught in the amber of her indecision and her confusion and the storm of conflict in her head and heart.

"The religious pressure groups have been battled into a corner these past two decades by ACLU-led attacks and antireligion rulings in the courts. Their mistrust of government has grown steadily stronger. They fall right into the hands of the money conservatives. These big-bucks guys have spent years learning to manipulate people. They use the religious conservatives for ditchdiggers during the campaigns, then feed them a few crumbs around voting time."

"You're saying I shouldn't get involved with them because nobody takes them seriously."

"See, I knew you were smart." Another deep swig. "These religious conservatives don't have any idea how to work as coalition partners. They think *compromise* is a dirty word. They're nobodies in the political process. They'll never amount to anything because they don't bend with the political winds." Satchell gave her the smooth smile, the one that never touched his eyes. "Do yourself and your career a world of good. Keep this religion thing to yourself. Treat it like a hobby, you know, like knitting. Never can tell, one day you might get tired of it. Then you'll be glad you didn't let on to anybody but me."

Linda started around him, knowing she had just heard her farewell song. "Sorry. I think you're wrong."

The smile vanished. His voice hardened in irritation at not being able to sway her. "You better listen up. It's the only warning you'll ever hear."

"Thanks for nothing, Rob."

"Outside of election time the only thing these religious groups are good for is acting as a safety valve for the conservatives' own lack of morality," he snarled as she started to walk away. "The power boys will never let them play with the real chips. Never. You get yourself involved with them, you're going to get yourself stomped into the dust of the arena."

-|| THIRTY-ONE ||-

☐ Linda considered her home to be a haven from all the world's storms. And there had always been a storm—some dilemma or crisis that threatened to bring her and all her hopes and dreams tumbling down. Her little apartment had remained the one place where she could relax and shut out the world of worries. Until now.

She owned a third of the fifth floor in a turn-of-the-century building on California Street, one originally constructed as a block of maisonettes for out-of-state congressmen and senators. The ceilings were high and the one in her living room was slightly domed. The floors were broad heart-of-pine, set in place with pegs and old-timey square nails and varnished to a ruddy shine. The renovators had sectioned the building to create a one-bedroom apartment with an entrance hall so large it also saw duty as a dining area. Linda had spent a small fortune having a carpenter build kitchen cupboards and built-in bedroom wardrobes and living room bookshelves, which matched the flooring as closely as possible. It was a warm place, cozy and snug and hers.

Sunday afternoon found her seated in her living room, the newspapers strewn haphazardly on the floor around her. She had scarcely moved since making her morning coffee, and was still in bathrobe and nightgown. Fuzzy slippers lay on the paper's front section, hiding yet more bad news about the economy. She had tried to read about the latest corporate bankruptcies, but the words would not make any sense. Then she had found the series of articles in the third section, the segment entitled "Religion" that catered to almost everything except what Buddy and Patrick and the others stood for. The headlines were about Buddy Korda and his latest prediction. That is what they called it. Prediction. The front-page articles pretended to hold an objective line. The second and third pages were filled with venomous attacks. Almost everyone was represented. The gays called the proposed amendment a threat to thirty years of progress. The National Organization of Women declared that the religious right intended to send all professional women back to the kitchen and the nation back to the dark ages. On and on it went, each more furious than the last. And every one of them felt aimed straight at her.

Linda uncurled one foot and used a toe to drag the disturbing segment of the paper under the sofa where she could no longer see it. Not that it would do much good. She stared at the rain-lashed window and felt as though the storm had not only invaded her home, but her heart as well.

When the doorbell sounded, Linda needed quite some time to decide whether or not she wanted to even see who it was. She walked over, peered through the peephole, and took another moment to recognize the face. Reluctantly she opened the door. "Mrs. Korda?"

"It's Molly to you, dear." The older woman was as diminutive as her husband. "How are you?"

"Fine." She kept the door barred with her body. "I'm . . . Well, I haven't dressed yet."

"Of course not. What else are lazy Sundays for?" Despite the livid scar rising from her collar, Molly Korda had the sweetest smile Linda had ever seen. "I'm sorry to be bothering you at all, but Patrick was worried. He's left a number of messages with your answering service, but received no reply. He asked if I would just stop by and see how everything was."

For some reason the words twisted her frustration. "I'm a big girl, Mrs. Korda. I can take care of myself."

"Of course you are, dear." Linda's ire did not seem to affect Molly at all. "May I come in?"

"I'm not . . . Oh, all right." Part of her wanted to shut the woman out, yet part felt a desperate need to let her in. The warring sides created only more coldness in her voice. "Everybody's probably wondering why I've been dragging my heels over the new video."

"No, that was yesterday. This morning before we drove back down the topic was you and Patrick." Molly stepped inside, took a quick breath, and exclaimed, "What a lovely place!"

But Linda felt trapped by the words. "Me and Patrick?"

"Yes, of course. Everybody wants to know if this is a romance or not." Molly proceeded through the dining area and into the living room, where she did a slow circle before declaring, "Dear, if I were a single woman, this is exactly the kind of place I would dream of having."

Linda felt her ire being defeated by this woman. "Would you like some coffee?"

"No, thank you. I had a cup when we arrived. I drove down with Alex and Agatha, you remember Buddy's brother and his wife."

Linda bent down and began gathering the papers, trying to make the question as natural as she could. "Patrick didn't come with you?"

"No, Buddy told him over the weekend that he should prepare to go on the road. It seems that Buddy is to wait here for God to speak again. Meanwhile Patrick and Reverend Wilkins and a young lawyer named, oh dear, I've forgotten. Is it Elroy?"

"Elroy Tommkins. He's an attorney specializing in constitutional issues."

"Yes, that's the one. Apparently they're to be the face the public associates with this effort. Patrick has been trying to call you to say he will stop by here later this week. Right now he's trying to decide if he should let the boys come down here and do volunteer work in the church."

Molly seated herself in the Danish leather settee Linda used for work. It had a swivel stand and padded footstool and was about the most extravagant purchase Linda had ever made. Molly swung back and forth in the chair and declared, "I want one."

Linda found herself fighting down a smile. "It is outrageously expensive."

"It feels like every muscle of my body is cradled." She swung around far enough to inspect the floor-to-ceiling books behind the wood-framed glass doors with beveled corners. Most of the books were about politics, economics, sociological and television trends, or autobiographies of newspeople she admired. Molly spent a long moment inspecting the titles before saying quietly, "You are giving up a great deal, aren't you?"

Linda tried to scoff at her words. "CBS kicked me out on the street, remember?"

Molly did not turn from her inspection of the shelves. "That's not what

I'm talking about and you know it. With a woman like you, another opportunity will come along."

"It already has." Abruptly Linda felt it all drain away. The anger, the commotion, the distress, the warring sides. All of it. She was left so depleted she would have sunk to the floor if the sofa had not been there to catch her. "I wish I knew what to do."

Molly turned to her, swinging the chair around so that she faced Linda square on. "There are two enormous differences between you and me. One, you are far more intelligent and have used your intelligence much better than I have or ever could."

"That's not true."

"Please, let's have honesty here between us, all right? I am a mother and a homemaker and very proud of both achievements. But I have nothing except admiration for you and your accomplishments. And I realize that it must be as hard for you to look your present choices in the face as it would be for me to, well, think about giving up one of my own precious children."

Linda remembered then. "How is . . . Was it your daughter?"

"Daughter-in-law. She's better. Making progress toward a full recovery, thank God. She and the baby both. The doctors are absolutely mystified at little Josiah's recuperation. They might even let them come home next week."

"Josiah, that's what you're going to call the baby?"

"Yes, but let's not get off the subject here." Molly slid the footstool over so she could prop up her feet. "There is another great difference between you and me. I have never felt the need to do it all by myself. Long ago I realized I did not have the strength or the wisdom to make all the right choices in order to raise a family, and participate in my community, and be a worthy partner to my husband."

There it was again. *Choices.* The word flung at her with casual power. The challenge she could not run from. "What did you do?"

"I accepted that I needed God's help. I learned to call upon Him whenever I was in trouble." Her smile was pulled slightly at the edge by the scar on her neck and cheek. "It was the greatest discovery I ever made."

Linda found herself unable to respond with more than a head shake. Back and forth, pushing at the emptiness and the lack of answers.

"Tell me, dear. Do you believe in God?"

That stopped her. The tug-of-war was clear now, struggling at the very base of her being. But she had no choice. Not here. This at least was clear. "Yes."

"Good. I'm so glad to hear you say that. Now let's take it one step further." Molly looked at the ceiling, then at the far wall, gathering herself. "We tend to think about God in relation to *things* in our life. What God has done for us means what He has brought—relationships, home, profession, or release from our unhappiness."

"Or our pain," Linda said softly.

"Yes, Patrick mentioned to me your upbringing. Your grandmother, is that right? Yes, for some it is a relationship defined by the things that are *not*. That which must be given up. That which must be lost."

The concern as much as the words themselves helped give voice to the struggle. "All this week, I've been worrying about how I am being forced to give everything up for God. Going away from all I've worked so hard to build for myself." Linda turned and stared at the storm-lashed window. "I had all the old nightmares again last night."

"Oh, you poor dear."

"Everything I'd fought so hard to leave behind. All the pain I knew as a kid, all still there with me. I lay there the rest of the night thinking how someday I'd be the one looking after the grandkids, telling my own stories of pain and loss. What it cost to believe in God."

Molly rose from the chair and came over to sit beside Linda on the sofa. She took one hand, held it in a grip as soft and warm as the heart that spoke, saying, "And now you don't even feel like you have any choice, do you?"

"No." The word was half laugh, half cry. "I'd like to fool myself and say, 'Okay, I'll walk away from this one like I have all the others.' But I know that's not the case. I'm in this. Stuck. Trapped. And I know it's going to cost me everything."

Molly did not deny it, did not offer the warm assurances Linda had half expected. Instead, she stroked Linda's hand and said, "Shall I tell you what my own studies have taught me?"

"Yes," Linda said, sighing the word to the rain-washed window.

"I have found that God's first and foremost concern is not the *things* at all. Not giving us the happy things. Not forcing us to give up other things. Not saving us from bad things."

Linda turned from the window, drawn by the words and the soft way they were spoken, soft and strong at the same time, filled with a lifetime of steady, loving assurance. Linda looked at the older woman, and in that sudden instant a thought flashed through her mind. One that brought the first hint of comfort she had known all weekend long. *I want what this woman has.*

"God's primary concern," Molly went on, "is the *journey*. His first concern is to draw us closer to Him. We are called home, walking the divine Way one tiny step at a time, day after day, all the way to His holy embrace. We must learn to trust Him more, through good and bad. We must walk closer. Listen better. Serve Him with deeper love."

They sat together, drawn by a closeness not even the cold, gray day could dispel. Rain drummed and trickled upon the window and the roof, but now the cold was banished. Now there was a new light to the room, and to her heart. Linda stared at Molly and realized she had found herself a new friend. "I wish I knew what to do about this job offer."

Molly did not ask what job she was speaking of. Instead she offered again the gentle smile and replied, "I know what Buddy would say."

"What's that?"

"Whatever step you take, make it on God's behalf. And make it boldly."

☐

Monday morning Linda arrived at the church guest house to find everyone crowded in the front room—Alex, Agatha, Molly, Buddy, Reverend Wilkins, Elaine Wilkins, Clarence. All conversation halted and all eyes turned her way as she entered. She smiled as best she could, but the telephone's ring interrupted the forming of her first word.

Clarence lifted the receiver, held it to her. "Our former boss wants to speak with you."

"I better take that." She sidled past the group, went into the dining room, and lifted the receiver. "Hello, Jackson."

The head of the CBS-Washington bureau did not waste any time. "I've been trying to reach you at home all morning."

"I went for a walk."

"I hear you had a chance to talk with Rob Satchell on Friday."

She heard Molly shushing the others as she answered, "That's right, I did."

"Well, I've had a couple of conversations myself. With the White House."

That was news. "About me?"

"About this whole mess you've gotten involved in. Apparently they feel there is a groundswell of support building for this amendment measure." Jackson Knowles's famed variety of false moods had for once been abandoned. He spoke in terse bits, chopping off the words. "Linda, this is huge. I'm not sure exactly what you're involved with, but from the sounds of things it's about to be launched into the national spotlight."

"I agree."

"Okay, here's the thing. We've done wrong by you. I agree. So does New York. We're prepared to make it up to you. Fifty percent raise over your old salary, plus full coverage of this issue as it develops. Are you listening good? You'd better be, because your train's about to arrive. Linda, you handle this well and you're guaranteed the number two anchor spot, and center stage for the weekend nightly news."

She did not answer. The offer appealed so strongly to her she was uncertain whether she could form any words at all. The morning's damp gray walk was still with her, the indecision and the tumult rising up to surround her yet again.

"Linda?"

She had walked through Kalorama to Connecticut Avenue, on to Dupont Circle, stopping for coffee at one of the little shops that had somehow managed to survive. And the whole time she had been reviewing her old life. The good and the bad, the mistakes and the triumphs. Wishing there were some way to have it all, what she had gained here, and what she had before.

Irritation at being kept waiting turned his voice harsh as dusty gravel. "It can't be taking this long to grab hold of the brass ring."

"I'm sorry, Jackson," she said, wishing she felt as easy inside as she sounded. "I can't accept just now."

"What?" The word was not quite a shout. "Just now? Did I really hear you say that?"

"You want an exclusive. I can't give it to you. My responsibilities here include fielding requests for Mr. Korda. He is not meeting with anyone just now. No exceptions."

A long silence, then, "Linda, do you realize what you're doing to your career?"

"Yes."

"No you don't. You can't. Satchell said he laid it out to you loud and clear. I should have known a political consultant couldn't add two and two and get anything under eleven. Linda, you're tying a lead weight around your neck and jumping overboard. You're going to drown in religious mania. Soon as this thing dies a dismal death, you'll be forgotten." When she remained silent, he raised his voice and shouted, "Do you hear what I'm telling you?"

"Thank you very much for calling. Good-bye." She hung up the phone and stood there looking at it for a long moment, hoping desperately this new faith and the choices it was requiring of her were not just another lie she was telling herself.

She turned back around. All the room was watching her, so she said, "That was my former boss. He wanted—"

The phone interrupted her a second time. Because she was nearest she picked it up and said, "Hello?"

"Linda, thank goodness. I've been getting worried."

"Patrick." The joy at hearing his voice was so strong she felt a burning behind her eyes. She sank into the chair at the head of the table, the one normally reserved for Reverend Wilkins. She waited a moment while Molly shooed everyone upstairs, then asked, "How are you?"

"Better, now that I've got you on the line. Where were you this morning?"

"Out walking. I needed to think."

"Are you all right?"

"Yes and no. Molly came over yesterday." Pitching her voice low. "It helped. At the time, at least."

Quieter this time, more serious. "Are you all right?"

"I just got a call from my former boss. He offered me the world on a string." She took a breath. "I wish I were stronger."

"Don't we all." A little pause. "Do you feel like you know what God wants you to do?"

"Yes." As clear on this point as she was yesterday over whether He existed at all. "I'm afraid."

"I understand." No prodding. No pressure. No judgment or holier-than-thou sentiments. "It's a point we're all brought to at one time or another, I'm sorry to say. When our own strength just isn't enough, and the future seems so hopeless and bleak that we are tempted just to give in and turn away."

The relief at being truly understood left her hand holding the telephone trembling along with her voice. "What do I do?"

"Take it one step at a time. Don't do anything unless you are certain God's will is reflected in your step." There was a shadow of ancient sorrow to his voice, a tone shaded by his own sleepless nights and savage fatigue. "Don't let anyone force you into anything. Don't be hurried, don't be swayed by what others think you should or shouldn't do."

She felt one liquid fragment of her internal tempest trickle down her cheek. She wiped it away with her free hand, and said, "Molly told me if I was going to make a mistake, do it for God."

"Let's hope you don't make any mistakes at all. Would you like me to come down?"

"Yes. Oh, yes." She didn't care how it sounded. She wanted to be weak, to be held, to be cared for by someone with strength for them both. "Can you manage it?"

"I'm hoping to make it tomorrow. Would you like to pray with me now?"

"Say the words for me," she said, wishing she had the ability to say what was truly on her mind and heart. But there was nothing in her background to prepare her for such a confession. "Please."

Yet as Patrick spoke the words, she felt as though a second voice were speaking as well, one that whispered the comfort she needed, and directed her to a course she already knew was there in front of her. His words illuminated the next step so strongly her inner storm could no longer hide the Way. So when Patrick finished, she was able to say, "I feel so much better."

"I'll see you tomorrow evening, God willing."

"I'll make you dinner," she promised. After hanging up, she almost ran up the stairs, not wanting to permit any further doubt or discord.

She arrived at the top of the stairs to find everyone standing in the midst of their electronic confusion, staring at the video in Clarence's hands. Now it was time. She was able to say, "Shall we show them what we've done?"

Clarence's face lit up with delight. "It's good, isn't it. Tell them how good it is."

Linda looked at them one a time, friends somehow old and new at the same time, and said with quiet confidence, "It is absolutely the best thing I have ever done."

"It's even better than that," Clarence agreed, his permanently tired features creased by an enormous smile. "It is inspired."

THIRTY-TWO

☐ Nearly a half hour later, Buddy's face faded from the television monitor. The room responded with absolute stunned silence. Linda took a full breath, then gave Clarence a small nod. It was as good as he had said. Better.

James Thaddeus rose slowly to his feet. "Miss Kee, you've taken the dream and made it real. I don't know what to say to you other than that."

She stared into that wise, dark face, and wished she had felt as certain about anything in her entire life as James Thaddeus Wilkins seemed to feel about everything.

He said to the room, "I got myself some calls to make." And to Buddy, "I can see why you wanted me and Elroy to get ready for the road. Gonna be a lot of people needing somebody to focus on."

Buddy asked, "Will your church be all right?"

"Patrick and I done talked this out." He walked to the phone by the second floor's front window. With the rain and the gray day as a backdrop, he dialed and said, "We both got good young men just waiting for a chance to grab hold of the Sunday pulpit. Now's as good a time as any to let them take on the Lord's burden."

Linda said to no one in particular, "There's going to be a need for a central office, a national news and information center."

"We done talked that through too," Reverend Wilkins said, then to the phone, "Afternoon, Samuel. James Thaddeus here. Hold on one minute, sir." To Linda he said, "You go over to the church office, tell the ladies there

I said to take whatever more space you need. We'll have enough volunteers reporting to you directly, I imagine."

She stiffened in her chair. "Reporting to me?"

"Who else, now?" To the phone, "Yeah, Samuel, I done seen it. The Lord's hand is at work, is all I can tell you. Hold on, I'll ask." To Clarence, "How long 'til I can let him see this?"

"Right now." Clarence gave Linda a sheepish smile. "I came in early and started making copies. I was sure you were going to see the light."

Linda kept her eyes on the tall, dark man by the window. Panic flickered like lightning at the edge of her heart's storm. "I'm to be in charge of the central office?"

"You said it yourself, ma'am. A central *press* office. An *information* office." To the phone, "I promised I'd call as soon as I saw it, and that's what I'm doing. And I'm telling you it's gonna knock you and the council straight into next week. Yes, all right. Fifteen copies. Tonight by express. You be sure and call me and tell me if I'm right."

James Thaddeus hung up only to start dialing once more. He did not need to look over to know that Linda was still staring at him. He said to her, "That was Samuel Ritter, former pastor of the First Baptist Church in Mobile, now minority leader of the state legislature. And a mover and shaker for our Lord. Gonna be a lot of others like him, tied to government and our Lord, yes. All needing somebody to feed information back to so it can be dispersed nationwide. Am I right?"

"If this thing takes off," Linda said slowly. But logic did not help. She wanted to scream her denial. She wanted to race from the room and the challenges and the demands being set before her. What held her, she could not say. But hold her it did.

"You seen this video, Miss Kee. You *made* it." To the phone, "James Thaddeus Wilkins for Senator Collins, please ma'am. Thank you." To Linda, "The Lord didn't have us go to all this trouble 'cept for *success*. That means your job's just started. Mr. Korda's done said it again this weekend. You got yourself a central role to play in the Lord's work."

Linda moved her whole body to look over to where Buddy was seated with Molly. "You said that?"

"On Saturday," Molly answered for her husband. "Or was it Sunday?"

"I don't remember," Buddy said, then to Linda, "That was truly powerful, Miss Kee."

"It was Saturday," James Thaddeus offered, holding the phone to his ear. "I know 'cause Patrick called me straight after. Man was worried when he couldn't find you, and told me 'bout what Buddy had said."

"It's just like I told you," Clarence said to her. "This work is dynamite."

"It's better than that," Alex said, speaking for the first time. "It's pure solid gold."

"Yes ma'am, I'm still holding," James Thaddeus said to the phone. He stood and watched Linda's expression, then gave a deep chuckle. "Don't tell me you thought the Lord raised you up just to use you for this here one thing, then was gonna set you back down."

"I don't know what I thought," Linda said faintly. She glanced at the door, wishing she could get up and walk away.

Another chuckle. "The Lord's done *called* you, Miss Kee. Ain't no time limit on a *call*." He turned to the window. "Senator, good afternoon, hope I'm not . . . Yessir, I seen it. It's sure something. A fire-lighter is what you said you needed, isn't that right? Well sir, this here video is high octane. Yessir. That's what I think. Twelve copies? Right this very afternoon." The gaze swung back to Linda. "We're setting it up as we speak. Gonna use our church's address. A name? Just one minute, sir."

James Thaddeus cupped the phone to his chest and said to the room, "Senator wants to know do we have us a name."

"New Jerusalem," Buddy said without hesitation. "Just like your church."

James Thaddeus looked at him for a long moment before raising the phone. When he spoke, his voice sounded slightly choked. "The New Jerusalem Council. Yessir, I think it's fine too. Fine name."

He listened, then smiled in Linda's direction. "Yessir, Senator, we surely do have ourselves a director. Her name is Linda Kee. You mightta seen her, she's been with CBS News. One thing for certain, you're sure gonna know her by the end of this video."

There was a pause, then, "What's she like?" The reverend's gaze seemed to reach across the room and shine directly inside Linda. "Well, sir, I'll tell you. She don't hardly know how fine a heart she's got. But God does. Yessir, He surely knew why He did His choosing where He did."

"Say it, brother," Alex said from his corner.

A gentle hand on her shoulder drew her around. Molly smiled down at her. "Come downstairs with me for a moment, will you?"

Linda followed her downstairs and into the front room. "I can't believe what I just heard."

"Don't let it frighten you, dear."

"I'm too terrified to be frightened." She halted. "That doesn't make a single solitary bit of sense."

"It did to me." Molly reached into the pocket of her sweater and drew out a pack of note cards. "I need to ask a favor. Each morning could you please put one of these on the mantel here?"

She accepted the cards, held together by a rubber band. "What are they?"

"Bible passages. Buddy likes me to give him one for each day. I feel better having this done from my hand to yours, if that's all right. I want them here so when he comes downstairs and greets the day, he finds a trace of me with him."

Linda read the first card with a voice that sounded meek and worried to her own ears, "'And God is able to make all grace abound toward you, that you, always having all sufficiency in all things, may have an abundance for every good work. 2 Cor. 9:8.'"

She looked up at Molly and asked, "How on earth am I going to do what they're requesting?"

Molly's smile did not waver. "With God's help."

"That's your answer? That's all you can offer?"

The gentle hand settled onto Linda's arm. "It is the only answer there is."

⊣| THIRTY-THREE |⊢

☐ Presidential Chief of Staff Ethan Eldridge leaned back in his chair and used the remote to turn off his office video machine. The television flicked back to its perpetual run of C-Span. He turned the volume down low, and muttered, "What an utter mess."

"I don't get it." Jerry Chevass, Royce's number two, was seated in the chair beside Royce. He still held to his skeptical demeanor, but it was being steadily chipped away. "The guy hires himself a television lady who got kicked out of the big time. They put together a second video. Okay, it's more professional-looking than the first, but so what?" He looked from one somber face to the other. "What am I missing here?"

Royce Calder found himself admitting, "I have a bad feeling about this whole thing."

"And *I* don't believe I'm hearing you say this," Jerry said. "Why in . . ."

His words trailed off with a single look from Ethan. The former banker continued his turn from the television until he was face-to-face with Royce Calder. "I'm afraid I agree with you."

"Our biggest asset in dealing with the religious wing is their disorganization." Royce felt a rising rage that was hard to keep from his consistently calm voice. "If they ever come close to being successful with this Constitutional amendment, they will discover what it means to flex their muscles."

"The entire political landscape will change overnight," Ethan agreed.

"Not to mention our own party," Royce reminded them both.

This was enough to silence even Jerry. Ethan muttered, "What a disaster that would be."

It was a known fact within Party politics that the religious voter turned out for *issues* and for *candidates.* Most had little interest in *Party* politics. This was of vast relief to the cadre of Party faithful. It was part of the creed by which they lived and breathed and operated.

The Party's core was made up of three distinct kinds of people. The first group was issue driven, and included the vast majority of religious conservatives. In the electoral process they could make up as much as *60 percent* of Party voters.

But in the Party process, they totaled less than five percent.

The second of the Party's core groups was made up of those interested in power for the sake of money and industry. Their goal was to utilize political access for their own gain. These bastions of industry, or their minions, used the Party and the candidates to support issues tied to their bottom line. Perhaps they wanted a pesky environmental regulation quashed. Or they wanted to accompany the secretary of commerce on a trade junket to China. They wanted the president to arm-twist a foreign government to lift a ban on their product. They wanted drilling rights, government road contracts, frequency bands for radio or television or cellular phones. The list was endless, their demands on an elected official constant. And despite the fact that they were the *smallest* portion of actual votes, their voices were heard the best. This group controlled as much as 85 percent of the most precious commodity of any election campaign.

Money.

The religious wing was seldom listened to at national Party level because they did not deliver money. They were recognized as great grass-roots volunteers, tireless campaign workers so long as their issues were recognized. Take them out of the campaign, and the Party would die on the vine.

But Party staffers who lingered year after year cared first and foremost about who gave the big bucks, and who wielded the big power sticks. Very few religious conservatives could walk into Party headquarters and write out a hundred thousand dollar soft-money check. As far as the Party's senior staffers were concerned, the man with wampum was king for a day.

The third group involved in Party politics was there because of power, ego, and status. These were the most faithful of all Party functionaries. These power groupies often had been involved in the Party and the campaigns since school. The Party was their social life. They viewed every issue, every battle, every headline from the standpoint of one essential question: *How will it affect the Party?* These people considered it the biggest thrill of their entire lives to be around power. They entered the state and national conventions as they would a temple, in trembling awe.

It was primarily because of these power groupies that the religious wing avoided Party conventions and Party politics. These two groups could not be farther apart, or more opposed to one another's viewpoint. The power groupies wanted nothing more than to see the Party get in power and stay in power. The religious wing wanted to gain power for a *purpose.* Without this purpose, there was no reason to have power. The power groupies considered this attitude as alien to the Party cause as an edict handed down from Valhalla.

Ethan Eldridge turned back to the television set, but he was not focused upon C-Span and the talking head. "You fellows weren't there when Korda was proved right the first time. I mean, certainly, you were around. But you weren't in the financial firing line. I can remember watching a tape of his performance on the CNN talk show, how we all sat around and laughed." Ethan shook his head. "There were six of us gathered that day. All senior bankers. Right now, three are walking the streets, their banks swallowed by the federal bailout. One took a high-dive from his twelfth-floor window. One fled to Canada with what remained of his bank's assets in a briefcase. I'm the only one who survived relatively intact, and my bank still walks the razor's edge."

Eldridge turned and focused on Royce. His face was as grim as Royce had ever seen it. "This is your second impossible."

"I understand," Royce said quietly. Wanting it and dreading it at the same time.

"Make this guy and his amendment issue go away."

Jerry looked askance across the desk. "This is hard? Excuse me, but we've spent years making toast out of guys a lot tougher than Korda."

"If that's the case, then you've been handed the easiest step up the ladder you'll ever have." Eldridge's gaze did not waver. "But I can't take that chance."

"We'll have a plan outlined in the next day or so."

"I don't want to hear," Eldridge snapped. "The White House will have to distance itself. Do I make myself clear?"

"We'll handle it through the Party," Royce assured him.

"The president will give his standard family values speech and then wash his hands of the whole affair. There will be too many of the religious wing involved for him to be seen as opposing this amendment issue." The eyes glinted dangerously. "That is, of course, until you succeed. Then he will join all the others in decrying this dangerous monolithic mania, which tears at the nation's fabric."

Royce looked at him in admiration. "Excellent. Truly a stroke of genius."

Jerry stared at his superior. "Sorry. You guys have lost me there."

"Explain it to him," Eldridge said.

"The church tax bill," Royce said, staring across the desk in awe. "This is the lever we've been looking for."

"Stifle them here, build massive public opinion against religious groups, then we strike. We'll demolish their financial base and leave them in a bigger mess than they were before," Eldridge said, the glint almost becoming a smile. "It could make this whole predicament worthwhile."

⊣| THIRTY-FOUR |⊢

☐ It was raining so hard when she arrived, Linda could scarcely make out the logo on the steel and glass doors. Linda paid the taxi, opened her door and her umbrella, and stood there on the sidewalk in front of the entrance to the CBS News Washington office. The offices were on Truman Avenue in Crystal City, just across the Potomac from the capital. Her office had been on the riverfront, fourteen stories above the traffic and the noise. From her desk she could look out over the green strips fronting the river, watch the joggers and the rowers and the glistening water, look over to Capitol Hill and be filled with the importance of her work. *Her* work.

Linda stepped forward so that she was sheltered from the downpour by the awning. She wanted to enter those doors. She wanted it so bad it filled her with a gnawing ache. March upstairs to the office of Jackson Knowles and say yes. Just yes. Slip back into the role she knew and loved.

But she could not move. The water dripped over the awning and surrounded her with the tears her heart wept with each broken beat. She ached for all she had lost and was now being offered again. She ached for it just as much as she was terrified by what loomed before her if she were to stay with Buddy Korda. Director of the New Jerusalem Council. It was not enough that she had made the video. No. That was just the beginning. It would go on and on and on, demanding ever more of her. This was to be her own endless march of faith, the path alongside the grandmother who had robbed her childhood of peace. Marching through the ruin of every dream she had ever known.

She stood there in the rain and yearned to walk through those doors.

The doors that had given her such a thrill just to enter. The doors that had declared to her that she had arrived. The doors that now seemed to mock her every time they slid back to permit someone else to enter. Always someone else. Never her. Never again.

For as she stood there, Linda knew she could not enter those doors. Not now. Not ever. She was defeated by this strange new choice she had made. This time she could not turn her back on her faith. She wanted to. She yearned to go back to where she had been before. Yes. She could not deny the truth here. She wanted to, but she could not, for something new was in her heart, so new and so alien she could not even define it. But this something was enough to keep her standing there, yearning and yet not moving.

A breath of wind reached beneath the awning and whispered into her ear. It was time to go. This place was no longer hers. Her farewells had been said. It was time to get back to the church. Patrick would be arriving soon.

Linda stepped from under the awning, so defeated she scarcely had the strength to raise her arm and flag a passing cab.

□

After Patrick had deposited the boys with James Thaddeus and Elaine, he checked in with Buddy, then returned to the guest house for Linda. He drove slowly through rain-clogged streets, following Linda's directions to her apartment. The drive was very quiet. Rain fell in misty curtains, the car drenched by every passing vehicle. Clouds hung heavy upon the surrounding hills. Overhead what sky she could see was a uniform gray.

Patrick finally said, "We missed seeing you this weekend."

"We?"

"The boys and I."

She cocked her head. "We?"

"Okay. All right. *I* missed you." He shook his head in mock surrender. "The professional interviewer pulls out the truth once more."

Linda turned back to the rain and the gathering dusk. "I needed a little time to myself."

"For what?"

"I'm not sure what to call it. All I know is, it wasn't easy."

Patrick nodded, not to her words so much as to his own thought, which was, *It isn't over yet.* He could feel the tension of unanswered need and unresolved worry there with them in the car. "Do you feel like God was there with you?"

She pointed through the rain-spattered windshield. "Take that parking space, it's almost in front of my building." She remained silent as he pulled in and cut the engine. When he turned to face her, she gave a tiny head shake and murmured, "A lot of sorrow for nothing. A lot of regret."

Patrick sensed her need to approach whatever this was in her own time, at her own pace. So all he said was, "If it brought you to a point of feeling closer to God, the weekend was not wasted. Nothing was."

Linda examined him with a gaze locked tight in tension. She started to say something, then opened her door and sprinted for the entrance alcove. Patrick sighed his way out of the car, wishing he knew what she needed.

Which was why, as he watched her fit the key into the heavy door, he asked, "Would you rather be alone tonight?"

"It wouldn't do any good," she said, and shoved the door open with her shoulder.

The interior hallway was high-ceilinged and decorated with art-deco mosaic tile. He followed her up the broad circular staircase, regretting that such anxiety marred his first glimpse of her home.

His compliments over her apartment were cut short by Linda's brusque thanks, as though somehow his words only made matters worse. So he worked alongside her in silence, setting the table and baking rolls and making a salad. He glanced her way from time to time, wishing he knew how to read this new side of her.

Throughout the meal Patrick battled against the silent tension by regaling her with information on the difficulty of fighting with two boys who showed the wisdom not to argue with him at all. He explained how he had first said there was no way he was going to permit them to come back down with him. None at all. They had merely accepted it and asked where he was going to spend his free time—in Washington or Aiden. Because he couldn't be in both places, not if he was going to be as busy as Buddy had said. Patrick started to add their final words, in Washington with *Linda.* But a single glance at the way she kept her gaze on her salad and avoided looking his way made him decide now was not the time to admit how that had been the deciding factor.

Patrick set down his fork, and fell silent.

The silence drew her gaze upward. "What's the matter?"

"Nothing." He had been struck by a sudden thought. The thought was, he wanted to spend time with her more than just about anything in the world. That he already knew. What had struck him so hard just then was, he wanted to do it even now. When she was revealing a side to him he had never seen before. One probably intended to shut him out. One that mystified him, especially after their telephone conversation of the day before. But here he was, uncomfortable on the one hand and happy on the other. Just glad to see her. Feeling that it was going to be all right, whatever it was that had her so silent. And somehow all those thoughts seemed to add up to only one thing—a gift. Patrick could not help it. He had to smile.

She saw it. And set down her fork, which was just as well, since she had done little except play with her salad. "What is it?"

He had to think, because he did not want to say anything but the truth, and yet could not tell her what he was thinking. Not then. Not yet. Then it occurred to him, "You owe me a long explanation."

Linda glanced at the night-streaked window. "Of what?"

"You know exactly what I mean." Trying to ease them into this with a light tone and another smile. "When we went out to dinner at that Italian place, I spent the entire evening spilling out my heart. It's your turn now."

She looked at him, revealing a stony gaze. "What if I don't have anything worth telling?"

He studied her, seeing beyond the frank beauty, realizing she had one of the most expressive faces he had ever known. "I think I ought to be the judge of that, don't you?"

Her features remained oblique. "What if I don't care to go in for the confession routine?"

Patrick realized then why he had been willing to accept her distance. "It's not me at all, is it?"

Clearly his words caught her off guard. "What?"

"Why you're feeling uncomfortable tonight." He forced himself to hold her gaze. "You don't have to tell me anything you don't want to, Linda. I just want to know about you, that's all."

She said slowly, "No, you don't."

"How can you be so sure about that?"

"The problem is, I can't gloss over the truth. Not with you. Not any-more."

"What is the truth, Linda?" He waited a moment, then said softly, "What are you afraid of?"

"You don't know who I am. You *can't.* Not and . . ."

More softly still, "Not and still care for you?"

The oblique gaze returned to him, eyes that shut him out entirely. Beautiful eyes, as blank as a locked vault. "You and your Alice and your kids, you're all so . . ."

"Perfect? Is that what you think?"

"*Protected.* Everything about you reeks of protection. You can't imagine what it's like trying to get ahead out there in the world. It eats away at everything. Relationships, time, ideals, motives, everything."

He waited. There was nothing to be said. For the moment he had enough on his hands dealing with the sudden blossom of sorrow at his heart level. He had known it would be something like this. And yet it was entirely different to hear the words spoken aloud.

Linda said to the window, "I can't remember when my relationships started becoming intertwined with work. But I can sure see how my think-ing went. Of course these relationships of mine were with people from work. How could they not be, when work was all I knew? Even if I was on so-called free time, I was doing something work-related. Receptions or junkets or courses, the works. Of course I became involved with men I knew through my profession. They were the only people I saw, the only men who understood what I was talking about."

The words spilled out, a confession spoken not to him but to the night. "It was so easy to ignore the fact that these were also people who could *help* my career. They were people on the rise, just like me—that's the way I liked to explain it to myself. In the dark of the night I felt so lonely I could die, dirtied by things that in the light of day were logical and rational and *fine.* Just fine. I was fine, I was doing everything great. A girl on the rise. A star in the making. But at night, especially this last year when the whole world seemed rocked by wrongness, I would wake up crying from dreams I couldn't remember. Does that sound like the actions of someone doing fine to you?"

When Patrick waited, comfortable now in the silence and the feeling that swept the room, she continued to stare at the empty darkness, her gaze as dry as her voice. "I don't know why I'm telling you this."

"Yes you do and so do I."

"You better be getting back," she said dully, but made no effort to rise. "Sorry to have ruined your dinner."

"You haven't ruined a thing." Somehow Patrick had the feeling that this was the best thing possible, though on the outside the evening seemed a dismal failure. "Linda, before I go, would you pray with me?"

It took a moment for the words to sink through the mire of her thoughts. Then she turned slowly, her eyebrows arched in astonishment. "That's your reaction to what I've just told you? To pray?"

"I just think God needs to be a part of this," he said gently. "I can't say any more than that right now. Maybe later. But right now that's the only thing that comes to me."

She studied him as though seeing his face for the very first time. In a small voice she said, "If you say the words."

"Thank you, Linda." He bowed his head, closed his eyes, and began to speak words that seemed to come from a very long way off. Words so much intended for her and not for himself that he felt like a telephone, merely passing them on, hardly able to remember what he had said as soon as the words left his mouth, the strangest experience he had ever known at prayer. What was stranger still was the sudden thought that came and lingered, resting there at the highest border of his awareness, so clear and yet so gentle that the thought did not disturb the flow of prayer. The thought was, Alice would be very proud of him just now.

☐ Party Chairman Jim Jenners slammed his fist down on his desk and shouted, "A national political alliance of the religious factions would be an absolute disaster!"

They had arranged the evening conference because Royce wanted to plot his strategy. The chairman's office was crowded with all nine of Royce's White House cadre, plus Jenners's three principal assistants. The atmosphere was as grim as the weather. Jenners swept a hand over the news clippings scattered across his desk. "The press is actually treating this thing as real."

"Part of them, in any case," Gladys Knight interjected. No one disputed her; she was the cadre's statistical mine, who daily read and collated data from newspapers across the country. "They seem to be caught as flat-footed as everybody else. The biggies are still treating this as they would a three-headed calf. But the locals are split between objective reporting and trumpeting this as the end of civilization as we know it."

"This Korda ought to be taken out and shot," Jenners muttered. He cast another grim look over the clippings, then focused across the desk and barked, "All right. What are we going to do about it?"

This was Royce's cue. "To begin with, we need to assume the worst. Indications are we have a genuine crisis in the making."

"It's like watching a lightning storm pass over parched earth." This from Gladys, who loathed the idea of the Party's religious wing gaining actual power as much as her boss. "Thirty-nine states have official centers now established to coordinate the Constitutional amendment's push."

"Thirty-nine in one *week?*" Jenners ruffled his normally perfect silver hair. "They must have a central organization to rival our own."

"Another surprise there." Royce looked to his assistant. "Tell them."

"They don't have *any* central organization to speak of," Elton reported. "I've been over a couple of times during the past week. They work from the guest house of the New Jerusalem Baptist Church over on P Street."

"Sounds like a black church," Jenners said.

"Yes sir. It is."

"Any political affiliations?"

"I've checked voting records. It's apparently pretty mixed."

"And they're leading a Party uprising?" Jenners looked askance across his wide desk. "Tell me this is a joke."

"I wish it were," Royce replied. "We're seeing a buildup that in most states cuts right across all established political lines. You saw their second video. The black pastor who spoke at the end is the guy in charge of this church. Remember what he said? This is not a Party issue."

"Not a Party issue!" The chairman stared at Royce as he would a bug in his soup. "*Everything* is a Party issue! Especially something that threatens our organization!"

Royce waited through a moment's calming silence before saying, "Not yet."

"Ah. You have a plan. I might have known." Jenners settled back. "All right, let's have it."

"We are going at this with all guns blazing." Royce opened the file in his lap. "Perhaps this movement will fizzle out on its own accord, perhaps not. But we can't wait around to find out."

"I agree."

"So does Eldridge, by the way. He remembers what happened the last time people underestimated the draw of this man Korda." Royce looked down at notes he had long since memorized. It was a habit too imbedded to break. "Gladys will handle the press."

"There's a national conference of editors next week," Gladys said. "A trusted ally is keynote speaker at the first luncheon. We've had a long chat and we see eye to eye on this. She's agreed to speak on the danger of fundamentalist fervor. Our intention is to stir up as much editorial heat as we can."

"Moving on to the rise of these councils, I've started assigning some personnel from here at headquarters," Royce went on. "We're pinpointing the states with the largest number of religious conservatives in both houses. Chevass is coordinating this."

"We don't have time to personally strike every state," Royce's number two explained. His voice was deeply embittered as well as worried; his cynical nature had finally been defeated, and he hated it. "So we need to find the pivots. Almost every state in the Bible Belt is a flashpoint. A lot of the Midwest as well. Wisconsin and Michigan and Massachusetts could fall against us. We've targeted twenty-four states that might go either way."

"More every year," Jenners muttered.

"Our goal is to make sure the matter never actually comes up for a vote before the state legislatures," Royce explained. "If there is sufficient opposition from the fence-sitters, the bill will never come out of committee."

"We're going after the middle-of-the-roaders," Chevass said.

Royce added, "But we need ammunition."

"You've got it," Jenners said instantly. "What kind?"

"Authority to offer campaign funding to every legislator who agrees to denounce the bill," Chevass said.

"Not just trinkets either," Royce said. "Enough to get them to come out publicly."

"Sixty, seventy thousand ought to be enough," Jenners mused. "To a state legislator, seventy thousand dollars in campaign funds is a genuine bonus. All right. Done."

"And access," Royce said. "We need to fashion a special junket for the party faithful. A banquet at the White House, an afternoon briefing with national figures. That sort of thing."

Jenners turned to his own assistant. "Book it in. And make an appointment for me to see the president. Soon."

"Yes sir."

The chairman turned back to Royce. "Is that all?"

"Not if you want to make sure this dies a swift and painful death."

"I want it buried," Jenners said, as cold as Royce had ever seen him. "I want this thing turned into a genuine humiliation for everybody who had a hand in it."

Royce turned and nodded at Gladys. "Go ahead."

Gladys straightened in her chair. "We've started a hit list. A number of these local councils are actually being headed by politicians—state legislators, mayors, even two governors. People we know to be part of the religious wing—and some we didn't—have started to back the constitutional convention publicly. We want to wipe them off the map. We'll start with rumors that the national Party is going to oppose them during the next Party nomination process."

Royce held his breath. This went directly against the Party manifesto. To even suggest it was a serious breach of protocol.

Jenners simply nodded. "Next?"

Gladys exchanged a glance with Royce. Her entire frame relaxed a notch. "I've had a word with the boys at IRS."

"Good, good." Jenners nodded. "I like it already."

"The Senate oversight committee has made the IRS a lot more sensitive to politically motivated requests," Royce said.

"We've asked them to take a particular interest in the personal and campaign finances of a particular group of state reps," Gladys explained. Her normally toneless voice held as much pleasure as Royce could ever recall hearing. "Even if they don't find anything, it will scare the pants off a lot of the possibles."

The Party chairman stared at the blank television screen for a moment, then said, "That woman. The reporter. What is her name?"

"Linda Kee. She's currently acting as the head of their central office." Royce nodded agreement to Jenners's unspoken idea. "We're going after her as well."

"See to it." Jenners rose, drawing the room up with him. "I am taking a personal interest in making this nonsense vanish, and fast. It is our number one priority."

"Jerry and I are hitting the road on Monday to start drawing the fence-sitters over to our side," Royce said, gathering his papers. "First I have to see a man about the law."

☐

Once he made it through the rainy evening traffic and was racing down the interstate, Royce used his car phone to call Rob Satchell. The political consultant did not seem at all surprised to be hearing from Royce after work hours. In fact, Royce had the distinct impression Satchell had been waiting for his call. Royce demanded, "You've seen the tape?"

"Watched it through twice."

"What do you think of it?"

"Mud bath was what popped into my mind." There was no hint of a smile to the consultant's voice. "You have any idea what would happen to the status quo if Korda and his gang pick up momentum with this thing?"

"Like a grenade dropped from the Gallery onto the floor of the House."

"I'm not talking about if they win," Satchell went on. "They don't need to make this amendment happen. All they need is to get a clear idea of just how much voting power they could muster if they were all to dance to the same tune." Satchell breathed heavy over the line for a minute, then growled, "You got to find yourself a way to stop the music."

"I'm working on it," Royce agreed. "But I need your help."

"Name it." No horse trading this time. Too much was at stake.

"The woman."

"Linda Kee." No pleasure in the name. Not anymore.

"She's become the head of their central office."

"Yeah, I heard something about that. Couldn't believe it."

"It's true."

"What do you want me to do?"

"Whatever it takes." Royce found it difficult to keep the thread of anger from lacing itself through his voice. "A woman with her combination of ambition and looks, you understand?"

"I'll call some people first thing tomorrow, start checking around."

"We don't have much time."

"Give me a couple of days," Satchell replied. "I'll have all the dirt you need."

"I don't want it. We haven't even spoken."

"Got you."

"A man in your position, you must have a list of people who would love to report the latest on this lady." Royce checked his speed, discovered the tension had pushed him over eighty. He slowed down to sixty-five. "Now that she is in the high-powered, visible position—"

"With the religious nuts." Satchell chuckled. "I love it and so will they."

"No connection to us, the White House, or the Party," Royce warned.

"There's no need. All it would take is one former boyfriend who is willing to stick in the knife." Satchell's tone had lightened perceptibly. "'Linda Kee, former rising television star reporter turned religious wacko, get the latest scoop at ten.' They'll be fighting for the chance to be first with the dirt."

"I knew I could count on you," Royce said, utterly satisfied.

"Are you kidding? This is going to be a pleasure."

□

"Come in, Royce. Come in." Supreme Court Justice Howard Hawkins pointed across the hall. "Let's sit down in my study, shall we?"

A woman's voice called from the back of the house, "Who is it, Howard?"

"Just a friend, dear. Court business. Never mind." To Royce, "Will you have something? A coffee? Drink?"

"I'm fine, thank you." The justice's redbrick colonial on a tree-lined Chevy Chase street was a million miles from the hurly-burly of downtown Washington. "It was very kind of you to see me this late, sir."

"Don't mention it. Some things should not be discussed in chambers." He pointed Royce to a leather sofa by the roaring fire. "Who on earth would believe this was actually springtime in Washington?" He seated himself across from Royce, easing down with the movements of a frail old man. "Do you know, this was the weekend last year when the cherry blossoms came into full bloom. Look at us now. I don't have the first leaf on my roses, much less a bud."

"Yes sir." Royce had no interest whatsoever in trading gardening tips with the Justice. "Have you had a chance to view the video I couriered over to you?"

"Terrible. Simply awful. I suppose you've seen the articles in the *Post.*"

"Yes sir." Finally the nation's mainstream press was awakening to the fact that this was a genuine threat, and not merely a misguided religious prank. "At least the editorials were in our favor."

"But thirty-nine states now running centers to press for a Constitutional Convention? Is that true?"

"I'm afraid so, sir." Royce examined the older man with renewed interest. He had seen the man under many guises, from imperious official of the highest court to pompous lecturer. But this was something new. The man looked genuinely scared. "Our information is that soon all fifty states will have some skeleton staff in place."

"But this is *outrageous.*" Justice Hawkins leaned forward. "The greatest power of the Supreme Court is the power of inertia. It takes so long either to bring most cases to our level, or to change the Constitution itself, that by this point most problems have erased themselves. But these people are not playing by the rules at all! They are *steamrolling* this thing. If I understand what the news is suggesting, this Korda actually intends to have the matter voted on within the current legislative term!"

"It certainly looks that way, sir." Despite the seriousness of the situation, Royce found himself enjoying this. A frightened justice was definitely one for the books.

"Well, you have to stop them!" Hawkins rose to his feet and stood facing the fireplace. "The world these religious fanatics are pointing to in their amendment is gone. It is past. It is *over.*"

"Not in their eyes, sir. We've had to deal with them within the Party for years. Every time something like that is suggested, they wave the Federalist Papers in your face."

Impatiently Hawkins flicked the words away as he would a pesky fly. "These people are living for a dream whose time has been gone for decades. We live in a pluralistic society, and the sooner they recognize this, the better off we'll all be."

"Unfortunately," Royce said, "given the power they currently wield, nobody seeking public office can safely make such a statement."

"This is absurd, totally absurd." Hawkins wheeled about. "The Constitution is a brief, concise, working document. It is not a desiccated piece of parchment. It is not frozen in time. Our interpretations must change as our nation changes. It must be flexible enough to adapt to our changing world. If this amendment passes, it will tie our hands totally!"

The justice was more than just worried, Royce silently confirmed. The man was borderline panic-stricken. "Not in the eyes of the church."

"What church?" Hawkins's face grew red with exasperation. "Just exactly which particular church are we talking about here?"

"We've used that argument for years, sir," Royce agreed, and found himself recalling something a colleague had told him years ago. The biggest advantage they had in dealing with the Party's religious wing, his colleague had said, was that their beliefs were a mile deep but only one inch wide. So they never could manage to agree on much of anything, and never for very long. "Our nightmare has always been that they would find some unifying cause. Something that would induce them to set aside their differences and unite under one banner."

This settled Hawkins back into his seat. "You're telling me this has happened?"

"I am saying that it is an ominous possibility," Royce replied. He waited a moment, then added, "Unless we all act in unison."

The justice eyed the man seated across from him. "You have a plan?"

"That is my job, sir. To find us a way out of crises."

"Good. Excellent." Hawkins hesitated, then said, "I don't want to know any more than that, do I?"

"Probably not, sir." Royce picked his way carefully here. "Actually, I asked to see you to find out if you were planning to rule in the next few months on any cases that the Party's religious wing might find controversial."

"Ah. I see." Hawkins mulled that over, then decided, "No. Definitely not. All such cases will find themselves postponed until after this crisis has been averted."

"This is certainly helpful to our cause, sir."

"No need to add fuel to an already explosive situation, am I right?"

"Exactly, sir." Royce rose to his feet. "Thank you for taking the time to speak with me. I'll see myself out."

⊣┃ THIRTY-SIX ┃⊢

☐ "Buddy?"

"I'm over here." From behind him, Buddy heard Molly stir in bed. But he did not turn around. "Go back to sleep."

"What are you doing?"

"Nothing. Listening to the rain." It drummed on the window and on the eaves overhead, soft beats threading through his thoughts and his fears. "You need to rest, Molly. Alex said he wanted to start back to Aiden first thing tomorrow."

"How am I supposed to sleep with you standing there staring out the window?"

When Buddy did not respond, she asked quietly, "Is everything all right?"

"Fine."

He heard Molly push back the covers. His back to the room, he listened to a quiet scratching upon the carpet, and knew Molly was searching the floor for her slippers. He knew her sounds so well, his wife of over thirty years. Just as she knew him. She padded across the room and stopped there beside him. "Things are not all right." She waited a breath, then demanded softly, "Are they?"

Buddy spoke to the rain-streaked window. "I thought the Lord was calling me to be His messenger."

"He is."

"Then why . . ." He stopped. He did not know the words.

"Why what?"

Buddy stood and stared out at the night. Beyond the church's silhouette, the streetlights' yellow globes were turned soft and ill-defined by the rain. All the world seemed asleep and calm and waiting. All but him.

"Honey?"

"It's strange how a place that is so foreign can seem so much like home," he said quietly.

Molly's hand slid around his back, and she leaned her head upon his arm. "I think it's because we have found here the same love."

Buddy nodded agreement. Overhead the rain patted like soft footprints upon the roof. It was a pleasant, comforting sound. "That night Patrick came over to our house."

She waited until she was certain he needed her urging to continue. Then she said, "The night Linda rang our bell and I didn't hear."

"I was so afraid . . ." It was hard to continue, but harder still to stop without the words being spoken. "I was so afraid I couldn't even see what it was that was frightening me."

Molly's tone lost the last vestiges of sleepiness. "And now you know?"

Buddy nodded up and down. Yes. Now he knew.

She stood there with him, leaning against him, waiting with him. Surrounded by the night, the two of them finding comfort in the closeness of the years and the love. But she did not ask. Buddy found himself waiting with her, understanding only after a time that Molly did not feel it was her place to ask. But she was waiting, in case he wanted to tell her. Which he did. Very much.

"All this time, I've been thinking that what was making me so afraid was the message. The message and the chance that it would make people more unhappy and more worried and more scared than they already were. But it's not that. Well, it is, but that is not what was at the heart of my fear. I think part of me knew this from the very beginning."

This time she could not hold back the question. "Knew what?"

"That God was going to call me to do something more. Something . . ." He closed his eyes, not against the night, but rather because he wanted to see the dream once more. And there it was, flashing against his eyelids with a power and clarity that made the night and the rain seem like the dream and his vision the reality. The one real part of this all. That and his love for Molly.

Buddy continued in a voice scarcely above a whisper, "I saw a figure bathed in light, standing upon the waters of a lake."

Molly lifted her head clear of his arm, and started to ask, "Who . . ." Then she stopped. There was no need to say more.

"He looked at me," Buddy went on. "I was sitting there in my safe little boat, and He said to me, 'Come.' Just that. 'Come.' He was telling me to step out upon the lake and walk over the waters to Him."

Molly's head grazed against his shoulder as she nodded her understanding. "God wants you to do something more."

"Something big," he agreed quietly. His eyes still shut, striving to hold to the reality of that shining vision, the arms outstretched, the impossible made real. And close. Very close.

Molly whispered, "Are you ready?"

Buddy opened his eyes, and allowed the night to stream in about him. The night and the rain. "I have to be."

─╢ THIRTY-SEVEN ╟─

☐ The North Carolina state legislature building was one of the finest examples of modern design Patrick Allen had ever seen. Designed by a French architect and dressed in white marble, the halls were full of light and the music of water. But on Saturday morning, when Patrick sat by the fountain of an interior courtyard, he was too exhausted and heartsick to care. Five days, seventeen cities, and the hardest week he had ever known. Patrick sat and listened to the fountain and wished he knew what to do.

Footfalls turned him from his musings. James Thaddeus and Elroy Tommkins walked over and dropped their cases at the fountain's edge. "Sorry to make you wait," the pastor said in greeting.

"The storm delayed our flight," Elroy added, his face almost gray with fatigue. "We didn't even stop by the hotel first."

Patrick studied his friend's seamed features, and saw the same concerns that were being etched upon his own heart. "How was Little Rock?"

"Ain't nothing I can put my finger on. But I got the feeling . . ." James Thaddeus sighed, and let his shoulders slump. More than fatigue was burdening this good man. "I hate to say it, brother. Feels like I'm being dishonest to my Lord even to shape the words."

"I know."

Elroy added, "It feels like we were flying along at a hundred miles an hour, when sometime about midweek we hit quicksand and started sinking." The young lawyer had been delighted at Reverend Wilkins's request for him to accompany the older man. James Thaddeus had explained that he needed a brother for the road, someone with the ability to speak the language of law. An educated man with a heart for God. But the five long days were etched deeply into Elroy's features now as he said, "I sure wish I knew where we went wrong."

"You haven't done a thing wrong. I'm certain of that." Patrick also knew the call could not be put off any longer. He reached into his pocket and pulled out his mobile phone.

James Thaddeus demanded, "Who you calling?"

He did not have time to respond, for his son answered on the first ring. "New Jerusalem. Can I help you?"

"Hello, Scott. How are you, son?"

"Dad! Hey, Jeff, it's Dad!" There was a moment's pause, long enough for Jeff to pick up on the extension and say, "Where are you?"

"Raleigh. Know where that is?"

"Come on, Dad, give us something hard."

Scott came on with, "We talked to Mrs. Korda last night. She's back in Aiden taking care of Veronica and Meredith. She said to tell you that Anne and the baby are doing good."

Jeff now. "She said to be sure and tell you to eat proper. She's gonna ask, Dad. Are you?"

"Yes." He wished he could be more sure he had done the right thing, letting them come down to Washington and help out. But they had been so eager, his boys. "How are things around the office?"

"Busy," they said in tandem. Then Scott added, "But not so bad as earlier this week."

"Things are calmer," Jeff added. "We've almost gotten caught up on our mailings."

"That's good, son." But it wasn't good. Not at all. He lifted his head and said to Elroy and James Thaddeus, "Things are growing quieter." He watched the two men nod slowly, understanding perfectly what it meant. Patrick asked his sons, "Are you keeping up with your studies?"

"Yes sir," they chorused, a little glummer now. "Linda is after us every night. She checks everything, Dad."

"She's worse than you are," Jeff agreed.

"Is she around?"

"She was earlier. She gave Clarence the morning off and has been over making more videos."

"Transfer me over, will you?"

"Sure. When are you coming back?"

"Soon as I can. I love you, boys."

"Love you too, Dad. Bye."

There was a series of clicks, then came a voice so familiar he was hearing it in his dreams. "Linda Kee."

"Hi. It's me."

"Patrick. Oh . . . Hello." Normally hearing the lilt she gave to his name was enough to raise a smile. But not today. There was a distance to her voice he had not heard since the dinner in her apartment. "Are you in Raleigh?"

"Yes." She had proved to be the perfect coordinator, helping with schedule changes and fielding a thousand impossible demands with deft precision. It had to be something very bad to have her respond like this. "What's the matter?"

"Nothing."

"Linda, please." He turned his back to the two men standing beside the fountain. "You're our only contact there. You have to tell me. Please."

A long sigh rattled the earpiece, then, "The press came out with an attack against me this morning."

He felt so hollowed by the week's stress it took him a moment to find even one question to ask. "The papers?"

"And television. I don't think anyone around here saw . . ." Another sigh. Shakier this time. "It was horrible."

Patrick was suddenly glad for the numb fatigue which swamped him. "I suppose we should have expected them to do something like this."

"They talked to my former boss at CBS. He was vile. Then they rounded up a couple of . . ."

"Boyfriends," Patrick said quietly, his mantle of exhaustion weighing even heavier now.

"Former ones. Yes. They said I was . . ." The words seemed to pile up, then pour out with a rush. "They said all the things I would say about myself, I suppose. Ambitious and grasping and calculating and manipulative. But it sounded horrible coming from them. And they loved it. One of them was asked what could have possibly driven me to work for . . . I never knew people could be so cruel."

He could only think to ask, "Are you all right?"

"I'll survive." A pause, then, "The question is, do you want me to stay on here?"

"Linda, we all need you. Of course we want you to stay on." He heard the murmur of voices behind him, so he said to her, "Wait just a second." Then he turned and cupped the phone and said, "The press has launched a personal attack against Linda."

"Oh, my." James Thaddeus's features folded even deeper. But Elroy's gaze remained steady. Patrick said, "You knew?"

"I read something about her in the paper on the way up from Arkansas."

He saw the answer in Elroy's face before he asked, "Was it bad?"

"They didn't pull any punches."

James Thaddeus said, "Tell the lady we'll be praying for her."

"Of course we want you to stay on," Patrick repeated to the phone. "I'm sorry, right now I'm so tired and so worried I can't think of anything else to say. But we'll talk as soon as I get in. Linda, I need to speak with Buddy."

More strained now. "I haven't seen him today."

Patrick shook his head at James Thaddeus. "Did you see him yesterday?"

A moment's hesitation, then, "I haven't seen him since Monday. He comes down at night after everybody's gone and raids the refrigerator. But I haven't seen him."

"I need to talk with him."

"Patrick, I'm not sure—"

"This is important. Go upstairs. Tell him that James Thaddeus, Elroy, and I are in Raleigh, and we'll be calling him back in thirty minutes. Tell him it's an emergency." He felt no pleasure when James Thaddeus confirmed his words with another single nod. "Will you do it?"

"But . . . All right."

"Good. I'll call you in thirty minutes."

When he clicked off the phone, James Thaddeus said, "You did the right thing."

Elroy confirmed, "It's time for Mr. Korda to be informed."

When Patrick did not respond, the older pastor went on, "Had me a thought on the way up from Little Rock. Felt like maybe the Spirit was speaking with me, even though I was so tired I felt like two bricks were tied to my eyelids. The idea was, maybe you should give my church the Sunday message."

"James," Patrick sighed his way to his feet. "I don't know when I've felt this tired." *Or this drained of anything worth saying.*

"I ain't pressing. Won't even say a word about it again." James Thaddeus fell into step beside him. "Just telling you how it felt, is all."

□

Linda stood looking at the phone in her hand. She could not deny what she had just heard. Patrick was not just tired. He was worried. He was *frightened.*

She felt a tension run through her, one of such force her entire frame seemed blasted by unseen winds. How *dare* he be frightened? He, the rock that she was leaning on, the man she had come to believe was always strong in his faith and his work. How dare he show her anything but confidence?

Slowly she set down the phone, a careful deliberate motion, and looked around the room, as if seeing it for the first time. The threadbare carpet, so worn in places the boards showed through, the sofa where the stuffing poked through one corner. The cast-off video duplication machinery purring along one wall. The haphazard pile of papers and addresses and mailing envelopes on what had once been a dining room table. The seediness of it all struck her so hard she felt it like a fist in her gut. What had she done? How had she ever thought it would be okay to give it all up and follow this crazy, stupidly illogical course towards . . . What? What was she doing? And why?

And the worst thing was, Patrick had not yet seen the press reports. It was one thing for her to tell him. But another thing entirely for him to see it on the screen or read it in the paper. When she had seen that first article in the *Post,* her stomach had churned so violently she had thought she was going to be physically ill on her doorstep. What would this pastor from a small Delaware town think of her now?

Linda squeezed her eyes shut with a force that knotted the muscles in her temples, pushing out all the confusion and the impossible choices and all the questions for which she had no answers. She had the strength to fashion only two words. They rose out of the tumult in a silent scream of her heart, *Help me.*

The answer was instantly there. *Call Molly.* Its immediacy was such a positive assurance in and of itself, she released a sob of relief as she dialed. She listened to the phone ring at the other end, gripping the receiver now with a fierce urgency. Molly had to be there. She *had* to *be* there.

The familiar voice answered on the first ring. "Korda residence."

"Oh, Molly." She had to stop and choke back the second sob. "I don't think, I never knew . . . I don't . . ."

"Linda? Honey, what's the matter?"

"It's not happening." She permitted herself to say what she had been sensing for two days, but had been able to ignore as long as Patrick had been strong for her. "It's a thousand different problems. Everything is coming apart."

"Wait, let me make sure the girls will be okay while we talk."

The phone was set down, and silence. Linda took a shaky breath, glad beyond belief that she was able to talk with someone. Really talk. Molly came back then, and said, "All right. They're fine. Now then. Start with the worst."

"The worst." A shaky breath. "The worst for me is what the press is saying about me."

"Yes." Still calm. Still there for her. "I saw something this morning. I was wondering whether I should call."

"You're not angry?"

Molly's voice seemed to echo her own surprise. "Dear, why on earth should I be angry?"

Her eyes threatened to spill hot tears. "Because what they're saying is *true.*"

"True then or true now?" Molly waited, and when Linda did not respond, she went on, "One simple fact you will find is, whoever has come to faith later in life will come to God with a past. And do you know what the Lord has said about this? Repent and I will remember your sins no more. They will be as far from Me as the east is from the west. Isn't that reassuring?"

"I suppose it should be, but, well . . ."

"You're worried about how Patrick will react." Molly sighed. "I wish I could answer that for you. He is human, like we all are human. But I do truly think he cares for you. Talk it out. Be honest. And pray."

"All right." Linda's voice was scarcely above a whisper. She was that scared over what she was feeling, and what she feared she was going to lose.

"Was that all?"

"No." She swallowed down the lump in her throat. "There are problems with the work. Not just with what they're saying about me. With everything."

"You're concerned that the amendment is not going to pass, is that what you're saying?"

"There isn't going to *be* any amendment. Things are trailing off. We had a tremendous amount of interest. A flood. But we're not picking up the backing we need from outside this core group. I can't tell you how I know. But I do."

"I won't argue with you, dear. You're the one with all the political experience. What does Patrick say?"

"That's just it." The crushing fear hurtled back. "He called me and said he had to speak to Buddy. I heard it in his voice. He knows it too. He didn't say, but I know, Molly. I *know.*"

"And now you're scared."

"Terrified." Another glance around the shabby house. Ashamed of where she was. "What am I doing here? Can you tell me that?"

"The Lord's work." Calm and placid as ever.

Her laugh sounded manic to her own ears. "Molly, that's not going to hold a lot of water when I go out there and try to find a job."

"Oh, somehow I don't think you'll be going back, at least not in the way you're expecting."

She reached for the nearest chair. Sank down. That or land on the floor. "What?"

"The Lord's call is not for a minute or an hour or a day, dear. It is for *eternity.* When you finish here, you must seek to find what He has planned next for you. He will reveal His purpose for you in time. You mustn't worry. I am absolutely certain He has great things in store."

She leaned one elbow on the table and set her forehead into her palm. A dark curtain fell to shut out all she could not fathom. "Don't worry?"

"Listen, dear. You have made the most common of mistakes. Something we all do from time to time. You have placed your confidence in another person. It is so much easier than trying to be boldly expectant for the invisible. But this is what you must do. You must pray. You must seek the Lord's guidance. You must have faith that He is behind this as well."

Linda did not fully understand, she could not even say if she believed all she was hearing. But she could not deny the peace that flooded her being. And once more she found herself thinking that she wanted what this woman had. "What about Patrick wanting to speak with Buddy?"

"Patrick did not want to hear from Buddy. Do you see? Patrick needed to hear from his Lord."

"But I haven't seen Buddy for days."

"I know. I haven't spoken to him since I left Monday morning. He asked me not to call."

Linda searched for a hint of exasperation. "That doesn't concern you?"

"You mustn't let Buddy's actions worry you. Many of the prophets were considered odd. Ezekiel had many habits that were far stranger than Buddy's. He did not mourn his wife when she died. He suffered a partial loss of speech, perhaps even some sort of seizure, because it is said that the Lord caused others to bind him with ropes. He lay on his side for forty days, and survived on a starvation diet of barley bread and water. He shaved his head with a sword and burned his hair in public." Molly's quiet confidence rang over the telephone line. "The Lord moves in mysterious ways, both then and now. I think Buddy will explain this sudden desire of his to shut himself away in his own time. For the moment it is our task to trust in his ability to hear God's call."

Linda forced herself back upright. It was not the answer she had hoped to hear, but it would do. "What about Patrick's request?"

"I agree with him. If things are as bad as you say, Buddy needs to speak with them. You go upstairs and tell him I said so." She showed a spark of humor. "Wives still have some sway, even when the Lord's hand is close."

□

Gloria Sessions was the senator representing Cabarrus County from North Carolina's farthest eastern reaches. She was also the key instigator of the move to put the constitutional amendment before both state houses.

In almost every state of the union, such a person had appeared. In many cases they had offered their coordinating services before the second video had been released; hearing Buddy's first message had been enough. Some were pastors, other civic leaders, two were housewives, four doctors, a graduate student, eleven state legislators, the mayor of Indianapolis—the list and its variety stretched the length and breadth of the nation. Patrick and James Thaddeus had spoken with almost everyone. Elroy's guidance on legal matters had made him an indispensable member of their little team. They had visited only those who said such a contact would be crucial. Such as here.

Gloria Sessions was in late middle-age, with hair dyed the color of old brass. She had the jaw of a linebacker, and a straight-eyed gaze that promised a will of solid iron. She welcomed them into her office with the question, "Have you seen today's papers?"

"Mr. Tommkins, our legal advisor, has." Patrick studied the woman's face as he eased into his chair. "Linda Kee has already offered to resign. I told her no." Then he waited to gauge the politician's reaction, hurting for Linda, for himself, for the project, for the world.

"I don't think it matters," Senator Sessions replied flatly to the three men seated across from her. "I'll tell you frankly. I just don't see it happening."

When neither Patrick nor James Thaddeus responded, she said for extra emphasis, "I am not speaking, gentlemen, of a Constitutional Convention at this particular moment. I am speaking of the amendment itself. Because I firmly believe that if we miss the mark this time, we will never get this close again. At least not in my political career."

Patrick could not bring himself to speak. A single glance at James Thaddeus and Elroy was enough to reveal that the two black men felt exactly the same—grim and beaten down. It was the same message Patrick had been hearing since Wednesday week. His own protests had been growing quieter with each passing hour, as he saw a true and total defeat. Their efforts were simply not enough.

"Let me spell it out for you." She cupped her hands together, shaping the air on the left side of her desk. "Here we have the believers. Make no mistake, they are eager. They are truly striving to work together. I have been amazed at the efforts I have seen over the past few days. People from every denomination and race, out there gathering signatures for petitions and organizing letter campaigns and personally pressuring their state representatives. Remarkable progress. Just remarkable."

She clipped off the words, "The momentum they created has been enough to get the amendment on the legislative docket. But unless we do something fast, it is going to die on the vine. Now let me tell you why."

She swung her hands to the opposite side of her desk. "Over here we have what I call the permanent opposition. I don't need to spell them out, you know them all by name I'm sure. As we speak, they are organizing their ranks for an all-out attack. Or I should say, they *were.* They can read the signs as clearly as I can, and they know we are headed for failure. So right now I imagine they're whetting their knives and preparing for the next election.

"Because the downside of this, gentlemen, is that I and many of my Christian colleagues have stuck our necks out on this one. We did what we thought God was directing us to do through Buddy Korda and through our own hearts. But with the defeat of this amendment, and all the adverse attention we will have brought on ourselves from those permanently opposed to us and our principles, well, my political career is headed for the disposal."

She shifted her hands to the center of her desk. "And here, right here, is the crux of our problem. The maybes. The people who have been elected on a broad platform, who probably believe in God when it suits them, but who are blowing hot and cold right now. They remember what Buddy's last message foretold. And what's more important, they know their voters remember. So they wait, and they listen. And if they thought this Constitutional Convention had a whisper of a chance, they'd back it. But right now they are patting one another on the head and congratulating each other for showing the good sense to hold back. Why? Because they can see just how bad it is going to be for those of us who supported it come next election time."

"The press has been terrible," Patrick admitted.

Elroy confirmed, "This attack on Linda Kee is just the latest step."

"Friend, this press is *nothing.* Right now they're still not sure what is happening. So they are being as negative as they can and still be *safe.* See where I'm headed?" She did not look weary. She looked old. Every one of

Gloria Sessions' years was vividly portrayed on her face and in her voice. Old and tired and deeply concerned. "Soon as they see that this is going down the tubes, they're going to swing the big guns over and attack us. The Christian crusaders, that's what they're calling us. As soon as the defeat is clear, they're going to start calling us a threat to society as we know it. A terrible danger to the nation's future. A throwback to the days of the scarlet letter. They're going to do their best to bury me, and everyone else they can get their hands on."

Patrick looked at James Thaddeus, wishing he could offer something hopeful. But the reverend looked weary and road-worn as he said, "I heard tell down Little Rock way that the Party has started working against us. Quiet and secret, but pushing hard."

"Doesn't surprise me a bit," she responded without hesitation. "They've decided to do what they've almost always done in the past, which is follow the money."

She looked from one man to the next, clearly wishing they had something positive to offer. When they remained silent, she rose to her feet, gathering them with her. "The proposed church tax bill was enough to stimulate an initial unified response, but now that the administration has backed off, the maybes have climbed back on the fence."

"This church tax," Patrick said, wishing he did not need to ask, wanting to avoid even more bad news, but needing to hear it from someone he could trust, "the administration will raise it again, won't they?"

"Absolutely. This proposed amendment of ours is the perfect galvanizing point, as far as they're concerned. They'll wait until the press has whipped itself to a fever pitch against these Christian marauders, these people who dared threaten the new pluralistic American way of life. Then they'll let this tidal wave of hostility carry their tax bill right through Congress and the courts." She walked around the desk and offered James Thaddeus her hand. "Our only hope is something to magnetize us and the maybes."

"I understand," Patrick said, accepting a grip as strong as his own.

"We need something to draw us all together," she said, walking them to the door. "Something big."

THIRTY-EIGHT

☐ Hesitantly Linda climbed the stairs to the church guesthouse's top floor apartment. She did not know why she was so reluctant, only that the man inside was almost as big a mystery as her own motives. She knocked on the door, and at the sound of a muffled response she opened the door and said, "Mr. Korda?"

"Come in." He watched her emerge around the corner, rising from the dining room table, smiling as best he could. "Don't you think it's time you started calling me Buddy?"

"Patrick just called," she said.

"Come over and sit down." He lowered himself back into the seat. "Would you like something? A cup of coffee?"

"No thank you. Patrick needs to speak with you."

Buddy nodded acceptance of the news, but seemed in no hurry to act. "How are you, Linda?"

"Fine. I'm . . ." She stopped and forced herself to slow down. She lowered herself into the seat. "No. That's not the truth. Not at all. The press started attacking me this morning. I thought you might want me to quit, so the fire storm doesn't take in the movement as well."

"No, no, that's not the answer." Buddy examined her, his gaze as soft as his voice. "It's hard, isn't it? The waiting. The *enduring*."

She looked at him then. Really looked. And saw him for what he was, a small, kindly grandfather. He was a good inch or so shorter than she was, and sparse in build. He wore a loose gray cardigan that matched his hair and seemed to swallow him up, as though he chose it because it would make him appear even smaller than he was. She said, "It's just terrible."

"I sit here and I read the Scriptures and I pray. Or I try to pray. And all I hear is the emptiness. My own lack. My own sins. And I ask myself, Why should God ever want to speak with me again?"

She felt the words echo through her. Of all the things she had expected to find awaiting her in the chamber of a divine messenger, weakness was not on the list. Nor fear. Nor an admission of sin. None of this. No. And yet, and yet, in hearing, she did not feel the same terror as she had from listening to Patrick. No. That was gone now, banished by Molly's quiet words. Instead, she felt that she was seeking to grasp something. Some essential kernel of truth was almost within reach, if only she could identify it. She confessed, "I don't know if I can stand it."

"Alone, none of us can." He waited then, offering her a chance to respond. When she remained silent, he went on. "The Lord said we were to expect difficulties," Buddy said quietly. "I remember how it felt when He spoke that message to me. I remember how clear it all seemed then. How *easy*." He tried to smile, but the sadness in his eyes kept his features from lifting. "It's so much harder now, in the silence, isn't it?"

"Yes." And it truly was a silence. A void. There was no power here and now. Only an apartment almost identical to the ones downstairs, one with a ceiling that sloped where it met the eaves. A silence filled the spaces, not in expectation of power, not in hope of change. Nothing at all. Just two people sitting across the table from one another, sharing all the doubts and weaknesses that came from being human.

Buddy traced a finger down the page of Scripture in front of him, as though seeking what he could not find or what he had lost. Linda studied the man, feeling as though there was something critical here. Something she needed to grasp. She *had* to find it.

Buddy said, "I was never any good at waiting. I live for activity. As long as I am moving, I am able to hide from my own weaknesses."

It hit her then. In one single flash of insight, she realized that here in this shabby little apartment set under the eaves of a prewar Georgetown house, she had finally found the answer. She *understood.*

It was not that they were stronger than her. Not Buddy. Not Patrick.

Not even Reverend Wilkins, with his face of stone and his will of iron. No. They were all weak. *All* of them had questions. *All* of them were afraid. *All* of them doubted.

Molly's message returned to her with a force the quiet woman's voice had not carried. They did not rebuke her for her past. Why? Because *all* of them had fallen short. The power of her realization catapulted her from her chair. She walked to the front window and stared at yet another gray and rainy day. If they were weak, just as weak as she was, what made them different? What was it that set them apart, that gave them the strength . . .

She reached out and traced the line of one falling droplet. The pane was a cheek for the tears of heaven, falling steadily upon the hurting fearful world. She understood now. Yes. It was not that they were stronger. They had simply learned to turn to God for what they did not themselves have. And in the moments when God was not there, their weaknesses and their fears and all the other frailties she had condemned within herself, they were all there.

She turned from the crying day and asked, "Why does God become silent?"

Buddy seemed to have been waiting for the question. Either that or he had been wrestling with it himself. "I wish I knew. I wish I had all the answers. The only thing I can say is that sometimes, when the waiting is over and I'm comforted by His presence once more, I feel as though He moved away in order to draw me forward."

Linda walked over and sat down again, comfortable now in Buddy's presence as she had never been before. She was drawn by the need they now shared—and always would. Always.

"I think He is quiet because He wants me to listen better. To prepare myself more fully for what is to come." Buddy's smile almost made it this time. "At least, that's how it seems when I'm not waiting anymore. Right now, it just seems excruciating."

"Ghastly," Linda quietly confessed.

"Horrible." Buddy nodded, a small man in an oversized cardigan, both hands spread over the Bible's open pages. "The longer I walk with Him, the harder it is to bear the times when He is silent."

Buddy looked away, his eyes seeing something far beyond the room's confines. "Every night this week I've been having a dream. It seems as though every time I close my eyes, the dream is there waiting for me. The image seems to be calling me to rise and walk into a new challenge. A new endeavor for my Lord. And yet when I awaken, there is nothing but this silence. The dream itself is full of peace, but afterward I am left so frightened." He turned toward her, his gaze pierced by his confession. "Every moment that I sit and wait for the Lord to speak, every instant that He keeps me trapped in this amber of silence, I am brought face-to-face with my own poverty."

"I understand," she murmured, tracing a pattern in the table's scratched surface. And she did. Weakness was not something to run from. It was something to *confess*. It was what would draw her closer to God, if only she allowed Him to enter in.

"Would you pray with me?" Buddy asked.

"Yes. Oh yes."

"I need to prepare for Patrick's next call."

Linda bowed her head and closed her eyes. "So do I."

☐

Buddy answered the phone on its first ring. "Hello, Patrick. How are you? Yes, you sound tired." Buddy seemed to shrink further, his shoulders rounding and his eyes closing as he bowed and listened. "I understand. Yes. Of course you've done all you can."

Another pause, Linda standing by the table, waiting and watching as Buddy then said, "No, Patrick. I wish I had something to tell you, but there's been no sense of anything further. No. Nothing at all. The only thing I have to offer is what we heard weeks ago, that the world would place obstacles in our way and . . . Yes, I understand how grave the situation is. I wish I had more to offer, but I don't."

Buddy listened a moment longer, then straightened with an effort. A stronger tone rose with the words, "Yes, Patrick, I understand how worried you and Elroy and James Thaddeus are. I also hear what you have left unsaid. You want me to make a decision. All right. Here it is. Come home. Right now. Come back here and rest."

A pause, then, "Patrick, wait—yes, of course I understand you had appointments scheduled for this afternoon. But what can you do in this frame of mind except share your worries with them? Nothing. So I think you and James Thaddeus and Elroy should come back here."

Linda watched as Buddy closed his eyes once more, accepting the worries and the burdens of his friend. "What will we do? We will wait together, that's what. Take strength from one another, pray, rest, and wait for the Lord to show us His will."

THIRTY-NINE

☐ Thankfully, the majority leader of the Tennessee senate was also the chairman of the state's Judiciary Committee. It meant Royce Calder could strike two birds with one stone. Which by Saturday, at the end of one of the longest weeks of his entire life, was not a bad thing at all.

In the course of his long career, certain adjectives had been used to describe Theodore Blythe—feisty, shifty, king of the pork barrel, argumentative. It was a fine introduction for Royce and Jerry, most especially because the description fit the man, not always the case in political circles. Teddy Blythe was smooth and gravelly in stages, moving easily from sleek pressroom tactics to the brawl of smoky backroom deal-making. He never committed himself without first extracting his pound of flesh. But when it came to pushing his agenda, Teddy Blythe moved with the force of a hurricane.

Which meant he fit Royce Calder like a tailor-made suit.

Teddy Blythe unbuttoned his jacket, loosened his tie, and leaned back in his seat. "Two senior party men with nice-sounding titles all the way down from Washington. And on a Saturday afternoon at that. My, my. Must be something big."

"That depends on you," Royce replied. He had no problem with the Teddy Blythes of this world. They spoke the same language, worked the political arena under the same terms. "You know why we're here."

"I heard something. Got me a call from a buddy in the Ohio senate the other day. Told me you fellers were running scared up there."

Jerry protested, "*Scared* is not the word I would use to describe—"

"We're scared," Royce said, breaking in, but holding to his mild tone. "And you should be too."

"Buddy Korda's a household name around these parts. Got lotsa people feeding their families through these hard times on account of his first message." Teddy Blythe's eyes were surrounded by padded folds, the result of thirty years on the campaign trail. "Hard times."

"If that's the case," Jerry countered, "why haven't you come out in favor of the amendment?"

Teddy kept his gaze on Royce. "Been thinking about doing that very thing."

Jerry started to rise from his seat. "This is a waste of time. Let's go see the others."

Royce remained in his chair, and kept his gaze fastened upon the older man. "But you haven't, have you? Come out. You heard we were making a swing, and you decided to wait and hear what we had to offer."

"Always ready to listen to reason," Blythe affirmed. He dug in his jacket pocket, came out with a thin cigarillo in a plastic mouthpiece. "You fellows mind?"

Jerry snapped, "Sure I mind."

"Go right ahead," Royce said.

"Thankee." He unwrapped the stogie, ignoring Jerry just as Royce was doing. "Reason comes in all sorts of packages these days. What kind of reason are you boys offering?"

"The best kind," Royce said.

Teddy Blythe lit a match, puffed hard, said through the smoke, "I'm listening."

"Jerry here thinks I'm making a mistake. But we've been on the road for six long days, and I'm tired. I don't want to make all the rounds in Tennessee. I want to find one person we can trust, someone with real clout, and let him handle the whole thing."

"Have to be a mighty powerful man," Senator Blythe said easily. "Being able to come up with enough muscle to stop this amendment locomotive."

"And I'm telling you," Jerry groused, "that it's a mistake to be sitting here at all."

"We've got us a package set aside for both Tennessee houses," Royce went on easily. "Seven hundred thousand dollars in campaign funds. Cash. No questions asked. Plus room for a dozen handpicked senators and reps to come to Washington at the president's personal invitation. And federal backing for a statewide project of your personal choosing."

Blythe's manner was as easy as Royce's. "That's some sack of wampum you put together there."

"We like to think so."

Jerry protested, "Look at this guy, Royce. You think he can actually deliver what—"

"Yes," Royce said quietly. "Yes, I do."

Blythe puffed a moment longer, then said, "Two."

"Excuse me?"

"Two statewide projects. A highway bridge we've been dancing with you folks on for nigh on three years, and something else. I'll have that one for you in a day or so."

"Two it is," Royce agreed.

"Always nice to have visitors down here from our nation's capital." Blythe's chair groaned as he shifted his bulk and rose to his feet. "Saw how this morning's papers were tearing into that lady reporter, the one heading up their Washington office, what do they call it?"

"The New Jerusalem Council," Royce said, rising to his feet as well.

"That's the one." Blythe walked around his desk, draped one arm around Royce's shoulders, ignored Jerry entirely. "You fellows responsible for loading the pressroom guns for bear?"

"I don't have any idea what you're talking about," Royce said, satisfaction clear in his quiet voice.

The senator gave Royce's back a congratulatory pat. "Give me until Tuesday. I'll have this thing sewn up tight by Tuesday night or my name's not Teddy Blythe."

"I knew we had chosen correctly." Royce moved through the doorway, easing out from under the senator's arm. "Good day, Senator."

Jerry waited until they had left the state building and rushed through the storm to the car before allowing his grin to show. "How did I do?"

"You'll never make it on Broadway."

"What are you talking about? I did great. Admit it. I was the perfect bad cop. Perfect."

"Maybe so," Royce said, starting the car. "But that guy was sold long before we got there."

"Yeah, ain't it nice to have others do the work for you." Jerry sighed down into his seat. "Man, am I ever bushed."

"I think it's time to go back to Washington."

"Oh yeah. My own bed. Home-cooked meal."

"You're a bachelor and you don't cook."

"A frozen dinner in my own microwave, then." He squinted at the fleece-lined sky. "Don't like flying in this weather."

Royce ignored the comment. Jerry had said the same words before every flight that entire journey. "I was thinking about stopping by that church of theirs next week."

"New Jerusalem," Jerry droled. "They ought to rename that council of theirs the 'Cemetery for Lost Hope.' You gonna wield the ax yourself?"

"Don't be absurd. I just want to offer these amendment organizers the hand of peace." Royce pulled from the curb. "Monday morning I am going by that church on P Street to see who has cost the Party so much in the way of money, favors, and lost sleep."

Jerry waited. "And?"

"And I want to see if I can enlist Korda in backing our church tax plan."

Jerry laughed out loud. "Talk about rubbing salt into their wounds."

"You never can tell. A man this far down might see it as a last chance to stay in the limelight. Get his picture taken with the president, maybe not for the bill he wanted, but up there just the same. The result's no different. He's still got a good picture for his power wall."

Jerry closed his eyes and laughed softly. "You're like a pit bull, you know that? Get a hold of something and you never let go."

Royce liked that thought so much it kept him smiling all the way to the airport.

⊣‖ FORTY ‖⊢

☐ That Sunday morning, the redbrick P Street church was packed. The vestibule was so full the ushers and deacons questioned each newcomer in turn, asking who they came to be with—Buddy Korda or the Lord. The elders' quiet solemnity was enough to turn away many of the journalists and sensation seekers. The remainder were swallowed by the crowd. They filled every seat, jamming the pews tight. They lined the side aisles, the taller heads turned a rainbow of colors by the stained-glass windows.

The congregation was mostly black, but there were enough whites and Hispanics and Asians that no one could feel isolated by their race. Linda sat toward the front in the row behind Buddy and Molly. She was seated between Alex and Agatha, with Jeff and Scott a little farther down the aisle along with a group of James Thaddeus' grandchildren. She breathed air scented with hair pomade, bath salts, and talcum powder, and hoped that today she might finally find some answers.

The understanding and the peace she had felt in Buddy's office had not solidified into lasting convictions. Linda felt as though she stood in the shadows of her own past, looking at a door she could not open. Frustrated and afraid and very aware of her own weaknesses. Knowing she would walk from the comfort of this crowded room, with the magnificent voices singing words of praise and peace, and enter anew the cold, harsh world. Knowing just how easy it would be to choose wrong again, as she had so often before. Yes. So often.

She had spent all day Saturday waiting for the ax to fall. Linda had forced herself to enter the offices and continue with her work, answering the phone and fielding the questions, even though every face and every voice seemed to hold a note of condemnation. She was not concerned about strangers' questions, however. She was waiting for Patrick to ask her to leave—for the good of the council. She could hear his words now, and knew what else would be behind it. How he did not want to see her any more, how he needed to protect his boys from the influence of someone like her. But he had only called to say he was taking the day off to rest, nothing more. Waiting had stretched the hours like taffy.

Even so, Saturday had held only two difficult trials, two moments when she had almost lost control. One was when Jeff had come up and said he was sorry. Just that. He was sorry someone had hurt her. His quiet voice and his caring eyes had threatened to rip her composure to shreds. She had been unable to do more than nod and turn away. But ten minutes later, one of the older women who staffed the phone lines had come up and taken Linda in a fierce hug, and in a honey-laced whisper had said, "We're all praying for you, honey. Every last one of us. Don't you forget. You can rely on God's shield." Linda had broken away and fled to the guest house, and spent the remainder of the day there in hiding. Waiting for Patrick to come and tell her it was over.

Now Linda sat among the congregation, looked up to where Patrick sat in the high-back chair by the podium, and studied him with the frankness of anonymity. She saw the wounds that the week had inflicted, and the wounds that were deeper still. He looked beaten down, exhausted. She did not know how he had been before, back in a world untouched by the current fierce winds. But seeing the raw power he possessed even now, she could well imagine the handsome football star gripping the podium with arms and shoulders bunched as if he were headed straight for the goal line. A powerful teacher. A winner. And yet, because of this power and this success, a little untouchable. Yes, it was possible to look at that tired face and see the man he had been before.

James Thaddeus rose to his feet and welcomed the crowd. He kept his prayer and his opening words simple and brief. Most of them knew his brother Patrick by now. The man was too tired to be up there. Yes. They both were. Tired and weighed down with the Lord's work. But James Thaddeus had felt that Patrick had a message to be shared. What it was, James Thaddeus did not know. But the man needed their prayers, yes, they all did, all of them working on God's purpose. So pray this man through his work today, and the work to come. Yes. Join with them all in prayer.

Patrick rose and approached the podium, and Linda knew that this time she was not listening with a journalist's distance. No. This time she was too desperate to maintain her lie of supposed objectivity. She was not there to criticize or analyze or scrutinize. No. This time she came looking for answers she knew she did not have, and knew she needed desperately.

"My guess is that everyone gathered here today is struggling to find a balance in their lives," Patrick began. "A balance between what they feel their calling to be, their *potential,* and still overcome all the problems that beset them." He waited through a quiet humming of affirmation, then went on, "We hunger to maximize our life and our talents, to become all that we can be. Yet we are caught in a constant swirling undertow of problems and failings and just plain human weakness."

A voice from the back called out, "Say it, brother!"

"The reality of life, especially in a troubling time like now, is that it is so easy to become caught in the mire of problems and difficult choices. Not only that, it is so easy to *focus* upon these problems. Extremely easy. Deadly easy. And the truth is, there is nothing that will rob you of life's potential faster than focusing upon the problem. Of looking at choices, and seeing only dangers."

Linda listened, and knew that the power was with Patrick still. But not the distance. He was bonded to those he taught by a shared understanding of pain. His wisdom of suffering was no longer merely of the mind. He *felt* for them. Perhaps his words were exactly the same as before, but certainly not his gaze. Nor his tone. He *cared* for these people. He *served* them. The crowd recognized this as well, and began singing out their chorus of punctuations, finishing each sentence for him, filling the hall with amens and clapping and urges for him to go on, take them further, show them the Way.

"God intends for His people to live *abundantly.* Even here, even now, God wishes for us, *all* of us, to realize our *full* potential." He waited through the response, then continued, "But not the potential we seek for ourselves. No. God wishes for us the potential, the direction, the *calling* He has chosen for us.

"But in a time of lack and worry and almost overwhelming problems, how are we to have this abundance? How do we know which choices to make? To find the answer to this question, I ask that you turn with me now to the book of Joshua."

From his place beside her, Alex thumbed the pages of his Bible with easy familiarity. He found his place and held it so she could read with him. Yet while she listened, her eye remained caught by everything else the pages before her revealed—Alex had underlined selected verses in two colored inks. He had highlighted other passages in yellow. Notes were scrawled along the top and bottom and in all four corners. Linda listened and read and wondered if she could even find her Bible, or if it was still somewhere in her apartment to be found.

"'Choose this day whom ye shall serve,'" Patrick went on. "In this one small sentence we find guidance for *all* our choices. Why? Because through-out the Scriptures we are told that whenever we are faced with a dilemma, we are to *choose God*. Whenever we are confronted with a problem or chal-lenge or fear, we are to *seek out our Lord*.

"We must keep our eyes upon the hills. Seek the everlasting answer. Desire first and foremost the divine wisdom that is God's and God's alone.

"When we accept this, we recognize that, in truth, we do not have a thousand choices to make. We have just one. We do not have a million problems. We have one. One problem, pressed upon us in a myriad of worldly guises. The problem may be masked within fear or worry or want or pain or loss or anger or a thousand other forms. Whatever the name we place upon this problem, when we focus upon it we are *instantly* threat-ened by defeat. Why? Because in that moment we are focusing upon God's *absence*. Instead, in *all* things, in *every* decision foisted upon us by this con-fusing world, we must make the *one* choice. We must turn toward our Lord, and seek His will."

The pastor kept on speaking, but Linda found herself halted. Stopped cold. Turned inward. The congregation and the words and the cross upon the wall, all became part and parcel of one giant mirror. Pointing inside herself.

Linda found no solace in looking down. Alex's Bible lay open halfway on his lap and halfway on hers. The only words she could focus on were those highlighted and underlined and starred, the ones that seemed to rise from the page and resound through her trembling heart. *Choose this day whom ye shall serve.*

Linda looked back up at the pulpit. She realized Patrick was winding down his sermon, but the words flowed about her without registering. Her mind remained caught by her response to this quiet command. She could not be sure of making the next right choice. This time, perhaps. But *next* time, no. She knew that now. All her focused drive and all her intelligence came to naught in the face of this constant challenge. Time after time she had been brought up short by the temptations of life and the pains of her past. Her ambition and her hunger to succeed and her desire to be recognized—and her fear of what faith might cost her. Yes. Even that. She studied the pastor whose words she could no longer hear, and silently she whispered to him the truth she had been unable to tell herself. *I am too weak. Sooner or later I'll get it wrong again.*

She stopped because there was nothing more to say. Defeat overwhelmed her to the point that she could not escape the next surfacing thought. The one that whispered to her breaking heart that she was not worthy of this man.

A tear seared its way down one cheek. She did not have the strength to lift her hand and wipe it away. Not because she was defeated. No. Because in that moment she had come to accept what her heart already knew. She was deeply, fervently, desperately in love with Patrick Allen. Yet she was not good enough, not strong enough. And her weaknesses were now out there on public display.

In the silence of aching inner sorrow, her mind focused once again on what lay beyond the boundaries of her own painful void. She looked up, and though Patrick's image swam now, she heard him clearly say, "This is not just an altar call for those who do not know the Lord Jesus. Today I invite all who are weak. All who feel unable, in and of themselves, to hold to God's course."

He opened his arms, his right hand sealed around the Bible, and spoke not to a congregation but to her. "Brothers and sisters, to come forward is not an admission of error. We are *all* weak. All of us have fallen short of God's call. But those who today face choices beyond their own ability to fathom, to those I say, Come! In your weakness will God's power be revealed. Come!"

The draw was so strong Linda was up and out of her seat before the choir had risen to begin the final song. Alex was in the process of reaching for his hymnal, but she brushed his hand aside and almost skipped over the feet of the next person in her haste to make the center aisle.

She was halfway up the aisle she could scarcely see before the first word was sung. She did not know what she would do when she arrived at the front. She only knew she had to go. She *had* to.

And Patrick was there to greet her. Tall, strong, and wounded Patrick. All she could see through the mist of unshed tears were his eyes. The caring. The welcome.

He knelt with her by the front step leading up to the altar. Put his arm around her shaking shoulders, placed his other hand upon her arm, and spoke words that seemed to wash over her with love and concern. His love and yet not his at all.

For the first time in her entire mangled life, Linda felt something more than that which she could touch and hold and define. As she knelt and wept and strived to hear what Patrick was saying to God on her behalf, she knew that they were not alone. She *knew* it.

And through the veil of her broken heart, she heard a second voice whisper to her. One so soft it did not speak to her ear or her mind at all. Rather, it whispered directly to her soul. A voice that revealed what had been missing from her vision of faith. A voice that disclosed what lay *beyond* pain. What resided upon the eternal altar, untouched by striving or sacrifice or earthly woes. The infinite gift, the everlasting mystery now revealed. That which was hers, now and forevermore.

⊣ǁ FORTY-ONE ǁ⊢

☐ Monday morning found Royce Calder so cheerful he did not mind the weather. Not even when he pulled up in front of the New Jerusalem Church on P Street and got out of his car and felt as though the wind had just been waiting for the chance to fling dirt into his face.

He squinted and raced for the church offices, just as the first big drops began pelting from a sky more black than gray. The place was a hive of activity. He straightened his hair and his jacket and looked around. The first impression came as a surprise.

There was none of the sense of gloom he had expected to find. He had seen his share of campaign centers caught on the losing end. In this hall, with its teeming activity and scurrying people, he found none of the weary defeat he was expecting. Just the opposite.

"Can I help you?"

Royce turned to find himself facing a black teenager in a blue blazer and gray slacks, with a white shirt and dark tie. The outfit was a good idea, but the kid did not know what to do with it. Clearly he had seldom worn anything like a suit before. Instead of proper shoes, he wore black sneakers. His tie was skewed hard to the left. One cuff of his shirt dangled almost to his fingertips while the other was tucked up somewhere inside his jacket sleeve. This kid would have lasted precisely three seconds in any campaign office Royce had been managing. "I'd like to see Mr. Korda."

"Oh. Right." The kid gave him a moment's hard stare, then scouted the room and shouted, "Scott, get over here."

A tall white kid rose from a computer terminal and walked over. He wore the same blue blazer and gray slacks, but was clearly more at ease with his outfit. Yet this young man's attitude was also far too casual. "What's up?"

The black teenager said, "The man here wants to see Buddy."

Royce held to his mild exterior. Inwardly he smirked. A truly amateurish operation. People this young should never be permitted to greet the public. "I tried to call a number of times this morning, but all your lines have been engaged."

"Yes sir, things have been busy around here." The kid offered his hand. "I'm Scott Allen."

"Very nice to meet you." Royce accepted the hand, wondering at the calm self-possession in a boy of this age, and he searched for some sense of failure in those clear eyes. "Allen, Allen, I know I've heard that name."

"My dad is Patrick Allen."

"Of course, the pastor who has been leading this campaign."

"He ain't the leader," the black young man huffed, "and this ain't no *campaign.*"

Scott silenced the younger boy with a single look. "I'm sorry. Buddy Korda isn't seeing anyone just now."

"I understand," Calder replied, keeping every vestige of satisfaction from his voice. Ignoring the hard stare the black boy was giving him, Royce handed over a card, one with the seal of the President of the United States embossed at the top, and the Pennsylvania Avenue address. "But perhaps he would like to make an exception in my case."

Scott's eyebrows shot up as he read out loud, "White House assistant director of domestic policy."

"My, my," the black youth said, sarcasm strong in his voice. "Ain't we just something else."

Royce shot the black teen a glance that would have frozen anyone who knew him better. The youngster just lowered his lids a fraction, and gave him a look that was straight from the streets. Sullen and angry.

Royce turned back to Scott and said, "I'd be grateful if you could please tell Mr. Korda that the president has asked me to convey a personal message."

Scott seemed caught by indecision, then said, "I better go see if Linda's around."

The black teenager's gaze did not shift from Royce's face. "Yeah, you do that."

Royce caught his smile before it reached the surface. Yes. Linda Kee. He wanted to see her too. It was time to spread some poison in that direction. Inject some genuine fear of what the future held for people who strayed into the religious fringe.

The black teen continued his squinty-eyed scrutiny, surprising Royce with his focused intensity. When Scott was well out of range, he hissed, "Don't you go sticking nothing you find 'round here in your pockets, you hear what I'm saying?"

Before Royce could recover enough to come up with a response, the youngster had wheeled about and sprinted from the room. Royce raised one hand to pat down his immaculate hair, his only external sign of irritation. He forced himself to put the teen out of his mind, and concentrated on the hall.

At closer inspection, he still found nothing that signaled downfall and defeat. Six young black ladies were stacking videos and filling out mail-forms. One of them was humming what apparently was a hymn. Across from them nine older women staffed a cluster of phones, many of them handling more than one line at a time. One of them finally hung up, saw no further flashing lights, and smiled over to him. "Can I get you a cup of coffee?"

"No thank you, ma'am."

"How 'bout a cola?"

"I'm fine, thank you."

"You just sit yourself down over there and make yourself at home. Scott won't be long." The phone in front of her started flashing. "I declare, it hasn't let up once all day."

Which was a tremendous astonishment. From his position Royce could look down the back hallway into a further trio of large rooms. All of them were hives of activity. This was not a campaign on the decline. These people acted like winners.

He turned around to mask his confusion, and stared out the window at the storm-clad sky. Either they had yet to discover that their little project was about to come crashing down around their knees, or they knew something Royce did not. Despite the fact that this was almost impossible, he could not escape a single shiver of apprehension.

□

In spite of all the logic her analytical mind could bring to bear, Linda found herself unable to focus upon the impending defeat—or give any more thought to the papers' vicious reporting of her private life. Her *former* private life. Nor was she able to worry about her future. Though she had every reason to chafe over everything that was going wrong, she couldn't. It was impossible.

Since departing the church, she had remained positively *filled* by the feeling that everything was going to be all right. The simple calm had pervaded her every waking moment.

After a long and happy Sunday lunch at the Wilkins residence, they had returned to the little guest house, where they had prayed and laughed and rested. She had left there only long enough to be creamed by Jeff and Scott and JT and Little G and Josh on the computer games in James Thaddeus's front room.

Without planning, without discussion, every hour or so they had gathered in the guest house's second-floor apartment. Sometimes they had talked, sometimes just sat in silence, sometimes spoke about their fears—but not often. Somehow the fears and the worries just did not seem to have any place in that incredible time. Even the lines on James Thaddeus's face had softened, and by Sunday afternoon he was smiling as much as the others. All part of something they did not understand, and for the moment did not need to.

That Monday morning they had gathered once more, and talked long and hard about what should be done next. Linda, Buddy, Molly, Alex, Agatha, Elaine, James Thaddeus, Scott, Jeff, Elroy, Clarence, JT, Little G, Josh, Patrick—a group growing closer and closer by sharing both prayer and their own weaknesses. She had never known it could be so good to be weak. Had never *imagined* anything like this could even exist. Yet here they were, seated together and waiting. Waiting in peace. Waiting and knowing it was right to wait.

They decided nothing should be done differently until they heard further direction from the Lord. It seemed the most natural thing in the world, as though there could not have been any other decision taken. As though it had been decided long before they had even gathered.

Patrick and Molly and Agatha and James Thaddeus and Elaine and Clarence and Elroy had all gone up to the third floor to start a long prayer session. Linda had declined, saying she was too restless, and she was glad to see Alex felt the same way. She saw the thrill on Clarence's and Elroy's faces when Buddy had personally asked them to come up and pray. And knew she was witnessing the power of a bonding that would remain with her for all her life. No matter where she might go, however far she might travel from this time and these people, they would forever remain a part of her life and her walk and her heart.

Which was why she was smiling and humming a little tune as she worked the video-duplicating machines, when Scott came in and declared, "We got company."

"Who is it?"

He read from the card he was holding, "Royce Calder, White House assistant director of domestic policy."

She stopped in mid-flow. "You have got to be kidding me."

"No ma'am. And he wants to see Buddy. He says the president sent him over with a message." The thought left Scott positively bug-eyed. "The president of the United States."

"Wait just a second." Linda glanced in the cracked mirror over the mantelpiece, straightened her hair, and wished she had worn something more elegant. She looked into her own eyes, and wondered how she could have lost the peace so swiftly. It made her feel as though she had spent the entire weekend lying to herself.

No, that wasn't right. She forced herself to stop and accept the truth of what she had known. What she was knowing now.

"Linda?"

"Just a minute." She bowed her head. If the weekend had taught her anything, it was that sometimes the best thing she could do was stop and admit she could not do this alone. That she had to turn and focus on God, and ask His help. Like now.

Her swift little prayer was interrupted by the sound of thumps up the stairs, and the sound of a voice complaining, "Stop your doggoned tugging!"

Josh came into view, hauling hard on the older man's arm. "I'm telling you, Mr. Alex, this here is *urgent business!*"

"It may be, son, but I won't do anybody any good falling down these stairs!" Alex leaned heavily on the doorjamb. A wide-eyed Jeff came bounding into view behind them. When Alex had gathered enough wind, he puffed, "This boy is dead-set and determined to weary me straight into my grave."

"I ain't doing nothing of the kind," Josh huffed. "Listen, Miss Linda, I got a feeling about that man. A *bad* feeling."

Scott protested, "He's coming from the White House!"

"And I'm telling you, you don't know nothing about *bad!*" Josh's eyes had a wild look to them. "I seen bad out on the street, Miss Linda. All *kinds* of bad. I *know* what I'm saying!"

Jeff spoke for the first time. "I think maybe you should listen to him, Linda."

Scott looked at his younger brother. "Who asked you?"

"Nobody." Not even his brother could rock Jeff's determined calm. "But I'm saying it just the same." Then Jeff said to Linda, "I think this is important."

Josh let go of Alex so he could use both arms for semaphoring danger. "Dead right, it's important!"

"Calm down, son," Alex said.

"Ain't no time for calming. This White House man, he's *danger.* He's *bad.* You got to listen to me, Miss Linda!"

She walked over and knelt down in front of the young teen. "All right. I'm listening. Now what is it you want me to do?"

Josh had to take a calming breath before he could say, "Don't you be going in there alone!"

☐

"Mr. Calder?"

Royce turned from his perusal of the window to face a woman of truly startling beauty. He offered a smile and his hand. "Ms. Kee. I would recognize you anywhere."

She seemed very hesitant, but in the end did the polite thing and accepted his handshake. Royce felt satisfaction. Finally here was a woman who knew the outside world. Of course she was uncertain. She was aware of what was going on beyond the borders of this little dreamworld. It was going to be a genuine pleasure to bring her down. Royce continued, "Thank you so much for taking the time to see me."

She replied with, "I'd like to introduce Alex Korda, Buddy's older brother."

"An honor, sir," Royce replied, which was an absolute lie. The man standing before him was genuinely bizarre. He wore a loud checkered jacket and rumpled shirt over a frame that was so thin it was almost skeletal. He leaned heavily on a cane, and wore what appeared to be a hand-knotted bow tie. Several odd tufts of red hair sprouted from what otherwise was a completely bald head. And he wore the thickest glasses Royce had ever seen. "I have been hearing your brother's name spoken with respect for years."

Korda gave his hand the quickest shake Royce had ever known, then pointed with his cane down the hall. "I believe there's a room free right along that way."

Royce said to Linda, "I was led to understand your operations were centered in a house somewhat separated from the church itself."

"And I'm telling you there's a meeting room we can use right down here," Alex said, and stumped away.

"Please, if you would," Linda said, apparently restrained by Alex's brashness.

"Certainly." He almost purred the word. Linda Kee was the weak link. He followed Alex Korda down the hall, knowing he had to get her alone. Then he would slip out the pincers and squeeze.

□

Perhaps it was just because Josh had been so alarmed. But Linda did not think so.

There was absolutely nothing on the outside to signal anything adverse about Royce Calder. He wore a pin-striped three-piece suit over a frame that was remarkably similar to Buddy's—small and slender and compact—though Royce was somewhat younger. His gray hair was carefully styled and held in place by hair spray—Linda knew because she could smell it as she followed Royce down the hall and into the empty conference room. There was nothing exotic about this, a number of male politicians used it to ensure they were ready for the camera at any time. But it added to the man's tightly controlled exterior. Everything about him seemed shellacked into place—the perfectly starched shirt, the carefully knotted tie, the bland voice, the mildly surprised expression, the careful brown eyes. Eyes as blank as a concrete wall.

Alex pointed Royce to a seat with his cane, then held out a chair on the table's opposite side for Linda. She noticed a tiny flicker of something on the bureaucrat's face, and realized he wanted her closer. It made her gladder still that Alex was there with her. She seated herself and said, "What can we do for you, Mr. Calder?"

"I was hoping that it might be possible to have a minute of Buddy Korda's time."

"I'm afraid that's not possible today."

His bland expression shifted with a slight raising of his eyebrows. "Don't you think an emissary from the president of the United States deserves to have Mr. Korda respond for himself?"

"The lady speaks for my brother, and so do I." Alex's voice grated cold and hard. "He is not in to visitors."

"I see. Well, perhaps you would be so kind as to say that the president would be grateful to have an opportunity to meet with him."

Linda could not mask her surprise. "President Gifford wishes to meet with Mr. Korda?"

"Most certainly. You yourself know how much attention this proposed amendment has received. There are certain aspects of it that the president is interested in seeing enacted into law. Not as an amendment to our Constitution, you understand. But some of the underlying concerns must certainly be addressed."

"I'm sorry, I don't follow you," she said.

"If anything, the sudden groundswell of support for this amendment has shown us at the White House just how great a concern the underlying issues are to a certain portion of our constituency." The man's tone was so bland as to mask the words within a harmless drone. The eyes held nothing but the mildest interest, the face nothing at all.

And yet Linda could not release the clench of nerves that tightened her gut. "Why would the president wish to meet with Buddy if he is already aware of these things?"

"Well, for one thing, we would like to know the position of this amendment's leader on a number of issues." Royce Calder lifted the edges of his mouth. The smile was like wax being pulled on a dummy's face. "To begin with, we are not certain of Mr. Korda's political views."

"That's easy enough to answer," Alex replied sharply. "My brother is a radical traditionalist. He fights against the slide away from God."

For Linda, the final word seemed to echo through the chamber. As though the air itself rang with the power of enacting the name. Royce simply turned his bland stare toward Alex. "I would certainly appreciate it, Mr. Korda, if you would pass on to your brother our interest in seeing his deepest concerns met."

Alex nodded slowly. "I'll tell you something, mister. I've been in business all my life, and I've met some sharp ones. And you are the sharpest. By a mile. But there's one thing all you sharp fellows have in common. You don't do nothing for nothing. You wouldn't cross the street unless it was to your favor. So I'm gonna ask you for the simple truth. What do you want out of seeing my brother?"

"Why, merely to see where we are in harmony." If Calder was ruffled by Alex's tone, he did not show it one iota. "There are so many possibilities for us to reinforce one another's objectives."

Then it hit her. The slight vibration within the chamber's atmosphere coalesced into a thought that was more than just an impression. It was a certainty. Linda said, "The church tax bill."

For once, Royce Calder showed genuine surprise. He jerked in his seat as though a current had been shot through the soles of his feet. "Excuse me?"

"That's it, isn't it?" Linda turned to Alex. "They are trying to bring Buddy in so they can apply some arm-twisting and horsetrading, and get him to come out in favor of this church tax of theirs." She turned back to Royce, and took great satisfaction in seeing the spark deep in those bland brown eyes. "I'm right. I know I'm right."

"Miss Kee . . . I came here representing the highest authority in our nation—"

"You sure got that one wrong," Alex interjected.

"—and I can assure you that the last thing on my mind is, as you call it, horsetrading."

Alex snorted. "Pal, I'll tell you something. Coming as close to death's door as I did has made me pretty impatient with nonsense. And that's what you're talking. Of a highly distilled variety."

"That, Mr. Korda, is your opinion."

"It sure to goodness is." Alex slid his cane out from the table, grasped the head, and pushed back his chair. "If somebody were to come up and tell me they were a new breed of poached egg, I'd believe them before I'd believe you. And I'd do the same thing I'm gonna do now, sir." Alex rose to his feet. "Which is get up and leave the room." He looked down at Linda and demanded, "You had enough of this man yet?"

She had never felt better about an ending than this very moment, which was why she could stand and look down at the astonished Royce Calder and say with genuine satisfaction, "Thank you so much for stopping by. Good day."

⊣| FORTY-TWO |⊢

☐ Linda awoke just before dawn on Tuesday, feeling as though a hand had shaken her hard. She stared into the quiet darkness of her apartment and wondered what it was. She rose from her bed, slipped on her robe, and walked into the kitchen to make some coffee. But as she started to pull down a mug, she had the strong feeling that even this was wrong. A sense of urgency gripped her. A need to be elsewhere.

Then it hit her. She raced to the back window, and stared out at the night.

The wind had stopped.

The predawn was utterly still. She could not see any stars, but after months of endless storm, the absence of wind left her unsettled. Yet it was more than just the night's silence. Something was pricking at her heart, something that left her feeling that she had to act, and act *now*.

She threw on some clothes and telephoned for a taxi. She was a true city girl and had not owned a car for some time. Her apartment did not come with parking, and these days a car left on the street overnight was a car gone forever. She stood by the front window waiting for the headlights to appear, and as soon as she saw the taxi's rooflight turn the corner she raced down the stairs. Even before she piled into the backseat, she said, "The New Jerusalem Church on P Street."

The entire journey she argued with herself, worried over arriving so early and waking the entire family. But when the cab pulled up in front of the church, it seemed as though every light was on—in the church, in the guest house, in the Wilkins residence. She paid the cab and got out, feeling a thrill at having gotten something very right.

She raced to the guest house and was greeted by the sound of singing. A woman's voice, one she recognized as belonging to Elaine Wilkins, was singing the old hymn "Amazing Grace." Slow in cadence, loving every word, holding the notes until she ran out of breath. In no hurry to go anywhere.

The music slowed Linda right down, calmed her so that she stilled her heart's frantic beating before opening the door. Elaine stopped her singing long enough to smile a welcome and say, "You hear the call, too, honey?"

"I don't know what it was."

"Uh-huh. I do believe your head's doing the talking just now, and not your heart." Elaine went back to cutting dough into biscuit shapes with a water glass. "That sound right to you?"

"Yes." Glad she was able to admit it to someone. "I didn't even stop for a cup of coffee."

"Got a pot simmering right over there. Help yourself." She settled the last of the dough into place and slid the tray into the oven. "Clarence and his wife just got here. Alex has gone back over to the motel to wake up Agatha. Says he don't want her missing all the fun, she can have her beauty sleep up in heaven." She humphed a laugh. "They make some pair, yes, they surely do."

"Can I give you a hand?"

"Thank you, but I got a kitchen full of helpers over at my place. So many cooking and talking, I came over here for some peace." She glanced through the oven's glass front. "These biscuits will keep everybody quiet 'til the big meal's done."

"Where is everybody else?"

"Up the stairs, honey. Just follow the sound of God's people calling out His name. You'll find them soon enough."

Linda took her mug and started back through the apartment. "Did you notice the wind has stopped?"

"Yes, I surely did." Elaine fiddled with the oven's dial. "I guess God wants to make sure He's got everybody's attention."

As she passed the fireplace, Linda's eye was caught by the little card leaning on the mantel. She walked over to read Molly's Bible quote for the day. It came from the fiftieth Psalm, and said, "Call upon Me in the day of trouble; I will deliver you, and you shall glorify Me."

She turned back to the kitchen and asked, "Attention for what?"

Elaine grinned at the younger woman. "Oh, I 'spect we'll be finding that out soon enough."

☐

Even in the crowded third-floor apartment, Buddy managed to find a place unto himself. He sat apart from the main gathering, more in the kitchen than in the living room. Molly was midway between the group and Buddy. Every once in a while she would reach over and squeeze his hand. Other than that, people left him alone, which was good. For while his body might have been there close to the gathering, his mind and heart still resonated with the power of what he had experienced before rising.

The dream had awoken him once more. The same dream he had been having all week. Yet this time it had been different. The light had shone so brilliantly over the water that Buddy had felt blinded by its power. Even so, he could not turn away. He had stood there in the boat, looking out over the waters to where the light shone and waited. This time, when the voice had called, *"Come,"* Buddy had stepped out onto the surface of the water.

And the light had flowed out to surround and consume him. And Buddy Korda had awoken, knowing he had done as God intended.

Yet at the same time, he had known that whatever lay ahead, it would challenge him in a most unexpected way. And every time he thought of this, he could feel his entire being tremble like a leaf in a hurricane. So he sat there with his back to the gathering and the Bible open in his lap, and he quivered. His fear could not be denied.

His prayer was constant, and one sentence long: *Lord, when it comes, whatever it is, give me the strength and the wisdom to get it right.*

☐

Linda walked up the stairs and was instantly gathered into the heart of the group. They prayed and they talked quietly about how God had worked in their lives. They gave thanks for many things. Molly spoke at length about her newest grandbaby, Josiah, and his miraculous recovery.

James Thaddeus spoke about the lessons he had learned from Buddy's disappearance into the storm.

Little glances were cast toward the small man with his head bowed over the Book in his lap. Despite her own curiosity, however, Linda found it hard to look at Buddy for long. Somehow she had the impression that it was wrong of her to disturb his privacy in any way.

After Elaine came up the stairs and passed around a basket of piping hot biscuits, Clarence described how much it meant to have worked on this project, how it felt as though all his training and work to that point had simply been getting him ready. Elroy spoke after him, describing how, even in the midst of the defeat and the fatigue, still he had felt sheltered out there on the road. He struggled to put into words how honored he felt to be a part of this, how *empowered*. The group watched and listened as this intelligent young man had difficulty finding the words. Heads nodding around the group. They surely understood.

Scott then gave thanks for Josh and his watchful eye the day before, spotting the White House man for what he was. Josh stumbled over the words, but gave quiet thanks for Jeff and what he had said the week before about loss and sorrow. Linda glanced at Jeff, saw a young man whose gaze seemed to finally be losing that wounded and empty central space. She then watched James Thaddeus reach over and grip Josh's hand. Holding it long and hard, saying only, "You did good, son."

Linda felt a growing need to speak. She did not want to, but the morning seemed full of an ability to overcome her logic and her objections. So when the group next grew silent, she swallowed hard, and looked at Patrick and said, "I need to thank you. I mean, I want to give thanks for you. No, not for you. For your sermon yesterday. Well, for you, too, of course." She found herself glancing at James Thaddeus. "I'm sorry. I don't know how to say it right."

"Ain't no right way or wrong way," James Thaddeus said in his gentle, deep voice. "If God's in your heart, that's all that matters."

Elaine echoed her husband. "Go on, honey. You're doing just fine."

So she took another breath and said, "During your sermon, I felt as though you were speaking just for me. As though the words were aimed straight for my heart. But at the same time I didn't feel I was listening to you at all. Not to you, Patrick Allen, my friend. I was hearing a teacher.

Someone who was talking for God. Talking from *inside* God." She hung her head. "Oh, I don't know what I'm trying to say."

But the laughter she expected did not come. Instead, James Thaddeus murmured, "You said it right, sister. You said it right."

Which gave her the strength to raise her head and find Patrick looking at her with a gaze as deep and open as she had ever seen. "That was," he said quietly, "the nicest compliment anyone has ever paid me. Ever. In my entire life."

Elaine rose to her feet, and announced, "I do believe breakfast ought to be ready by now."

□

Buddy did not join them for the meal, and the plate Molly took over came back untouched, which left everyone more subdued than would have been expected, seeing as how the Wilkins home was now packed to the gills with people. Linda sat in the living room surrounded by strange yet friendly faces, the plate balanced on her knees. Smiles greeted the newcomers, but few words. Linda understood perfectly the need for quiet. There was the sense of all of them having gathered in a hallowed place. She did not know why she felt that way, but the sensation was too strong to be denied.

When she returned to the guest house, she was part of a group that numbered somewhere between sixty and a hundred. A few younger kids tried to race around, but they were quickly stifled with looks and soft words. Reluctantly several of the mothers agreed to stay behind in the Wilkins home and watch over those too young to be trusted to stay still. Molly greeted them on the second-floor landing to announce that Buddy had moved back upstairs, and did not want to be disturbed just then. No one seemed surprised by the news. Linda certainly understood.

Daylight strengthened, gray and quiet. The whole world seemed to be holding its breath. People kept filing in, drawn by the same invisible voice that continued to speak a message of peace to her own heart. There were so many people gathered now, they could not all enter the two apartments. People seated themselves on the stairs, on the floor, down the halls leading into the ground-floor and second-floor bedrooms, and still there was not enough room. The remaining people stood outside on the porch. And still they came.

The second floor grew close with all the people. Someone opened the windows, and the brisk, dry air filtered about them as they sat and waited. Patrick led them in a prayer, and James Thaddeus in another. But there was little need to speak.

Linda found herself looking around the room, searching out faces she had come to know. Some were from the church, people she had worked with over the past few weeks, people who had accepted her as one of their own. Scattered among them were other faces, ones belonging to people of her more intimate heart. Patrick was there, and Scott and Jeff. They seemed surrounded by a light all their own, and she knew the love from her heart was adding to their light. And she did love them. All three. They were part of her now. Even in a gathering this huge, she felt the intimacy of a bonding beyond earth and time.

Patrick felt her eyes, and lifted his gaze to fasten with hers. He did not smile. Did not speak. But across the room he reached with his eyes, and his gaze cradled her heart and spoke to her with a power that was both his and not his. His, and yet something far beyond the ability of an earthly heart to hold. His, yet only because he wished to share it with another. With her.

Then the moment passed, and she looked down at her hands. Not because she wanted to, but because the mood had changed. Even with all those people, the air became still. The silence was no longer merely an absence of words. It was a *presence.* It pressed down upon the room and the gathering, silencing even the squeals of children filtering in through the open window. The pressure grew and grew until Linda's heart felt as though it were on fire.

Somewhere in the room, a man groaned. She shivered, as though the sound had been pulled from her own throat, her own heart. Another groan, something that sounded almost like an amen, but not truly a word. Then nothing. She closed her eyes, the pressure building and building still. A tear was pushed from her eye, and traced its scalding way down her cheek.

A murmur built in the room, a rise and fall of voices like the sound of a human current, a tide of emotion that was forced from throats who did not even realize they were speaking. It rose, it fell, it vanished. And still the pressure grew.

She did not need to lift her gaze to know what she saw. Through her closed eyes Linda witnessed a room and a house filled with hearts on fire for God. Their spirits burned in unison, lit by a holy flame. Black and white, young and old, yet strangers no more. There was no room for alienation or difference here. Not now. The power was too great. They were joined by the divine hand, one that continued to grow and strengthen until it felt as though her heart were going to melt away—that her earthly body would perish, and she would rise to join with all the others who were gathered with them that day.

Like a wind that rose and fell unseen, the feeling began to diminish. It could have been hours or minutes, days or weeks, Linda could not tell. But finally, finally, she was able to draw an easy breath. And raise her eyes. And find other heads lifting all around the room, and other hands wiping at cheeks. All of them focusing upon where Buddy stood on the stairs leading to the upper room.

Buddy searched the room, and found Patrick. He said softly, "It's time."

FORTY-THREE

☐ White House Chief of Staff Ethan Eldridge set down his phone and turned to stare out the window, gathering himself. He tried to tell himself it was just another crisis. Just one more problem in a problem-filled world. But this one weighed heavy. There was a touch of something new to this, something that left him more than just unsettled. Ethan Eldridge rose from his seat and started for the door, wondering why this particular crisis had him feeling so afraid.

He walked past the security man parked midway along the hall between the Oval Office and the doors leading to the president's private quarters. He saw Jerry Chevass, Royce Calder's number two, leaning into the doorway of what had previously been Ken Oakridge's office. The former security chief's health had declined faster than anyone had expected, and the previous Friday he had decided he could no longer remain in office. Ethan had seen no reason not to allow Royce to move in.

Jerry Chevass turned and spotted Eldridge's approach, and tried to wipe the grin from his face. But he could not manage it entirely. "Just stopped by to shower the man with envy."

"No promotion is complete without it," Royce said from behind his new desk. Boxes were piled everywhere. Royce's blond assistant was busy arranging books and plaques on the shelves, while Royce fiddled with the wires to his computer. Royce looked up and instantly knew something was wrong. "What's the matter?"

"The president is giving Oakridge his send-off in the Green Room." Ethan's words came out tipped with ice. "He's supposed to go straight from there to a meeting with the governor of Ohio. After that it's a picture session with somebody, I can't remember—"

"The Ohio Chamber of Commerce," Royce offered. "I stopped by his secretary's office this morning and checked the schedule. They're down to make a pitch—"

"It doesn't matter. Go find the vice president. He's supposed to be hosting the prime minister of Malta. Cancel that. Your job is to take hold of the president's schedule and shepherd the vice president in his place. Got that?"

"Yes." Royce was already up and making notes. "I could see if one of our tame senators could handle the delegation from Malta."

"Whatever. Tell them we have a crisis on our hands. The president has been pulled away. You know the drill." He turned to where Chevass stood by the doorway. "There is a press conference scheduled an hour from now. We were intending to formally announce the church tax measure. Find the press attaché. Tell her to prepare them for a different announcement."

"She won't like it," Chevass predicted. "The release will already be passed out and—"

"I couldn't care less what she likes or dislikes," Eldridge snapped. "Have her retract the release. Tell her this comes straight from the top."

"On my way," Chevass said, and made tracks.

Eldridge looked back to Royce. "The Oakridge event finishes in five minutes. The governor will be waiting in the Oval Office antechamber. I have no idea where the vice president is. Check with security. Move."

Eldridge turned and started down the hall. He did not run. Too many people were watching. Soon enough they would hear of the crisis. There would be plenty of running after that.

He arrived at the main entrance to the Green Room just as the applause was sounding. Eldridge made his way around the edge of the gathering, and waited as the president stood for the final pictures, one arm draped around his former security chief and the other around Oakridge's wife. Friends and family milled about the grand salon, first used by Thomas Jefferson as the main dining hall. Eldridge kept his eye upon his boss and friend, and tried to fashion exactly how he was going to put this news.

That Bradley Gifford was president at all remained one of the great mysteries of fate. Ethan Eldridge had been part of the backroom negotiation team that had finally nailed the man's platform together, and he knew just how close a call it had been. The truth was, they had come within a razor's edge of having someone else in the chair. Someone who would have altered the nation's and the Party's course for good.

For the first time, the Party's religious wing had almost managed to put forth a candidate of their own. The nation, scarred by the scandals of the previous administration, had been looking for a moral voice. The Party hierarchy had watched in tight-lipped panic as the presidential race had almost come unhinged. Ethan had chosen his moment carefully, then come forward with Bradley Gifford as the alternative. The only alternative with the chance of winning.

After the strains of the scandal and the economic collapse, Ethan had argued, what the nation needed most was someone who could reassure them. Someone whose voice and face were well known, who stood for integrity and unity. Someone who would harken back to the fireside chats of President Franklin D. Roosevelt.

Bradley Gifford was a man the public had known for years. He had been in politics longer than the majority of voters had been alive—thirty-eight years in the Senate alone. He was a patriarch of the political system, a father of four and grandfather of nine. He was fit and jogged five miles a day. He spoke with authority and kindly concern. Throughout the campaign he had calmed fears and promised reform—and he had won.

Although the economy continued its faltering downward spiral, Bradley Gifford's popularity remained strong. He promised results. He worked for the nation as a whole. The road ahead was still tough, but the end was in sight. President Gifford was a master of the short sentences television required, and the warm concern people needed. A master.

President Bradley Gifford was also a delegator. He had been his entire political career. It was his defining characteristic. His staff was selected upon the premise that they would each run their own show, and without his interference. One top person was all he wanted to hear from—one general, one secretary for each department, one congressional whip, one chief of staff. According to President Gifford, ruling this nation was too big a job for any one person. As he had grown older, his propensity to filter the world through one principal aide had only grown stronger. Ethan Eldridge had accepted his current position precisely because of this. His job was to be the primary voice the president heard. And when other voices played a role, his was to be the *last* voice. The one that counted most.

President Gifford noticed his chief of staff's grim visage, and extricated himself from the crowd. He walked over and said in greeting, "Whatever it is, it must be bad."

"Let's move next door, Mr. President," Ethan said, opening the door behind him.

"Don't I have the governor of Illinois waiting for me?"

"Ohio, Mr. President, and that's being seen to. We have a crisis in the making." Ethan ushered the president into the neighboring Blue Room, now empty.

President Gifford walked over and leaned against the marble-topped center table, part of the original furniture purchased by President Monroe in 1817. "All right, I'm listening."

It seemed a shame to have to speak of such things in this wonderful setting. The Blue Room had always been Ethan's favorite. It was another elliptical salon, like the Oval Office. Yet now the empty chamber seemed to take his words and fling them back in his face. "Mr. President, I am sorry to have to report that this morning a number of our elementary schools have been taken over by gangs. The children are now being held for ransom."

The grandfather in the president showed pain over the news. "How many is 'a number'?"

"The reports are still coming in. Nineteen at last count."

"This is a coordinated attack?"

"We have no idea, sir. To be honest, I don't see how it could be otherwise."

He scratched his cheek. "I seem to recall something, a movie, wasn't it?"

Ethan gave a somber nod. "*Final Showdown.* This is definitely a copycat situation, sir. The attacks seem to be almost identical to the one portrayed in the film."

"No doubt the studio has already released a denial that their work had anything to do with this." He did not expect an answer, and Ethan did not respond. The president sighed and seemed to age before Ethan's eyes. "Do you have any knowledge of the first Great Depression?"

By now he was long used to such digressions. It was the president's way of buying time to mull over news. "A little. Mostly what I read in books."

"I remember my father talking about it. He was just starting his own family, and he lost everything. My dad carried the scars of those times all his life. He always pinched pennies, even when we were living good. Drove his cars right into the ground. Learned electronics so he could repair all the stuff around our house. Made my mother shop the sales and buy bulk groceries. When he died he was worth, oh, a lot. But he still owned only four suits, two for winter and two for summer."

Ethan waited, knowing there was no way he could pressure the president when he took off on these tangents. The president continued, "I remember how Dad used to talk about the depression. It was a sad time, but it was also sedate. Bread lines, but no riots. Hunger marches, but the people were singing hymns. Now what do we have but street disturbances, riots, robberies, crime of all kinds gone straight through the roof. Gang violence exploding in every city. And now this."

When the president did not continue, Ethan started in with, "We have the National Guard standing by. We also want to send in our special Green Beret terrorist hit squads. Supposedly the gangs have wired the doors and windows with explosives, and taped more to some of the children—"

"Those poor kids," President Gifford murmured. "Those poor parents."

"Yes sir. But you need to go in front of the nation immediately. The White House press corps is scheduled to assemble within the hour—you were supposed to give the speech announcing the church tax measure. I've already taken the liberty of changing that. You need to prepare a statement. Something that will keep the nation from going into a major panic over this."

"Of course." President Gifford pushed himself erect, turned to his chief of staff, and said the same words Ethan had heard ten thousand times before. "Can you handle this?"

The question was how President Gifford had approached every major crisis since taking office. Ethan had always come back with a glib response, something to help the president move into the public spotlight with confidence. But this time the words stuck to the roof of his mouth.

"Ethan?"

The chief of staff hesitated a heartbeat more, then replied, "I hope so, sir. I truly hope so."

⊣| FORTY-FOUR |⊢

☐ Because time was so short, all the adults staffed phones and made calls. The core group restricted themselves to contacting every council around the nation. By Linda's fifth call, the questions were as predictable as her responses, and given just as quickly. "Yes, Buddy feels this is somehow a part of God's plan. I'm sorry, no, I can't tell you why. But Buddy seems absolutely certain that God's hand will be at work . . . No, the only details we have are those coming in over the radio. As far as we know, there has not been a school taken over in your area, we contacted all those places first. Yes. Yes. Please just pray. Gather together all your people and pray for the children, for the parents, for us, and for our nation. Yes, those are Buddy's instructions. Pray. Pray as hard as you know how. Thank you. Yes, just as soon as we know something more. Of course. Thank you. Good-bye."

She hung up the phone to find Patrick standing over her. "Buddy feels that you should come."

"All right." There was no time to question the comment. Not now. "Where is Clarence?"

"Loading the rest of his gear into the church van."

"Did Buddy say why he wanted this filmed?"

"He hasn't even said *what* we'll be filming."

She craned to one side so as to inspect his face as she followed him out on the porch and down the guest house stairs. "But you know, don't you? You do."

Patrick held the car door for her, and said only, "We'll all know soon enough."

□

Buddy sat in the backseat of the second van, all alone. Molly was seated to his right and Patrick to his left, but even so, he was alone. More alone than he had ever been in his entire life. And more frightened.

His heart seemed to hammer louder and harder with every passing mile. But there was nothing he could do. He did not know what lay ahead. Only that he had to do it.

Molly reached over and gripped his hand. It felt as though she had reached out from a million miles away. He licked dry lips, kept his eyes closed, his attention fastened upon the single thread of prayer that kept spinning through his mind and his heart: *Lord, whatever it is up ahead, give me the strength and the wisdom to get it right.*

□

The gang had chosen well, taking over a Bethesda elementary school right in the heart of one of Washington's wealthiest suburbs. The traffic halted their forward progress four blocks from the school. They pulled the van and the car onto the curb, picked up the equipment handed to them by Clarence, and joined the stream of people milling forward.

Buddy moved within a bubble of isolation. They surrounded him, but did not touch him. Not even Molly seemed willing to make physical contact. Nothing seemed to affect him in any way, not the weeping mothers or the shouting police or the stream of troops or the helicopters roaring overhead. Nothing. Buddy remained as silent and enclosed as the cloud-covered sky.

They were halted by the first cordon. People stood seven and eight deep around the sawhorses, which were backed up by soldiers with guns at the ready. A funnel moved slowly through two checkpoints, permitting in only those with press passes and parents with children inside.

Patrick looked at the mob and demanded, "What now?"

"We have to go in there," Buddy said, speaking for the first time since leaving the guest house.

"But how?"

"The Lord will make a way."

"But . . ." Patrick halted himself in mid-sentence. He then pointed with his chin, since both hands held Clarence's equipment. "All right. Let's head for the checkpoint."

They joined the throng slowly moving forward to where an officer flanked by several dozen men was carefully checking IDs and licenses, going through what was clearly a list of children before admitting the next cluster of weeping parents.

Progress was slow—too slow for some. Frustrated rage was building with the tears; Linda could feel it surround her.

Finally one man standing directly in front of her shouted, "I have had just about all I am going to *take* of this!"

The officer looked up as the man started jamming his way forward. "Hold it right there, mister."

"You shut your trap!" The man kept one hand gripped tightly on his wife's arm as he pressed through the throng. "My *baby* is in there!"

"Sir, we have to check—"

"You get out of my way!"

And suddenly there were a thousand furious voices shouting together, pushing together, propelling themselves forward. Like a dam broken by an overwhelming wave, the soldiers were pushed helplessly aside as the mass of parents surged forward. Linda and the others had no choice but to allow themselves to be hurtled forward with the others.

Suddenly they were through and running. They passed tanks and water cannons and soldiers in SWAT gear and police and special forces with charcoaled faces. Radios squawked and people shouted at them and several officers tried to stand up to the rush with hands outstretched. It did no good. The parents screamed and shouted their helpless rage, and they ran straight for the school.

Linda's side was burning from the sprint and her hands and arms ached from carrying the heavy equipment. When they finally reached the second cordon, this one topped by barbed wire and flanked by more police and soldiers than she had ever seen in one place, she was grateful for the chance to stop and set down her gear.

"Linda? Linda Kee?"

She turned to find herself facing Attie, the newsroom receptionist. "What on earth are you doing here?"

The woman frowned. "Are you kidding? We're *all* here. All but the ones over covering the White House. Everyone who survived the grim reaper." She looked over Linda's shoulder, and said, "Hey, Clarence, how you doing, man?"

"Fine, Attie, fine as anybody can be on such a day."

"Yeah, this is something, ain't it?" She looked over their crew. "Who you here with, anyway?"

"Buddy Korda."

Her eyes widened. "The man who had the message? He's here?"

"Right over there."

"Wait, wait, I gotta get Jackson on this. You don't move, you hear me? Stay right there." Attie hurried away.

Linda turned to Patrick and said, "I hope I did right."

But it was Buddy who answered. "You did exactly right."

She examined the little man. And yet little no longer. The fire in his eyes was so bright, so *overwhelming,* his physical size mattered not one whit. He looked from one face to the next, and said, "Could we join together in a moment of prayer?"

And that was how the news cameras found them. The film footage was played over and over the whole world around, starting with that one moment. Molly and Patrick and James Thaddeus and Clarence and Linda and Elaine, the six of them huddled in a tiny circle. No one knew whose camera it was that picked up this first image. By the day's end it had become property of the world.

For as they stood there, heads bowed, listening to Patrick form words meant to join them with the invisible, the Lord's hand descended upon them all.

□

Buddy did not hear a single word that Patrick spoke. Even so, this was the most powerful moment of prayer he had ever known.

He stood and he waited and he felt the power build. There was nothing else to be done, except wait. Wait and listen. Listen for the Lord to tell him what to do.

Then his head lifted. It felt to Buddy as though his vision were drawn up and outward by unseen hands. Directed to look beyond the second cordon. Beyond the barbed wire and the soldiers. Out to the sterile concrete pavement that had now become a killing ground. Out to what had once been a school, and now was a building that shouted menace.

Buddy saw none of it.

There was no light, no figure standing there. Even so, he knew he had arrived at the point where he was called to step out upon the water. To do the impossible. To move entirely beyond the realm of logic and worldly power, and follow the will of his God—wherever it took him.

And in that moment, made of a silence and a power so great there was only one voice Buddy was able to hear, he listened with all the intensity that his meager human frame was able to draw together. And he heard the Voice say just one word.

Come.

□

The silence Linda had felt in the guest house was *nothing* compared to this moment. *Nothing.* It felt as though the air were being squeezed from her lungs. Her heart burned so brightly that when she raised her head, she saw the entire silent gathering through a sheen of tears. Impatiently she wiped at her face, determined not to miss an instant of this. Not one second.

Buddy stepped gingerly around the cordon of wire and wood. He did not look at the police and soldiers. Nor did they try and halt him. It was doubtful any of them could have moved. The only sound was from the flicking of police car lights, and the squawk of one lonely radio somewhere off in the distance.

Buddy stepped into the dead man's zone between the cordon and the school. And as he moved, the first ray of sunlight lanced through the clouds and blazed upon his graying head.

He stood there, a single, small figure in rumpled pants and the same shirt he had worn since the day before and a sweater two sizes too big for his little frame. Yet nothing could detract from the light that shone from his face. Nothing could diminish the sense of *majesty* that surrounded him.

"It is not your guns and your worldly might that conquer here this day," he said, and his voice rang through the silence that held them all. The sunlight was magnified by television spots swinging toward him, until he was lit by a worldly illumination almost as powerful as that which shone from him. Almost. "This day does not belong to you. This day is the Lord's.

"Behold the work of His hand, and know it is a sign. A sign given to an undeserving people, calling to one and all throughout our tired and wounded nation. His call is this: Turn this wounded nation from its evil ways, its self-centered walk! Make this a national day of turning! Make yourself a part of His divine plan. Help our nation turn back toward God! And accept this as a sign of His intentions."

Buddy stood there a moment longer, then raised one hand and swept it out toward the school. "Behold the hand of God!"

The silence lasted through one tense breath, two, three.

Then there was the rustle, as of the wind. And yet the day remained still. Still and breathless and silent. Silent save for the rustling sound. The sound of an army on the march. An invisible horde descending, marching, rushing, *invading* the school.

"Get me out of here!"

The scream was so wrenching Linda jumped. Before she could recover, a second shriek rose from the school, this one wordless, panic-stricken.

"Open the door! Do it now!"

More and more noise, shouts, scrambling, screaming, shrieking, wailing clamor. Then the doors *burst* open and the gang members flooded out. Faces terror-stricken, so frightened they saw nothing but that from which they fled. Straight into the arms of the waiting soldiers, who flattened them onto the ground and slipped them into hand-cuffs and flung them into the back of waiting wagons. Still screaming and staring back at the school, horrified by what they had seen. What they had witnessed.

Then the first child appeared in the doorway, and a woman in the crowd screamed out a name and flung herself through the cordon and rushed for the stairs. And suddenly the soldiers were busy trying to get the wire out of the way before somebody got injured, for hundreds of parents were now scrambling and fighting and pushing their way forward, screaming out a chorus of names.

Children poured from the doors and down the stairs, ushered by soldiers who were trying to rush them away from the explosives planted at each arm of the entrance. Despite their best efforts to get them away from the school, the front lawn became packed with a hugging, weeping mob.

Buddy slipped unnoticed back through the mob and into the waiting group of friends. He glanced back at the parents and children, his features tired but satisfied. Then he looked at them and gave his little smile. In his quiet voice he said, "Let's go home."

☐ The hammer came down on the podium, and the boom echoed over the microphone and out through the crowded hall. Patrick leaned forward and intoned, "The Philadelphia Constitutional Convention will now come to order!"

The throng dispersed swiftly to their respective seats, the areas marked by state and region. Patrick waited until all were seated, the television lights were on, and he was the focus of all attention.

He then shouted, his voice ringing with triumph, "The votes have now been counted. The measure to amend the Constitution of the United States has passed as written!"

The news was greeted with a single huge shout of acclaim. Sunlight streamed through the row of windows high overhead, forming giant golden pillars that streaked across the convention floor. Patrick moved aside, opening his arms to hug his two boys. Their grins were as brilliant as the sun. The convention's co-chairman, Reverend James Thaddeus Wilkins, stepped forward and waited for the clamor to diminish enough for him to announce, "The vote was unanimous in favor of our amendment!"

The pandemonium threatened to overwhelm the arena. People sang and shouted and danced in the aisles, embracing strangers, raising hands to the ceiling, laughing and crying all at the same time.

With one hand, Linda Kee directed Clarence to pan out over the audience a final time, then come back in for a close-up. "There you have it, ladies and gentlemen. What may soon become the Twenty-Seventh Amendment to the Constitution will now return to the states for a final vote. If a simple majority of voters in three-quarters of our states votes in favor, it will immediately become the law of the land."

Linda put a hand to her earpiece, listened to what her producer was saying, then spoke to the camera, "We are almost ready to take you to Washington, where the president of the United States is preparing to address the nation. But before we cut over, we have just enough time for a reaction from our two guests."

She swiveled her leather chair so that she faced the man seated across the small central table. "With me now is Mr. Royce Calder, formerly a member of the White House staff and now assigned to cover the convention for the president. Mr. Calder, what do you anticipate the president will have to say to the country?"

The man's complexion was as gray as his hair, his gaze as bleak as his voice. "I am certain the president will want to congratulate the convention for having demonstrated the will of the nation."

For some reason, that caused the television reporter to smile. She then asked, "Just prior to the amendment issue gathering steam, reports circulated that the current administration had planned a measure to strip away the finances of America's churches. Do you have any reaction to this?"

Royce Calder shifted uncomfortably in his seat, and a flicker of genuine pain seemed to pass over his features. "The administration has no plans to change the current tax status of America's churches, now or in the future."

"Thank you, Mr. Calder." Linda then turned to the man seated on her opposite side. "With me also is Buddy Korda, the man who has been responsible for both this amendment and the remarkable resolution of the gang conflict that threatened so many of our nation's schools."

As the camera backed up to include all three people, the similarity and the difference between the two men seated alongside her became striking. Calder and Korda were almost identical in build, both graying, compact men. But when seen together like this, Calder became a parody of the other man. A bitter, empty shell in a neat pin-striped suit.

With the pandemonium on the convention floor as a backdrop, Linda continued, "Mr. Korda, your divine message resulted in an instantaneous release of hundreds of hostages who were held for ransom in twenty-two schools. Now your message has resulted in the first successful Constitutional

Convention of this century. How does it feel to be the divine messenger of God?"

Buddy smiled at her as she held the microphone toward him, then turned his smile toward the camera. "Being a messenger of God is a responsibility given to every believer. God's voice is never silent in our lives. God made us so we could *all* know Him and love Him. Everything we are, everything about us, invites us to come closer to the divine. It is the eternal binding force of the universe. If we allow, every experience will speak to us of Him."

Linda drew back the microphone. "Thank you, Buddy Korda. Words of divine importance from a man who carries the mark of God. This is Linda Kee, reporting live from the Philadelphia convention center for the Christian Broadcasting Network, handing you over to our correspondent in the White House."

When the camera's light turned off, Linda found it the most natural thing in the world to ignore Royce Calder as he glared at her and rose to his feet and stalked from the chamber. Linda dropped the microphone to her lap, leaned back in her chair, and gave Buddy a grandly satisfied smile. "Thank goodness that's all over."

Buddy stared at her in quiet astonishment. "What on earth makes you say that?"

"Why . . . "She waved a tired hand out over the convention floor, to where Patrick stood on the stage hugging his two boys and James Thaddeus and Elaine Wilkins, to the cheers of a wildly enthusiastic crowd. "Look for yourself."

"I am," Buddy said quietly, his gaze fastened solely upon her. "And what I see is that for you, my dear sister in Christ, this is only the beginning."

⊣∥ AUTHOR'S NOTE ∥⊢

☐ While many people have aided in the research required for this book, two people in particular require special thanks. The first is my wife, Isabella. Thank you, sweetheart; as always, your love and your wisdom shine from these pages.

The second person is Mike Ferris. Mike is a Constitutional lawyer based outside Washington, and currently serves as Director of the Home Schooling Legal Defense Association. He has so many different honors to his name it is hard to know what to mention here. He was very narrowly defeated in a race for the lieutenant governorship of Virginia. He is a well-known author in his own right. He has tried a number of cases at every level of federal court, and is a champion of Christian rights and issues. Mike went out of his way to help me grasp the inner workings of party politics. With a few stories I feel the essential kernel has been transformed into diamond brilliance principally through the aid of one particular person. In the case of this book, that person is Mike Ferris.

Because my wife and I live in England, mail from readers has remained a vital component of my writing life. Hearing from readers, particularly those whose walk has been aided in some small part by my work, has meant more than words will ever say.

You can send correspondence to me as follows:

Davis Bunn
c/o Thomas Nelson Publishers
P. O. Box 141000
Nashville, TN 37214

⊣| ABOUT THE AUTHOR |⊢

☐ Before becoming an award-winning author, T. DAVIS BUNN earned a master's degree in international finance and worked as a business executive in Europe, Africa, and the Middle East. He has written fifty books, including such bestsellers as *The Great Divide, The Book of Hours, Tidings of Comfort and Joy, One Shenandoah Winter, The Warning,* and *The Ultimatum.* In July 2000 his novel *The Meeting Place* (coauthored with Janette Oke) won the Christy Award for Fiction. Davis and his wife, Isabella, live in Oxfordshire, England.

Kingdom Come

Larry Burkett and T. Davis Bunn

Central North Carolina hasn't seen much change in more than 50 years, but suddenly people who have lived there for generations are leaving the small farming settlements lock, stock, and barrel. When massive warehouses surrounded by prison-regulation fencing seem to go up overnight and more than six thousand families establish residence in a community named Kingdom Come, the FBI begins to suspect cult activity. Agent Ben Atkins is sent to investigate, and though he does not sense something major happening, he is not convinced that it is not sinister. In fact, he begins to wonder if those inside the community are working to keep evil out. But time is running short for him to discover the truth, as unexpected enemies threaten the community's existence.

ISBN 0-7852-6770 • Paperback • 324 pages

The Book of Hours

After his wife's death, Brian Blackstone's days had become a meaningless blur. But now, recovering from a tropical fever, he arrives in the English village of Knightsbridge to confront the inheritance he doesn't want to claim. His wife had insisted that Castle Keep was a place of enchantment, and urged him to hold on to the crumbling property. Impoverished and alone, Brian feels only the despair of trying to honor her dying wish.

Then a mysterious letter sends Brian on a search to find the secrets of the ancient estate. And the local doctor, Cecilia Lyons, though suspicious of him at first, soon becomes an ally in the fight to save Castle Keep before it can be auctioned.

ISBN 0-7852-7088-4 • Paperback • 324 pages

One Shenandoah Winter

It's late autumn in the mountain town of Hillsboro, and assistant mayor Connie Wilkes has her hands full. She's concerned about her beloved eighty-three-year-old uncle, Poppa Joe, and his ornery insistence that he can still be as independent as a man half his age. She's also worried about a young friend's hasty plans for marriage. And now the new doctor, Nathan Reynolds, may not even stay to help the town that so desperately needs him.

But before the first winter snowfall, a chain of events is set in motion that will transform Connie, the doctor, and the town forever. By Christmas Day, the greatest sorrow and the greatest miracle will bring reminders of th glorious possibilities of Emmanuel, "God with us."

ISBN 0-7852-7217-8 • Hardcover • 272 pages

Tidings of Comfort and Joy

It started with an old photograph. One of Marissa's grandmother, younger and more beautiful than Marissa had ever seen her. But the officer who was embracing her with such passion didn't look like her grandfather!

As the questions begin, an extraordinary story unfolds—a story of love and loss, of separation and reunion. Of small acts of heroism half a century ago in a distant and war-weary English village.

As her grandmother shares this story with Marissa, the two discover that the most precious gift of Christmas is that of the present, and that the season of giving is not limited to once a year.

ISBN 0-7852-7203-8 • Hardcover • 324 pages